An Evans Novel of Romance

TAKE THIS WOMAN

JOSEPHINE COX

M. EVANS & COMPANY, INC. NEW YORK

Library of Congress Cataloging-in-Publication Data

Cox, Josephine.

Take this woman / Josephine Cox.
p.   cm.
ISBN 0-87131-644-7 : $17.95
I. Title.
PR6053.09676T35   1990
823'.914—dc20   90-49291
CIP

M. Evans and Company, Inc.
216 East 49 Street
New York, New York 10017

Manufactured in the United States of America

9 8 7 6 5 4 3 2 1

Dedication

This book is for Jean Brindle, a darling little lady who was loved by many people, and is sorely missed by all of us. There was no one more proud and delighted when my first story was published. She was an angel on earth, a wonderful sister-in-law and a dear, dear friend.

To Bernard, Gary, Christine and Craig, I can only say that the Lord must have something special for her to do by his side.

We have precious memories of our Jean, and in our hearts we'll always have her also. Each one of us is a better person for having known her.

> 'Heaven and yourself
> Had part in this fair maid; now heaven hath all,
> And all the better is it for the maid;'
>
> *Shakespeare*

There are many ways in which a woman can be taken. Laura was taken first in rape then in treachery.

How can she now trust herself to be taken in love?

Contents

PART ONE

1947

BETRAYAL

I remember, I remember
The house where I was born,
The little window where the sun
Came peeping in at morn;
He never came a wink too soon,
Nor brought too long a day,
But now, I often wish the night
Had borne my breath away.

Thomas Hood

Chapter One

'Aw, Netti darling! Why would a little angel like you need to go to confession?' Laura gave the small girl a loving hug as she lifted her onto the low wall which fronted the church. 'No. You wait here ... I'll not be long,' she said, quickly turning her back on the child for fear of more probing questions.

Hurrying along the flagged pavement, Laura did not look back. Instead, she hastened towards the small picket gate which would take her up the church path and on into the stark grey building, where she hoped to find a measure of comfort.

In the dim interior of the church, Laura stood for a while, her dark brooding gaze sweeping the empty pews, the white-clothed altar and the magnificent golden crucifix high up on the wall behind. Finally, her gaze came to rest on the confessional box to her left. With a surge of relief she noticed there was no one waiting to see the priest, although a glance at the heavy velvet curtain drawn across the cubicle nearby told Laura that she would have to be patient for a few minutes at least.

With a small impatient sigh, she moved forward, the splitting facets of light shimmering through the tall stained-glass window onto her lovely face and illuminating the troubled look in her amber eyes.

To the outside world, and to those who knew her, Laura's calm and composed countenance was an indication of her great strength of character, remarkable for her tender years. Yet inside, Laura's peace was shattered and her strength sorely tried. Night or day, there was no stemming the grief or crippling resentment which tore at her heart and racked her faith for her father, whom she loved fiercely, was losing his fight for life. It was a bitter justice, which Laura found hard to accept.

Laura edged into the pew, then undid her headscarf, and allowed her wayward auburn hair to fall about her shoulders in a luxuriant mass. Next she bowed her head forward and collected the straying hair beneath the confines of her scarf, then tightened the knot beneath her chin and sank to kneel into the plump red cushion on the flagstoned floor before her. She leant forward and rested her elbows on the wooden hymn-book rack, lowered her head and muttered a heartfelt prayer.

The echo of departing feet made her turn around and the sight of a woman's figure retreating from the now empty cubicle told her that the priest would be waiting.

Laura suddenly felt afraid and unsure of herself and she made no move to rise from her knees. Instead, she watched the departing woman, taking stock of the stout black walking shoes and the long, like-coloured skirt that swirled against the dark-stockinged ankles. The woman turned just once at the head of the aisle, where she bobbed down quickly on one knee, to face the altar and make a small sign of the cross on her forehead. Then she lifted the heavy grey shawl that draped her figure and wrapped it about her hair. She clutched it tightly at her neck, and nodded a friendly greeting towards Laura, before disappearing towards the outer door and in a moment she was gone.

Laura had absent-mindedly noted that the woman, aged about sixty, was of the old Lancashire stock who dressed as their parents and grandparents before had dressed, and who would never be persuaded to discard their long flouncing skirts and shawls to follow the 'new-fangled' fashions that the younger women liked so much. This stubborn resistance amongst the old to fight any change seemed to Laura to have strengthened since the end of the War in 1945, two years ago.

Laura closed her eyes, summoned up a semblance of courage, and focused her wandering thoughts on the purpose of her visit to the church. Rising from her knees, she moved slowly towards the confessional box, entered quietly and reached out to pull the curtain across behind her. She sat on the hard wooden chair and hoped that the rest of the world had been effectively shut out.

'Yes child?' The voice, with its soft persuasive tones, broke

14

the silence and Laura looked up. The small grill, inserted at face level in the partition that separated her from the priest, was made of narrow, twisting pieces of wood that curled and snaked to form an intricate pattern. Laura was thankful that it concealed the face of the priest from her and protected her own anonymity.

For a long moment, she didn't reply, and it crossed her mind to leave as silently as she had arrived. How could she tell this devoted priest that she had come to doubt his God? That the awful war, responsible for her father's pain and imminent death, could have been created by a powerful evil over which even his God had no control. If there *was* a God who believed in compassion, then why had he allowed such a thing to happen, and why did she feel that her searching questions were sinful?

A great anger took hold of her heart, and drawing a deep weary breath, she got to her feet. There is no peace, she thought, not even here. Pausing only to lift the curtains aside, she murmured, 'Forgive me, Father', and stepping into the aisle to face the altar, she bowed her head as though in shame and turned to walk away.

Outside in the cold light of a February day, Laura felt surprised and not a little afraid at her boldness in leaving the confessional box. It was only when the voice of Father Clayton called out to her, that she realized the extent of her deep anger. Laura paused, waiting for the priest who hurried towards her, his long black frock billowing slightly from the cold gusts of wind. The long rosary hanging around his portly waist whipped and danced in the air, and the thin strands of greying hair that belied his youthful face were being blown about in feathered chaos.

'Laura . . . Laura,' his pale eyes filled with concern as he asked quietly, 'so you couldn't find it in your heart to confide in me, eh?'

Briefly, their eyes met and neither of them spoke, and the priest was both saddened and inspired by the sorrow and proud defiance that scarred those beautiful searching eyes that stared at him with such accusation, making his heart heavy. The same questions that had brought this young girl to his church and hurried her angrily away from it, often raked his own mind with painful persistence, for he too needed answers.

'I know what's in your heart, Laura, and you are never far from my prayers, but the answers to your questions aren't so easy to find. It's in yourself and in the strength of your faith that you'll find peace. You must believe that.'

Laura kept her eyes fixed on his kindly face and she listened to his words, but she found nothing there to comfort her. His words were firm and there was no doubting his concern. But his words held no conviction, and in spite of herself, Laura recalled the talk that had been rampant in Blackburn town these last few months. Father Clayton had served his country as countless other men had done during the War years. But there were those among his faithful and forgiving flock who claimed that the priest had gone to War a brave, dedicated man and had returned disillusioned, filled with crippling doubt and aged before his time.

Laura's heart ached for him, but if this priest didn't believe in what he was saying, then how could *she* be expected to? Her voice was strong and cold as she said, 'And my father? What of him?'

'How is Jud?' The priest smiled at her and Laura despised him for avoiding her question.

'He's dying,' she said quietly, 'my father's dying.' She turned from him. 'I have to go now.'

As she closed the gate behind her, Laura heard him call out, 'I'll be along shortly. Tell your father, Laura.'

Laura nodded and hurried away, the sturdy heels of her shoes cutting an angry pattern into the thin layer of snow beneath her feet. A short way along the low wall that fronted the church she collected the small, bright girl who had been patiently waiting for her sister's return.

The priest watched the two young girls as they went away down King Street, and when he could no longer see the bright blue headscarf and well-worn grey woollen coat, or the smaller girl with long flowing fair hair, tightly clasping her sister's hand, he shook his head slowly, rolled his eyes upwards and murmured, 'Will you be there when they need you?' Then with a heavy heart, he made his way back up the path towards the sanctity of his church.

Once out of sight of Father Clayton, whom she felt was

16

watching her, Laura slowed down, but it was only when the small child at her side almost stumbled, that the thoughtlessness of her angry retreat dawned on her. She stopped and looked down on the girl's anxious face. 'I'm sorry, Netti. Are you alright?' she said, pulling the girl into her embrace.

Netti ignored Laura's question, shook free from her sister's arms and asked in a firm, accusing voice, 'Can we go to the canal now?'

'Oh Netti! I think we ought to be getting back to our dad.' Laura pictured her father watching the door of his sickroom, looking for her. But then she remembered that he had stopped recognizing her these last few weeks; indeed, she often wondered whether he even knew that she was there at all. In a way, Laura knew it was a blessing that he wasn't aware of how his own wife avoided the sight of his wasting away, his diseased lungs gasping for every breath. Ruth Blake was only too willing to let that unpleasant burden fall onto her daughter's young shoulders, and for Laura's part, she wouldn't have wanted it any other way.

'Please Laura, you promised!'

Laura felt Netti's determined fingers tugging at her own, as she continued towards home. Yet her conscience bothered her. It was true, she *had* promised to take Netti along the canal; but she begrudged every minute spent away from her father who needed her. However, she was painfully aware of her sister's needs too. Ruth Blake's love had shrivelled not only from her dying husband, but from her two daughters as well, and so it was to Laura that Netti now looked for warmth and guidance.

'Come on then,' Laura shouted, and the glowing smile of gratitude that greeted her decision was more than reward enough.

Tugging the girl behind her, Laura drew up at the kerb-edge where they waited patiently for the assortment of traffic to trundle past. Then with a shout of 'Run, Netti!' they quickly crossed to the far side. Saturday was always a busy day and King Street was a lively thoroughfare of trams, various horse-drawn flat carts and wagons. Countless folk still plied a living by carting and rag-a-boning in Blackburn, and the trusted horses remained a familiar sight. But the more adventurous of the small tradesmen were beginning to desert the old ideas, and it saddened Laura to see the increasing volume of cars and lorries whose belching fumes tainted the air.

Laura and Netti walked almost the length of King Street; past numerous pubs, which were said to draw more of a congregation on a Friday night than Father Clayton's church ever did on a Sunday; then along by the devastation that Laura remembered to be a neat little row of terraced buildings before the War; over the bridge that spanned Blakewater, filled now with rubble from the adjacent derelict and since neglected buildings, and onto Brown Street.

The canal and surrounding open fields were a delight to Laura, who hadn't forgotten the wonderful times before the War, when her father would bring her here; the last time just before he'd gone to be a soldier.

Laura had cried for weeks after his departure and it was only when she was told of Netti's impending arrival, that she began to look forward with determination to her father's return. But that was to be years later, and the man who came home after a long torturous confinement in a Japanese Prisoner of War camp, was only a broken shadow of the father she remembered. Yet she loved him all the more, and it was only in these last few months that Laura had been forced to accept that her prayers for his recovery were not to be answered; and that knowledge sorely tested everything she had ever believed in.

At the sight of the open steps leading down to the canal, Netti ran ahead, laughing and shouting with excitement to Laura, who urged, 'Watch the steps! It's slippery.'

Sitting herself on a boulder embedded in the snow-covered grass of the bank, Laura watched the sparrows pecking at the isolated patches of bare earth and she sympathized with their busy and futile antics. 'Poor little things,' she said out loud. She looked towards Netti, who was scraping up the fast-thawing snow and kneading it into small round balls; some of which she promptly threw into the water and the others she piled into a neat little pyramid. As Laura watched, a great surge of love moved within her. She mustn't begrudge her sister's innocent laughter and joy, for Netti had never known their real father, not the man he had once been. Netti had only ever known the tortured delicate soul in a sick-bed from which

18

he could find no strength to rise.

As she listened to her sister's bubbling laughter, Laura could vividly remember her own. It was here, to this canal, when she was younger than Netti was now, here to this very spot that her father had brought her, that day before he went away. All that morning they had chatted to the kindly barge-people, who'd invited them into their small gaily painted houses in the end of their boats. Then she and her father had run beside the great horses along the towpath, watching them pull the barges through the water. It had been a wonderful day and that night when her father had spoken of going away, Laura was enthused by his obvious excitement at what he said was 'a worthwhile job that must be done'. Neither of them could have envisaged what that 'worthwhile job' was to cost him — him and countless others.

Laura pushed the painful thoughts from her mind. It was at the very moment she got to her feet that she saw the dog, a small brown and white terrier. The dog was bounding towards Netti, and close on its heels was a man whom she recognized as a friend of her father's, now selling papers and rat-catching. The man's face was a deep purple shade of anger as he waved and shook what looked to be a sack. His voice was angry and hoarse. 'Yer bloody fool! Come back 'ere or I'll 'ave yer sodding arse!' As he drew closer, he caught sight of Jud Blake's two daughters and momentarily looked sheepish. He grabbed the cap from his head and murmured, "Ow do, lasses. My regards to Jud.'

Just then the dog doubled back round in a circle, ran at Netti's legs, bowled her over, then streaked past Laura, carrying in its mouth what she took to be a rat. Netti got to her feet as Laura ran forward to steady her, and the two of them stood staring after the dog, who seemed to think it was all some sort of game.

'Bloody silly cur!' In spite of his obvious rage, the man looked a comical sight. Ramming his flat nebbed cap well over his ears, he stopped, gasping for air greedily. 'Five bob! Five bloody bob I forked out for that there dog! Grand rat catcher, I were told! Well, I intend to 'ave me money back, I'll tell thi!' His enormously fat belly rose and fell as he shouted, 'That sodding dog's no more a rat-catcher than yon lass,' he nodded towards Netti who, to Laura's consternation, had started to giggle. He wiped his nose with the back of his hand, then pointed to the dog, who had turned in its tracks to race back towards them, and shouted, 'Look yon! The bugger's mekkin back!' He then opened the mouth of the sack, whereupon he proceeded to scrape it along the ground, in an effort to line it up with the approaching animal. 'Watch out,' he shouted, 'for Christ sakes, don't let the bugger get past yer! You see what the silly sod's done, eh? Don't even know what a bloody rat *looks* like! That's my prize ferret caught 'atween 'is teeth. I'll 'ave the bugger fer that I will!'

At that point, everything seemed to happen at once. The man, over anxious to catch the dog in his sack, lost his balance, and with his legs hopelessly entangled in the trailing sack, he fell over. As the dog shot past, Netti began jumping and shouting 'Go on dog! Go on!' and in spite of the poor man's distress, Laura found herself laughing out loud.

'It's no bloody laughin' matter, young Blake!' The man struggled to his feet and took off in pursuit of both dog and prize-ferret, leaving Netti and Laura to find their way from the canal, still helpless with laughter, and for the briefest of moments, Laura's sorrow was pushed aside by the rare experience of pure childish joy.

Skirting the busier part of town, Laura took the way past the clutch of cotton mills that stood high on Cicely Banks and looked down over Blackburn town like monstrous sentries of Victorian times, then on through the narrow ginnel that would take them into Penny Street and home to No 9.

Penny Street was a long snaking cobbled road, flanked by terraces of shops and two-up, two-downers, each with its own identical white-stoned front doorslab at the top of a flight of steps leading down to the cellar; and at the back of each house was a small flagstoned back yard and the privy.

Netti caught sight of a long rope hanging down from the arm of a gas-lamp standard in front of No 9, perhaps left there by some forgetful child. 'Can I play swinging, Laura, eh?' she shouted, then without waiting for a reply, she left Laura's grasp and looped the rope into a seat beneath her. 'Just a few goes,' she promised, levering her feet against the lamp-standard to push her weight into a dizzy swinging spiral around and around the metal column.

Laura didn't reply, but shrugged her shoulders, wondering why it was that two-thirds of Blackburn had been graced with tall elegant columns of new electric lighting, while poorer areas such as Penny Street appeared to have been forgotten.

Pulling at the string hanging in the letter-box, Laura grasped the key which dangled on the end, then glancing along Penny Street, she thought how unusually quiet it seemed. It crossed her mind that folk had probably kept the noisiest of their children inside, as a mark of respect for the ailing Jud Blake. Laura let herself into the narrow front passage and took off her coat and scarf. Then she hurried towards the bottom of the passage, cautiously entering the first of two rooms to the left of the stairway.

The air struck cold as Laura quickly crossed to the small canopied fireplace, where she collected two knobs of coal from the black iron scuttle, placing them onto the dying embers in the firegrate and opening out the damper some way up the chimney. And now the coal caught fire, emitting a degree of warmth and lending a cheery air to the miserable room which skulked in the dim light from the tall narrow windows, almost smothered by the lace curtains and heavy tapestry drapes.

Laura looked towards the huge bed, its glossy brass surround twinkling like gold in the slit of light that struggled in from the window. That same daylight bathed her father's face, yet Laura could see no twinkle there. Crossing to kneel beside the bed, she gazed lovingly at the sallow complexion of his lean features and some deep inner instinct told her that he had gone further away from her. She moved the thick brown lock of hair from his forehead and, taking a hankie from her pocket, she wiped away the beads of sweat that covered his brow. He gave no response, and Laura walked to the window where she looked out at Netti still swinging around the gas-lamp, and the whisper of a smile brightened her face. Laura turned back to the room and looked about the parlour.

'I should hate this room,' she murmured softly, taking stock of the faded flowered wallpaper and the narrow chest of drawers, upon which rested a huge jug and matching bowl and a neatly folded towel with a bar of carbolic soap on top. Nearer to her father's bed stood a well-polished sideboard of dark

21

mahogany. It held three clocks; two small mantelpiece clocks of sturdy design and a beautiful tall chiming clock, arched at the top and scooped into dainty little claw feet at the bottom. In the centre of the sideboard stood a magnificent bronze scuplture of an eagle in flight. These things were Jud Blake's pride and joy. The only other piece of furniture in the room was a rush-seated stand-chair by the head of the bed, on which rested a copy of the Bible, and a half-burned candle securely wedged into a circular brass holder with a hook for carrying. It was a room without hope, and it had about it an air of desolation that flooded Laura'a heart whenever she entered it. She could have hated this room, for she needed to fix her rage and frustration onto something. But then she recalled all the precious, private hours spent in here with her father, when the two of them would talk until he became too tired to go on; then Laura would tell him things of the outside world, stories that she had gathered from the 'carting round' that had been Jud's, and he would listen gratefully, often falling asleep before she could finish them. Those times belonged only to her, and she knew she could *never* hate this room.

Laura sensed the door opening, and she raised her eyes to meet the disapproving scowl on her mother's face.

Ruth Blake, even in her condition of advanced pregnancy, was a woman of considerable beauty, with the same wild profusion of auburn hair as the girl whose gaze now met her own. The eyes too were the same deep-speckled amber, but where Laura's eyes were steadfast and strong, her mother's were shallow and weak, filled with doubt and fear. Dressed in a woollen calf-length skirt of bottle-green, and a pretty high-necked blouse of paisley print, loosely gathered into the wrists, she boasted a vibrant figure that belied her imminent birthing and her thirty-ninth year. Yet Laura could remember some eight or nine years back, when her mother had dressed not unlike the woman she had seen in the church; her slim straight shoulders draped in a finely crocheted shawl that covered a dress of fitting bodice and full swinging skirt. The memory was a pleasant one, because her mother had been a much happier person then, and life was warm and wonderful. Things were so very different now, and even though her mother was much the same in appearance, if a little older, there was no joy or

22

warmth to light the beauty of her face, and often in her mother's unguarded moments, Laura had glimpsed a dark expression that portrayed some terrible haunting anxiety, and at those times Laura was filled with inexplicable dread.

Ruth Blake stepped into the room, then suddenly seemed to become aware of the fact that she and Laura were not the only two people there. Her eyes narrowed, and she furtively glanced towards the bed where Jud Blake lay still as death, his breathing intermittent and rasping. Ruth Blake recoiled from the sight of her husband and stared at Laura, a look of contempt twisting her features. Stepping backwards out of the doorway, she gestured with a pointed finger down the passage and towards the back parlour. She spoke but one word, 'Out!' yet the menacing tone of her voice and the wrath that had darkened her eyes, spoke volumes.

Laura looked once more at her father and, satisfied that she could do nothing further for the time being, she crossed the room, and in a moment she had passed her mother to hurry the few yards along the passage into the back parlour. She waited by the one small window that overlooked the outer yard. Retreating footsteps told her that her mother was moving up the passage and towards the front door; then there was the sound of the door being opened, and Ruth Blake's voice cut sharply into the quietness of the parlour. 'Netti! Get yourself in here!'

Laura hoped there wasn't going to be another scene, especially not in front of Netti. But when she heard the determined shrillness of her mother's voice and Netti's mumbled replies, Laura knew that there would be no escape from yet another ugly confrontation.

Setting her slight shoulders in an attitude of defence, Laura sighed, waiting for the imminent verbal whipping, and took strength from the familiar and well-loved things that surrounded her in this room. The small circular table for example, with its drop sides and pretty barley-twist legs, one of two, that her father had collected on his first carting round the streets some fourteen years ago. He had sold one, but this particular table he had kept to strip, mend and wax until it was restored to its original beauty. Then he had presented it to his young bride, as a mark of love and gratitude on the birth of the first child, Laura. The table, draped now in a cream lace cloth, stood in the far corner, a resting place for the round topped wireless that had stood silent these last months. The only light came into the room through the one tiny window and there was a certain hostility about the cold flagstone floor, the faded cream emulsion on the walls, and the glass lamp-shade blackened by the fumes from the coal fire.

To Laura, however, this room was the heart of the house and she loved it. She loved the big black shiny fire-place with its deep side oven, the colourful rag-pegged rug in front of the hearth, and the clothes' rack high above, ever filled with neatly folded clothes for airing. Laura enjoyed polishing the long narrow sideboard that stood against the far wall, and she even remembered the day some kind person on the carting round had given her father that green cornice cloth, whose big silken bobbles danced and leaped in the heat from the fire. Strange how the cloth had exactly matched the one that covered the huge square table in the centre of the room, surrounded by four hard wooden stand-chairs, and decorated with a pot jardinière containing a large fern plant. Situated on either side of the fireplace were two tall backed chairs of black prickly horsehair and deep rolled arms; the one on the right her mother's place, and the one on the left her father's.

It occurred to Laura at that moment that she might never again delight in the familiar sight of her father resting in that chair by the fire, and with the thought came an unbearable sadness that cut deep into her mind, causing her to lose awareness of the present situation. It was only when Netti pulled at her hand that Laura sensed her mother's presence.

Ruth Blake shook her head in anger, spitting out the words, 'Answer me, my girl!' She thrust her face towards Laura's. 'And don't lie, because I've already talked to that one!' She pointed an accusing finger towards Netti, who had run to half hide behind Laura, and who was now pushing her tearful face deep into the folds of Laura's skirt.

'I won't lie, Mam.' Laura stood up straight, moving one hand behind her to stroke Netti's hair in a soothing manner.

'No, and you'd better not, if you know what's good for you! Is that right you've been to see Father Clayton, is it, eh?'

'I went to confession. Father Clayton followed me outside.'

At Laura's words, Ruth Blake's mouth fell open and in an instant, she raised her hand way above her head, then with a shout of, 'You little bitch!' she brought the flat of her hand down in a sweeping arc that thudded hard into the side of Laura's head. 'What are you up to, eh?' She raised her hand again, to swing it with vehemence into Laura's face; then undaunted by the sudden gush of blood that spurted from Laura's nose, she demanded, 'You've been talking about *me*! You have, haven't you?' She stood over Laura now, her eyes bulbous and accusing.

'No Mam! No!' Laura was shocked and confused, and suddenly afraid for this demented creature that was her mother. 'Nobody even mentioned *you*.'

'Leave her alone! You leave my Laura be.' Netti had dived from behind Laura, to grasp at her mother's skirt and shake herself back and forth, swaying them both off balance, the tears borne of fear now replaced by a fierce love and anger. 'Leave her alone!' she screamed. 'I hate you!'

Laura pulled the child away, and clutching her face to stem the steady trickle of blood that now stained her nostrils and mouth, she looked up to meet her mother's hostile glare, and in a quiet steady voice she told her, 'Father Clayton just asked after Dad, that's all.'

'Well I'll not have you talking to no priest! D'ya hear me? You're nobbut fourteen, Laura Blake. You'll learn to do as you're told! And in future, *I'll* tell you when to burn precious coal in that sickroom — it doesn't come free!'

Laura recalled the dampness of the front parlour and the fire almost dead in the grate, and at that moment, she felt nothing but contempt for this woman before her. Yet she didn't reply. Instead, she drew herself up, took the sobbing Netti by the hand and walked away into the adjoining scullery with as much dignity as she could muster.

The scullery was a cold forbidding place, separated from the parlour by a heavy brown curtain at the door-way. It was some eight feet square, consisting of an old gas-cooker, a single wooden cupboard with several shelves above it, and a deep stone sink beneath the window. Built into the corner was a brick container, housing a copper washtub and closed at the top by a large circular lid of wooden slatted design.

Releasing her hand, Laura reached down to lift her small sister up onto the washtub. Then she washed her face clean, wiped a wet cloth over Netti's tear-stained face and bent to kiss the shining forehead, saying in a secretive whisper, 'If you give us a smile, I'll take you down to the corner pub next Friday and we can stand near the window. Old Peg-Leg Tandy plays the piano of a Friday night. We'd be able to hear right well if we stood right up against the window,' she nudged the girl's shoulder playfully, 'but I don't expect you'd want to go, would you, eh? Not feeling miserable like you are, and too mean to give us a smile.'

Netti looked up and Laura was gratified and relieved to see a broad grin spread across her sister's face.

'What time will we go? Can we stay longer than last time? Will you lift me on your shoulders, so I can see the piano, eh? Will you, Laura, will you?'

Laura reached out to embrace the child before easing her down to the floor. 'We'll see,' she promised, 'We'll see.' There! She hadn't been wrong; the possibility of listening to Peg-Leg Tandy bashing away at that old piano had brought the smile back to Netti's face, just as Laura knew it would. Netti had always had a real appreciation of music, of anything that sang, rattled or whistled. And whenever there was an opportunity, whether it was watching the cymbal clanging of the Sally Army, or standing for hours fascinated by the band in the park, she would think of nothing else. It was said that she got this love of music from her grandma on her mother's side who had apparently been the only one of the family who had managed to master the pianola with some dignity.

The two girls looked up as Ruth Blake came into the scullery. There was no trace in her features of the rage she had displayed earlier, and when she spoke, it was in a quiet voice, which although it seemed contrite, held the merest suggestion of defiance.

'Happen I were just a bit sharp,' she told Laura, unable to meet Laura's forthright gaze and so fixing her attention on to Netti, who had stepped a pace closer to her sister's side. 'As for you, young madam! Another display of that vindictive temper, and mark my words, you'll not be able to sit down for a week!'

Laura was glad that her mother had come into the scullery,

for Ruth Blake was well known for her stubborn pride and it could not have been an easy thing for her to admit that she might have been in the wrong. And now, as her mother turned to leave, Laura realized just how much she loved her. She thought of the child soon to be born, and she thought of its father; *her* father, lying in the front parlour. A small tight sob strangled her throat and with tears fast in her soft brown eyes, she ran forward to place a loving arm around her mother's waist. 'It's alright Mam,' she told her, 'I'm sorry too.'

Ruth Blake spitefully twisted herself free from the unexpected embrace and stood glowering at Laura's surprised expression, and through closed teeth she hissed, 'Don't you touch me! Don't you ever touch me!'

Laura visibly cringed beneath the naked hatred in her mother's wild eyes, and for a moment, there was real terror in her young heart. What was wrong with her Mam? Was it *her* fault? What had she done?

Ruth Blake snatched the curtain aside and quickly departed, leaving Laura staring after her, not sure what to do next.

'I want to go to bed, Laura. I don't want to wait till bedtime.' Netti's voice was trembling, and she was very obviously afraid.

Laura turned to look at the small figure cowering now against the sink, then in an instant, the child was safe in her arms. And it was painfully clear to Laura that when God had taken her father from them, they would be alone in this world, she and Netti. They would have no one else but each other.

Laura felt more afraid and alone right now than at any other time she could remember, and for a while, as she held and comforted the trembling figure clasped tight against her, the awful heartache she had fought against so valiantly was let loose, to run through her like a tidal wave. And there in the silence of that depressing scullery, with tears of defiance hardening her amber eyes to steel, Laura made a promise. A bitter determined promise to herself, that whatever happened from that day on, she would look to no one else to do what she instinctively knew had to be done. It was up to her and her alone, to provide the love and security that Netti needed, and if it was within her power, she would make it up to her sister for the unhappiness and fear of these last months.

'I want to go to bed, Laura.'

'Bed? Already?' Laura sank to her knees before the child, and lifting both her hands, she tenderly placed them either side of Netti's head, then smiling into the tired blue eyes, she leaned forward to place a kiss on the sorry little face. 'Alright then,' she said, in as bright a voice as she could find, 'you *have* had a long day and we've walked a few miles.' Then as an after-thought and in a bid to prompt a giggle, she added, 'But not so far as that man after his best ferret, eh,' and at the recollection she found herself stifling an impulsive burst of laughter.

But Netti laughed out loud and throwing herself into Laura's arms, she cried, 'Oh, I do love you, Laura, I do.'

Laura blinked away the tears that had risen to sting her eyes after Netti's affectionate outburst, and she got to her feet. 'Get yourself washed at the sink — stripped to the waist mind! None of your half-measures, and I'll see you off to sleep with a story. Right?'

'Right!' came Netti's quick reply.

Laura watched Netti as she fled to the sink and proceeded to undo the buttons at the shoulders of her dark blue pinafore dress. Satisfied that Netti would do the job properly, she went out of the scullery and into the back room.

Ruth Blake was sitting by the fire, her hands crossed on the bulge of her stomach and her eyes flat and expressionless as they stared into the flames.

Laura called her twice, 'Mam, Mam, are you alright?' There was no response and for a while, Laura stood there, watching and praying that things could be different. She wanted so much to help her Mam; she would have done anything, *any-thing* for that stiff unyielding figure to turn towards her now and hold her fast in an embrace. But she sensed in her deepest heart that it would never be.

With a deep sigh Laura left the room to make her way into the front parlour. The brightness of day was already ebbing, shrouding the room in twilight, so Laura went quickly towards the stand-chair by the bed, collected the candle, lit it and placed it on the sideboard, and then put another knob of coal onto the dying embers in the fireplace. Finally she drew the curtains together carefully, so as not to make any sudden or startling sound.

'Laura, Ruth, is that you?' The voice was faint and confused, but to Laura it sounded wonderful.

She hurried towards the bed and eased herself ever so gently onto the edge, reached out to take the hand that had proffered itself to her, and whispered softly, 'It's me Dad. It's Laura . . . '

Jud Blake focused his weakening eyes on the girl before him, and he cursed the sickness that was taking him from her. He gazed at the perfection of her heart shaped face; with its aristocratic high cheekbones and round generous mouth. He saw those wonderful amber eyes and the depth of love within them, and he marvelled at the thick auburn hair. Who on this earth would watch over her when he was gone? Not Ruth; no, not Ruth — who had never wanted her. God above, he cried in angry silence, is this your way, to punish the innocent?

'Dad?' Laura was deeply disturbed by those empty brown eyes staring at her with such intensity, and yet appearing not to see. 'Dad, is there anything I can fetch you? Shall I run for the doctor?' When he shook his head, she asked, 'Do you want me to fetch me Mam?'

This time he answered, 'No, lass,' and just for a moment Laura saw a certain fire in his eyes. Then he whispered, 'Come here, Laura,' and raised his arm, and she lay down beside him, a skip of happiness lightening her heart.

Oh, please let him get better, she pleaded to herself, let him get better. Yet even as she begged it of some unknown almighty power, Laura expected nothing, for she had already forced herself to come to terms with the knowledge that he *wouldn't* get better. Not now. And the tears that had built up inside her chest like a solid painful lump, rose to tumble from her eyes and to run quickly down her face, onto her father's hand.

Jud Blake mustered what little strength he had and pulling her towards him, he murmured, 'Lord bless you, Laura. You shouldn't be left to shoulder such a burden.' He stroked her hair gently, his quiet voice reaching out to comfort her. 'Shush your crying, little 'un.'

'Don't leave me, Dad, please don't die.' The plea came as a sob.

He didn't answer. Instead, he drew her close and for a while, father and daughter took solace in each other's arms.

Outside, a busy day was coming to a close and the cold February night was growing thick and dark. The familiar sounds of Penny Street threaded their way into the twilight of the tiny parlour; the clip-clop of Shire horses pulling their carts along the uneven cobbles; and the echo of hurrying feet over the flagstones. And Laura thought how unreal it all seemed.

'Laura, listen to me, lass . . . ' His voice broke away beneath the pain which racked him, and Laura sat up, her watchful eyes encouraging as he went on. 'You're some'at very special. I've allus known that, ever since the night your Mam birthed you,' his eyes grew bright from the memory, 'a strange, beautiful night it were. The moon lit the sky like it were magic. Your poor Mam 'ad a bad time, lass. That's why she's allus favoured Netti to you. That's a cruel thing, but I've never been able to alter it.' His eyes drew on her loveliness, seeking to find peace and comfort to soothe him. 'It saddens me that I'll never see you grow to a woman. I've allus loved you best of all, and one day, you mark my words, you'll tek this 'ere tired old world an' you'll mek it sing! 'Cause you're Laura Blake, my lass.' The tears he'd been holding back flowed unashamedly down the gaunt lines of his face, as he whispered, 'I don't mind dying, lass. It'll be a welcome release, but as God's my judge, it pains me most to leave you. Oh,' his voice petered away, then with new found strength he pleaded, 'don't let the warmth in you grow hard and bitter. Sometimes, when a body has to fight for survival, the best things inside get trampled; don't let that 'appen.' His voice grew faint and closing his eyes he sucked in breath with a rasping sound, then in a moment he looked at her again. 'Your poor tormented Mam'll be looking to you more an' more now. She can't 'elp it, she's not as strong as you. She's a leaner, an' there'll be times when you wish to God *you* 'ad somebody to lean on. Oh, you've a long lonely way afront o' you, lass. Life won't treat you easy, you've already learned that, an there'll be enemies, enemies . . .'

The passion of his outburst seemed to have drained him, and he leaned back onto the pillow, his eyes closed, his breathing laboured.

'Dad!' Laura's concern stirred him, and for a while he just gazed at her, his eyes filled with pride and the mask of death already grey on his face.

She could find no words to comfort him, and when he cried softly, 'I've no priest, no priest,' she soothed him lovingly as one might soothe a child. 'Ssh, we'll say the Lord's Prayer together.' Settling gently against him, she brushed a kiss over his tired eyes, gathered him into a tender embrace and began, 'Our Father, which art in Heaven, Hallowed by thy name . . .' Her small voice was strengthened by that of the dying man's but halfway through Laura found she was alone in her praying.

She gathered her father closer into her arms, hardly able to utter the words because of the tears flowing down her face into her mouth, and finished, 'For thine is the kingdom, the power and the glory, for ever and ever. Amen.'

Long after her father's frail body had grown cold in the loving strength of her arms, Laura stayed to hold him closer. The little parlour grew black as the night, and the smell of death shrouded the air; but she made no move. This was her father. And she loved him. Nothing can hurt him now, she told herself, nothing ever again can cause him pain. She was thankful that her father's suffering was over; but she knew instinctively that her own ordeal was just beginning.

Laura looked up to see Ruth Blake standing in the doorway, and she searched for something in her mother's face that might ease her awful pain. But there was no unspoken message of love or compassion. Her face was a blank stare, betraying no glimmer of emotion. Then she lowered her head and turned away quietly, closing the door behind her.

In the dim glow of candlelight, Laura stared at the spot where her mother had stood, and in a voice that was strong and firm, she declared, 'I'll help her, Dad. I'll look after me Mam and Netti, and after the birthing, I'll look after the babby too. I promise.'

31

Chapter Two

'What's to be done?' Ruth Blake stared hard at her daughter, Laura. Her voice was broken and trembling. The dark eyes, although heavy with sorrow and reddened by tears, were still strikingly beautiful. She continued to stare at Laura, her wild expression hardened into a glare of accusation. 'You! You and your dad forever whispering! Don't think I've not seen the two of you. Whispering about me, were you?' Her eyes glazed over as she seemed suddenly preoccupied with a new train of thought. 'Makes no difference now, we're all left to fend for ourselves.'

Laura hated seeing her mother like this, but whenever she had gone to comfort her, Ruth Blake had moved quickly away. The message was painfully clear to Laura. Her mother wanted nothing to do with her and for some reason that Laura couldn't fathom, it was she who was being blamed. And yet she still didn't know what she was being blamed for.

She spoke up now, her voice deliberately reassuring and belying the fact that she had no way of knowing whether things would be alright for her, Netti and her mother. The new baby would maybe take their minds off the unhappiness that now filled their little house, and should be looked forward to. 'We'll be alright, Mam,' she urged her mother towards the armchair, 'come and sit down. We've allus managed, and we'll manage now. Dad wouldn't want you crying and worrying. I'll look after us, honest. It'll be alright.' She was surprised and heartened by the fact that her mother had not shaken away the touch of her hand.

'Now then young Laura!' The thin wiry voice pierced the air, as the busy little figure of Lizzie Pendleton bustled towards them, her long dark skirt swishing smartly about wholesome ankles. Turning her hawkish features to indicate the small gatherings in the parlour, she said, 'Away an' see to these 'ere folks! Your Mam's in no fit state to attend them. It's *your* place and *your* duty, my girl, so off you get an' see to 'em. I'll tek care o' your Mam.' She pulled her mottled shawl tightly about her and fetched a dark scowl to rest on Laura's face. 'Go on then!' she ranted. 'Take yourself off!'

Laura didn't care for Lizzie Pendleton, and neither, she knew, did her mother. There had been bad blood between the two women for many years, but the cause of the feud was not common knowledge. Certainly Laura had no inkling of its making. But occasionally, like now, one or the other would make an effort to communicate.

Both women were obstinate and secretive; yet in their outlook they were as far apart as it was possible to be. Lizzie Pendleton, unlike the smart and fashionable Ruth Blake, had clung to tradition and had never deserted the long skirt and shawl of her ancestors. Some six years older than Ruth Blake, she had never married and was well known hereabouts for her quick temper and selfish ways.

Laura resented her taking charge of her mother, and when she spoke it was with a certain degree of rebuke. 'Mebbe me Mam wants *me* to see her upstairs.' Laura looked to her mother for support and confirmation, but none was forthcoming.

'Don't stand there gawping, lass!' Lizzie Pendleton shook her pointed head with its thin scraping of greying hair. 'Are you looking to aggravate me, young woman?' she demanded impatiently, 'You'll 'ave to wake your ideas up! You've a family looking to you now.'

'Well, it'll be nowt new to the lass, Lizzie Pendleton!' A well-endowed woman beamed at Laura. 'Laura 'ere's been the little breadwinner long enough now, I'd say. Can't see as 'ow she needs any lessons in that direction, an' it'll be no new experience if folks find a need to look up to 'er, now will it, eh?' She smiled kindly at Laura, who had recognized the woman as Tilly Shiner, a big-hearted and forthright character from Clayton Street, and she was thankful for the intervention.

'I've not minded,' Laura told her, 'and somebody's to fetch food to the table.'

'Oh, I know that, lass. Bless you, we all know how proud Jud was to have you for his daughter.' She smiled quietly. 'But you're on your own now.'

Tilly Shiner's last remark heralded a fresh outburst of loud sobbing from Ruth Blake. Her tormented cries rose above the general murmurs, and Lizzie Pendleton's tight face scraped a hostile glance over the offender. 'Tilly Shiner! I shoulda' thought you'd choose your remarks with a bit more care! Let the poor man's memory rest with 'im.' Turning her back with deliberate disapproval, she collected Ruth Blake from Laura's care. 'Go on, lass. I'll away upstairs with your Mam. She needs a bit o' quiet I'm thinking,' and casting a sharp raking glance at Tilly Shiner, she chided, 'Away from tactless remarks!' And in the privacy of her own thoughts, she added, 'An' where I might softly loosen her tongue as to who spawned the child in her belly. For I'll be hanged if it's Jud's.'

Laura looked at her mother as though searching for strength, perhaps for help. But there was no room in Ruth Blake's private grief; not even for her daughter. Laura marvelled that even in her grief and swathed completely in black, there was no more beautiful woman in this room.

Her careful dark eyes never left Ruth Blake's downcast face. But there was no intimate smile or knowing glance to make her feel as though she belonged. Her mother did not look up. Her gaze was vacant; her every thought back in the bleak church yard with her man, a man she had once loved so long ago, a man who had known her failings, a man who had been good to her; a man she had badly wronged. Even the swollen shape of the unborn child she carried seemed to diminish beneath the dreadful guilt which enveloped her.

Lizzie Pendleton guided the bent trembling figure across the parlour, towards the small slatted door which led immediately to a narrow flight of stairs.

The quiet murmur of voices filtered through Laura's thoughts, as she gazed around the parlour. There was a sadness in her that weighed heavy; but it wasn't a new experience. It seemed always to have been with her. Watching her dear father struggling to breathe and wasting in long, slow agony had brought a terrible kind of awakening to her young life. She hadn't minded leaving school early, in order to help support the family. She'd been glad to do so. She didn't even mind the long hard hours trudging that cart round the streets of Lancashire, until her feet were blistered and her heart sore.

She knew her duty, and she would never fail it. Her father had taught her well. But oh, what she would have given to have had things differently. Her thoughts were tinged with a measure of relief; Jud Blake's suffering at least was over. But somehow, even that thought brought small consolation.

Laura sighed, suddenly conscious of the long narrow sideboard set against the back parlour wall. Yesterday, it had borne her father's coffin. Today, it bowed beneath the many lardiecakes, baps and sweet baking, which the women had produced through a long lonely night, while she had kept vigil beside the thin wasted remains of her father.

In an effort to shut out the crowding memories, she studied the few remaining mourners that now stood about in small quiet groups. Her attention was captured by a dark haired young man, who returned her gaze with a boldness.

Pearce Griffin was some five years older than Laura, a good-looking fellow, with deep expressive eyes and an air of arrogance and blatant conceit. He was neither admirable nor reliable in character, being of devious and predatory nature. Yet for some reason she had never understood and that had often caused her some anxiety, Laura found him disturbingly attractive. His father, Parry Griffin, was an old enemy of Jud Blake's. His stepmother, Molly Griffin, was Ruth Blake's sister, but they shared no sisterly love. Her absence here today was conspicuous, for she was a loud and vulgar person whom it was impossible to ignore. Laura wondered at the reason for Parry Griffin and his son attending. She hardly believed it to be Parry Griffin's conscience that had brought him; yet she could see no other reason.

Pearce Griffin was moving towards her now, his stride determined, his manner confident, and at once she felt the colour growing hot in her face. She was angry at her inability to control the wave of excitement that quickened her heart the nearer he came. She made a strong conscious effort to draw her gaze from him, but there was a magnetism about his smile that held her fast.

Mesmerized, she followed his movements as he weaved his way around the mourners to get to her, and Laura thought begrudgingly that there could be no man as handsome as he. He wasn't unusually tall, but there was something very striking and commanding about the lithe easy way he moved. Like a lion, thought Laura, stalking his prey. His dark brown hair, worn longer than most men, was thick but silky, falling from a natural centre parting to half cover his ears and form a perfect frame for his even features.

When he had come to stand before Laura he said in a low voice, 'I'm sorry about your dad.' But Laura sensed the cold indifference in his voice, and she knew at once that he was *not* sorry. There was no compassion in those wicked dark brown eyes. They were fathomless and inviting, and Laura felt they could see right through her, to that most secret part. His brows were the most perfect that Laura had ever seen on a man, and the slight arch gave the impression that he was engaged in some private contemplation that amused him.

She offered no resistance as he reached out to cup his hand beneath her elbow, saying, 'I've been sent to collect you.' He gestured towards the far end of the room, where several faces were turned in Laura's direction. 'You shouldn't be left on your own right now.' He propelled her before him and Laura, although resenting the intimate touch of his arm around her waist, felt powerless to disengage herself. She wished that Mitch could have come today, but he was deep in the work that had made her Uncle Remmie's shop such a success. Mitch was steady and reliable, and every bit as handsome in his own way as this arrogant fellow. Why was it then she wondered, not for the first time, that she felt nothing special for Mitch?

'Oh, I'm not saying as Churchill didn't know 'is stuff! There's no denying 'e's got more titles than I've got teeth, but a good leader in wartime isn't allus as valuable when peace comes.'

'An' isn't the fact that we'd a'lost the bloody War without him to count in the man's favour at all?'

'Oh, aye! Aye! But that damned War near sucked this country dry, an' nigh on two years later, we're not free on it! No, my own thinking is that Atlee's the man to see us right.'

'Well, time'll tell. Aye, that it will.'

Laura neither knew nor cared about who was best at leading the country. Her thoughts were upstairs with her mother. She wanted to go up there and offer comfort, yet she knew it would not be welcomed.

Raising her eyes, Laura looked at the man who was speaking now. She never knew what to make of Big Joe Blessing. He had been a companion of her father's before the War, through it, and then afterwards, when he had been a constant visitor to his sickroom. Joe Blessing was a commanding figure, and many was the time that Laura had heard both her father and her mother refer to this fellow as 'a fine figure of a man, and a good friend'. Tall and proud, with a thick crop of healthy blond hair, a strong military bearing and attractive enough face, Joe Blessing towered above everybody in this little group.

The injuries he sustained during the Second World War were evident in the empty sleeve pinned across his chest, and in the slight limping gait when he walked. Looking at him now, Laura thought how ill at ease he seemed in the navy blue striped suit stretched tight across his muscular body. Strange, she contemplated, looking around the room, how most of these men here today had exchanged one kind of uniform for another. They were all dressed in dark suits of broad lapels and baggy trousers, with those hideous broad stripes and buttoned-up waistcoats. She'd heard Mitch say they were 'Demob suits', and all some of them had to show for serving their country. A storm of envy rose in her heart. Well, at least they were alive! Her father wasn't.

'Aye, that's Jud to a tee.' Remmie Thorpe was speaking now and Laura shifted her attention to him. He was a man of kindly countenance in his mid-forties, brother to Ruth, and a fond uncle to Laura and Netti. There was a gentleness about his face that had always drawn Laura to him. He winked cheekily and nodded his head towards her, saying, 'An' this 'ere lass is a chip off the old block.'

Remmie's wife, Katya, some twenty years his junior, stood beside him, a small clinging person with shifty eyes and a nervous disposition. Her china-delicate features and rolled halo of blond hair gave her the appearance of a pot doll. Dressed in a fitting two-piece of pure wool, with a jaunty narrow-brimmed hat adorning her head, she seemed too precious to be real. She was not one of Laura's favourites.

'Penny for your thoughts,' Pearce Griffin asked Laura.

'You'd best watch out for my lad.' Parry Griffin clasped his son's shoulder firmly and with a disrespectful guffaw of laughter which terminated in a cough, he told Laura, "'E's got a real taste for pretty things like you.' He turned to look into Pearce's laughing eyes and added quietly, 'But the lad's clever though. 'E intends to go places does this one.' He playfully shook his son, and added seriously, 'Oh aye! This lad's got a right sharp 'ead on 'is shoulders. An' that's what's needed if you're to get anywhere these days.'

Parry Griffin was in his late thirties, some five years younger than Joe Blessing, and although he stood almost level with Joe Blessing's shoulders, his bearing was of much less consequence. His shifty expression seemed to spread through his stocky body, to find outlet in constant fidgeting and shoulder-shrugging. Parry Griffin was his own worst enemy, and found little support when he'd chosen to set himself up in business against the well-liked Remmie Thorpe.

'It's a cruel world we live in, young Laura,' Joe Blessing was saying, and his sad eyes grew pained. 'Your Dad and me, we set off together, to fight in a war nobody really wanted. There's not a day or night goes by when I don't think on Dunkirk; crawling across blood-spattered and broken bodies, deafening guns and whining shells to drive a man crazy!' The awful memory showed deep in his eyes. 'What a soldier your Dad was! Brave as a lion and reckless as a twelve year old. Me, I was never so keen, but your Dad . . .' A small choking sound broke his words, as he sniffled hard and laughed out loud. 'Both on us inherited souvenirs from that God-forsaken war! Your Dad with his diseased lungs, and me left with a stump for an arm.' He made no attempt to conceal the tear that slipped from his eye to trickle down the strong lines of his face. 'But we walked away from that bloody hell! A lot o' good lads didn't. Me and your Dad, we've been friends ever since, right up to his last breath.'

Laura couldn't trust herself to speak at that moment; so she swallowed hard and smiled understandingly at the man whom she knew her father had always looked on as a true friend. Joe Blessing was guilty of nothing but kindness, but somehow she had never really taken to him, although she had always managed to hide that fact from Joe Blessing himself.

'Once Jud made a friend of you, he were allus a friend,' Parry Griffin shifted from one foot to the other as he gazed round the group, before resting his eyes on Joe Blessing's face, "course I didn't know Jud for the same length o' time *you* did, Joe, being that much younger an' all. But it were Jud as got me started tatting after the War. Found myself out of a job, not a penny nor a trade to me name, an' no ideas on 'ow to earn a living.' The easy smile shifted to Laura, 'Your Dad told me to go door-knocking. Get yourself out tatting, he told me, get yourself an old pram an' buy rubbish in. Do it up, then sell it out again! Just like *you* do now, Laura. It's a crying shame that your Dad were struck down. The two on us were just beginning to do alright an' all. Shame that you're having to start all over again. You know you're allus welcome to come an' work for me. What with your sharp brains an' my experience, we could turn over a tidy penny.' His voice was quietly persuasive.

'I do alright, thank you Mr Griffin.' although he had married her Aunt Molly, Laura couldn't bring herself to call him 'Uncle'; and as for working with him, it had been common knowledge that his relationship with her father hadn't been as honest as it should have been, and there were those who claimed that he'd never really forgiven Jud Blake for marrying Ruth. It was Ruth he'd always wanted, and marrying Molly, her sister, had been a poor consolation. But it was all speculation as far as Laura was concerned; she had no time for such gossip. She'd once confronted her father with it, and his denial had been enough for her to dismiss it. Laura continued, 'I earn enough to keep us, and that's all we need. Anyway, I work better on my own. But thanks for the offer, Mr Griffin.'

'I'd like a shilling for every time I've tried to tempt the lass to come an' work in *my* shop, Parry. But she'll 'ave none of it,' Remmie Thorpe wrapped a friendly arm round Laura's shoulders, 'and who can blame the lass? She prefers to be 'er own boss — that right?'

Laura nodded gratefully, but the sullenness in Parry Griffin's watching eyes made her feel uncomfortable. She wasn't surprised when he turned to attack Remmie's comments with bitterness. 'Well, I can't say as I blame 'er for refusing to work with *you*, Thorpe!'

Remmie's sharp response made everyone turn their attention to him. He was facing Parry Griffin; his strong features drawn up into a scowl. 'You're a wily bugger, Parry Griffin! An' that's a fact. This 'ere lass 'as got the folks o' Blackburn eating out of her hand! They trusted Jud Blake to treat them fair, an' they trust his lass, Laura, to do the same! There's not one o' Laura's customers as'd look happy on the lass coming to work for you. If you hadn't been so fond o' your gamblin', you wouldn't be in danger o' losin' your shop now; the very shop as Jud paved the way for!' The anger in his face was belied by the deliberate calm of his voice. 'Won't be long now I'm thinking, afore you're back on the streets again! But if you're lookin' to earn some ready brass, you'd be well advised to stay out of young Laura's patch.'

'Uncle Remmie . . .' Laura didn't want this, not with her father so fresh in mind; it was no secret that Remmie Thorpe had little time for Parry Griffin. 'I don't own the streets of Blackburn. Parry Griffin, Pearce or anybody else come to that, they've got as much right as I have, to tat for custom.'

'That's the truth of it!' Parry Griffin beckoned to his son Pearce to follow him out. 'If a thing's there, then it's there for the taking, eh? And if me or me lad 'ere see the need for taking, then *you'll* not stop us, Thorpe! No, I'll be damned if you will!'

Pearce turned to follow his father, and his parting words were meant for Laura; 'It's true my Dad's about to lose the shop.' Anger darkened his face as he told her quietly, 'But we won't be down for long. I'll see to that. I do hope though that you won't need to get hurt in the process.' A contented smile spread over his face as he moved away.

'By God! They're a devilish pair an' no mistake! Knife their own mother for a shilling, that they would.' Joe Blessing shook his head slowly.

'There's no call for that sort of talk, Mr Blessing.' Laura's heart was still too full of her father to tolerate such wrangling.

She looked up as Remmie Thorpe pulled her round to face him. 'There's no wonder you're well liked, Laura, lass. You've a sharp sense o' fairness an' honesty about you, an' it's to be admired.' His eyes narrowed and his voice took on a menacing tone which frightened her. 'But be warned by me that loves you like you were 'is own. Yon Pearce Griffin's tainted with 'is father's brush. He's a wrong un! You be on your guard, lass, or the buggers'll take the bread from your mouth.' He shook her firmly. 'D'you mark me?'

'I mark you, Uncle Remmie.' And she did. Because her instincts told her that Remmie's warning was the truth.

Chapter Three

'Get yourself off to school, Netti! You've less than five minutes afore the tram goes.' Laura pushed the protesting girl out of the front door, thrusting a package of jam-butties into her hand.

'Oh, Laura, let me stay home with you, please!' In these last three weeks Netti hadn't mentioned the death of her father. Laura had followed suit and avoided the subject. After all, there was nothing to be gained by causing Netti to remember. All the same, Laura couldn't help a sneaky feeling that Netti was missing her father. No matter, thought Laura now, if she finds the need to talk, I'm here. Tightening the falling slide in her sister's long fair hair, Laura told her firmly, 'No! You can't stay with me. Look, it's for sure *I* won't be doing any more learning.' For a second her dark eyes looked sad, but quickly brightening them with a smile, she said, So it's up to *you*, young 'un. Don't waste your schooling, Netti. Make something of yourself, for me, eh?'

'Is Mam gonna be alright, Laura? She were crying again last night. I'm allus frightened when Mam starts to cry.'

''Course Mam's going to be alright, you silly! The birthing's near that's all. Go on, off you get, and see 'as you come right home from school. I might need you quick, to run for Mabel Fletcher.'

She watched Netti out of sight, before returning to the parlour and the breakfast things. It didn't take long to clear the table. There were no fancy breakfasts in this house, nor anything else fancy come to that! She put the last spoon in the drawer, then looked around the scullery to satisfy herself that everything was clean and orderly. The grey flagstones were still shining wet, where she'd scrubbed them, and the makeshift cupboard was wiped and presentable.

Laura relaxed for a while in the deep black armchair that had been her father's. A warm smile melted the tiredness in her face, as she recalled the night she'd brought the chair home. It was broken and losing its stuffing, but between the two of them, they'd stripped it down, repaired and reassembled it in less than an evening. The heaviness returned to her heart. That had been over a year ago, before the illness had gained its terrible crippling hold.

She missed her father; oh, how she missed him. She hadn't realized just how much, until these last few days. It seemed as though it was only just beginning to dawn on her. He was gone for good now. She would never look at his dear face again, or hear that soft soothing voice that pleased her so.

Oh, she felt tired. Her mother's constant complaints and endless demands had wearied her well into the early hours. But she couldn't blame her mother. The birthing was very near, and the loss of her man played hard on Ruth Blake's emotions.

The summoning knock on the floor of her mother's bedroom scattered her thoughts. She fleetingly glimpsed the way things had been, and she recalled that in spite of their poverty, this little house had seen some happy times, secure in a man's love and pride for his family. Yes, there were things she could always remember and treasure. But they were things of the past, and it was the present and the future that was calling her now.

The muffled sound of the knocking-stick on the ceiling above became insistent, angry. Laura chided herself. Enough of all this maudling! What with her mother swollen like a pea-pod about to burst, and her a good two hours behind her carting, it was high time she got a move on.

'Where've you been? Takes you long enough to climb them stairs!' Ruth Blake levelled her accusing eyes at Laura. 'You can't be going off carting today! You've to stay an' watch me. D'ya hear me, Laura Blake? Somebody's to stay an' watch me. Me time's near. It's right near, I tell you!' Her voice trailed away in a rush of sobs, as she buried her tousled auburn head in her palms.

'Oh, Mam.' Her mother was right! The time *was* near; even *she* could tell that. But if she didn't go out carting today, there'd be no money to feed them, or pay the rent, let alone pay for the goat's milk her mother would need. 'I can't stay to watch you. But I've fixed it for Mabel Fletcher to visit you every now and then. I'll leave the back door on sneck, so if you need owt, just holler and she'll come a running.' She looked with concern at her mother's scowling face before bending to kiss her. She wasn't surprised when Ruth Blake resisted, drawing her head deeper into the pillow. Her affection towards her mother, rejected so often, seemed lately to have begun to wither. 'Don't fret, Mam. I'll do the carting in double quick time. It's going on ten o'clock now. I'll be back afore you know it. Mabel Fletcher's at the ready. She knows your time's near. She's got everything on hand.'

Ruth Blake emerged from the depths of her pillow. 'Go on then! Tek yourself off! That's all you care. Serve you right if I die up here, and the child along o' me!'

'You *know* I've to go carting, Mam!' There was nobody to scrape a bit o' money in, nobody but her, and if she didn't do the carting, they'd like as not all starve. But she mustn't get angry. It would only serve to make matters worse, and she could do without that! No, her Mam would just have to stop expecting her to be in two places at one and the same time so, collecting the pob-bowl and tea-mug, she said in a firm quiet voice, 'You've everything you want, Mam. Mabel Fletcher's coming round to get you a bite to eat later on, and she'll hear you well enough if you shout, or knock loudly with your stick. I'm leaving the scullery door open, it's only a stride from her back door. So behave yourself and I'll be back as quick as I can. I shoulda' been gone ages back, so I'm going now, Mam, alright?' She looked for a kind response in her mother's face, but there was none. The expression remained stiff, and disapproving, so Laura left the room, quietly closing the door behind her. Oh Mam, Mam, she thought impatiently, if only you'd talk to me proper.

She hurried down the stairs and made her way out of the back door to cross into the next yard.

Mabel Fletcher had chided Laura once before when she had stopped to knock on the back door, pointing out in no uncertain manner that, 'There's no closed doors 'ere, lass! An' I'll not 'ave you knockin' an' scrattin' at that door like you was a stranger!' It was something Laura had never forgotten, yet, pushing the back door open, she still felt the need to tap quietly as she entered the scullery.

Mabel Fletcher was a big spreading woman, with large smiling eyes and a broad happy face topped by a chaotic mess of steel grey hair. As always, she was surrounded by little folk, all tugging at her skirts and loudly moithering for this or that. When Mabel Fletcher caught sight of Laura, she emitted a piercing shriek that sent them scurrying in all directions to hide behind the furniture. All except the smallest, who scuttled beneath her skirt and out of sight. Yanking this one up into her arms, she laughed a low rumble, her ample cheeks pitting with deep dimples. And Laura laughed too as Mabel roared. 'Little sods! No wonder folks call me old bloody Mother 'Ubbard, eh?' She suddenly quietened and asked, 'Yer Mam's not started, 'as she?'

'No. Not yet, Mrs Fletcher,' and not till I get back, prayed Laura, 'but she's carrying on some'at awful about me leaving her. I *have* to go carting today! She knows that.'

'You go on lass!' Putting the child on the floor where it joined the others who were standing quietly now, she shook her head in exasperation, declaring loudly, 'A body'd think it were 'er first! I'd like a shillin' for every little 'un I've fotched into this 'ere world, I'll tell you, lass. But I've never known such a mard 'un as your mam!' Catching sight of the defensive look on Laura's face, she quickly added, 'I expect it's losin' 'er man. That's what it is, lass, can't get over it, eh?' She leaned towards Laura and said with kindly encouragement, 'You get gone. You've money to earn, an' you needn't fret, you've left yer Mam in good 'ands. I'll watch 'er like she were me own.'

'Thanks, Mrs Fletcher. I know you'll watch her.'

Returning to her own back yard, Laura loaded the split firewood bundles onto the cart. Taking stock of the dwindling pile, she made a mental note that she and Netti would have to collect more logs from the timber yard. And by the look of it, that axe needed sharpening.

She manoeuvered the lumbering wooden cart out onto the cobbled back-alley; then she settled herself between the long curved shafts, and took a firm grip with each hand. Trundling it behind her, she started out towards Preston-New Road, by way of Back Salford. Her Monday route was always the same;

45

up through Preston-New Road, then back towards Remmie Thorpe's shop, and a few shillings. Preston-New Road often brought good pickings. That was where the mill owners lived. Back Salford, narrow and cobbled, soon lay behind her, home for rats and filth of all descriptions, and frequented at night by homeless lovers and folks of dubious character. Ahead of her stretched the wide tree-lined expanse of Preston-New Road, where even the air seemed to taste fresher and the sky appeared much brighter.

There were only six houses on Laura's patch, all along one side and looking out over the grimy depths of Blackburn below. Set well back from the road, they boasted leaded patterned windows, and wide curved doorsteps decorated on either side by fearsome stone lions or dancing cherubs. Reached by long gravel drives, bordered left and right by green lawns and colourful flower-beds, they were grander than anything Laura had ever dreamed of.

Laura's first sight of these houses had stirred something in her that she hadn't even known existed. She craved for the day when she herself could live in such a house. The desire had started as a passing notion which she'd dismissed as fairy-tale nonsense, but then somehow, without her being aware of it, the notion had grown into an ambition, and then into a driving compulsion, the fierceness of which sometimes frightened her. Even though she couldn't begin to imagine how a poor no-good like herself might achieve such grandness, still it comforted her. It was something to dream about, a goal to believe in.

'Laura, I've been waiting for you. You're late this morning.' The tall grey-haired woman approached from the side gate, her fine brows drawn together in a frown. 'You nearly missed me, you know! I'm going to Manchester to do some shopping.' She beckoned Laura to follow her.

'I'm sorry, Mrs Enderson.' She dragged the cart as far as the gate, where she brought it to rest. Rubbing her hands together to restore feeling where the constant grip of the shafts had rendered them numb, she chased after the hurrying figure.

A few minutes later, she stood before the woman in the back of a small outer wash-house. The woman had delved into a deep wooden box to withdraw a green blouse which she held up for Laura to see. 'I knew you wouldn't take offence,' she said confidently, her sharp eyes taking stock of Laura's brown threadbare skirt and black wollen pullover, 'but you're such a pretty little thing, it does sadden me to see you in those same clothes all the time. There are other things in the box; a coat, frocks and I do believe you'll find a pair of smart brogue shoes in there as well. They're not mine. My clothes would probably hang loose on your dainty figure.' A spread of smug satisfaction gathered on the woman's features as she informed Laura in a grand voice, 'I went round a few of my friends. Of course, they wanted to know all about you, but when I explained about your poor dying father, and you left to fend for your family, well, they all contributed something.' She held the blouse against Laura, cocking her head to one side with a snort of satisfaction. 'It suits you. Yes, it suits you.' Ramming the blouse back into the box, she beckoned Laura to the other end of the wash-house. 'Look,' she pointed to what looked like a small wooden seat set against the wall, 'that's been standing there long enough now. You can take it. It's an old commode. I had thought to give it to the Old Gentle-woman's Home, but they've sent no one round for it, and I have no intention of *taking* it there, I can tell you!'

Laura had always thought Mrs Enderson to be a nice woman, a little bit swanky, but not as bad as the rest of the 'stuck-ups' who lived along Preston-New Road. Now though, she found herself close to tears. She hated that awful sickly green blouse, and the way Mrs Enderson had made her feel. Fancy asking her posh friends to give something! They owed her nothing, and she certainly didn't like feeling obliged to strangers who knew all of her business, while she knew nothing of theirs. No! She'd thank Mrs Enderson politely, and she would take the clothes. But they wouldn't find their way on to *her* back! She hadn't offered herself as a charity-case, not yet she hadn't and not ever, while the saying was hers.

She realized that for the very first time she was actually reckoning on working for Uncle Remmie. She'd always resisted *that* before. It wasn't that she found the idea of working at the shop unattractive. Oh no! She was fond of Uncle Remmie, and she'd always felt comfortable in his old shop. But if she were to take him up on his offer, she'd not have her independence any more. She valued her independence more than anybody could guess, and it was *that* she didn't want to give up.

'Thank you Mrs Enderson. It was right kind of your friends to think on me.'

'That's perfectly alright, Laura. We've got to dip in our pockets now and then, to help those less fortunate than ourselves.' She turned her back on Laura, calling out, 'Make sure you fasten the gate on your way out.'

For a while Laura just stood there, her lovely dark eyes sad as she gazed dreamily at the house and gardens. There was a stone ornament in the middle of the back lawn, shaped like a boy holding up a round table. From where she stood, half-hidden by that lovely tree whose branches scraped the grass, she was able to watch the birds as they grabbed at the food on the table. It made her feel happy and sad all at the same time. She looked back to the house and the lovely pink floral curtains at the kitchen window, then across to the flagged area and the numerous pots of flowers scattered about.

She couldn't look anymore. Acting like a silly fool! Fancy thinking *I* could ever live in a place like this! Not for the likes o' *me*, is this. Stop your dreaming Laura Blake; there's work to be done, and folks at home counting on you!

When she finally pulled her cart out of Preston-New Road she had very little to show. There had been no answer at three of the houses, and the other two had, 'Already given to a young man. Thought you weren't coming today, not like you to be late.' So apart from a hall table with one leg missing, and two leather-bound volumes of *Stately Homes of England*, the week looked set for a bad start. But she couldn't grumble. She *had* been late, and if Pearce Griffin had beaten her to it, then she'd just have to bear the losing, and get herself out on time of a morning.

Clayton Street might have been a million miles away from Preston-New Road. A narrow cobbled alley with tightly packed rows of thin grubby doors that opened straight out onto the pavement, it was noisy, dirty, swarming with people, but wonderfully welcoming. The women, all turbanned, laughing or talking, and nearly all pregnant, were busy white-stoning the steps, washing the windows, or watching young 'uns, who spent their days sitting on the kerbs with sugar butties; sailing matchstick boats down the gutters; and dropping loose stones into the stinking drains.

'Hey up!' Smiling Tilly Shiner was the first to spot Laura and her cumbersome cart. 'It's young Laura!'

'Tongue 'anging out for a brew, I expect.' The broad-faced Belle Strong waved a fat dimpled arm towards Laura. 'Get your arse into my kitchen, young 'un!' she shouted coarsely, her numerous chins waggling and bright round eyes laughing. 'Leave yon cart agin the kerb. They'll 'ave it filled in no time, lass!'

Laura was glad of the chance to free herself from the shaft. There was no pleasure to be found in dragging that cart along the cobbled back streets. Not that the odd articles she'd collected today were anything like a weighty load, but the wooden cart was heavy to pull after a while, tugging at her arms and stretching her back till she thought she couldn't walk another step. As she brought the cart to a halt outside Belle Strong's house, the women had already started bringing their contributions out to fill it.

'Good pair o' clogs 'ere, lass,' Tilly Shiner held out a pair of brown iron-clad clogs for Laura's inspection, 'the ol' fella, well, 'e 'int got no use for these 'ere. Don't wear clogs like they used to. Shame! But Remmie'll likely find a customer as can't afford no fancy shoes, eh?' She then produced a white enamel pot. 'Piss-pot 'ere an' all! 'Appen worth ha'penny to somebody. One thing's for sure, lass, it'll not do any good sittin' i' my back yard!' She pointed to the bundles of kindling wood lying in the cart. 'D'you reckon these 'ere bits is worth *two* bundles, eh?'

Laura smiled gratefully. ''Course they are!' These folks hadn't got much, but they always managed to sort out a few things that Remmie might see fit to take from her; though truth be told, she couldn't see him forking out good money for that pot. But she'd not offend Tilly's good nature by refusing it. Still, the old folks still swore by the use of clogs, and like as not they'd fetch two bob.

Following Belle Strong's instructions, and leaving the women to the cart, Laura made her way into the narrow parlour — a deal smaller than the one in No 9, Penny Street — but cosy and welcoming for all that.

'Folks 'ereabouts 'ave allus 'ad a soft spot for your dad, bless

49

'is 'eart an' may the good Lord welcome 'im! No, there's not one o' these lasses as 'int 'ad a kindly word from Jud Blake, when their menfolks 'adn't the work.' Belle gestured for Laura to sit at the table. 'Sup the tea while it's warm. I've 'ad that bloody kettle on and off sin' two hours back!' She slurped noisily at her own pint mug. 'Might 'a thought as you'd forgotten us,' a broad smile exposed the blackened teeth, 'but we know better, eh? Monday morning'd show a strange kind o' face without you an' yon cart.'

Laura had a particular soft spot for this little woman. There were no fancy airs or back-biting habits about Mitch's mother. Nor any about Mitch, she mused, and felt irritated that Remmie's assistant had infiltrated her thoughts.

Belle Strong was a familiar sight about the streets of Blackburn. Measuring less than five feet high and packed solid like a little round ball, she was surprisingly active and agile. Her age was not known, and when quizzed on it, she would simply reply, 'twixt fifty and sixty!'

There was something very pleasing about this busy woman, always wrapped in an oversize floral pinnie with huge pockets invariably bulging from the paraphernalia kept in them. Her features were well-padded and ever cheerful, and her brownish grey hair always rolled into a thin scraggy halo. She was a good neighbour and had shown herself to be a true friend.

'Netti was playing up this morning.' Laura sighed as thoughts of her young sister plagued her mind. 'Since Dad . . . died . . .' Even now, it hurt her to say that. 'She's got it into her head that she should go tatting with me, instead o' going to school, but she'll *not* come tatting! She's to make some'at of herself, Belle. Oh, I so much want Netti to do well at school. You know *I* liked school. I liked the learning and thinking. But I were never clever, not like Netti is. She'll not waste it either! I'll watch out for her and my Mam. She mustn't bother her head about *anything*!' It was a craving of Laura's, to see Netti high up in the world. There was nothing she wouldn't do to that end, and somewhere in the back of Laura's mind she believed that Netti's mark in the world would be in the field of music. Well *she* would help her. She would help her in every way she could, when times got better. And they would, they would!

Now, as she spoke to Belle, the conviction in her heart spilled out; 'Our Netti's to leave the worrying to *me*!'

The look of sorrow in the older woman's eyes was too fleeting for Laura to glimpse, but it showed in her quietened voice as she told the girl; 'The lass'll not let you down, Laura. She's a good little thing, an' Lord knows, she loves you. Your dad med a lot o' friends; well, they're *your* friends now lass, an' they'll see you right.' A tear sparkled in her eye as she clamped a chubby hand over Laura's. 'We 'int got much, but we'll allus watch out for them that's been good to us.' She slurped quietly on her tea, her eyes fixed thoughtfully on Laura's face as she churned something over in her mind. Then she spoke; 'Yon Pearce Griffin's been out on the streets this morning. 'E got a right roasting from these quarters, I can tell you! Offered folks money 'e did! Huh! A grand shop like them Griffins own, prime spot an' all. Well, they should wake their ideas up an' that's a fact. It's an easy road down'ill, but a slippery one back up, eh? Offering money indeed! That lad knows full well as any bits an' pieces kept down Clayton Street, are kept for Jud Blake's lass, an' there's no need to talk o' money! What scraps us folks sort out 'int worth but mealy coppers, 'e knows that well enough!' She set her chin hard into the bulge of her waggling throat. 'After tekkin' the shirt off yer' back, that's *'is* little game, lass, an' you'll do well to watch that one! Teks after 'is dad 'e does.'

Laura was grateful for the concern her dad's old friend was showing; but she felt it was unnecessary. Pearce Griffin's father got little from his shop, and it wasn't for her or anybody else to starve anybody out of earning a living. 'Blackburn's a big place, Belle,' she said reassuringly, 'there's streets that I've never seen, as might be glad of a tatter to clear their stuff away.'

'Aye lass, that might well be! But yon Pearce Griffin 'int concernin' 'imself wi' *them* streets! 'E's on *your* tail, following the streets as've allus been yours an' your dad's afore you.'

'But they were streets as my dad followed with Parry Griffin, and his son has just as much a right to take them up, as I have.'

'No, lass! The lad's father gave that right up, when 'e went off to open 'is shop.' A deep scowl hardened her face. 'Deserted

51

your dad 'e did! Used 'im, then deserted 'im! Travelling the right road now, though, eh? Gambling an' booze 'ave 'im by the bloody throat! No more than 'e deserves!'

'Haven't seen Mitch lately, Belle, he's alright isn't he?' Laura felt the need to change the subject. She knew there'd been something bad between her dad and Pearce's father. She'd always been wary of that, even though her dad would never talk about it. But she couldn't believe that Pearce would deliberately set out to ruin her, because of something that might have happened years ago. No, Pearce was maybe strongheaded and ambitious, but that wasn't enough for her to condemn him.

'Changing the subject, eh lass?' Belle Strong laughed out loud. 'Shrewd! That's a bit o' yer dad . . . 'e could be a sly one, could your dad. Alright then, lass. You've a right 'ead on your shoulders. 'Appen you'll best tek care o' your own affairs.' She struggled out of the chair, collected Laura's cup and ambled towards the scullery. 'Mitch's doing fine. Oh, 'e's a grand lad, is my Mitch. Remmie's allus telling me 'ow the lad is like 'is right arm in that shop.' She lowered her voice as she came back into the parlour.

'Our Mitch could show Pearce Griffin a thing or two. Right proud I am o' that lad.' A thought seemed to cross her mind suddenly. 'Won't be long now afore yer Mam's birthing, will it?'

'No.' It had been on her mind ever since she'd set out that morning, causing her to miss out Rosamund Street altogether, which would show when the cart was unloaded. 'I'm just on my way home now.' She rose and walked towards the door. 'Thanks for the tea Belle.'

'Hey up, lass!' The little woman scurried round the table, her long skirt caught up in two chubby fists. 'I nearly forgot! Yon Joe Blessin' fotched himself in 'ere this morning.' Her tight little mouth set itself into an irritated tut. 'Lord only knows what's got into that one. I expect it's sittin' at 'ome on 'is own all day, frettin' an' broodin'! I told 'im to get out an' find some'at to do! But 'e's not in 'is right-thinkin' mind at the minute, poor soul. That bloody war's got a lot to answer for, but I expect 'e'll pull 'imself together, eh?' Aware of Laura's hurry to get home, she told her quickly, ''E's asked you to call

52

in, lass. Got some'at as 'e reckons you could mek a few coppers on.' She pushed Laura towards the front door. 'Go on lass! Leave the cart 'ere. I'm sure it's nowt too big to carry.'

Laura had already passed Joe Blessing's house on the way in, expecting to see him on the doorstep as usual on a Monday morning, but when he wasn't, she'd put it down to the fact that she was late, and he'd probably made off towards the pub.

When he opened the door, Belle's reason for concern was very apparent. The sight of his unshaven face and scruffy appearance shocked Laura.

'Hello, Mr Blessing, Belle said you had some'at wanted taking away?' The bleary eyes focused to recognize her. 'Is that young Laura, eh? Come in, lass, come away in.'

She stepped into the front passageway, the immediate smell of stale booze and damp air filling her nostrils with such pungency that it almost made her vomit. 'I haven't much time, Mr Blessing. I've to get back to me Mam.'

'It's alright, lass,' Joe Blessing passed her, his thick heavy frame leading the way to the back parlour, 'It'll not tek a minute. I'd a' fotched it to Belle's 'ouse for you, but it needs a young 'un like you, to get it from the shelf where it's sat these long years.' He pulled a small table towards the wall, and pointed to a high shelf. 'Up there, lass. There's a big old meat plate, been there long as I can remember. 'Int doing anybody a bit o' good lyin' up there. Get it down, lass, an' tek it away. It'll 'appen fotch you a few coppers.' His voice trailed away, and Laura thought he was crying. 'Your dad, well, 'e were my best pal.' He coughed loudly, and the spittle from his lips sprayed the air, as he gripped her arm. 'Stand on this 'ere table, you'll reach it easy, then. But don't drop it, mind!'

Laura felt uncomfortable. Something didn't seem right; Joe Blessing had changed. She didn't want to admit it, not even to herself, but she felt frightened. But what was there to be frightened of? Joe Blessing had been a good friend to her dad. He was only concerned to help Jud's family.

She clambered up onto the table, then standing on tip-toes, she ran her hands along the shelf, until the hard edge of the plate touched her fingers. She was so engrossed in manoeuvering the plate from the shelf that the increasing pressure of Joe Blessing's grip on her ankles didn't alarm her straight away.

It was when she had the huge blue and white plate safely in her hands, and attempted to pass it down to him, that she found difficulty in moving. Bringing her startled glance down to his upturned face, she asked him in a deliberately calm voice, 'Take the plate, Mr Blessing, please.'

The bleary eyes had grown wide with a haunted look that made him appear almost demented, and the long broad fingers around her slim ankles now moved menacingly along her shapely calves. He didn't speak, but just looked up at her, his mouth open and eyes narrowing until she could hardly see them.

'Let me down,' she demanded, the nervousness within her now evident in the sharper tone of her voice. But still he made no move.

'Laura! Laura! Where are you, lass?' Belle Strong's agitated voice cut the brooding air, as they both turned to greet her rushing, breathless figure. 'Oh, lass! You've to tek yourself 'ome this very minute. Mabel Fletcher's lad's come lookin' for you. Your Mam's asking after you, she's in a bad way.'

Laura felt physically sick; although she couldn't be sure whether it was Belle's news, or the result of Joe Blessing's strange behaviour. She held the plate towards him. Without looking at her, he collected it and laid it on the table by her feet. Then, looking downwards, he shuffled to an armchair, and sank quietly into it.

'Come on, lass!' Belle reached out to help Laura down from the table. 'Leave the cart an' all. I'll get Mitch to tek it to Remmie's in the morning. You'll need to run, lass, run all the way! Things must be worrying, 'cause Mabel Fletcher don't often want to send for the doctor, but yer Mam'll 'ave none on it! She'll not 'ave no doctor! Keeps screamin' as it's *your* place to be there! Lord 'elp us! As if you 'int got more than enough on yer plate, you poor little bugger.'

Chapter Four

When Laura turned into Penny Street, her lungs felt near to bursting and deep inside her troubled heart, she was afraid. All the way home she tried without success to shut out the insistent thought that kept creeping into her mind. Suppose her Mam died? Oh God! She mustn't let such terrible thoughts frighten her. Her Mam was strong. She'd had two babbies already, so there was nothing to be afraid of. But supposing this time was different? Everybody knew her Mam hadn't been the same since losing her man. There'd been days on end, when she would lock herself up in the bedroom, not talking, unless it was to attack Laura with vicious abuse.

She'd never realized before just how long Penny Street was. The line of terraced houses and the military precision of the old gas lamps seemed to stretch endlessly before her, as she hurried along, half-running, half-walking to ease the sharpness of the jagged pain in her breast.

She was only vaguely aware of the odd groups of murmuring women, all of whom called out encouraging remarks, urging her that, 'she wasn't to worry', or 'she knew where to come if she wanted owt'. Her gratitude was automatic, but her thoughts were up in that bedroom, with her mother.

The front door was open, and as she pushed herself past the huddle of women whose joy it was to appoint themselves guardians, the unearthly scream which came from Ruth Blake's bedroom brought immediate silence.

Her mouth dry with fear, and all manner of thoughts bursting in her mind, Laura ran up the narrow flight of stairs. Pausing only long enough to compose herself so as not to alarm her mother, she pushed open the door.

The familiar portly figure of Mabel Fletcher was standing over the bed. She turned seriously towards Laura, gesturing for her to stay where she was. Then reaching down, she collected the blood-spattered child by its tiny legs and holding it upside down, she proceeded to slap its bare buttocks with unusual vigour.

Laura held her breath. The silence was ominous, broken only by the low sobbing of the woman in the bed. Something was wrong! Laura felt deeply disturbed; but she couldn't, wouldn't accept that the baby was dead. But it wasn't crying! Through tear-filled eyes, she looked at her mother's face. The sobbing had stopped, but the eyes seemed dead, wide open and staring vacantly.

Mabel Fletcher sharply slapped the baby's buttocks, time and time again, until Laura felt each blow as though it was being delivered to her own skin. Then, when sweat and tears were running down the homely woman's face, it happened. The baby cried. The small thin voice pierced the air, weak at first, then lustily as though protesting against the battering it had received.

'Lord love an' bless us.' Mabel Fletcher could say no more. Grasping the new-born babe to her heart, she opened her arm to enfold Laura, who had almost collapsed with relief at hearing that wonderful cry. The two of them almost crushed the child between them, their joy equally as enthusiastic as the child's loud anger.

'Right then, lass, I'd best get your Mam washed an' comfy.' She nodded towards the new-born babe. 'Like to wash this little mite, would you? It's another little lass.'

Laura didn't know how to thank this dear woman, who'd saved her new sister's life. There was nothing she could say just now. Her heart was too full of the wondrous thing she'd just witnessed. Wiping the tears from her eyes, she held out her arms, as Mabel Fletcher lifted the naked child towards her. It was only then she realized why her mother had screamed with such terror; and why Mabel Fletcher had looked at her with unspoken concern. The baby's right arm was hideously deformed. There was no forearm, and the tiny hand was fixed to the elbow at a peculiar angle, the minute fingers perfectly formed.

It was a terrible shock. She hurt inside; not for herself, but for this tiny little creature who was undeniably beautiful, and who had fought for its right to live in a cruel world.

'She's so lovely, isn't she?' The baby had stopped crying, and she bent to kiss its face. 'I can wash her,' she said quietly, her strong dark eyes smiling warmly, as she looked up at Mabel Fletcher.

A tide of admiration transformed the homely woman's features. 'If this little lass grows up to be even a patch on you, Laura Blake, then she'll cope well enough.' She sighed heavily. ''Appen your Mam's ready to 'ave a proper look at 'er new-born now, eh?'

Laura sensed the fear in Mabel Fletcher's voice. 'Let *me* show her,' she said. Then, taking a blanket from the cot, she wrapped it cosily around the baby, before approaching Ruth Blake, whose eyes were now following her every move. 'Mam,' she knew how much of a shock it must have been to her mother, who was never one to accept imperfection. 'Mam, look at her. She's beautiful, like you.' She sat on the edge of the bed and held the child out towards her mother. 'Do you want to hold her?' The ensuing scream startled her. She got to her feet to console the child, who had begun to cry fearfully.

'Take it away!' Ruth Blake dragged herself up in the bed, her eyes bulbous. 'A monster! If you give it to me, I'll kill it! D'you hear me? I'll kill it!' She then began murmuring quietly; occasionally raising her voice to ask why *she* was being punished, it wasn't just *her*! All the time, Laura was painfully conscious of her mother's insistent question, 'That Laura! Why weren't she here? Why?'

'Mam, it's alright, Mam.' Laura felt confused. Her mother was ill. She didn't mean what she'd said. She couldn't mean such a thing. Yet remembering the terrible look on her mother's face, she realized that just at the minute, she wasn't responsible. It was too soon. She needed time.

'Come away, lass.' Mabel Fletcher eased her from the bed. 'You go an' wash the little mite, then wrap it up warm an' lay it abed in yon cot.'

'She won't feed it, will she?' She was afraid. The baby mustn't be allowed to die! It mustn't! She'd heard about babies, babies with *two* good arms being smothered for the price of a penny death policy! 'I can earn enough to keep us all. I'll work a bigger area. I can do it.'

'Hey!' Mabel Fletcher shook her gently. 'Nobody's gonna let this child die, Laura Blake! D'you think I tired me'self out smackin' its arse, so we could let it die? No, lass,' she gazed down at the child held tightly in Laura's protective arms, 'I've never 'eld wi' such things! Seven kids I've 'ad, an' every last one's been cherished.' She weighed her heavy bosom in the palm of her hand. 'My young un's goin' on two now. It won't 'urt the lad none to come off the breast.' She winked at Laura. 'There's plenty in these 'ere tits to fill that little mite. Now, come on! Get the poor thing washed, while I see to yer Mam.'

Laura wrapped an arm round the podgy neck. 'I love you,' she said simply, brushing the fat dimpled cheeks with a kiss.

'Gorn, you soppy thing!' came the embarrassed response. But there was a warm smile on Mabel Feltcher's face as she turned towards the woman in the bed. 'Now you can stop yer rambling, Ruth Blake! You'll not be troubled wi' that child, 'cause there's a lass 'ere as makes you look downright shameful!'

Ruth Blake gave no response, then as Mabel Fletcher turned her back to drop the soiled sheeting into a bucket, she reached her arms up behind her and grasping the wooden struts along the bed-head, she silently hoisted herself up, her eyes fixed on Laura.

Besides the wooden framed bed, the only other furniture in the room was the deep bulky wardrobe of strong oak and the matching oblong dressing table, upon which Mabel Fletcher had placed a large enamel bowl, half-filled with warm soapy water. Next to this, a cotton towel was spread out, doubled under to make it softer, on which Laura was now placing the baby, keeping it well supported with one hand, while with the other she reached into the bowl to squeeze out the flannel.

As she looked up, her face filled with pride and looking for Mabel's approval, Laura saw her mother, and for a brief moment, she hardly recognized the staring eyes, alive with hatred, and the mouth pinched and spiteful.

Laura sensed something terrifying and evil, and she instinctively cradled the child to her protectively. All manner of thoughts churned about her mind. Was it the poor helpless babby that her mother hated so much? Or was it *her*? And if it was her, then why? All the pleasure that had shone in her face

58

quickly disappeared. She turned away, and when she had washed the baby and wrapped it up warm again, she returned it to Mabel Fletcher, then without a backward glance she hurried out of the room.

Chapter Five

'Mam doesn't love us any more, does she?' Netti looked with sad blue eyes at Laura, who caught her into a fast embrace.

'Tell me what you've been doing at school today, Netti.'

'She *doesn't*, does she?'

The question was insistent, and Laura knew she would have to try and dispel her sister's anxiety. Taking the girl by the shoulders, she set her at arms' length, not really sure what to say. Netti, in her childish innocence, had sensed what was no less than the truth. Ruth Blake *didn't* love them. During the three weeks since little Rosie's birth, she'd stayed in her bedroom, growing more withdrawn and morose by the day. She hadn't spoken a single word. There was never a thank you for being washed and fed; and what was more hurtful to Laura, her mother hadn't asked about little Rosie, not once. Laura was concerned that arrangements should be made with the priest for Rosie to be baptized, but her mother would not even discuss it. It preyed on Laura'a mind, and she'd decided that if it wasn't arranged soon, then *she* would take it into her own hands. And now, here was Netti, waiting to be satisfied that her own mother really did love her.

'Mam's ill, Netti.' but even *she* doubted the truth of that. A better description might be sulking. 'She's had a lot to put up with. She's missing our Dad, an' Rosie's birthing was hard. Mam'll be alright, Netti. She'll be alright.' Laura prayed every night that her Mam would get better, but as things were, it didn't seem likely. If only she would help herself! But she just lay up in that room, not caring whether it was day or night; and yet there were times when she'd look at Laura with bright wary eyes, as though she wanted to talk, to ask something. But when Laura spoke quietly to her, she'd suddenly look away, her mouth set tight and hard.

'I don't want to go to school anymore, Laura.' Netti stepped out of the tin bath, and waited patiently for Laura to towel her dry. 'I want to stay with you an' Rosie.'

Laura slipped the nightgown over her sister's long fair hair. She wanted to take the girl in her arms and reassure her. But that would only make matters worse. Right now, Netti needed a firm hand.

'You listen to me, young madam! You made me a promise, didn't you? You promised me that you'd work hard at school, so's I could be proud of you!'

'I *am* working hard, and I'm nearly top of the class!' Netti was justifiably indignant.

Laura smiled. It was just the reaction she'd wanted. 'Well there you are then! You see, some folks are good at one thing, and some folks are good at another. When I were at school, I was a right dunce.'

'You weren't! Mrs Tomlinson said you 'ad the makings of a . . . a scholar!'

Laura remembered Mrs Tomlinson. She was a good teacher, and when she found out that Laura was leaving to tat the streets, she caused such a fuss that in the end Laura had been glad to go. 'Well, poor old Mrs Tomlinson was never very hard to please. *You're* the scholar, Netti, an' I'm the tatter. I can't go back to school now, not ever. So if *you* don't learn, we'll *all* be ignorant, won't we, eh?' She was relieved to see the pouting expression giving way to understanding. She pointed to the pram in the corner of the parlour. 'I'm counting on you, and so is little Rosie. Just think, Netti, when she's able to talk, she'll be asking you all sorts o' questions. I won't be able to tell her, 'cause I won't know. But you will! Now then, that'll be grand, won't it, eh? You'll be able to tell her about all the kings and queens, and sums, and all sorts o' clever things. An' you'll be able to tell me an' all.'

'I can, I can, Laura!' The blue eyes lit up, and her voice became excited. 'Just today, we learnt all about multi . . . multi . . . clation, and making sums get bigger. I'll show you, Laura, let me show you, eh?'

Half an hour later, after suffering tens of multiplication sums and hearing all about King Harold, Laura left Netti fast asleep in bed.

Opening her mother's bedroom door, she walked quietly to her bedside.

'Mam, are you asleep?' Ruth Blake moved slightly, but gave no response. Laura collected the empty tea mug, and tiptoed out.

This was the time of the day she loved best. In about an hour's time, at ten o'clock, Mabel Fletcher would come round to give little Rosie her last feed. It was a wondrous thing to watch, and always made her feel humble. She knew she would never be able to thank Mabel enough.

She carried the small tin bath through to the scullery, where she opened the back door, and tipped the dirty water out into the yard. Then with the hard brush she swept the water into the grubby yard corners, swishing and brushing until she'd covered every single flagstone. When the water began to trickle away through the criss-cross of nicks, she hung the tin bath on the nail in the wall and went back inside.

With the washing-up done and the house quiet, she drew the deep armchair up to the fire-grate, and collected the sleeping baby from her pram. Holding the baby close to her breast, she settled into the chair, and gazed at her sister. So many times she'd looked into that tiny face, and each time she was surprised by its innocence and beauty. The hair wasn't fiery like her mother's, but gold and fine like silk. Her eyes were the same colour as all babies, but deep in the blueness there was a mottling of green, which made them especially beautiful.

Laura lifted the baby to her shoulder, savouring the velvety smoothness of the face which nuzzled against her. She couldn't find words to describe how much she loved little Rosie. Sometimes when she was out tatting, she'd think of her at home with Mabel Fletcher, and her heart would fill with such love that it hurt. Little Rosie was special. For some reason she still couldn't understand, the Lord had seen fit to mar such an innocent; but in every other way, He had blessed her with perfection and beauty. Laura had taken it on herself to give little Rosie all the love and care that her mother had denied her. From that very first day she'd loved this baby. And although she hadn't yet admitted it, something deep inside her could never forgive her mother for rejecting what was after all her very own flesh and blood.

The familiar tap on the door preceded the busy and capable figure of Mabel Fletcher. Striding towards Laura, she held her arms out. 'Marding 'er again, eh? You'll 'ave the poor little bugger spoiled rotten! I've telled you afore, one o' these fine nights, she'll start screaming an' 'ollering for a feed afore I'm 'ere! Then what'll you do, eh?'

'Sorry.' Laura gave up her place in the armchair, and watched as Mabel Fletcher manoeuvered herself into a comfortable position, before undoing her blouse to reveal an ample nipple, upon which little Rosie automatically fixed her searching mouth.

'Greedy little sod, that she is,' Mabel Fletcher laughed. 'Can't bear to be parted from this little 'un, can you, eh?' Her voice grew quiet, and she gestured for Laura to sit on the chair opposite. 'Mek a grand mother, you will. But listen to me, lass. It's well known as yon Pearce Griffin 'as an eye for you! Be careful, that's all I'm saying.' She looked at Laura with unusual directness. 'You've a liking for 'im too, 'aven't yer?'

Laura felt concerned. She knew what Mabel Fletcher was asking, and she couldn't deny it. 'I've never had cause *not* to like him.'

''Ey! You know right well what I mean, an' when all's said an' done, who could blame you? 'E's a fine looking lad, with a right sharp 'ead on 'is shoulders, but there's a lot o' Parry Griffin running through them veins. There's talk that young Pearce is a right one for the lasses! All I'm sayin' lass, is be careful. 'E'll 'ave yer drawers off soon as look at yer! Nay lass, what you want is somebody like young Mitchell Strong; now there's a grand steady lad, good-looking too!'

Laura began to think that folks seemed to know more about her than she did herself. 'I'm not looking to fix myself up with no lads, I don't know why folks need to keep stirring things up.'

'Aye, well, you're a right bonny lass, an' what with your dad gone an' yer Mam the way she is, folks like to think as Jud'd want 'em to watch out for 'is lovely lass.' She looked down to draw little Rosie from her breast, then she buttoned her blouse, and handed the child to Laura. 'Pat 'er gentle-like in the small of 'er back, mind to support 'er little 'ead!' She watched Laura for a while, then her voice quiet, she asked, 'Yon Lizzie

Pendleton 'asn't shown 'erself, as she?'

'No.' She didn't look up. Her attention was given to burping little Rosie. 'Haven't seen her since the funeral. Why?'

'Nowt, lass. Nowt to bother yourself over. But it might be as well if she stays away. Your Mam's not right fond on 'er, is she? An' that Lizzie Pendleton never 'as a kindly word to say for anybody!'

'What?' She thought she'd missed a part of the conversation.'You mean she's been spreading tales?'

Mabel Fletcher got to her feet. 'Oh no, nowt like that, lass. But it's as well she doesn't see yer Mam as she is. Now then, are yer in need of owt? Managing alright, are yer, lass?'

'Yes, we're fine thanks. I've fetched the rent square, an' the tatting's keeping us fed. I'm managing well enough.' She didn't want Mabel Fletcher to know about the rent-man's threat that the arrears had been bad enough to set them on the street. Squaring up had meant less food on the table, but they weren't starving.

'You're a grand 'un, Laura Blake! There's many a lass'd been long gone by now, lookin' after theirselves!' She shook her head slowly. 'It's a long road we all 'ave to tread, but you'll do alright I'm thinkin'. Aye, I reckon a lass wi' your spunk'll do alright.'

She stood for a while, taking pleasure from Laura's handling of the child, then she declared, 'Right! I'll be off to see to me own brood!' and with a cheeky wink, she was gone.

It was the following night, just as Mabel finished feeding Rosie and was about to leave, when Ruth Blake made her way down to the parlour. Laura had been running up and down stairs ever since coming home from her tatting, but not once had Ruth Blake given any inkling that she was thinking of leaving her bed. Laura had seen Netti off to sleep and was now engrossed in fetching up Rosie's wind.

Mabel Fletcher was talking. 'You're Mam ought to be out and about by now, seeing to young Netti at least.' She gazed sorrowfully at the child in Laura's arms, a great sigh lifting her swollen bosom. 'Then there's this poor little bugger. Lord knows, she'll 'ave a bigger cross than most, an' only you to 'elp 'er.'

64

'And me, Mabel. She'll have me.' Ruth Blake had entered the room so quietly that neither Laura nor Mabel Fletcher had been aware of her presence.

As they both turned towards the sound of her voice, she moved further into the room, her eyes sweeping the scene before her.

Laura was the first to recover from the shock of Ruth Blake's silent entrance. 'Oh, Mam.' She got quickly to her feet, the glad warmth she felt at her mother's appearance written into the welcoming smile that lit her face. She would have rushed to her mother's side, but something warned her against it. Perhaps it was the previous rejections that made her hesitate; or perhaps it was that strange piercing look that forbade sympathy and friendship. Her arms instinctively grew tighter about little Rosie's squirming body, as she gestured towards the chair. 'Sit here, Mam.' She dared not suggest that her mother should hold the child, the child that she had birthed in such violence just a few short weeks ago.

''Ere! Give the little 'un to me, Laura.' Mabel Fletcher's voice was unusually quiet, as she watched Ruth Blake settle in the chair. 'You go an' mek your Mam a fresh brew.' She reached out towards Laura, but was halted by the firm interruption of Ruth Blake's voice; 'I'll take the child.' She looked up, to meet Laura's eyes, as she held out her arms confidently.

'You want to hold little Rosie? Oh, Mam, she's so beautiful.' Laura felt close to tears as she wrapped Rosie into her mother's arms. But when she stepped back to gaze at mother and child together, a stab of disappointment spoiled the pleasure she felt. Her mother's expression showed no warmth or compassion, although she held the child firmly enough and looked at its tiny face with a degree of curiosity.

Somehow, Laura felt cheated. But for the moment, as she delighted in her mother's sudden appearance and desire to cradle the poor deformed creature she had so wickedly rejected, it was enough. There would be time later for them to get to know each other. At least, for the first time, her mother had brought herself to claim little Rosie; and for that, she could feel only gratitude.

'It's grand to see you out o' bed, an' cuddling yon little 'un.' Mabel Fletcher leaned towards Ruth Blake, a broad smile shaping her features. 'She's a right little darling.' Suddenly conscious of the fact that her encouraging words were falling on deaf ears, she straightened herself up, and not a little peeved, she told Laura, 'Well I'll be off then, lass.' Looking back at Ruth Blake, who remained in the same rigid position, she said, perhaps a little too loudly, 'I'll be round first thing in the morning, eh? Mek sure you've everything you need. Little Rosie'll want seeing to an' all.' She gestured for Laura to follow her into the scullery. 'Come an' mek your Mam a fresh brew, lass.'

Once in the scullery, she pulled Laura away from the parlour door, her voice lowered so as not to be overheard, 'Look, lass, if you need owt, owt at all, you're to send Netti for me! Don't matter what time it might be.' She glanced furtively towards the parlour. 'I'm not saying as you *will* need me, but you're not to put too much weight on your Mam 'aving come from 'er bed. She's not well. Oh, it's grand that she's tekking an interest, but you're not to forget 'ow poorly bad she's been. It's not some'at as a body gets over in a minute.' She shook her head as though talking to herself. 'Will you be alright? I'll stay an' see your Mam back to bed, if you want.'

'No thanks, that's alright.' She didn't want anything to separate little Rosie and her mother; not yet. She'd waited too long for it to happen, almost despairing that it ever would. Wrapping her arms around Mabel Fletcher's considerable waist, she hugged her gratefully. 'I'm so happy,' she told her, the tears bright in her soft dark eyes, 'she'll love her now, won't she? She'll not want to be parted from her, you wait and see.'

The thoughtful expression on Mabel's features squashed Laura's enthusiasm. But when the little woman caught hold of her hand to squeeze it affectionately, the conviction in her kindly voice helped to dismiss any qualms.

'You're right, lass! Your Mam's been through a fair share o' troubles, an' I dare say she'll mek fine fettle now. Lord knows we all want 'er to mend, if only for your sake. Anyroad, what I said still stands; if there's any need of me, you know where I am.' She gave Laura a reassuring cuddle. 'I'd best be away to me brood. Goodnight, lass.'

'Goodnight, and thank you.' She closed and bolted the door,

before making a fresh brew, a cup of which she took into her mother.

Ruth Blake didn't thank her, but she supped it with enthusiasm, her eyes taking in every tiny detail of little Rosie's features. She looked at Laura just once to tell her in a matter-of-fact voice, 'Not like us is she? I expect folks 'ave been quick to notice that, eh? Well, I thought it was time *I* took a proper look at her.'

'No, she's not like us, Mam,' Laura agreed, 'but she's so pretty. Me and Netti are real proud of her.' She couldn't help but notice that her mother had covered little Rosie's deformed arm with the shawl, and it looked as though she had it drawn tight so it couldn't be freed. It wasn't an observation she liked very much, but she knew she'd have to be patient, and give her mother the time she so obviously still needed. At least, the first step had been taken, and for that, she was more than thankful.

Lying in bed some time later, Laura thought about how her mother had recoiled from the suggestion that she might enjoy bathing little Rosie, and how while Laura tenderly bathed the tiny deformed creature, Ruth Blake had sat unnaturally upright in the chair, to stare at the two of them. After only a few moments, she had got to her feet, then without a word, she had hurried from the parlour.

Laura realized that she no longer knew her own mother; and even more disturbing was the strong feeling that Ruth Blake had extended her hatred of Laura to include little Rosie. The only hope that Laura could cling to was to lay the blame on the sequence of tragic events that had led up to her mother's illness. She desperately needed to convince herself that it was so, and that her mother's recovery *would* be complete in every respect; because she wanted, *needed* her mother back again.

She looked across to where little Rosie was sleeping in her cot, and her heart grew lighter. Just three weeks ago, Ruth Blake had violently rejected her new-born babby; yet tonight, she had held that same little creature in her arms. Surely, her heart *must* have been stirred with motherly feelings? Yes, Laura promised herself, her Mam *would* come to love little Rosie. How could she not?

These thoughts must have preyed on her sleeping mind, for when she woke the next morning, she hadn't rested well and she felt tired, almost irritable. Something had disturbed her in the dark hours; not enough to wake her, and yet she didn't feel it had been a dream.

Leaving the warmth of her bed, she reached out for the straight grey dress and brown woollen cardigan on the back of a nearby stand-chair. It was with a little stab of horror that she read the time on the small mantel-clock. Ten to six! If she didn't get a move on, there'd be no goats' milk left. Jacko was along the street by now, and probably all but sold out.

She heard the voices at the same time as she noticed with a rush of panic that little Rosie's cot was empty. 'There's no call for you to concern yourself, Mabel Fletcher!' Her mother's voice sounded unusually determined. 'It isn't that I'm not grateful, because you've done a lot for me,' the voice paused before going on in quieter tones, ''appen *more* than was called for. But I'd like to be left alone now! I think I know how best to deal with things.'

'Well, if you're sure?' Laura recognized the voice of Mabel Fletcher, and by the sharp pitch of her reply, she wasn't any too pleased. 'I dare say you *'ave* got a trickle in your breasts, but it'll tek more than a trickle to satisfy little Rosie.' She fell silent as though waiting for confirmation. But when none was forthcoming, she declared sullenly, 'Well if you're determined there's no need of me?'

'I am, and there isn't.' Laura couldn't remember her mother's voice ever having displayed such crisp authority. It didn't sit right; and it worried her. Although she hated to admit it, even to herself, she was more than a little jealous. She'd have to remember that little Rosie was her mother's child, not hers! Slipping her bare feet into the flat ankle-strap shoes, she called Netti, who assured her she was out of bed, then she quickly made her way downstairs.

Normally, first thing in the morning, she'd spend a few minutes cuddling little Rosie. But she had to catch Jacko. It was enough to see her mother cradling the child in her arms. There was time enough for her to have a cuddle when she'd fetched the goats' milk.

'Hello, Mam.' She leaned forward and would have accompanied the greeting with a kiss, but she retreated at the stern accusing expression on her mother's face. 'You're not so keen to leave your bed of a morning, are you? Half the night this child was crying. I dare say it was Mabel Fletcher's milk. She's not the cleanest of women!' Her eyes smouldered. 'Screaming half the night, an' you ignoring her. Snoring like a dying pig!'

'Are you sure, Mam?' She didn't want it to seem that she was calling her mother a liar, but she would have heard. Little Rosie only had to turn over in her cot, and she'd be by her side. If she'd been screaming, it would most certainly have woken her. She could never have slept through that! How had her mother come into the bedroom and taken little Rosie, without her knowing about it; especially if, as her mother claimed, little Rosie was screaming? She felt confused, and angry. But the accusing look on her mother's face and the fact that there was no milk, urged her to leave things be.

'I'd best get after Jacko.' She grabbed the half-gallon churn and the coppers from the sideboard. Then with a surge of warmth she turned to the woman, whose narrowed eyes still glowered at her. 'It's nice to see you out of your bed, Mam. I'll see to little Rosie when I get back, eh?'

Jacko hadn't gone. His horse and cart was down the bottom end of Penny Street, and judging by the queue of folk waiting, he still had a drop of milk; although looking at the depth he had to sink his ladle, she thought she'd be lucky if there was any left for her.

Jacko was a mountain of a man, whose jutting craggy features were half hidden beneath a forest of ginger hair that hung over his ears and fell into a great sprouting moustache, which then joined forces with the profusion of his beard, to form an impenetrable fortress.

'Hurry thisel' up, young Blake!' he shouted as she approached, 'thar late this morning!'

The women in the queue turned to greet her and a bevy of voices joined chorus; ''Ello, lass.' 'Mam an' babby keeping well, eh?' 'Overslept did you? Easy done is that.'

Laura smiled and returned their greetings. Strange, she mused, how things can seem the same yet be so different. But these folk here hadn't changed had they? No. It were only her Mam that had changed.

'Woa up there!' Jacko calmed the horse, who appeared to be doing a tap dance.

Now it was Laura's turn for the milk, and she held up her churn. But as she did so, a scampering cat startled the horse, who took off in such a hurry that not only did Laura's churn end up clattering on the cobbles, but so too did Jacko, his ladle and a number of empty churns that rolled away along the road, to the tune of Jacko's cursing. As for Laura, who daren't let loose the laughter bubbling inside her for fear of retribution from the mighty Jacko, well, *her* main concern was that she should get the milk she came for.

In a minute, the whole street was in uproar, as folks came out to investigate the pandemonium. With the many willing hands, it didn't take long to restore order; although the same couldn't be said for Jacko's temper as he threatened the inattentive horse, 'I'm buggered if I'll not tek thi' to the knacker's yard! Be a sight better off I would, an' that's a fact. Is this the way tha repays me for not following old Trench's example, is it, eh? Got 'issel' one o' them nice new motorized milk-carts, 'as Trench! An' it don't give 'im no bother at all.' He heaved a mighty sigh and gave the horse a playful thump that was more forgiving than spiteful. 'Fancy runnin' away fro' a bloody cat!'

As Laura made her way back to the house, the incident seemed to have had a remarkable effect on her. With the four-pennorth of milk swishing and splashing in her can, she felt a little happier. Things were never as bad as they seemed. She'd just woken up in a strange mood, that was all.

But her lightheartedness was quickly dispersed, when Netti came running down the passage to meet her. 'Mam was here when I came down! She wouldn't let me cuddle Rosie.'

'I expect she was feeding her.' The tightly drawn mouth and trembling chin told Laura that Netti was close to tears. 'She'll probably let you cuddle her before you go to school.' She followed the pouting girl back into the parlour.

'She won't.' Netti threw herself into a chair. 'She *won't* let me cuddle little Rosie, 'cause she's gone back to bed, an' she's taken our babby with her!'

'She'll be down in a minute or two, Netti.' Laura's head was throbbing now.

'She shouted at me!' The quivering mouth suddenly relaxed to emit a rush of sobs. 'She says we've to stay away from her,

70

you an' all!' the wide blue eyes filled with tears, which spilled out over her lashes as she looked up at Laura. 'An' she smacked me hard!'

Now that Netti's face was turned up towards her, Laura could see the bright red finger-marks just beneath the cheekbone, and there was a faint nail-scratch across her nose. 'Oh Netti, I'm sorry.' She caught the sobbing girl up in her arms. 'It's my fault! I should have waited till you'd come down, only I was afeared there'd be no milk.' She didn't know how to deal with this. What had her mother been thinking of? Netti was a good girl, quiet and helpful. She always held Rosie for a little while before going off to school. She'd come to look forward to it, and she was so careful. 'Look,' she held Netti at arm's length, 'you go an' get yourself washed, an' I'll make your pobs especially milky, eh? Honest, Netti, Mam didn't mean to hurt you. I should have told her that I always let you sit an' hold little Rosie for a while. You see, she didn't know, an' I expect she thought you were too young.'

'She *did* know! 'Cause I told her you allus let me hold the babby, an' she said *you* weren't fit either,' Netti looked away, 'she called you some right bad names.' Her lips set in a hard determined line, then looking at Laura with a challenging expression, she said quietly, 'I hate her! I don't want her for my Mam. I only want you!'

'No, no, you mustn't say things like that.' She was beginning to feel out of her depth. She'd never seen Netti like this before. 'Tell you what! How would you like to miss school, an' stay with me? Just for today mind!' She didn't want Mrs Tomlinson to start asking questions about that nasty weal on Netti's face. 'I'll give you a note tomorrow, to say you were poorly.'

'Yes, yes, Laura! I want to stay with you. I don't want to go to school.'

'Only for today! You're not to ask again. Promise?'

'Can I ride in the cart?'

'I'm not going tatting today. I'm helping at Uncle Remmie's shop. He's off to a posh sale at Chorley Manor.'

'Well, I can serve the customers, eh?'

'No, you can't do that, you're too little. But you can dust the books an' look at the pictures.'

71

She kissed the tear-stained face. 'Now go an' splash some cold water on your face, an' get your pobs. I'm going to see Mam.'

'You're not to! She'll smack you an' all if you don't do as she says.' Netti looked really frightened.

'Go on.' Laura pushed her gently towards the scullery door. 'We've to be at the shop by eight o'clock.'

Half-an-hour later, after seeing to Netti's breakfast, Laura climbed the stairs and she began to wish her mother hadn't got out of her sick-bed at all. Then her heart flooded with shame and she prayed silently for forgiveness.

Outside her mother's bedroom door she paused, not sure what she might say, or whether she even ought to be there after what Netti had said about her mother's claim that she wasn't fit. Fit to do what? To look after little Rosie? Mind the house? Fetch the food to the table and see the rent was paid? She'd been fit enough to do all those things since her dad had been taken. So what was she not fit to do? And smacking Netti like that had been spiteful and uncalled for! She *had* to say something, and yet she didn't want to spoil her mother's interest in little Rosie. She and Netti could wait for their share of affection. It was little Rosie that really mattered.

She took a deep breath. Time was wasting. Yes! She *would* go in. But what would she say? What if she tried the door and it was locked against her?

'Who's that? Who's at the door?' Ruth Blake's voice scattered her thoughts.

'It's me, Laura. Can I come in?' The long pause made her feel sick.

'If you want!' The tone was surly, but oddly submissive.

She opened the door and edged her way in. She didn't expect to find her mother fully dressed and looking as though she might be getting ready to go out. The hair that less than an hour ago had hung dull and lifeless, was twisted up into a fancy coil, and the black dress she wore clung to her slim figure, accentuating its youthful lines. When she turned to look at Laura, her eyes seemed more alive than they had been for many a long week.

'Are you going out, Mam?' Maybe she intended to take little Rosie out in her pram. 'Do you feel well enough to go out?' She didn't think her mother should be going out so soon after leaving her sick-bed. But if she felt well enough, that would be grand, and it would do little Rosie good too.

'I might. They won't talk about me to my face! Only behind my back!'

Laura sat gently on the bed, to gaze at little Rosie's sleeping face. She didn't make any response to her mother's peculiar remark as she didn't rightly understand it. 'You think she's lovely, don't you, Mam?' She realized that she didn't really know whether her mother thought her child lovely or not. 'You *do*, don't you?'

All of a sudden, her mother slid on the bed to face her, a strange expression shaping her features. 'That day when they fetched you, when I was birthing,' she looked quickly at little Rosie, then looked away again, 'her. What were you doing in Joe Blessing's house, eh? That Fletcher woman told me, I kept asking for you, asking and asking, and when the lad came back, 'e said Belle Strong had gone to fetch you from Joe Blessing's house!'

'Joe Blessing's house?' She'd all but forgotten. Then it came back to her; the way he'd grabbed her ankles and stared at her. She'd been frightened, and now her mother was making her remember.

'Yes! Don't try denying it.' Ruth Blake's eyes narrowed and the painted mouth stretched into a sneer. 'I don't miss much. And I'm watching you. So keep away from that Joe Blessing! D'you hear? Keep away!'

Laura could feel the hot blush creeping up her neck and face. Her mother couldn't know how he'd frightened her! No; but she might know something about Joe Blessing, and was trying to warn her. But there was no need. 'I won't go in his house again,' she said decisively.

'Good, you'd better not.'

'Mam,' she thought it a good time to mention it, 'Mabel Fletcher's been right good.'

'I know that!' Ruth Blake moved from the bed. 'I don't want to talk about Mabel Fletcher. Get yourself off to work.'

Now she was sorry she'd brought it up, because her mother had withdrawn from her; just like she'd done before. Well, it *was* time she was going. Little Rosie stirred contentedly as she leaned over to kiss her. Looking at her mother again, she realized there was little point in trying further conversation, and there was the washing-up and cleaning to be done yet. 'I'll see you when I get home then, Mam.' There was no acknowledgement. Then just as she was about to close the door, she heard her mother call, 'Tell the lass I'm sorry I slapped her.'

Netti wasn't impressed with the apology, and when Laura asked her to go up and see her mother, she hurried out of the front door and went on ahead, almost running down Penny Street.

Laura closed the door and followed her, a slight frown creasing her forehead. She hated this rift between Netti and her mother. But in a way, she couldn't really blame her sister. She'd probably react in the same way if she'd had *her* face marked, just for asking to cuddle little Rosie. Things had been hard these last few years, and she couldn't remember the last time she'd really laughed, at least not like she used to before her dad had to take to his bed. But she hadn't minded too much; there were always things to do, and folks to talk to. She'd never felt unhappy, not like she did now. Funny that; all this time, she'd been praying that her mother would get well and take an interest in little Rosie; and now that her prayers seemed to have been answered, she felt really miserable. It was daft really, and time she learned to be thankful!

'Laura,' Netti stopped at the end of Penny Street, 'which way are we going?' She pointed down Spindlers Passage. 'Can we go that way?'

'What d'you want to go that way for?' She wasn't too keen on the idea. Spindlers Passage was a narrow back alley, closed on either side by high back-yard walls and steep cobbled banks that ran down to a stinking centre gulley. A lot of the houses backing onto the alley were vacated ready for demolition, and the gaps where the back-yard gates had been now led into mountains of rubble. The many cavernous gaps beneath and between the rubble often served as homes for old tramps and runaways. But it was the quickest way to town and Uncle Remmie's shop, and it *was* broad daylight.

'Alright, Netti, but you wait for me! I don't want you running off in front.' As she drew alongside Netti, she caught her firmly by the hand. 'You're *never* to come down here on your own, and don't you forget!'

The alley was quiet. She wasn't really surprised though; it was a night-time place. She wrinkled her nose in disgust — there was always a strange smell in these narrow alleyways; sort of sweet and rotten.

'Pooh!' Netti squashed her hand deeper into Laura's. 'Stinks like it's bad!'

'Well, it were *you* as wanted to come!' She had to smile at her sister's little face tightly twisted with revulsion.

With the smile still on her face, she glanced absent-mindedly into the open yard of a bombed house. A man had his back to them, and from his splay-legged stance and directed concentration, it was obvious that he was peeing over the bricks. Then just as they drew level, he turned towards them. With a rush of horror and total surprise, she recognized the man. It was Parry Griffin, Pearce's father. Grateful that Netti hadn't seen him, Laura hurried her steps, pushing the girl along past the yard.

'Will Uncle Remmie let me polish the wooden things?' Netti obviously had her mind on other matters.

'I'll ask him, eh?' Laura didn't want to launch into a busy conversation just now. She still hadn't got over the shock of seeing Parry Griffin like that. She'd heard talk about how he'd sunk low from the drinking, and how there was real danger of him losing the shop. It was said too, that out of pig-headedness, he was smothering Pearce's efforts to retrieve their old customers, who had quickly turned to Remmie.

Laura found it difficult to picture the smart confident Parry Griffin as a loser. She never liked to see a body brought down like that; even if he *had* been guilty of cheating her father some years back. Well, she didn't know the truth of *that*, but they do say the Lord always takes vengeance. And yet, she couldn't help but feel sorry, especially for Pearce and Auntie Molly. Still, Pearce was clever. He had a good business head. Everybody admitted that, even though they had little else good to say about him. He'd see his family right; hadn't he said as much himself, at her father's funeral?

'Look, Netti pulled on Laura's hand, 'look at him!'

The man was obviously drunk. Whether it was a hangover from the night before, or a fresh dousing of booze, she couldn't tell. But it was a sorry fact that he couldn't put one foot before the other. His flat cap was askew on one side of his head, while the uncovered side sprouted rampant wisps of hair that looked as though they'd never seen a comb. His long demob coat had slithered down his narrow sloping shoulders, and the belt of his trousers dangled against his leg.

'Just walk quickly, Netti,' she gripped the trusting hand tighter and edged the girl over to the far wall, 'don't stop, an' don't look at him! Just keep walking.'

When the man heard them coming he looked up, half-smiled, then proceeded towards them in an ungainly fashion. ''Ey! What we got 'ere, eh?' His bleary eyes lit up and the hanging mouth transformed itself into a broad grin. 'Two little angels.' When he saw Laura's serious face, he grew quiet for a second, then hurrying to keep after them, he said sorrowfully, 'Threw me out she did! The bugger threw me out. My bloody 'ouse an' all! I should'a kicked 'er sodding arse, eh?' He was tumbling and falling about in his efforts to keep up with them. 'Said I were nowt but trouble! I'm a soldier, I am, a bloody soldier! Kicked me out, said I were drunk. It's *'er* as is trouble!' All of a sudden, he started to laugh. Then as if the effort was too much, he fell into a doorway, and began to sing. 'Pack up your troubles in your old kit bag an' smile, smile, smile. While you've a lucifer to light your fag, smile boys, that's the style . . .'

Laura thought it must be the relief she'd felt not being attacked, because she burst into laughter at his singing. And as she and Netti hurried away, they could still hear the words of his song.

'Does that man live there?' Netti was still straining her neck to keep him in sight.

'Sounds like he don't live anywhere! Been kicked out, he reckons. Nearly there,' she said, her cheery voice reflecting her lightened spirits, as they passed the tightly packed rows of millworkers' houses. The women were already out on the street, white-stoning the doorsteps. Turbanned heads nodded in friendly greeting as they passed, and toddlers settled themselves on the kerbing, to share their jam butties with the many dogs who wandered the streets hereabouts.

A left turn at the bottom of Union Street brought them out

into the cobbled square, which led off to the huge open area where the weekend markets were held. Across the square towards the three brass balls high up over Fella's Pawn place, along the row of tumbledown shops, and they arrived at Lord Street, and Uncle Remmie's pride and joy.

The shop had stood strong for a hundred years; its advancing age boldly displayed on the wooden plaque fixed to the top of the door-frame. It was hand-carved in rapidly fading numbers depicting the year 1847.

Its great age was increasingly evident in many ways; the gentle sag of the brown-tiled roof and the tell-tale bulge of the brickwork, which jutted out above the bay window. The stone step from the pavement into the shop had sunk beneath the level of the floor and regular customers carefully stepped over it. The rear of the shop backed on to Blackburn's busiest Market Square, a high brick wall dividing the two. The old shop consisted of the yard, a back store-room, and the crammed quarters of the front shop with its deep bay-window. The three rooms upstairs had been converted by Remmie, into self-contained and comfortable living accommodation.

Eighteen months before the shop had been broken into and several valuable framed prints had been stolen. Usually anything of value was taken home by Remmie, and carted back to the shop each morning; but on this particular occasion, he'd been out buying, and Mitchell had been left to lock up. But on Mitchell Strong's sixteenth birthday, over a year ago, he had proudly taken possession of the newly appointed living quarters over the shop, and since then there had been no attempt made by anyone to break in.

The arrangement suited one and all; Remmie Blake because he valued Mitchell's dedication and realized that while the shop was being lived in, it obviously served as a very effective deterrent to prospective thieves; and Mitchell because it gave him the responsibility and independence he so highly treasured. Belle and Tupper Strong were content with Mitchell's enthusiasm for the arrangement, claiming that, 'The lad looks after issel' at 'ome so there'll be nowt spoiling!'

These two loveable old rascals had found young Mitchell as a 'tied up bundle o' skin an' bone'. They had collected the cold little mite from the pub doorstep where they'd all but tripped over him, after rowdily celebrating Tupper's forty-fifth birthday. As there was no indication of the lad's age, they'd hummed and hawed and discussed it over many a pint pot, before deciding that it was unlikely a mother would abandon her child after months of loving it and growing close to its needs, so finally the baby's name was declared to be Mitchell, and his age to be 'as near four months as didn't matter!' Later on, as the baby grew into a young boy, and the boy displayed a healthy claim to approaching manhood, his considerable strength and size suggested that they may have under-calculated his age; but it was of no real consequence and certainly didn't warrant a fuss.

Over the years, nobody ever stepped forward to lay claim to the boy, so Belle and Tupper brought him up as their own, saying little if nothing about the circumstances, yet never hiding the facts from the boy himself. He had grown to love and respect the old couple, and never once did he entertain notions of his rightful parents; they had left him on the doorstep of a pub, and that was all he needed to know.

Mitchell had enjoyed his share of girl admirers; but that was before Laura. He had never met anyone so beautiful and forthright and for him, there had never been anyone else to fill his fanciful dreams in quite the same way as she did.

'Uncle Remmie's got lots of special things in the window, Laura!' Netti released herself from Laura's hand to run and squash her nose against one of the bullions. 'Look! Look Laura, a big doll!'

'Don't wipe your snotty nose all over the glass, Netti!' It warmed her heart to see the girl's excitement. That miserable business this morning didn't seem to have sunk too deep, thank goodness. But then Netti was only a real young 'un, and things were soon forgotten. But *she* wouldn't forget! Things had somehow altered between her mother and herself.

She thought of little Rosie, and the warmth it brought showed in her shining brown eyes and sounded in her voice, as she called, 'Come on then, Netti, let's away in, and see what us duties are, eh?'

As she hurried Netti into the shop and turned to close the door behind them, Laura instinctively looked through the window to where Parry Griffin's lock-up occupied a prime corner position, straddling King William Street and a good section of the market-square. With twice the frontage and more than double the floor space of Remmie's shop, Laura had never really understood why it didn't have at least twice the number of customers. It was a pitiful fact, but that shop had never reached its full potential, and now, judging by the flaking paintwork on the wooden window frames and the rotting front door, it wasn't likely to do so.

The sound of the bell dropper as it hit against the top of the door echoed the rising happiness in her heart. Things would get better. Little Rosie would bring them all together again. Her Mam had *three* folks to love her now, and a new babby needed its own Mam; she realized that. Maybe she *had* felt some jealousy, but she knew better now and she'd be glad to tell her Mam so when she got home today.

'That me favourite lass?' Uncle Remmie's voice preceded his appearance from the back store-room. 'Thought it were a bit early for customers.' His kindly brown eyes alighted on Netti. 'Well I'm beggared! 'Ello young 'un, what's to do wi' school today then, eh?' He held his arms out to greet her. 'Thought they could manage wi'out you today, did you? Well, your Uncle Remmie's glad o' your company, lass.' He kissed her firmly, then holding her hand, he looked meaningfully at Laura. 'So long as it's not to be a regular 'abit, eh? Can't 'ave a clever lass like you throwin' away your schooling.'

Laura shook her head quietly, gesturing for him not to take the matter any further. The least said, soonest mended, to her way of thinking. 'Did you manage to sell that green blouse and the other things?'

'I did that, lass. Old Madge Arkwright took the lot, needed 'em an all! Got 'erself a right little army, she 'as; an' big as a barge for another!' He laughed. 'They'll often go short on things o' the world, but they'll not go short on love, not with old Madge.'

Laura was eager to get started, 'What do you want us to do then, Uncle Remmie?'

'Well, I'm leaving the shop to you and Mitch,' he looked down on the attentive Netti, 'an' this 'ere lass, eh? There's a lot o' shifting to be done, 'cause I fotched a load in yesterday. It's all to be stripped down, scrubbed and made ready for mending. Mitch knows what to do, lass. If you can mind the shop, no doubt the lad'll tek care o' the rest.' He looked beyond Laura, to the slim fair-haired figure passing the shop window and making for the door. 'Hey up! It's Katya. She's coming to Chorley Manor wi' me. A day out'll do 'er good.'

Katya entered the shop and Laura thought how elegant she looked in the fitting brown calf-length coat, with its deep revered collar and swirling hem. Over the crook of her arm, she held a shiny brown leather handbag, and on her head, with just the slightest suggestion of an angle, was a brown wide-brimmed hat, from which jutted a long waving feather of irridescent colours.

Remmie smiled at his wife. 'I'm ready, love, just putting Laura right.' Placing an encouraging arm around Laura's shoulders, he pulled her close, and Laura thought she detected a pained expression on Katya's face as he said, 'She's a grand little lass, my Laura. Mitch an' 'er between 'em, well, they'll tek right good care o' things while I'm gone.'

'Hello Auntie Katya.' Laura always felt uncomfortable beneath Katya Thorpe's ice-blue cold eyes. She couldn't rid herself of the feeling that this delicate pretty woman disliked her intensely; and yet this impression had never been conveyed by an unkind word or gesture.

'Good morning, Laura.' She turned to Remmie, and her voice softened to a caress. 'Will you collect me from Stacey's? I must get a packet of Cephos powders.' She brushed a long dainty black-gloved hand over her forehead. 'I've got the most awful headache.'

'O' course I will, love. The van's all ready out in the yard. I'll be right be'ind you.'

'Would you like me to run down to Stacey's?' Laura asked politely, suddenly feeling sorry for Uncle Remmie, who was so obviously besotted with his helpless little wife.

'No, thank you. It's only round the corner.' She waved a dismissive hand. 'Don't keep me waiting, will you Remmie love?' Then, with quiet mouse-like movements she left.

'Poor lass, never been blessed wi' good 'ealth.' His eyes took on a soft distant look. 'Seventeen she was when we married. Loveliest creature for miles.' A gentle laugh marbled his voice as he looked at Laura. 'But I've a feeling it might be an altogether different tale since the lass afront o' me started blossoming. Katya could 'ave 'ad any fella she fancied, but she chose me. Oh aye, I've a lot to be grateful to Lizzie Pendleton for. If she hadn't 'a taken Katya as a babby when her own folks died, well, 'appen I'd 'a never met 'er.' Sadness crept into his voice, 'Pity your Mam an' Lizzie never got on. Pulls me two ways, one being my sister an' all.'

'Mr Thorpe . . .' The voice was youthful, yet strong and decisive. Mitchell Strong entered the shop from the yard. 'I've swept the van out. She's ready when you are.' Catching sight of Laura, he leaned against the door jamb, his strong lithe frame relaxed and capable. Surveying her with his intense green eyes, he flicked the tumbling fair hair from his forehead. 'Nice to see you, Laura.'

'Hello, Mitch.' She liked him a lot, and she wasn't unaware of folks' speculation hereabouts. It seemed to be expected that she and Mitch would wed when the time was right. A fleeting glimpse of Pearce Griffin passed through her thoughts and with it came sharp irritation. Folks always seemed too quick to take on too much of other people's business! She wasn't fifteen for another few months, and getting wed did not figure in her thinking, not yet, and definitely not to a man of somebody else's choosing.

'If you'll just tell me what I'm to do' Laura's voice was quiet and encouraging as she met Mitch's gaze, 'you can leave me an' Netti to it if you like. We'll not want to keep you from your own work.'

Mitch straightened his shoulders and adopted a defensive stance. His pleasure at seeing Laura now hardened into contempt. It had always been a characteristic of Mitchell Strong, that he was at his most handsome when riled. And now, his mouth set stern like chiselled rock, he told her, 'I don't need *you* to remind me of my work, Laura Blake, an' I'll thank you to remember that!'

''Ey!' Uncle Remmie's twinkling brown eyes turned to Netti's upturned face. 'Rowing already they are! Like they've been married for years.' He gathered Netti into his arms and took her to the window, where he put her down to the floor. 'Bet you'd like that doll, eh?'

'Oh, Uncle Remmie, she's beautiful!' It was the one she'd

noticed through the window.

'Right then . . . on two conditions. One, you'll need to give it a name.' He reached into the window to collect the doll, which he put into Netti's outstretched arms. 'And two, keep an eye on these two 'ere, he gestured to Mitch and Laura, 'way they've started, they could end up fighting afore the day's out.' He laughed out loud. 'I'd best be off, or Katya likely as not'll be ready to fight wi' me, eh?' After issuing a quick round of instructions, he was gone.

The following silence made Laura feel uncomfortable. Netti had settled herself into a corner, where she proceeded to undress the large pot doll, talking to it in quiet happy tones, and obviously content to slip into a little world of her own. Laura shifted uneasily, acutely aware of Mitch's handsome green eyes searching her face.

'Laura.' He was standing close to her now. She could smell his sweat, and her heart grew quick within her. He reached his broad capable hands up to grip her shoulders. 'What's wrong? Aren't you glad to see me, Laura?' His quiet voice stirred some deep strange emotion, which seemed to excite and frighten her all at the same time.

Looking up she found herself resenting his confidence; yet at the same time, she was surprised by the intensity of other unfamiliar feelings.

He repeated his question. 'You *are* glad to see me, aren't you?' Her hesitance seemed to inflame him, as he suddenly released her to mutter in a low angry accusation, 'Sorry I'm not Pearce Griffin!' His features hardened, as he told her, 'There's a new batch o' furniture in the back to be made ready, and this lot here to be polished. I've the yard to clear, an' the back store-room to clean out. I'll get on with that. In between serving customers, I'd be glad if you could give 'and to the other jobs!' Without waiting for an acknowledgement, he stormed out through the back door.

Laura stood for a moment, her anxious dark eyes staring after him. Her emotions were all stirred up. She toyed with the idea of going after him. But what good would that do? Mitch was right. Although she'd liked the feel of his hands on her and the nearness of his manliness, she *had* thought of Pearce Griffin.

Taking a deep breath, she looked about her. Well! There was plenty of work to be done, and standing about wouldn't make it any the less. While she was still debating where to start first, the shop door rang open, and the first customer settled her decision.

'D'you have a small display cabinet?' The woman looked to be from the better part of town. Dressed in a smart two-piece topped by a beady-eyed fox fur, she looked able to pay well for her indulgences. 'I've got a few small ornaments I want to keep safe, so it'll need to have a glass front. Oh, and do you deliver?'

Uncle Remmie found his way back to the shop just before half-past two. He'd bought some pictures and a couple of china figures. 'Paid the earth for them!' he moaned. 'If I'd stayed any longer we'd all a' been outta work!'

Laura thought he'd bought well. She didn't care much for the china figures herself, but there was always a ready market for such items. 'But the pictures are lovely,' she told him, filled with enthusiasm at the beautiful old engravings; one of a cherub, the other portraying lovers talking by a blossom tree.

'Knew you'd like 'em,' he smiled appreciatively, 'sharp little 'ead you've got, an' that's a fact.' He looked at her closely. 'Tired are you, lass?'

'Only a bit, but the furniture's all ready for you to start on it.' The broken night's sleep was beginning to tell.

'Get your coat on, lass. I'll run you 'ome in the van.' He waved her protests away. 'We've to tek your cart back anyroad, an' there's that cabinet to deliver, bless you. Netti can bide 'ere a while, wi' Mitch. I'll fotch 'er on later. You've worked 'ard, lass. Get yourself off an' see to your Mam an' that little babby o' yourn.'

She had to admit that little Rosie had been on her mind all morning, and it might be a good idea if she could talk with her Mam before Netti was brought back. 'Thanks, Uncle Remmie, if you really don't mind.'

He pushed two half-crowns into her hand. 'Mind! You've been a godsend today. I only wish you'd mek your mind up to coming for good.'

She just smiled patiently. He knew she wouldn't make it a permanent arrangement. She liked the shop well enough, but

83

the cart had been her Dad's. It was hers now, and she liked the freedom of being in charge of herself. She reached up to kiss him gratefully. 'I love you,' she said simply, 'and I know you're only trying to help.'

Uncle Remmie took himself off to the van, while she went through to the back store where Mitch and Netti were busy waxing some renovated furniture. Netti was pleased to be staying a while longer; but Mitch had little to say. Laura felt responsible for his quiet attitude. She wanted to apologize, to tell him how much she'd liked him being close to her. But the thought of actually saying those things made her face burn. No, it was best left alone.

Within half an hour, Uncle Remmie had delivered the cabinet and they were on their way to Penny Street. As she'd suspected, the woman had come from the Cherry Tree area. Judging by the grand house and the description she prised from Uncle Remmie of the inside of the house, the fortunate woman didn't want for anything. Laura didn't like the little squirm of envy that wriggled into her thoughts and so she closed her mind to it.

As the van turned into Penny Street, she became instinctively aware that something was wrong. Her fears were confirmed as they drove nearer to the house.

A number of women were clustered about the door in busy little groups, serious expressions on their faces. The sight of a black car, and a tall ambulance with open rear doors, struck fear into her heart.

'Quick! Stop, Uncle Remmie, let me out!'

'Keep the door shut till I stop!'

The quiet strength in his voice seemed to convey a little calm to her, yet she wasn't altogether unaware of his own well-disguised anxiety. As Uncle Remmie drew up behind the black official-looking car, Laura sprang from the van, to push her way through the sombre women who were milling about the door issuing warnings; 'Don't go inside, lass,' 'Let your Uncle Remmie see to it.'

She tried to push the awful meaning of their words from her agitated mind. Something terrible had happened; she was sure of that. As she ran down the passageway towards the parlour door, she was vaguely aware of Uncle Remmie in pursuit.

84

The little parlour seemed crowded, although at first glance, she could see only two people; a burly constable, whose helmet was wedged securely beneath his arm, leaving him free to scribble into a small note-book; and a thin bespectacled man in the uniform of an ambulance driver. He was talking quietly into the constable's ear.

As she moved further into the parlour, nervous and afraid of what she might find, Laura's heart grew cold at the scene before her. In the far end of the parlour were three women. Mabel Fletcher, whose reddened eyes and stained face showed she had been crying, sank onto the stand-chair and proceeded to sniffle loudly, her hands covering her face. A small well-dressed woman of official appearance eased Ruth Blake from the sofa to guide her towards the passage door, her voice emitting low reassuring sounds to the silent bent figure.

Then the terrible truth of what had happened here burst into her mind, as she gazed at the small bundle secure in the stranger's arms. The corner of the shawl that covered little Rosie's face had slipped away. The tiny familiar features were still and quiet, tinged an odd shade of grey.

Later, Laura had no clear recollection of what happened next. She could only remember crying out in terrible anguish. Then her mother's wild crazy eyes as she surged forward, tearing at her face, her hair, accusing her daughter of such dreadful things that Laura knew would always be in her memory, to torment and haunt her. Things that must have preyed on her mother's mind since the day of the birthing, and which she had nursed in her fevered thoughts until they'd eaten into her sanity; of how Laura had not been there when she needed her most; of how Jud and Laura whispered together, plotted against her; and how on that terrible night when Laura was born, the night had been as day, and the moon so bright and big it threatened to fall on them. She was a witch! She'd been the curse on them; and it was *her* who'd kept the deformed creature alive, when everybody knew it would have been better off left to die!

It was some time later, when the house was quiet and Uncle Remmie had bathed the scars left by her mother's tearing nails, that Laura began to remember. The remembering became too

85

much to bear, and the sobbing broke the pain within her.

'Go on, lass,' Uncle Remmie's soothing voice reached into her tired mind, 'you cry as much as you need to. It's all over now.' He lifted her head, raising the cup of tea Mabel Fletcher had brought from the scullery. ''Ere lass. Sip it gentle like. Tek your time.'

Sipping the warm liquid, her senses grew sharper, more able to recall the awful events. Little Rosie was dead. But she still didn't know how, or why, and what had made her mother attack her. Her questions remained unanswered.

'I'm afeared your Mam's lost 'er right mind, lass,' Uncle Remmie said. 'I can't say what med 'er come after you like that, but you've done nowt wrong. Nowt! An' you rest on that, lass. There's not a single soul as doesn't feel for you. You've done more than anybody else in the same place would 'a done, an' you've never set a foot wrong. No, lass. I'm proud o' you. Your Mam was going down'ill long afore little Rosie's birthing. It was just, well, when a body's sick in the mind, nobody ever rightly knows which way it'll go. She meant nowt in them awful things she said to you, lass; 'cause your poor Mam, my poor sister, well, she didn't know what she was saying. You just think on that, an' you'll come to no 'arm.'

'Little Rosie?' She had to know. What her mother had said to her was something she'd have to live with, but what about poor little Rosie?

'Seems like it were an accident.' Uncle Remmie looked at the anxious Mabel Fletcher before levelling his comforting eyes on Laura's distressed face. 'Some'at as couldn't be 'elped. Some babbies choke in their sleep an' nobody knows why. There's many a 'ealthy young 'un goes the very same way.' The tears grew bright in his eyes as he caught her to him, 'You'll do well to forget it, lass. Little Rosie's gone, an' 'appen it's for the best. Yer Mam'll be looked after. Think on little Netti lass, an' yourself. You've to promise you'll try an' forget it, eh?' Placing a gentle finger under her chin, he lifted Laura's tear-stained face to meet his gaze, 'Promise?'

Laura couldn't bring herself to speak, but the nod she gave seemed to satisfy him, as Uncle Remmie sighed deeply, then visibly relaxed. Yet in his head there was a stirring of memories — haunting visions which carried him back over the years to his own mother, and Laura's grandmother. He recalled the day which had never left his mind — the day his and Ruth's mam herself had been taken away in much the same manner as Ruth had been led off just now. That demented look on Ruth's face, had also been on their mam's when she had attacked Ruth — just as Ruth had attacked *her* daughter, Laura. After all these years, history had cruelly repeated itself. Remmie could hear the doctor's words just as clearly as if the man was standing beside him now; 'Mental derangement,' he had said, 'a condition often hereditary.' Later it had been confirmed that their mam was suffering from a peculiar form of mental disturbance which gave delusions of persecution and a fixation of inexplicable hatred often directed towards a close, loved one, and for no apparent reason. It was a condition suspected to be hereditary, although there was no real evidence of this yet. Only time itself would tell, they said.

Remmie betrayed none of the black feelings coursing through him now. But there was no escaping the awful truth of what had happened here. And poor unsuspecting Laura had been cruelly caught up in it. His heart went out to Ruth. But more than that, he felt great compassion for the bewildered girl before him. He prayed she would be strong enough to bear the frustration and heartache which he knew must follow. And which to a certain degree her father Jud had borne. For it was he who had been instrumental in securing his mother-in-law's 'safe' custody in an institution. And although Ruth at the time had recognized it was for her mother's own good, there had crept into her heart a crippling hatred of her husband which intensified with the death of her mother and the deterioration of her weak-willed father, who not long after had followed Ruth's mother to her grave. In all these years, Ruth had never really forgiven Jud.

Chapter Six

The white-frocked woman gestured for Laura to follow her, then she led the way through the big double doors and into the long narrow corridor that smelled of disinfectant. About half-way down the seemingly endless corridor, the woman stopped by a polished wooden-slatted bench. 'You sit there.' She offered a stiff grimace for a smile, and her voice was sharp and frosty. 'I'll see what I can do.' She watched Laura sit down, before striding off down the corridor, the stiff hem of her frock rustling against her legs.

Laura sat on the hard wooden bench, and looked about her with wide sad eyes. She gazed at the green distempered walls and many plain brown doors placed at regular intervals. It was a depressing experience, no less miserable than the two previous occasions she'd been here.

She so much wanted to talk to her mother, to say how in spite of everything she missed her, and hoped she'd soon be well enough to come home. There were things she hadn't been able to understand; things that stalked her sleep and preyed on her waking thoughts. The house seemed empty with little Rosie gone and her mother not there making demands on her time. She sighed, a deep weary sigh that settled quietly on the undisturbed air. Today was her fifteenth birthday, but she had told nobody. She didn't see any need to. Her birthday wasn't important, not to her, not to anybody else. She'd always made a little cake and stirred up a fuss on Netti's birthday, but that was different. Netti's birthday mattered.

Perhaps today her mother might be glad to see her, to talk to her. Yet somehow, Laura doubted that. What was so different about today? Oh, she'd set out with the eager belief that today she wouldn't be turned away. She'd taken extra trouble to look nice — brushed her wild hair into some sort of order and dressed in her best grey dress and smart black jacket. But it seemed that her mother was still refusing to see her, or anybody else; and according to the kindly well-meaning doctor who'd assured Uncle Remmie that his sister was not aware of her own actions, the mention of her daughter Laura had caused Ruth Blake to lapse into a violent tantrum.

Laura's wandering thoughts were stopped by the reappearance of the white-frocked woman. Judging by the stern expression on her face it was obvious to the anxious Laura that her visit had not been successful this time either.

'Dr Harper would like a word before you leave,' she waited for Laura to get to her feet, 'this way, please.'

Laura nodded and once again followed the woman deeper into the building. In spite of the fact that she'd half-expected not to see her mother, she felt close to tears. For the first time she felt angry, and the little core of bitterness she had tried so hard to suppress rose in her heart to smother her gentler feelings. What had she ever done to drive her mother away from her? It was hard to accept that her own mother had turned away in hatred. It was true that six weeks ago, on that dreadful day of little Rosie's death, she'd found it hard to find any love or forgiveness in her heart; but she hadn't understood. She *still* didn't understand even now. But she wanted her mother's love, not her hatred; and she wanted to tell her how she'd come to realize that little Rosie dying hadn't been anybody's fault.

Dr Harper meant well. His words were soft, gentle even. But the meaning behind them was clear and firm. 'It would be best, Laura, if you didn't come here again, not for a while at least. We'll keep in touch with your Uncle Remmie. No doubt he'll let you know about your mother's progress.' He paused. 'I'm sorry. She's very ill, and these things do take time.'

So that was it. She'd been warned off, until Uncle Remmie thought the time was right for her to come here again, to plead to see the mother who had rejected her. Well, she wouldn't! She'd learn to do without a mother who didn't want her! She had Netti to look after, and she'd do that without anybody's help.

All the way home on the tram, Laura inwardly gave vent to the bitterness within her. But once inside the house, she remembered what her father had said; 'Don't let the warmth in you become hard and bitter . . . sometimes when a body fights for survival, it can happen.' She thought of his dear suffering face, and oh how she missed him, would *always* miss him.

She ventured softly into the front parlour where his unused bed and the things he had collected were; the chiming clock she'd mended and waxed to a brilliant shine, that lovely bronze sculpture of an eagle in flight. They were still there, standing where they had always been, close to his bed where he could see them.

'Oh, Dad! Dad.' She threw herself across the narrow bed, her arms enfolding his pillow, and the tears she'd held back ran down her unhappy face to soften her heart and ease the pain within her.

By the time Netti arrived home from school, the front parlour door was firmly closed and the table in the back parlour was laid for two. In the centre of the table was a plate filled with freshly baked baps, there was a brown stone jar containing plum jam, and a wedge of marge on a saucer.

While Netti was tucking into the lovingly prepared food, Laura brightly chatted to her of this and that, never once mentioning her visit to the Sanatorium that afternoon.

Later, when the table had been cleared and the pots washed and put away, they sat around the big old table, and Laura helped Netti with her sums.

'You're good at sums, aren't you, Laura? Mrs Tomlinson told me that today. She said you were a bright one.'

'I never were!' Laura herself had been told that countless times by Mrs Tomlinson, but she didn't want Netti to dwell on it too much. It might give her ideas that what Laura threw away, then so could she! And that would never do.

'Right, are you sure you know how to do these dividing sums now?' She pointed at the book, which Netti promptly closed.

''Course I can! I can *now*.' She leant forward on the table to rest her head in her hands, looking for all the world like a little old woman. 'You know, Laura, that Mrs Tomlinson's nice enough, but she's no good at telling me these sums. Not like you are.' Her thoughts suddenly elsewhere, she looked straight into Laura's face. 'Bet you don't know what *else* I did today,' she prodded Laura, 'go on! Guess.'

90

Laura did guess, several times and all unsuccessfully. And when Netti could stand it no longer, she blurted out, 'I played Miss Fordyke's piano! I played it, Laura. I played it *proper*, and everybody in the assembly clapped me.'

Laura was at once intrigued. '*Proper?* How could you play it *proper*, Netti?' She knew from Netti's chatter before, that Miss Fordyke, the headmistress at the school, had taken it upon herself to start giving music lessons, but she hadn't been aware that Netti had achieved such status as being able to play a piano *proper*. Well, it was a good thing! Yes, a good thing if it showed up a special talent in her Netti.

Right up until bedtime Netti was full of nothing else but how she played that piano proper. Her bright chatter instilled a feeling of love and contentment in Laura, and long after the child had gone to sleep, Laura lay awake, thankful that she had Netti. She'd make it her business to go and have a chat with Miss Fordyke.

During the following few days, however, there was no time to visit the school. The normal carting round wasn't fetching enough money to pay for rent and food, coal and light, and generally keep things going. Laura had been forced to extend the round, but even then it hadn't improved matters much. Her loyal friends in places like Clayton Street still tried to do her proud, but other folks had taken to selling their bits and pieces directly to the shops, where they were worth a few more pence.

Laura had come home today disillusioned and bone-weary, and while she set about getting Netti's tea her mind was searching for a way to improve her takings. In fact, it had crossed her mind more than once to take out that Family Allowance book that had lain untouched since her Mam had been taken. But her instincts had said no. The orders in that book were made out for ten shillings; that was five shillings for Netti and five shillings for little Rosie. Ten shillings was a fortune to her right now, and, oh, what she could have done with it. But Mabel Fletcher had given her cause for concern, when she'd warned that the authorities would be sending for that book, now that circumstances had changed. Well, they hadn't sent for it so far, and taking it to have little Rosie's name removed, might stir up a nasty kettle of fish. No.

91

However badly off they were, she'd best leave it be.

Laura had been in only twenty minutes when the knock came on the door. It was a determined unfamiliar knock, which caused her to hurry to the door, a fearful urgency knotting her stomach.

'Laura, is it?' The woman was inclined to plumpness, her cheeks already rounded beneath the bright wary eyes. But she had a kindly countenance which straightaway put Laura at ease. 'Laura Blake?'

'Yes, Laura Blake. That's right.'

'I need to have a word, Laura.' She poked her head towards the passageway. 'Alright if I come in?'

'What is it you want?' Laura had no inclination towards strangers right now. Netti would be home soon looking for her tea.

'It's alright, Laura. I'm Miss Fairchild, from the Welfare. We're aware that your father died a while back and your mother's been taken ill.' A slight feeling of embarrassment at the girl's unwavering stare made her glance along Penny Street, 'It *would* be better if we could talk inside?'

Laura was aware of the cluster of gossiping women some doors away. 'Alright. But my sister's home soon. I don't want her frightened by no strangers.' Stepping back, she waited for the woman to pass, before quietly closing the door.

'It's alright. I just want a quick word.' She followed Laura down the passageway and into the parlour, where at Laura's invitation, she sat on the stand-chair by the table.

Taking a sheaf of papers from the narrow case she'd carried under her arm, the woman took a moment to examine the wording. Then smiling at Laura opposite, she said, 'Netti, that's your younger sister, isn't it? Eight years old?'

'Nine next month.' Surely the woman must know Netti was nearer nine than eight. She had the air of a person who knew everything.

'Now then, you and Netti, you're here on your own since your mother took ill? It isn't a situation that can be allowed to continue, you know, Laura.'

'What d'you mean?' There was that knot of fear again,. 'Who says?' There was something very unnerving about her presence.

'Well, you're only just fifteen, and there's Netti still only eight. Supposing one of you were to be taken ill or have an accident? Who'd be able to look after you, feed and clothe you and pay the rent?'

'We manage. I'm never ill! And if Netti was took bad, I'd look after her, like I've allus done!'

'But then, how would you manage? How would you fend for yourselves?'

Laura felt cornered and she didn't like it. 'Mabel, Mabel Fletcher next door, she'd see to us. But it won't happen! I won't be took bad, and neither will Netti.' She wanted this conversation brought to an end. She felt disturbed by it. 'I'm sorry Miss Fairchild, but I've to get Netti's tea ready.' She rose in a deliberate effort to encourage the woman to leave.

'Very well, Laura,' she slid her papers back into the narrow case and stood up, 'but I'll have to go and see your mother's sister, Molly Griffin. I'm afraid it might be found necessary to take Netti and perhaps you into care, if your mother's to be away for some considerable time.'

'No! I'll not have Netti in no home!' She felt so angry, she could have pushed the woman all the way down the passage and out of the front door. 'I'll look after her, like I've allus done, and Auntie Molly can only tell you the same!'

The woman seemed pleased to leave, but her parting words only confirmed her intentions. 'I'll need to see you again, Laura. But first, we'll see what your Auntie Molly has to say.'

Laura thankfully closed the door against the departing figure, her cheeks burning brightly beneath the rising anger. Blasted cheek! Coming here, threatening to take Netti away; and maybe even her! She was more than capable of keeping things going, till their mother got well. That was all very well though; what if her mother *didn't* get well? What would the way of things be then?

Her face grew tight with determination. No matter! They would manage without help from the Welfare busy-bodies. All the same though, deep nagging doubts had already started to eat into her stubborn refusal to accept defeat. What with one thing and another, she hadn't been fetching enough money home to meet their needs; and the biggest worry of all was the arrears on their rent. Twenty-four shillings by the week after next, the rent man had said, or they'd be served notice to quit. Well, she'd just have to get herself out earlier in the morning; but then, who'd see Netti off to school? Oh, there *had* to be a solution to it all, things were never as bad as they seemed.

She wandered absent-mindedly into the back scullery, her amber eyes depressed and thoughtful. She'd give it more thought later, after she'd seen to Netti. But one thing was certain. She would ask nobody for help! Nobody at all.

The following evening, after the supper things had been washed and put away and Laura was just testing Netti on her times-tables, Molly Griffin arrived.

She was a large forceful woman, whose awesome stature and wide straight shoulders held an air of authority. She had piercing eyes, brown like her brother Remmie's. But where Remmie's eyes were appealing and gentle, hers could be unnerving and evil. Even in their quietest moments they were spiteful and accusing. And it was then that Laura would see the sisterly likeness between Molly Griffin and Ruth Blake.

She was dressed in a tight-fitting coat of grey herring bone, whose padded shoulders broadened her already considerable frame to almost grotesque proportions.

'Fine thing, I must say!' She settled herself into Jud's old chair and pulled it close to the small but cheery fire crackling in the grate. 'Strangers knockin' on me bloody door in broad daylight! Gave the neighbours a right bone to chew on, an' that's a fact.' She hoisted her skirt up a little higher, so as to feel the heat on her thick unattractive legs. 'What's a body to do, eh? *I'm* not responsible if me sister goes off 'er bloody rocker an' leaves two young 'uns to fend for theirselves, now am I?' She threw a wounded glance at Laura.

'No, Auntie Molly. You're not responsible.' She realized Netti had suddenly deserted her learning, to pay attention to Auntie Molly's loud complaining. 'I'll just get Netti off to bed.'

'I don't want to go to bed yet, Laura!'

'Well, you're going! It's near enough your bed time anyroad, an' I've to be up early an' off to Uncle Remmie's shop while he goes off to Accrington.' She urged the protesting girl to bid Auntie Molly goodnight, before propelling her upstairs, where she tucked her into bed and kissed her fondly.

94

'Straight off to sleep, mind.'

'Night and God bless, Laura.'

'Night, God bless, Netti, sleep tight.'

Auntie Molly glared at Laura when she returned. 'I've brewed some fresh tea,' she told her grudgingly, 'it'll be mashed now. Fetch us a mug, would you?'

Laura had never really known what to make of her mother's older sister. There had been times when she had suspected that Auntie Molly positively disliked her; yet she'd never had any real cause to imagine such a thing. All the same, it was there, that uncomfortable feeling, and it always put Laura on her guard. Auntie Molly and her mother had always seemed to antagonize each other, using every opportunity to belittle each other. And tonight appeared to be no exception.

'Your Mam's allus been a weak-willed woman, an' it were never in 'er to be maternal. I mean, can you tell me when she ever showed *you* any affection, eh? Can you? No, o' course you can't! Mind you, she could *pretend* a sort of affection when it suited 'er, oh yes!'

Accepting the tea that Laura held out to her, Molly carefully noted the warning in Laura's darkened eyes, and she murmured quietly, 'Aye well. That's all water under the bridge, I suppose. So, off to your Uncle Remmie's tomorrow agin, eh? Calling on you to leave your carting a fair wack these days 'int 'e? Not that I'm complaining! Oh no. What wi' my Parry not well — been bad 'e 'as — it's all up to Pearce now. More *you're* carting, an' less 'e's carting. So you be off to Uncle Remmie's, an' leave the streets to the lad, that's what I says!'

'It's only now and then, Auntie Molly.'

'Aye, oh, aye.' She slurped noisily at her tea. 'Now then! What's to be done about this other business, eh? Made to feel like a bloody criminal, I was. I don't like them Welfare folks! Never did 'old truck wi' nosey do-gooders like that. I told the woman straight! 'T'int my business to fotch other folk's kids up, even if they *are* me own sister's.'

'We've not asked anybody to fetch us up. Auntie Molly. Me an' Netti, we can look after ourselves . . . ' She could feel her anger and resentment rising. 'If it comes to it, we'll sell a few of my Dad's things. He wouldn't mind. He'd want us to.'

'What things?' Molly was on her feet all of a sudden. 'What

did your poor dad ever own that was worth anything, eh?'

'His silver watch, that big eagle, an' there's three good clocks.' Though how she would ever be able to sell her father's personal treasures, she didn't know. These things had been her father's reward for trudging the streets, and she could never part with them; no more than he'd been able to when times were bad. 'There's other things,' she added, eager to forget she'd even mentioned her father's well-beloved belongings. 'Bit o' furniture an' few good clothes I brought home for my Mam. But she never did like them. Wouldn't touch them.'

'Oh, clothes eh? Molly Griffin's features had suddenly grown softer. 'What sort o' clothes? Upstairs now are they?' She inched towards the parlour door. 'Like to show me, would you, Laura?'

'Can do. But walk quiet, 'cause I don't want Netti woken up.'

A few minutes later, they were in Ruth Blake's bedroom with the articles of clothing laid out on the bed for Molly Griffin to inspect. Laura watched her as she stroked the rabbit fur wrap before slipping it round her shoulders.

'There's some smart pieces here.' Molly Griffin slid her greedy eyes over the frocks and hats on the bed. Then she slyly glanced at the dark oak dresser and matching wardrobe, and the good solid wood bed with its deep soft eiderdown. Laying the rabbit fur over the bed with delicate reverence, she smiled at Laura. 'We'd best go downstairs an' talk things over, Laura. There's things to be seen to, an' that's a staring fact.'

Laura wanted to get off to bed. The events of the day and the worry on her mind just made her want to sleep; maybe with the foolish notion that when she woke up again, all the worries would have gone and they'd have nothing to fear.

'Now then, young Laura.' Molly Griffin flounced into the parlour and squeezed with some difficulty into a chair positioned at the table opposite Laura. She looked at her sister's child with some curiosity, before announcing with obvious irritation, 'I'm here to sort things out. After all's said an' done, your Mam is still my sister, an' I've a duty to you young 'uns.' She reached out to lay a podgy hand over Laura's. 'I keep a nice 'ouse, an' I make few demands. It's a sure fact yon Welfare won't leave you be, not now they've got wind of you! Like a dog wi' a bone, that bloody lot. No, what you've to do, Laura lass, is to think o' little Netti. Now you don't want 'er tekken to no charity home, do you? An' they'll 'ave 'er away, you mark my words.'

'They won't! I've told them. Me an' Netti, we'll take care of ourselves.'

'Oh, but they will! An' there's not a blind thing us poor folks can do about it. Except o' course, *I* can put a stop to it.'

'*You* can put a stop to it? How? How can you do that, Auntie Molly?' If there was any way at all to stop the Welfare from taking Netti, she'd be grateful.

'Well, that there woman as good as told me. If I was to tek you an' Netti in, till your Mam was to come 'ome, well, they'd not bother you. Now I've thought on it, an' it'll be strange 'aving a little 'un like your Netti about the place, an' I dare say it'll do me 'ealth no good at all, but I can't see the poor mite dragged off to no council 'ome! I'll tek you in, *both* on you, an' that's only what I consider to be the right an' proper thing.'

Laura hadn't expected this. That's what the Welfare woman meant then, when she said she'd see what Auntie Molly had to say. But she wasn't sure. This little house was her home, hers and Netti's, and she didn't want to shut it up and leave it. But how could she stop the Welfare from taking Netti, if they stayed here? She needed to think, to work things out.

'Can I come an' let you know tomorrow, Auntie Molly? I'd like to talk to Uncle Remmie; I'm not right sure what to do for the best. This is my dad's house, an' by rights, me an' Netti should stay here till my Mam comes home.'

'But your poor Mam could be a long time coming home yet. Your Uncle Remmie knows that, an' you've to let me know *now*, 'cause that Welfare woman's mekkin 'er way back to me first thing in the mornin'. If the answer's not enough to satisfy 'er, well you know what she'll be up to, don't you? She'll be off to yon school an' tek the lass from 'er desk! I know that for a fact, 'cause I've 'eard tell on it many a time. The law's on their side, you see. Folks like us 'int got no say in the matter.'

Laura felt sick. Deep down she knew Auntie Molly was telling the truth. She'd heard such awful things herself; and the thought of Netti being taken away was too terrible even to think about. Besides that, the way things were, it wouldn't be too long before she'd need to start selling things to pay the rent and keep them fed and clothed. A lot of the posh neighbours had deserted her in favour of Pearce, whom they referred to as 'that charming young man'. She bore him no grudge. It was his right to earn a living, and there was no doubt that he was sharp. Pearce Griffin would do well. She was sure of that; and if she was to tell the truth, the idea of staying in the same house as him did afford a degree of pleasure. But what about his father, Parry Griffin?

'I don't know, Auntie Molly. What about Mr Griffin? Have you talked to him about us?'

'O' course I've talked to him! My Parry's as pleased as anything. Mind you, like as not 'e'll seem a bit moody now an' then, 'cause of 'im not 'aving been too good lately. But 'e's on the mend now, so don't concern yourself. You an' Netti, well you'll both be very welcome.'

Laura still wasn't sure. But the way things were, she didn't see much of a choice, 'Thank you, Auntie Molly. Yes, we'll come and stay with you, but only till my Mam comes home!'

'That's right, Laura,' Molly Griffin had already taken stock of the various ornaments and solid reliable furniture, 'just till your Mam comes 'ome.'

Later, after Molly Griffin had taken her leave, and Laura lay restless in her bed, she hoped they'd done the right thing. But when she reflected on the possible consequences, she was convinced there had been no other way. It wouldn't be so bad. Auntie Molly was to charge only eight shillings a week each for her and Netti. There'd be nothing else to find, and with Auntie Molly being there all day, Netti would have somebody to see her off to school. So it wouldn't matter if she made an early start with the carting. She'd already mapped out a new route, so as not to cross Pearce's path. She'd soon make Auntie Molly's sixteen shillings, and have enough left to see the rent paid on the house, till her Mam came home. Then, when they were all together again, things would soon be sorted out.

By the time she fell asleep, Laura felt a little more content about the decision to accept Auntie Molly's offer. It was done now, and probably for the best.

Chapter Seven

'Well all I can say is, I'm glad you came to your senses, Laura. You're a sight better off working here for your Uncle Remmie, than trudging that cart round the streets.' Mitchell Strong leaned his broad back against the heavy double wardrobe, to ease it steadily up against the wall.

Laura lifted her eyes from the brass jug she was polishing; but she made no reply. Mitch seemed to have taken it upon himself to dictate her every move. He meant well, she supposed; but lately she'd begun to resent his protective manner. She was having to mind so many other folks' opinions now, and life seemed to have grown more complicated. She'd been at Auntie Molly's house just four short weeks, and already she felt suffocated. Parry Griffin had proven himself to be a pig of a man, and she wondered how it was that Auntie Molly could ever stand it; let alone defend him at every turn. She rarely saw Pearce. He'd taken to staying out at nights, and often he didn't find his way home for days on end. The Griffins were a strange kind, she'd decided; but Netti seemed content enough, and they didn't go short.

Uncle Remmie hadn't been too pleased about the arrangement. He'd made her feel a bit of a traitor for having rejected every offer of help he'd ever made, and yet she moved in with Auntie Molly before even consulting him. She'd finally accepted his offer that she should come and work at the shop, but it had really been to console his wounded pride and keep the peace between them. But she wasn't really happy. In her deepest heart, she would have liked to get back to the carting, where she had nobody else but herself to answer to; and yet there were compensations in working at the shop. Uncle Remmie paid her thirty-five shillings a week. After she'd given Auntie Molly the sixteen shillings for lodgings and the rent money for the little house each week, there was the best part of seven shillings left. Out of that, there were a few shillings to see Netti properly dressed for school and given a threepenny piece spending money. The rest was carefully put away in a sock, hung halfway up the chimney in her bedroom. Her Mam would want a start of sorts, when she got well enough to come home, and Laura kept that well in mind.

'Penny for 'em, young Laura!'

'Oh,' she looked at the sharp-faced woman looking down on her; she hadn't even heard Lizzie Pendleton come in, 'hello, Miss Pendleton.' She scrambled to her feet, straightening the crumples in her dark blue pinafore dress. 'I didn't hear the shop-bell.'

'I can see that! Miles away you were. Still, you've a lot to be thinking on, eh?' Pulling her dark shawl about her, she sniffed hard. 'Katya tells me as your Mam still refuses to see you. Shame on her, that's what I say!'

'What is it you're looking for?' She hated folks knowing that her mother was still turning her away. It made it seem so final, being common knowledge. But Uncle Remmie had told her to take no notice of what folks had to say. It was her mother's illness that made her act that way. It was only temporary, and she'd just have to be patient.

'A coal-scuttle. There's one in the window for two and fourpence. Mine's neither use nor ornament since I dropped it down the cellar-steps.' With a self-satisfied smile she said, 'I could have one o' them there 'lectric fires, but I'm not one to be changing just for the sake on it. I could afford it though! Oh yes, I'm not short of a bob or two.'

'That's nice.' Laura had often wondered where Lizzie Pendleton's money had come from, as did all the other folks hereabouts. There was talk of a man hidden away somewhere; but that didn't sit right somehow. The gossip about her dad having left her well off was probably nearer the truth. Lizzie Pendleton lived along Ribble Road. The only company she enjoyed since Katya's marriage to Uncle Remmie was a pretty green budgie, who declared loudly to everyone that, 'Lizzie's gone to catch the tram.' It was hard for Laura to imagine that the hard-faced and strict Lizzie Pendleton had actually raised Katya from a baby. But she had, and it did deserve some measure of admiration.

'It's no secret that I've little time for your Mam,' she harped on, 'but I feel right sorry for you and Netti; bad enough losing your dad and little Rosie, then having to leave your home. But it can't be any comfort to see your Mam in an asylum, even if she's in the right place.'

'Brew up time, Laura,' Mitchell Strong took the coal scuttle from her, 'I'll see to Miss Pendleton.'

If she'd ever been grateful to Mitch, it was at that very moment. The tears were already smarting her eyes, and the anger bubbled hot inside her. That Lizzie Pendleton! She just had to keep on and on, obviously getting particular enjoyment out of it. Her hands shook as she held the lighted match against the gas-ring.

'Don't let folks like Lizzie Pendleton rile you. They're not worth a tinker's cuss.'

She turned as Mitchell Strong came into the back room. Then, just for a brief moment as he stood looking down at her, she would have liked him to wrap her into his arms. All of a sudden she felt very sad, and oh so lonely. Poor Mitch. She always took offence when he made it his business to watch out for her, and it was a fact that she dared not reveal her affection, for fear of his misconstruing it. But when it came right down to it, besides Uncle Remmie, he was probably the best friend she had.

'Hey.' He laid his hands on her small shoulders, then gently lifting her face towards him with his work-worn fingers, he seemed to search beyond the shining tears brimming in her wide dark eyes. His voice, though still that of a boy, held the vibrant passions of a man. 'You're so beautiful, Laura Blake. Don't cry, I've never seen you cry before, and you've had more to cry about than the spiteful tongue of Lizzie Pendleton.'

'Sorry,' she was more than surprised herself. Crying wasn't something she admired in folk. 'It was temper really. She made me that mad!' Her anger had melted into shame at her own behaviour. With a determined twist of her shoulders, she moved from beneath the warm strength of his hands. 'I'll make the brew, eh?'

'Right.' The intimacy had gone from his voice. 'I'll be out in the yard. There's that shelving to be moved yet.' He brushed past her without another glance.

Laura filled the pan with cold water, then lined the mugs up and dropped half a spoonful of tea leaves into each. The water seemed slow to boil, and she was just toying with the idea of going out to the yard, to thank him properly, when the shop-bell rattled.

'A-ha! So this is where you spend your days, eh?' Pearce Griffin's presence seemed to fill the shop, and in spite of herself, Laura blushed at the persuasion in his voice.

Dressed in a grey jacket and black trousers, he looked unusually handsome and prosperous. 'Seems I've been neglecting you lately, Laura my sweet,' his brown eyes twinkled as he stepped up close to her, 'but I've been casting my net about, so to speak. Found a couple of geezers in London who've put me onto a paying caper. Seems they can find buyers for all the good stuff I can get; period furniture, paintings and such. What with dad letting the shop go to rack and ruin and fighting all my ideas for improvement, well, all the old customers are looking to your Uncle Remmie, and *I'm* forced to look elsewhere to line my pockets!' He dug his hand into the inside of his breast-pocket. 'What d'you think o' that, eh?' His fist was wedged with pound notes. 'Not bad for a couple o' days work.' He moved closer, until his jacket brushed against her face, and his breath ran along her neck.

'Does that mean you won't be carting any more?' She wasn't really interested in his answer. But she felt the need to say something to disguise what she was really feeling. Her throat had squeezed up so tight, she thought she'd choke; and she couldn't move away from him . . . didn't want to!

'No need for carting. I've enough ready brass to look further afield. Told you I'd do it, didn't I, eh? Let's celebrate!' He ran his fingers through her thick auburn hair. 'It's Friday night, an' in case you didn't know it, in exactly seven months and two weeks to the very day, I'll be marked officially to be a man!' He leaned towards her, his mouth drawn into the softest of smiles. 'But a body doesn't need to be twenty-one to prove himself a man, you know what I mean, eh?'

Laura wasn't sure how it came about, but suddenly she found herself in his arms, and it seemed the most wonderful and natural thing in the world when he brought his mouth down on hers. She gave herself up to him eagerly, tasting the excitement of her first real kiss, yet not feeling awkward or embarrassed. It was a lovely feeling, and one which she never wanted to end; not even when his hands began to move about her body, to search out the shape of her breasts and the warmth of her thighs, and when as though in a dream, she heard Mitch call out, 'You rotten swine!' she resented him for what he had spoiled. Then she felt herself wrenched from Pearce Griffin's embrace, as Mitchell Strong separated them with a vicious lunge. Ramming both fists into Pearce Griffin's chest, Mitchell sent him stumbling backwards. Reeling beneath the strength of the younger man's attack, and caught off guard, Pearce Griffin balanced himself against the sideboard into which Mitchell had sent him crashing. 'Are you bloody crazy, or what?' He ran his fingers through the thick dark tumble of hair disturbing his vision. Levelling angry narrowed eyes at Mitchell, who stood over him with doubled fists, he straightened himself up. 'What the sodding 'ell's up with you, man?'

'If you don't want a right good tanning, Griffin, you'll keep your grubby hands off Laura 'ere, an' tek yourself off!' There was fury in his green eyes and in his trembling voice, but he made no move, as they stood facing each other in equal defiance.

'Since when has Laura made *you* her keeper, eh? I'll leave her alone, when she tells me to, not at *your* bidding!' He made the mistake of smiling at Laura, then as the smile eased into a leer, he dropped his voice out of Laura's hearing. 'Fancy her yourself, do you? Well, there'll be plenty left for you when I've finished with . . .'

The words disappeared beneath the clenched knuckles, as Mitchell let out a roar and launched himself, fists flying, to bundle both Pearce Griffin and himself on to the floor.

'Stop it!' Laura's scream fell on deaf ears, as the two young men scrambled to their feet. Pearce Griffin's nose was running blood, and Mitchell's forehead had received a deep cut from the corner of the sideboard.

'What in God's name!' None of them had heard Uncle Remmie enter the shop. The anger and disgust was evident in the flare of his nostrils and the disturbing quietness in his voice. 'Get out!' He threw the shop door open and glared at the dishevelled bleeding Pearce Griffin. 'Get out an' don't ever let me catch you in 'ere again!'

Pearce Griffin shuffled to the door, where he stopped and turned around to survey them, his final glance resting on Uncle Remmie. 'Think you're a big man, don't you, eh? My Dad's right about you. You're just a small timer, going nowhere.' He straightened himself up, lifting both hands to flatten his unkempt hair. 'We'll just have to see if we can get you there a bit quicker, won't we?'

'Out!' Uncle Remmie took a step forward.

'Don't worry! I'm going.' He took a last look round. 'Do me nicely, this shop would. We'll see, we'll see.'

Slamming the door hard, Uncle Remmie glared fiercely at Mitchell and Laura, who were standing close together, looking more than a little ashamed.

'What were you thinking of? The pair on you, what the 'ell were you thinking of?' His words were addressed directly to Mitch; but Laura knew she was just as much to blame. And as she recalled the pleasure which Pearce Griffin's embraces had created in her, Laura's neck and face flushed pink and hot until she felt the urge to flee the room. Instead, she addressed Remmie in a subdued voice. 'It were *my* fault, Uncle Remmie.'

'No it weren't!' Mitch stepped forward. '*I* started the fighting, the jumped-up swine. Pity you came in when you did, I were all set to kill 'im!'

'Hey! Whoa lad!' The merest whisper of a smile flitted across Uncle Remmie's strong features. 'I reckon you'd best get out back, an' wash yoursel' down — in *cold* water might be best!' He watched Mitch out of the shop, then he turned to Laura, a serious look creasing his kindly face. 'I don't think it's wise for you to stay at your Auntie Molly's any longer, lass.' He stroked his chin thoughtfully, 'I'd like you an' Netti to move in wi' me. I'll broach it to Katya tonight. She'll not want you staying at Parry Griffin's 'ouse any more than I do.'

'Katya doesn't care for me, Uncle Remmie, an' we're alright at Auntie Molly's, honest.'

'You're *not* alright! It weighs on me mind, you being there,' he took her two hands in his, aware of her obstinate nature, 'an' I'll not 'ave you saying as Katya doesn't care for you. You're not to think such an unlikely thing, d'you understand?'

'Yes, Uncle Remmie.' But Katya *didn't* like her. She never had and Uncle Remmie knew the truth of it, just as much as she did.

Mitchell kept out of her way for the remainder of the afternoon, and Uncle Remmie looked to be deep in thought, as he busied himself taking stock and shifting the window display around.

About half an hour before closing time, he suddenly snapped his note-book shut. 'Mitch!' He waited for Mitch to appear, a sullen look weighing his handsome features. 'We're closin' shop, lad. See to the locking up, while I run Laura home in the van.' His thoughtful brown eyes sought her out. 'Get yoursel' ready, lass. I'll drop you off at your Auntie Molly's, then I'm away to 'ave a word with Katya. I'll not 'ave you in that 'ouse any longer than needs be.' He dug into his breast pocket, to withdraw a small brown envelope. 'There's your week's money, lass. Now go an' get your coat. I've some sortin' out to be done, an' as far as I'm concerned, the sooner the better!'

Laura climbed into the van, aware that Mitch was watching from the window. She looked away, conscious that she herself was not entirely blameless in the incident concerning Pearce. But maybe things wouldn't have escalated the way they had done if Mitch had shown caution. Things weren't ideal at Auntie Molly's; but she had an instinctive feeling that life in Katya's house could be even worse; in spite of Uncle Remmie being there.

Looking out of the van window, she gazed up at the restless April sky, silently praying; Please God, let Mam get better, so me and Netti can go home.

Chapter Eight

'Don't like me, do you, eh?' Parry Griffin wiped his dribbling mouth with the flat of his hand, his drunken eyes reduced to reddened slits through which he glared at Laura. 'Think old Parry Griffin's beneath the likes o' you, that's it, 'int it, eh?'

Laura chose not to answer him. The man was blind drunk; had been ever since he'd walked through the door not twenty minutes after she had said goodnight to Remmie. Remmie had wanted to come in to approach Auntie Molly with the idea of the two girls moving in with him and Katya; but Laura's earnest plea for him to see Katya first had persuaded Uncle Remmie to leave her outside the miserable little house.

Butler Street, where the Griffins lived, was little more than a back alley, squashed up tight with rows of narrow little ginnels and minute houses. There was nothing in the alley to brighten the appearance of the dwellings, and nothing in the dwellings to brighten the cramped quarters or the poor creatures that lived there. And Molly Griffin, in spite of her fondness for telling folks otherwise, did *not* keep a tidy house.

Unlike No 9 Penny Street, these houses had only one parlour. The front door opened straight into this room, with nothing to separate the two but a tall wooden panel which served as a draught excluder. At the rear of the parlour were two doors; one led to a small passageway and stairs; the other led directly into the scullery. What first struck Laura when she entered this house was the clutter. In the centre of the parlour was the familiar big square table, clothed and bearing a centre ornament, a huge bulbous vase filled with all manner of objects, such as cotton bobbins, bits of cloth, numerous buttons and other articles that seemed of little use.

Around the table stood four arched-back chairs, and scattered about the parlour stood even more chairs. Chairs of every

106

description lined the walls; ladder-back stand-chairs and old carvers of Queen Anne style that had seen better years; chairs with arms, chairs without arms, and even one or two that somewhere along the way had lost their backs altogether. All of these left only enough space for one other item; a Victorian sideboard whose back-shelving reached right up to the ceiling and whose thick deep drawers and fathomless cupboards settled down on the brown linoleum floor. Laura thought it an ugly thing, but a fitting piece of furniture for Molly Griffin, whose far-reaching dimensions seemed in total harmony with those of the sideboard.

Laura had not found Molly Griffin's house to be a homely place, and she had wondered why Parry Griffin hadn't taken up residence in a better area of town. At one time there had been money enough, and judging by the tales that were told, this house and the shop were bought and paid for. But it was a fact that when Parry Griffin had been taking good money at his shop, it had not been spent on improving his life style; only on extending his gambling and drinking.

Earlier, when Auntie Molly had opened the front door to her, Laura had wondered whether Pearce had been home with a tale to tell. But there had been no sign of him, and judging by Auntie Molly's usual greeting of 'Oh, it's you', after which she turned away into the parlour, Laura guessed that Pearce had not been back; and he was still not back.

Laura's heart had sunk at the sight of Parry Griffin, standing with his back to the fire-range, his trousers low and wrinkled, his shirt collarless and opened to the waist, exposing a bulge of unsightly beer-belly. He was obviously in an advanced state of drunkenness.

All through the meal of rabbit-stew, Laura had felt his eyes on her. And now he was talking, demanding her attention. "Ey! I'm bloody asking you! Not fond o' me, are you, eh? Glad to stay under me sodding roof, but can't stomach the sights o' me, can you?'

Molly Griffin's quick eyes had gone from her husband to Laura, and then back again. She had no illusions about her man. But he was *hers*! And she didn't care for the way he watched her sister's girl. Laura Blake carried far too much of her mother's beauty, and remembering the strong bond that

107

had once drawn her sister Ruth and Parry together, Molly Griffin didn't like the way of things. Not one little bit! Getting to her feet, she shouted, 'Leave 'er alone!' and gestured for Laura to help her clear the plates away. 'You'd do a sight better if you could keep your lad at home! Lord only knows where he is. I never know from one day to the next whether he's coming home or not!'

'Shut yer bloody blatherin', woman! Pearce 'as 'is wits about 'im. Teks after 'is dad, does my Pearce, don't give a sod for nobody!'

'Teks after you? Aye that he does, more's the pity.' Her tone was condemning, but her critical eyes betrayed the truth of her affection. 'I expect you're off out are you?'

Parry Griffin didn't answer at once. His piercing eyes followed Laura's slim figure as she busied herself collecting the supper things. Her need for a new set of clothes was obvious. Over the last few months, her slim girlish figure had given way to the soft roundness of approaching maturity, evident in the tighter fit of her pinafore dress, which clung to reveal the thrusting shape of her breasts. Her legs too, had begun to lose that awkwardness of childhood. The ankles were fine and shapely, the long legs smooth and amply curved.

'I'm talking to you!' Molly Griffin slammed a spoon on the table. 'I said, are you off out?'

''Course I'm off out!' He jerked his face towards her. 'You don't think I'm stopping in wi' you, d'you? An' I'll need a few quid.' His voice suddenly lost its surliness, 'got a bet to pay off, Molly.'

'For Christ's sake, Parry! I can't keep up with you. I gave you the last few bob yesterday.'

Laura touched Netti on the shoulders. 'Come on, young 'un. Get yourself washed.' It was painfully obvious there was another row brewing. She led Netti to the scullery where between them they washed up the supper things. Neither Molly Griffin nor her husband took any notice of them; such was the passion of the row that continued to rage long after Laura had marched Netti up to her bed.

'Why are they shouting and screaming, Laura?' Netti slid in between the sheets, her blue eyes already heavy with sleep.

'Some married folks are like that, Netti. They seem to enjoy

108

allus rowing and sparking.' She was thankful that Netti was a sound sleeper. Most nights, the shouting and arguing went on into the early hours, making her turn restlessly, unable to sleep, while Netti lay blissfully undisturbed.

Turning the light out, she groped her way back to the bed, where fully clothed, she lay on top of the eiderdown. Normally, she would have stayed downstairs until Parry Griffin was out and Auntie Molly had gone to her bed. It was always a tricky business having to wash at the scullery sink, for fear of being disturbed. That was why she never stripped off, but merely washed one part of her body at a time. She'd reduced it all to a fine art, and the most she ever exposed were her shoulders and arms.

The rowing seemed as though it might never end. Laura couldn't remember it ever being so bad. As usual, the raised voices bickered over money. Parry Griffin wanted more. Auntie Molly argued that she had none. At one time, it sounded as though Auntie Molly was crying, but that was something difficult to imagine, so she quickly dismissed the idea. Molly Griffin was not easily given to crying.

Netti had been asleep some time, and there was no sign of peace from downstairs. Laura decided that she may as well get into her nightie and lie in the bed. The room was cold, and Netti's quiet rhythmic breathing made her feel tired. She could always have a wash in the morning, but then there was no telling who might be about early. Pearce had been known to let himself in the front door at all hours. No, there was nothing else for it. She was tired, and they were still going at it hammer and tongs. She'd make do with a splash in the morning, and a quick comb run through her hair. There was the back room at the shop, with a sink and a kettle to warm some water, if needs be.

Cuddling up to Netti, she closed her ears to the row downstairs and gave herself up to sleep.

Whether it was the sudden silence that woke her up, she didn't know. But her throat was dry and her head throbbing with a dull ache. A quick glance told her that Netti was still fast asleep.

The house was quiet as she crept out along the landing, save for the rumble of Auntie Molly's snoring. She had to have a drink of water to quench her raging thirst. She supposed it must have been the stew they'd had for supper. She'd mentioned that it seemed salty, but Auntie Molly had quickly instructed her not to be ungrateful for decent food, especially as most things were still rationed. As she entered the parlour, and flicked on the light switch, Laura was surprised to see that it was already five o'clock. So she'd slept well, and yet it seemed only minutes to her.

Thoughts of Pearce entered her head as she made her way to the scullery. That fight between him and Mitch had been awful, and it was her fault! She found herself wondering where he'd gone. Strange, how she missed him when he wasn't around. But then she'd always liked him, in spite of his dubious character; or maybe because of it. A half-smile warmed her features as she replaced the mug. She supposed he *was* a shady character. But there was no harm in him, she was sure of that. She switched out the light and moved towards the parlour, aware of the cold stone floor beneath her bare feet. As she opened the door leading from the scullery, the parlour light went out, plunging her into thick blackness.

Cursing under her breath she edged forward to grope her way towards the sideboard and nearby switch. The disturbing sense of someone else's presence made her stand still. 'Who's that?' She could feel her heart beating in the dryness of her throat, as she listened intently in the darkness.

There was a quick shuffle in front of her, then a low laugh. In an instant, the figure was on her, clamping a hand over her mouth to stifle the rising scream. The other hand tore viciously at her nightie, shredding it to reveal her nakedness.

The pungent smell of booze filled Laura's nostrils as she hit out blindly in the darkness, her feet kicking desperately against the strength of her assailant. A fervent prayer struggled against the stark fear in Laura's mind as she lashed at the unseen face, scoring his skin beneath her nails, and causing him to cry out. The fury of her resistance only served to incite him, as he brutally fought her to the floor, his hand firmly clamped to her mouth.

Laura's assailant lunged at her time and time again; one hand clutching the pliable inner flesh of her thigh, the other tight about her throat. His wide open mouth smothered hers,

110

suffocating the screams which cried out in the hysteria of pain and terror flooding her mind. Laura's drowning consciousness was alerted twice during the relentless attack on her; once when the crazed voice against her mouth murmured, 'Ruth! Oh, Ruth,' and again when her eyes were forced open by the pain that sliced into her.

It was then that the narrow chink of light from the lighted passageway silhouetted the face which loomed over hers. It confirmed what Laura in her heart already knew. The monster tearing at her was her uncle Parry Griffin.

There was no-one to help her, no-one to stop this nightmare, as Parry Griffin took her virginity; without love, without tenderness or mercy. But with every vicious invading thrust, Laura marked this man in her darkest thoughts. Her fear and pain became a loathing, and the loathing shaped itself into a vow. One day, one day in the future, she would see him dead!

It was almost six-thirty when Molly Griffin made her way downstairs, her eyes still heavy after an undisturbed night's sleep. But when she came upon Laura seated by the fire-grate with the look of hatred still etched into her face, Molly Griffin's eyes grew wide. She sensed that her fears had not been unfounded and her mind quickened to her husband's defence.

Laura waited until Molly Griffin was standing before her, then she stood up to discard her clothes. In her nakedness, even though she had earlier washed the bloodstains from her face and body, she felt ashamed and dirty beneath the glower of this woman, her own aunt. Lowering her face and fighting back tears, Laura stared at the floor, and in a quiet voice said, 'Look at me, Auntie Molly. See what he's done.' The voice that spoke seemed not to be hers.

Molly Griffin stared at the young vulnerable girl, whose body bore the marks of a brutish attack, and who now looked back at her with such control and dignity. There was no deny-ing that Laura was of strong character and equally strong in mind. And in that instant Molly Griffin sensed a deadly enemy, and the fear she felt caused her to scream out, for she must not be seen as the weaker of the two. 'You're a liar! A slut! Just like your Mam!' Her face was distorted with rage as she went on,

111

'Oh, I know your sort. Set in the same mould as Ruth Blake! God-given looks to lead men on, an' the divil's own wickedness to bring 'em down!'

Laura was astonished that Molly Griffin should deny what was here before her eyes. And yet something inside her had warned of it; she had half expected Molly Griffin to side with her husband. When she spoke, the accusation in her voice was clear. 'You *know* Parry Griffin did this to me, Auntie Molly.' She wondered how her voice could be so calm.

Some while after Parry Griffin had left her, she had got up from the floor to wrap herself in the tablecloth and to sit in the chair. She had shed no tears, for there had only been a core of hatred, cold and still, within her.

The clock had struck six when she'd gone to the scullery and boiled the water for a strip wash. Then quietly, so as not to wake Netti, she'd returned to the bedroom and dressed herself. After that, knowing that Molly Griffin would be making her way down soon, she'd gone to sit in the chair again to wait; and to pray in the darkness that she would forget the horror that scarred her mind.

Ignoring Auntie Molly's blustering accusations, Laura spoke quietly, her eyes defiant. 'I'll be leaving this house, with Netti. We're going home; but when I leave here, I'm going straight to the police.'

'The police, eh?' Molly Griffin thrust her face close to Laura's, the tears bright in her eyes. 'You do that, Laura Blake! I've got plenty to tell an' all. There's bad blood runs through you, bad blood from your Mam. Everybody knows as that little cripple babby weren't Jud's!' She laughed as the astonishment showed on Laura's face. 'That's right. It were a bastard, born out o' wickedness. Now then! How would you like Netti to know about that, eh? Or how *you* lured my man on? Oh yes, that'd make good telling in the town, so it would!'

Laura turned from her. She knew that Molly Griffin was well aware of what her husband had done. It was there, in her tearful eyes and in the cruel threats. In a quiet voice that betrayed nothing of her real feelings, she said, 'Me and Netti, we're going home, where we belong.' That thought alone brought a glow of happiness to her heart, and she added sharply, 'If you take it into your mind to make trouble for us with the Welfare, you'll find that you're not the only one as can tell a tale!' Quickly pulling her clothes on, she demanded, 'Give me what's mine, the house-keys and the rent book.'

The cackle that issued from Molly Griffin's sneering mouth struck a new kind of fear into Laura, and when the woman threw back her head in scorn shouting, 'House-keys! Rent book! They've been gone long since,' Laura was horrified, and for a moment she couldn't take in just what unspeakable things those words were telling her.

'You think sixteen bob a week's enough to keep the two on you, eh? Well, you can forget your bloody 'ouse, an' your precious belongings, 'cause they're gone! It's tekken more than them to keep the pair on you.' Snorting, she backed away from Laura's hostile glare. Then from a safe distance she began shouting, 'So get out! Now!'

Laura felt murder in her heart, and for the first time she felt tears threatening. She *had* to believe that Molly Griffin had told her lies about her mother and little Rosie. But she was not telling lies now. No doubt the real person responsible was Parry Griffin, whose insatiable appetite for gambling had probably taken all the money that the furniture could bring, and every penny of the rent money for her father's house. The thought of that man brought a rush of nausea to Laura's stomach. The pain which still racked her body was more bearable than the horror of it all. She was out of her depth, and Molly Griffin knew that. Oh, what kind of fool she had been, to trust such a creature!

She stood to face this woman who had betrayed her, realizing with deep anger that there was nothing she could do. Not yet! She would have to bide her time. But there would come a day when Parry Griffin would pay for having spoilt her, and this woman, his wife, would regret the hour she had been born.

'What d'you intend to do then, eh?' Molly Griffin could not completely disguise the fear in her voice.

Laura eyed her with contempt, 'I'll collect Netti and we'll be gone as quickly as we can.' She couldn't bring herself to say any more. With a heavy heart, she turned from the parlour and Molly Griffin. The sooner she got herself and Netti out of here, the better.

As Laura moved towards the passage-way and the stairs beyond, the sound of the front door opening and Pearce's voice as he crossed the parlour made Laura stop.

'Ah! So it's running off at the sight of me, is it?'

Laura made no move to come back into the parlour, yet neither did she immediately leave it. Half turning, she looked first at Molly Griffin, whose face registered both apprehension and challenge, the sharp bright eyes directing a warning at Laura. As Laura looked towards Pearce, something must have shown to him. For when she replied in a deliberately controlled voice, 'No, Pearce, nothing of the kind. It's time me and Netti left, that's all,' he said, 'Time you left? Why? What's brought that on all of a sudden?' His voice suddenly fell quiet, and he looked at Molly, and at once perceived the look of guilt on her face. '*Why* are they leaving, Molly? It's you, isn't it? What dirty little games have you been up to, eh?'

'Watch your mouth, me lad! You're not past 'aving it swiped! She's leaving of 'er own accord!' Butting her face towards Laura, she urged, 'tell 'im! Go on, tell 'im as 'ow you've decided to find pastures new.'

Laura felt she was at this woman's mercy, for now anyway! Yet just at that moment, she might have blurted out the truth to Pearce, whom she sensed to be on her side. She was convinced that had he been aware of the truth, there'd be hell to pay! But the fact that he was his father's son, and the knowledge that Molly Griffin was more than capable of spreading the poison she'd threatened, stopped any outburst Laura might have made.

'Is that right, Laura, you're going of your own accord?'

'Yes,' she answered, going quickly from them to make her way upstairs.

At the top of the stairs she stopped, her eyes dark with hatred as she looked at the room where Parry Griffin lay. His woman had shielded him, but the strong desire in Laura to see him dead had not abated.

Sighing deeply, Laura went to stir Netti.

'Am I not going to school, Laura?'

'No, not today, love.' Laura quickly helped the child to dress.

'Where am I going then?' Her voice dragged with sleep still.

'I'm not rightly sure, Netti. But we're not stopping here.'

'Are we going home?'

'No. We'll not be going home any more. Just stop asking questions. Get your hair combed and let's be gone.'

Going through the parlour was a trial. Molly Griffin's glowering face followed Laura's every step, and in the brief exchange of farewell that passed between her and Pearce, Laura was aware that he was not entirely satisfied with the situation, for his eyes were alive with suspicion. Yet he said nothing further, other than to wish her well.

Out in the street Laura wasn't sure which way to go. She knew that Mabel Fletcher would take them in, or even Mitch's adopted mother, Belle. Then into Laura's churning thoughts came the image of that Welfare woman, who would take Netti away at the slightest opportunity. And the one person who would put a stop to that was Uncle Remmie.

The spring sunshine bathed Laura's face with its gentle warmth, and there was a brightness about the early morning that promised a pleasant day. The sparrows were already out, fighting and squabbling in the troughing along the roof tops. And the sounds of their chattering brought distant thoughts into her mind. They were sad thoughts, taking her back to the night her father had died. Yet murmuring in the sadness was a measure of joy. She could remember every word he had said to her. His voice seemed now to whisper in her heart. 'You'll tek this tired old world, an' you'll mek it sing! 'Cause you're Laura Blake, my lass.'

She blinked hard to dispel the tears smarting her eyes, and in that same instant she knew that her dad had seen something in her that she hadn't recognized. She *would* take the world, but she wouldn't make it sing! She'd make it *pay*, for its cruelty, for its injustice, and for taking everything and giving nothing! Her way was clear now. She had to fight back tooth and nail, for her share of happiness; hers and Netti's — and fight she would! *Nothing* was going to stand in her way.

Gripping the small warm hand into hers, she tugged the tired child, urging her, 'Come on, Netti. Come on. You'll have to walk a bit faster than that, Netti.' They had quite a way to walk through the dark and narrow back ways before they got to the better part of Blackburn and Uncle Remmie's. She didn't feel comfortable about their destination because she knew if Katya had been warm to the idea of them going there, Uncle Remmie would have fetched them last night. Oh dear God, if only he had, if only he had.

But there was nowhere else she could turn, and one thing at least was comforting. Katya didn't seem to mind Netti being around. So the thing was for *her* to keep out of Katya's way as much as possible.

The coins she'd retrieved from up the chimney pressed against her leg. At least Parry Griffin hadn't found them, and she wouldn't be going to Katya Thorpe empty-handed. It was only now, as they approached the grander terraced houses on Ribble Road, where Uncle Remmie lived, that she began to realize their true predicament. Their home was gone for good, and so was their furniture, and all of her parents' personal things. She could never forgive Molly Griffin for that. Then there was her mother to think of. Strange how she'd come to believe that she probably wouldn't care if she never saw her mother again. Molly Griffin had said some cruel things about little Rosie and her mother; and while she dismissed most of them as blatant lies, Laura knew all too well the truth of one claim. Her mother *had* turned from her. She *had* threatened to see her dead, and even though Uncle Remmie had told her that fixation of hatred was all to do with the illness, she hadn't been able to accept or forgive the vehemence her mother felt towards her. Ever since that day when little Rosie had died, she'd tried with all her heart to understand and forgive her mother's attitude. Now, she didn't care. From now on, she would only concern herself with Netti.

'Are we coming to live with Auntie Katya?' Netti's blue eyes seemed to light up.

'We'll have to see what she says. Uncle Remmie says we can, but I don't know.'

As they passed Lizzie Pendleton's house, Laura saw her peeping from the curtains. Well, one thing was for sure. If that miserable woman had her way, Katya Thorpe would certainly close the door on them.

But the door wasn't closed on them; yet neither were they made to feel very welcome. Uncle Remmie ushered them in with genuine warmth, but Katya's voice was cool as she told them, 'Well I must say, I hadn't expected you round this early, but now that you're here, I suppose we'll make the best of it.'

Laura eyed the slim fair woman, who was no more than ten years her senior. Clad in a corded dressing-gown of the same weak blue as her eyes, Katya Thorpe looked at the two girls.

Laura squeezed Netti's hand reassuringly. Her face burned with shame, as Katya's gaze fell on the well-worn coats that were the only outdoor garments the girls had.

'You can see to them, can't you Remmie?' She reached up to place a kiss on Uncle Remmie's kindly face. 'I'm going back to my bed. Oh, and see if you can make them more presentable.' She smiled weakly at Laura, whose tight expression conveyed defiance. 'Don't be offended. You can't afford to be proud, can you, and your Uncle Remmie has to think of appearances.' With the smile still sweet on her china features, she wafted away up the stairs and out of sight.

'Tek no notice, lass,' Uncle Remmie smiled heartily, 'she means no 'arm. It's just 'er way, the way Lizzie Pendleton brought 'er up, I expect, eh?' He moved forward to place a comforting arm about her shoulders. As the strength of his embrace pulled her to him, Laura was suddenly filled with blind panic. Since the horror of Parry Griffin's attack, she'd tried to bury the awful memory deep in her mind, away from her conscious thoughts. But the touch of Uncle Remmie triggered off a wave of fear and nausea, which rose to suffocate her.

It was only Uncle Remmie's quick reaction and her own self control that got her to the bathroom just in time to spew out the churning anger of her stomach. And then she cried, cried bitterly, until the ache in her heart had lessened, and the way of things grew clearer to her.

She washed her face in the small white basin, then looked up to examine herself in the wall mirror. She looked long and hard at the face before her, and the luxurious auburn hair, wild and rich against the creamy smoothness of her skin. It was true. She did look like her mother. Even the eyes, which before seemed soft and friendly, were now hardened by new resolve and determination. Yet the hardness rendered her dark eyes even more beautiful, filling them with fire and excitement.

The whisper of a smile moved across her mouth. Oh yes,

she'd make the world pay. However hard she had to work, or however much courage and scheming it took to raise her and Netti above the measure of those who'd looked down on them, she'd find it within herself somehow. Straightening herself up to tidy her dishevelled appearance, she uttered a heartfelt vow. Never again would she be made to feel ashamed, or be brought to bitter tears; not by any woman, nor by any man!

Jud Blake had left a young girl behind, a warm loving daughter whom he had idolised. The reflection in the mirror would have astonished and saddened him. The child was no more. The innocent young creature that once was had been devoured by circumstances that were her only heritage. The image in the mirror showed an emerging woman, shaped in the wake of tragedy and driven by the bitter-sweet taste for revenge.

A few minutes later, feeling calmed and more sure of herself, Laura made her way downstairs to the kitchen, where Uncle Remmie and Netti were waiting.

When she greeted them, her voice was quiet, controlled. There was no trace of the tears that had racked her. Instead, her fine features were confident and proud, disguising the storm that still raged in her tormented heart.

'There you are then, lass.' Uncle Remmie placed a mug of tea on the table, next to where Netti was sitting tucking into a piece of chicken. Pulling out a chair, he gestured for Laura to sit. 'Drink that. Then we'll sort your rooms out, eh?'

Laura nodded and smiled. At least here was a friend. Uncle Remmie was a good sort and he'd not let any harm come to them. Yet she felt sure that he had questions on his mind, questions she would rather not have to answer. Had he guessed at Molly Griffin's treachery? Oh, please let him keep his questions to himself, she prayed silently. But as he lowered himself into the chair opposite, he asked, 'What's to be done about yon 'ouse, Laura? The furniture an' such, eh?'

Laura did not hesitate, and she didn't look up as she replied, 'The house has been let go, and everything sold.'

There was silence for a minute. 'Sold? What, *everything*! What about your dad's things, the sculpture, an' them beautiful clocks 'e cherished?'

'All sold!' Reaching into her pocket, she withdrew the sock

of money and placed it on a table. 'There's the money. Please give it to Katya, Uncle Remmie, I don't want her to look on us as beggars.'

'She'll not do that! An' I'll not 'ave you paying money.'

'Then we'll not stay.'

'But, Laura, I can't bring me'self to believe that you sold your dad's things?'

'I had to, Uncle Remmie, he'd understand the need.' And she prayed that he would. For it was *her* doing that they were gone! And it was through her own stupidity and misplaced trust that she and Netti were thrown to the mercy of other folks.

Chapter Nine

On a brilliant day in July Laura was driven by her torment to seek out her old neighbour and friend.

'Well if it i'nt Laura, an' little Netti.' Mabel Fletcher threw open the door and tousled Netti's bright blonde head as the two girls came forward into the passageway. 'I'm right glad to see you, that I am!' she declared with a broad grin. Then catching sight of Laura's thin pale face that, in spite of her returning smile, was devoid of any gaiety or colour, she reached down to playfully smack Netti's rear end and said 'Get yer arse down that passage, an' look in yon scullery cupboard lass. I'm not saying as you'll find any treasure, but unless my greedy brood 'ave swall'ered the lot, you might just come across a meat an' tattie pie!'

'Ooh, thanks, Mrs Fletcher.' Netti glanced at Laura and at Laura's quick nod, the girl was away down the passage and on into the parlour. And now Mabel Fletcher turned to ask in a quiet intimate voice, 'Is 'owt amiss, young un'?'

'What d'you mean, Mabel?' Laura forced a half-smile and a bright curious innocence into her voice. 'We've come to see you, we miss you, that's all.' She didn't say, 'I've come to ask your help because I'm desperate.' In fact, Laura suspected that she would not now be able to tell Mabel Fletcher the real reason for calling, because already her nerve had gone. The courage she had mustered to bring her here had dissipated beneath Mabel's pointed question.

'Oh, aye? Well, that's grand, Laura. That's good enough for me, lass.' The look she gave Laura betrayed the fact that she suspected more. Then the look relaxed into a grin and she said, 'Close the door then an' come away in. Me ol' man's tekken Sally an' the young 'uns to Corporation Park, so I'm on me own.'

Laura closed the door and followed Mabel Fletcher's ample figure as it ambled towards the parlour. Once there, Laura was ushered into a chair next to the big centre table, and Mabel Fletcher told her smartly, 'You'll 'ave a mug o' tea, my gel, an' a thick wedge o' bread an' drippin'! You look as if you could do wi' fattening up . . . what! You're not as far through as an empty bobbin, an' that's a fact, I've seen more fat on a starvin' cat!' With that, and satisfied that Laura was offering no resistance, she quickly waddled into the scullery and out of sight.

Laura hadn't the heart to tell her that at the mention of bread and dripping, her whole stomach had come up into her mouth, and how she'd kept it from spilling over, she did not know. For of late, she had little control over the workings of her insides. Something strange and uncomfortable was happening to her body. And Laura was frightened. She wasn't altogether naive in such matters, because hadn't she seen her mother growing big before producing both Netti and little Rosie, and hadn't she seen things with her own eyes on that day of little Rosie's birthing?

The knowledge of conception and pregnancy was a natural and wonderful thing, and it was never hidden away, especially not from girls of Laura's age. Indeed, women the like of Mabel Fletcher and Belle Strong considered it to be a vital part of a girl's upbringing, and whenever Laura found herself in their company, like as not they'd relate a most recent death or a long complicated birthing, with such vigorous detail that Laura could almost imagine herself to have actually been there. There was no fear attached to such events, and certainly no shame!

But now, with the stark truth staring her in the face and memories she had prayed to forget running through her mind, Laura was filled with shame. And the fear was magnified a thousand times, because it was a fear she dared not share.

She was with child. Of that, Laura was in no doubt. Instead of the usual monthly functioning of her body and the discomfort that came with it, she had been experiencing a far greater discomfort, the worst of which was being sick. This had started three weeks ago in the mornings, and had only now begun to subside. Luckily, most times she'd been able to suppress it long enough to get out on the moors at the back of the house, where only the bushes and the birds bore witness. And on the odd occasion when she'd just made it to the bathroom in time, only Netti had heard and she had been quite happy to accept Laura's assurance that it must have been, 'Something I ate'. Fortunately, Laura made so little of it, that Netti gave the matter no further attention.

Laura, however, was at her wits end, and more than once she had been on the verge of confiding everything to Remmie. Yet she did not. What stopped her was the thought of how he would react, and the sure knowledge that Katya would purge her house of the shame, by putting both her and Netti out on the street. And Laura in her own mind was certain that Remmie would have murder in his heart if he ever found out that Parry Griffin had done this terrible thing. God help her! Oh, dear God help her. What on earth was she going to do?

Suddenly, Laura was forced to attend to the question that Mabel Fletcher had already asked once and now asked again, 'What's to do, lass?'

The warmth and concern in Mabel's softly-spoken question brought to Laura's throat a tight painful lump, which she instantly swallowed. Then with bright tears threatening her eyes, she actually gave a little sound of laughter, saying, 'Oh, Mabel, there's nothing. Honest.' The lie was as abhorrent to Laura as was her situation, and when she concluded, 'Like I said, I've missed you,' she was unable to hide the tremble in her voice. And when the tears swam into her big dark eyes, Mabel Fletcher was quick to notice.

'There bloody well *is* some'at, my gel! An' you'll not leave this 'ouse before you've telled me!' With a swish of her skirt and a resolute nod of the head, she was on her feet, and after giving Laura's hand a pat of encouragement, she went over to the dresser and called out, 'Netti! Netti, lass. 'Ere with you, this minute.'

Netti appeared from the scullery, still clutching her half-eaten pie. 'Yes, Mrs Fletcher?'

'Tek this.' Mabel thrust a ration book and a few coppers into Netti's hand. 'Jessup's keeping a few bacon bits for me, you know, the little shop at the corner of Albert Street. Tek this'el off, eh! An' mind the old sod don't take more than one coupon!'

'Bacon bits?'

'Aye! 'E knows right enough. Just tell 'im I sent yer.'

With Netti gone and the front door safely closed, Mabel came back to where Laura was supping her tea, her eyes deliberately averted from Mabel's quizzical look, and her heart weighed down with the burden of her shameful secret.

'Now then, me lass. You tell old Mabel what's ailing you. I'm not blind an' there's nowt as'd please me more in this world than to 'elp you. You know that, don't you, eh?'

There it was again, that great straddling lump in Laura's throat and this time, try as she might, she couldn't stop the hot smarting tears from spilling out of her eyes to run unchecked down her face. Then of a sudden, she was in the fat comforting arms of this dear woman, and the tears became sobs that broke from her like a dam. So bitter was her crying that for a while she couldn't speak. She could only cling to Mabel and take wonderful comfort from the gentle voice which soothed, 'There, there, lass. Mabel's 'ere, you go on an' cry, young 'un. It don't pay to keep it bottled up inside.'

When Laura's fearful sobs began to subside, she kept her head buried in Mabel's neck, and in broken gasps she poured out the terrible fear that was haunting her, her belief that she was with child and that the future was filled with horror for her and Netti. And when she had finished the silence, broken only by an intermittent sob, was unbearable to Laura. Then she felt herself being lifted from her hiding-place in the dark squashy comfort of Mabel's neck. And as the two chubby hands cradled her head, Laura found herself looking at Mabel's face. And what she saw filled her heart with immense love and gratitude, for the wise old eyes that looked into hers were soft with compassion and bright with tears.

Sniffling hard, Laura murmured, 'I'm sorry, Mabel, I don't know what to do.'

'Oh, lass, lass! Don't be sorry. It's strong you've to be, strong and unafraid.' And quickly now, her voice still soft but charged with insistence, she demanded, 'Who was it? Give me 'is name, child! 'Is name!'

'No!' Laura pulled away, and now she was on her feet, her heart suddenly swamped with fear. Molly Griffin's warning echoed in her mind, and Laura knew only too well that there

123

would be folks quick to believe that evil woman's deliberate lies. And Netti must never know! Nobody was to know, please God. She had to give herself over to Mabel Fletcher's mercy, for there was no one else to whom she could turn. The only other had been Belle Strong, but dear as she was, that little woman was a born chatterbox.

'So. You'll not tell me, Laura?'

Oh God, I shouldn't have come here, thought Laura. But now that she had, and Mabel knew, Laura would have to beg her to help and not to question as to the identity of the scoundrel who had put her in such a dreadful predicament.

'Sit yourself down 'ere, Laura, an' we'll talk quiet like, eh?' Mabel Fletcher patted the floor beside her chair. 'You tell me as much or as little as you feel the need to, an' I'll not press you, child. No, I'll not press you.'

A great surge of relief drained through Laura. She *would* help. Mabel would help. Thank God, she had a friend in her.

Chapter Ten

The summer was a difficult time for Laura. There wasn't a day
when she didn't feel unwell, and the worst part was trying to
appear as though she was on top of the world. Both Remmie
and Katya had remarked on her unusually pale complexion,
and Mitch had teased, 'They're not starving you up at that
house, are they? I shall have to take Remmie to task unless you
start filling out.'

And fill out she did. Though thankfully not as much as she
might have done — some women were fortunate in that way,
she knew. Her condition was easily concealed by winding a
length of binding linen tightly about the bump in her middle,
and by covering this with loose fitting frocks and baggy cardi-
gans. Yet while her middle was suitably contained; though
uncomfortable; her face and the rest of her body became thin
and peaked, until at one stage Remmie declared, 'There's
some'at ailing you, Laura lass. 'Appen a trip to yon doctor's
might not go amiss.'

Laura had been thankful at Katya's intervention, when
she'd greeted Remmie's remarks with 'Don't fuss over the girl!
It's a stage they all go through.' Then she had gone on to chide
Laura for dressing so sloppily, adding in that superior way she
had, 'I can see it will be left to *me*, to educate you in the
manner of dress and the art of grooming!'

Quickly following this had come Remmie's enthusiastic
promise to Laura that he too would contribute to her learning,
by teaching her everything he knew about the different types of
wood employed in the creation and restoration of furniture.
Then growing excited at the task of instructing his protégé, he
had risen from his place at the table to stride over to the sideboard, and from the drawer he had withdrawn a catalogue

depicting detailed and beautiful pictures of fine pieces of furniture throughout the different periods; showing splendid examples of Tudor, Regency, Georgian and Jacobean design, together with descriptions of every piece, and the craft of restoration. The catalogue was a long-treasured possession of Remmie's, but now he proudly thrust it into Laura's hands saying, 'Read that, lass. Read and study it from end to end, an' we'll make a master of you yet!'

Katya's peevish glance had not gone unnoticed by Laura, who over the next few weeks had found a degree of solace in studying the catalogue. And to her surprise, she found immense pleasure in the knowledge it imparted; a pleasure which in future years was to grow into a fervent passion.

It was towards the beginning of January, some four weeks before her time, when Laura felt the onset of her birthing, and the dreadful fear which she had suppressed all these long months came flooding back with a vengeance.

On her last visit to Mabel Fletcher, who had kept Laura's secret and had never ceased her vigilant attention to Laura's condition, mental as well as physical, she had been given strict instructions. Mabel had told her, 'Some time before the babby intends to start its journey, you'll feel it shift inside you. It'll slip to a lower position, and you'll like as not feel sore and uncomfortable, lass. Then when it's almost ready, you'll begin to feel as though you're filled with a gurt surge of energy, an' you'll grow hot and restless inside.'

Laura had recently marked these very changes, and now there was something else. Mabel had warned, 'When you get a curious sensation of your whole body being gently squeezed, and when that particular feeling gets stronger an' comes in regular stages, you get yoursel' over 'ere as fast as yer legs'll carry yer, my gel!'

The 'squeezing' had started that very evening at the supper table, right in front of Remmie and Netti. Katya had retired to bed early with one of her 'crippling headaches'. Laura had been worried that either Remmie or Netti might notice her acute discomfort. But they had not, and Laura was grateful for the fact that her middle had not grown as much as she had feared and, therefore, her careful and systematic 'letting out' of the clothes she stubbornly wore in the face of Katya's disapproval, had been disguise enough.

Once or twice Katya had cuttingly remarked, 'You're letting yourself go to pot, my girl! You want to smarten your ideas up, and quickly!' Laura had been swamped with self-conscious embarrassment. She had fervently promised herself that once this awful business was over, she would take Katya's offer up of teaching her niece how to dress with style and discover the art of grooming. Yes, she would gladly follow Katya's every word, for although Laura had found little else in Katya to admire, there was no doubt that she was an extremely smart and proudly turned out woman.

Laura could hardly contain her relief when Remmie bade her and Netti goodnight, adding, 'I'll be off to Katya. She's not well again.' Then with great effort on her part, she helped Netti to wash up the supper things. After which Netti went off to bed, saying she was glad it was Sunday tomorrow and she could lie in.

Some minutes later, Laura went upstairs, deliberately making enough noise to assure each of the others in their bedrooms that she too was having an early night. Laura sat on her bed in the dark, holding her breath and listening for any sound that might indicate the others were still awake.

For a long time now, the house had been quiet and Laura's discomfort was growing more extreme by the minute. It seemed as though they were all asleep, but even so she would *have* to risk making a start right now! There were peculiar movements going on inside her, and suddenly she felt the urge to be sick. She *must* get to Mabel's house. Quickly!

How she came through the streets to Mabel Fletcher's house, Laura would never know. And when Mabel quickly answered her feeble knock on the door, Laura was under the impression that the dear soul had been waiting for her. It was only later that she learned of Mabel's recent nightly vigils sleeping in the front parlour, ever alert for Laura's knock. 'I *knew* t'would be early! Quick, lass, bless yer 'eart.' With gentle caring hands, she ushered Laura into the rarely used front parlour, where there had been got ready a small iron-framed bed, and in the grate there was a cheery fire burning. With quick skilful hands, Mabel helped the frightened girl out of her clothes, and when she had her laid out on the bed, she took just one quick look, saying with quiet urgency, 'By God, lass, you've not med it 'ere a minute too soon.' Then she threw a heavy shawl about Laura's top half, bent to wipe away the sweat on the girl's brow, and in a low encouraging whisper, she said, 'Trust me, Laura lass, I'll not let any 'arm come to you, nor the babby.'

Laura did trust her, with all of her trembling fearful heart, and she knew that whatever happened this night, she would always love this woman, this dear kind soul who was her only salvation. But oh, she was afraid, so very much afraid of what was happening. And the 'squeezing' which Mabel had described, was swelling into crippling pain that came in relentless rhythmic surges and left her gasping for breath. She was being swept along on a tide of events over which she had no control, and in her young inexperienced heart, Laura was convinced she was about to die.

'The water's broke!' Mabel dabbed again at Laura's face, murmuring over and over again, 'Breathe easy, me lass, easy.' Then she told Laura, 'I've to fetch Sally. It's alright, lass. She can be trusted to say nowt. Don't fret yourself, just keep doing what I said; breathe easy, an' don't push, not till I tell you.' Then she left Laura's side and turning to the parlour door, she said, 'I'll be nobbut a minute. The water's broke, it'll not be long now.'

But she was wrong. An hour later, on the chime of midnight, there was still no sign to end Laura's suffering. And for all she had been determined to be brave, Laura was forced to cry out more than once at the savagery that was gripping her body; and when the tears spilled out of her eyes to run away down her face and onto the pillow, Laura took comfort in the gentle hands that stroked her brow. It was Sally, Mabel's eldest daughter, who had been given the task of soothing Laura in the throes of birthing, who was not much older than Laura herself.

Three long arduous hours later, the little parlour came alive with the sound of a child's cry. Laura cried too, but they were tears of gratitude and relief.

'It's a little lad!' Mabel cried. 'A right bonny little lad.' Her eyes were bright with emotion as she instructed the delighted

Sally to get fresh hot water to wash Laura and her son. 'The tiniest mite I've ever clapped eyes on!'

'Oh Mabel, let me hold him please.' Laura raised herself up on one elbow to peek at the little bundle in Mabel's arms. And for the moment, all fear of the future disappeared beneath a great tide of love and curiosity for this little new born person that was her own son.

But then, when Mabel came forward, her broad face beaming as she lowered the child into Laura's outstretched arms, a strange and frightening thing happened. Laura held the tiny bundle close to her heart, looking at its small perfect features.

That tiny pink face seemed to grow dark before Laura's eyes, and a new terror assailed her heart, which had been warm and loving, but now seemed to freeze. The face of her son was superimposed with that of Parry Griffin. Laura was in that dark parlour with the monster, reliving the horror, and now, as then, she could feel her body being torn apart. She wanted to scream out, to frighten the terrible feeling away, but she could not open her mouth. Her body was trembling, then shaking uncontrollably, and she was helpless to stop it.

'Good God in 'eaven, child!' Mabel Fletcher had seen the shaking which had convulsed Laura, and she recognized the onset of a fit, as the girl's eyes grew wide and staring then rolled upwards in her head, at the same time strange unintelligible noises came from her half-open mouth.

When Sally came back into the room, she saw her mother almost running with the new born to place it into the makeshift cot shaped from an orange-box. And one swift look at Laura told her why her mother was in such panic. Even before Mabel cried, 'Sally! Get yer dad, quick! Be careful not to wake the young 'uns,' Sally was already on her way upstairs.

There followed feverish activity, during which time, Mabel Fletcher offered more than one silent prayer. But thanks to her skilful knowledge and experience, the crisis was quickly brought under control, and there was no need to summon the doctor.

Laura knew little of what had happened. But when some two hours later she regained her total senses, she knew one thing beyond any doubt; it was as though *she* was being punished for Parry Griffin's sin, because in her heart she knew that she had been cruelly denied ever knowing the tender wonderful love which motherhood should bring.

Twice at Laura's request, Mabel Fletcher brought Laura's son to her. And twice, Laura made a desperate effort to take him in her arms. But she could not. And the awful knowledge that she may *never* be able to hold him, tore her heart almost in two.

Mabel Fletcher dismissed her husband and daughter and held Laura tight against her bosom, soothing the sobbing girl with words of assurance. 'It's not your fault, lass. These things can't be explained, an' it's not surprising after all you've been through. Leave the lad 'ere amongst my brood, an' to all an' sundry 'e'll be *my* lad. Sally an' me old man'll say nowt. It'll be our secret, lass. An' when the day comes as you want 'im, you know where 'e'll be, eh?'

'Oh, Mabel!' To Laura, it seemed the only thing. She had so much in her heart and on her mind. Later, there would be time for clear thought. Now the very thought of having Parry Griffin's child near her made her cringe. Oh, God forgive her and help her! 'I know you'll look after him, Mabel. And one day, I'll fetch him.' But if by instinct she knew anything, it was that she could never lay claim to Parry Griffin's child.

After a few hours sleep and against Mabel's strict advice, Laura got from her birthing-bed before the first light. At six-thirty she was being taken home by horse and cart by a reluctant Mr Fletcher, a man older than Mabel and given to deep silences, but a good man. Half an hour later, she had entered the house silently to creep up to her bedroom, where she undressed, and in the weakness of exhaustion fell into bed and a sinking sleep.

A week later, with Remmie cursing the virus that had struck her, Laura was well enough to resume her duties at the shop.

The awful catalogue of events was ever alive in Laura's mind. And the love in her heart for her son, whom she had called Tom, was strong and vibrant. Yet so too were the memories that never ceased to plague her; of her Aunt Molly's treachery, of Parry Griffin, and of revenge. And God help her, so real were these emotions that they overcame and suffocated her need for her child.

It was a terrible thing for Laura to realize that her heart had grown cold, like a wonderful summer's day might shrivel and die when the sun was smothered. And in her loneliness, she wondered whether in all her life she might ever know the real meaning of love.

PART TWO

1952

REVENGE

I don't want to stand with
the setting sun
And hate myself for the things
I've done.

Edgar A Guest

Chapter Eleven

Mitchell Strong stood by the fire-grate, his arm crooked over the mantelpiece. There was a quiet strength about his presence that seemed to fill Mabel Fletcher's little parlour. Coming up to his twenty-second year, he had acquired a fine maturity, portrayed in the broad capable physique and strong steadfast green eyes, whose thoughtful gaze now held a deeper awareness. It had been over a year ago now since he had returned to Remmie's shop from his duties as a soldier. Mitch was no longer a boy, but a man. And he had left behind that narrow vision with which a youth of tender years viewed the world about him. In this year of 1952, a nation still fettered by food shortages and ration books had been brought to new sadness by the passing of George VI, a good and faithful King. The young successor, Elizabeth II, was now Queen and Head of the Commonwealth, and a new era had begun.

Mitch had secretly hoped that during his absence Laura might have discovered in herself a need for him as great as his love for her. But while he believed the sentiment shown in her words, 'I'm so glad to see you home', he despaired of ever hearing her whisper those special words of love that would make his life meaningful. And now, what he had discovered on this cool September day had left him both shocked and enraged.

He went to the table where Mabel Fletcher sat with her head bowed low. Putting a comforting hand on her shoulder, he told her, 'Laura would never find a more loyal friend than you. You did right in sending for me Mam, and I'm glad I insisted on fetching her, or I would not have known the way of things.'

'Well, it's a fact *you* weren't meant to be told. But 'appen it's just as well.' Mabel thought Mitch to be a grand young man, a man she'd be proud to have for a son-in-law. Her Sally would

135

be a grand match for such a fine fellow as Mitchell Strong. There had been a time when she'd even wondered whether Mitch was the one who'd violated Laura and made her with child. But she had rejected the speculation, reproaching herself for the very thought. No! Whoever had done that dreadful deed, it was never Mitchell Strong. But who? Somebody had spawned little Tom, and Laura, though she loved and provided for the youngster, could not bring herself to let him invade her heart. And it was a sad, pitiful thing.

'Who was it, Mabel?' Mitch stood taut before her, his fists clenched hard against his sides. 'Who? Did she tell you that?'

'No lad, she wouldn't name the culprit. And these last four years, Laura's son 'as been our secret; mine, Sally's an' my man's, Lord rest 'is soul. 'Twas a natural thing for the lad to be lost amongst my brood as one o' me very own.' But she wondered what would happen when she herself took the same path as her beloved man? Nine months at worst, a few years at best, the doctor had said. And it was to the future, and the boy's future that she needed to look now. Laura wasn't the answer, she knew that, because when Tom had first breathed life, something in Laura had died. And over these last few years, it had not been rekindled. Many a time Mabel had wept for what Laura had lost, for a worse fate could not be fall any woman than to be denied that wonderful precious bond between mother and child.

Mitch and Belle's first thoughts were that Laura would shun the gossips, brave the ensuing storm, and claim the lad.

'No, an' it's not that she doesn't love the boy,' Mabel had explained, 'because she does! It's some'at as goes much deeper, like a door's been slammed inside 'er to shut out the things as could bring 'er pain. She's afeared, awful afeared is Laura. Aye! An' I can understand. But the lad's wanted for nothing, an' Laura's never stinted with the money for 'is keep.'

Mitch's face darkened to a glower, as he hissed through closed teeth, 'If ever I find out the devil that violated her, I'll tear him limb from limb!'

'Oh an' you'll 'ave yer work cut out lad.'

Belle sat up now, her eyes riveted onto Mabel's face. 'What d'you mean by that, Mabel?'

Mabel meant a lot by it, but she instantly regretted blurting out the words. She'd had her suspicions about too many things these past years. Yet all she said now was, 'There's more than *one* divil 'as violated Laura. 'Er own mam, refusin' to see the lass these three years an' more. Oh ay! an' Laura would 'a *starved* 'erself afore sellin' that little 'ouse o' theirn. All I'm sayin' is, it meks a body wonder, the two lasses turning up sudden-like on Remmie's doorstep!'

At this, Belle grunted, but Mitch made no comment. Instead, his lips grimly pursed, he stared into the fireplace. He could hear Mabel addressing Belle, describing what everyone knew, that the Griffins were a strange lot. And what a waste of good premises, with Parry Griffin recently taken to living alone at the shop, living by the bottle and sharpening his gambling wits. In Mitch's mind, his thoughts of Laura and the love he felt for her, mingled with Mabel Fletcher's earlier comments. And suddenly, as though he had no control over it, his mouth opened and out tumbled the name, 'Pearce! Pearce Griffin!' He turned to see Mabel and Belle looking at him, with Mabel quietly nodding, as though in agreement with his thoughts. God almighty! Was it that swine, Pearce, who'd shamed Laura? He couldn't shake it out of Pearce Griffin, because after a public stand-up fight with his drunken father, he was rumoured to have gone off to London to seek his fortune. He'd find out though, but he knew Laura wasn't one for confiding. He'd have to step very warily.

His thoughts ran on amidst the quiet chatter of the two women. And it was only when Belle cried out, 'Lord love us, Mabel! The lad's the living image o' Jud Blake,' that Mitch looked up. He saw Sally Fletcher and a small boy coming into the parlour. Seeing Mitch and Belle, the boy became shy and ran straight away to hide behind Mabel Fletcher's chair. But not before Mitch had recognized Laura's late father in the child's large eyes, coloured the deepest brown, and in the thick dark hair that framed a heart-shaped face.

The young woman who followed was somewhat ordinary in appearance. She had long straight brown hair that fell prettily from a centre parting, and her eyes were a little too small, although a becoming hazel colour. She had a wide generous mouth and pleasant even features, and when she smiled her face was at its prettiest, showing a warm affectionate nature.

137

The soft brown dress with straight pleated shoulders and long fitting sleeves was of a style that had become increasingly popular with the young. It suited her small trim figure, and the matching brown ankle-strap shoes with their wedged sole and tall chunky heel, added complimentary height.

After inclining her head towards Belle and Mitch with a smile and a greeting, she addressed her mother in a quiet resolute tone. 'Mama, I know you sent for Belle to ask her to look after the lad should anything happen to you, God forbid. But my mind's made up! He'll be *my* responsibility when the need arises.' She turned towards Belle adding, 'It's not meant to be personal to you Belle, but he's one of us, an' I could only see it otherwise if Laura herself was to claim him.'

Belle looked at Mabel, whose eyes were shining with pride and tears. Then she said heartily to Sally, 'Don't you fret yourself, lass. I'd do the very same, but I'll not be far should you ever 'ave need on me.'

Mitch was silent as Mabel thanked Belle and protested that she hadn't wanted to saddle Sally with fearsome responsibilities, but Sally had a stubborn streak and a yard-full of compassion.

Just before he and Belle left, Mitch exchanged an intimate smile with Sally, and seeing her protective attitude towards the boy, he was inclined to agree with Mabel's assessment of Sally's character. He'd known her from school. She was a warm reliable person, just like her Mam.

Mitch had found it difficult to take his eyes off the lad who was Laura's son. And when Mabel said, 'Surprising 'int it 'ow beautiful 'e is for a lad? A breath of spring after a dark foul winter you might say?' he replied, 'You're right there, Mabel. But it's his Mam's beauty, an' she's always been something special.'

His parting words had been delivered quietly, as though for his own ears.

Nobody noticed Sally Fletcher's pained expression as she turned from them.

Chapter Twelve

Laura emerged from the back storeroom, and in an instant, the dowdiness of the shop paled beneath her awesome beauty.

No full-blooded man hot for love, nor maturing boy eager to fulfil himself to manhood, could look upon Laura Blake and not fall helplessly beneath her spell. Yet she showed no interest in them; and so they retreated, their fanciful dreams and ambitions withered.

The last few years had seen Laura grow from a lovely undemanding creature of gentle moods, to become a magnificent young woman, who had taken the worst things in life and shaped them to her own advantage. She possessed the ability to be the most sensitive and caring of all creatures, but because such traits had invited others to scorn and cause pain in her formative years, she had cultivated the art of self-protection, and a discerning control over her emotions.

Her magnificent beauty was not of the ordered kind, for she enjoyed a bewitching quality, which set her apart from others. Her slim shapely figure breathed with the passion of emerging maturity, and she moved with a confidence borne from the inner secret knowledge that she had it in her to become her own master.

Laura had denied herself the emotional ensnarement of romance, and so she had also denied herself the joy, tenderness and companionship which love could bring. Yet in deliberately hardening her heart against such involvement, Laura had achieved at least a measure of inner sanctuary.

She had made few friends, for that would have been an indication that she needed other people; and she didn't! There was little value to be found in young people of her own age. They were too frivolous and demanding. No. Far better to keep one's own counsel.

Netti however, was a different matter. She appeared to have perception far greater than her thirteen years, and Laura found endless pleasure and satisfaction in their long intimate exchanges. Even Katya Thorpe's half-hearted attempts to wedge the girls apart, had only served to bring them closer together. The security of Netti's future was ever uppermost in Laura's thoughts. She had never lost sight of the fierce desire that her sister should make something of herself. She wanted her to attain that respect that had always seemed to evade the daughters of Ruth Blake.

Laura had long ago ceased to crave the love of her mother. For she knew from Uncle Remmie's disguised comments that Ruth Blake in her ravaged mind still saw everything in terms of fear and loathing. Even now, after all this time, Ruth Blake still vehemently refused to see the girl who had once vigorously defended her. But time had eased Laura's pain and now she could accept the truth that her mother had irretrievably disowned her. She didn't fully understand why; she never would. But she had finally come to accept it. What she couldn't, wouldn't accept, was that she herself had played any part in bringing about such a situation. It had crossed her mind so many times lately, how the image of her mother, who was still alive, grew more and more blurred; while the image of the father she kept close to her heart, stayed true and sharp in her memory.

It had been that memory, and her devotion to Netti, that had seen her through that first difficult year at Uncle Remmie's.

Katya Thorpe had proved herself to be a thoroughly pampered woman, who sought to have her own way in every matter. Uncle Remmie, who doted on her, could see no wrong in her actions. But Laura had sensed from that very first day a real animosity that had not diminished with time. While Katya Thorpe sought Netti's favour at every opportunity, she rarely wavered in her efforts to belittle Laura on every possible occasion, deriving extra delight when doing this in front of Remmie. And oddly enough, Laura had not only learned to live with Katya's sharp tongue, but had formed a rewarding alliance whereby the two of them actually found pleasure and satisfaction in their mutual love of clothes, with Katya the teacher and Laura the ever-attendant pupil. It was an odd truce initiated some months following Tom's birth, when Laura was discovered in Katya's bedroom trying on one of her dresses.

Laura prepared herself for a terrible scene and was astounded when instead of indulging in one of her tantrums, Katya quite purposefully made herself responsible for Laura's instruction in the rudiments of self-grooming and skilful clothes' sense. It was an art in which Katya herself was a perfectionist and she revelled in boasting her expertise to someone of Laura's inexperience and exceptional beauty.

In spite of the circumstances which had dictated her continued presence in Katya Thorpe's home, Laura took small offence at this woman's dislike of her, for she suspected that it was based on envy; envy of the way Uncle Remmie entrusted her with an increasing share of responsibility in the shop, and envy because in spite of all Katya Thorpe's efforts to win Netti's undivided affection, the girl's love and loyalty belonged, first and foremost, to Laura.

Busying herself now about the shop, surrounded by dusty pictures and woodwormed furniture, Laura Blake's beauty seemed all the more striking as her features radiated contentment. The piles of secondhand chairs, musty articles and various paraphernalia bedecking the shop represented the coveted trade of Remmie Blake, whose love and appreciation of old and beautiful furniture and works of art had enthused Laura so that she too had come to develop a strong passion for these things.

She intended to learn this trade in all its detail, seeing the acquisition of such specialized knowledge to be the greatest chance she was ever likely to get. Her intention was to better the station she and Netti had found themselves in, and she was learning fast. Uncle Remmie had said as much. She already knew the difference between a worthless piece of junk and a highly priced antique. She could buy and sell with confidence, and every day taught her more. The day she really looked forward to was the day when Uncle Remmie would allow her to bid at the auctions. Bidding at the auctions called for a special kind of confidence and true judgement of the piece you'd committed yourself to. You needed a quick eye and a large slice of luck in order to avoid buying what Uncle Remmie described as 'a pup in a manger'. She had argued that she was ready, if only he'd give her the chance to prove it. But Uncle Remmie would just smile and tell her to be patient. But like everything else, she viewed it as another milestone on her way to the top; and she found patience an elusive virtue. He'd taken her to the auctions many times, and she loved the colour and excitement. She always looked forward to them, and she watched every procedure with the greatest attention. She knew every auctioneer, every regular bidder, and they didn't possess a nod, a sign or a particular fancy that she didn't immediately recognize. Uncle Remmie had taught her much. She was grateful, and she knew instinctively that her first chance to bid wasn't too far away.

Deeply engrossed in thought, she failed to notice the sudden appearance of Mitchell Strong.

Emerging from the back storeroom, he paused on his way into the shop. From his easy vantage point by the big Jacobean wardrobe, which partly hid his presence, he gazed for a long moment at the beautiful girl who so determinedly rejected his every advance. She was wearing that straight black corded skirt and full-sleeved blouse, whose shades of autumn brought out the colour of her eyes, and plain grey high-heeled shoes, that complimented her perfectly shaped legs. There was no disguising the love that Mitch felt for her. It shone in his steadfast eyes as they caressed her every move.

There was a tiredness about his handsome features, that betrayed the anguish and sleepless nights he'd suffered since last Friday when Mabel Fletcher had found the need to reveal young Tom's background. A whole week! And he still hadn't been able to broach the subject to Laura. The shock had hit him in two ways; firstly, the knowledge that another man had forced himself on Laura when she'd been no more than a child, stealing her virginity and leaving her with a burden in more than one sense. Mitch's disappointment at Laura's obvious inability to confide in him had been tempered by his compassion for her and his pride in her courage.

Secondly, and this he could not come to terms with, was Laura leaving her own child in someone else's care. Laura,

142

herself a loving sensitive creature, being so *in*sensitive in this particular matter. Yet maybe he was cruel to use such a word. He had thought long and hard on Mabel Fletcher's defence of Laura. Although Remmie paid her a regular wage, Mitch suspected that it must be a constant struggle for Laura to eke out her money. Most of it, he knew, went on Netti. Yet Mabel had said that Laura provided well for the lad and saw to his every need. Every need but one, and that was the need for his own mother.

But through all of this he had come to see one particular issue more clearly, and that was Laura's constant rejection of his approaches. He had not been aware of the burden which Laura kept secret and which by its very nature must have coloured her attitude towards men. But it seemed as though he had loved Laura for all his life, and even in the face of her disinterest, he would not give up, because he felt in his heart that one day, Laura Blake would be his, willingly, lovingly. And when that wonderful day came, he would open wide his arms to gather in both Laura and her son.

As Laura straightened up from her task at the counter, she became aware of someone's presence, of a pair of eyes following her every move. It was with a little shock that she swung round to see Mitch now in the shop, and her tone registered both surprise and pleasure as she cried, 'Oh, it's *you*, Mitch! You startled me. I thought you were still busy in the yard.'

'I've done there. Next job is to shift them crates out.' Keeping his eyes on Laura, he jerked his thumb to the back entrance where a number of crates were stacked.

For a moment, Laura felt that Mitch was about to ask her something, so intense were his searching eyes on her face. But the moment was lost as he suddenly turned away and went towards the crates. Then in a savage movement, he swung the topmost one up onto his shoulder and disappeared out towards the yard. She looked after him until she could no longer hear the sound of his footsteps, then her brows drawn together in an expression of puzzlement, she shrugged her shoulders and returned to the stock-ledger. Laura had been sure she had known every one of Mitch's moods. But this last week had proved her wrong, for he had suddenly become unpredictable, a trait hitherto totally outside his nature. On more than one

143

occasion, she had looked up to find him silently studying her in such a way that she had not seen before. And like just now, when he had stared at her so intently, she had been made to feel decidedly uncomfortable.

'It's no good, Laura! I've *got* to talk on it.' Mitch had come quietly back into the shop.

Laura straightened up from the counter. 'Something's troubling you isn't it, Mitch?' But if she had been ready to listen sympathetically to his problem, Laura was totally unprepared for the cause of it.

'The child is *yours*!' he said, and the very manner in which his statement was uttered, represented an outright condemnation. 'And for the life of me, Laura, I'm at a loss to understand how *any* woman could leave her own child to be fetched up by another!'

As Mitch arraigned her with remarks that he meant to be firmly reproachful, but which emerged as cruel and scathing, opening up painful wounds in Laura that were not yet healed, she stood with her mouth half-open, eyes wide with astonishment and all manner of thoughts racing through her head. He knew! Mitch knew about Tom. How? How had he found out, and what did he intend to do with the information? Her first reaction was not one of anger that he should take it upon himself to be judge and jury over her. No, he had brought the fear back into her heart: the dreadful fear of herself; of a son from whom she still cringed, because he was the living reminder of a nightmare that stalked her waking hours; and of the very real prospect that should Katya ever discover her secret, she and Netti would surely once again find themselves homeless.

Laura said as much now, to Mitch. And his answer was to grab her by the shoulders, torn with emotion as he cried, 'Oh, Laura, Laura! While I live, you and Netti would never find yourselves homeless. I don't mean to crucify you because of the boy. I know well enough that you've been caused a lot of pain.'

'No, you don't! You don't! How can you?' Laura looked up at him, her eyes pleading with him not to torment her any further. Mitch didn't understand. She hardly understood it herself. How could she explain the deep unfulfilled longing to hold her child tight against her, to be able in one moment to blot out that darkness which shadowed her? But she could not! Because inexplicable and cruel as it was to her, and seemed now to Mitch, something within her reacted, overpowering and paralyzing every other natural instinct. Instincts which had taken her to Mabel Fletcher's many times in the first few months following the birthing. But each time had resulted in the crippling guilt and frustration which were to cause endless sleepless nights and made Laura suspect that she was going the way of her own mother.

She had stopped going round to Mabel's and that dear soul, blessed with great perception, had seemed to understand, 'Don't you fret, lass,' she had said, 'I'll keep the lad as me own. 'E won't be the one to come off worse.' And Laura had often wondered whether it was a sorry prediction that she herself would probably 'come off worse'.

A great hopelessness now engulfed Laura, and when she felt herself being roughly pulled in to him, a rush of terrible panic took hold of her. 'Don't touch me! Leave me be, Mitchell Strong. You're not *my* keeper!'

But his hold on her did not relax. Instead, he held her from him and said in a hard angry voice, 'You mean everything in the world to me! Can you understand that? Can you?' He emphasised his last words by shaking her back and forth.

Laura did not flinch beneath his accusing glare, but spoke with a calmness that belied the feelings raging within her. 'Don't, Mitch. Please don't say those things, I can never return your love.'

' *Won't!*' His fury hissed out, as he demanded, 'Isn't that the truth? You *won't* let me get close to you.' His voice broke as he moaned, 'Laura, you're so lovely.' He seemed for the briefest moment to kindle a response in her, and it crossed Laura's mind that there was many a girl who would gladly trade places with her right now, to be in Mitch's arms.

Only when he brought his head down and she felt the dry warmth of his breath caressing her mouth, did she find the strength to twist herself from his grip that was becoming an embrace. 'No!' She scrambled backwards to stand flat against the wall, her whole attitude defying him to move in on her again. 'I mean it, Mitch! I don't want you to touch me.' The taut anger in her heart suddenly relaxed at the sight of Mitch, who stood quite still, his expression quiet now and resting on her face.

'Alright, Laura. I won't touch you again. And the business of the boy is yours, not mine. I'll say nothing more. But one thing I *would* like to know. Who was it, Laura? The one as took you against your will?'

Over the years Laura had cultivated a defence, and it rose now as she retorted, 'Don't pry, Mitch. Some things are best not raked up.'

'I'll find out, Laura,' Mitch clenched his fists tight against his sides, 'and when I do!'

'You won't.' Her voice was quietly confident, for she had told no one but Molly Griffin, and she would keep the silence on her own terms. She supposed young Tom would know one day. And just as she had found the need to shut him out of her life now, he too would have a choice to make. It was strange though, how after all this time, she still could not identify Parry Griffin's child as being hers. She had grown away from him, and that in itself had brought a measure of peace to her.

Mitch moved towards the stack of crates, lifting the nearest one on to his capable shoulders with effortless ease. Before striding out towards the yard, he turned to watch as Laura came back to the counter. Then his features hardened and he told her, 'I hope you get what you want out o' life, Laura, but I'm afeared you're heading for an almighty fall.'

His words incensed Laura, and the anger she felt now betrayed itself in her words as she retaliated, 'I'm heading for no fall, Mitch! I intend to carve a path that doesn't lead downwards nor backwards. Me and Netti, we've always given full value for our keep, and we've never asked for charity.'

Mitch's reply was a stony glare. Then he was gone. Laura felt both angry and humiliated. If only he would leave her alone! If only he would stop trying to run her life, as though he had a right! But deep down, she supposed he meant well, and in a way she was grateful.

Determined to put the whole incident out of her head, she deliberately busied herself re-arranging the window display. A grey cloud of dust took flight as she shifted the pile of books aimlessly from one corner of the window to the other.

Lost in the torment of her thoughts, she suddenly found her

eyes being inexplicably drawn to the pavement side of the window.

Even before she looked up, his presence whispered itself into her heightened senses. The man, a stranger, seemed unabashed when she found him looking upon her with such blatant curiosity. His face relaxed into a warm easy smile, which seemed to pierce and mellow the lingering umbrage within her. The man was strikingly handsome. His face had a gaunt strength about it, which somehow reminded her of her father, and the eyes, now soft and smiling, held a disturbing magnetism in their black depths. His lips were fine and sensuous, the confident smile with which he shamelessly raked her lovely face, drew her to him persuasively and his dark hair was straight and thick.

Laura knew at once that he didn't belong to these parts. The cut of his black roll-necked sweater and expensive tweed jacket were not the type worn by any of the local men. Still clutching the willow-patterned meat plate she had intended to reposition, Laura straightened herself back out of the window. The stranger entered with a confidence she had only ever seen in Remmie Thorpe. She felt apprehensive; almost shy. She guessed the stranger to be in his early to mid-twenties.

'Good evening. Can I help you?' The question was marbled by the curious excitement she was feeling.

'You must be Laura?'

'Aye! that's right; and who might *you* be, eh?' The cutting remark caused both Laura and the stranger to look towards the back doorway, where Mitchell Strong stood arrogantly looking at the dark-eyed stranger. 'Can't recall seeing you around these 'ere parts.'

The sharp jangle of the bell above the shop door shattered the brooding atmosphere, and the broad figure of Remmie Thorpe entered. The past few years had been kind to him, for he was still a handsome figure of a man. The quiet strength was still there, set in the resolute squareness of his shoulders and the assertive authority of his features. The smiling mouth was topped by the now greying 'tache which straddled his top lip. His hair was thinner, lighter in colour, yet effectively complimenting the alert brown eyes set deep beneath the jutting protection of his brows.

147

Winking at the dark-eyed stranger, he laughed out loud. 'Med' yoursel' known then, I see.' Propelling the smiling young man forward to stand before Laura and the angry Mitch, Remmie introduced him. 'This 'ere's a buyer, a buyer from London way.' A broad smile crinkled his features. 'Only met the lad a few months back, but by God, the young bugger's caused me some battlin' at yon sales! Sharp 'e is! Sharp as a tack, I tell you!' He laughed out loud again. 'Thought it were time as I fetched the enemy into our camp, so to speak, eh? Keep 'im on our side!' Moving over to stand beside the thoughtful Laura, he told Mitch, 'Best get ready for locking up, lad, it's time we were off an' left you to it.' Bringing his attention back to Laura, he grinned happily. 'I've asked young Thackerey back to dinner, lass. He's off to London first thing in the morning, and we've a thing or two to talk over afore he goes.'

'I'm staying at The Bull,' Jake Thackerey said, 'been there a week now, on this last trip. It's getting to be like a second home; it's a nice enough place, but the food's none too special, and keeping your own company can get a bit lonely.'

Unlike Uncle Remmie, Laura didn't miss the meaningful look that accompanied his words. 'Well, I suppose it's only to be expected when you travel about a lot, Mr Thackerey,' she said quietly, releasing the full dazzling effect of her smile, 'but I can promise you you'll enjoy your meal tonight. Katya's a marvellous cook.' There, at least, she could speak the truth. After living on scraps and make-do for so long, she still hadn't got used to the luxury of Katya Thorpe's table. Cooking was her one and only interest; apart from her concern for the demanding Lizzie Pendleton. Everything else left Katya bored and impatient.

Aware of Jake Thackerey's dark brooding eyes drinking in her every detail, she suddenly felt vulnerable; and such a feeling made her impatient. Remmie Thorpe seemed to sense her irritation, as, taking her by the arm, he pointed her towards the back store room, 'Go and get your coat then, lass! Being as we've company tonight, I expect you'll need extra time for washing and fancying yourself up, eh?'

Laura eyed him accusingly, 'Give over, Uncle Remmie.' A fetching pinkness suffused her face; what did he have to go and

148

say a thing like that for? She was only too conscious of the state she was in, covered with dust and looking anything but her best.

'Come on then, Mitch!' Remmie Thorpe said. 'Stop your day-dreaming. Let's have you away to start locking up.'

Mitchell Strong looked back just once, his narrowed green eyes directed towards the stranger in glaring hostility. He'd been quick to notice the undivided attention Laura was paying to the stranger as she came back into the shop, and the pain it brought him was evident in the surly expression with which he greeted her. 'Right you are then, Mr Thorpe,' he acknowledged grudgingly, 'I've one more crate to shift before the job's done.' He hoisted the last remaining crate up onto his shoulders, before disappearing through the door and out into the back store-room.

'Now then, Jake,' Remmie Thorpe draped an affectionate arm around Laura's shoulders, meeting her pleasured smile with warm response, 'so what do you reckon to this lovely little lass 'ere, my niece, Laura?'

'She's very beautiful, Remmie,' Jake Thackerey gazed at Laura, his deep eyes filled with admiration, 'you've every reason to be proud.'

Remmie gestured for the stranger to direct his attention towards a painting. 'This is the painting I was telling you about, the weaver woman, by that Yourelli chap you're so fond of. It's a grand 'un, sure enough, an' if it were mine, you could no doubt persuade it from me, for the right figure. But't ain't mine.' He looked at the painting with admiration. It was a magnificent painting, depicting the shawled figure of an old woman at her weaving. There was a special air of timeless magic in the creases of her face and the soft delicacy of her half-blind eyes. To gaze upon it was to experience the love and passion which its creator had breathed into its inanimate canvas.

'It's the most striking painting I've seen,' Jake Thackerey seemed excited and entranced, as his eyes greedily enveloped the painting, 'if it isn't yours to sell, then whose is it?' he turned to meet Remmie Thorpe's forthright gaze.

'It's mine!' So she had something that this man wanted! Oh, she liked that, indeed she did!

Remmie Thorpe had given her the painting as a starting present when she'd first come to work for him. Giving her the wide freedom of choice from the many items of value, Uncle Remmie had not been surprised when without hesitation, she'd chosen the painting. She had been drawn to the dark sombre colours and the inherent transience of the subject; its appeal was instant to her discerning taste. The fact that this disturbingly handsome stranger nurtured the same aesthetic appetite for precious things as she did, intrigued and excited her.

'Yours?' Jake Thackerey's utterance emerged in a breath of surprise, which he quickly disguised to ask more briskly, 'I wouldn't have thought it the kind of painting a young woman would want. How much will you take for it?'

'It's not for sale.' Laura glanced at Remmie, whose amused expression heightened the urge within her to torment and manipulate the stranger into offering an unrealistic price. She suddenly found the idea of toying with him wickedly appealing. But there was something else too. Deep in the back of her mind, an idea had begun to take shape. It was obvious that Jake Thackerey was a wealthy man. It was evident in his clothes, his poise, his whole manner; and he was attracted to her. She could sense it, almost smell it. Wasn't this the chance she'd been waiting for? Jake Thackerey could be the ticket to a better life, a new start for her and Netti. Yes! She felt sure that if she played this handsome man along, she'd be able to secure more than a fancy price for a painting. Selling the painting to him would be easy; selling herself would call for much greater skill. But the rewards could be everything she had ever wanted. And oh, the doors which could be opened for Netti!

A dark shadow fell over her thoughts, as she remembered. No! She wouldn't let Parry Griffin or any other man cause her to hide herself away any longer. Men were not to be feared. They had used her, and by God, it had to be her time now. Time to use them, to make them pay. She'd play them at their own game, and if anyone was to be the loser, she'd have to make damned sure it wasn't her!

Lifting her eyes, she met his bemused gaze. Oh yes, he wanted her, and when *she* was good and ready, he could claim her. But he'd find she wouldn't come cheap. If he wanted

Laura Blake, then he'd need to offer much more than his manly charms. She felt his black eyes searching deep into her face, and she knew that he was within her grasp. She sensed the self-protective reflex which stiffened his next words, directed at Remmie.

'Have you anything else by the same artist?' He had deliberately averted his eyes from Laura's bewitching face; but she never once lifted her compelling gaze from his features.

"Fraid not. I've never come across this 'ere painter afore, never even heard of Yourelli, but when I saw this hanging in that old dying house, I couldn't leave without it; sort o' grips a body, don't it, eh?'

Jake Thackerey looked up to admire the old weaver-woman. 'It's certainly one of the most magnificent examples of his work that I've ever seen.' He turned to meet Laura's uncomfortably direct gaze. 'I'm willing to pay a good price for it.'

'How much? That is *if* I was intending to sell it, and I've not yet made up my mind on that particular score! It's a much treasured gift from my Uncle Remmie.' She quickly shifted her fiery glance towards Remmie Thorpe, whose proud expression reflected the deeply held belief that his niece was first a shrewd business type, and only next, a woman.

'I think a fair price would be in the region of say, five pounds, but to tempt you, I'd be prepared to go to seven.'

'Away with you!' Laura thought he was being over-generous at five, but she knew he was hooked. Her passionate eyes burned into the black piercing gaze which brazenly challenged her.

For the space of a moment, no one spoke. The young girl and the dark stranger stared at each other; each confident in their own strategy.

Mitch came back into the shop, his bewildered expression reflecting both curiosity and resentment. Remmie put out an arm to halt his intrusion, and gave a sharp glance to allay any questions.

'You know it's not worth even the seven I've offered, don't you Laura?'

'Oh, is that a fact? Well now, my own thinking doesn't run along such lines,' her eyes played with his, 'I don't go by what folks *tell* me,' she tapped her heart, 'I go by what I feel in here!

151

That painting could have been sold time and time again,' she tossed her rich auburn hair at the delicious thrill of such a blatant lie, 'but I've no mind to sell the painting after all!' She half-turned to leave.

'Nine pounds, and I'd be a fool at that!'

She rounded on him. Her instincts told her that he was almost at his margin, but not *quite*, she decided. 'Twelve pounds, and it's yours!'

'Twelve!' He stepped forward quickly, grabbing her hand into the lean strength of his own, 'Done! Before you change your mind.'

The touch of his skin made Laura shiver, and as he looked down at her, she suddenly felt afraid. She knew now, without any doubt, that what had begun as the merest germ of an idea, had become a compelling intention. She wanted this man and everything he stood for. The memories of poverty, degradation and humiliation demanded that she should succeed.

'Well Jake,' Remmie Thorpe collected the painting, 'I don't know which o' you got the best bargain, but by God, I enjoyed watching Laura give you a taste of your own medicine!'

'Laura!' Mitchell Strong accused her, his green eyes blazing, yet moist with tenderness. 'Your uncle's present? What in the name o' goodness made you part with it?'

Laura might have retaliated more swiftly to Mitch's dim view of her selling the painting. But truth be told, amidst the exhilaration which had lifted her spirits, there did lurk a semblance of regret; she consoled herself with the fact that when Remmie had given her the painting, he had instructed her to look on it as an investment.

Mitch waited for an answer, but before Laura could bring herself to give one, Remmie intervened. 'Now then, Mitch,' Remmie's quiet firm voice dispersed the charged atmosphere, 'Laura can do as she likes with her belongings, an' it makes not one penn'orth o' difference *who* gave them to her.' The pride still burned brightly in his eyes. 'She'll go far will my Laura. I couldn't have been better blessed if I'd had a son!' He held the painting out towards Jake Thackerey. 'There's your spoils then. It's time we were all away from here, eh?'

And there it rested, with Jake Thackerey handing Laura the twelve pounds, before taking his leave with the promise of seeing them up at the house later that evening.

On the way home with Remmie, Laura recalled how strangely disturbed she had been by the deep compelling look which had passed between herself and Jake Thackerey. Somehow, he had seemed to touch emotions within her, that she didn't recognize, didn't want to recognize, for they left her feeling unsure of herself and oddly vulnerable. These were the very sensations she'd vowed to bury; for her one aim in life now was to always be in charge of her own destiny. There wasn't room for fear or hesitation, and if she ever again allowed full rein to her conscience, then she'd be lost. She would need to be determined and objective if she was to be her own woman.

'Penny for 'em lass.'

Sighing quietly, she turned in response to Remmie's pointed remark. In the darkness of the old ramshackle van, she was glad he couldn't see the unhappiness which had drawn itself across her face. 'Oh, I'm just thinking, Uncle Remmie,' she told him in a matter-of-fact tone of voice, 'thinking how quickly it gets dark now,' she lied.

She felt uncomfortable and guilty in the ensuing silence, before Remmie commented, 'Oh. Not thinking about Mitch then, eh?'

She knew he was waiting for her to reply, but what could she say?

'Mitchell Strong's a grand young fellow, Laura,' Remmie concentrated on manoeuvering the rattling van over the jutting cobbles, 'I'm fond on him; you know that lass, don't you, eh?'

Laura sensed the plea in his voice. Snuggling up to him, she pulled the loose coat tightly about her. Although it wasn't yet November, the air was sharp and clean. 'Sorry,' she reached up to kiss his face, 'but he just makes me that mad! He's got the idea that I belong to him, he's got no right! No right at all!'

Remmie chuckled at the indignation of her retort. He turned his head, to look quietly at her brooding face. 'Mitch thinks the world on you, lass. He's only looking out for you; 'allus has done, making sure as you come to no harm.' He returned his concentration to the bumpy roads which led out of town towards the Ribblesdale area, and the open Moors.

Laura didn't reply; there was nothing to be said. She knew

how Mitch felt about her, for hadn't he conveyed it countless times; until she'd nearly come to suspect that she might feel the same way towards him. Physically, he was a strong handsome figure, proud and angry; but in terms of ambitions, he was small. His outlook was small, and so were his demands; except where *she* was concerned. She'd never really seen Mitch as a man of business; he lacked that special kind of drive. Jake Thackerey possessed it; and according to Uncle Remmie, so did she. During these past five years, she'd made herself many promises. But no vow had ever been uttered with such passion, such deep conviction as the one that grew strong within her now: Jake Thackerey, whether he knew it or not, whether he wanted it or not, would be hers! If she was to realize her dream of becoming rich and powerful, then he was her best chance; maybe her *only* chance, and she could not afford to ignore it. He had given her just a small glimpse of another way of life; and now she wouldn't rest until Jake Thackerey and all he stood for was brought to heel.

She smiled to herself in the disguising darkness of the van; her heartbeat racing so furiously that she feared it might betray her. One thought seared her mind with its fervent promise: tomorrow, Jake Thackerey would be going back to the bright lights and comforts of his own way of life; but tonight he was hers, and she wouldn't waste a single moment of it!

The night enveloped them in her darkening mantle, as they journeyed away from the lighted centre of Blackburn town and on towards home. The piercing halos of ghostly light emanating from the street-lamps grew scarcer and scarcer as they followed the outward route; along endless miserable terraced houses that led them through territory that was painfully familiar; past the house that had been her father's pride and joy, and which had been so cruelly stolen from her by the selfish and devious Molly. Strange disturbing thoughts of Parry Griffin's child, living next door with Mabel Fletcher, preyed on her mind. She supposed the child would grow into the image of that devil Parry Griffin. And with that supposition came the fervent hope that he would not be cast in his father's character.

'Come on, old gal.' Remmie pointed the old van at the daunting climb up towards Ribble Road. 'Keep your foot down, Uncle Remmie,' she urged, the flush on her cheeks reflecting a mounting anticipation, 'don't let it stop!'

Remmie afforded a speedy glance at his niece. 'One of these days, lass,' he told her half-seriously, 'we'll not make it up this blessed brew!'

'We'll *always* make it!' she declared in a sudden violent explosion. 'It'll take more than a steep brew to beat us!'

A curious smile twisted Remmie's mouth as he murmured in such low tones that Laura could only just hear. 'You're a strange creature, Laura Blake, an' that's a fact. I sometimes think you want the entire world in the clutch of your dainty little hand.'

Laura moved close to him. Reaching up to brush a light kiss against the roughness of his face, she whispered, 'No I don't; I don't want the world in my hand,' the sharp handsome image of Jake Thackerey sat coveted in her thoughts, 'I want the world at my *feet!*'

Remmie's great throaty roar of appreciation vibrated through the van. 'A lass after my own heart! I'm buggered if you're not the best bloody son a man could ever have!'

Laura smiled into the darkness. Her natural affection for Remmie had strengthened with the years, and he'd come to lean on her more and more. He seemed to search out in her the child Katya had never given him. During the years he'd shared his home with his sister's tragic daughters, Laura's determination to become as important to him as the son he'd always craved for had healed and finally erased his longing, as though it had never existed. Her devotion to him secured the deepest place in his heart. Netti he loved dearly; but Laura he adored.

His voice was calm and serious as he told her, 'You'll need to search long and hard to find a man able to match *your* fettle, that you will, my beauty! There's only one as comes quickly to mind; and that's Mitch. He'll make good account of himself to any lass,' the enthusiasm in his voice trailed off at Laura's brooding silence, 'not for you though, I'm thinking, eh? Got your sights set a good deal higher I dare say, although you're nobbut nineteen, and there's time enough to waste.'

Laura smiled secretly into the darkness. 'No,' she murmured, 'Mitch isn't for me, and you're wrong Uncle Remmie, there's never time to waste. I'll be twenty soon, and wanting the best!' Mitch was certainly a good looker, and she wouldn't deny those moments of curiosity and excitement in his presence. But they'd meant nothing and brought her no real comfort, and eroded her peace of mind and determined ambitions.

Rounding the top of Montague Street, and edging the spluttering old van into Ribble Road, Remmie manoeuvered it to the opposite side before jerking it to a halt in front of the house. The house was reminiscent of the solid and generously ornate Victorian period; not especially grand or pretentious, but a vast improvement on what Ruth Blake's girls had been used to. The brickwork was already showing signs of decay where the incisive winds swept unhindered across the moors, driving relentlessly against the vulnerable properties. The houses formed a small terrace, of which the Thorpe's abode was the most exposed at the farthest extremity.

'This poor old van's just about buggered,' he yanked the hand-brake on and slumped wearily across the steering-wheel, 'like me I expect — seen better days.'

Laura knew of Remmie's frequent visits to the doctor of late, and she had not missed Katya's pointed references to his heart condition and her sly insinuations that his, 'worrying over somebody else's children doesn't help matters!' Now the sight of him obviously so weary filled Laura's heart with dread. 'Come on, Uncle Remmie,' she gently urged, 'let's be getting inside.' Satisfied that he was merely tired and probably hungry, she got out of the van, and waited for him.

This particular stretch of the road was always steeped in menacing shadow. The solitary street lamp flickered a weak yellow light from the decayed mantle within its lantern-shaped house. The house was set back from the pavement by a short area of shrubbery enclosed by a red brick wall with a small wooden hand-gate.

Laura loved the house; she loved its elevated position and robust strength. But most of all, she loved the untamed moors that stretched away from the rear of the house, where over these past difficult years she had found a measure of uneasy peace and welcome isolation. There was a power, a magnificence about the bleak sweeping moors that filled her with a deep sense of awe; seeming to ease the terrible pain of her loneliness, and the burden of guarded secrets.

Holding the door open for Remmie to pass, she stood poised to shut out the night, her dark eyes piercing the blackness before her. She was suddenly alerted by the quickness of a figure across the road. In the fleeting uncertainty of the moment, she strained her eyes towards the rushing movement. It appeared to be a woman, shawled and bound against the cold biting air. Then as her eyes focused in the dark, the figure was just as suddenly gone.

Laura thought little of it, as she peered for a moment into the night, before closing the door against the enveloping darkness.

Allowing her mind to fill with thoughts of other, more exciting matters, she grew pleased with her recent impulsive extravagance in buying the dark blue dress that Katya had spitefully claimed made her 'look like a tart'. The dress was her one and only claim to shameful luxury, and she knew instinctively that Jake Thackerey would appreciate its slender clinging quality.

'Laura!' Uncle Remmie's call melted her thoughts as she made her way down the passage, towards the kitchen.

'There's a note here,' he moved from the cooking range, to hand her a sliver of white paper, 'Katya says we're to get a sandwich or some'at. Seems Lizzie Pendleton's had a bad fall, and Netti's gone with Katya, to the hospital.'

Laura quickly scanned the note, which confirmed what Uncle Remmie had told her. The sympathy she instinctively felt was quickly swamped by thoughts of Lizzie Pendleton's vindictiveness. And Laura wondered whether a measure of justice had at last been served on that woman for the wickedness of her tongue, and the sharp spite of her lingering malice towards Ruth Blake and the daughter who had inherited her striking looks.

'I'll get you a bite to eat, Uncle Remmie.' She wasn't unaware of Remmie's weariness as he slumped into the broad ladder-back chair by the table.

As she placed the fresh ham sandwiches and pint pot before him, he ran a broad comforting hand over his tired features. 'Can't seem to do a full day travelling about, lass, not like I used to.' He sounded tired, but then the familiar rugged smile won through as he told her stoutly, 'It'll be nice to have young

Jake Thackerey at the table tonight, eh? D'you know, he's not yet thirty, and he's already on his way to being a wealthy man.' He slurped the last of his tea, wiped a finger along his 'tache and stamped his pint pot on the table. 'Works hard though, and by God he makes some o' them veterans at the auctions look right useless! Oh aye, has 'em running round theirselves in circles, he does; he's a sharp 'un, there's no doubt o' that.' Getting to his feet, he glanced at the clock on the mantelpiece. 'There's time for a lie-down afore dinner. Give us a shout when Katya gets back, will you, lass?' A frown creased his forehead as he asked, 'Don't mention about yon Jake Thackerey, eh? Leave that to me.'

'I'll not say anything at all.' Laura knew that Katya enjoyed showing off her cooking skills, but she didn't welcome sudden surprises. She liked plenty of warning when it came to strange visitors. 'You go and lie down, Uncle Remmie. It's been a long day.' She was painfully aware of his dragging steps as he left, turning just once to smile at her. 'You're a grand lass.' His voice betrayed the deep affection he held for his sister's girl. 'You've had nowt easy, and you've even less to thank some folk for. But you've turned out grand, aye, that you have.' Blinking to disguise the brightness in his eyes, he heaved a sigh that straightened his shoulders and filled out his thick chest. 'You'll give us a shout then, lass?'

'Go on!' Laura shook her head at him. 'You know I will.'

After he left, the smile left her face and she scowled about the roomy kitchen. There was many a woman living in squalor in the alleys of Blackburn who'd spend her miserable days dreaming of a kitchen like this. It covered a bigger area than a regular parlour and scullery together, and there was everything a body could ever need. The magnificent black cooking-range boasted a king-size oven and sizeable hob, and standing alongside was a new gas cooker, which Katya used more frequently.

Laura smiled, as she thought of their expected visitor. If Katya had been given proper notice, that cooking range would have been in full use all day, fairly hopping with energy. But even so, she didn't doubt for a minute that Katya Thorpe would produce a splendid meal to delight her guest; in much the same way that a practised magician might produce a rabbit out of a hat.

On the far side wall by the back door stood a huge pine dresser, its tall spreading back festooned with deep scalloped shelves, decorated by china plates of every shape and colour. Numerous cups hung from beneath the shelves, all of the daintiest blue design and as fine-lipped as Laura had ever seen. By the door that went into the passage, a bench-type chest of drawers stretched almost the full length of the wall. At one end stood the mesh-covered meat-safe, always filled with tender hams and freshly made black-puddings. At the opposite end stood the huge bread-bin, in which Katya kept her store of biscuits and cake-loaves. Filling the considerable space in between were the highly treasured tools of Katya's trade: the various sized wooden and pot rolling-pins; baking tins of every assorted size and shape; thick wooden dough-rolling platforms and a huge barrel of spoons, ladles and other whisking tools. Hanging along the wall above the chest of drawers stretched a range of magnificent cast-iron pans, all lovingly scraped and cleaned ready for the next session.

In the very centre of the kitchen stood an oblong pine breakfast table. Along both sides of the table, and one at each end, stood eight ladder-back chairs with latticed wicker bottoms.

The window behind Laura was not the original one. Katya had deplored the narrow pane that had been the only source of light to the kitchen; so Uncle Remmie had paid to have a huge window knocked into the wall. It had instantly transformed the kitchen. On a summer's day, the sun would flood in to bathe everything in light, consequently making this room the real heart of the house, and a place that Laura loved.

Coming here to live in Katya Thorpe's domain had brought about a strange mixture of gratitude and resentment in Laura's bitter young heart. All of this was Katya Thorpe's; as she was constantly reminded by the woman herself; and she was no more than a lodger. It was true that Remmie had gone out of his way to make her and Netti feel that this was their home. But nothing could disguise the real truth. It *wasn't* their home, and it never could be.

She lifted her eyes towards the window, and the night thrust black and thick against the reaching light from the kitchen, and her aching heart sought peace, as it bathed in gentle recol-

159

lection of the moors beyond. In her mind's eye, the bleak expanse of untamed beauty served to temper the bitterness that raged within her. All of a sudden, and for no reason that she could identify, she wanted to cry. But she'd long ago given up the futile luxury of tears. They brought no comfort, nor did they serve any purpose. Tears were for dreamers, and dreamers believed in fate. Well, up to now, fate hadn't given her very much to believe in, so she had decided to take charge of her own destiny; and to believe only in what she alone could achieve. A half-smile whispered about her lovely mouth. It did seem strange though, that Jake Thackerey should enter her life just now, at a time when she was convinced of her readiness to strike out and grasp the security she so craved.

Her brooding thoughts were interrupted, as an insistent pounding on the front door suddenly echoed through the house. Afraid that Remmie might be disturbed, she hurried from the kitchen.

'It's alright, lass,' Remmie was already on his way down the stairs, 'I'll see to it.'

Laura cursed herself for having allowed the knocking to bring him down and at the same time was angry with whoever had pounded the door with such deliberation.

'I'm sorry.' The man stepped forward into the light of the hallway. He was painfully thin, with a long tired face and brown receding hair. 'I saw the light on, but I didn't seem to be able to make anyone hear.'

'That's alright,' Remmie stepped aside, allowing the man to enter, 'what is it you want?'

Laura shivered as Remmie closed the door. The cold night air had invaded the hall. The man was talking to Remmie as she excused herself and started to make her way back into the kitchen. His quiet words followed her, striking surprise and fear into her heart.

'It's your sister, Ruth Blake. I'm afraid she's gone missing. In view of her aggressive tendencies we have serious cause to fear for her own safety, and possibly others.'

Laura stopped, and as she turned towards the man whose empty eyes had shifted to rest on her face, he asked, 'Forgive me, but the resemblance is remarkable — not now, of course, but Ruth Blake was once a very beautiful woman.' He reached out a hand in formal greeting, 'You're Laura, I think?'

She didn't respond immediately; she couldn't seem to make herself move. 'Aggressive tendencies,' he'd said, 'her safety, and others.' She smiled at the man. 'Yes,' she told him, 'I'm Laura.' Fool that she was. The past had been buried long since. Ruth Blake was a sick woman, representing a threat only to herself. She'd wanted no contact with her daughters five years ago, and as far as Laura could tell, there was nothing now to suggest anything different. Ruth Blake had disowned her; discarded her like some worthless object. There might have been a time when the child Laura could have forgiven and forgotten; but not now! Not *this* Laura who, in spite of all that Ruth Blake could do, had survived. This Laura was different; stronger, wiser, and not so easy to frighten!

Turning to Remmie who stood deep in thought, a shadow of fear in his kindly brown eyes, she told him in a calm, deliberately matter-of-fact voice, 'She'll be alright, Uncle Remmie. If anybody can take care of herself, it's Ruth Blake.' Speaking to the man now, she explained, 'You'll have to excuse me. We have a guest arriving this evening, and there are things to see to.'

'Yes, please go ahead. It's really Mr Thorpe I came to see.' If the man was surprised by her dismissive attitude, he didn't show it in his reply. But once Laura had disappeared into the kitchen, the tone of his voice took on a sharp urgency as he told Remmie, 'I didn't want to frighten her, you understand. But we've every reason to believe that Ruth Blake has it in mind to harm somebody.' He nodded at Remmie's acknowledging gesture. 'I don't need to tell *you* about her blind hatred for the girl; you've witnessed it for yourself many a time.' He glanced with concern towards the kitchen door. 'Watch out for her. Until we find Ruth Blake, and be assured we will, you'll need to keep a sharp eye out.' He gave Remmie a look of sympathy. 'It's not a pleasant thing to have to say, but I'm afraid your sister is past all help. She's become a very dangerous woman; just how dangerous, even we hadn't recognized.' He sighed, then moving to open the door, his parting words were delivered in a soft but unmistakeable warning. 'Ruth Blake isn't just insane, I'm afraid. She has a devious calculating mind, and I have to tell you for your own safety,

161

Mr Thorpe, that she is the most evil creature it's ever been my unhappy lot to try and help. I'm sorry.' As he stepped out into the black of night, he called back, 'If she does show up round here, don't be fooled by her. Get in touch with us, or the police, straight away! We'll let you know of course, when we have her safe in custody.'

Remmie watched until he was out of sight, before closing the door and returning to the kitchen and Laura.

Chapter Thirteen

The clock on the mantelpiece chimed nine, as Laura took her place at the heavy circular dining table.

The room, like the house itself, echoed the stalwart dependability of its master. Each piece of heavy Victorian furniture had been hand chosen and lovingly restored by Remmie Blake.

The monstrous dark-brown sideboard against the back wall seemed to throw its looming shadow across the room. In a strange overpowering manner, it could lay claim to a thick-set beauty, which boasted character rather than grace. Its lines were straight and stiff, reaching upwards in the shape of bleak pillars and narrow arched mirrors; the shallow drawers and deeper cupboards were magnificently symmetrical in design, and extremely functional in practice.

The table, always draped with a deep green overcloth of heavy corded design and long silken tassles hanging from the edge, was constructed in the same sturdy design as its partnered sideboard. The table served as an eating surface, a playing surface, a sewing top, and mostly for Remmie Blake's benefit, a writing desk. The eight polished stand-chairs that skirted the circular table were now well-worn, and here and there in the stiff uncomfortably ridged seats, straying black horse-hairs stood up in little petrified clusters.

There were two other chairs, deep floral armchairs, set one either side of the firegate. The only other item of furniture was a small table with drop-down flaps and highly polished barley-twist legs. This was conveniently pushed out of the way into the corner by the window; 'for safety's sake,' Remmie had declared, ever protective of the arched-top wireless which perched on the narrow surface in a most precarious fashion.

Everyone knew their place at meal-times, and it never varied. Remmie Blake sat at the head of the table, before the

163

window. Katya sat on his right, and Laura to his left, with Netti beside her. The remaining four chairs were reserved for visitors who might be honoured with a request to stay for a meal. But that was a rare occurrence, as Remmie Blake placed a high value on his own company, his family's dependence, and the privacy of his living-room. But there was always the odd occasion, like now, when Lizzie Pendleton might invade their privacy at Katya's request; or Remmie would take it upon himself to invite a respectable business colleague.

Katya had seated Jake Thackerey on Remmie's left, shifting Laura and Netti one seat down the table. Seated beside Katya and directly opposite Laura, was Lizzie Pendleton. The seating arrangement offered anything but comfort to Laura; who was excited by the closeness of Jake Thackerey, yet painfully aware of the piercing disapproving glare of Lizzie Pendleton. Deliberately ignoring the hostility of the ailing woman, she smiled reassuringly at Remmie who, by the preoccupied expression on his face, was still dwelling on matters as yet known to only him and Laura.

The delicious aroma of freshly cooked hot-pot assailed their nostrils and sharpened their appetites as they waited for the man of the house to start grace.

The darkness outside had deepened to impenetrable blackness, and the wind from the neighbouring moors blew relentlessly against the house, shuddering the windows and forcing its penetrating gusts through the open chinks in the frames, where time and weather had successfully rotted any resistance. Rising from his seat at the table, Remmie drew the heavy brown cord curtains across the penetrating draughts, which played in through the windows to dissipate the warmth from the cheery blazing coalfire. As he brought the curtains together with a rippling swish he shivered noisily. Rubbing his hands together, he turned to smile vaguely at one and all, before resuming his position at the head of the table. Satisfied that everyone present was paying attention, he bowed his head, waited until all heads were so respectful, then in a smooth commanding voice, he delivered a prayer of grace before the evening meal.

With his head bowed, the weight of his thoughts seemed to sit heavy on his broad shoulders. He sighed deeply, and as he looked up just long enough to search out Laura's returning look, she saw the fear that unwittingly showed itself to her. She knew instinctively that he was thinking of Ruth Blake, and she wanted to assure him of her own confidence.

After grace, the pile of plates set before Katya Thorpe were systematically filled with the steaming hot-pot from the big brown casserole. The plates were then passed quickly and carefully around the table to everyone in turn.

Usually, there was little talk during meals. It was not a pastime Remmie normally approved of; but he had not entirely forbidden such exchanges and tonight, after all, was a special occasion.

'So you're from London way then, Mr Thackerey?' Lizzie Pendleton toyed with her fork over the hot-pot as she pinned Jake Thackerey beneath a quizzical gaze.

'That's right, Mrs Pendleton, a place called Woburn Sands.'

'It's *Miss* Pendleton! I'm not Katya's mother, I've never been married, you understand; but I've been the only mother Katya's ever had, since her own parents died when she was but a child in arms.' Having made known her embarrassment and disapproval at his misunderstanding, she registered pain and discomfort with her narrow sharp features. Ignoring Jake Thackerey's prompt apology at having jumped to the wrong conclusion, she turned towards Katya, her voice almost a whine. 'I said it wasn't a good idea for me to be hobbling about. My leg's giving me some gyp, Katya. I'd be obliged if you'd take me home.'

'But you've eaten nothing.' Katya left her seat to move towards Lizzie Pendleton.

'I *want* nothing! I told you I wasn't hungry. Just get me back to my bed.'

After some quick gentle talking from Uncle Remmie, Laura was relieved to see Katya return to her seat, and Lizzie Pendleton at least seem to enjoy her food, and even initiating the conversation at one point. 'Were you an admirer of our lately departed King George, Mr Thackerey?'

'Indeed I was, *Miss* Pendleton,' Laura enjoyed Lizzie Pendleton's indignant expression at his exaggeration of her title, 'they do say that during the war, King George travelled over half a million miles by train, sea and air, to the bombed

165

cities and to the munition factories.'

'An admirable man,' Uncle Remmie was speaking now, 'and I dare say his daughter Elizabeth will show the same qualities.'

'Well, *I* can't see how a snippet of a girl can take on such responsibilities!' Lizzie Pendleton snorted, looking to Katya for support.

'Oh, hardly a *snippet* of a girl,' Katya told her gently, 'and she is twenty-six, you know.'

'That's right, Katya,' Uncle Remmie beamed at his wife, 'and the lass did 'er share in the ATS during the war. She'll mek a good queen, 'ave no fear o' that, an' there'll be folks already counting the days to 'er coronation.'

Laura was relieved when the meal was finally over, and Katya considered it her duty to return the ever-complaining Lizzie Pendleton to the security of her own bed.

When Katya returned half-an-hour later, the two men were engaged in earnest conversation, occasionally stopping to enjoy the mugs of strong tea that Laura had brought them.

'He's right good-looking, isn't he?' Netti washed the last plate and handed it to Laura. 'And he likes you. I've been watching him. He hasn't taken his eyes off you all night.'

Laura gave her sister a gentle nudge. 'You're imagining things, Netti.' But even as she spoke, the truth of Netti's remark was equally obvious to her. Jake Thackerey was the most handsome man she'd ever seen, and he *had* watched her closely all evening. She hadn't yet decided how she might use the situation to her own advantage. He was obviously used to the attentions of attractive women. No doubt he was a man of the world, who would be more than a match for any woman who set out to trap him. A man as attractive and wealthy as Jake Thackerey could no doubt have his pick of beautiful women. If he was to be the one who would take her and Netti up the social ladder and into the finer strands of social life, then she'd need to play him carefully; to find out what he really wanted from a woman, and what that woman would need to offer in order to build up more than a physical bond. She didn't just want a pointless flirtation; even if that was all he had in mind. She wanted him, his wealth and the social standing he obviously enjoyed. In short, she would settle for nothing less than to be the wife of Jake Thackerey.

As she watched Netti stacking away the crockery, her heart was full and proud. She thought how lovely her sister was, and how the fine braids of hair wound delicately above her ears shone like spun gold against the overhead light. She marvelled at Netti's gentleness and her endless reserves of patience and understanding, and looking closely at the trim figure and pale delicate features, that odd realization, which had struck her so often of late and which she'd chosen to ignore, presented itself with increasing persistence in her mind. But, of course, the staring fact that Netti resembled no one else in the family meant nothing at all. It often happened like that, and there was nothing unusual or sinister about it. But all the same, it was a situation that caused Laura a degree of puzzlement, if nothing else. It would have been nice to have recognized a like feature of herself in Netti. But that was childish and vain, and such a notion didn't even deserve to be entertained. Netti was unique in more ways than one. She had an open generous nature, and in every way Laura could wish she was a loyal sister and friend.

'I'm afraid Lizzie's worn me out,' Katya Thorpe appeared at the kitchen doorway, 'I'll have to take myself off to my bed.' She sighed heavily and brushed the fair hair from her forehead, her sharp blue eyes set deep beneath a frown, as she asked Netti, 'You'll be able to finish up here, won't you?'

'O' course we will. You get off to bed, and we'll see to everything.' She waved an arm towards Laura, who'd grown used to Katya's policy of deliberately ignoring her. 'Laura's just about to make a fresh brew; shall I fetch you a mug upstairs?'

'You're a thoughtful little thing.' Katya reached out to draw Netti into a quick embrace. 'Yes, you can; I'll take a couple of sleeping tablets with it.' She sighed again. 'I get that tired lately, I don't know what to do with myself.' Still muttering, she turned towards the parlour, where she could be heard issuing apologies, and receiving condolences from Remmie and Jake.

Laura could not fathom Katya Thorpe. In the early days, when she and Netti had first come to this house, Katya Thorpe's malicious tongue had been the prime cause of many a sleepless night. Time and practice had hardened Laura's heart towards her; but now, as she watched the thin fair-haired figure moving along the passage and up the stairs, she realized

167

for the first time that perhaps Uncle Remmie knew more about Katya's health than he let on. There was certainly no denying the fact that she'd grown painfully thin, and her movements, which had once been quick and purposeful, were now tired and slow. Laura was moved with compassion, even though Katya Thorpe and that awful Lizzie Pendleton had gone out of their way at times to hurt her. And try as she might, Laura could not easily forgive such deliberate spite.

Placing the knives and forks into the drawer, she realized that there was more than one reason for her frustration. In that moment when Katya had drawn Netti into her arms, a startling observation had disturbed her peace of mind; Netti and Katya were alarmingly similar in build and feature, even their colouring was the same. Good God! What was she thinking. It was coincidence, pure coincidence, and she'd do well to put such nonsense out of her mind!

She deliberately turned her thoughts towards Remmie. He and he alone was her hero, stout-hearted, daring and occasionally ruthless. He had fire in his veins, ambition in his heart and passion in his soul, and it was said by all that she walked in his strong shadow.

A surge of pride filled her breast as she recalled some of his business deals. She had seen him bargain a man down to one third of his original asking price; and in her capacity as assistant, she had shared his pride in acquiring some particularly valuable and beautiful pieces of furniture fervently sought after by his growing number of competitors. Nigh on eight years had passed since the end of the war, and the latter years had seen a gradual increase in the demand for better things. It was a good time for the furniture dealers, especially those who could provide a higher standard of property, and the opportunities were there for the taking.

The drone of voices drifting in from the parlour told her that Jake Thackerey and Remmie were still discussing business. Of a sudden, she wanted to be part of it all; to judge for herself the true measure of Jake Thackerey, and to include herself in any future plans that might be taking shape.

'I'll take this in to Katya,' Netti said, 'then I'm off to bed myself. It's gone eleven, and I want to be bright and fresh for that interview with Miss Fordyke in the morning. They say she's right particular who she takes into that class of hers.'

Laura closed the drawer, her whole attention now concentrated on Netti and that forlorn expression she always had whenever something particular was playing on her mind. 'Netti Blake! If Miss Fordyke was to interview a hundred lasses tomorrow, she'd be hard pushed to find one anywhere near as good as *you*. She knows you're the best, and if anybody's likely to win that music scholarship, it's just *got* to be you!'

'If I'm able to play well, it's only thanks to you, Laura. I'd *never* have got the practice in for this exam if it hadn't been for you buying me that piano last year — all your hard-earned money.'

'That's right, Netti! Hard-earned for *one* reason, and that's to see you better yourself. Oh, one of these days, Netti Blake, folks'll come from miles around just to hear you play.'

Netti smiled, a patient mature smile that caressed her gentle beauty and belied the tenderness of her years. 'Honestly, Laura! To hear you talk, you'd think I was the best pianist in the whole world.'

'Well, you are!' Laura could never understand Netti's complacency about her special musical ability. Oh, if only *she* had such a talent! She would shout it from the rooftops until the whole world knew about it. But she had no special talents, and she had accepted that long ago. But Remmie had said she had a sharp eye for a unique piece of furniture, and *that* was a special talent not many folks could lay claim to. Right then! If that was to be the measure of her ability, then she'd not waste it. She'd use it, develop it, until she was better at it than anybody else.

Affectionately placing an arm around Netti's shoulders, she walked with her to the door. 'I'm telling you, one of these fine days, Netti,' she brushed a soft kiss against the girl's golden hair, 'I'll be done up in all my furs and jewels, and I'll be on my way to see you play in a grand concert. You'll be the star, and I'll be that proud.' Just thinking of the dream she had always cherished for Netti brought tears to her eyes and shattered the firmness of her voice. 'Miss Fordyke's no fool. Just play like you've never played before, and she'll be eating out of your hand.'

'Do you really think so, Laura?'

'Oh, Netti, Netti, I *know* so. I've *always* known.' Her mind sped back over the years, as she thought of something her father had said with his dying breath. Drawing the girl close to her, she whispered, 'I've never told you this — I've never told anybody — but our Dad said something to me once. He told me that I'd take the world and make it sing,' she smiled as the memory filled out in her mind, 'said we all had special powers. Well, maybe we have and maybe we haven't,' she caught Netti by the shoulders and turning her round, she looked deep into the clear innocence of her bright blue eyes, 'but he was wrong about *one* thing. It's not *me* that'll make the world sing! It's *you.* That's your special power, Netti, and you'll want for *nothing* while I can work and help you. You're not to worry about *anything* but your music. Be grateful for the marvellous talent God's given you, and don't let anything or anybody sway you!'

'All I can say is, it's a right shame it's *me* that's being interviewed tomorrow, and not you! I bet you'd make their hair stand on end. I wish I was more like you, Laura; more confident and determined.' Breaking away from her sister's arm, Netti headed for the stairs, turning just once to tell Laura quietly, 'And our Dad wasn't wrong. There's more than one way to make the world sing, and he was talking about *your* way Laura.'

'*You're* my world, Netti, and every ambition I've ever had is for you.'

There was a slight tremble in Netti's voice as she said, 'Don't expect too much of me, Laura. Sometimes when you talk about me the way you do, I get frightened.'

'Go on,' Laura was eager to get back to the parlour and Jake Thackerey, and she was quick to impatience when Netti showed doubt in herself, 'take yourself off, Katya won't thank you if that tea's stone cold when she gets it. Goodnight, God Bless.'

'Goodnight, God bless, Laura.'

'Ah!' Remmie got to his feet as she entered the room, 'Here's the very lass herself.' He walked over to the fireplace where the fire had burned down to a few blackened pieces of charcoal. Standing with his back to the dwindling warmth, he gestured for her to sit down. 'I've just been telling Jake here how you've got some right smart ideas for expansion.' A throaty chuckle interrupted his words. 'Told him how you kept on at me to open out that back wall from the shop yard into the Market Square. Couldn't see it myself, could I, eh? But you kept on till I gave in; and you were right.' He looked at Jake Thackerey, whose dark thoughtful eyes had come to rest on Laura's face. ''T'aint the first time she's been right neither!'

Laura remembered the incident. She'd spotted it straight away. On market days, when the square was teeming with potential customers there was no direct access into the shop; although the wall backed straight on to the busiest thorough-fare. Now, when the gates were opened on market day, even the curious who wandered into the yard to delve about in the cheaper secondhand items invariably found their way through to the shop, where they'd buy much more valuable pieces. Business had quickly trebled; although Uncle Remmie and Mitch had good-humouredly justified their own failure to spot the potential by claiming that the customers came to feast their eyes on the beautiful Laura, rather than on articles of furniture and paraphernalia. Remmie was saying as much now to Jake Thackerey.

'And who's to blame them?' His dark desirous eyes strayed over Laura's beauty. 'I only wish I had a few more days in which to enjoy your company, Laura, but I've to be off down the road, and back in the gallery first thing in the morning.'

'Gallery?' Laura thought that sounded grand.

'That's right, lass, ours is a shop, theirs is a "gallery". Jake travels about — off to Amsterdam in the next few days.' Remmie smiled, but Laura could see a shadow darken his eyes. 'Sounds exciting, eh? Not like round here; the same old faces, same old stamping ground.'

'Ah!' Jake Thackerey got to his feet. 'But that's up to you now, Remmie. I've put the proposition, all you've to do is say "yes", and it's done.'

'Aye, and it's a grand proposition.' Remmie sighed and shook his head slowly. 'I tell you, if there weren't . . . things . . . on me mind right now, I'd 'a given you a straight answer,' he sighed again, obviously weighing up the 'things' in his mind, 'but you'll have my word on it when we see you again, I promise you.'

'Well, Remmie, I hope to see you next summer.' He came to stand by Laura, to gaze down on her with his dark searching eyes. His voice grew quiet as he addressed Remmie, even while he gazed at her; but she knew the inherent meaning was meant for her alone. 'I'll look forward to it; I only wish it could be sooner, but they do say a pleasure postponed is a pleasure to savour.'

She found him exciting. He was poised, confident, and had a quality she hadn't experienced before: sophistication. He was worldly and well-travelled; in fact, he was everything she was not. Everything she intended to be.

Remmie stood up and held out his hand. 'I'll leave Laura the pleasure of seeing you off.' Gripping the hand which Jake Thackerey thrust into his, Remmie told him, 'But I'll shake on our discussion and give you a straight yes or no when you find your way back, eh?'

'I hope it's yes, Remmie, because an opportunity like this only comes once in a lifetime. I can't go it on my own, and it's hard to find a fellow in our business who can be trusted. I can trust *you*, Remmie. I respect your experience and the careful straightforward way you go about your business. We could do very well, you and me,' he turned to look at Laura, 'and look who we've got on our side. If we don't keep hold of her, she'll end up as the competition, then *none* of us will stand a chance!'

Remmie laughed out loud. 'Aye! You've got a point there.'

Laura got to her feet. What was this proposition that Jake Thackerey had put to Uncle Remmie? If she hoped he was about to tell her, she was disappointed.

'Goodnight then, lass,' Remmie leaned across to accept the kiss she placed on his cheek, 'I'm afraid I'm feeling the worst for wear tonight,' he gave her a meaningful look, 'an' I've things on me mind, things I need to talk over with Katya.'

Laura sensed that he was referring to the news of Ruth Blake's disappearance. But how he could imagine Katya would be able to help, she couldn't even begin to guess. She supposed though, that just discussing it with his wife would give him a measure of comfort. As for her own peace of mind, she wasn't too deeply disturbed. Ruth Blake had long ago ceased to worry her.

With Remmie on his way upstairs to seek Katya's confidence, and Netti probably lying in her bed fussing and worrying over her appointment with the dreaded Miss Fordyke, Laura felt strangely uncomfortable left alone in Jake Thackerey's close presence. Quite suddenly, all her calculated plans concerning him seemed fanciful and over-ambitious. Even so, a hard knot of determination prompted her to ask, 'Have you ever seen the moors, Mr Thackerey?'

'Jake, please.' He moved closer, his dark eyes searching her face. 'No, I've never seen the moors. Remmie tells me you've claimed them as your own?'

'No one could ever claim them.' She lifted her head until the fiery amber of her eyes mingled with his gaze. 'Would you like to see them? There's a moon tonight, and that's when they're most beautiful.'

She didn't wait for his answer, and he offered none. There seemed to be an understanding between them, and quickly sensing it, she led him from the room and out towards the back of the house, and the moors.

It was a strange evening, so still and brooding. The moon was bathed in gently shifting clouds which filtered its rays, causing them to flicker across the moors like bright scurrying shadows.

'It's as though the moors are breathing,' Laura's voice was reverently low. Turning to the man standing close to her, she told him, 'Lots of artists have tried to sketch these moors, you know. They often come up here during the different seasons, especially in early summer, when it's really beginning to wake,' a warm contented sigh accompanied her next words, 'but they can't capture the beauty of these moors. They're wild and free; they're not meant to be pinned down on a canvas or a sketching pad.'

She heard Jake Thackerey catch his breath as though in surprise; then as she turned back towards him, he bent his head slowly, and she knew he meant to kiss her. Some odd sensation quickened her heart and burned her face, and it was with a small inner burst of anger and sense of amazement, that she found herself thinking of Pearce, Pearce Griffin, of all people!

The touch of Jake's warm moist mouth on hers was unexpectedly pleasant; nothing more. Then as his arms grew tight about her, drawing her slim bending form into the arch of his

173

own, something erupted in her mind, causing her to break out in a cold sweat. It was the old memory, the scar which had not yet healed and which seemed always to haunt her. When she stiffened against him, Jake soothed her with the softness of his voice, 'Be still, my lovely.' His mouth breathed against hers, and she was aware of the urgency within him.

With a determined effort, Laura drew herself away from his encircling embrace. That one kiss, so passionately intended, had told her two things. Firstly, Jake Thackerey's handsome looks had not affected her deeply. She could never love him. But the most important thing she had learned was that this man, wealthy and powerful by her own standards, was hers for the taking; and take him she would. And in the taking, she would strive to bring him contentment, even though she was certain that their union would bring her none; save for the material element.

'Don't rush me, Jake,' she whispered, a world of promise in her quiet voice.

For what seemed ages, he looked down on her, his eyes black with the passion she had raised in him. Then, lifting his hand to gently stroke her hair, he murmured, 'You're bewitching, Laura. I've known many kinds of women, but never one like you. Believe me when I say that you're the most beautiful creature I've ever seen.'

Later, when Jake Thackerey had gone, and she was making her way upstairs, Laura thought of his words and smiled to herself. She remembered how Jake's closeness had prompted her to think of Pearce. Pearce, who had questioned Molly Griffin's treatment of her, and who in spite of his reputed badness, obviously had a measure of decency in him. She wondered about him, his activities and whereabouts. Yet Laura did not ignore that deep instinctive warning, which told her to stay clear of him and his family.

Entering her bedroom, she quietly closed the door against the dark, already sleeping house. Switching on the light, Laura restlessly looked around the confining room. The air struck cold and damp, and the sweet musky smell clogged her throat. The room was small, sensibly but unattractively furnished. To the left of the door stood a great heavy wardrobe, stripped of any relieving decoration, and rendered to a flat, easily main-

tained surface of high polish. Remmie had bought and renovated every piece of furniture throughout the house, retaining
decoration and intricate carving only where it was still worth
saving. The ruthlessness he so often employed in his business
transactions was just as fiercely applied to any dilapidated
piece of furniture which might in the long term benefit from a
complete change of appearance and personality.

Matching the wardrobe, and set in such a position as to hide
the little iron firegrate, stood a narrow serviceable tallboy.
That too, had been flattened to a smooth polished surface. The
four iron-handled drawers were deep and accommodating, and
Laura's well kept secrets were satisfactorily embedded in the
depths of those drawers, hidden from prying eyes.

The secrets were those of a lonely person; articles of private
interest and enjoyment. They had been stolen away from the
nearby moors, to lie coveted and protected in her jealous
possession. Wild flowers, plucked while enjoying the full
strength of colour and beauty, lay pressed and preserved
forever between the stained pages of her small bible. Bright
coloured stones of weird shapes and smooth comforting touch
bided in the dark corner of the drawer, lovingly placed in a long
white box. Her most recent acquisition was a most beautiful
and tragic thing. During one of her long meandering walks
across the windswept moors on a summer morning, she'd
alighted upon a spider's web. Within the luminous dewy
strands of the delicate creation, struggled a small butterfly. It
was the most magnificent creature Laura had ever seen. Striking in appearance, with spreading fingers of crimson and bright
yellow fashioning the opened span of tiny wings, it fought for
life until completely exerted.

She had watched from a distance, admiring the valiant
determination of such a tiny creature; yet she'd been loath to
interfere with Nature's primeval pattern. She'd often
wondered afterwards whether death was inevitable, asking
herself whether she was never meant to save it from its own
careless blundering.

Its struggle for survival must have started long before her
untimely arrival, for it was hopelessly exhausted and had
already begun to cease its futile wing-flapping. By the time she
had hesitated over her right to intervene, death had collected

its last fluttering heartbeat, and the beautiful creature lay empty and still within the grasping girdle of the spider's lair.

Her heart heavy with remorse, she had collected the poor dead butterfly, with such tenderness that the spider's web remained hardly disturbed; then holding it reverently within the hollowed palms of her hands, she had taken it home. Every thought in her mind on that funereal journey had been cruelly pierced by the conviction of her own guilty part in the little creature's demise. It had lain in the drawer since that day last summer, swathed in her softest white handkerchief and protected in an old silver watch-case.

Laura hated the confines of her small bedroom. This was evident now in the hard glint of her critical gaze as her restless eyes swept round the tiny room. In a typical gesture, Netti had given Laura free choice of the two rooms placed at their disposal by Remmie. For anyone else, the choice would have been easy; for the front-facing room besides Remmie's and Katya's was a large welcoming room, whose wide bay-windows caught the very last essence of daylight which constantly bathed the room in a warm smiling atmosphere.

But Laura's wild restlessness had allowed her no real freedom of choice. At first sight, she had been drawn to the open spaciousness of the front-facing room, and the decision to settle for that one had already formed itself in her mind, only to be suffocated by the view from the window; overlooking Ribble Road and the steep slope of Montague Street, the room had seemed quite suddenly to be stripped of its grandeur and become irreversibly tarnished.

Now, as she stood before the window in her own cloistered room, the panoramic view which stretched away transported Laura beyond her miserable surroundings, and into a strange restless kind of peace. On such a night as this, the heathland steeped in thick darkness and raked by the driving winds, she felt at one with its untamed spirit. She shifted the latch across to release the window, which she then slid upwards, allowing the full force of the cold wind to invade her bedroom.

Lifting her face to enjoy the rush of air, Laura began to undress. With slow deliberate movements, she removed her clothes as though taunting a lover of impatient passions. Only when the biting cold had viciously chilled her body and reduced her to trembling, did she reach out to close the window against it.

Shivering uncontrollably, she collected the deep red cover from the bed and wrapped it tightly about her. She felt exhilarated. The day had been very rewarding, and she murmured the name of Jake Thackerey gently as she moved towards the long mirror embedded in the wardrobe.

'Jake Thackerey,' the feel of his name gave her a sense of great excitement, 'Jake . . . Jake Thackerey,' she murmured over and over.

As she stared into the yellowing mirror at her reflection, a strange sensation of power surged through her. Straightening her shoulders, she let the bed-cover slither from her body to settle around her feet. For a long time, she just stood before the mirror, staring at the image before her.

Her eyes travelled the curves of her body's reflection critically. She felt the power of her unquestionable beauty, and her full sensuous mouth moved into an easy satisfied smile. There could be no denying her magnificence. The slim lean shape of her figure had matured into the attractive fruition of womanhood. The breasts were full and thrusting; culminating in the darker pigmentation of deliciously rounded nipples of inviting prominence. The straight shoulders were strong yet unmistakeably feminine; a perfect setting for the wild profusion of auburn hair that settled tantalizingly across them. Her smooth shapely hips followed a proud natural line, down through the dark obvious signs of womanhood and into the slender beauty of long graceful legs.

She never wondered at her exquisite form. She was Laura Blake, a person unique. That Laura Blake was as perfect in figure and feature as anyone had a right to be, did not occupy her thoughts. It was merely a fact, and one that she took for granted.

Stepping forward to touch the reflection of her face, she ran a sensuous finger along the proud high cheekbone, over the rich temptation of her mouth, then down the white perfection of her throat. The deep intense gaze that looked back at her promised a world of pleasure, and Laura knew with striking certainty that she had it within her to achieve anything. She had known terrible poverty and degradation. She had experienced pain and fear. But the fear she felt now was a strange new emotion, which for a fleeting moment caused her to panic. 'What if he never comes back?' The urgent exclamation was spontaneous, startling her into the need for assurance. 'Oh, but he *must* — he will!' Her deeper instincts told her so. She had felt the passion within him, and she had seen the tormented desire in his eyes.

The slow smile of satisfaction returned to light her splendid features as she slithered, still gloriously naked, between the cold enveloping sheets. 'Oh, yes. Jake Thackerey will come back. And when he does, I'll be ready!' she said softly, but with determination, into the darkness.

The following morning gave Laura little time to dwell on Jake Thackerey, for Netti was out of bed early, nervous about her imminent interview and dreading the prospect that Miss Fordyke might ask her questions to which she might not have the answers.

For a solid hour — and even before being allowed the comfort of a cup of tea — Laura found herself pinned into a chair, with a list of questions and answers thrust into her hand. Netti sat nervously before her sister, all ready with what she prayed were the right responses.

'Go on, Laura, I'm ready. Start anywhere,' she urged, her eyes bright with anticipation, and fidgeting so excitedly on the edge of the chair that Laura could see her landing on the floor at her feet any minute.

'Alright. Just calm down my girl! Now then . . .' Laura cast her eyes down the list of questions prepared by Netti — all about the great composers, their lives and their music. And all of it strange and fascinating to Laura. Yet this was *Netti*'s forte, Laura reminded herself, shaking off a niggle of inadequacy and concentrating on the task in hand.

'Was the famous musician Richard Strauss related to the Austrian composer *Johann* Strauss?'

'No.'

'Good girl! Right then, staying with Richard Strauss, what year was he born, and where?'

'Munich — 1864.'

'Name two of the instruments he played.'

178

'Piano and violin.' Here, Netti gave a little giggle, obviously pleased with herself.

'Hmm — these are too easy my girl!' smiled Laura, running her eyes further down the sheet. 'Ah! Stravinsky — what was the *first* work to win him notice?'

There was a slight pause before Netti answered, with perhaps a little less of her previous confidence, 'Er — *Scherzo Fantastique* — based on Maeterlinck's *Life of the Boe*.'

'Which instrument did Bach mainly compose for?'

'That's easy! It was *my* instrument — the piano.'

And so it went on, with Laura asking the questions in as roundabout a way as possible. And Netti bouncing back with the answers, until her nervousness had completely disappeared.

When Laura saw her sister out of the front door, she was pleased to see that Netti positively *glowed* with confidence. 'Go on with you, Netti Blake!' she chided, 'You've done your work well. Miss Fordyke won't know what hit her.' And as Netti kissed her goodbye, Laura felt that she too had acquired just a little insight into Netti's world. It gave her a curious feeling of well-being as she took herself back inside, to indulge in a well-deserved cup of tea.

Chapter Fourteen

'Get off an' make your own bloody mark in the world, an' leave me an' my shop alone!' Parry Griffin leaned forwards across the table towards his son, his fist doubled tight and thumping the air. 'I'll mek my way up again. Aye! Wi'out *your* soddin' interference an' all.'

'Some chance!' Now Pearce Griffin was on his feet, glowering back at his father with equal vehemence, but when he spoke it was with control and with an authority that seemed to fuel the other man's rage. 'You've managed to hang on to that shop up to now, and this house. But the way things are, it's only a matter o' time before you lose the lot.' He leaned forward, thrusting his face upwards in defiance as he said, '*I'm* the only one as can help you, and I will. My ideas can put that shop back on its feet in no time. But I want a free hand; don't want no drunkard telling me what to do!'

'Aye! You want a free 'and alright, an' like as not I'll lose everything that much quicker. I may be a drunkard, but I don't associate wi' the likes o' Johnny Street, gamblers an' scum with it! No, you'll not get your 'ands on yon bloody shop! Not while I've breath enough to see you off! I'm not finished yet, not by a long chalk. That shop were got wi' sweat an' blood, an' I'll 'ave it thriving again, I tell you!'

'Got with sweat and blood you say? Well, maybe, but not *your* sweat and blood. That was rightfully Jud Blake's and it was only your cheating that got it from him. By rights, it belongs to Laura.'

Molly Griffin had retreated to the scullery. She'd witnessed these scenes before and she had no taste for them. And now she stopped her pot-stirring, for she knew what the mention of Laura would do.

Parry Griffin had his son by the scruff of the neck, a look of fear on his face. But when he opened his mouth to issue a warning, there was no fear in his voice. It was calm and threatening. 'As God's my judge, son or no son! If you so much as whisper 'er name, or talk on matters past, I'll flay you alive!' He tightened his grip about Pearce's throat, and when he'd seen the mouth fall open to gasp for breath, and the look of a coward return, he released his hold. Then stepping back to watch as his son gasped air back into his lungs, he laughed out loud. 'Got the message right enough, I can see that.' He set his mouth in a downward line as though seeing something repulsive. 'You were never 'ard to convince. Never did 'ave any spunk!' He turned away, as though unable to look on Pearce any further, then in a low threatening voice, he said, 'Get out! But think on what I've told you! An' don't show your face to me again, you're no son o' mine.'

Without saying a word, Pearce Griffin slunk across the parlour and out of the front door. Ten minutes later, his father followed suit.

Molly Griffin came to sit by the table, where she sat quietly for a long time, her mind dwelling on things long gone. It was true that her sister's furniture and clothes together with Jud Blake's personal things had fetched a tidy sum, which she'd salted away at the time. But now, what with Parry's demands and nothing coming in but a few shillings from her sewing, it was all gone, and so were most of her own things.

She lowered her eyes and opened her fist, then having satisfied herself that the forty shillings were still there, she closed her fist again, thinking it was a good thing that Pearce slipped her a bit of cash now and then. Oh, if Parry 'ad seen this, he never would 'ave settled for the five bob just now.

She began to chuckle, and just as quickly, she stopped. For a moment, she stood very still, listening for the sounds that she fancied came from the cellar. There it was again. Like scampering rats. That might have been the answer, but for the rat-poison she religiously fed them. Didn't like rats. And she'd never stand for them sharing her abode. Not rats? But what then?

In a moment, she was into the scullery, out of the back door and down the steps. She fetched the candle and matches from the niche in the cellar-wall, then with the candle lighted and clutched tight in her hand, she moved forward treading softly as she went.

She hadn't known what to expect. But what she saw made her scream out loud and drop the candle, which instantly fluttered out. With her hand clutched to her heart, she stood stiff in the pitch black, murmuring, "Eaven preserve us, oh, 'eaven preserve us.'

When her courage returned, she bent down, feeling about to retrieve the candle. When her hand touched it, she breathed a sigh of relief, stood up and dug into her pocket for the box of matches. Her hands shook and fumbled and a small pile of burnt matches lay at her feet, before she'd managed to light the candle.

Had her eyes deceived her, she wondered? Stepping forward and holding the candle higher this time, she knew they had not. For there in front of her, crouched tightly into the corner and the look of terror in her mad eyes, was a figure that looked like her sister, Ruth Blake. She was enveloped in a long dark coat that was draped about her head and shoulders like a shawl.

It took fifteen minutes of coaxing to get Ruth Blake out of the cellar, and another half hour of feeding and grooming, before she was sitting at the table with some semblance of dignity.

Molly Griffin had been mortified at the sight of her sister cowering in that cellar. But she had been equally horrified to find that even with her face clean and auburn hair combed, there was a savageness, a demented look about Ruth Blake that struck fear into her heart.

'You'll not send me back? I'll *not* go back there! I'll not,' Ruth spat out, from lips which had once been desirable to men, but which were now stretched thin and tight against her stained teeth. The fear tainting her voice drove her to scramble to her feet and to pace back and forth across the floor like a wild animal caged.

'No, I'll not send you back.' Molly Griffin caught the frantic woman in her arms, then led her forward to seat her in the big armchair. She'd said she wouldn't send her sister back to the asylum, and she wouldn't. Mad as Ruth Blake had become, there was no other family for Molly Griffin — no one to give a blessed damn about her! Suddenly a wicked thought presented

182

itself to her, bringing to her ungainly features a sinister satisfaction. There was a certain characteristic of that madness which she *could* use to her own advantage; the delusion which brought about a vicious hatred of a particular person. It was *Laura* who had attracted Ruth's loathing — *Laura* upon whose person Ruth would wreak vengeance were she able to.

Here was her chance! Her way of repaying Laura Blake for the trouble she'd caused. An opportunity which she'd be a bloody fool to miss!

Displaying her sweetest smile and her voice soft with concern, she told her sister, "T'aint *me* as would put you away fer good. Oh no — it's that girl o' yourn. That divil, Laura!' When Ruth Blake's eyes were wide with fear, Molly Griffin pulled her chair closer. She lowered her voice and warned in a menacing tone, 'Oh, I'm tellin' you, me beauty! That one's *already* 'ad the law searchin' fer yer — 'igh an' low they've looked. Ready to root yer out an' lock yer away fer ever more!'

For just the swiftest moment, Ruth Blake looked almost normal. But then with startling transformation, the madness began to creep back, until so terribly distorted were her features that even Molly Griffin felt the need to inch away. But she listened with satisfaction when her sister said, 'You're right! That Laura — she *is* a devil!' Her voice dropped to a whisper. 'I know where she is! I've *seen* her — watched her. She's at Remmie's — Penny Street weren't grand enough for the likes of her.'

'That's true, Ruth! And do y'know she even got rid of all your stuff? Would you believe she sold every last one o' poor Jud's belongings!'

The mention of Jud's name struck a guilty chord in the sick woman's mind and she began to cry. Molly Griffin made no effort to comfort her — she'd known well enough of her sister's illicit affair with Joe Blessing, a weak bugger of a man if ever there was one! No, she had no inclination to comfort Ruth. Instead she leaned back in her chair, a curious gleam in her eye as she warned, 'You'll not be safe, Ruth! Not in this 'ouse — nor in any other. Not till Laura's got out o' the way fer good.' She waited to let the words sink in. ''Ow long you been down i' that there celler, eh?' There was no reply, so she leaned back again and, added, 'Ah well. Don't mek no difference at all.

You'll be alright there fer a little while longer I dare say — till Laura sends 'em lookin' 'ere fer yer.'

'No! I'll not let her!'

'That's right — don't you let 'er, eh? You an' me, we've plans to talk on, aint we? We've to see what can be done about riddin' us-selves o' a few enemies, don't you see?' She watched until Ruth Blake gave an agreeable nod, then resting back into the chair, she beckoned the other woman to kneel beside her.

And there they stayed; the one crouched on the floor, her head resting against the chair, the other with a fearsome smile on her face, stroking her sister's dark hair. And each with a look of madness in her eyes.

Chapter Fifteen

Laura looked around the packed auction room and it amused her to see that as usual, all eyes were on her, as though they'd never seen a woman before. She smiled and nodded at them in turn, and they grinned back, touching their caps and shifting about uncomfortably, their thoughts as busy as hers. There wasn't a man in the room who wouldn't have given his soul to bed Remmie Thorpe's niece. Yet they knew that such dreams were fanciful, for Laura Blake, who had blossomed into a creature of incredible beauty, was not for the likes of them. She was a woman of quality, a rare queen brought up amongst peasants.

Uncle Remmie was gazing down at her, with a distinct look of pride on his half-smiling face. Leaning towards her, he whispered, 'I'm the envy of every manjack 'ere!'

Laura laughed, then replied softly, 'Give over, Uncle Remmie. They don't like me being here, invading their territory.'

'Aye, well, 'appen there's a sniff o' the truth in that an' all. A grown woman standing 'ere alongside these men, well, that's a rare old sight. But you'll not let that bother you if *I* know it. Laura Blake might be a woman the likes of which they'll never see again, but in business, she's man enough to match the lot on 'em, eh?' He laughed and stretched himself to stand upright, intent now on the man who was making his way to the rostrum. He didn't hear Laura say quietly, 'No, Uncle Remmie, they *don't* bother me. Not any of them.' And lowering her eyes to check the catalogue in her hand, she thought of the painting they were trying to buy, and consequently, she was reminded of Jake Thackerey.

Jake Thackerey's return to Blackburn — and Laura — had been repeatedly delayed. The weeks had stretched into months, until Laura thought she would never see him again. It was less than a week before her twenty-first birthday when Remmie had a letter from him, asking him to 'root out any Yourelli paintings' as he expected to arrive before the weekend.

Laura had received the news with mixed feeling. Unbeknown to Remmie, she'd telephoned the gallery at Woburn Sands no less than eight times since Jake Thackerey's visit to Remmie's house. The smooth female voice on the other end had politely informed her, 'I'm afraid Mr Thackerey is abroad on business . . . not expected back for some time.'

Laura had grown to resent the voice, and its cool dismissive authority, so that eventually she stopped ringing. Instead, she immersed her every working day in the increasing and profitable business assets of the shop. She derived great pleasure too, from the time increasingly spent watching Mitch at work. There was a special magic in the way his clever hands moulded new life into an old neglected piece of furniture. Another pleasing development was Netti's growing commitment to her music.

In her leisure hours she walked on the bleak moors, thinking of Jake Thackerey and what seemed to be a lost dream. She had initially viewed his absence and now the curtness of his letter to Remmie as a personal insult. But once the anger had subsided, she finally came to see it all as an inevitable setback. After all, he was coming back.

She sighed quietly, her thoughtful mood suddenly pierced by Remmie's exclamation, 'This is it, lass!' He was clearly excited, as he nudged her with quiet urgency. 'Keep your fingers crossed, lass, it's the only one in the sale!'

She looked upwards, towards the auctioneer's rostrum. The man with the hammer was seated behind a heavy panelled wooden table. His furtive conversation with the person standing slightly to his left caused him to tilt his chair sideways in a remarkable feat of balancing. Laura couldn't help but smile at his unusual appearance. She likened him at once to a walrus; certainly, the thick white 'tache sprouting from his top lip resembled that of a walrus with absurd accuracy. His face was narrow at the top, gradually increasing in width, eventually culminating in a broad flat chin which merged into the thickness of his bloated neck. Tiny rimless spectacles with half-lens balanced in constant danger of slithering from the top of his nose; and perched on top of the damp white hair which fell in delightful disarray around his head, was a narrow ill-fitting hat of speckly tweed pattern.

He finished his conversation and brought his chair back to a safer position, then opening his hairy mouth, he addressed the gathering and at the same time gestured for the porter holding the painting to step forward.

'Lot 42,' he waved the hammer above his head, 'a painting of exceptional beauty. This, friends, is the best piece of merchandise today.' He hesitated, looking down at the written information before him. '"Cottage in the Mist", by Yourelli. It isn't often we get paintings, and this is a really nice one.' He lifted his head and focused pea-small eyes on various prospective purchasers. 'Right then! Who'll start me, eh?' His request was greeted with silence.

Laura sensed Remmie's impatience, but she knew he wouldn't be the first to bid. It was a game of skill, where each player waited for the other to make the first move. She looked up at his face, and felt admiration for the clever expression of indifference which shaped his strong features.

'A guinea? Who'll start me at a guinea?' The auctioneer tipped his hat back on his small head. 'Come on! We all know it's worth more than that!'

Someone in the crowd must have decided that the delaying tactics had gone on long enough. Suddenly, the air was brisk with activity and the bidding reached five guineas with frightening speed. This was the part Laura loved, and she would have given anything if only Remmie would trust her to bid. *She* knew she was capable, but Remmie had insisted that she must wait until her twenty-first birthday.

A small doubt in the back of her mind grew as the bidding hovered at twelve guineas. Had Remmie left it too late? Surely he couldn't be losing his touch, not Remmie!

'Going once . . . twice . . .' The walrus raised his hammer, threatening to strike the table.

Laura closed her eyes, unable to watch any longer. Then as the rush of air brushed her burning face, she knew that Remmie had entered a bid, and she breathed a sigh of relief.

'Thirteen guineas . . . fourteen, do I hear fifteen? Do I hear fifteen guineas?'

Laura followed the direction of his gaze. The walrus was looking at Remmie. 'Yes! Fifteen, I have fifteen guineas! Have I got sixteen? Thank you sir, sixteen I have!' The Market Hall was hushed as all eyes searched out the new bidder, who was leaning confidently against the exit door.

It was with a rush of alarm that Laura recognized the tall dark-haired man. It was Pearce Griffin, his lean handsome face set in thought, seemingly unaware of the girl across the room. So he was back! Pearce Griffin, whom Laura had last seen over five years ago. He was back and looking prosperous. She had heard talk that he'd been seen on occasions visiting the house on Butler Street, and more than once she had wondered whether he might seek her out.

When suddenly his deep eyes lifted to meet her gaze, Laura cursed herself for the feelings that surged through her. Meeting his arrogant gaze, she half-smiled, unable to completely disguise the confusion that threaded its way through her turbulent emotions; then turning away, she deliberately concentrated on the bidding. She wanted this painting for Jake Thackerey.

There was a pause in the bidding, and Laura looked towards Remmie. He had seen Pearce Griffin, but apart from a fleeting expression of surprise, he displayed no emotion. Raising his catalogue, he entered a new bid.

'Thank you sir.' The walrus addressed Pearce. 'Eighteen?' he asked quietly, then to the audience, 'Do I hear eighteen?'

Pearce Griffin lowered his eyes to concentrate on his catalogue. Then just as Laura was convinced he'd stopped bidding, a slight nod of his dark head enthused the proceedings.

'Eighteen guineas I'm bid!' The auctioneer lifted his hat to quickly set it back again on his head. It was obvious that the figure had gone way beyond his expectations.

Laura looked up at Remmie. He's giving it away! she thought, he's giving it away! In the background, she could hear the auctioneer raising the final call, and her heart thumped painfully; he couldn't give it away, not now! He couldn't! She knew they'd come to purchase that painting for Jake Thackerey. What was Remmie thinking of? He'd get his money back, and more!

'Uncle Remmie!' Her voice was quiet, but pressing. 'Please!'

The rising tears almost choked her. Remmie looked down at her, and in that instant, she knew his trust in her was complete. Meeting the steadfast gaze of his gentle brown eyes, she smiled beneath the warmth of his love and the strength of his commitment to her. All she needed was his encouraging murmur, 'Go on, lass!'

'Nineteen!' Her voice rang out loud and triumphant.

'Nineteen guineas!' The exhilaration she felt was so complete, that she wondered whether she'd ever experience such glory again. The painting was theirs ... was Jake Thackerey's! Pearce Griffin caught her eyes, and with a curt nod, he lifted his catalogue to tap his forehead in admiration. Then he smiled a lingering smile, before losing himself in the departing crowd.

'Done like a good 'un!' Remmie's pride shone fiercely in the adoring look he bestowed on her. Then glancing about the room, he said in a low voice, 'Beat 'em at their own game, lass. That's the way. They'll not tek kindly to a woman dipping 'er thumb in their pie,' he laughed.

And when she smartly replied, 'Well, they'll just have to get used to it, won't they?' he laughed again and shook his head. 'Aye! I think they will, lass, I think they will!'

Laura had earlier caught sight of two other lots, which she had seen to be both beautiful and valuable. Lot No. 46 was an extremely pretty antique Sheraton mahogany Pembroke table inlaid and crossbanded with a light-coloured tulip wood.

Lot No. 47 was an unmarked set of fine willow-patterned serving dishes. Remmie firmly endorsed her opinion of these two items, and did not prepare to leave until these had been secured at a satisfactory price.

It had been a gratifying afternoon. But for Laura, the real highlight of the day was the acquisition of that lovely painting.

All the way back to the shop, she held the painting safely on her knees, loath to let it lie in the back of the van.

'Funny thing, lass,' Remmie cast a sideways look at the painting, 'this Yourelli artist was born and bred in Blackburn, but I'd never 'eard on 'im, till yon Jake Thackerey pointed 'im out.'

A sense of futility gripped Laura as she replied, 'I think it's cruel that such a talent can just die. Still, he's not forgotten, is he? Not like I'll be when I'm gone.'

Remmie laughed heartily, then sensing her self-consciousness reached across to stroke her hair, saying, 'You're a strange one. However you an' Netti came to be so different, I'll never know. There's allus some'at pulling at you, isn't there? Tugging and pulling, giving you no peace.' He sighed heavily. 'There's never any good comes o' fighting what life deals you, lass! Aspiring out o' your station can fetch its own grief!'

Laura patted his hand. 'We did well today, didn't we?' she asked brightly.

'Aye, lass. We did,' agreed Remmie, marvelling at her ability to close a subject so astutely.

They drove the rest of the way in silence. But it was a warm communicative silence, which drew them together in comradeship and faith. As they drew into the yard, Mitch was waiting to greet them. And in spite of her conviction that Mitch often complicated her life, Laura could not help but admire the man he'd become. The handsome features were shaped now by rugged lines of deepening maturity. His strong athletic figure commanded confidence; and he had grown quieter of nature, yet somehow more striking and authoritative.

'Good fella!' Remmie threw open the doors at the back of the van. 'Watch how you go, Mitch,' he'd stopped calling him 'lad' these past twelve months, 'there's some breakables under that lot somewhere.'

Laura was carefully manoeuvering the painting out of the van, when Mitch came to stand before her. Beneath the intense glare of his green eyes she felt uncomfortable. Then in a proud confident tone, she told him, 'We got the painting.'

'So I see,' he murmured. His voice was cold and accusing as he went on, 'It *is* for Jake Thackerey though, isn't it?'

Laura could have snapped out a suitable retort, but chose not to. With the greatest effort, she kept her composure, then swiftly departed beneath the intensity of his watchful gaze.

Remmie satisfied himself that the purchases were secure, then stroking his 'tache in that thoughtful manner he often adopted when troubled, he reached inside his waistcoat pocket, to draw out the Bill of Sale. 'See that!' He handed it to Mitch. 'Never paid so much for a painting 'afore. It's to be hoped it's

190

not me first real pup! You tek that painting upstairs; small fortune, that.' He retrieved the Bill from Mitch, who retorted, 'Let's hope that Thackerey fellow doesn't let you down, eh?'

Laura scowled at Mitch. She didn't care much for his sullen jealous mood, and she would have preferred to watch the painting herself. But when she asked Remmie, 'Can't *I* take the painting home? It'll be safe enough with me . . .' he replied promptly, 'No, lass!' And Laura knew that when he used that particular tone, there was no arguing the point. And in all truth, she knew it would be far more secure left in Mitch's care, here at the shop.

All the way home, she could think of little else but Jake Thackerey. Would he still find her bewitching? Had he thought of her since their last meeting? She found herself wondering who it was that answered his telephone with such bright feminine tones and cool efficiency. In an odd, detached way, she began to grow jealous. But it wasn't an angry, heated emotion. It was more the possessive attitude with which a person might regard a valuable chest of drawers, purchased as a calculated investment and treasured only because of its growing value. Jake Thackerey was such an investment, and she would leave no way open to other interested bidders.

Her private thoughts slipped away, as Remmie held the van door open, 'Thought you'd gone asleep on me, lass. Never known you so quiet!'

Laura smiled, but gave no answer. At the front door, she slipped her key into the lock, opened the door, then stepped back to let Remmie pass on into the house.

Katya emerged from the kitchen to greet Remmie. 'Oh, I'm so glad you're home, Remmie.'

'Are you, lass, bless you, an' I'm glad to *be* home. It's been a rare ol' day.'

Laura watched Remmie gather the slim fair-haired woman into his outstretched arms. He reached down to brush his mouth over hers, then still hugging her to him, he went towards the kitchen. Laura didn't follow them, but made her way directly upstairs.

After washing and changing, Laura collected Netti from her room where, as usual, she was deep in study and surrounded by numerous neatly stacked piles of notepaper and sheet-music.

The two of them made their way to the dining parlour, where the tea had already been prepared by Netti and Katya. The freshly baked pies and scones had obviously taken a great deal of time and effort, but for some reason, Laura didn't feel hungry enough to do them justice.

'Go on then, Netti, tell Laura your exciting news.' Katya's words made Laura turn towards Netti. 'News? What news?'

'I wasn't going to tell her until later, Katya.' Netti looked at Katya, an expression of slight disapproval shaping her features. 'Miss Fordyke called me into the office today, Laura. I got the best marks for the mock tests. She says if I'm willing to pursue a teaching career, she'll make sure there's a post waiting for me, with her.'

'Teaching!' Laura was painfully aware of the half-smile of satisfaction lighting Katya's face. 'Teaching's not for *you*, Netti, you're too good! Miss Fordyke knows you're made for better things. You want to be a concert pianist, don't you? Isn't that what you've always set your heart on?'

'Laura! Leave the lass alone for now, eh? She's old enough to make up her own mind.' Remmie stood up to push his chair back, then addressing himself to Netti, he said, 'Mebbe we can talk on it later, eh?' And the tone of his voice left Netti in no doubt that he too had been shaken by her announcement.

'Yes, Uncle Remmie.' Netti quietly excused herself, then avoiding Laura's searching eyes, she collected the plates and left for the kitchen, where the sound of running water and busy movement indicated that she had started the washing-up.

Normally, Laura would have followed her to lend a hand, but even after Remmie and Katya had left the table, she remained in her seat. Netti had confided in Katya before her! That would account for the gloating expression on Katya Thorpe's face. Perhaps Remmie was right. It wouldn't be wise to talk to Netti just now. Laura found it hard to believe that Miss Fordyke could really be serious! What? Shut Netti away in a classroom and condemn her to anonymity? Never!

Later, in the parlour, Remmie remarked on the pointed lack of conversation. 'Well! You two 'int got much to say, an' that's a fact.'

'I'm tired, Uncle Remmie. I'll not be long before I go to bed.'

'It's all that studying, lass, seems you do little else these

192

days. Still, if it's what you want, then likely it won't seem too much of a bind, eh?'

Laura had seated herself on the floor, her back comfortable against the sideboard. To all intents and purposes, she appeared to be studying a catalogue on a forthcoming sale, but her mind was alert to the conversation, and she was already speculating how she could make Netti see the futility of Miss Fordyke's offer.

A high wind blustered fiercely about the house, roaring and moaning in the chimney, and occasionally sending little puffs of black choking smoke into the room.

'Pull the damper out, Katya, afore we're all suffocated!' Remmie asked his wife, who was seated on the nearest floral armchair to the fire.

'It's that tiresome wind,' Katya leaned forward to grab the long poker, with which she reached above the back of the fire, to open the dampening ledge, 'it never seems to stop moaning and wailing, like some demented soul! You wouldn't think it was coming up to spring, would you?'

Remmie sat up straight in his chair, looking with concern at his wife. 'Alright, are you lass? You're not looking so well, I'm thinking?'

Laura too had noticed how much paler than usual Katya was. Her blue eyes were drained and dull, and there was a weariness in her voice. The only vitality about her shone in the golden braids of her lovely silken hair, set snugly in the nape of her neck in a perfectly round coil.

'I'm fine, Remmie,' she assured him, settling back into the comfort of her chair.

'It's that troublesome Lizzie Pendleton, isn't it?' Remmie was suddenly angry. 'She's nobbut a spoiled old woman, phlebitis or not! She has you dancing attendance every blessed turn!' He got to his feet and strode angrily to the fireplace, where he stood deep in thought for a long moment, before calling their attention to his next words. 'This concerns all of you.' He waited until all eyes were on him, then he continued, 'some time back, I was made an offer, a good business offer, by Jake Thackerey.' Turning to Laura, he explained, 'I've said nowt about it 'afore, because I'd already made my mind up against it, so there seemed no point in fetching it up. Now, well Katya,

I think it might do you good in particular.'

Katya looked at Laura, rested her eyes a little longer on Netti, then urged Remmie, 'Go on.'

'Jake Thackerey's clever, right clever in matters o' business. He's a buyer for an antique gallery down south, that much you know. What you *don't* know is that the fella as owns the gallery looks to retire soon, an' he's put a proposition to Jake Thackerey. The old fella's offered to sell the business to him at a very attractive figure, providing he gets a cut o' the profits up to his death. He'll be what's called a sleeping partner. He'll have no say in running the business at all. Now, even though he's offered it at a price below market value, Jake Thackerey needs a partner. He can't raise the capital on his own.' Remmie paused to stroke his 'tache. 'For all I know, he might have managed to fix himself up by now. But if he's *still* looking to make a deal, I'm half-minded to tek him on. I reckon Laura's gone as far as she can with me, and there's much better pickings for *all* on us down south. The folks that way place a higher value on antiques.'

'Remmie!' Katya was on her feet now. 'What exactly are you saying? What will all this mean to *you*, and me?'

Remmie regarded her closely. 'It means, lass, that I shall sell out here, and buy a half-share o' the antique gallery.'

'Will it mean us moving down south, away from here?'

'It will.'

'No, Remmie! I'll *not* move!'

All this time, Laura had listened attentively to Remmie's words. Now, as Katya glared at her with open hatred, she had to look away.

'You're doing it for *her*, aren't you?' Katya glared once more at Laura, before bursting into tears and rushing from the room.

'Katya! It's for *you* I'm doing it, lass, can't you see that.' He hurried after her. 'I'm thinking o' *your* health . . .'

'Leave me be!'

Laura waited until the sounds of their voices had disappeared into the bedroom, then she went to stand beside Netti. 'I had wanted to talk to you, Netti. But it can wait, eh?'

'Oh, Laura, what's made Uncle Remmie think of such a thing?' Netti relaxed into Laura's comforting embrace. 'He

194

belongs *here*, in the North. He'd never settle anywhere else.'

Laura placed the guard before the fire, then turned the lights out as they made their way upstairs. 'I know he's very worried about Katya's health, Netti, and Lizzie Pendleton being so self-centred and demanding where Katya's concerned. And he *is* a good business-man, don't forget. He must see the venture to be a good one, or he would never entertain it; *you* know that.' Yet Katya's words, 'You're doing it for *her*!' had dampened Laura's own enthusiasm. There was no denying that Remmie was strong-minded enough not to be really swayed by anybody. But deep down, Laura hoped that his decision *had* been prompted by the right reasons; that he was doing it for his *own* sake, and for Katya's. It would be unpleasant to have Katya's unhappiness on her conscience, however deep their differences.

Suddenly, and for a reason that she could not fathom, Laura didn't feel as excited about the prospect of actually working and living alongside Jake Thackerey as she would have liked. Instead, she felt apprehensive, yet didn't really know why. She quieted her restless thoughts by telling herself it was most likely that Netti's news had disturbed her.

After saying goodnight to Netti and getting ready for bed, she stood for a long time, just looking out of the window. All manner of things crossed her mind in turn, to be thought over and then dismissed. The idea of actually moving from the area, brought first a degree of sadness, and then a kind of exhilaration. She thought of the past, and the people who had shaped her future, either directly or indirectly. Then, at last, her mind came to dwell on Ruth Blake, and on the poor deformed little Rosie, whom she'd loved so very much. Even in her innermost thoughts, she dared not dwell on the question of Rosie's untimely death.

As she stared out at the dark merging stretch of moors and sky, a small flurry of alarm penetrated her pensive mood. Straining her eyes against the thick shroud of darkness, she detected a movement, quick and low against the profusion of bushes by the back wall. Holding her breath, she watched as the crouched figure scurried along. For the briefest moment, the light from her window bathed the dark shape. Then, with a shiver of horror, she thought she recognized the long unkempt hair and the broad craggy face of old Joe Blessing! But it couldn't be, could it? Since Ruth Blake's disappearance, there was talk of Joe Blessing having hidden himself away. 'Not in his right mind,' they said. Certainly, *she* hadn't seen him for years; not that she wanted to! And the thought that he was out there stalking the moors seemed preposterous! Yet, there had been something.

The night had closed in again, lying still and undisturbed. But her mind couldn't rest. In one way and another, it had been a strange day, and the knowledge that Ruth Blake was still free, together with the feeling that somebody was watching the house, left her imagining all manner of things.

Lowering the curtains, she looked towards the open doorway, and the landing light beyond. She wondered whether Netti would mind if she slept in her room for tonight. She felt angry with herself for being so foolish, but at the same time, she felt unsettled and apprehensive. On bare soundless feet, she went quickly down the landing towards Netti's room.

The low murmur of voices was easily recognizable, as she drew nearer to Remmie and Katya's bedroom. She felt uncomfortable, as though eavesdropping; but she had to pass the door in order to get to Netti's room down at the end of the landing.

Remmie's stern voice filtered out through the half-closed door. 'Katya, you're too soft, lass. You're letting Lizzie Pendleton wear you out! You know what the doctor said, you're to tek things easy.'

'You can't blame Lizzie! I've never been strong, and nobody knows that more than she does. She's been like my own mother, Remmie. I can't desert her now, when she needs looking after!'

'Aye! That's as may be, but there's times when she treats you like her own personal servant, and just as you want to look after *her*, lass, I want to look after *you*! It grieves me to see the way she uses you. What about the Welfare? Have they been told she's laid up?'

'Oh, Remmie! You know she'd not have no Welfare at the door.'

Laura could sympathise with Katya's exasperation in the deep silence that followed, and she imagined the two of them looking at each other, each one convinced of the justification for their own arguments. Moving on careful but hurried foot-steps, she made her way down the landing. Suddenly, she heard her own name on Katya's lips, and stopping to squash herself against the wall, she found the accusations painful to her ears.

'It's not me *or* Lizzie, is it?' Kayta's voice sounded agitated, close to tears yet vehement as she continued, 'You're thinking of *her*, of your precious Laura. She's your *sister*'s child, Remmie, not yours! And what's more, she *hates* me, do you hear, hates me?'

Laura might have been struck by lightning, such was the shock she felt at Katya's words. So Katya imagined that *she* was hated! When all this time, Laura had seen Katya's vin-dictiveness as being a kind of hatred. And now it seemed more likely that it was a form of defence, born from the fertile work-ings of a jealous mind. There and then, Laura resolved to speak to Katya tomorrow. There was peace to be made between them. And at the prospect, Laura's heart became much lighter.

Remmie's voice echoed Laura's sentiments. 'Nay, Katya, don't get yourself into a state, lass. Laura doesn't hate you. 'Appen she's become a bit too defensive of late, but that's all. There's no hatred in her.'

'There is! Towards *me*, anyway. Can't you see how she clings to you, Remmie? How she tries to come between us? I don't like her! It's her that's put you up to this idea of moving, isn't it? Isn't it?'

Remmie was quick to assure Katya that what she was saying was not the truth. Not at all, because Laura had known noth-ing of it. And to Laura, who felt defenceless against Katya's verbal attack, Katya's insistence that she did not believe Remmie was abominable, because there was no man alive more truthful than Remmie Thorpe!

The silence following Remmie's assurance that if Katya *really* wanted it, they would stay where they were, gave Laura to imagine that Remmie had taken Katya in his arms. Poor Katya, who had let her possessiveness of Remmie become an obsession. And Laura could not blame her, for it was probably Lizzie Pendleton who had poisoned her mind.

Laura tiptoed on to Netti's room, hoping that the raised and angry voices had not reached her sister's ears. She found Netti

197

still awake, but undisturbed. Closing the door, she crossed to the bed and slipped in beside Netti. Settling back against the bed-head, she said, 'Thought you'd be asleep by now.'

Netti smiled, moving along in the bed to make more room for her sister. 'No. I've been lying here thinking.' Her long fair hair fanned out in a bright silhouette against the low lights from the beside lamp. 'I'm sorry I didn't talk to you first, Laura, about Miss Fordyke's offer.' Her gentle features hardened to emphasize the truth of her next words. 'But I promise you, I won't give her an answer, until *we've* discussed it first.'

Laura slid down in the bed, a half-smile shadowing her face. That was all she needed. Miss Fordyke would need to look elsewhere for a new teacher. 'Turn the light out, Netti. We'll talk about it tomorrow, when I get back from the shop.'

'Goodnight, God bless, Laura.'

As she lay in the darkness Laura began to examine the way of things. It had been quite a shock seeing Pearce Griffin at the auction, and although she would have wished it otherwise, the sight of him had definitely unnerved her. With Jake Thackerey coming here this weekend, and Remmie half-minded to think about his offer of a partnership, she should have felt good; but she didn't. There was a churning inside her that distorted her well-laid plans. Jake Thackerey was still her best bet; hers and Netti's. She had no reason to doubt that, but still she felt somehow discontented and unsure of things. Katya's emotional outburst just now had been very hurtful, and Laura was not sure how to allay Katya's fears. There was only *one* sure way that Laura could see, and that was for her and Netti to move out.

Such a step would cause difficulties, because for one thing, although Remmie was fair in the wage he paid her, Laura could not see how to stretch it to make do. Netti needed things for her studies, and they both had to survive. And what of Mabel's weekly allowance for young Tom? It was completely out of the question for *that* to be diminished in any way! No, if anything, Laura would have liked to give Mabel even *more* money, now that the lad was nearing school-age.

And even if she could manage to find a house, how in God's name would she find enough money to pay the rent? And apart from that, no landlord would offer tenancy to a female, of her age particularly. He would probably insist on someone signing for responsibility over her.

It was all a terrible predicament. And when Laura eventually fell asleep, she had not been able to find an answer. Except to wonder whether Jake Thackerey might be the saving of it all?

It was some time later, just before the dawn broke, when Remmie woke them, the tears streaming down his solemn face. Astonishingly, neither Netti nor Laura had heard anything of Remmie's anguish in the night.

The sombre-faced doctor assured them that Katya's heart had just given out while she lay sleeping. Then, by way of compensation, he announced that it had been a very peaceful passing.

To Laura, death was no stranger. She had seen him more than once, and too close to home. But the tears she shed for Katya were heartfelt, and her own sense of loss was unexpectedly acute. Knowing how Remmie had idolized his wife, Laura's deepest compassion went out to him, and she prayed that he would find the strength to cope.

Chapter Sixteen

It was a bright, crisp day when they buried Katya Thorpe; and it was Laura's twenty-first birthday.

Katya's poor delicate body had been transported to Blackburn Infirmary, where the cause of death was officially reported to be heart failure. The body was then brought back to the house, in a dark wood coffin decorated with gleaming brass handles and clutches of fine carving at the head and feet. It had stood on trestles by the window in the front parlour for the two days prior to the funeral.

Remmie had cried until his eyes were so swollen they were almost closed. Then he'd fallen into a deep silence, oblivious to all but the sight of his beloved Katya lying so still and alone in her grand coffin. From the moment her body had been returned to the house he hardly moved from her side. Laura couldn't persuade him away, and the food she brought to him was later removed by Netti untouched and unnoticed.

It was left to Laura to make all the necessary arrangements. The irony of fixing Katya Thorpe's burial on the same day as her own twenty-first birthday didn't escape her, and she felt sure that Katya would have somehow squeezed a degree of satisfaction from it.

Laura did what she could at the shop, but what with the funeral details and Remmie helpless in his grief, a great many business transactions were successfully concluded by Mitch, whose unswerving loyalty to Remmie raised him in Laura's esteem.

There had been a good turn-out at the funeral, for both Remmie and Katya had some good friends and acquaintances. Laura had asked Mitch to go round and inform Molly Griffin, but apparently she had kept him on the doorstep, showing little interest in the news he carried. She had not attended the funeral, and Laura was glad of that. So that left Laura and Netti as the only real relatives, although Lizzie Pendleton, who reportedly hadn't been sober since Katya's death, made repeated garbled efforts to dispute that claim. 'There's more than one dark secret lying in the ground with my poor Katya,' she was heard to tell various departing mourners.

Most of the visitors and sympathizers had gone, and Laura stood now by the parlour door, quietly surveying the plates of half-eaten sandwiches and well-drained glasses that haphazardly decorated every available surface.

She glanced back towards the kitchen, where Netti had already started the washing up. Then moving into the parlour, she made a mental note that Lizzie Pendleton was still seated in the armchair by the fireplace. Some three-quarters of an hour she'd been there, half-asleep, then half-awake — and more drunk than any sick old woman had a right to be. Laura left her there, and busied herself collecting the crockery. It might be as well to leave Lizzie Pendleton where she was; let her sleep it all off. At least while she was asleep, she was not hurting from Katya's passing.

The two other people in the parlour, Mitch and Sally Fletcher, raised their heads from deep conversation. Mitch made his way over to Lizzie Pendleton concerning himself with her obvious condition, and Sally came to stand before Laura. Taking the black beret from her head, she shook the long brown hair free, and addressed Laura in a softly spoken voice. 'Laura, we need to talk; it's about Tom.'

One look at Sally's troubled face told Laura that something of a serious nature had taken place. Then as Sally went on to impart the cause of her concern, that her mam, Mabel, was ill and deeply anxious about Tom's future, Laura too, grew increasingly apprehensive. Mabel, who had been more than a friend, was poorly, and it was *that* thought which was uppermost in Laura's mind. She did not want Mabel worrying at a time when her thoughts should be for herself and for her family. 'Tell your mam that I'll be round to see her the first minute I can,' Laura reached out a comforting hand to Sally, 'and tell her not to worry, Sally.'

'And Tom?'

For a moment Laura was quiet, her mind grappling with

Sally's question; a question which had to be answered.

The years had fled since Mabel had taken Tom into her own home, giving Laura that time which she had so desperately needed, and *still* needed. Yet here it was, that same insurmountable problem, compounded by the passing of time and her estrangement from the boy, now caught up with her, and demanding to be resolved. And resolved it would have to be, for Mabel's sake and for the boy's sake.

Laura had no plan, no easy answers, and even though her voice conveyed confidence and reassurance for Sally's benefit as she replied, 'I'll talk to your Mam. It'll be alright, Sally. You'll see,' her heart was racing and all the old fears had come back to haunt her. Whatever she decided now would be no easy task. The boy himself saw her as a virtual stranger and a threat. And people of Molly Griffin's character did not mellow with the years, and should all be revealed, Laura was in no doubt that trouble and sorrow would come of it.

The sight of Mitch making his way towards them prompted Laura to end the conversation. But not before she had quickly assured Sally, 'I'll do what's best, you've got my word on that.' Judging by the relief that lightened Sally's face, Laura's word was good enough.

As Mitch drew level with Sally and she turned to look up at him, Laura couldn't help but notice the softness with which she gazed at him, and it caused her heart to make a little skip.

'Laura, I'm not so sure we ought leave Lizzie Pendleton sitting in that chair. Do you want me to get her home to her bed?' Mitch asked.

'No. She'll be fine there for a while.'

'You could be right, happen she's best sleeping it off. And Remmie?'

'Upstairs. He's alright, just tired.'

'I did want a word . . . what do you think?'

Laura was satisfied that Remmie was beginning to cope a little better now, although she knew it would take him a long time to accept Katya's death; if he ever did. He needed some rest, but he'd been so morose and silent these last few days, maybe a few words with Mitch might be just what he needed.

'Let me go up first,' she answered, 'if he's sleeping we'd best leave him.'

Mitch nodded, his eyes intent on her face as she turned and headed towards the stairway and Remmie's room.

He wasn't sleeping, and as she tapped gently on the door and entered at his bidding, her heart went out to him. It seemed as though he'd aged almost overnight. Even the smile with which he greeted her gave the impression that his thoughts were elsewhere. He was seated by the dresser, a large framed photograph of Katya lying face up on his knee. As Laura came to stand by his side, he raised his gentle brown eyes to look upon her face. The noise of his weary sigh seemed to fill the room as he told her quietly, 'She spent many a time sitting here where I am now. I'd watch 'er from me bed, while she brushed 'er lovely hair till it shone like pure gold.' His voice broke away for a second, and for no reason Laura felt plagued with guilt and remorse.

Sinking to her knees beside him, she said softly, 'I'm sorry, Uncle Remmie.' Then as he reached out an affectionate hand to smooth her hair, she could see the expression of surprise on his face. It had been a long time since she'd called him 'Uncle'.

While Remmie reminisced, Laura sat quiet for a while, just listening, and before long, she was relieved to see the light return to his eyes. Getting to her feet, she told him that Mitch was waiting downstairs to see him. She wasn't surprised when he waved his hand in a gesture of impatience, saying, 'No. Not now, lass. The others all gone, 'ave they?'

'Yes, apart from Sally Fletcher, who's giving us a hand. Oh, and Lizzie Pendleton, stretched out in the chair, as drunk as a Lord!'

'Drunk, eh? Well, we all 'ave us own ways o' coping with grief, I suppose, lass.' The great sigh which swelled his chest, seemed to lift him out of the chair, as he rose to walk over to the window. 'I'll not come down, lass. Not just yet, you understand?'

Laura understood, and as she made her way back to the parlour, she was ashamed to find herself wondering whether Remmie might still go ahead with his plans to take up Jake Thackerey's offer. After all, it was a good one, and a brand new start might be just what Remmie needed. She couldn't deny her own renewed enthusiasm for the prospect, nor for Jake's arrival some time this evening.

She knew she ought to have telephoned the gallery and informed Jake of Katya's death, and asked that he should postpone his visit; but she had not been able to bring herself to do it. Obviously Remmie had forgotten Jake's impending visit, but there would be time enough to remind him after Mitch and Sally had gone.

Thinking of Sally, and the news she had brought, cast a shadow over Laura's features. It was still there when she entered the parlour, and it deepened when she saw that both Sally and Mitch had gone. There was only Lizzie Pendleton mumbling to herself, straddled uncomfortably in the chair.

'We're in here!' Mitch's voice came from the kitchen.

As she turned, Mitch was there, right beside her, and from the look on his face, Laura knew that he would have liked to take her in his arms and press her close to that loyal heart of his. It struck Laura, how much easier life would be if only she could bring herself to respond with honesty. But when she spoke, there was no betrayal of her innermost feelings in her quiet voice. 'Mitch, do you think you could please take Lizzie Pendleton home now?'

Lizzie Pendleton was suddenly alert, her pink watery eyes staring fixedly at Laura, as though she was trying to satisfy herself about something. 'S'pposing I don't *want* to go? S'pposing I want to stay here, in Katya's house?' Hoisting herself into a half-upright position, she cackled and shook her head. 'Wouldn't like that would you, eh? Might cramp your style with Remmie. Oh yes! Don't think I haven't seen you, told Katya I did! You watch that scheming Laura, I told her, we mustn't forget she's Ruth Blake's daughter.' She made an effort to get out of the chair, but only succeeded in sinking further back into it, her drunken eyes rolling. 'Bad blood! Folks don't know half, but they will, as God's my judge, they will.'

Laura wasn't inclined to place too much importance on what Lizzie Pendleton's befuddled mind conjured up. She knew, everybody knew of the ill-feeling between Ruth Blake and this woman. With Ruth Blake out of sight, Lizzie Pendleton had chosen to direct her malice at Laura. And Laura for her part, thought Lizzie Pendleton to be contemptible. Turning to Mitch, she asked again, 'Please Mitch, just take her home would you?'

'What about Remmie? Did you tell him I wanted a word?'

'Yes. But he's best left alone right now . . . wants to be quiet for a while.'

'Well, it won't hurt till Monday, when I see him.' All of a sudden he grew silent, and Laura sensed that his mood had changed. Reaching into the deep pocket of his suit coat, he produced a small oblong parcel, neatly wrapped in pretty coloured paper. Holding it out towards her, he said with a smile, 'Happy twenty-first birthday, Laura.' At the look of surprise on her face he said, 'You surely didn't think I'd forget?'

Laura didn't know *what* to think. But she might have guessed! Mitch had no intention of allowing Katya's funeral to overshadow her own twenty-first birthday. Taking the box, she thanked him, and this time, when he brought his strong hand-some face down towards her, she did not resist. There was something very pleasing about his nearness, and when his mouth touched hers, it brought a warm comforting feeling with it. But that was all. Parry Griffin had taken much more than her virginity and innocence; he had viciously deprived her of hope, hope that one day she might be part of a warm loving relationship, as she had witnessed between Mabel and her husband, Belle and Tupper, and more closely to her, between Remmie and Katya. As she remembered being in Mitch's arms, a great feeling of sadness came over her.

After she'd seen Sally and Mitch out of the door, with Lizzie Pendleton clinging to them as though her very life depended on it, and Netti bringing up the rear, Laura started to make her way towards the kitchen.

'Laura!' Remmie's voice brought her to a halt halfway down the passage. He was standing at the foot of the stairs. 'Is Mitch coming back?'

'No. He's off to the shop. There's that sofa-table to be stripped and ready for french-polishing. Mr Carruthers wants it first thing Monday morning.'

Laura watched him reaching up for his jacket from one of the hall-pegs. Then he shrugged himself into it and came down the passage towards her. 'I've a mind to spend a while in the shop.'

Laura was relieved to see him more alert, and after

embracing him, she waited until he had taken his leave. Then she paused for a moment and then gazed at the parcel Mitch had given her. Quickly, she removed the paper to reveal a box. It was made of leather, dark and beautifully grained, and it felt smooth against her fingers. Clicking open the lid, she looked down at the fine gold chain and oval shaped locket, then taking it gently between finger and thumb, she opened the locket case. Inside, engraved in the back were the words. 'To Laura. Happy twenty-first, All my love, Mitch.'

Gazing at it, Laura's eyes began to smart and a tight lump straddled her throat. That Mitch! Would he never give up? Fancy giving her such a present! Oh, but it *was* lovely. Indeed it was. Suddenly her thoughts of Mitch became merged with the image of Sally, and her mind grew troubled. Things had taken a turn and by its very nature, all the signs were that it was a turn for the worst. All this time her secret had been safe with Mabel and her daughter, Sally. And young Tom had been secure under Mabel's wing. But now? Oh, what now?

Well, first thing in the morning, she would go to Mabel's house, and when she had talked to Mabel, her course of action would hopefully be much clearer. But if Laura was to heed the deeper feelings which insistently murmured beneath her conscious thought, she would know without question that to admit Tom into her own life now was no more possible than it had been on the day he was birthed. Later, as Laura sat alone in the house, after rushing around in preparation for Jake Thackerey's arrival, she took time to weigh up the situation concerning Tom, and the emotions that began to swamp her became urgent and frightening.

It was with relief that she heard the sound of the front door opening, and at the same moment, she heard the clock strike seven. It suddenly dawned on her that Remmie was still not aware of Jake Thackerey's impending arrival. She'd best tell him now, and hope that he would not be angry.

But the news didn't anger Remmie. In fact, if anything, it seemed to Laura that he was glad. 'I like that young Thackerey. Katya liked 'im, an' all. You an' Netti sort some'at out for a meal. Nothing grand, mind! It, it wouldn't be respectful. But he'll be in need of a hearty meal after travelling all that way. Right! I'm off for a bath.' Wrinkling his nose, he sniffed at his hands. 'That blessed french-polish gets everywhere!'

'Where's Netti, Remmie, did she come with you?' Laura had expected to see her return before now.

'Netti? Oh, she stayed to see to Lizzie Pendleton.' As he turned to make his way towards the stairs, he muttered, 'Going wrong is that one, aye, going wrong.'

When Netti returned some ten minutes later, Laura thought she detected a worried look on her face. But when Netti saw her sister eyeing her thoughtfully, she laughed. 'What a handful she's getting. Won't let you undress her, doesn't want to be washed, moaning and complaining.'

'What about?'

'Oh, this and that, nothing in particular. At least, nothing that makes sense.'

Laura thought for a while, then shrugged her shoulders and suggested, 'You go and make yourself look lovely, while I see what I can conjure up for a meal. We've a visitor, you remember? Jake Thackerey's arriving this evening.'

'Oh, Laura. Can't you put him off? I mean, what with Katya, and everything; and what about Uncle Remmie?'

'It's alright. It'll do him good to have somebody here, taking his mind off things.'

'How long is he staying?'

'Overnight, if the original arrangement still holds. So, while you're waiting to get to the bathroom, I'd be grateful if you'd take the sheets off the spare bed, and wrap them round the tank to air. I'll make a start on the meal, fish I think, then you can take over while I get ready.' Glancing at the clock on the shelf, she said with some surprise, 'He'll be at the door inside of two hours.'

In fact, Jake Thackerey arrived just over an hour later, and he wasn't alone.

Laura heard the voices in the hallway, just as she was brushing out her hair, trying to tease the wayward strands into some semblance of discipline. As she took stock of herself in the long mirror on the wardrobe door, she wasn't displeased with the result of her labours.

She'd chosen to wear the black dress that she knew complimented her colouring. The slim fitting dress, with its fine pleated yoke and profusion of swirling hem at the calf, clung

207

seductively to the smooth curves of her attractive figure. To complete the effect, she threaded a fine black bandana through the deep waves of her hair, tying the ends so that they dangled down her neck and across her shoulder, in a way that attracted the eye, exaggerating the comparison between the smooth silky blackness of the bandana and the soft creaminess of her skin. The black high-heeled shoes served to accentuate her small perfect feet and the long graceful lines of her silk-stockinged legs. Black suited her, and it was with some surprise that she found herself wondering whether Katya would agree.

Certainly, when she made her way downstairs, appreciation was immediately obvious.

'Laura, even more lovely than I remember you, and grown into a woman.' He came towards her, looking exactly as she had kept him in her mind. He had an easy charm that seemed to relax the atmosphere, yet at the same time charge it with emotion. The dark jacket and trousers made his tall figure seem somehow slimmer than she remembered, and the stark white of his shirt was no more striking than the strong straight smile with which he greeted her. Strange though, how his dark expressive eyes reminded her of Pearce Griffin, then the image of him at the auction sprang into her thoughts and dulled her pleasure.

'This is Ria, Ria Morgan.' Jake held out his hand to bring the young woman to his side. 'Ria, this is Laura Blake.'

It was only now that Laura became aware of Jake's companion. She hadn't noticed her seated by the door, and she was angry that the surprise and disappointment she felt at that moment must surely have been evident on her face.

Ria Morgan was extremely attractive. She wasn't striking in appearance, but there was a beauty, a softness about her, that Laura immediately perceived. Short, dark hair cropped close and a small oval face lit up by large brown eyes, gave her the appearance of a child; that gentle helpless appearance that men seemed attracted to.

Laura forced a smile to cover the hurt and embarrassment inside her. At once, she discreetly appraised the small dainty form and noticed with no small degree of envy the expensive lines of the other woman's green silk dress. Simple and sophisticated, without frills or fuss, it was well chosen and extremely flattering.

Ria Morgan stepped forward, and Laura thought she detected a slight whisper of alarm in the smile which greeted her. 'Jake said you were beautiful, and he was right, you are.'

Laura waited, for she had the impression that Ria Morgan hadn't yet finished speaking. She felt impatient and somehow cheated. Jake had no right to bring this person here, and what was worse, Laura immediately recognized Ria Morgan's voice. It was the same smooth voice that had informed her so often over the telephone that, 'Mr Thackerey is not available.' She wondered whether Ria Morgan had guessed that she was the persistent caller desperately trying to contact Jake Thackerey. There had been times when Laura really began to believe that she might never see him again; and yet here he was. It did seem as though their paths were meant to cross.

She sensed that Ria Morgan was watching her closely, and a quiet surge of confidence warmed her heart. She could handle this woman. Life had taught her to be prepared for anything. But in spite of her self-assurance, Laura was *not* prepared for Ria Morgan's next words.

'Jake holds you in high esteem, Laura. I've looked forward to meeting you.' She shifted her brown eyes to fix on Jake, who still appeared to be entranced by Laura's stunning presence, then having successfully drawn his gaze back to herself, Ria Morgan continued. 'Jake didn't give me a full introduction.' She held her hand out, taking Laura's in a firm grip. 'He foolishly forgot to mention that I'm his fiancée. We're engaged to be married.'

Laura's smile froze on her face, and she inwardly congratulated herself on disguising the rush of alarm that greeted Ria Morgan's words. She managed to maintain her self-assurance throughout the evening meal, articulately keeping the conversation on a light-hearted and congenial level. The fact that she could do so Laura readily attributed to Katya's example, and she was grateful for it.

At one point, Remmie got to his feet to address the gathering, and Laura, seeing the lines of grief still deep in his kindly face and his soft brown eyes on her, suddenly realized that in spite of his losing Katya, he had not forgotten his niece's twenty-first birthday.

'It's a day of mixed blessings; my Katya was laid to rest

today, an' Lord only knows how I'll miss her. But I'm not left alone.' Again, he looked at Laura, his eyes bright with threatened tears. 'I'm a lucky man. I've been given the company of two lovely young creatures to lighten me life,' the suggestion of a smile creased his face, 'an' to keep me on me blessed toes!'

After raising his glass to them all, Remmie took a sip of wine and lowered himself to his seat. There was a moment of quiet, when Laura was afraid that Remmie was close to tears. Then lifting his head and glass simultaneously he said in a firm voice, 'Raise your glasses to Laura, please; it's her twenty-first birthday!'

Laura couldn't find it in her to say anything. Instead she went round to where he sat, and wrapped her arms around his neck, hiding her face in the crevice of his shoulder.

Remmie made a small sound before easing Laura free, and in a voice meant for her hearing only, he said, 'When you get a minute, lass, tek a look in yon top drawer. Get yoursel' from round me neck then! You'll 'ave me embarrassed.'

That comment raised a sound of laughter from the onlookers, and everybody started talking at once and offering birthday congratulations. Laura was delighted by Netti's thoughtful present of a lovely silver pin in the shape of a sprig of heather, but she was surprised and thrilled by Remmie's hidden gift. Laura had discreetly looked into the sideboard drawer indicated by Remmie, and there she had found a long brown envelope, simply addressed, 'Laura'. When she went into the kitchen to prepare more coffee, she had taken a moment to open the envelope, and had learned of Remmie's intention to increase her wages.

No sooner had her eyes scanned the page than Remmie's voice came over her shoulder, 'That's right, lass. Another five pounds a week. Since you first turned a hand in yon shop, trade's prospered. You've turned over more goods than me an' Mitch put together!' He leaned over her shoulder to nod at the letter still in her hand. 'That's a token o' my gratitude, an' it's no more than you've earned, lass.' Then squeezing her shoulders affectionately, he whispered, 'Bless you.' Then he left, leaving Laura to appreciate what his gift would mean to her. In her already restricted budget, she assessed it to mean a great deal. Some of it would help Netti, and Tom. But a slice of it would swell her little nest-egg.

By careful and calculated scrimping, Laura had managed to put a modest sum of money by. It was nowhere near enough to finance her dream of owning her own business; but it was a start, and whatever happened, Laura was adamant that nothing should encroach on her ambitions to succeed. It struck Laura that her life was not, nor ever had been, her own. Yet she felt no resentment; only a strong sense of purpose towards her intention that one day she would be a woman of consequence, and Netti an accomplished musician. Her thoughts took her on to Miss Fordyke. Yes, she would need to go and see Netti's tutor. There were things that must be put right straightaway.

Laura remembered that Netti had fallen unusually quiet during the meal, and she had made a mental note to seek out her sister for a close conversation at the first opportunity. At the back of her mind was the suspicion that Lizzie Pendleton's spiteful tongue might be the cause for Netti's brooding mood.

In the wake of her thoughts following Remmie's kind gesture, Laura had almost forgotten Ria Morgan's claim on Jake Thackerey; but she remembered it now, and grew quiet.

It was only later, when she slipped out of the house and onto the moors, that she led herself to believe it was just another challenge; an obstacle to be overcome. She intended even now that Jake Thackerey would be hers, and she could not allow Ria Morgan, nor anybody else to stand in her way.

It wasn't until she felt the grass damp beneath her, that she realized she was kneeling. The sound of the narrow beck that meandered its way around the skirt of the Moors reached her ears, and calmed her mind. Almost without thinking, Laura took off her shoes and stockings, and locating the beck she stepped into the water. It was cold and biting, sending a small shock through her confused thoughts. Giggling softly to herself, she wondered whether she was intoxicated. Certainly, she had drunk more wine than she intended, and it did seem to have a strange delicious effect on her.

Suddenly Laura resented the confining elements of her narrow life with more than a little irritation. She thought of the wild birds that chose to live on these beautiful primitive moors, and she envied them. She thought of the winding streams that sparkled and danced beneath the light of the moon; she recalled the free-growing heather and the tiny flowers which peeped from the crags and scattered boulders hereabouts; and she would have given all of her life just to be an infinite part of it.

The ache in Laura's heart grew until it seemed like a stone weighing her down. But after a while she stepped from the water, used the swirling hem of her black dress to dab her feet dry; collected her shoes and stockings in a tangle, and started for home. The wind had risen, and it teased about her now, seeming to play hide and seek between the dark corners of night and the intermittent light from the moon. She enjoyed the way it snatched at her hair and caught the hem of her dress in a swish of urgency.

Carefully picking her way over the roughness beneath her feet, Laura was oblivious to everything but the magnificence of these moors when cloaked in moonlight, and did not perceive the figure coming towards her.

Jake Thackerey was searching for Laura, whom he had seen wandering from the house. But now, as she drew nearer, he stopped, and before she could become aware of his presence, he marvelled in silence at this woman; this devastatingly beautiful creature that had haunted his thoughts since their first meeting, and whose compelling nature had caused him deliberately to stay away.

He had taken Ria as his fiancée, and brought her with him to Remmie Thorpe's house, thinking such a course of action would rid him once and for all of his desires for this creature called Laura. His future plans had no place for personal involvement with her. He had *other* plans, more urgent and calculating, that involved both the respectable, trusting Remmie Thorpe and his niece. There was no place in his plans for the complications that entanglements of the heart might bring. Yet looking at her now, barefooted and breathless, her wild auburn hair a dark profusion and her eyes aglow, she reminded him of a primeval goddess delivered from the depths of night, and every other ambition was driven from him, but his craving to have her, to hold her, to take this woman here! Now! And to keep her forever. This longing within him churned and hardened until it became a frenzy, and when

Laura came upon him, he struggled to fight the devil that clawed at his insides.

'Jake!' Laura's cry shook him to his senses, and when he saw how his sudden appearance had alarmed her, he smiled reassuringly and put his arm out to steady her, saying, 'I thought I'd come out and breathe some of this clean fresh air. I'm sorry if I startled you.'

Laura did not take his arm as was his obvious intention. Instead, she took up step beside him, a half-smile lighting her face as she recalled his expression just now. She sensed that he had not come out to 'breathe the air', but that he had followed her, had been deliberately seeking her out.

As they reached the back gate, he caught her fiercely in his arms, moaning, 'God, you're enough to drive a man crazy!' He pulled her to him, his mouth searching out her half-open lips. Then when he tasted their richness, his low moans became filled with agony and Laura, held tight against his body, could feel the urgency of his passion.

Struggling to release herself from him, she smiled up at him, saying in a whisper, 'We'd best go in, Uncle Remmie'll be out looking for me.' She was unsure of herself, and of him. Just at that moment, he had raised a feeling of resentment in her. What *was* his game? And what of Ria Morgan?

Her insinuation that they might be discovered had the desired effect, for he took his arms from her and silently nodded his head; yet he made no move to follow her as she began to cross the yard towards the house. He just stood quite still, his handsome face flushed and his dark head slightly bowed.

Laura didn't look back. But when a flurry of movement in the window above caught her eye, she guessed that it was Ria Morgan who quickly dropped the curtain and retreated when Laura looked up. A feeling of shame engulfed Laura. Then just as quickly, she felt the need to defend herself. It was obvious that Jake was deeply attracted to her, and why shouldn't she take advantage of that? Hadn't that been her intention all along? And as for Ria Morgan, surely she was able to look after herself in matters such as these?

Letting herself into the house, Laura made her way through to the front hall, where she swiftly and silently mounted the stairs. Netti had moved into Laura's room for the night, having given up her own room to Jake Thackerey. Ria Morgan had been allocated the spare room. Netti was asleep, and Laura was glad of that, for she had much on her mind; not the least of which was young Tom.

It was with a sharpened sense of determination that Laura eventually drifted off to sleep. Life was a battle. But she would face it *without* losing her dignity, and without shirking her duty.

Chapter Seventeen

Following a restless night and much mind-searching, Laura's course of action regarding Tom was unexpectedly taken out of her hands and decided for her.

She had risen early on the morning of Jake and Ria's departure, taking extra trouble to look her best. The clear sky and bright promise of a sunny day had prompted her to wear a simple fetching white top and yellow swirling skirt that Netti so admired.

Breakfast had not been an easy encounter, because throughout the meal and in spite of Jake's warm smiles and Netti's bright chatter, Laura had felt decidedly uncomfortable beneath Ria Morgan's hostile glances. They were a clear warning to Laura that she should steer clear of Jake, but to Laura's surprise, Ria's meaningful signals had the adverse effect, for she found herself even more determined that Ria Morgan would have to take her own chances against a challenge for Jake. After all, the final choice must surely lie with Jake, whose parting words to Remmie had reinforced Laura's view that he had already made a choice. 'I want you in with me, Remmie, you and Laura. I reckon we've got up to eighteen months to take the offer up. After that, the old man'll be looking to sell outright on the open market.' Then he had looked meaningfully at Laura, his dark eyes smouldering as he murmured, 'I'll be counting the days, Laura.'

Those quiet words and the meaning she had construed from them stayed with Laura as she made her way from Ribble Road, through the narrow alleyways and familiar streets to Mabel Fletcher's, her step lighter and a feeling in her heart that life was good.

It was only when she tapped on Mabel's front door and pushed it open to enter the darkened passage, that a heavy foreboding entered her spirit. Here was one problem that would never go away.

Laura had been deeply disturbed to learn that Mabel was ill, yet not for one moment had she expected to find her slower in movement or woeful of countenance, for such indulgence was not in Mabel's make up. And when a voice called out, 'Is that you buggers back agin? You'd best be gone afore I change me mind!' Laura laughed out loud.

She pushed open the parlour door and showed herself carefully, for she knew well enough that Mabel had a good aim when it came to flinging soft missiles at one or the other of her brood. And sure enough, there sat Mabel with her arm upstretched, preparing to release the squashy cushion grasped in her fingers.

'Well! Bless me, if it 'int Laura. I thought it were my wayward kids changed their intent for going to the park.' She lowered the cushion and quickly issued instructions. 'Get thi'self in 'ere then, lass. Sally! Light the gas under yon kettle, mek a fresh brew o' tea.'

Laura crossed to where Mabel sat with a tousle-haired lad on her knee. For a moment, Laura was lost for words as she gazed down on the boy. He was a handsome child, and like Mitch, Laura saw her own father in him. As she looked at him, watched his small chubby fingers entwining themselves in and out of Mabel's greying hair and saw the look of joy and contentment on his face, Laura felt within her a great sadness and a sense of loss. She felt emotions that were alien to her; she was a stranger to this child, who might have been Mabel's own son.

Sally greeted Laura, then following Mabel's repeated instructions, she departed to the scullery.

'How are you then, Mabel?' Bending to kiss the older woman's face, Laura felt the boy's hair softly brush against her cheek. Suddenly, it was back, that creeping anxiety she had sought to conquer.

'Well, sit thi'sel' down! Don't stand about like a knocker-up's stick on a day off, lass.' Mabel watched as Laura lowered herself into the chair opposite, then taking the cup that Sally offered, she waited until Laura had done the same, before eyeing her steadily and asking in a low voice, ''Ave you a mind

216

to let the lad know you're 'is Mam?'

There was no clear purpose in Laura's heart just then, save one, and it was that Mabel should be asked to do no more, not for her and not for Parry Griffin's son. He was *her* responsibility! There was only one answer to give to Mabel's question, however difficult it might be to utter, and whatever the consequences to follow.

Laura slowly straightened and lifting her eyes to encompass Mabel's thoughtful face, she said quietly, 'Yes, Mabel, I think it's time.'

At this, Mabel's whole body appeared to relax and in that instant, Laura saw the years roll into the dear woman's face. Then Sally said under her breath, 'That's good, Laura, he has every right to know the truth,' and Laura felt a strange calmness within her.

But it was a calm that was quickly shattered. In the gentlest of manners, Mabel told the boy that Laura was his mother, and that she herself would be happy if he could give to Laura some of that love which he had shared with her. When Tom looked her in the eye and stated in a firm voice, '*You're* my Mam,' Laura had called his name and reached out to hold him. 'No! You go away! I don't want you, I want my Mam!' The words tumbled out, becoming incoherent in the boy's growing hysteria, as he fended off Laura's attempts to embrace him. When in desperation she abandoned her coaxing, her son ran to bury himself in Mabel's lap, his deep racking sobs pitiful to hear, and each one echoing painfully in Laura's heart.

'Lord love us.' Mabel rocked the boy soothingly, her eyes bright with unshed tears. 'I'm sorry, lass. It's too late, don't you see?' The tears toppled down her face as she turned to Sally. 'Tek the lad, Sal, fetch the others from the park, eh?'

Laura's heart was heavy as she watched the sobbing boy wrap his arms about Sally's neck. The tables had turned on her, for this was her son, afraid and rejecting her in the same way that she herself had rejected him all these years. It was painful and cruel, but Laura took it for the justice it was. Not even Sally's encouraging words, 'Give him a while, Laura,' or Mabel's comment that Laura was 'Still afeared, an' the lad can sense it,' could still the murmurings which told her that Tom didn't want her, didn't need her, and probably never would.

When Laura left, her instincts telling her that Tom was out of reach were echoed in Mabel's sad eyes as she clung to Laura's embrace, the reassurance in her voice empty as she whispered, "'Appen 'e'll come round in time, lass. But don't set yer 'eart on it, eh?'

Laura didn't, for she knew what Mabel was really saying. Tom had his own identity, and to wrench him from the family he saw and loved as his own would be to punish him for what Laura now saw as her own weakness. They were strangers, her and the boy. And maybe, after all, it was better that it should stay that way.

That evening, Remmie and Laura sat in the front room, listening to Netti playing the piano. It was a beautiful piano of highly-polished walnut wood, its natural grains creating exquisite designs within the panels along its front. In the centre panel was the most delicate handcrafted cameo depicting the perfect rose. Lizzie Pendleton had a similar piano which Netti had been allowed to play whenever Katya had taken her on a visit. However, it soon became obvious to Laura that Lizzie Pendleton and Katya had begun to use that piano as a lure to Netti — drawing her increasingly from Laura's company. It wasn't long before Laura was peeling her eyes at every sale and auction that took place, and within a matter of weeks she had acquired the piano from a woman who was selling up her father's house in order to move him into a nursing home. It had cost her dear — over three weeks' wages. But the look on Netti's face at its arrival and the pleasure she'd got from it since had repaid Laura many many times over.

Now, Laura glanced to where Remmie sat. But he didn't see her. His mind was carried back by the music — back to when as a lad he had listened to his own Mam playing the pianola. It saddened him to think of it, for in spite of the ensuing madness, his Mam had been very gifted — and sometimes it frightened him to see how intensely Netti had inherited that same gift. Laura was puzzled by the look of sadness on his face — which she attributed to the music, yet in a strange way, she knew how he felt. After the trauma of Tom's hostility towards her, there had emerged an odd sort of contentment in her heart, and as she listened now to Netti playing and bringing

218

that piano to life, her fevered thoughts had melted away and her heart was soothed to quietness.

The music was a lonely, haunting melody — a composition of Netti's which had taken a prize at school. Whenever Netti played it for her, Laura was invariably moved to emotion by its simple beauty. The music swelled first to a crescendo, then fell gracefully away to such a whisper that was painful in its strength. The room came alive as Netti's fingers played skilfully across the keyboard, her whole being merging as one with the instrument — which without the persuasion of her deft and talented fingers was just as inanimate as a table or a chair.

Suddenly, Laura was aware of Remmie looking at her, and the sight of his proud tears made her ache inside — strengthening her fast held vow that Netti's music should thrill the world!

Some time later, lying in her bed, Laura's thoughts turned to Jake Thackerey. He had said he would be counting the days — and so would she! But Laura could not get Ria Morgan out of her mind. How strong *was* that woman's influence over Jake? Certainly she was in a much better position to persuade him to her way of thinking, and Jake must have some affection for her, otherwise why had he taken her as his fiancée? Laura realized that Ria Morgan was clever. Clever enough not to reveal to Jake that she had seen him and Laura locked in each other's arms. She had obviously realized that her greatest strength lay in her silence. Oh yes, Ria Morgan might be more of an obstacle to her plans than she had at first thought.

Laura forgot her fears for a moment to recall the deep longing in Jake Thackerey's eyes when he'd gazed at her one last time before moving off. A quiet confidence filled her heart. Time would tell, she promised herself — time and fortune would tell.

Oh, but what of Tom, who now knew her to be his mother? Laura could not expect that the knowledge alone would bring her his love. Yet oh, how she prayed it would not instil in him a terrible hatred of her. But she was only too well aware that Mabel's revelation — however kindly put — had brought the boy considerable fear and pain. And God forgive her, for it was all *her* fault. She had lacked courage, and had left it all too late.

Chapter Eighteen

'Where in God's name are we to put all this stuff? This back room's fair bursting and if we cram any more in yon work-room, there'll be nowhere for you to do your building an' polishing.' Remmie blew out his cheeks in exasperation, then falling back onto the chest of drawers that he'd manoeuvered into the corner, he splayed out his legs, exhaled his breath in a wearisome sigh and looked at Mitch and Laura for a solution.

'We've no cause to grumble, all the same,' Mitch declared, taking a small circular table and heaving it up to stand on top of a nearby sideboard, 'we're shifting as much stuff as we're taking.'

Laura stepped forward from her place at the doorway that led into the shop. 'There's no mystery about what's needed,' she said, placing her hands on her hips and looking about at the piled-up furniture, 'bigger premises! That's what we need.'

At once there were protests. First from Remmie, who stood up straight saying, 'It's not as simple as that, lass. A good shop near Blackburn centre's not all that easy to get 'old of, them as 'as 'em, 'int in no 'urry to let go.' He put his hand up as Laura prepared to speak. 'I know what you're about to say, an' aye! That new row o' fine shops they're building on that prime site opposite the boulevard, *is* grand, an' one o' them *would* suit us fine!' He shook his head and declared stoutly, 'But they're not for us. For a start, they're not for sale, an' the rent's a crippling figure, knock your profits sideways it would! An' secondly, I've 'ad this 'ere old shop for more years than I care to remember. Paid for lock stock an' barrel, an' I'd be loath to see it in some stranger's 'ands.'

'And so would I.' Mitch had gone to stand by Remmie, as though joining forces. They both looked at Laura, and Mitch said, 'We've been crammed in here afore. And we've shifted it, and the problem disappears. I don't go for this talk of moving. We've a good spot here, the best!'

Remmie nodded, and Laura knew she would be battling for a lost cause if she pursued the matter any further. So she shrugged her shoulders and went out to answer the call of a customer. It was plain enough! If there was to be any expansion, and it was her intention that there *would* be, then she'd have to do it on her own.

The customer was a young woman, of slight build and pretty dark features. She was dressed in a plain black two-piece that Laura thought was a bit too severe. It crossed her mind that the woman might have been to a funeral and her deduction soon proved to be correct. 'I don't know whether you're able to help, but this establishment comes highly recommended. Apparently, you did some reparation on some of my Uncle's furniture a while back.'

'Your Uncle?' Laura asked, and already she had associated this well-dressed, politely spoken person with the grand houses out Freckleton way.

'Mr Adamson, the dentist at Freckleton.'

'Ah, yes that's right. I remember now. Regency secretaire, two new drawers and the whole thing stripped and polished?'

The woman smiled. 'You have a good memory, Miss . . .?'

'Blake, Laura Blake. My Uncle Remmie owns the business. How can we help you?'

'My Uncle died a few days ago. I've always known that the house and everything in it would be mine.' She paused for a moment, then went on, 'I would have sold it all just as it stands. But my husband is a dentist in a large practice in the Midlands. Well, it's the ideal opportunity for him to acquire a practice of his own now that . . . Anyway, the thing is, some of Uncle's furniture is not to our taste; heavy, ornate, you know the kind of thing. So I want to sell some, and there are other pieces that we would like fully restored. Also, do you make furniture to order?'

'Of course.'

'Then we can do business on all three counts?'

'Most certainly. When will it be convenient for us to call?'

The arrangement was quickly made and Laura mentally calculated that there was a good sum to be made out of such a transaction. At the same time, her subconscious mind had been churning over their problem of limited storage space. An idea took shape in her mind and she hurried out to the back room where Mitch and Remmie were still shifting things about.

'We'll have a sale!' she told them.

'A sale? What sort of sale?' Mitch demanded.

'An auction. Folks bidding against each other'.

Remmie stood up and walked across the room to stand in front of her. 'By! Why in blazes didn't *I* think o' that?'

'You mean you *will*?' Laura had expected opposition. After all, they'd never done it before, and these two men seemed to say 'No' automatically to anything new.

'Can you get them auctioneer folks to come to a little shop like this, eh?' Remmie stroked his chin, warming to the idea of uncluttering the shop and perhaps getting Laura off his back with her idea of finding new premises. 'You know, they're used to bigger places than this; manor houses an' the like.'

Laura reached up to kiss his cheek, 'I'll get them, don't you worry. Just you decide what you want to sell and what you want to keep. Leave the rest to me.'

'Right!' Remmie swung round to Mitch. 'Get pen an' paper. We'll mek a list, eh?'

For most of the day, between serving customers and brewing tea, Laura was called upon to give her advice to Remmie about what they should get rid of and what they would need to keep. She also telephoned Weathercocks, the firm of auctioneers, who agreed to come and talk to her. But they were very busy at the moment, they said, so would next week be suitable? Laura made it quite clear that it would not, so they promised to come out to the shop to discuss her proposition before the weekend.

The day was a busy one, and three o'clock soon came round. Laura had made arrangements that morning to go along to Miss Fordyke after school hours, at approximately four-fifteen, when, Laura knew, Netti would be on her way home.

Bringing the counter cash-book up to date, and making sure that everything was in order, Laura went in search of Mitch, whom she found in the back store-room perusing the list they had made.

'Any problems?'

'No! Why should there be problems? Haven't *you* already

decided what goes and what stays!' Mitch said sharply.

'And don't you agree?'

'If you *really* want to know, I'll tell you what I've already told your Uncle Remmie. I think you're stripping this place of too much. We have got a business to carry on, you know! When the customers come through that door and see a half-empty shop, they'll be off up that road yelling to all and sundry that Remmie Thorpe's gone bust.'

'No they won't!'

'Oh? And how's that, then?'

'Because the shop *won't* be half-empty. I'm off to the school just now, so I'll not be able to do it today. But I have it in mind to visit that furniture warehouse along Dock Street. I've heard tell that they supply a few of the shops about here *and* in Manchester.'

Mitch towered over her, an expression of utter disbelief and fury written across his face. 'You have it in mind to do *what*? You're *never* contemplating buying that muck! Furniture? It's never furniture! It's utility rubbish! Cardboard!' he thumped his right fist down hard into the open palm of his left hand, and Laura got the impression that he would rather have been thumping her.

'There are houses being built at a pace hereabouts now,' she told him, 'and newly-weds need cheaper furniture. They haven't got the liking nor the money for the heavy solid stuff, and if *we* don't start supplying this new brand of customers, then they'll go elsewhere! I'm not saying we abandon our present line, Mitch, there's money and custom enough there as well.'

'But not for you, eh?'

Laura shook her head saying, 'That's not a fair comment, Mitch, and well you know it! What's wrong with trying to expand the business?' Mitch's grim expression told Laura that he would never come round to her way of thinking. It seemed like a lost cause, and so she brought the subject to a close. 'Oh, Mitch, we could argue till the cows come home, and you'd never see it my way.'

'That's the truth of it!' Mitch declared stoutly, and Laura let it be.

Laura's attention was drawn to where Remmie stood out in

the yard, and she saw that he was talking to a dishevelled man. It was with some disgust that she recognized the man as Parry Griffin, shabby and unshaven, and in deep agitated conversation with Remmie.

The sight of these two men, one whom she loved and one whom she would always loathe, made Laura think. She could see no reason why they should be together in this yard thrashing out some particular matter. It was not an agreeable matter either, judging by Remmie's frantic arm-waving and Parry Griffin's glowering expression. Laura continued to watch with interest, and now Mitch had turned his attention on the two men, his expression showing that he too thought it strange.

Remmie was shaking his head at Parry Griffin, obviously in refusal of something. Then as Remmie came striding angrily back towards the shop, Parry Griffin shook his fist and stormed out of the yard through the big open gates.

'What was *he* doing coming round here?' Laura was waiting by the door for Remmie, and now he gestured for her to go back inside, saying, 'The man's become a bloody menace. I were fool enough to feel sorry for 'im . . . lent 'im a few quid for the asking, an' now 'e's round 'ere after more! Well 'e'll get no more from me. I told 'im to shake 'is feathers; come to 'is senses an' get back to working, not begging!' He was standing looking at Mitch, whose anger was still dark in his face. Remmie stopped, then turned back to look at Laura, then again at Mitch, demanding, 'What the bloody 'ell's been going on 'ere? Thought I 'eard you ranting at each other. Come on, what's up?'

Mitch looked away, and in a defiant manner that was unwise in Remmie's present mood, Laura explained her intentions about buying and selling utility furniture in bulk. As she suspected, Remmie's answer was swift and in keeping with Mitch's. 'Not while I'm alive! This shop sells quality, quality I tell you.'

'But we can *still* sell quality,' Laura argued, 'we can open out the back storeroom to show the new stuff. There's a ready market for it.'

'I said no, an' that's an end to it,' Laura winced beneath the stare he gave her. 'I thought you took *pride* in this 'ere shop, an' all it stands for.'

'I do! Oh, Uncle Remmie, I do.' She stepped towards him and would have embraced him, but he took a step away, saying, 'Thought you were going to yon school for some'at today?'

Laura knew when she had been dismissed, and he left her in ho doubt of that. So she nodded her head, saying, 'I'll see you later. Oh, and please don't tell Netti I've gone to the school.' Then she left the shop, her own anger evident in the heavy-handed way that she allowed the door to clatter shut. Stuck in a rut they were, she silently fumed, the *pair* of them! Stuck in a rut and *nothing's* going to shift them! By! She wished she had a shop of her own, that she did. And she *would*, she *would* have a shop of her own, because there would be no peace inside her until she was a woman of property. Yes, that's right, that was just what she intended to be, a woman of property, a person of some consequence. She'd work towards that end, plan and build towards it. And when she was on the way up, it would give her the greatest satisfaction to knock Parry Griffin down. Yes, and to see his woman beggared and homeless; the same way she had seen her and Netti! Oh! What a prospect, what a thing to look forward to.

The day seemed brighter as Laura covered the mile to the school, out through Blackburn centre and up by the church. There was a spring in her step and a smile on her face as she thought on the right way to set about the downfall of Parry Griffin and his cheating wife. It would have to be planned, and it would need to be inescapable for them!

But now she was at the gates of the school, and not rightly sure how to tackle this Miss Fordyke. According to various chit-chat that had taken place both at home with Netti, and in the shop between customers, Miss Fordyke, who had taken on the headmistress-ship of the old school in recent years, was quite a formidable character, who considered the school and her music to be the ultimate achievements in her life. Certainly, she had attracted a rising number onto the school roll, and her prowess as a teacher of musical instruments was undisputed. It was said that she was so proud of her instruction and success in this particular field, that she had even extended the hours of tuition into her own private time, and that there wasn't a competition she had not entered, or trophy she had failed to win.

Laura had gone through the big iron gates and across the flagged yard that served as a playground, and now she was standing just inside the open doors which led into the spacious hall. To her left, there was a little window beyond which was an office, and in front of the window, there was a shelf containing a large brass hand-bell. Propped up against this were two typed notes in black capitals. One instructed, 'All foods for the party to be left here.' Laura deduced this to mean contributions towards the planned celebrations which would mark Queen Elizabeth's crowning in Westminster Abbey. Folks all over Blackburn, and indeed the country, were busy planning street parties and festivities for June 2nd, in three weeks' time. And, according to little Belle Strong, both Laura and Netti were to be involved in the one along Clayton Street.

The second note instructed, 'Please ring the bell loudly.' This Laura did, and at once, the pealing echo summoned a pair of feet that hurried noisily towards her along the facing corridor. A tall gaunt woman appeared, with piles of grey hair caught up on top of her head and a look of open-mouthed surprise on her painfully thin features. She was wearing a small pair of rimless spectacles, and as the woman drew nearer, Laura could see that the spectacles were a bad fit, for the gold link between the two lens dug so tightly into the bridge of her nose that bulges of reddened skin had swollen up to almost bury it. The same had happened to her temples, where the spectacles' arms stretched tight to reach the ears. She was dressed in a grey gored skirt and stark white blouse buttoned down the front and decorated at the throat by an enormous Italian cameo brooch. Her hands were joined together across her stomach and now as she addressed Laura, she clasped and unclasped them in a nervous fidgeting manner, which lent confidence to Laura and her errand.

'Yes?'

'Good afternoon. I'm Laura Blake, to see Miss Fordyke.'

'Ah! You're Netti's sister.' She extended a hand, adding, '*I'm* Miss Fordyke,' and gesturing for Laura to follow her, she swept away.

They turned into the office on the other side of the window, and in a moment they were seated; Miss Fordyke behind the desk, and Laura before it. Now the headmistress was smiling,

226

and Laura was astonished at the pleasant transformation it brought to the hitherto stiff unyielding features. 'What's on your mind? No trouble with Netti, I'm sure.'

Laura readily returned the smile, replying, 'Oh no, no trouble, Miss Fordyke. It's just I'm concerned about Netti's future, and I would like to discuss a particular matter. Also, I would very much like to thank you for developing Netti's musical talents in the way that you have.'

'Netti's *considerable* musical talents. I understand she inherited them from her grandmother?'

'Yes.' Laura was impatient to get to the real issue and the best way, she decided, was to come right out with it. 'Miss Fordyke, I feel it only fair that you should know that I am strongly opposed to the idea that Netti should become a teacher. Netti and I, well, we've always hoped for something grander for her.'

For what seemed like ages to Laura, the woman sat staring at her in silence, her face set like stone, giving no indication of what effect Laura's statement might have had on her.

But behind the expressionless features, Miss Fordyke was examining the implications of what had been said. Her instincts confirmed what she had already suspected concerning Netti's sister, about whom the child chattered incessantly. There was no secret about the background of the Blake girls; and this Laura had to be admired for the way she had cared and provided for Netti. Yet it would seem that Laura had paid the price, for the indications were that she had been moulded harder by the responsibilities put on her, and by the consequence of having to grow up more quickly. It was small wonder that Laura Blake would not settle for second best where her sister was concerned.

Miss Fordyke put aside her own reservations for the moment, and asked Laura, 'If not a teacher, what then?'

'A concert pianist.' Laura's confidence was gradually being eroded beneath the sharp searching eyes that never wavered in their piercing stare.

'There is no doubt that Netti has the *talent* to become an excellent pianist. What she does *not* possess, is the right temperament; that dedicated single-mindedness and iron will that can effectively shut out all else but her goal.'

'What are you saying?' Laura's back stiffened and she leaned forward to place her hand on the desk, asking a question that required no answer, for wasn't it plain enough what this woman was telling her? She was saying that Netti had no backbone! How dared she say such a thing!

'Netti is basically a gentle creature. She plays well, and she loses herself in her music because it has become a means of escape,' Miss Fordyke continued.

'A means of escape? From what?'

'Who knows why people want to escape? From reality, from memories? I can't tell you that. But what I can tell you is that there are two kinds of musicians; there is the one that I've just described, who plays to escape, who derives a great deal of personal pleasure from music. And there is the other one, the ambitious one, who excels in what they do and who revels in the adulation of others.' She leaned forward and her voice took on a warning tone as she told Laura, 'That isn't your Netti. Push her, try and mould her to your own will, and you'll break her. I've seen it happen so many times.'

'Netti does have a mind of her own, believe me, Miss Fordyke. She has it in her to be a great pianist, you said as much yourself just now.'

'She has the *talent,* yes! And she has a deep appreciation of the work of great artists such as Strauss, and most particularly, of Beethoven; I must admit she interprets his music on the piano like no other pupil I've taught. But having an appreciation of music and the ability to play with excellence is not enough.'

'It *is* enough. It *must* be!' Laura was on her feet now, defiant and adamant. Yet there was a measure of anxiety in her heart; this woman couldn't be right. She didn't *know* Netti, she had no idea of what went on in Netti's mind. Why, Netti only lived for her music!

Miss Fordyke had also risen to her feet, and she told Laura quietly, 'In view of the way you feel, perhaps Netti ought to discontinue her studies with me.' There was a look of sadness in her face, and it was this emotion which Laura manipulated as she replied, 'That would be the cruellest thing you could ever do to her.' Laura was aware that throughout the whole of Blackburn, even if it cost every penny she could find, there was no one who could bring Netti on like Miss Fordyke could. But how to ensure that she would? Laura realized that there was but one way. Just as Remmie held a great pride in his shop and in the quality of his merchandise; so this woman held her reputation and her music as the most important things in her life. *That* was her security, hers and Netti's, and so she said, 'Netti could not have achieved anything without your help, Miss Fordyke. And it isn't just you, me and Netti who know that. It's everyone in Blackburn, who matters. It's the mill owners, who send *their* children to you for private tuition. It's the Doctor and all the other professional people who look to you to raise their children as accomplished musicians.' Laura sensed that her words were striking home.

'Very well, Miss Blake. I won't desert your sister. But neither will I drive her beyond her capacity. I may be wrong, we'll see. We'll see.'

Laura was visibly relieved as she asked, 'And the scholarship?'

'She shall have her chance.'

There was nothing more to be said, and when Miss Fordyke saw her to the door, Laura took her hand in a firm grip, saying, 'Thank you for your concern, Miss Fordyke. Netti won't let you down.' When Laura left, it was with the conviction that she had done the right thing; the best thing in the world for Netti.

Hurrying back to the shop, where she knew Remmie would be waiting to take her home, Laura's mind was overflowing with plans. There were so many things she wanted to do, so very much to be properly thought out. Jake Thackerey and Ria Morgan were ever present in her thinking; Netti's future; the excitement of the auction at the shop, and oh so much more.

High on her list of priorities, was Parry Griffin. But she wasn't anywhere near ready to deal with him yet. She had a tidy sum put by, but needed a great deal more. The bigger the carrot, she reasoned, the more irresistible the temptation. So, she would just have to be patient, for she must not fail!

The next ten days saw Laura, Mitch and Remmie putting long hard hours in at the shop in preparation for the forthcoming auction. It was Tuesday now, and the auction had been fixed for the approaching Saturday morning. All the necessary advertising had been done, and all that remained now was to shine up the brass and silverware, dust the paintings and set all the pieces out in the back store room and shop; both of which had been fully distempered in a soft shade of green by Laura. In the meantime, Mitch and Remmie had cleared up, mended and french polished any furniture that needed doing.

Every article would be set out to its best advantage; Laura had the sharpest eye for that, and Mitch and Remmie would give credit where it was due, following her directions to the letter. There was no quick way of carrying out the final preparations; not if it was to be done properly as Laura insisted; and not when there were customers in and out of the shop all the time, stopping to chat and ask cumbersome questions.

But even if it *was* tiring and demanding, Laura loved every minute of it. Even Mitch and Remmie were enthused by her state of excitement, and Remmie had remarked more than once that she would have them all down with a heart-attack.

The day had gone by swiftly, and now Mitch, sleeves rolled up and beads of sweat glistening on his temples, pulled, pushed and heaved the magnificent mirror-backed sideboard into position. He had spent the best part of two days renovating this particular piece of furniture, and now he stepped away from it, his critical eye surveying its tall angular lines and the deep burnished hue. His mouth lifted slightly at one corner, indicating to the watchful Laura that he was pleased with the results of his labour. As for her, she found no such pleasure in ornate Victorian monstrosities, with their numerous barley-twist poles, great square mirrors and myriads of small useless cubby-holes.

Mitch turned to look at her, and as always when his eyes alighted on her face, they deepened with emotion. The passion she stirred in him took many forms; anger, impatience, pride and the strongest of love. Now, as he came to her and said, 'It's been grand having you at the shop these long days,' it was his love for her that shone in the sincere green eyes.

Laura was aware of it, but she gave no recognition of it as she walked away to lock the display cabinet that held the silver items; muffin-dishes, candelabras and various other bric-a-brac. 'There's still a deal to be done yet,' she told him with a smile, yet consciously avoiding his gaze.

Mitch nodded, and in his love for her, there was a hatred at her deliberate evasion. 'It'll get done,' he said, turning now to greet Remmie, who had entered from the back store room. 'Off then, Remmie?'

Remmie's answer was to lift a finger, which he crooked at Mitch, saying in a whisper, 'Come 'ere. Quiet, mind.'

Mitch and Laura exchanged looks, then they followed, Mitch first, with Laura a cautious distance behind.

Once out in the yard, Remmie brought them all to a halt, then looking down at the oblong manhole cover beneath his feet, he said in a loud whisper, 'Them's bloody *rats* down there!'

'Rats?' Laura took a step backwards.

'Aye!' Looking at Mitch, Remmie went on, 'Fetch yon shovel fro' behind that timber. There's only one way to deal wi' these mangy creatures, an' that's to flatten the sods!'

Laura didn't much like the idea of rats beneath her feet, but neither did she go along with 'flattening' them. Stepping forward, she grabbed Mitch's arm. 'You'll not hit them with no shovel, Mitch, that's vicious!'

'Vicious! Vicious!' Remmie wasn't about to admit his innate fear of the blighters. 'They're nowt but bloody vermin! Aye, an' they'd not think twice 'afore ripping out yer bloody throat, let me tell you.'

'Remmie,' Mitch could see the funny side of it, but with a straight face he said, 'I don't even think there *are* rats down there.'

'There are! I 'eard the buggers, I tell yer!' Remmie made a loud shivering noise, before stalking over to collect the shovel, which he held out over the manhole. 'Now then, you 'old that cover up, Mitch. I'll 'ave the bugger when it scarpers for freedom.' Turning to Laura, he said, 'You get off inside, lass.'

Laura was having none of it, 'I'll do no such thing! Put that shovel down, it's like Mitch said, you're just imagining there's rats down there!' In a swift movement, she had bent forward, her legs straddling the manhole cover, and with her fingers inserted beneath the levering bars, she hoisted the cover up.

What followed was pandemonium. Remmie was the first to see the rat, which he claimed later was 'the size of a bloody

231

'orse!'. When he shouted, 'There it is!' Mitch fell backwards into the timber and Laura, seeing Remmie's shovel about to descend, screamed and let go of the heavy cast-iron cover.

Remmie's standing joke in the shop for many days afterwards was how *he* had only wanted to give it a swift painless blow on the head, whereas Laura did no less than chop the bugger i' two with the manhole cover! Mitch very wisely made no comment; but once or twice, Laura caught him quietly smiling to himself. Finally, she herself could no longer hold back the giggles, and the three of them ended up roaring with laughter, not so much at the poor rat's demise, as at their own comical antics in the matter.

Two days later, on Thursday evening, Remmie and Laura were in the front room, having enjoyed some twenty minutes of Netti's piano-playing. She was just bringing the final melody to an end, when a matter close to Laura's heart was brought into the open.

At the close of the melody, Remmie rushed to embrace Netti, and when he spoke, his voice trembled with emotion, 'By God, lass, you've a rare talent an' no mistake. That's the loveliest thing I've ever 'eard.'

'Thank you, Uncle Remmie.' Netti hugged him back. Then looking at Laura, who was sitting with the pleasure brought by Netti's music still evident in her face, she said, 'Miss Fordyke has entered me for the scholarship.'

At once, the atmosphere in the room became charged. Remmie stood bolt upright, looking open-mouthed from Netti to Laura and back again. Laura was out of her seat and quickly across the room, to grab Netti in her arms. Her voice left the tightness of her throat in a thick cracked whisper, 'You'll win that scholarship. Oh Netti! You will!'

Remmie let out a 'Yahoo!', rushed to the sideboard and retrieved a bottle of sherry and three glasses. He filled up all the glasses, handing one each to Netti and Laura and raising the third, he blinked back the threatening tears and shouted, 'To the best bloody pianist in the world!' Then with a proud shake of his head, he tipped the glass to his lips and quickly emptied it. Netti and Laura did the same, after which ensued much coughing, spluttering and laughter.

Later, after Netti and Remmie had gone to their beds, Laura sat for a long time in her chair. She couldn't possibly go to bed, not yet. She was too filled with excitement to sleep. Netti was entered for the scholarship, and the day after tomorrow would see the very first auction at the old shop. On top of all that, she had Jake Thackerey in mind, and she felt confident that he had *her* in mind also.

Suddenly, she had a deep longing to walk on the moors. There was a wildness in her tonight that wouldn't rest. Going through to the kitchen, she took her mackintosh from the hook on the back door, and pulling a scarf from its pocket, she wrapped it round her head and knotted it securely beneath the chin. Then she let herself out and made her way across the yard and out onto the moor's edge. She didn't intend to go far. She just wanted to taste that jagged bracing air and feel the whip of it on her face.

Laura thought it was a strange sort of evening. There was little moonlight and the sky seemed ominous, and all around was the most unusual silence. Normally, there would be a rushing and scurrying of night creatures going about their business, and the occasional giggling and whispering to suggest that a courting couple had found their way up to the spinney across the beck. They were always comforting sounds to Laura, but tonight there was only an uneasy silence. It's *me*, she thought, it's me that's fidgety and uneasy, not the moors.

Her thoughts rambled on. Was she hoping for too much in thinking Jake Thackerey was her knight in shining armour? Would Ria Morgan use her strong position to keep him away? With some surprise, Laura found that she had crossed the beck by way of the stepping-stones, and she was almost to the spinney. The wind had gained momentum, whipped up now to a force that caused a low moaning noise in the tops of the silver birch trees just ahead. 'I'd best get back,' Laura murmured, sitting for a moment on the tree stump by her feet. She felt tired, worn out. These last two weeks had been very demanding, and it was only now, when all but the small finicky issues had been organized, that she felt able to relax. And in relaxing, she discovered a great tiredness within her. Suddenly, she thought of the Griffin family and she recalled her father's words; 'And there'll be enemies.' Well, she had enemies right enough. But she would see her day with them!

While Laura brooded on her enemies, so too did the dark-clad figure that had stalked her from the house, and was now hidden by the trees and observing Laura from behind.

Ruth Blake had enemies that tortured her fevered mind; Joe Blessing, who had persuaded her into adultery, fathering two of her offspring, one a cripple to punish them. And Laura Blake — the divil's own spawn! Molly was right; there was a job to be done before she, Ruth, could rest easy. There were enemies to be got rid of once and for all! Joe Blessing, and this one. While those two walked the earth, she would know no peace.

So carefully, silently, she crept up on Laura, the thick stumpy branch raised high in her hand. She brought it down and clubbed her daughter unconscious. As Laura fell face down into the earth, it was merciful that she couldn't feel the blows that rained across her back and shoulders.

The first time Laura regained consciousness, she thought the enveloping darkness was the pit of Hell, and that the tall swaying trees that loomed above her were the Devil's angels. Her body was numb and stiffened by the cold, and her head felt like two, each separate from the other.

The second time she came to, she saw the sky, whose twinkling stars appeared as though through a mist, each star blindingly bright and grotesquely misshapen. She rolled onto her side and clutched at the air in an effort to get hold of something that would lever her up. But there was nothing. She tried to cry out, but the effort of opening her mouth brought such unbearable agony that she brought her hands to grasp either side of her temple, and for a long time she lay still, drifting in and out of consciousness. Somewhere, far off in her mind, she heard the voices, but was not able to recognize them.

'Thank God! Oh, thank God.' Mitch gathered her into his arms, as gently and lovingly as one might a very small child, and as he gazed down on her pale blood-stained face a great tide of love surged through him with such an almighty force that he was made to cry out in agony, and with tears streaming down his face, he called to Remmie and Netti who were searching the other side of the spinney, 'I've found her! Laura! Laura!

I've got her!' Then holding her close to his heart, he stumbled towards the others who had broken into a run and were now almost upon him.

Chapter Nineteen

Laura had spent four days in the Infirmary, and the first two of those had passed without her knowing it. But on the third day, she was awake, uncomfortable from the clutch of stitches behind her ear and from the stiff aching back and shoulders where the skin was not broken, but bruised and battered.

She was able to sit up in the ward amidst all the bunting and decorations to watch the Coronation ceremonies in Westminster Abbey. One of the doctors had kindly donated a television for the event. The nurses too, excitedly related news of the colourful street parties; the best of which, according to Netti, was the one in Clayton Street. Laura enjoyed all the colour and spectacle of the televised event, but her heart wasn't really in it.

Remmie had resisted all Laura's pleas to take her home, where, she promised, she would religiously adhere to the doctor's instructions and stay confined to bed. But such was her cajoling, that a week after her hurried admittance to the Infirmary, he came to take her to her own bed. Mitch, who had not allowed a single day to pass without coming to sit by her side, carefully escorted her along the ward, down the marble steps, and then out to Remmie and the waiting vehicle.

Netti was waiting for their arrival home, and with much protesting from Laura, she directed the men out of the bedroom and got Laura smartly into bed declaring, 'The doctor has given strict instructions that you're not to leave that bed for at least a week, and for once, Laura Blake, you'll do as you're told!'

Laura smiled, murmuring, 'Oh, I see. I've only been in that Infirmary for a few days, and here you are taking over, Miss Bossy-Boots, is it?'

Netti finished emptying the small portmanteau, then she

lifted it up onto the wardrobe and came over to the bed where she leaned down to kiss Laura. 'Oh, Laura. You can't know how good it is to have you back home. This house is empty without you in it, and those first few days, you were so ill.'

Laura reached up to stroke Netti's fair hair, and asked the question that had constantly bothered her, and that she had asked both Remmie and Mitch, yet had received no intelligible answer. 'What happened, Netti? How did I come to be unconscious on the moors, like Remmie said?'

Netti straightened up saying, 'Nobody seems to know. It's said that it could have been some wandering vagabond who laid into you, or being a windy night, possible that the branches of a tree could have broken off and . . .' She paused for a moment, seeming to examine the possibilities herself, then she reached down to pull the bedcovers over Laura, who had slid comfortably into the pillows. 'I doubt if we'll find out for sure. But you're on the mend, and that's all that matters now. You sleep quiet for a while, eh? I'll be up later.'

Laura didn't protest, for she felt the need to sleep. But in her tiredness, there was a strong measure of resentment at having been injured by something or some person unknown, and at having missed the auction, which Remmie had told her was a huge success. Mitch had added that it was all thanks to her. Mitch, that big handsome loyal man, who had the knack of bringing out the very worst in her. What was she to make of him? What was to be done about him? She couldn't think now. Every part of her body felt sore, but she was content to be home, and she just wanted to rest, to sleep and wake up strong and fit. There was much to be done, and it wouldn't get done with her lying here in this bed! She could hear the movement of busy feet downstairs, and the clattering of crockery from the kitchen. Groaning, she turned over to bury her face in the pillow. She hoped Netti didn't intend to bring her anything to eat. The thought of food made her feel nauseous.

Downstairs Netti played quietly on the piano — a rendering of Beethoven's overture to Fidelio. But her heart wasn't in it and after a few moments she busied herself about the domestic tasks, taking pleasure in them. She liked having Laura dependent on her, instead of always the other way around; it made her feel useful.

237

Remmie was seated by the table, supping thoughtfully on the pint mug of tea. Laura being injured like that, well, it had put the fear of God in him. When he'd heard her go out that night, and then when he'd watched the dark hours mark her continued absence until he had been forced to raise the alarm, the awful realization that something had happened to her struck his heart with terror. Oh, and when she had been found! Dear God, when she'd been found . . .

Remmie placed his mug back onto the table, and lifting both his hands with the thick worn fingers spread out, he ran them through his hair, letting his head fall forward to clasp it between his fists. Closing his eyes, he breathed in a great gulp of air, then slowly exhaled it through his nose. The noise it made caused Netti to turn round and ask, 'Are you alright, Uncle Remmie?'

'Aye, lass.' He opened his eyes and sat up straight against the back of the chair. 'Aye, I'm fine.'

'She'll be alright now. Laura'll be alright.'

'I know that. Don't fret yourself, lass. I know that.'

Satisfied, Netti turned back to her baking, and Remmie resumed his thinking. Laura *would* be alright. He did know that now. And he knew something else as well; or at least he had come to believe it beyond any doubt. It was Ruth Blake that had harmed his Laura! Meant to kill her no doubt. And by God, if he ever got his 'ands on that demented sister of his, well, she'd be put out of her misery once and for all, God forgive him for such wicked intentions. But now that Katya was gone, Netti, and Laura in particular, meant all the world to him.

His immeasurable love for Laura had grown stronger with the years. He'd done his best by the lass, but if he did tenfold more all the days of his life, that would never be enough. Nothing about Laura's life since her dad passed on had been what anybody could call 'natural'. It had raised a force in Laura that was vengeful and often self-destructive. She drove and punished herself day after day, and even *he* couldn't seem to reach her. Did she really think he didn't know what Molly Griffin had done to her and the child? Oh, it were known to him right enough, but if Laura thought it best to keep him in ignorance, then so be it. And how many more secrets had she thought to protect him from, eh?

He got to his feet now and went to put a comforting arm about Netti, telling her, 'I'll just peep in at the door an' see if she's asleep, eh?' On quiet footsteps he made his way out of the room and on up the stairs thinking, 'Netti's said it more than once, an' by God she's right. This house *is* empty without Laura's vitality to fill it.' His mind was made up! If that business with Thackerey were still on, they'd move from these parts. Laura was the one 'as mattered, and them damned police were mekkin' a poor job o' tracking Ruth Blake down. He'd said as much to that police constable, who'd been at the Infirmary bothering Laura with his fool questions; did she have any idea as to what had happened? Did she see anything at all? Stupid buggers! If she'd seen owt, then she'd have said so! Instead of questioning Laura, their time'd be best spent ferreting out that Ruth Blake! Still, a rat knew where to go underground, an' that were a fact.

On stealthy footsteps, Remmie opened the door of Laura's bedroom and opening it just a chink he peered inside, looking towards the bed. Observing at once from the stillness of her body and the rhythmic breathing beneath the bedcover that she was soundly asleep, he drew away closing the door noiselessly. Then he headed towards the stairway, thinking with satisfaction, that's just what she needs, plenty o' quiet healing sleep. Aye, our Laura'll be up and about in no time at all.

In fact, by the end of that week Laura was out of bed, dressed and stubbornly picking up the reins of her duties; in spite of the doctor's insistence that she had suffered a nasty blow to the back of her head which entailed a regime of little movement and quiet for a great deal longer than she was prepared to accept.

Laura had thanked him and promptly dismissed his services, saying that now her stitches were out and the blinding headaches had receded, she felt that his talents could be put to much better use elsewhere. Eventually realizing that he had indeed been well and truly dismissed, he departed, complaining to Remmie that his niece was ungrateful, obstinate and totally uncompromising. Remmie had smiled at him, but secretly he agreed wholeheartedly with the doctor's diagnosis, and he told

Laura as much on his return to the kitchen, where she was standing gazing out of the window.

'The doctor's right. You should still be in your bed. There's not an ounce o' colour in your cheeks at all.'

'Rubbish!' Laura turned round to face him, her impatience etched deep on her face. She might not feel as fit as she would have liked, but the quickest way to that was to get back to work. And after Jake Thackerey's telephone call to Remmie yesterday, she needed to be alert and in control. With that in mind, she asked Remmie, 'Tell me again, what did Jake Thackerey say? What *exactly* did he say?'

'Good Lord! If I've gone over that conversation once, I've gone over it a 'undred times.'

Laura came to sit by the table, and looking up at Remmie, her dark amber eyes large in the pale thinness of her face, yet luxuriant and dancing now with excitement, she demanded, 'Again, tell me again!'

Remmie laughed and then so did she. She grasped his arm and bowed her head as though in embarrassment, before saying, 'I'm sorry, Remmie.' She raised her head to look at him again, smiled and asked him, 'Is it true, though, he's coming here next weekend?'

'Aye, just for the Saturday. Coming to talk a bit o' business.'

'And you're *really* thinking of taking him up on this deal? Moving away from here?'

'I am. But I'll not set my 'and to nowt, till it's been talked through first. After that, there'll be more talking wi' the accountant and such likes. Then, if all seems ship-shape and promising, we shall make arrangements to go an' see this 'ere business. But it isn't some'at as can be done overnight, lass. It 'as to be tackled right, and viewed from every possible angle. I'm too old to get involved with a pig in a poke.'

'And your shop? Will you not mind selling your shop?' Even now, she found it hard to believe that he was actually prepared to contemplate such a thing. Why, there was nothing he loved more than his old shop. Deep inside, Laura guessed that it had something to do with her having been injured. She'd thought long and hard on that business herself, but it was not something that she'd been able to fathom. She had the feeling that if she was to work at it, she could dissuade Remmie from

240

abandoning his beloved Blackburn and the business he cherished; but she was not about to do that. Oh no! Not when she was convinced that Jake Thackerey promised a better future. For *all* of them, and in more ways than one.

Remmie had been thinking about Laura's question regarding the shop. He looked at her, his mood darkening as he replied, 'There's plenty o' time, plenty o' time, lass. We'll tek it all slow an' careful.'

Laura's sharp business instincts told her that Remmie's cautious attitude was the right one. But she felt like leaping and dancing in her impatience.

There was almost a week to wait before Jake Thackerey's arrival and although she needed the time to get back her strength and to look her best, Laura wondered how she would stand the waiting.

Chapter Twenty

During the weeks following Laura's mysterious attack, the talk in that part of town had been of nothing else. But now there was a new interest and the whole town was agog about the up and down fortunes of Parry Griffin. Because here was a scoundrel that had come as close to bankruptcy as was possible, and now, thanks to a straight win accumulator and three outside horses shooting past the winning post, he was back in business. There was even speculation that his son, Pearce, was home.

'Well, it's to be hoped that he doesn't show his face round these parts again. Like as not he'll help to spend his dad's new found wealth, then he'll be on his way again, looking to relieve some other unsuspecting blighter of his wallet.' Mitch was up the ladder, retrieving a large red and brass tilly lamp from the top shelf. Then when he'd securely grasped it he came down the ladder and placed it on the counter. The customer, a man of advanced years and impaired hearing, had his hand cupped to his ear, where it had been all the time Mitch was talking. Sorting out a pile of silver from his pocket, he slapped six half-crowns down on the counter, and added a ten-shilling note which he extracted from his waistcoat pocket. Collecting the tilly lamp by its handle he said, 'That's a fact. Aye, allus been a bad 'un, that Pearce, never change neither.' Then with a nod of his head, he ambled towards the door and away out into the street.

Almost at once, the door opened again and Laura came in dressed in a cream jumper and deep beige skirt of pencil-slim design and with her hair simply combed into its natural style. She looked stunningly attractive and fresh and, as always when he saw her, Mitch's day took on a new meaning.

Coming round the counter to greet her, he collected the shopping bag from her hand and led the way through the shop

242

and into the back room, where he put the bag on a table and proceeded to fill the kettle. 'I expect you're after a cup o' tea, eh? It's no fun trekking round that market of a Saturday.'

Laura thought how handsome he looked, in those black trousers that made his legs seem even longer than they were, and how perfectly that green open-necked shirt suited his fair hair and almost exactly matched his eyes. She recalled with gratitude how concerned he'd been during the time she'd been confined to the house, and how these last few days since she had been back at the shop, he'd danced attendance on her at every opportunity. She for her part had found a deeper measure of contentment in his company. But always, whenever a closer relationship had threatened, Laura had retreated, invoking his anger and frustration. Maybe, after all, she thought, the level of their involvement would be best kept on a business footing. The last thing she wanted was for Mitch to be hurt. They had no future together. Their needs were too far apart, and she would never be able to give him the love he deserved. But what could she do? The only thing was to keep her distance as before.

Deep in her thoughts came the image of Parry Griffin and the recollection of how he had influenced the moods of her heart. She thought about his new found fortune, and of its effect on her plans for revenge. Yet she took comfort from her strong belief that he had gained this new security from his compulsive gambling, and that he was still as much a victim to that particular disease as he had ever been. What could be won could just as easily be lost. Especially if he was given a helping hand in that direction!

'Laura,' Mitch held out the cup and came to stand before her to look down on her with intensity and to say in a quiet voice, 'I've been meaning to talk with you. There's something in particular that I want you to hear.' She sensed that he was about to take her in his arms, and while such a prospect was not unpleasant, it didn't stir any deep desire within her, so avoiding his gaze, she moved away into the shop, saying brightly, 'Can it wait, Mitch? We'd best lock up now. Uncle Remmie'll be back any minute to take me home.' It was with relief that she saw Remmie's van pull up outside, and when he came into the shop, she hurried past Mitch to replace her cup on the table and collect her shopping-bag.

'Ready are you, lass?' Remmie looked towards Mitch, saying, 'You can lock up when you like, an' we'll expect you up at the 'ouse about eight-thirty. We'll 'ave a long talk on Monday, Mitch. I'd value your opinion on a few matters.'

'Right you are then, Remmie,' his voice was quietly firm, betraying nothing of his emotions, 'I'll see you later.'

It was eight-fifteen when Mitch arrived at the house, and Laura welcomed him warmly. Leaving Mitch and Remmie discussing business over a drink, she returned to the kitchen, where with Netti's help, she prepared a splendid meal of rabbit-pie with baby carrots and small crispy potatoes baked in stock, and apple pancakes and sauce to round the meal off.

'It'll all be spoiled if he doesn't soon get here.' Netti sank into a chair and nibbled on a biscuit. 'I thought he was supposed to arrive at eight o'clock? Do you think Uncle Remmie will ask Lizzie Pendleton to come round if Jake Thackerey lets him down? There's oceans of food.'

'I can't say, Netti. I did mention it to Remmie earlier, and he didn't seem too keen for her company, and to be honest, I can't blame him; and besides, don't forget that it's *her* who's decided to keep her distance.' Laura could just imagine what sort of gathering there would be at the supper table if Lizzie Pendleton saw fit to show herself.

Still, since Katya had been gone, that miserable old woman had seemed to find more pleasure in her own company, for she hardly ventured out of the house. Visitors were rare, except for the occasions when Netti ran errands or looked in on her. Laura shook her mind free of Lizzie Pendleton, because even the mention of her had cast gloom over the evening. Turning to Netti, she chided, 'Stop picking at the food, and Jake *will* be here. He's got important business to talk over with Remmie.'

'That's not the *only* reason he's coming though, is it? He's besotted with *you*! He rang every day when you were in that hospital.'

Secretly, Laura took pleasure and satisfaction from that remark, but choosing not to discuss it, she told Netti, 'Come on, go and set the glasses out. Everything else is ready. I'm sure he'll be here any minute.'

In fact, Jake Thackerey arrived half an hour later, full of apologies and complaining that he had been held up by heavy traffic for the last eighty miles.

'Don't apologize for some'at you couldn't control,' Remmie told him. Then re-acquainting him with Mitch, he plied him with a shot of whisky. 'Get that down you. We'll get straight into supper and then we've some talking to do.'

'Suits me fine.'

The atmosphere over supper was strained at times and Laura quickly attributed that to the fact that while Mitch freely engaged in conversation with her, Netti and Remmie, there was a definite reluctance on his part to pursue any particular matter with Jake Thackerey; although it could not be said that he didn't reply to Jake's questions with admirable courtesy. Nevertheless, there was a distinct frostiness between the two men, and much to Laura's embarrassment, Netti took great delight in whispering to Laura, 'They hate each other, because they're both crazy about you.'

Laura was pleased that Remmie had been careful not to allow the meal to be used as a background for business discussions. The chat was kept on more of a social level, Remmie praising the accelerated programme of council house building, and Mitch arguing that there were still too many folk living in condemned dwellings. Jake Thackerey for his part had little to add to the subject, except to say, 'It does seem to me that progress in the northern part of the country lags a good deal behind that of the south.'

Laura found nothing stimulating about council house building and government subsidies, and she was happy to leave the men with their views.

It was eleven-thirty when she and Netti came in from the kitchen, where they had quickly washed and stacked away all the utensils. Laura would have liked Netti to play for them, but the girl looked tired and said to Remmie, 'I hope you don't think it rude of me, Uncle Remmie, but I think I'll be off to my bed.'

'No, you go on, lass,' Remmie replied.

'Take no mind of us, Netti, and thanks for a lovely meal,' Mitch said.

Jake seconded Mitch's appreciation, adding, 'I'll see you in the morning before I go.'

Netti bade them all goodnight, and when she had left the room Mitch addressed himself to Jake Thackerey, inquiring in a stiff voice, 'So you're staying here for the night?'

'That seems to be the plan,' replied the other man, meeting Mitch's forthright stare. 'Remmie kindly suggested that it might serve our purposes better.'

'Quite right!' Remmie brought the bottle of brandy from the sideboard and going first to Mitch and then to Jake, he topped up their glasses, adding for Mitch's information, 'Soulless place that Bull, besides, Jake's an early riser like me, an' we've a good deal to tidy up concerning this 'ere business proposition.' He returned to his seat and pitched a querulous glance at Jake Thackerey. 'That right, young man?'

'True enough, and I have to get an early start back; strange how the work piles up when you're not there to see to it.'

Laura had sat quietly during this quick exchange of words, sipping on her coffee. But now in a soft voice that made them all look at her, she asked Jake Thackerey, 'Not in *your* case surely? I should have thought your efficient Ria would keep the business smoothly ticking over in your absence. Isn't that why you left her behind this time?'

Jake Thackerey seemed momentarily lost for words, his eyes fixed on Laura's beauty and his hands nervously rolling the brandy glass to and fro.

'Aye, where is that pretty fiancée o' yourn?' Remmie called out, then in a gust of laughter, he went on, 'I allus thought once a fella were promised, 'is intended never left 'is side!'

'Fiancée, eh?' murmured Mitch, and Laura could almost feel his relief.

Jake Thackerey's gaze travelled from Mitch to Remmie and back to Laura. With a meaningful smile spreading over his dark handsome features, he said to Laura, 'Ria is *not* my fiancée, not any more. It wouldn't have worked between us, and I believe I've managed to convince her of that.'

Immediately, Remmie took up the conversation and in his usual straightforward, no nonsense fashion, he launched a volley of questions at Jake Thackerey concerning the proposed joint business venture; and for the moment, the matter of Ria Morgan was of no consequence.

Of no consequence to Remmie, thought Laura, but of considerable consequence to me.

For the next hour the conversation was deep and earnest, Laura answering particular questions put to her concerning the new venture's possible success, and she in turn putting questions and well-received suggestions of her own. All this time there were glances between her and Jake Thackerey that had nothing at all to do with the business venture. Occasionally she would become aware of Mitch closely watching her. It was almost as though those searching green eyes of his could see right inside her and could pick out the very worst of her intentions.

Yet Laura admired the skilful manner in which he mastered the conversation, drawing information about Jake's affairs from him with such superb discretion, that Remmie finally left the negotiating almost entirely in Mitch's hands.

Laura too followed the developments very carefully, and she had to admit to herself that even though she was biased in favour of the merger, it did seem to be a good move on its own merit. The only drawback was that Ria Morgan would be staying on. That arrangement was apparently on the express insistence of the old man who was the present owner of the galleries.

It was in the early hours when Mitch stood up and declared, 'Right, well I'll be making my way off home.' He looked directly at Remmie and added, 'Unless there's something else?'

'No. There's nowt as can't keep. There's no question o' this being brought to a conclusion.' He turned to Jake Thackerey. 'Lot to be done, you understand? Least of all, a trip down south to give these 'ere galleries the once over, formalities an' so on.'

'I understand. The best deals in the world were never done overnight.'

Laura watched as Mitch stretched back his shoulders and drew himself up to his full height, saying in a voice that was filled with meaning, 'Act in haste, repent at leisure; isn't that how the old saying goes?' His question was directed towards Jake, who appeared none too pleased at its implications, but it was Remmie's fist that he took hold of to shake firmly. 'Goodnight Remmie, see you Monday morning.'

'Goodnight, Mitch.' Remmie stood up to grasp Mitch's hand. 'Laura'll see you out, won't you, lass?'

247

Laura followed Mitch towards the door, where he turned to say to Jake Thackerey, who was still seated and watching Mitch and Laura, 'Goodnight then, Thackerey.' When the other man simply nodded, Mitch made no move to go from the room. He looked at Jake Thackerey before asking pointedly, 'You *did* know that Laura was injured? That she was in hospital and laid up for nigh on a fortnight?'

'O' course Jake knew,' Remmie intervened, 'told 'im mesel' when 'e telephoned the very day after.' He looked surprised that Mitch should have raised this particular matter.

'I have purposely avoided that subject tonight, not wanting to raise unpleasant issues,' answered Jake.

'Quite right!' Remmie sat back down in the chair, calling out, 'See you Monday then, Mitch.'

Laura guessed that Remmie sensed a degree of antagonism between the two men and was at a loss to fathom why, bless him.

Outside Laura told Mitch, 'That was a spiteful thing to ask Jake just now. It was *my* wish that he shouldn't come to the Infirmary. I didn't want him to see me ill,' she lied, adding quietly, 'Goodnight, Mitch.'

She would have turned away then, and left him there. But she felt herself snatched forward as Mitch caught her by the arm, and pulled her into him with a rough determined movement.

His arms closed tight about her, pressing her into the warmth of his body, and Laura felt powerless to move. He buried his mouth in the softness of her hair and his murmurings stirred a deep emotion inside her; an emotion that was painful in its intensity, and that erupted in fury. Struggling against the iron grip that held her, she lifted her face and for that split second when Mitch brought his gaze on her with such tenderness and with such wonderful love, there was a response in Laura's heart that she could not recognize. But what she *did* recognize was her secure future with Jake slipping away from her. Laura saw the danger of Mitch swallowing up everything she had planned for her and for Netti. 'No, Mitch! No.' Her clenched fists pushed hard against him, coming like a wedge between them. 'Why won't you let me be? Please, Mitch.'

Mitch didn't answer, but his eyes blazed into Laura's and for a moment, she thought he was going to kiss her and that made her desperate to be free of him. She renewed her attempts to break from the deadlock of his arms, and when he suddenly threw her from him, she stood panting and gasping, her heart flooded with rage and tears very close, as she looked at him before preparing to go back inside. 'Leave me be, Mitch,' she told him, in a strangely subdued voice, 'Jake Thackerey's the man I want, can't you understand that?'

The mention of Jake Thackerey caused Mitch's face to harden and when he spoke, it was in a fierce growl, 'You're a fool, Laura Blake! Jake Thackerey is no *man*! He's weak and unreliable. But that doesn't matter to you, does it? As long as he's well-off!'

Laura moved backwards now, as his manner suddenly changed and his voice took on a gentle tone. 'I love you, Laura. I've *always* loved you and that'll never change, not in a million years. *I'm* the man for you, and by God, I might not give you the grand rich life you're forever craving after, but I'll cherish you like no other man ever could.'

'No!' Laura felt real animosity in her heart as she faced him, her shoulders set square and straight and her head held high in defiance. 'I *know* what I want! And it isn't *you*!' Her protest was forceful, but not loud, yet even to her own ears it sounded deafening, and in the thick silence that followed, she could almost hear her own heartbeat. Mitch hadn't taken his eyes off her, not for a moment, and now he was studying her as one might study an impossible puzzle. Then with a curt nod of the head, he told her quietly, 'Like I said, Laura, you're a fool. Your own worst enemy, God help you.' Then he bade her goodnight. He didn't look back as Laura watched him climb into the car that he'd recently bought. Then she stared after it until it disappeared from her sight.

She felt alone and empty. It was an uncomfortable feeling that had the effect of strengthening her determination to use her own life as she thought fit! Mitchell Strong was not her master, and he never would be!

As she made her way back inside, she remembered how Mitch had skilfully drawn attention to Jake's marked absence during her stay in hospital and then afterwards at home. She had to admit to herself that she too had taken a poor view of that. But she had purposefully dismissed such notions by reminding herself that Jake had been promised in marriage to another woman. He was not obliged in any way to commit himself publicly to Laura Blake. She hadn't expected that he would, and therefore had not been disappointed. Mitch could say what he liked, and *she* would believe what *she* liked!

All the same, when Remmie went off to his bed, leaving her and Jake alone downstairs, Laura pondered on the subject that Mitch had stirred in her mind. Mitch must also have been in Jake Thackerey's thoughts, for now he said, 'He's a forceful character, that Mitchell Strong. It's obvious that he's in love with you.'

Laura said nothing, but her eyes followed Jake as he came to stand in front of her, got down on one knee before her, at the same time holding her gaze and reaching out to touch her face. 'I wonder half the men in Blackburn aren't in love with you.' He laughed softly, before continuing, 'Poor fools. I can imagine them dreaming over you night after night, craving for you and looking at you in the same way a cat might look at a king. They do say that a woman who's too beautiful actually has the effect of driving men away.'

Laura sat still and quiet, enjoying his words, her dark pensive eyes appraising his face. She was thinking how good-looking he was, with that deep-coloured hair and those black eyes. And hadn't she got him right where she wanted him, here, on his knee before her? Yes, all of that was very satisfying, but something was missing. Maybe it was his eyes, which, though deep in colour, were shallow and devoid of fire or expression; or was it that his chin was not square and strong like Mitch's? She couldn't pinpoint a particular weakness. But she could sense it, and in her heart, she suspected that Mitch was right. And when she heard Jake telling her, 'I had intended to come and see you, but I have an aversion to illness, and hospitals,' Laura found the laughter beginning to bubble in her throat. She could have taunted him, laughed in his face at such a pitiful confession. But instead, she found herself murmuring, 'It's alright. I'm glad you didn't. I'd rather we forgot about the entire incident. I don't want to talk about it.'

'I understand.' He got to his feet, and Laura felt herelf being drawn up into his arms, and he whispered into her neck, 'Oh, if only you knew how I've wanted you, needed you.' He brought his hands up to cradle her face, and Laura was taken aback by the lustrous passion in his eyes, as he whispered, 'How could I ever marry Ria? It's *you* I want. You will marry me, won't you. Laura? Say you will.'

Laura heard his words, and she secretly savoured them, but at the same time she was surprised at her own cool reaction to his proposal. This was her moment of triumph, wasn't it? This was what she had schemed and manipulated for. So why wasn't she ecstatic? Why didn't she cry out her acceptance with wild enthusiasm? Yet she didn't. What she did was to fold herself into his arms and offer herself up to his kiss, a long passionate embrace that kindled no like emotion in her own heart. Then, when he drew away, she told him, 'Yes, Jake. I'll marry you.'

'Oh, Laura, I knew we were meant for each other the first time I laid eyes on you in Remmie's shop. You were meant for better things, and you shall have them. You'll have everything you want, I promise you that.'

He gripped her shoulders now, his voice alive with excitement. 'Remmie won't hesitate on our deal now, and Netti will be well provided for, I'll see to that. There are people in London who can take her right to the top in her music.' He looked straight into her face now, and seeing her quietness, he asked, 'It's what you want, isn't it?'

Laura thought of Netti, and what all this could mean to her. And at once, her heart warmed and a rush of gladness went right through her. 'Yes! Yes, it's what I want. It's what I've *always* wanted.' When he pulled her into him and covered her mouth with his, she gave herself freely.

But when his fingers closed around her breast, and she could feel the hard urgency of his need for her, Laura withheld that ultimate sacrifice. Putting her hands on his chest, she gently levered herself away from him, saying in a whisper, 'Not here, not like this. It doesn't seem right.' But what she was really saying was that she doubted if it would *ever* be right, *anywhere* or any time. She heard his low groan and felt his reluctance to let her go. But when she looked up at him, she saw nothing at that moment to keep her. 'Goodnight, Jake,' she said, 'we'll talk in the morning.' Turning away, she walked from him, out

251

to the passage and on up the stairs to her room.

It was some time later, when she was lying in her bed unable to sleep, that she heard Jake going first to the bathroom and then back down the landing to his bedroom. She felt confused, cheated and angry; angry at herself, for withholding what she now saw to be rightfully Jake's, who was to be her husband. But most of all, she felt angry with Mitch and his incessant probing into her life. It was *him* who had set off the doubts that had already begun to torment her. As always when she thought about Mitch, she grew more and more restless and her irritation became a storm that engulfed her. So Mitchell Strong thought Jake wasn't the man for her? Yet he was conceited enough to think *he* was! Did he *really* think that she could ever entertain a man who chose to spend his life dressed in overalls and breaking his back over someone else's treasured furniture? What a fool! Couldn't he see that she wanted more, that her plans for revenge on the Griffins demanded it? And was he too blind to see that her ambition to get Netti recognized as the talented musician she was also dictated her every move, like it always had? Jake Thackerey was her future, hers and Netti's. *Nobody* would be allowed to stand in the way of that! Not Mitch, not anyone!

The intensity of Laura's thoughts had made her get up from her bed and pace the floor. Now, she was at the door and quickly on to the landing. She quietly closed the door behind her and leaning against it, her breathing sharp and fast, she listened for a moment. All was silent. So on swift determined footsteps, her bare feet making no sound on the carpet, she made her way along the landing to the spare room, and Jake Thackerey.

Turning the door handle, she wondered whether he might have slipped the bolt on the other side. When the door opened into the darkness, she breathed a soft thankful sigh. Standing with her back to the closed door, she allowed her eyes to accustom themselves to the darkness, before she moved forward, silently, carefully.

The light of the moon through the window settled on his sleeping face, throwing strange shadows beneath his eyes, until Laura thought he had opened them and was looking at her. With a shiver of excitement, she suddenly realized that he *was* looking at her. There was no surprise, no anger or reproach in the dark emotion of his gaze; only a deep passion of wanting.

An answering smile spread across her face, then without taking her eyes from him, she reached up to release the flimsy nightgown, allowing it to slither quietly to the floor where it settled about her bare feet. She enjoyed the way her beauty seemed to startle him, for his dark eyes widened and then narrowed with desire, as he drank in the magnificence of her nakedness. Without speaking a word, he reached out to lift the covers beside him.

Laura wondered why she didn't feel afraid. But she didn't; yet neither did she feel passion, or love. She felt only power and revenge in her soul, and this man was the means by which she would be made free; free like the birds on the moors, and free from the chains of her past.

The moist caress of his searching mouth pleasured and tormented her and the warmth of his body flooded over her, as he covered her with the searching demands of his manliness, knowing that at long last he was to experience this magnificent woman; to take her into himself and to make her truly his.

Laura was surprised by his gentleness, and consoled by the discovery that at last some of the demons that had haunted her for so long seemed to melt into the dark interior of her mind.

Yet some time later, when she emerged from Jake Thackerey's bedroom as silently as she had entered it, Laura would have liked to deny the tears that stung her eyes, but she could not. Neither could she deny that beneath the probing touch of Jake Thackerey she had experienced nothing to soften her heart. There was a coldness within her that could not be melted. She had shared her body, allowed him to invade it in order to satisfy his love for her. But there had been no love in her own heart, and nor could there ever be. But there was hatred. Black hatred for Parry Griffin, who had created the memories that, although they would never be allowed to haunt her as before, were still alive in her darkest thoughts.

Shivering now, she deliberately pushed such matters from her mind. So she was committed to Jake Thackerey, and the fact that it was a cold commitment brought no remorse to Laura's heart. In this world of surprising twists and turns, she'd learned that in order to survive, you had to grasp greedily at every opportunity. There was no room for compassion. It was not a luxury she could afford!

Laura crossed to the window in her room, where she looked out into the blackness beyond, allowing her thoughts to embrace the memory of Jake Thackerey's closeness. She began to wonder what it might be like to feel love, real deep love, for a man. Almost without realizing it, she found herself remembering the trembling excitement she'd felt that day at the shop, when Pearce Griffin had kissed her. Pearce Griffin! The very last person she should allow into her mind. Was he not his father's son?

Angrily dismissing the run of her thoughts, Laura indulged in her urge to bathe. Later, lying in her bed, there came over her a terrible feeling of shame and revulsion at what she had done, and she saw herself as little more than a prostitute. The tears that followed were bitter and self-recriminatory. Laura realized that the price for success was a very high one.

Chapter Twenty-one

The summer had been glorious, but the winter had been one of the hardest Laura could remember. The steep brews and narrow ways leading into various hamlets surrounding Blackburn had been virtually impassable, and business at the shop had suffered as a result. But now it was May, and the weather had changed at last.

Laura came into the shop and looked about her. She felt pleased with what she saw. They'd picked up some very nice pieces of furniture from the big houses out Wigan and Cherry-Tree way. All good stuff, some Regency and one or two heavy Jacobean pieces. But what pleased her most was that they'd managed to find another Yourelli painting.

She let herself into the large cupboard at the back of the shop, reached up to one of the shelves and pulled down a parcel wrapped in sacking. After removing several layers of sacking, she lifted the painting out into the light. It showed a tumble-down cottage, whose thatched roof had been ravaged by weather and in the foreground, leaning over a fence, was a woman of ample proportion. Dressed in blue and wearing a white frilly cap, she was chastizing the small child who cowered on the other side of the fence. Two other small children were happily amusing themselves on a makeshift see-saw by the gate.

Laura gazed at it for a while, the pleasure she felt evident on her smiling features. Jake would love this painting. It was magical, and she had been so entranced by its beauty, that for a while she had been tempted to keep it for herself. But it was Jake's, therefore she would keep it safe for him.

As she returned the painting to the cupboard she thought of Jake Thackerey. His trips back to Blackburn had been frequent and productive in more ways than one. Her engage-

255

ment to Jake Thackerey had been initially received by Remmie and Netti with less enthusiasm than she would have liked; Mitch had made small comment on the matter, but his very silence had been an expression of condemnation.

However, as she had suspected time had mellowed their opposition, and her plans of marriage to Jake had become an accepted intrusion into their hitherto close-knit lives.

Laura hadn't seen Ria Morgan since that day at the house when Ria had warned her to keep away from Jake. Yet she still felt uneasy at the knowledge that Jake and his ex-fiancée continued to work in close proximity. In spite of Jake's assurance that it was all over between him and Ria, the thought of that woman being in a position of influence remained a constant source of irritation to Laura. No doubt Ria Morgan thought her position at the gallery to be secure, because of the present owner's wishes. Well, Laura had secretly vowed to change all that when the gallery came into their hands; and it was envisaged that this would happen some time during the autumn.

It had been arranged that some time within the next few weeks, Mitch would look after things at the shop, while she and Remmie made a trip south, to see what they might be letting themselves in for. If all was as Jake had said, then negotiations would be started to sell the business at this end as working capital for the new venture. Laura was filled with optimism that at long last, things were beginning to look up for what was left of the Blake family.

The loud jangle of the bell over the shop door cut sharply into Laura's brooding thoughts. There was no time now for thinking! In less than an hour, the market place would be teeming with potential customers.

'A bright mornin' to you, Laura. We're on us way to set up wi' these 'ere carpets and rugs. Is the lad about?'

Laura wondered at the remarkable change in Belle Strong, over the years. She and Tupper had given up the sturdy walls of their little house for the freedom and vagabond life of wanderers. Their home was an old gypsy wagon, pulled about until its final visit to the local knacker-yard some eight months back, by an ancient Shire of dubious origin and gentle nature. Mitch had long since given up trying to persuade them that in their twilight years they should be thinking of security and a quiet life. Instead, he'd settled for the obvious fact that they were happy, and raised no further objections, at least in *their* hearing.

'Hello, Belle. What brings you out so early?' She'd never lost her affection for Belle, although she felt estranged by the older woman's increasing eccentricity. Even her appearance was unpredictable. The bright little eyes were still alert, and the tongue still as rasping; but the fat little figure seemed to have grown shorter and to have spread outwards in a wobbling mass.

When she spoke now, her voice was all a-flutter, the urgent words stumbling one over the other in her haste, 'We've a bit o' bother wi' yon bloody truck,' she gestured towards the ancient black pick-up truck parked outside the shop, 'coughin' an' splutterin' an' threatenin' to stop at every turn.' She took a white hankie from her pinny pocket and thrust it around her nose with a determined flourish. 'You'd best explain, Tupper,' she instructed the man by her side.

'Morning, Tupper,' Laura encouraged, acutely aware of the poor man's shyness.

'Mornin' Miss Laura,' he returned, his eyes directed away from her. Grasping the flat grey cap from his head, he held it tightly, glad to have something on which to fix his gaze. No man of vanity, he ignored the disturbed hair which stood up around his head in straggly grey clusters.

Laura thought he *must* be uncomfortable, for the black jacket which stretched tight beneath his arms was fastened unevenly, leaving a spare button at the top and a spare hole at the bottom. His great shiny boots looked exceedingly heavy and ill-fitting, and the little silk scarf at his neck was tied in a fashion fit to choke him.

'I've allus said as you can't beat a good hoss an' cart!' The subject was obviously a favourite one, judging by the quick confidence in his voice. 'Didn't want no truck! Hoss an' cart, I said, same as we've 'ad for many a year; but no! Belle 'ere said it were time we bettered ourselves. Now, we've bettered ourselves an' we live in fear that we'll be stranded one o' these days! Hoss 'ud never let you down, faithful things is hosses!' He turned sideways to look at Belle. 'We don't need to bother

257

these 'ere folks, Belle lass. They've enough to do of a Saturday mornin' as it is.'

Laura sensed their reluctance to ask the favour they obviously needed. 'Mitch's out in the yard . . . ' She did hope though, that they weren't about to take him from the shop. She really needed him this morning, especially with Remmie out buying.

As though reading her thoughts, the little woman's features wrestled into a dimpled smile. 'I've not come to fotch 'im away!' she declared stoutly. 'We just thought as 'ow 'e might look inside that there truck an' see what's ailing.' She looked around the shop. 'Remmie's off out, is 'e lass?'

'Yes, but he said he wouldn't be too long. He's gone to fetch a writing desk from Doctor Street's surgery. Seems that new doctor's got no use for such a big article.'

'There you are, you see!' Belle Strong nodded towards her husband. 'Even them posh folks get movin' wi' the times; can't stand still, doin' the self-same thing year in year out, got to move wi' the times!'

'Aye, well.' Tupper Strong looked more uncomfortable by the minute. Running a bony finger between the rim of his shirt collar and his poor strangled neck, he told her, 'You'd best go and see the lad, Belle.'

'Why didn't you tell me, Dad?' Mitch followed Belle back into the shop. 'I said the truck were making a peculiar sort o' noise; sounds like it needs new plugs.'

Tupper Strong scratched his head and threw his cap up, to squash it tight over his wrinkled forehead. 'Damned fangled vehicles! Gimme hoss an' cart any time!'

'Come on, you miserable ol' sod!' Belle laughed as she manoeuvered him out of the shop. 'Jealous! That's what's up wi' you! Jealous 'cause our Mitch knows a bit more about some'at than 'is old dad! *You* couldn't fix it, med' it worse if 'owt!'

'Don't be so bloody daft, woman!' The sheepish expression on Tupper Strong's embarrassed face reflected both the truth of Belle's words, and his shame at their utterance.

They were still busy arguing, as Mitch assured them he'd be along to see to the truck after the shop was closed. Laura watched as Belle pushed and shoved the protesting Tupper out to the truck, then sensing Mitch's eyes on her, she set about dusting the furniture with excessive zeal. She was determined not to give him the satisfaction of turning round to meet his gaze. Only when the outer door slammed behind him did she relax.

Remmie's van pulled up about half an hour later, loaded with some choice pieces.

'That's a grand old desk.' Mitch had developed a good critical eye for quality furniture. The desk was constructed in solid dark oak, boasting a beautiful ridged roll-top and several deep drawers capped by figured brass handles.

Remmie stood in the van, his hands securely placed round the back of the desk. 'You're right,' the strong broad smile reflected his approval of Mitch's observation, 'it is a grand old desk. I don't expect this to set long afore it's sold!'

Laura cleared a path through the jungle of paraphernalia, as they carried the considerable weight to its chosen position in the foreground of the shop.

Remmie smiled at her. 'Don't like it, do you lass?' He followed her critical gaze towards the desk. 'Not your style, eh?'

Laura crossed to his side, placing her arms around his thick waist to hug him to her. 'Sorry,' she said decidedly, 'but I hate it! Mind you, it'll bring a good price.' She looked at the square solid strength of the desk. It reminded her of Mitch; reliable, handsome, but totally staid and predictable. 'I expect some dreary old man will buy it, to stuff his dreary old papers in!'

Mitch slapped his fist on the top of the desk. 'This 'ere desk'll still be useful when all your pretty flighty rubbish is long gone!'

For an uncomfortable moment Laura realized that his thinking wasn't too distant from her own! He too was drawing a parallel; making comparisons between himself and Jake Thackerey!

Remmie let out a bellow of laughter, and Laura thought how good it was to see him growing more like his old self; although she knew he would never completely get over Katya's death. 'Now then, lass. Shall you manage if I take Mitch away for an hour? There's that stuff to be taken up to the Convent. I'll not be able to manage them great beds on me own, an' that's a fact.'

Laura knew it wouldn't be any good reminding him, as she'd done so often before, that he could well afford to employ a man for labouring and heavy lifting. He was too stubborn; always insistent that he wasn't ready to be 'put out to pasture!' She watched them go and as always she was glad when Mitch was out of the shop. Remmie wanted to take Mitch south with them when the shop was sold. It was a prospect that troubled her.

Laura wasn't ready to give in on that point just yet; and not at all, if there was any possible way of avoiding it. To this end, the germ of an idea was taking shape in her mind. Some time back a man of means had come into the shop — a southerner who had travelled north in search of antiques and *objets d'art*. He had offered good money and after browsing through the shop, had purchased several small items. This man's visit had told Laura a good deal, and she had churned it over in her mind ever since.

It seemed as though the antique trade — which was only just gaining real recognition in the north — had become a fast-growing and lucrative business in the south. But what was more interesting was confirmation of what Jake had already told them; the antique business looked to the north for supplies of older and more sought-after items. That being so, then there was a strong case for keeping the shop. It would be a valuable source of supply.

Jake and Remmie had already discussed the need for regular buying trips to this area, so what better than to have their own outlet, one that people were already accustomed to, and had come to trust. And who better to manage the shop here, than Mitch?

The more Laura thought about the idea, the more she liked it. It would solve two problems; that of looking for a new and reliable source of antiques, and the personal problem of Mitch.

But the matter did, however, create its own problem. The sale of the shop was to provide the capital they needed in order to buy partnership with Jake into the gallery. It *was* a problem, there was no denying that; but she'd find a way, somehow!

With a steady influx of customers into the front of the shop, and the market people entering the yard at the back, Laura found herself far too busy to even think about capital. But the

260

issue stayed quietly insistent in the back of her mind, until Remmie and Mitch got back just before the lunch break. The shop remained open, each of them taking it in turn to attend to the customers. Laura had set up a table and chairs in the back room where they could enjoy their lunch in a semblance of civilized surroundings. Mitch had offered the use of his upstairs flat, but from there, they wouldn't have been able to hear customers coming in. From the store room, they could attend to the front shop and keep an eye on browsers wandering in from the market square.

'You're right, lass. It's a grand idea, an' if I were to tell the truth, I'd say that it *had* crossed me mind.' Remmie took a deep gulp of tea, then sat quiet, a far-away look in his eye.

Mitch was in the shop, seeing to a customer. When she heard him return, Laura told Remmie, 'Let's not say anything in front of Mitch. We'll talk about it later, eh?'

'As you like, lass.'

Laura knew from the tone of his voice that he held out little hope of them being able to keep the shop. But *she* wouldn't give in so easily. There *had* to be a way, and she intended to find it. She'd discuss it with Jake. He might have an idea or two.

After the lunch break, when Mitch was busy in the yard with customers, and Remmie had taken a phone call in the back room, Laura had a visitor.

As it was a warm, still day, she'd wedged the shop door open, and she was on her knees, carefully stacking some Wedgewood crockery in the bottom of a cupboard, when she became aware of someone standing over her.

'Still as beautiful as ever, Laura Blake.'

Laura didn't need to look up. She knew who that smooth persuasive voice belonged to.

'You!' She stood up to look straight into the handsome arrogant face of Pearce Griffin.

'That's right. Pearce Griffin at your service, as blatant as ever! Been waiting for me, have you?'

Before she could spill out the retort on the edge of her tongue, he slid his free arm around her waist and pulling her to him, he brought his mouth to cover hers, and although he claimed her viciously, Laura suspected a degree of real love in

261

his kiss. Through her dress, she could feel the warmth of his body and she felt herself relaxing against him. But when he caressed her ear with his mouth, and murmured, 'Are you gonna show old Pearce a good time tonight, eh?' Laura was instantly alert.

With a determined effort, she struggled against him and a minute later she had freed herself from him, only to have him grab at her again. Backing away, she seized an evil-looking knife from the cabinet and held it before her. Then she told him in a low threatening tone, 'I'm promised, Pearce Griffin! Promised! Do you understand? So remember that, and keep your distance!'

Pearce Griffin's answer was a low chuckle, but all the same he backed away from Laura, his eyes fixed warily onto the knife-blade. 'Well! Well! Promised, eh? Still, that don't mean a thing, especially not with you enjoying my kisses.'

Before disappearing through the door and away down the street, he paused to look at her with admiration. 'You're a magnificent woman, Laura Blake,' he murmured, 'you and me, we can't stay apart; we're too much alike, me beauty! I'll be seeing you.' Then he was gone.

As though it might shut him out of her mind, Laura rushed to the door and closed it behind him, even slipping the bolt. She was actually trembling as she leaned against the door; but whether from anger, or from some other more disturbing emotion, she daren't even contemplate.

After a while, she unbolted the door, but left it closed, and went out to the yard where Remmie and Mitch were now in the throes of dealing with customers.

It was less than an hour before closing time when Sally Fletcher came in. Remmie and Mitch were out delivering a consignment of chairs and a heavy regency table.

Laura knew straight away, from the misery in Sally's face. 'Mabel?' she asked softly.

'Yes. Late last night.'

Laura came round the counter, her heart heavy for Sally. 'Oh, Sally, I'm so very sorry.'

Sally remained by the door. She didn't speak for what seemed to Laura a long time. Then drawing in a long weary sigh, she said in a quiet voice, 'I sat with her for hours, and I was there at the end. I'm glad of that. We've known for a long time that she wouldn't get better,' it was only now that her voice flattened, 'expected it. But oh, I still can't believe it.'

Laura moved towards her. Thinking back on the way she felt when little Rosie died, she could partly understand how Sally must be feeling. But Mabel had been Sally's mother; a good mother; and that kind of love and devotion was something outside her own experience.

'Oh, Laura!' Sally fell into Laura's open arms. 'Things can never be the same now, can they, not now Mam's gone?' Her voice fell away beneath the stifled sobs, and all Laura could do was to hold her fast, in the same way that she herself had often been held fast in Mabel's arms. Only when Sally straightened herself up, wiped her eyes and said simply, 'Laura, leave me Tom,' was Laura forced to think of the boy. But in her heart, she had already given him over to the Fletcher family.

For a while after Sally had left, having promised to send details of the funeral, Laura stood deep in thought. So, Mabel Fletcher was gone! Mabel Fletcher, a friend indeed, a great pudding of a woman with a heart of gold and an honest capacity for loving. Oh, she would be sorely missed, not least of all by Laura herself. Most of all, Laura's heart went out to Sally, dear Sally, whose first thoughts had been that Tom also, would be wrenched from her. Well, that would not happen. Laura accepted that Tom was where he now belonged. And where he wanted to be.

Going out to the back yard, Laura deliberately concentrated her attentions on bringing the various items in and under cover. She locked the gates and bolted the store room before she returned to the shop, her thoughts still blurred by the news of Mabel's passing.

She had just finished cashing-up and completing the entries, when Laura's attention was caught by someone staring at her through the window. The small figure appeared to be an old traditional Lancashire woman; for she had a dark shawl wrapped around her head and shoulders, almost hiding her face. When Laura moved towards the window, the figure hurried away, showing the out-dated length of her flouncing skirt.

Laura was intrigued, especially since there were very few

women in Blackburn who still dressed in such a manner. Lizzie Pendleton was one of them; but Laura knew it wasn't her. She would have recognized *her*. And anyway, these days Lizzie Pendleton was always too drunk to put one leg before the other.

She mentioned it to Remmie when they arrived home that night, but he just shrugged and told her, 'Lots of women like that still about. Cling to their clogs an' shawls like it's their own identity. Traditions die hard for some, lass.' And the subject gave way to Remmie's distress on hearing of Mabel.

Later, after the evening meal was finished, Netti voiced her condolence on learning of Mabel Fletcher's passing, after which she related news of her own; startling news that took Laura completely by surprise.

'I'm giving up my studies.'

'You're what?' Remmie was the first to recover.

'You're doing no such thing!' Laura got to her feet; her eyes bright with anger as she rounded on Netti.

'It's no good, Laura. I've made my mind up.' Even now, she couldn't lift her eyes to look at Laura. She remained in her seat by the table, her head bowed, her face half-hidden by the long fair hair that was draped forward.

'Look at me Netti!' Laura stood before her, her hands gripping the edge of the table, as she leaned across it.

'Now then, Laura,' Remmie said quietly, 'let the lass have her say.' He folded the newspaper he'd been reading, then laid it down on his lap. 'What's happened, Netti? We thought you were doing so well.'

'I am,' she lifted her head, and Laura saw that the blue eyes were filled with tears, 'it's not that.'

'What then?' The sight of Netti's distress made Laura talk in a gentler tone. She pulled a stand-chair out and sat to face Netti. 'You can't give up your studies, Netti. We won't let you.'

'Hey! Let's hear what the lass has to say first.'

'I'm sorry, Uncle Remmie. There's nothing to say, really. I just want to do something else.'

'I won't hear of it, Netti Blake!' Laura got to her feet again. 'It's all we've worked for, you and me, to get you through your studies.'

'Laura! Leave this to me for now, eh? You go an' brew us a pot o' tea.'

Laura's mouth felt dry too. But it was from anger, not thirst. Perhaps it *would* be best if she took herself off to the kitchen.

A few minutes later, she was standing by the back gate, looking across the moors. From the kitchen, she'd heard Remmie trying to reason with Netti, and she'd heard Netti skirting the issue and giving no answer at all.

Funny how she hadn't noticed this change in Netti. It couldn't have happened overnight. No! Wait a minute. There had been something. Netti *had* grown quiet of late, seeming to brood and draw things into herself. But what with her own obsession about Jake, and moving south, she hadn't taken as much notice as she should have done. Well, it wasn't too late. Whatever the problem was, they'd work it out. But for the life of her, she couldn't think what might have unsettled Netti to such an extent that she wanted to give up her music studies. It was all she lived for.

Slowly, a thought came into Laura's head, and she couldn't dismiss it. It became obvious to her that Lizzie Pendleton, that drunken vicious old woman, was behind this! The day of Katya's funeral when Netti had come back from seeing Lizzie Pendleton home, there had been something *then*. But what? That vile woman was well-known for evil gossip. Netti surely couldn't have taken anything she'd said seriously?

There was only one way to find out!

As Laura made her way to Lizzie Pendleton's house, she was seething. It was easy for her to see how the wicked tongue of this woman might distress such an impressionable sensitive soul as Netti.

She pushed open the kitchen door and was immediately struck by the silence. Usually, if Lizzie Pendleton had been at the bottle, there'd be a faint humming and moaning coming from the house. The passageway was freezing, and as she hurried towards the front parlour, Laura wondered whether the old woman had made her way to an early bed. She hoped not! For the things *she* had to say wouldn't wait till morning!

As she pushed the parlour door open and her eyes strained against the darkness, the stench of booze filled her nostrils. Lizzie Pendleton hadn't gone to her bed! She was here, in the darkness. Laura found the light switch and clicked it on. But she wasn't prepared for the sight that greeted her.

'Whadd'ya want? Who the bloody hell?' The voice was slurred and incoherent. Then, as Laura approached, Lizzie Pendleton tried to drag herself into a sitting position.

She was lying on the floor in front of the easy armchair, her bare feet straddling the brass fire-fender. The fire had long since died, leaving a grey heap of brittle cinders, from which the heavy poker protruded at an uncomfortable angle. Laura looked down at the hunched figure, and in spite of everything, she felt a small pang of guilt. How could something like this happen? Katya would have been horrified at the terrible demise of this woman, who had brought her up from a babe. But then, if Katya hadn't died, it probably wouldn't have happened.

'Oh, you! Don't want *you*!' Lizzie Pendleton was looking at her now, her hand searching for the half-empty bottle resting against the chair. Laura reached it first, and as she leaned over the figure of Lizzie Pendleton, the smell became almost unbearable. It swam into her mouth and filled her lungs, until she thought she'd have to be sick.

'Come on! Get up, you disgusting old woman.' As she lifted the protesting body into the chair, the reason for the terrible smell revealed itself. A puddle of urine had dried in a shapeless ring on the carpet, but the bottom of Lizzie Pendleton's nightie and the back of her legs were running wet.

Laura managed to get her into the chair; but suddenly, as though being seated upright had restored her sense of decency, Lizzie Pendleton noticed Laura's grimace of distaste.

'Pissed meself, 'int I? Well you needn't look so bloody pompous, not *you*!'

It seemed to Laura as though the old woman had been asleep rather than drunk, because now she appeared to be more alert and certainly back to her vindictive form.

'Don't want you in my house. Get out! Go on!' She lifted her eyes to look at Laura, then blinked as though the effort was too much. 'Go on. . . out!' she mumbled.

'I'll go when you've answered a question or two.'

'Question? What question?'

'I want to know what you've been saying to Netti.'

'I've said nothing! Not to Netti, not to nobody.'

'You're a liar, Lizzie Pendleton. Now tell me. I want to know!'

The old woman wriggled deeper into the chair and closed her eyes. 'Clear off!'

Laura could so easily have wrenched her from the chair, but the thought of touching her again was too sickening. 'I'm not leaving! Not till you've told me what I want to know. You've been saying things to Netti, haven't you?'

Lizzie Pendleton dragged herself back up in the chair and pointed her bloated face at Laura. The leer that started at her mouth spread over her face until it glowed viciously in the pink, half-closed eyes. 'Telled her the truth, didn't I?'

'What do you mean?' Laura moved forward until she could actually feel the warmth from Lizzie Pendleton's awful breath. 'What "truth"? What have you been saying? You spiteful crazy old fool!'

'Old fool am I?' She pushed her face towards Laura, an evil glint in her narrowed eyes. 'Do *you* want to know the truth, eh?' She cackled. 'Well you go and see Joe Blessing. He's the one as wronged your dad, bedded your crazy mam, bedded me.' All of a sudden, she started to cry. 'Katya's gone, and I never told her.'

Laura watched her reach out to snatch the bottle from the small table by her arm where Laura had placed it. Lifting it to her mouth, she gurgled the liquid down until Laura thought she'd be bound to choke. For a long moment, she stood over Lizzie Pendleton, a cold rage dark in her eyes. Then, as though finally accepting that there would be no sense in pursuing the issue tonight, she turned away.

Halfway down the passage, the impact of the old woman's words and their inherent meaning suddenly struck her. She'd said that Joe Blessing had wronged her father, bedded her mother. Laura's heart grew cold at the implications. Was Lizzie Pendleton saying that Joe Blessing was her father, and not Jud Blake? Oh God! She didn't know *what* to make of it all.

Closing the kitchen door behind her, she wandered across the yard and out towards the moors. She'd be able to think clearly there, about poor Mabel, and about the things Lizzie Pendleton had said.

She stopped by a small clump of shrub, where she sank down into the soft willowy grass. For a moment, there was no

267

thought in her mind. She just gave herself up to the stillness and the black of night and a sense of peace filled her confused mind. The thick clean perfume of running water and wild flowers took away the stench of Lizzie Pendleton from her nostrils. For a while, thoughts of Mabel's kind loving nature filled her heart and eased the pain inside her.

Some time later, in a calmer mood, Laura made her way back home. She'd been a fool! Netti might be fooled into believing Lizzie Pendleton's mad ramblings; but *she* ought to have known better. That woman's hatred of Ruth Blake must have turned her mind; and what with Katya's death and all the boozing, it was no wonder if she began to imagine things. She'd tell Netti so; advise her to stay clear of Lizzie Pendleton. Remmie would need to call in the authorities and have the old fool put away.

She felt deeply disturbed, and very frightened. It had been an odd sort of day. The unsettling part of it had really started with Pearce Griffin forcing himself on her. Then Sally's news of her mother's death; and that strange woman lurking outside the shop, watching her. There had been the shock of Netti's news, and the broken incoherent claims of Lizzie Pendleton. But she wouldn't believe anything that drunken sop might say! She was long past seeing things as they really were.

Yet if her thoughts told her one thing, her aching heart told her another. In spite of her determination to treat it all as drunken imaginings, Laura found herself curious as to Joe Blessing's whereabouts, and how he might answer the charges laid at his door.

When Laura got back to the house, Netti had gone to bed. 'Leave her be, lass.' Remmie stroked his 'tache thoughtfully and sighed wearily. 'Happen we could all do with an early night.' He walked across to the door and then turned back to ask, 'You'll not disturb the lass will you? Some'ats got to 'er, an' that's a fact. I might go in an' see yon Miss Fordyke.'

Laura scotched that idea by telling Remmie that in her opinion it was nothing to do with school, and that she herself would deal with it.

Remmie shook his head. 'Funny little thing, our Netti. Teks things to heart. Too serious by half; it's all that blessed study-ing!'

Laura reached up and kissed him gently on the cheek. 'Don't you worry.' There was no sense in Remmie puzzling and making himself miserable. It would all be sorted out, and by her! She knew how to handle Netti, and she suspected the strain which Netti was under right now.

After Remmie had retired to bed, Laura sat downstairs for a long time. The things Lizzie Pendleton had said must be causing Netti a great deal of pain, for they were giving *her* no peace. She thought of her father and her heart grew heavy. 'I'll always love him!' she said out loud. Then the thought of her father being betrayed by Joe Blessing, whom he had always regarded as a friend, hurt so much that Laura was forced to pace the room.

By the time she was on her way upstairs, one thing stood clear and bold in her mind. She *would* find Joe Blessing and face him. She'd be able to tell whether he was speaking the truth, or lying through his teeth!

Chapter Twenty-two

It was June when Joe Blessing's whereabouts were made known to Laura.

She was in the shop, waiting for Remmie and Mitch to get back from a house sale. As it was nearly closing time and business had slowed right down after a hectic day, she had it in mind to slip the bolt on the door and display the 'Closed' sign. As she turned from the china cupboard, she caught sight of her reflection in the polished glass doors. It was a pleasing image. The russet coloured slim fitting dress seemed to highlight the warm amber of her eyes, and as she looked at the perfect features and luxurious auburn hair, it came to her that at least one of Lizzie Pendleton's claims was true. It might have been Ruth Blake looking back at her; the young vivacious woman that Laura had known as a child. Now, she was insane, and out there somewhere, hiding. Or, for all Laura or anyone else knew, maybe dead.

She turned away from the reflection and slid her hand into the hip pocket of her dress and took out a neatly folded envelope. Opening the envelope, she withdrew a letter and started to read:

'My Darling Laura,

Three days gone and less than a week before I'm on my way home. I won't be sorry to leave Amsterdam this time. I miss you, my love. Next time, we'll see this lovely old city together.

I've been trying most of the day to get you on the phone, but couldn't get through. Keep the arrangements as discussed. You'll all travel down on the 18th. Remmie has detailed directions, which should bring you straight to

270

Aspley Galleries. As you know, I occupy half of the house as my private quarters. Ria's been organizing redecoration of them in my absence. She has very good taste, so I think you'll like it. I must say, I'm surprised and delighted that she's being civilized about the whole thing.

We've arranged that party I promised you. All the best people will be there, and they are all looking forward to meeting you. Ria's offered to take you round the fashionable shops for a suitable evening gown. She seems to think you don't have such places up north. But for my money, just wear your black dress, and I'll be the most envied man there.

You don't know how much I'm looking forward to seeing you again, and holding you in my arms.

Till then, my love, take care. I'm thinking of you.

All my love,
Jake.

Laura stared down at the letter, reading it again and again. Each time she became more aware that Ria Morgan's name seemed to dominate the letter. She'd have to be on her guard against that woman! On this trip, it had to be made clear once and for all, that Jake Thackerey belonged to her! The sooner the wedding date was fixed, the better. The day after tomorrow was the 18th, and she would have the whole weekend with him. She didn't intend to waste a single moment.

'Must be a good letter.' The thin beady-eyed woman of advancing years and the small boy had entered the shop without Laura hearing them. 'Used to get letters meself during the war.' Her tight glittering eyes grew sorrowful. 'Love letters they were, from my fella. But what bloody use is love letters, eh? That soddin' war! Left me with a drawer full o' love letters, four kids, an' nowt to look for'ard to! My fella, well, never came back did 'e? But I 'int the only one. I keeps tellin' meself that.' She reached down to prod the boy, who was opening and shutting a desk drawer. 'Get your bloody fingers off, afore I trap 'em inside o' that drawer. I telled you, didn't I? I said if you didn't be'ave, I'd tan your bloody arse!'

Laura smiled at the woman, trying not to laugh out loud. She knew Nan Barker, but only by reputation. It was true what she'd said. She had been left destitute with four children. But they were all grown now, and this boy must be one of her many grandchildren. Before Laura could ask what she wanted, the woman was talking again.

'No good, these bloody letters! I'll bet there 'int one woman in Blackburn as don't 'ave a bundle o' love letters. Mind you! Some on 'em would likely cause a stir or two, eh?' She broke out laughing, 'Not all o' them soldiers were 'usbands!' Then she grew serious. 'Sad to think what war did, eh? When you think on 'ow some of our lads came back to us. Some left their arms and legs back there in them there bloody trenches! An' some lost worse than limbs, eh? Lost their dignity. I mean, yon Joe Blessing's an example o' the like. Half bloody daft now 'e is! Living in filth you'd not believe.'

'Joe Blessing?' Laura was suddenly attentive.

'Aye, lass. Old Joe Blessing, as used to be a fine 'andsome figure of a man, dossin' down in one o' them derelict places along the alley. Disgraceful, that's what it is! That place shoulda' been cleaned up 'afore now. Bloody 'ell! War's been over long enough, eh? There's even talk that we'll soon be seeing the back o' them bloody ration books!'

Laura nodded, recalling Lizzie Pendleton's words, and her own vow to seek Joe Blessing out. She looked at the woman's face, trying to concentrate on what she was saying.

'Shame about Mabel Fletcher though. Nice woman that, one o' the old sort. Saw you at the funeral, didn't I? Allus close to your mam, was Mabel, as I remember? An' a good friend o' yourn, I gather? By God, that were a lovely wreath o' flowers you sent, lass. Oh, I do enjoy looking about the flowers, an' reading the cards.'

'She did have lots of lovely flowers,' Laura recalled. But what had been paramount in her mind then was the way Tom had glared at her in hostility throughout the service. Only once had she approached him, and his reaction was to half-coil like a snake about to spit out its venom. She had been hurt by it; until she reminded herself of the hurt she had caused him. Laura decided that she would not approach him again.

The woman was talking to the boy again, 'Shut thi' bloody moithering! I'll not fotch you out again, an' that's a fact!' Jerking her head back to Laura, she asked, 'What'll you give

272

me for that?' She opened her palm to reveal a small star-shaped medal, decorated by a ribbon of red, white and blue. 'T'aint no use to me, any more than them bloody letters.' She bowed her head, and Laura suspected that she was crying.

A slight sound behind Laura indicated that Remmie had returned. He just stood there, watching. Laura knew he would leave the matter to her. It wasn't his policy to interfere. She looked back to the woman, who seemed unaware that Remmie had entered the shop. She had recovered sufficiently now to repeat her question. 'Well! What's it worth, eh?'

Taking the medal from her, Laura knew at once that it would not sell. People didn't want to buy them, and there were more medals lying in the window now than she was hopeful of ever selling.

'Well? What'll you give me for it?'

Laura was aware of Remmie's eyes on her. She hoped he would not intrude, because what she was about to do went completely against her business sense and, she knew, against Remmie's. She turned the medal over in her hands. Then Laura said, 'It's a very nice medal. How will ten pounds suit you?' Laura was not surprised when the woman's mouth fell open in astonishment. She quickly collected ten pounds from the till and handed it to the woman, assuring her that the medal would not be put in the window, but would be put aside for her to collect when times got easier.

The woman's mouth drew itself into a tight trembling line, then reaching out to grip Laura's hand, she whispered, 'God bless you.'

Laura watched the door close firmly behind the woman and her grandson, and when Remmie stepped forward to say, 'That medal's worth *nothing* to us, and you know it,' she simply answered, 'Don't tell me you wouldn't have done the same?'

At that moment, Remmie threw his arm about her shoulder and pulled her roughly to him. 'You've a warm generous heart, Laura, lass, if only you could put the bad things out of it, the bad things that won't let you rest contented.'

Laura would have denied what he was saying, but Remmie put up his hand, and went on to confess that he wasn't sure whether this move with Jake Thackerey was the right one, and how he had always seen Mitch as the right fellow for her. He

273

also related his admiration at Mitch for having saved a considerable sum of money towards a shop of his own. When Laura expressed surprise at this, not having seen Mitch as an ambitious man, Remmie accused her of seeing only what she *wanted* to see.

But just at that moment, Laura was seeing things in a very clear light. It suddenly dawned on her that here was the answer. If they were to offer Mitch a half-share in this shop, it would provide them with a lump sum, and give Mitch half of the business! That way, with Mitch looking after their interest here, there would be not only the outlet needed to provide them with a source of goods, but also a regular income. And it would please Remmie to retain a half concern in his old shop.

She briefly outlined her idea to Remmie, and it was obvious from his reaction that he was indeed pleased. 'But I'll not give Mitch the go-ahead until we've been and measured the lay o' the land, so to speak, see whether it's what you really want, lass.'

Laura had no doubts on that score. But it was agreed to say nothing to Mitch just yet. Squeezing her arms affectionately about his shoulders, Laura pecked a kiss on his cheek, then released herself from his embrace and asked if she could go out for a while. 'I thought I might go along and see Sally,' she lied. And as she had hoped, Remmie thoroughly approved.

Leaving the shop, Laura turned right towards the old part of town. The sun on her face was still warm and it promised to be light for quite a while yet. Mid-summer was always a lovely time. It was now when the moors seemed at their best, and everybody went about their business in a happier frame of mind.

Strange though, how the sky seemed to grow darker the nearer to the old part of town she got. It made her feel uncomfortable heading for the area Nan Barker had mentioned. Even when she had lived in the endless maze of narrow cobbled streets and miserable back-ways, she'd always avoided that particular alley where Joe Blessing was said to be living. If her memory served her right, she could recall only one instance when she'd been down there. It had been a long time ago, and she'd had Netti with her. It was when that drunken tramp had frightened them. Her thoughts paused for a second, almost as though they didn't want to acknowledge the emerging image of Parry Griffin relieving himself over the rubble.

Hurrying now, she crossed by Merchant Street and turned off to the left. Then straight down Water Street and into the narrow ginnel alongside. It was quite a walk and after the long day at the shop, she began to feel weary. The only reason she didn't turn back was because she had to know whether there was any truth in Lizzie Pendleton's ramblings. Normally, she would have paid no heed. But suspicions that had lain dormant in her mind had been triggered off. It wasn't something she could just ignore. She had to know!

When she reached the end of the alley, she leaned against the stones that jutted from a half-demolished wall. She was appalled by the filth littering the whole stretch before her. Dog-muck, empty beer bottles and filth of all description paved her way. The stench was nauseating, and she instinctively clamped a hand across her mouth and nose. Visions of Joe Blessing as she remembered him at her father's funeral made all of this seem even more unbelievable. Then she remembered that day when Belle Strong had sent her to his house. He had already started on his downward path, even then. And how could she forget the way he'd looked at her, the way he'd touched her.

She had looked into almost all of the derelict houses and yards, and now, three-quarters of the way along, she began to wonder if it wasn't all a waste of valuable time. She was just debating whether to go, when she heard voices, and the name Joe Blessing.

There was a man's voice and a woman's, loud and angry. Picking her way through the brick-bats and rubbish, she climbed into the yard and squeezed herself tight against the old lavatory wall. She could see the two people through what was once the parlour window, and hoped they couldn't see her.

The woman, a vagabond, was shouting, her face contorted with rage, her eyes bulbous and wild. 'You're a liar, Joe Blessing! You've allus been a bloody liar!'

Laura was shocked at the sight of the man. Surely to God, that couldn't be Joe Blessing? He was sitting on what looked like an upturned orange-box. His face was swollen like the meths drinkers Laura had seen so often as a child, and the eyes had almost disappeared into the puffy flesh around them. His silver hair was long and hopelessly matted. When he spoke, Laura thought he could be crying.

'Leave me be, woman! That were all a long time back.'

'Not so long I've forgotten!' came the retort, 'and not so long I'll forgive! It weren't just *me* as cheated Jud Blake — it were you alongside o' me, beckoning me on till I were as tainted as yourself. We committed a cardinal sin against the man who was married to me in the Church of God — and though that same man had me own Mam locked away, I had no call to sin in the eyes of the Lord! That's why I've been punished, don't you see? — and that's why I've to carry out fit punishment on others. You'll not escape, Joe Blessing. I can't allow it — nor can I let the other one go on spreading her evil — that Laura, the divil 'imself!'

'Lord 'elp us! You *are* mad — mad as a bloody 'atter!'

What Laura heard next turned her heart to stone.

'Will you repent, Joe Blessing? Will you help me get rid o' the other one — the divil in disguise?'

'Get away from 'ere! Tek yoursel' right away from 'ere — go on.' His voice was desperate. 'I'll promise I'll not give you away.'

'Oh no. I can't do that. Not while there's a breath left in you.'

'Oh aye! *Kill* me, would yer? Well, you've done it afore, aint yer, eh? Murdered a 'elpless babby as were crippled!'

'I *had* to, don't you see? That deformed one — that were punishment for what we did. The two of us spawned that creature in sin, just like we'd done before with the girl, Netti.'

There followed a torrent of hideous abuse, during which three things became painfully clear to Laura, who had listened in horror and disbelief. God above! That wretch in there with Joe Blessing was her own mother. The two of them had been lovers the years her father had been alive. Could she really believe that *Netti* was Joe Blessing's child — as was baby Rosie! And oh, worst of all — that the helpless little mite had been smothered to death by her own mother? All these facts emerged like frightening images to blind and torment. But still, Laura was forced to listen — mesmerized by the nightmare she found herself in.

'They did right to lock you up! You're *mad* — completely insane.'

276

'And you're *bad*, Joe Blessing! You even sinned with Lizzie Pendleton. Oh, don't think I didn't know! That lass, Katya, — she's yours — isn't she, eh? *Yours* — deny it if you will!'

'I'll not deny it. And I'll not stay 'ere — get outta me way!'

Ruth Blake's dark eyes gazed on the cowering man before her, and he began to shake and fear for his very life. It was true that he'd coveted Jud Blake's wife, given her two children and, in spite of calling the man his best friend, had enjoyed the whole sordid affair. It was also true that Lizzie Pendleton's girl, Katya, was his — the result of his insatiable appetite for the tempting and cruder things in life. Oh, but at this very moment in time, he'd give *anything* to turn the clock back!

Yet, repentant as he was, there was more fear than regret in his voice as he told Ruth Blake, 'I'm warning yer! Tek yerself off — afore I fetch 'em to come an' lock yer up again!'

The ensuing screams of abuse came to Laura, as she fought down the waves of nausea churning inside her stomach; but she couldn't, and not caring where she trod or whether they might see her, she moved into the niche further down the wall, where she emptied the contents of her stomach.

Standing with her back to the wall, she looked up towards the window. Ruth Blake and Joe Blessing were now both on their feet and it appeared as though Joe Blessing was trying to defend himself against wild blows aimed at him. Suddenly, the struggling figures fell from Laura's sight. There came a sickening thud, then silence; fearful silence which echoed in Laura's ears until she thought she'd be sick again.

With the truth of what she'd learned still glaring in her mind, she ran from that place. In her haste she left her shoes behind and the jagged stones cut into her feet.

Once away from the alley the awful weight of her thoughts drove her on, sometimes running, sometimes walking. So! Netti was Katya's half-sister. That explained the similarity between them. The thought hurt her, but then, it made her love Netti even more. Poor Netti — to have a man like Joe Blessing for a father. At least *she* had Jud Blake's fine clean blood in her. A sob caught in her throat as she thought of his gentle trusting manner, and her anger bubbled at what those two creatures had done. Oh God! And Rosie, little Rosie. Oh dear God! She wanted to cry, *needed* to cry. But she could not.

It was all too terrible and it only confirmed what she had come to believe. In this world, you had to trust nobody! You had to watch out for yourself.

But Netti? What about poor Netti, whom Lizzie Pendleton had taunted. It was all so clear now. Netti knew. And she would seek the truth, of that Laura was sure. But what to do? Should she tell Netti everything? Oh no! Oh God, why was life so awful, why was it always such a struggle? And what had happened back there? God in Heaven, what awful thing had happened? She felt in her heart that Joe Blessing had been murdered. Murdered! Yes, Ruth Blake was a self-admitted murderer. Laura shivered as she realized that her mother's blood as well as Jud Blake's ran thickly through her own veins.

Tormented and deeply immersed in her thoughts, she didn't hear the car pulling up alongside her. She'd wandered well away from town, and was following the road out to Cherry Tree. In her confusion, she had been instinctively drawn along the route she used to take as a child with her hand-cart.

'Well, well! Wild, beautiful, and bare-footed. A devastating combination. One to draw the beast from any man!'

As she turned towards the voice, her eyes showed the awful pain and sorrow in her heart, and she couldn't speak.

'Good grief, Laura. What's happened?' Pearce Griffin threw the car door open. 'You'd best get in.'

When she just stood, staring at him, he got from the car to gather her in his arms. She didn't resist. There were other things, more horrible.

When she thought about it later, Laura couldn't remember riding in the car beside him. But she remembered sitting as she was now, a glass of wine in her hand and Pearce Griffin sitting on the bed in his hotel room.

'So you won't tell me?'

'Nothing to tell.' How she prayed that could be true.

'Alright, Laura.' He came to refill her glass. 'You look to me as though you've had a shock. And where's your shoes?'

Laura didn't reply. Instead, she gave him a hard look, then drank the wine from her glass. It helped her to forget.

'Never saw *you* as one for drinking.' He filled her glass

278

again, and his own. 'But I'm not complaining. Don't think that.' Suddenly he burst out laughing. 'You and me, eh? Sitting here together. You not trying to scratch my eyes out.' He walked quietly across the carpet, keeping his eyes on her till he reached her side.

Laura felt his hand in her hair, on her shoulder. She didn't resist. The wine made her feel warm and good inside. It fogged her mind so she couldn't remember.

'God! You're so beautiful.' His words caressed her ear. His open mouth moved down her neck. 'I've never wanted anybody, like I want you.'

Laura tingled beneath his touch. She liked it. She had always liked it. When he carried her to the bed, she held on to him and said teasingly, 'You're bad, Pearce Griffin! But I must be bad too.'

His voice was thick now with the passion filling his veins. 'Bad? Maybe just a little, eh? But then, think on the pleasure that a little badness can bring.'

As he undressed her, she laughed softly. Then she watched with admiration as he took his own clothes off. It came to her that she'd never really seen a man naked. She had felt the nakedness of Jake Thackerey, and she'd known the raw passion of a man's desires. But she was almost twenty-three now, and this was the first time a man had stood before her, completely naked.

She let her eyes move over his body, drinking in the magnificence that was about to be hers. She knew, as she had always known, that he was the most devilishly handsome man she had ever met. And she wanted him, oh yes, she wanted him with a fierceness to match his own.

When he came to take her in his arms, she clung to him. And when his mouth searched hers, she kindled his passion with her own. She wrapped herself around him, folding him into her with a cry of triumph, and her want became a compulsion. Then the compulsion became a frenzy that knew no satisfaction. Beneath his touch, she felt awakened, and it dawned on her that this man, to whom she was deeply attracted, had a way of bringing out the very worst in her. But now, with the warmth of his nakedness close against her, and his soft persuasive tongue whispering smooth endearments into her mind, she could think of nothing else but her desperate need for him.

It was only later, when he left her at the end of Montague Street, that she loathed that part of her that was drawn to him. It was a side to her character that she had never understood. It showed a savage streak, and it frightened her.

Laura had left him to the sound of his soft laughter and his promise that he would see her again.

Laura gave no answer, except to assure herself that he would *not* be seeing her again. Not if *she* could help it!

Chapter Twenty-three

Laura spent the following day in a kind of trance. She couldn't rid her mind of the scenes she had witnessed in the alley. Nor could she come to terms with the awful realization of having lain in Pearce Griffin's arms of her own accord. What in God's name had she been thinking of? But then, that was it. She *hadn't* been thinking, had she? The very last thing she had wanted to do when Pearce Griffin came across her in the street, was to *think*, to think of the awful things she had learned; that Joe Blessing had fathered Katya and Netti, and little Rosie. Oh, and what sort of monster was Ruth Blake, to take poor little Rosie's life?

All day long, Laura's mind was tortured and she couldn't settle, couldn't apply herself to anything. Finally, after supper, when Netti was working at the piano and Remmie was engrossed in calculating figures, she put on her coat and scarf and embarked on a long walk that took her a good way along Ribble Road, then down the brews that led into Penny Street. When she got there, she stood for a while, looking at the house that had been home a very long time ago. When she began to feel cold, she started on her way back to Remmie's house, her mind no calmer now than it had been when she first came out. Thank God they would all be away from here soon, away to a new life.

Turning into Ribble Road, she saw a police car stationed outside Remmie's house. She hurried, instinctively suspecting that it had to do with the violence she'd witnessed in the alley. But how could that be? No. It must be Lizzie Pendleton, she reasoned, remembering Remmie's recent comments on the old woman's deteriorating health.

The front door was half-open. She went in quietly. There were two of them; a policeman and a policewoman and they were in the parlour with Remmie. There was a sound of soft crying coming from upstairs. Remmie turned to see her standing in the hallway.

'Laura!' He went towards her, followed by the police officers. 'It's bad news, lass.' His voice sounded broken, and Laura thought he looked haggard. 'It's your Mam, Ruth. She's, she's been found murdered.' He was crying and the policewoman led him back into the parlour, where she eased him into a chair.

The other officer said to Laura, 'We *suspect* murder. Nothing's so, until it's been proved, you understand. We've got a search underway for a Mr Joe Blessing. He was known to have inhabited the place where Ruth Blake was found.'

Laura could hear him; the words came to her plainly enough. But there seemed to be something not quite right. Wasn't it *Joe Blessing* who'd been killed? She'd been sure of it. She wrestled with her conscience. Should she tell them what she'd seen? No. Better not. They'd want to know what she'd been doing down that alley. And there was still Netti to think of.

For a while after they had gone Remmie sat by the fire, his head cradled in the palms of his hands, and every now and then a low moan would escape him. Laura stood watching him, knowing that whatever she said or did, it would not ease his grief. He was a man of principles. He'd always looked to himself for part of the blame regarding Ruth Blake's demented mind. But he was not to blame, and everyone knew that.

Laura held a deep affection for this man, who had given her and Netti so much love these past years, and it hurt her to see him in so much pain. Quietly, on tired feet, she crossed to kneel before him. Gently lifting away his hands, she persuaded him to raise his head and look at her.

'Remmie. There is *nothing* you can reproach yourself for. Ruth Blake's downfall was her own doing, and no one, not even you, could have prevented it. I know that now.' Her voice was soft. She looked at him and spoke to him as one might comfort a child.

A great shudder ran through his body, and his eyes became a little brighter. 'You're right, lass.' He ran his fingers down her face. 'You've a way of saying things, a straight for'ard way, but it grieves me to think on it all.'

Laura could say no more. She recalled the scene between Ruth Blake and Joe Blessing, and she was glad the monster was dead. She watched Remmie rise from the chair and walk away towards the door.

'I'm sorry, lass. But you'd best get in touch with Jake. We'll not be seeing him this weekend, not with your Mam to be buried.' He looked at her intently, as though waiting for a protest. She made none, so he bade her goodnight and left to make his way upstairs.

With Remmie gone, the room suddenly felt cold and empty. So she wasn't to see Jake yet? Visions of Ria Morgan grew large in her mind, and she examined briefly the possibility of travelling down alone. There were coaches leaving regularly for the south. Yet even as she thought of it, the futility of such a notion could not escape her. Much as she resented the idea of attending a funeral for that, that *murderess*, Ruth Blake, she knew how distressed Remmie would be at her absence. She couldn't deal with the important issue of the Gallery on her own. There were things to be discussed; finer details that only Remmie could handle. And even though he had come to trust and respect her judgement, he would never finalize any business transaction without first going into a detailed investigation regarding sales, stock, marketing and accounts. There was too much at stake. Even she knew that. No. There was nothing else for it. She would have to contact Jake and explain the situation. With a sense of purpose she went upstairs and quietly into Netti's room. She was more determined than ever to be rid of this way of life. She had to get away from old haunts and crippling memories. And she had to get Netti away. There was much here that was rotten. It had been part of her growing up, and she had coped. But now, it was beginning to touch Netti's life in a dangerous way, and she could not allow that to happen.

The room was dark as she entered, and for a second, she thought of turning away. Instead, she went silently towards the bed, where she sat carefully on the edge. The curtains were still open, allowing a measure of light into the room. The sight of Netti's face still marked by her tears saddened Laura. She stood up and reached over quietly to move the strand of fair hair from her sister's face, then leaned over to kiss her.

'I'm not asleep, Laura,' Netti moved to a half-sitting position against the pillow.

'Was it me? Did I wake you?' Laura sat beside her.

'No. I've been trying to sleep. But I can't.'

'Because of Ruth Blake's death?'

'Because of the *way* she died. Murder, they said.'

'*Suspected.*'

'I know. But it wasn't *just* that.' Her voice faltered, and Laura noticed the tears running down her face.

'What then, my darling?'

It was some time before Netti could bring herself to talk. Then she said in a whisper, 'Laura. Lizzie Pendleton told me that I'm not your sister. She said I'm . . . a bastard.' She was sobbing now, her voice rising in hysteria. 'She said Jud Blake didn't father me. She said I had a *coward* for a father, and a crazy woman for a mother. Oh, Laura! Laura! Is it true? Tell me she was lying. I'm *not* a bastard, I'm your sister, aren't I! Aren't I?'

Laura knew that the decision she made now, would have to be the right one for Netti. Who could prove that Netti wasn't Jud Blake's daughter? There were only three people as far as she knew, who held that particular knowledge. There was Lizzie Pendleton, who could easily be discredited; there was Joe Blessing, who was now on the run for murder and who would be too concerned for his own safety to bother about the children he'd fathered; and she herself was the last. There was no decision to make. 'Listen to me, Netti. Lizzie Pendleton is a drunken, vicious old woman. What she's told you is nothing but a pack of lies! Me and you, we're sisters! You're as much Jud Blake's daughter as I am!' She could still see the doubt in Netti's sad blue eyes. 'Tomorrow, we'll go to Lizzie Pendleton together. We'll face her, make her tell you the truth, that she was lying to cause mischief. She's just a wicked, spiteful woman.' It was a bluff, and she prayed it would convince Netti.

'Neither of you are ever to go near that woman's house again. Never!' Remmie's voice came from the open door. Clicking the light switch on, he moved towards the bed with slow deliberate footsteps.

'Did she mention any names, in her fanciful accusations?' he asked.

'Names?' Netti was calmer now.

'You said she mentioned a "coward"?'

'Yes.'

'That was all?'

'Yes, Uncle Remmie.'

Laura saw the relief in his face and in the sudden sag of his shoulders. He knew! Remmie *knew* that Joe Blessing was Netti's father! It crossed her mind that he must also have known that Katya was Joe Blessing's daughter too. If there was any room for doubt in her mind, it vanished beneath the truth in his eyes as he looked at her.

He told Netti softly, 'Netti, lass. You had a fine honourable father in Jud Blake. There's nothing for you to concern yourself about. Ever! Ever, do you understand? Lizzie Pendleton is everything Laura says, and more. From now on, this family's to have nothing at all to do with her. She was right about *one* thing. Your Mam was crazy, there's no denying. But what kind of a woman is Lizzie Pendleton to sit in judgement. There's many a thing can drive a body crazy.' He bent down to take Netti in his arms, then kissing her gently, he wiped her eyes. 'So think on! Neither of you are to go anywhere near her house again. I *mean* that. You'll pain me, if you don't do as I ask. And when your Mam's been laid to her rest, I'll set about the authorities to do some'at, mebbe get that woman put where they can properly look after alcoholics.'

Laura watched him straighten up from the bed. So he'd known all along? She was sure of it. As he came forward to kiss her goodnight, he caught her hand and squeezed it reassuringly. 'There's nothing for *either* of you to fret on. Just think on what I said,' he went towards the door, 'you're to stay away from Lizzie Pendleton's altogether!'

The door closed quietly, and Laura felt as though a great weight had been lifted from her shoulders. They did say 'a trouble shared was a trouble halved', although she somehow sensed that it would never be openly discussed between Remmie and her.

'There you are, Netti Blake!' Laura lifted the covers and persuaded Netti to slide beneath them. Laura thought how like a child she looked, with her soft tearful blue eyes and long fair hair fanned out over the pillow. She would never let anything hurt this sensitive, loving creature. 'Now you know! And the devil take Lizzie Pendleton for putting such rubbish into your head.' Her next words were whispered encouragingly. 'And perhaps we'll see you back to your studies, eh?'

'Laura, I'll need to study for four more years at least. I'll be twenty then. I really don't know what I want. I need to think.'

Laura knew it would be foolish to discuss it any further tonight. Netti had been brooding too long on what Lizzie Pendleton had told her. Now, as her eyes met Netti's, she realized that there was still a semblance of doubt lurking there. But there was no more that could be done. She and Remmie had offered reassurance in the only way possible. Now, all that remained was for Netti to believe in herself; to recapture all that had been lost.

A pleasing thought occured to Laura; Lizzie Pendleton was no longer a threat. Remmie had disowned her. That meant two things; firstly, she would no longer be in a position to poison Netti's mind; and secondly, Remmie would not have her to consider when the time came to move away. And if they were to retain part-ownership of the shop, then gradually, all possible obstacles were being removed. The pattern was coming out right at long last.

When she left Netti's room, the horrors of these last two days and the turmoil which had pained her mind had lessened. She felt a kind of peace in her heart. Tomorrow, she would talk to Jake; there was much to be said. And, beyond Ruth Blake's funeral, much to look forward to.

Chapter Twenty-four

The week passed quickly, and during that time Ruth Blake was buried in a patch of ground some way from Katya. All Saints Church was small, and there was little choice of a resting place, for the graveyard was filling up fast. Laura had never hated anything as much as she hated attending that funeral. She thought several times during the service and afterwards at the lowering, that she should stand up and denounce Ruth Blake for the murderess she was. But the ordeal was quickly over. There were no guests and no gathering afterwards.

Remmie arranged through the Welfare for a woman to attend to the needs of Lizzie Pendleton. He informed the authorities that she had no kin and was incapable of looking after herself. Then he'd forbidden any further mention of her name.

Today was Friday, and in view of the fact that they were due to travel south the next day, Remmie had given Laura the day off; to 'get yoursel' poshed up an' ready', was how he had put it. Netti was attending her music tuition again. But although she had resumed her studies, it was painfully obvious that her heart was no longer in it.

Laura spent the morning going through her wardrobe and trying on the garments she'd bought from the big fancy store in Manchester. She must have taken one particular purchase from its box at least four times, just to gaze at it before carefully wrapping it in tissue and returning it to the box. The garment was the most expensive item she had ever bought. It was a gown; a beautiful creation in cornflower blue silk, and as flimsy as gossamer. It clung to Laura's smooth shapely figure as though moulded to it. The front was shaped into a slender halter neck, and the back dropped low to flatter her tiny waist. It was only after she had bought it and was leaving the store that Laura realized with a little shiver of horror just how much it had cost. With a rush of guilt she calculated its cost to be only a few shillings short of the forty-five pounds that Remmie paid Mitch for a week's work. She decided then and there not to tell Remmie. She could easily imagine what his reaction might be.

Now, as she packed it away for the fourth time, she smiled quietly to herself. It was *Jake*'s reaction she was really concerned about. Everything depended on what happened this weekend. Her whole future could well be at stake.

What *did* happen, however, was totally unexpected, and affected her future in the most decisive way possible.

It was four o'clock. She had sorted out the clothes and shoes she was taking and spread them out on the bed, to take a last minute stock of them. Then she'd put the green two-piece and slim high-heel sandals to one side. She could travel comfortably in those. And now, she had stopped and gone outside to stand by the back gate and enjoy the view across the moors. She would miss these moors. They knew all of her secrets, for she'd spent many a night whispering them to the wind that whistled constantly over the heathland, carrying her innermost thoughts to the deepest and most hidden crevices. These moors had been her salvation when she'd felt most desperate; it would be like leaving a friend behind.

Drawing in a long breath of the cooling breeze, she made her way back into the kitchen. Remmie and Netti would be in shortly. She'd best make a start on the meal.

The knock at the front door started as almost a tap, then while she was on her way up the passage to see who it was, the knocking became more urgent.

Laura flung the door open, agitated at such impatience. Such was the shock when she recognized the caller, that the curiosity in her face turned to astonishment and her mouth fell open to say in a small voice, 'You!'

'Yes, me. May I come in?' Ria Morgan smiled sweetly as she noticed Laura looking about. 'Jake isn't with me. You'll understand why, when we've had a chance to talk.'

Laura could say nothing. Ria Morgan here, alone! She opened the door wider and stepped away to one side, the other woman's perfume filling her nostrils as she wafted by and on into the front parlour. Even in the midst of the many questions already shaping themselves in her mind, there lurked a reluctant admiration of Ria Morgan's natural elegance. The white coat, which fell from her shoulders in a yoke of slender pleats, was of the finest and most expensive material. Her shoes were patent leather and of the most wonderful shade of burgundy. Laura calculated that her own entire wardrobe upstairs wouldn't amount to the price of Ria Morgan's single outfit.

'I'm sorry I didn't let you know I was coming,' Ria was standing by the fireplace, her hands thrust deep into the pockets of her coat, 'but that would have defeated the object, because you probably wouldn't have seen me.'

Laura was suddenly afraid. 'Jake? There's nothing wrong?'

'No, there's nothing wrong, as you put it.' A look crossed her face that reminded Laura of Katya Thorpe. 'Jake hasn't come to any harm. Not *yet*, that is.'

'What do you mean?'

'I think you had better sit down.'

'I'll stand, thank you.' Laura didn't like this woman, and she liked even less the suspicious thoughts crossing her mind at that minute. 'Why are you here?'

'I'm here to stop you making your trip this weekend. It won't be necessary now; Jake and I were married two days ago.' She held her hand out, moving forward so that Laura could see more clearly the sparkling gold band on her wedding finger.

'You're lying!' Laura felt sick and angry. Why? Why would Jake do this?

'I blackmailed him.'

'You what?' Laura could hardly believe what she had just heard. Was it a joke? The look on Ria Morgan's face told her it was not.

'Jake Thackerey is a crook! I had suspected for some time that he was involved in gem smuggling. Too many trips to Amsterdam, and too much money. He even adjusted the gallery's account books, in order to cover it all up. But I'm a very thorough person. It wasn't difficult to see that the goods we sold did not tally with the goods entered.' She stopped and half-smiled at Laura. 'So you see, in a way, I've done you a favour. The gallery is a 'front', and not all of Jake's wealthy clients come to purchase fine art. You *do* understand what I'm saying?'

Laura understood. Oh yes! She understood.

'You're saying he intended to use Remmie and me?' She found all of this hard to believe.

'Oh Jake does love you! Mr Alderney, the owner, might be old, but he certainly isn't stupid. It would only have been a matter of time before he too became suspicious. When he offered the gallery to Jake, it seemed heaven-sent. You and Remmie would have been perfect. Respectable, honest and totally trustworthy. And of course, Jake is hopelessly bewitched by you. But he'll get over that. He'll *have* to!'

'Get out!' Laura gestured towards the door. She intended to telephone Jake. She felt confused and bitter; and she didn't know just how much of this to believe.

Ria Morgan moved towards the door, talking over her shoulder. 'I'll tell you what I told Jake. I have positive proof that would put him away for years! Make no mistake. I won't hesitate to use it. Oh, and don't get in touch with him. Not that I think you would want to. He had every intention of making you and Remmie an important part of his operations.' A sneer curved her mouth, as she went on. 'He even had a few trips to Amsterdam lined up for you. *His* little trick was to hide the gems in the back of small engravings. No doubt *you* would have made an excellent courier.' Her voice seemed to grow softer as she told Laura, 'You know I really *have* done you a favour. Jake is no good. But I've always loved him, and I'll settle for having him this way, than not having him at all.'

Laura didn't reply. Instead, she turned away from her, and only when she heard the front door close did the tight defiance in her shoulders relax and the bright spark of anger in her eyes mellow into a kind of bewilderment. Was this some kind of nightmare? Jake and Ria Morgan married? Yes. They were married, and she had been right to feel wary of that woman. But Jake, a gem smuggler? She knew that such things went on. It happened all the time. The gallery, a front to hide its real purpose? And Ria, she had evidence that would put Jake away. Well, if that were true, she had no doubt that Ria Morgan *would* put him away, rather than see him in another woman's arms.

All of a sudden the thoughts churning in her mind came to a halt. One thing stood out clear now; all her ambitions, all her dreams, had come to nothing. The anger returned, and with it came a new determination. She needed to substantiate all of this, and the only version she would accept was Jake's.

She looked for his number in the small notebook by the telephone, then quickly dialled it. When Jake answered, her heart skipped, and she found herself convinced that the whole thing had been part of some elaborate plan designed by Ria Morgan.

'Jake. It's Laura. I had to ring you. Ria Morgan's just been here.'

'She's told you, then?' His voice was flat, empty of the passion which normally filled it when he spoke to her.

'Jake,' Laura was afraid now, but she went on, 'you and Ria, you're married?'

There was a silence at the other end, then, 'Yes. We're married.'

'And she had threatened to tell the authorities that you had been smuggling gems?'

'It's true, all of it. Laura, please believe me, I had no choice. Prison would kill me.'

Laura chose to ignore him. 'Just tell me one thing, Jake. She said you would have used Remmie and me.'

'No! She's lying. I would *not* have done that! I love you, Laura. I'll find a way for us to be together. Listen, please listen, Laura. Next Wednesday, I'm flying out to Amsterdam. Ria expects that my business should take me a week, but I'll conclude it quickly, and arrive back at London airport on the last flight on Friday. Meet me there! We'll book in somewhere for the night.'

When she greeted his suggestion with stony silence, he began to shout. 'Laura! I *must* see you, to explain.'

'To explain why you had to marry Ria? To explain why you've made a fool of *me*?' She was shocked at her hostility, but what he had done was cowardly and despicable.

Laura held the phone away from her. She felt contempt for him, together with a burning desire to see him degraded, just as he had degraded her in allowing Ria Morgan to bring the news to her in person. So the whole business was not a lie as she had hoped. Jake Thackerey was deceitful and he was a criminal.

She could have forgiven him for being those things. What she could never forgive him was his cowardice. And Thackerey had maybe intended to use her! The irony of the situation had not escaped Laura; how could she condemn Jake Thackerey, when all the while, she had been using *him*? It would seem that they were two of a kind. No! No, not quite, not quite, she prayed.

She composed herself and asked quietly, 'We'll book in somewhere for the night, you say?'

'Yes! Give me that, Laura. One more night with you, and Ria will be none the wiser. We'll work something out, you'll see.'

'Alright, Jake. I'll be there to meet your flight.' Laura listened for a moment, hating his gushing gratitude and his expression of regret that Ria had the upper hand. 'Till next Friday,' she said, quickly replacing the telephone.

Laura stared down at Jake's telephone number in the notebook. The tightness in her throat was threatening to choke her, and the burning sensation behind her eyes melted into tears. The emotion had to emerge either as tears or laughter, and thinking again of the way she had planned to use Jake to get what *she* wanted, Laura began to laugh. Softly at first, and then helplessly, until she knew it was bordering on hysteria.

When the telephone rang, Laura had already brought her emotions under control, and she resisted the impulse to pick the receiver up, and let it ring. Tearing the page from the notebook, she took it between finger and thumb, and with slow deliberation she tore it into small pieces. What kind of fool did he take her for? All kinds, if he thought for one moment she really intended to be eagerly waiting for him when he arrived at London airport!

From now on, she had better things to do with her time, and Jake Thackerey did not fit into her future. Let him think she would be waiting open-armed for him. Yes! Let him look forward to that, and then let him suffer the same disappointment and humiliation that he had caused *her* to suffer. The prospect gave Laura a measure of consolation. Ria Morgan was welcome to him!

However, Jake Thackerey had triggered off an idea in her mind. She *would* go to London. She had an impulse to see the big city furniture stores, to walk about them and to cast an eye over quality and prices. Her instincts told her that Remmie would not sanction such a venture or be keen on her wandering about London alone. Nevertheless, she intended to go!

The telephone rang constantly during the next hour, and Laura guessed it was Jake. She hated him! She toyed with the idea of informing Her Majesty's Customs officers of Jake Thackerey's smuggling activities, and of his impending return visit to Amsterdam. But after much deliberation, Laura found that she could not bring herself to do such a callous and spiteful thing, not even to a person of Jake Thackerey's dubious character. No, there would come another time, and when it did, she would not let it pass by.

When Remmie arrived home, the phone was silent. Laura knew that he would have to be told, and she didn't relish the idea. She waited until he had eaten the hurriedly prepared ham salad; then she told him.

She had not expected it to be such a shock. Remmie's gentle brown eyes grew wide and he kept saying over and over again, 'Well, I'm buggered!' Then he quietly put pen to paper, telling Jake Thackerey that if he ever showed his face in these quarters again, or attempted to contact any member of his family, then he would inform the police himself, without the slightest qualm!

Remmie sealed the envelope and fixed a stamp onto it. Then he propped it on the mantelpiece, silently staring at it for a long time, before asking Laura, 'Don't mention any of this to Netti, not yet. She's 'ad enough to cope with recently. You know lass, if I was to tell the truth an' shame the divil, I'd say I smelled a fox a long way back.' He breathed in a long gulp of air, and held it till Laura thought he would burst; then he blew it out again, saying, 'You've not to let this business sit heavy on you, lass. I never thought Jake Thackerey were our kind, and by God, he's proved it! Look here, lass. We don't need his sort. And I'd bet my right arm that his gallery won't be any grander than the one *you'll* have! Aye, *and* in less time than you think. You've already increased our business too much to contain it in yon little back market shop.' He got up and faced her squarely, as though it gave more emphasis to his words. 'You're *already* going places, lass, an' tekkin' me with you. If you want to tap these markets down south, then by God, you'll do it! And we

293

none of us needs the likes o' Jake Thackerey to tell us how!'

If she had planned it herself, Laura could not have done better; for there in Remmie's outburst was the opening she wanted, and she quickly told him, 'I've been thinking along those very same lines myself. Would you object to me being away from the shop for a couple of days? I have it in mind to go to London — have a look around, so to speak.'

'To *London*, eh?' Remmie appeared to be quietly thinking, then he said, 'No, lass! You tek yoursel' off for a spell. We'll manage.'

Laura thought she had never loved him more than she did at that moment. Stepping forward, she clasped herself against him. 'You've always believed in me, haven't you?'

'Only because you've always given me cause.' He bent towards her and said quietly, 'But you've got to understand Laura, lass. You'll not find happiness, real happiness, until you find yourself. And you'll not find yourself in the hard, impersonal world that makes for business deals.'

'But that's where I *am* happiest.' Yet even as she answered him, her heart protested.

Remmie gripped her by the shoulders, then gently pushed her from him. For a brief tender moment, he looked into her face. Then he sighed wearily and kissed her lightly on the forehead. 'God bless you, lass. I'm off to an early bed. Goodnight.'

Laura watched him until he reached the door and she thought how very tired and worn he looked. Pulling his mouth into a closed smile, he started through the door, then turned to remind her, 'Think on! Leave it to *me* to tell Netti. It'll be for the best, eh?'

Netti arrived home less than half an hour later. She was in such a state of excitement that she pushed her food to one side. When Laura told her that they wouldn't be making the trip south and that Remmie would explain, Netti just nodded as if it was the most natural news in the world. 'I've made the most marvellous friend, Laura. Her name's Judy, and she works in that new dance place in Mill Hill.'

Laura was at once on the defensive, 'Dance place? You surely don't mean that dive where all the roughnecks end up?'

'It's *not* a dive! They teach ballroom dancing and they've just done it all up.' Her eyes sparkled and the words came tumbling out one after the other.

Laura had never seen her like this. 'You're not telling me that you've been inside that place?' When there was no answer, she cried out, 'Answer me, Netti! Have you been inside that place?'

'Yes. I have!' There was no defiance in her voice. 'Please Laura, don't be angry. It's alright. Honest. Judy's got a job there. She and three others play there most nights in the band. It's called 'Nightime' and Judy plays the piano. Oh, you should hear her, Laura. You should just hear her!'

Laura wasn't quite sure how to handle this. She listened without comment while Netti told her all about her new found friend Judy. She had apparently tutored under Miss Fordyke, who had already made her disapproval of this 'misuse' of talents very clear. In fact, it had been through Miss Fordyke that Netti had learned of Judy and she'd gone along to the 'dance place' just out of curiosity.

Laura realized that Netti was not the timid, helpless little creature Jud Blake had left in her protection. She had become a young woman of gentle trusting beauty, and she was beginning to develop real individuality. It was with deep-seated fear that Laura realized Netti was growing away from her. She was losing her! Suddenly, Laura heard the words that only confirmed her fears.

'Laura, do you think Uncle Remmie would mind if . . .' She hesitated and looked away from Laura.

'Yes?'

Netti lifted her bright blue eyes and said in a rush, 'Judy's got a flat in Mill Hill. I want to move in with her.' When she'd finished speaking, she sat with her head bowed, as though suddenly aware of what she had just said and the effect it might have. Then she looked up again. 'I know I'm not old enough. But if he says no, I'll go anyway!'

Laura couldn't trust herself to speak. What she *wanted* to do was to take Netti by the shoulders and shake her! She wanted to shout out and protest at the selfishness of her request. She ought to do that! She ought to tell Netti how stupid and ungrateful she was being; and how Remmie wouldn't allow it. And neither would she! But she knew instinctively that such a reaction from her would prove disastrous. So, mustering all her self-control, she forced her mouth into a half-smile, and she looked at Netti's wide eyes staring defiantly into hers.

'You're obviously very fond of this girl, this Judy.' She must be careful to say the right thing. 'I'm pleased you've found a friend, Netti. And Remmie will be pleased as well. But don't you think it would be nice for us to *meet* Judy? Then we could talk about this flat business.'

'You mean you'd both want to look her over, don't you?'

'If that's the way you want to see it, then alright. It's not so much to ask, is it? And moving out of a secure home, without thinking carefully and weighing up all the disadvantages would be irresponsible and stupid. And you're neither of those.' She looked for a response in her sister's expression. But there was none, so she went on, 'Netti? You surely can't object to bringing Judy round?'

There was a long pause. 'Oh, alright then.' A sullen note came into her voice. 'But if you don't like her, and you say I can't go, it won't make any difference!' Then, as Laura attempted to discuss Netti's forthcoming music exam, she flounced out of the room and up the stairs, leaving Laura deeply disturbed and even more despairing of the fact that Netti's piano was little played these days.

That night, long after Remmie and Netti were fast asleep, Laura paced the floor of her bedroom. Then she went to stand by the window and gazed thoughtfully into the night and across the moors. It had been a day of shocks: a day that had eaten away at her innermost ambitions; a day that had left her feeling drained and, yes, she felt *old*. Some people were born to good things, which got better as they lived through childhood, adolescence and maturity. She couldn't even remember the separate stages of her life. There had only ever been one stage, that of survival. And now, if she was to lose Netti, and if Netti was to discard all of her wonderful talent, to play in some sleazy 'dance place' . . . she couldn't think of it any more. Netti was too young to know what she was about. Something would have to be done; and quickly.

As she climbed into bed, the thought came to her. Yes. She would do it; first thing in the morning. And Netti need never know.

* * *

296

When Laura awoke, it was early. She got out of bed and she threw back the curtains. The summer sun shone in on her, and she made her way to the bathroom with a much lighter heart. Strange how one could see things more clearly after a night's sleep. Remmie was right. They *didn't* need Jake Thackerey. And once she could sort out this affair with Netti, there would be time to concentrate on expanding the business.

She quickly washed and dressed, then went down to the kitchen, where she made herself a brew of tea. She couldn't face breakfast as she was too occupied with what she had planned to do.

She remembered that Netti would be kept busy with Miss Fordyke all day. They were in the final stages of rehearsal for a concert to be performed on Monday evening, in Blackburn Town Hall. It was to be a small public event before the important examinations; and apparently, the students' individual performances would be marked as a percentage of their final marks. Netti had only told her and Remmie about it a few days ago, and they had been looking forward to it. Laura now admitted to herself that the planned visit south had probably been allowed to overshadow Netti's big moment. She wondered whether that was the reason Netti hadn't told them earlier.

She scribbled a note explaining that she would see Remmie at the shop later. She wrote an encouraging but discreet word or two for Netti, then placed the note in a conspicuous place on the mantelpiece and collected the letter addressed to Jake Thackerey.

A few minutes later, after letting herself out of the house quietly in order not to wake Remmie and Netti, she was boarding the early bus into town. Ten minutes after that she alighted at the Boulevard, walked across the Market Square and past Parry Griffin's shop. She didn't stop, but slowed her step and cast a critical eye over the front of the premises. She saw that the long fascia boards and deep sills were already losing that freshly painted look, the bare exposed patches where the paint had quickly peeled off showing signs of advanced decay. That wood should have been replaced, thought Laura, but knowing Parry Griffin, he'd probably cut costs by plastering a layer of paint over the top, seeking to disguise the rot beneath. Looking into the window and at the area beyond, Laura saw that he had indeed replaced most of his stock; and in spite of the obvious fact that his merchandise was of poor second-hand quality, the word was that he was turning over a reasonable living. It was also known that what he earned, he quickly spent, on booze, gambling and women. That knowledge gave Laura cause for comfort, because as sure as night followed day, Parry Griffin would topple from his new found perch. And when he did, she would be there waiting.

She crossed the square to Remmie's shop, and the big market clock was just striking seven as she knocked on the shop door. It wasn't open yet, but she knew that Mitch would have been up long ago.

When he opened the door, and stood before her with a look of concern on his face, it struck her just how handsome he was. But then, she'd always thought so. Usually, he'd stay up late working in the back, renovating and french polishing, then in the morning he'd dress suitably for delivering and seeing to the shop. This morning, though, he was wearing the blue overalls that he normally wore for the dirtier work. It was obvious to Laura that he was wearing very little underneath. The top half was open to the waist, revealing a broad masculine chest. His hands were stained by french polish, and some of it had found its way up to his face. With the back of his hand, he rubbed his forehead where the fair hair had stuck to beads of sweat.

'Laura! Come in.' The pleasure in his voice at seeing her made Laura feel grateful to him. Closing the door behind her, he excused his appearance. 'Thought I'd get that dining-room suite finished before I opened up. I kept at it till midnight, but it's a big job; finished now though.' He was standing before her, and the intensity of his gaze made Laura feel strangely uncomfortable. His eyes were so strikingly steadfast, that it made her errand seem shameful.

'What's brought you out so early? I thought you were leaving for the south, this morning?' His voice became quiet and his eyes held her face. 'You're not going?'

'No. We're not. That venture is all finished. Remmie can tell you about it.' For the first time, she felt humiliated and she couldn't bring herself to look him in the face. Why was it that

298

he could make her feel so uncomfortable? He always seemed to be silently accusing her of something. Or was it all in her imagination? Perhaps he stirred her conscience somehow.

'You mean you *won't* be moving away.' He couldn't hide his pleasure. 'Oh, Laura! That's grand, grand.'

'It means you won't be able to buy into this shop.' She felt the need to test him.

His response was immediate; 'No matter. You'll be staying. *That's* what matters.'

'Mitch. I need five hundred pounds. And I need it now if possible. Can you help me, please?'

He didn't answer, but she could see that her request had caught him unawares. Yet he asked no question, but one, 'You're not in any trouble?'

Now she smiled at him. How like this man to think only of her. Not to question her as he had a right to, and not to look for reasons against handing over such a sum, but to be concerned only with her well-being. She could trust him, and she knew that whatever she confided in him would be kept secret. Yet she also knew that he would be horrified at what she was about to do.

'It's Saturday, I can't get any money. You'll have it back as soon as the banks open on Monday.'

'Alright, Laura. I keep a sum of money ready for any emergency. You know that, and you're welcome to it.'

'You'll not mention it to Remmie?'

Again, he looked at her, and all the questions were there, in his eyes. But he simply assured her, 'Don't worry. I'll go and get the money for you.'

While Mitch was upstairs she did two things. Firstly, she took Remmie's letter to Jake from her pocket, tore it into small shreds and dropped it into the waste-bin beneath the counter. Then she made a phone call. The manager of the 'dance place' was only too pleased to help, and Laura wrote the girl's address on the piece of paper, which she quickly thrust into her pocket as Mitch came back.

Some five minutes later she left the shop with the money; she hoped it would be enough.

Mill Hill was so named because of the many sprawling cotton mills surrounding the maze of streets and back-ways.

Situated to the north of Blackburn centre, it wasn't a place where wealthy folk lived. The endless terraces of narrow houses belonged to the Corporation. The mills that paid the meagre wages of the people who abided in those houses belonged to the fat prosperous men who enjoyed the luxury of the grand dwellings along Cherry Tree.

It didn't take Laura long to walk the distance out to Mill Hill, and she soon found the street which was written on the piece of paper. The house was just like all the other houses in the row; and it took her memory back to things best forgotten.

She stood in front of the grimy door for quite some time before she summoned up the courage to knock. But once she had rattled the door, she kept on rattling it, until a girl answered. Laura calculated that she was about twenty. The rattling had obviously wakened her from her bed, and the scowl on her face made her look hard. She was of slim build, almost too thin, thought Laura. And at one time, she had probably been very pretty. Her hair was dark and caught up at the top of her head by a pin-comb. The scowl on her face changed into a look of surprise at the sight of Laura.

'Is there a bloody fire, or what?' She drew hard on the newly-lit cigarette which she raised to her mouth. Then as she spoke, she released a measure of smoke with each word. 'Three o'clock I got to bed this morning! I hope this is important.'

Laura gave her a direct look. 'Can I come in? I'm Netti's sister.'

'Oh! Laura, eh?' All of a sudden she seemed conscious of her appearance. 'You must be Laura? Yes, now you've wakened me up, you might as well come in, I suppose.'

Laura followed her down the passageway and into the back parlour. The place was a tip. There were clothes heaped on the backs of stand chairs, and raked-over ashes strewn across the grate. The carpet was a pattern of stains and there were empty glasses decorating the mantelpiece.

'Sorry about the mess,' the girl said in an offhand way, 'there 'int much room here. I've got the downstairs, this room and the front parlour — that's my bedroom — and the back scullery. It does me though.'

'And Netti?'

'What? Oh, that's right. Netti's all for moving in with me.' A

300

meaningful smile tightened her features. 'Well! *Now* I know why a la-de-da like you would want to visit me.' She drew hard on the cigarette again before adding, 'I'm right, eh? You don't want Netti in a place like this?'

'No. And yes, you're right. That is why I'm here.'

'Huh! Won't do you no good. And anyway, you've only yourself to blame. You *push* her, push her all the time!'

'Did Netti tell you that?'

'Yea, she did! Netti don't want no cissy career. She wants to see a bit o' life.' She laughed coarsely. 'She'll see it with me, right enough!' Then her voice grew quiet. 'Nice little thing is Netti. Fancied her I did, right from the start. Never been interested in boys, has she?'

Overwhelming rage engulfed Laura. This morning she had started out with the express intention of bribing this girl to leave Netti alone, to let her pursue her studies. But then, she had decided to be cautious and see whether in fact this particular friendship might be good for Netti. But what she had encountered here appalled her.

Laura waved the bundle of notes before her eyes. 'Leave Netti alone,' she said, her voice cold and stiff. 'Here's five hundred pounds, more than enough for the likes of you! Take it!' She saw the girl's eyes light up with greed. As she snatched the money from her hands, Laura insisted, 'Tonight! You'll go tonight?'

The girl nodded, slowly and deliberately. 'Sure,' she laughed, 'me an' the fellows, we've been thinking of moving on for some time.'

Laura walked towards the door. 'I'd better not find out that you've been in touch with my sister. I don't want to hear of you, or see you again! Is that clear?'

Now the girl was standing behind Laura with a look of arrogance on her features. 'You needn't worry, *sister* dear!' She waved the money triumphantly. 'This'll do me. Netti was just a novelty.'

As Laura looked at this creature, she could not trust herself to stay another minute, but she recoiled from going back to the shop just yet. So her path followed the high ground circling the town, taking her back towards the house, and the moors.

All the way there, her fists remained clenched, her mouth set in a grim line. Then when she reached the solitude of the

301

moors, she sank to the grass, and a feeling of nausea swept over her. The tears smarted in her eyes and gathered in her throat like a hard knot. But she wouldn't give in to the release they might bring. Instead, she looked at her part in the miseries of this day. Had that girl been right? Did she push Netti against her will, driving her in a direction she didn't want to go? No, she couldn't believe that. Netti loved her music, and until Lizzie Pendleton had unsettled her, she had thought of nothing else. And *that* was why boys had never really interested her.

The small spiral of doubt inside her grew until it became almost overwhelming. But she pushed such unwelcome speculation to one side. Having seen that girl, she was more than convinced that she had done the right and only thing. But she felt no pride in her actions. Instead, she felt shamed and degraded.

Looking out across the moors, she drank in their beauty and as always, it soothed her. Then the anguish within her found voice, and she whispered into the breeze, 'Oh, Netti! Netti! What possessed you to be drawn to such a low creature?' And quickly, like a cruel echo, the answer came to her.

Hadn't she herself been drawn to such a low creature? Hadn't she freely given herself to Jake Thackerey for thoughts of gain? And allowed herself to be seduced by Pearce Griffin? No! Not allowed, but enjoyed, knowing that to him, she was a mere plaything. Dear God, could it be that Ruth Blake had bred something evil into her and Netti?

A recollection of something that Remmie had imparted to her came into Laura's confused mind. It was an awesome description of the ocean's tide surging through a narrow strait. The effect was a turbulent and menacing force, which only found peace when it had expended all its energy and came to rest in calmer waters. Remmie had read it in one of his old books, and Laura had been fascinated to hear it. And now, she thought of it long and deep. The conclusion she came to was that life itself could be likened to such a phenomenon, her own particularly. Turbulent and menacing, yes, but would there ever be calmer waters?

It was only when her bones began to stiffen from her uncomfortable position that Laura realized with a shock just how long she had been there. It was almost eleven o'clock.

Mitch and Remmie would wonder where she'd got to. Especially Mitch, who had played a small but important part in her conspiracy. Dear loyal Mitch, who had always loved her. Oh, how she envied him that capacity. At this moment, Laura resented all the blind ambitions that drove her; the fierce desire to see Netti make something fine and grand of herself, and the relentless force that impelled her to seek the kind of riches and power that would make people look up to her. These things would allow her such freedom, that never again would she have to depend on others. These things were her own private passions, and whatever she had to do to bring them to fruition, then she would do!

The bad things, like that girl, and yes, like Pearce Griffin, would never go away. Laura knew instinctively that she would be called upon to face them, or something just as evil, in the years to come. But whatever happened, she intended to survive.

Yet there were still those who would use her, who waited to drag her down, Laura knew that. With this thought in mind, she followed the path home, her mind weighing up Jake Thackerey's arrogant proposition and her intended trip south. Wasn't it said that behind every cloud there was a silver lining? Yes of course! She would keep that thought uppermost in her mind.

Chapter Twenty-five

Laura had been up almost since first light that morning, and yet she found herself rushing to pack an overnight bag and now having to run for the train. She let herself into the carriage just as the train shuddered into motion, and with a thankful sigh, she lifted her small blue oblong portmanteau up into the net racking, and eased herself onto the seat beneath. The carriage was empty apart from a bowler-hatted gentleman in the far corner of the seats opposite who appeared to be deeply engrossed in his copy of *The Times*. In actual fact, he had taken time away from his newspaper to cast an appreciative glance at this astonishingly beautiful woman who looked every inch a lady. Laura had chosen to wear a pale blue cotton coat that hung straight from the padded shoulders before flaring out to the calf in a generous hem. The high neck was of mandarin style and the deep turn back reveres that ran from collar to hem fell away as she sat to reveal a plain slim-fitting dress of matching material. Her high heeled shoes and slim beret placed atop her auburn curls in a jaunty side-saddle fashion were also blue but several shades deeper than her dress and coat.

Laura was unaware of the man's surreptitious ogling, as she relaxed into her seat, letting the rythmic rumble of the train infiltrate her busy mind. But her insistent thoughts gave her little peace and rose above the noise of the train, to remind her that yet again the path of her life had changed direction.

She smiled softly to herself as she recalled Remmie's parting words that morning. 'London 'int all it's cracked up to be. A body can get lonely an' lost in the crowds of a big city, that they can.' Laura believed that. She also believed that a body could be lonely and lost *anywhere*. But it allayed at least some of Remmie's anxieties when she had allowed him to make her hotel booking. He had reserved a room for her at one of

London's better hotels, The Hotel royal, and he had justified the expense by telling her, 'I wouldn't rest in me bed if I thought you were down some side street in one o' them cheap nasty places!' Laura hadn't protested, but his remark had caused her to think that after all this time, Remmie really didn't know her. The last thing in her mind would have been to stay in a cheap nasty place. Oh no! She was going to London, and she was going to see it in some style. She had no intention of pinching pennies, because she had decided that only the best would be good enough!

A slight frown creased her brow as she thought of Netti. These last few days, her sister had seemed to withdraw into herself and Laura suspected that it had something to do with that girl, Judy. But Netti hadn't mentioned that her friend had gone from the area, and Laura thought it best to leave well alone. That creature Judy had been a very real threat to Netti's future and it would surely only be a matter of time before Netti realized that herself.

Laura had toyed with the idea of taking Netti to London with her. She would have valued her sister's company and a visit to the city would have probably done Netti a great deal of good; but Laura eventually decided against it. She considered that the very worst thing she could do just now, when Netti appeared so unsettled, was to encourage her away from her studies.

Laura concentrated now on her immediate arrangements. Today was Thursday, and she planned to spend tonight and tomorrow night at the hotel. That would give her all of Friday and part of Saturday to locate the very best furniture stores and take measure of her competition. If there was time left over for sight-seeing, that would be marvellous, but she must not lose sight of her real purpose in coming to London. Her business instincts told her that there was money to be made from establishing a contact, an outlet, through which goods from Remmie's shop could be channelled towards the discerning purchaser.

Laura had told Remmie that she hoped to be back in Blackburn late on Saturday night, and she knew that he would be watching out for her arrival. But for now, she was leaving Blackburn behind. Laura settled back to look out of the window at the sights and scenes which quickly flashed into view and then out again. She felt like a small child on a birthday treat. Some time later Laura got out of the train at Crewe and found her way to platform six, where she boarded another train that swiftly carried her over the second lap of her journey.

On her arrival at Euston Station, Laura was horrified at the sad plight of an ex-soldier who was seated on the floor at the exits from the platforms. The two ribboned medals pinned to his khaki coat seemed to Laura to serve as receipts for the loss of a limb; betrayed by his empty trouser leg carefully folded back and tied to his belt. He was blowing on a mouth-organ, and the thin soulless lament brought all to silence as they passed.

Laura stood back to fish a note from her purse. She discreetly dropped it into the hat on the ground beside him, smiled into his eyes and whispered, 'That's a lovely tune,' and was warmed by the cheery wink he gave her.

The trip had taken nearly all day and when Laura finally arrived at the hotel, she was not only weary from the journey, but incredibly hungry. Stepping from the taxi, she thanked the driver, gave him a pound note and told him to keep the change. It was not that she was feeling especially generous, but when he made a big fuss over having no change and searched all his pockets in slow motion, she decided that the four and sixpence change was hardly worth the aggravation.

Laura watched him draw away, and for a while, she stood still, taking in the impressive hotel fascia. The building itself, constructed mainly in light coloured bricks and acres of glass, was of modern design. There were two broad marble steps that curved in to join with the marble platform. Laura went through the huge double glass doors into the spacious foyer and was astonished by the luxury: the deep domed ceiling above, from the centre of which hung a shimmering crystal chandelier of immense proportion and consisting of thousands of multi-coloured droplets that gently moved in unison; the floor and wide sweeping stairway swathed in a deep plum coloured carpet that almost swallowed her feet up to the ankles in its expensive deep pile; the highly polished wooden doors leading off in all directions; and directly in front of her the reception desk of the same highly-polished wood, with raised oblong panels along its curved front, and two attractive ladies smartly attired in white blouses and cherry-red skirts with matching cherry-red ties.

Laura made her way over to the desk and at once, one of the young ladies smiled in a warm greeting, 'Good evening, Madam?'

'Good evening. I have a two-night reservation. Miss Blake.'

There was another smile and a quick consultation of the desk ledger. 'That's right.' She turned away to collect a key from the rack of pigeon-holes that covered the wall behind her. Handing the key to Laura, she said, 'Room 202 on the second floor. Would you like someone to take up your luggage?'

'I have no luggage,' Laura replied, lifting the small portmanteau into view, 'just this. Thank you.' She half-turned away, then looked back to ask, 'Oh, is there somewhere I can get a meal?'

'Of course. You can get a snack at the bar, through there,' she indicated towards the frosted glass door to Laura's left, 'or if you'd care to wait until seven pm,' she consulted the clock over the main doors, 'just over an hour, you can get a main meal in the upstairs restaurant. I can book you a table now, if you like?'

Laura calculated that by the time she had rested and bathed, it would be gone seven anyway. 'Yes, I should like that. Thank you.'

As Laura walked away towards the lift, the second receptionist came to stand by her colleague, and her eyes on Laura's departing figure, she uttered but one word and that word was 'Wow!' to which her colleague replied, 'Wow, indeed! What wouldn't I give to look like that? She's beautiful.'

'Beautiful, yes. Happy, no.'

'She *does* look rather sad, in spite of her confident air of authority. Perhaps being a beautiful woman *isn't* the be-all and end-all of everything?'

At this, the other girl laughed softly. 'Perhaps not, but if *I* looked like her, oh, but I'd lead the men a merry dance!'

'Well you don't look like her, not many of us do. But *we* get our fair share of what's going, and some women don't like men enough to lead them a dance, so stop griping and get back to

307

your work,' she finished good humouredly.

Upstairs, Laura found her room to be comfortable, yet not of the same luxurious appearance as the hotel foyer. There was a wide, beige-curtained window at the far end of the room; a double-bed covered in a beige quilted eiderdown; a long narrow dressing table of veneered wood, with a square padded-topped stool beneath it; a built-in double wardrobe; and a sizeable bathroom leading off from the bedroom with spotless and adequate facilities.

She hung her coat on one of the wardrobe hangers which she then slid over the rail. There were a number of fine creases around the seat area, but the material was such that they would fall out in a short while. She opened the portmanteau and unpacked her cream two-piece; a straight pencil-slim skirt and short fitting jacket that nipped in at the waist before bouncing out again in an elegant little frill. Then came the light grey dress which had a blouse-like top and long full sleeves, and a skirt that fell in a gentle flare from the belted waist. The two pairs of shoes, one black and one white, and each with a matching box-style hand-bag, she left in the case for a moment, together with her toiletries. Then she kicked off her shoes and fell onto the bed, sighing with relief at having reached her journey's end.

At a quarter to eight, Laura entered the dining room. It was a long airy room with white-clothed tables, buffet dressers bedecked with baskets of fresh rolls, gleaming artefacts and rack upon rack of best wines. Every wall was a sheet of decorated glass, which appeared to be a particular feature of this hotel. As she head waiter hurried towards her, Laura sensed that everyone was staring in her direction and she was thankful to sit down at her appointed table, which was inconspicuously tucked into the far corner. All the same, people continued to stare at this slim shapely woman in a most becoming dress of soft grey, whose mass of auburn hair shone like gold beneath the overhead lights, and whose strikingly lovely wide dark eyes held the appeal and fascination of a child — yet were wise and filled with strength and determination.

Laura enjoyed a meal of grape and orange salad with ham and a glass of Lambrusco, followed by a delicious helping of Charlotte Russe. She wasn't used to dining in such style, but quickly decided that she could very easily adapt herself to such gracious living.

Afterwards, feeling somewhat refreshed and filled with a degree of contentment, Laura signed the receipt with her room number, conveyed her thanks to the waiter and returned to the welcome privacy of her bedroom where, after gazing out of the window across the unfamiliar skyline for a while, she slipped out of her clothes and gratefully into bed, to give herself up to the luxury of closing her eyes and thinking of little other than a good night's sleep.

When Laura awoke, it was with a startle. Sitting upright against the pillow she allowed the shrill telephone-bell to sound just long enough for her to acclimatize herself to these strange but lovely surroundings. Then she lifted the receiver to her ear and quietly thanked the desk clerk for calling her as requested at seven am — afterwards replacing the bedside telephone and rising from the silky comfort of the sheets. She eased the curtains back on their runners and at once the room was filled with glorious sunshine which promised a wonderful day.

Wasting no time, Laura went quickly towards the bathroom. Breakfast was served from eight am and she wanted to be one of the first. Her intention was to be quickly in and out, because she envisaged exploring the shops the minute they opened. After bathing, she attempted to persuade her wild hair into a semblance of order, but the thick auburn locks seemed as usual to have a mind of their own. When Laura entered the breakfast room at eight-fifteen — looking fresh and cool in her cream two-piece — her hair was a profusion of deep burnished waves and stray curls that teased waywardly about her lovely face.

The breakfast menu was comprehensive; an endless list ranging from fruit, cereals, fresh hot rolls and buttered toast, to kippers and the usual full english breakfast. Laura settled for grapefruit, coffee and a lightly poached egg.

'Ah! Miss Blake.' Laura was stopped short as she prepared to leave the foyer for the street outside. She turned to see the bright enquiring face of the desk clerk and retracing her steps she went to stand before the bright-eyed young lady and asked, 'What is it?'

'There's a message for you.' The girl consulted the note-pad

309

on the desk by the phone. Mr Remmie Thorpe rang about five minutes ago. He wondered whether you would telephone him sometime this morning.' She pointed to a row of three kiosks to the right of the main entrance. 'You can use one of those. Would you like me to get the number for you?'

Laura gave her the number of the shop, entered number one kiosk and closed the door behind her. In less than a minute, the telephone on the shelf in front of her began to shrill insistently. 'Hello, is that Remmie?' A female voice intruded to announce, 'Go ahead, you're through now.' Then came Mitch's voice, 'Thorpe's here.'

Laura had a mental picture of Mitch standing by the counter. It was good to hear his voice. 'Mitch, is Remmie there?'

'Laura!' The joy in his voice and that special way he had of saying her name, reached across the miles.

'Mitch. Remmie rang the hotel, can I speak to him?'

Mitch's answer was curt, and Laura guessed that he would have preferred to talk on. 'I'll fetch him.'

Within a moment, Remmie's voice came on the phone. It took but a minute for Laura to reassure him that she was perfectly alright and safely installed in the hotel.

'Right then,' he concluded, 'go on, an' get yoursel' off to where you're itching to go, an' I'll see you tomorrow night. I'll meet the ten pm train as agreed. If there's any chance o' getting back earlier, I expect you'll give me a ring or some'at, eh?'

'Yes. Is Netti alright?'

'Fine, lass. Now, tek care!'

There was a new warmth in Laura's heart as she stepped out through the main doors and into the sunshine. She was glad that she'd come to London, because inside her there was a conviction that special things were going to come of it.

Some three hours later, a few minutes after twelve o'clock, Laura was sitting at a table in the back of a sandwich bar. Her feet were tired and hot and she greedily gulped down the tea which the plump Italian lady had placed in front of her. Laura leaned back in her seat and closed her eyes. Miles she'd walked, miles and miles, up and down Oxford Street, Regent Street, and countless other streets whose names she could not even call to mind. Down the Underground, off and on those whistle-stop carriages where everybody sat staring at everybody else and every station looked exactly the same as the last one.

She must have been into at least a dozen stores, stores that were divided into departments and sold furniture only as part of a conglomerate package, and stores that specialized in furniture alone. Two particular things had happened on each occasion. Firstly, Laura had browsed leisurely amongst the stock, making notes in her small pocket-book of what she considered to be astronomical prices for choice pieces of furniture, that nowhere equalled the quality and superb craftsmanship of Mitch's products. And secondly, when she had asked to speak to the manager, who was always a man, her well-presented proposition that she could provide them with an excellent range of furniture, reproduction Regency or in fact any period of their choice and of the most superb detail, his immediate and irretractable decision was, 'I'm sorry Madam, but we are not open to new contracts for supply. We have our regular people, you understand.' Oh yes, she had definitely begun to understand. It was because she was a woman! These narrow-minded conventional men were mortally afraid of admitting a woman into their hallowed chambers. Well, she had no intention of giving up! Her *feet* might be screaming for surrender, but the more of a brick wall these men of business constructed to keep her out, the more fiercely she would fight back to break it down!

Laura had a second cup of tea, and then went to the cloakroom where she splashed her face in cold water at the handbasin, renewed her make-up and lipstick, ran a comb through her hair and emerged from the sandwich bar like a trooper refreshed and eager for battle.

Bond Street was a revelation to Laura. She had no previous knowledge of how the other half lived, but the beautiful shops bedecked with exquisite and priceless artefacts filled her with envy. She wandered from shop to shop, imagining herself dressed in this designer dress of pure silk, or that matching array of glittering priceless diamonds. There were galleries lined with the most beautiful and rare paintings and delicate engravings by people like Lewis and Landseer. There were furniture shops too, displaying only the best and most traditional examples of leather suites, and tasteful items of furni-

311

ture in only the best rosewoods, mahogany and walnut.

Laura had been into several of these shops, but the managers' responses had been exactly the same as all the previous ones. She had covered almost the whole length of Bond Street, criss-crossing from one side to the other, and now, she was standing outside a shop called Weston and Favers, which had a small frontage, but a deep and elaborate showroom space.

Laura entered the highly-polished door, which was solid at the bottom and glass at the top, and once inside the shop she let out a small unchecked gasp at the outspoken luxury that surrounded her. All about her were deep rich chairs and settees of soft pastel colours in figured silk; magnificent grandfather clocks of choice grained wood; exquisite rugs of intricate oriental design and such splendid pieces of furniture that Laura thought she had now seen the like of Mitch's superb craftsmanship. The walls were festooned with glorious gilt-framed paintings, a number of which depicted fierce battles and honourable death at the hands of an enemy. Laura followed the burgundy carpeted aisle, until she came to a further showroom that ran from where she stood, to curve away to her left and out of sight. And this too, was a wonderland of treasures.

'Can I help you, Madam?'

Laura had not noticed the two men standing by what looked to be an office. When the shorter of the two stepped forward to address her, Laura swept aside the doubts telling her that she would be wasting her time in such an establishment, and looking him boldly in the eye, she asked, 'Could I see the manager?'

The tall man came to stand between them, saying to the other man, 'Alright, Bob, I'll see to it.' He turned now towards Laura, 'I'm the manager.' Extending his hand in greeting, he added, 'Mr Craven. What can I do for you?'

Laura took his hand and when he shook it in friendship, Laura noted how firm and tight his grip was and how human his open kindly face was in comparison to the stiff mouthed unsmiling masks that had greeted her elsewhere.

'I'm not a customer,' Laura offered, determined to put him right straight away. If he thought she had the kind of money to shop here, then he was a *long* way out!

'Oh?' His pale eyes studied her face for a moment, then

312

stepping to one side, he gestured towards the half-open door behind him. 'Perhaps we'd better go into the office.'

Laura nodded and he hurried before her to push wide open the office door. In a minute they were seated, him behind the big oak desk and her in front of it.

'What exactly is your business then?' he asked.

'The same as yours, well almost.' Laura thought the best way in was the quickest, and anyway she did not now have the patience for frills and dressing-up. She leant forwards and rested her hands on the desk. 'We have a business in Blackburn, Lancashire and we've all but exhausted the possibilities in that immediate area, so I'm here in London to try and establish an outlet for our high-quality furniture.'

'Let me stop you before you go any further.' He made to rise from his chair, and Laura's heart sank at his tone, for she had heard it so often that day. But this time, she would *not* be deterred, and deliberately cutting in on his words, she said, 'Please let me finish, Mr Craven. I'm sorry, but I've heard all the arguments and quite frankly, they stink!' He had closed his mouth which had fallen open at her outburst and now he was leaning back in his chair. She could see that behind his bemused expression, there was a spark of interest, and it spurred her on. 'There isn't one piece of furniture in those showrooms out there that is in any way superior to what *we* can supply you with, except perhaps in the price you have to pay. I won't ask you what colossal sums you pass to your contractor, but I can virtually guarantee that ordering from *us* you can make an initial saving of fifty per cent. Not only can we provide you with *new* items of period reproduction, but quite often we come across the *genuine* article, and on top of that, we provide a restoration service that is second to none!' Laura paused for a moment, breathless and excited, but when the man opposite leaned forward in his chair and seemed about to speak, she took up a new line in her argument. 'If you're going to decline, then do it because you don't need a supplier who will keep up your standard of quality and keep *down* your outgoing monies! Decline because your contractor is so suitable in every way, that you do not need to contemplate opening out your options.' Her fiery eyes were alive as she saw the astonishment on his face. Her voice lower now, she finished, 'If you

313

must show me the door, Mr Craven, do it for the *right* reasons. Don't do it because I'm a woman!'

The ensuing silence made Laura feel self-conscious. Or was it, she wondered, the fact that since she had finished speaking, the man, Mr Craven, had not taken his eyes off her. He had sat deep in his chair, his fingers moving to and fro across the balding patch behind his forehead, crinkled now into numerous furrows. Laura pretended to be examining the many watercolours hung about the walls, but all the while she was conscious of his attention to her. She felt as though she was being examined herself, scrutinized. Well, let him scrutinize all he wanted. She wouldn't budge from here so easily!

All of a sudden, and in a way that caught Laura off guard, Mr Craven leaned forward, to ask, 'What's your name?'

'The name of the business?'

'No. Your name.'

'Laura Blake. The business is my uncle's, but one day I hope to have my own.'

'I have no doubt, Miss?' he paused and when she affirmed the title, he went on, 'Miss Blake.' He half-smiled, then settling back into his chair again, he said, 'Now tell me about your business, every little detail. Leave nothing out.'

It was five minutes to three when Laura emerged from Weston and Favers, and as she went down Bond Street, she wondered whether her feet were actually touching the ground. And if they were, then they had no right to be. She wanted to skip, to run or fly! Because she had done it! She, Laura Blake, had formed the first contact that would elevate Remmie's little business beyond its present confines! If they could establish themselves firmly with Weston and Favers, there was no telling *where* it might lead! Mr Craven had even bowed to her insistence that it should be in writing; that he would take delivery of one reproduction secretaire in best grained walnut.

It was to be on approval only, and any future contracts would be dependant upon satisfaction of quality, delivery and agreeable terms. Mr Craven had emphasized that it was a big step for him to be taking and it was done with much apprehension. Well, it was an even *bigger* step for Laura, and she was not in the *least* apprehensive!

When she jumped into the taxi-cab, it was with a feeling of immense excitement and a sense of accomplishment. She deserved a treat, she told herself. 'To the Savoy Hotel, please,' she said, deciding that tea in one of London's grandest institutions was a treat indeed!

Seeing the almost iridescent glow on her lovely face, the taxi-cab driver was sure she was about to burst into song. When she didn't, enthused by her happiness he broke forth in a rush of melodic whistling.

Back in the office of Weston and Favers, Mr Craven was addressing his colleague. 'Well, it's done, down in writing. I hope it's not a costly mistake.'

'Can't think why you did it, Mr Craven. Bartering with a *woman* of all things! A tasty piece like that should be in some man's bed, taking his mind off his troubles and keeping him happy, not trying his shoes on for size.'

Mr Craven laughed out loud, and it must have been a rare sound, for the other man stared hard at him. Mr Craven slapped him on the back and said through his laughter, 'Well, all I can say is that this fellow's shoes must fit her well, because she led *me* a pretty dance, and no mistake.' The little man called Bob also accepted the funny side of it and he too exploded into laughter.

Laura's sense of elation had carried her through the rest of the day. She indulged in much unashamed luxury and pampering of herself, that would have caused both Remmie and Mitch to raise their eyebrows in astonishment — and *that* had given as much pleasure to Laura, as the events themselves.

Later, when she was lying in her bed unable to sleep for the excitement coursing through her veins, Laura reflected on the day. Oh, and what a time she had had! She'd fed the pigeons in Trafalgar Square, peered through the railings at Buckingham Palace, where she imagined the young Queen Elizabeth to be free from the kind of worries that beset the multitudes, yet bothered by problems of a much higher plane. Problems that came with a crown and the title of Monarch. Laura had looked at the splendid Palace, at its regal stature and historic properties. She had imagined the fine and beautiful artefacts within, and for all that, she had not envied the young Queen.

Instead, she had pitied her, for now that the burdens of crown and country were squarely placed on her shoulders, Elizabeth's life would never be her own again.

She dwelt momentarily on the plush surroundings of the tea-lounge in the Savoy Hotel, where she had supped tea from best china cups, chosen dainty little cakes from the most exquisite three-tiered silver and china cake-stand; and all to the music of a harpist who had constantly showered her with smiles. Oh yes, it had been an adventurous day, completed by a candle-lit dinner in a small intimate restaurant by the River Thames, a charming little place where her being alone seemed quite acceptable.

Laura closed her eyes now, and tried to will herself to sleep. But she wasn't tired and after a while of tossing and turning, she got up and padded to the window, where she opened the curtains and gazed across the rooftops of London. Blackburn was approximately two hundred miles away, but to Laura just then, it was another world completely.

She was in an odd restless sort of mood, a mood for remembering. She remembered the dirty narrow alleys of her hometown, the rubble of dwellings that even to this day had not been cleared for rebuilding. She thought of the awful poverty that had always been a way of life and the utter frustration it bred.

Laura stood by the window for a long time, her thoughts sweeping through her life. Then she searched ahead for the pattern of her life to come, and with it came the comfort that in her handbag was a sheet of paper, drawn up and signed by the manager of a swank London shop. One solitary piece of furniture on approval might not amount to much at first sight. But to Laura, it was the beginning of something wonderful. For even the mightiest of buildings must by necessity start with one brick. That was a fond saying of Remmie's and if she hadn't seen the implications of its message before, she did now. She thought now of Remmie, Mitch and Netti, and decided that she would change her plans and catch the first train home.

Feeling more relaxed within herself, she suddenly felt the need for sleep. She drew the curtains and went back to bed, where she climbed in and snuggled into its cold embrace. It wasn't long before she felt the waves of sleep engulfing her,

316

and in her sinking consciousness, she murmured out loud, 'Wait till Mitch and Remmie hear what I've done, *our* furniture being sold in a posh place like Weston and Favers. There'll be no stopping us now!'

Chapter Twenty-six

'What in God's name were you thinkin' on, lass?' Remmie said to Laura, who was furiously polishing the display cabinet, and deliberately keeping her back to him. He was going to start again! He'd been like it ever since she'd rushed from the train on Saturday, eager to show him the paper signed by Mr Craven. He had whipped up a storm of protest that had taken her completely aback, and if it hadn't been for the fact that she would give no man the satisfaction of causing her to shed tears, she would have bitterly sobbed then and there! But she had told herself, *convinced* herself, that there must be a way round his sudden change of heart, which to her mind amounted to nothing less than mutiny! And now, he was going on again about it, and except from running from the shop, she had no alternative but to be bombarded once again with his objections.

'I'm not about to expand out o' Blackburn, we're not ready! How in the blazes d'you think Mitch can make up more new furniture, eh, on top o' the mountains o' work created by renovating! No, lass, put it out o' your mind. One o' these fine days, Laura, the shop, the 'ouse, everything'll be yours, yours an' Netti's. Wait till then, eh, an' you'll be free to expand all you like.'

Laura turned to face him now, her eyes vivid and angry, and Remmie felt a flood of shame that was reinforced by her accusing words. 'You've gone back on your word, and you've *never* done that before.' She could have ranted on at him, made him feel small and ashamed; but Laura sensed that nothing would ever convince him to expand out of Blackburn. Not now. Not since Jake Thackerey's treachery had eroded the foundation of his trust. And there was something else too; she had seen it in his fading brown eyes and in his slower walk. 'Don't think too harshly of me, lass. I'm not as young as I used to be; new ideas don't sit too comfortable on these 'ere shoulders. Bide your time, eh? To please me?'

Beneath the strength of his love for her, Laura was loath to maintain her fury at what she still considered to be his treachery. It only took a second to recall what this kindly man had done for her and Netti, and her features softened into a half-smile, albeit a reluctant one. Yet the anger still tight in her throat would not allow her to speak. Remmie seemed to understand, for he grasped her in his arms and muttered, 'Sorry, lass. But you don't want to go searching for responsibilities that could bring their own heartaches, eh? Time enough, there's time enough.'

Laura was glad when he took his arms from her and moved away, for there was still a part of her that had stiffened against him and refused to yield. Time enough! Was that all he could say? There *wasn't* time enough. There was *never* time enough, for it was gone all too quickly!

Laura made a swift mental calculation. She had amassed close on a thousand pounds in her bank account. It wasn't anywhere near enough to set herself up. What she would dearly love was one of those shop units in that new building in the centre of town. There were still two left. But oh, it was impossible. It would take many more thousands than *she'd* got, to fit a place like that out, and then to stock it properly. And how could she keep her option open with Weston and Favers? Mitch was the only person in these parts who could create the most splendid furniture out of a pile of seemingly dead wood. And he would never desert Remmie, not in a thousand years. But what to do? How to break out on her own?

Like a flower opening to the sunlight, a thought moved from the dark interior of Laura's mind, into the light. The bank manager. She would go and see the bank manager! After all, lending money was their strength, wasn't it? Setting people up in business? Yes, of course it was.

Laura decided not to let Mr Craven of Weston and Favers know how Remmie felt. There might still be a way round it. What the way was, she didn't know, but that piece of paper safely tucked away in her wardrobe had been hard to come by, and she wasn't about to let it go if she could help it!

319

During a quiet moment towards closing time, Laura satisfied herself that both Remmie and Mitch were busily employed elsewhere, then she looked up the number of the bank, dialled it through on the telephone, and in a quick exchange of words with the desk clerk, made an appointment to see Mr Dewhurst the manager at two pm on Thursday. She returned to her work and her thoughts but was jolted out of the latter by a voice directly behind her.

'Sally came to see me last night.' Mitch had waited until Remmie was out of earshot in the yard. He slid a newly repaired drawer into its slot in a kneehole desk, then watching Laura carefully in order to gauge her reaction, he repeated, 'I said Sally came to see me last night,' adding in a stronger voice, 'It was really your business she came about.'

'Oh? My business? How's that then?'

'It was young Tom she came about. It seems he's cutting up rough at school, forever fighting. I told her I'd get the lad a punch-bag to take his frustrations out on.'

Laura looked at Mitch, her mind going over his words. Tom had taken to fighting people? Tom, whom she had let down so badly, and who could not forgive her. And now, was he taking it out on others? Oh, Tom, Tom! 'Does Sally want me to go and see her?'

'No! Worst thing possible according to Sally. Yes, Laura, she explained the way of things.' He had seen the look on her face, the look that asked him whether he knew that Tom didn't want her near, and his heart went out to her.

'Thank you for telling me, Mitch.'

'I just thought you ought to know how he's faring.'

With a heavier mood pressing down on her, Laura waded into the mountainous stack of timber that had just been delivered and needed checking. Drawing the pen from behind her ear, she started scribbling furiously into the small note pad in her hand, deliberately filling her mind with matters that were as far removed from Parry Griffin's boy as was possible.

Laura checked that the yard gate was securely locked and retraced her steps to the back store room. When she drew level with the outer door, Mitch appeared and blocked her way. He made no move to clear her path, but put out an arm to stop her. 'Remmie told me, Laura, about the London thing. I'm sorry you've been let down on it.' Laura was amazed at the pride with which he suddenly blurted out, 'A contract with a posh London shop, that must have taken some doing. You're a special kind of woman, Laura, there's no denying that.' He looked down on her for a moment before moving off, leaving her to ask herself why Mitch of all people should have appreciated the effort she had put into acquiring Mr Craven's signature, for like Remmie, Mitch was rigidly opposed to business expansion. But then Mitch was a straight-forward man. He would always give credit where it was due, whether he agreed or disagreed with a particular transaction.

After the excitement of London, the mundane routine of the next two days was almost unbearable, especially in view of the fact that all Laura could think of was her approaching appointment with Mr Dewhurst the bank manager. She had never met him, and she found herself plagued with doubts. Would he be sympathetic to her business proposition? What was his attitude to loans of the considerable size *she* would require? She had all the figures, calculated in the secrecy of her bedroom, away from the inquisitive eyes of Netti and Remmie. She would have confided in Netti, but the girl had enough on her mind at the moment, keeping up to the demands made on her by Miss Fordyke. Laura had decided in any event that, for the moment, she was best keeping her own council.

And now here she was, sitting in this stuffy office, with its ancient wicker chairs and drab atmosphere, compounded by the brown walls and lack of light. Laura's spirits might have sunk beneath the depressing and forbidding atmosphere of the room, but for her heightened sense of purpose and promise of what a successful interview here could accomplish. The possibilities excited her so much that she dared not contemplate them, when the door opened to admit a dimunitive male figure. Laura was so engrossed in her thoughts that she did not become aware of his presence until he said, 'I'm so sorry to have kept you waiting; pressures of being a bank manager I'm afraid.' He smiled, and as Laura stood up to meet him, she couldn't help but inwardly smile at his appearance.

Mr Dewhurst was some five inches shorter than she, with a bulbous stomach that was decorated by the tight waistcoat of his blue pin-striped suit and emphasized by the remarkable

321

length of silver chain that stretched from his button up to the top pocket where Laura assumed his pocket watch lived. He had the reddish-purple features that were peculiar to heavy drinkers, that supposition endorsed by his brightly mottled nose and pink eyes. His small pointed head was completely devoid of hair and by the shine of its crimson skin, Laura was convinced that he must spend many hours polishing it.

After they had shaken hands, Mr Dewhurst retreated to his large swivel seat behind the mahogany desk and gestured to Laura to sit on the stand chair before it.

'Now then, Miss Blake. What can I do for you?' He gave a patronizing grin which Laura resented and immediately put her on her guard.

Withdrawing the sheaf of papers from her bag, she spread them out on the desk before him. 'I'd like you to look at these facts and figures,' she said with a crispness that made Mr Dewhurst sit up and lean forward in his chair, his quick beady eyes darting over the sheets of paper she had offered. As Laura explained them, he studied the figures closely. 'These papers represent a breakdown of a prospective business that will return excellent profits,' she went on, 'though not straightaway of course. I calculate that it will take three years to come to full strength. But it will stand on its own feet after an initial injection of capital, and as you can see, I have forecast the outlay as six hundred pounds for the first year's rent, another six hundred for carpeting, decor and so on; two hundred for advertising, which I intend to cover a very large and carefully chosen area; four hundred pounds to cover miscellaneous bills such as heating, lighting and telephone etc.; two hundred pounds for a decent delivery vehicle; four thousand pounds wages for myself and one assistant; and the largest figure being for stock; some will initially have to be bought in, but I anticipate arranging a situation whereby at least part of my merchandise will be craftsman-built in our own workshop. That will come later though, and is not reckoned in the initial stock figure of five thousand pounds. My intention, Mr Dewhurst, is that Weston and Favers, an eminent and lucrative business in London with whom I have already transacted an agreement will in time be one of my major outlets.' Laura lifted her eyes from the desk, expecting the man before her to be deep in concentration. When she saw that he was *not* and that he was displaying more interest in the top button of her blouse, she brought him up sharply with, 'Mr Dewhurst! I trust you can see the tremendous potential of my business proposition?'

'Why yes, of course!' He leaned back in his chair, the flush of pink to his face leaving Laura wondering whether he was excited by the figures on the desk, or embarrassed that he had been caught Tom-peeping.

'Then you'll help me?'

'Hmmm!' He got up to walk just once to the door and back. Then he returned to his seat and looked up at Laura. 'I was told that you were looking for a loan from us?' he said.

'Yes. I have about a thousand pounds deposited here. I shall of course invest that into the business. What I'm looking to *you* for, is a loan for the remainder, over say a period of five years.'

'But Miss Blake, are you telling me that you intend to embark on this adventure on your *own*?'

'It is *not* an adventure, Mr Dewhurst! This,' she waved her hand impatiently over the desk, 'this represents a very sound business proposition, and yes, I *do* intend to embark on it alone!'

'But you are talking of a loan in the region of . . .' He leaned across the desk to peer at the papers and shift them about, his sharp eyes scanning the figures that Laura had so meticulously prepared.

'Ten thousand pounds!' She had no need of reckoning, for didn't she know those figures inside out! 'Subtracting the thousand I already have, I still need ten thousand.'

'It's a great deal of money I'm afraid, and I don't believe we've ever done business on this scale before with a woman, especially of your young years and with no man behind you.'

'I don't need a *man*, Mr Dewhurst, it's a loan I want.'

'But what you have to realize, Miss Blake, is that we will not be in a position to take out a mortgage on the property, as it will be a rented one, and you are offering us no alternative collateral. Now, if you could get a business man of some reputation to guarantee . . .'

'Mr Dewhurst! Please let us proceed on the understanding that I want to do this on my own. Your guarantee is *me*, my stock and personal references.' Laura had still not closed her mind to the possibility that the bank would help her, but her fear was strong that here in this man she had come up against all the old prejudices. She had no doubt that if it had been a member of the *male* sex sitting here in her place, he would have left the bank ten minutes ago with the agreement safely in his pocket!

'I'm sorry, but we need more than personal references when making a loan of this consideration.'

'Then you *won't* help me?'

'I'm afraid it isn't a matter of *won't*, Miss Blake, more a matter of *can't*.'

He began to shuffle her papers together, and Laura could have swiped that stupid benign smile from his face. Getting to her feet, she grabbed the papers from the desk, the biting tone of her voice causing the smile to slip from his face. 'I will of course be closing my deposit account. Please arrange it and notify me.' Folding the papers up, she returned them to her handbag and ignoring his efforts to reach the door before her, she stood with her hand on the door-knob and turned to look back at him. When she addressed him again, the little man was overawed by the air of authority and quiet dignity with which she told him, 'Remember this day, Mr Dewhurst, mark it well, because I intend to set up my business somehow, and to prove that the decision you've made this afternoon will be one you'll bitterly regret.'

After Laura left his office, Mr Dewhurst fell into deep contemplation, and when it grew into depression he went to the wooden cabinet in the corner and took out a bottle of whisky which he uncorked and took a great comforting swig from.

Laura made her way back to the shop smarting from her brief but stormy encounter with Mr Dewhurst. How could it be that such an insignificant little creature like that had the power and authority to thwart her plans? Well, they would *not* be thwarted! She meant every word she'd said; she would prove him wrong and make him regret having turned her down. What if she *was* a woman in a man's world! All it meant was that she would just have to work that much harder to compete.

As she went past Parry Griffin's shop, Laura noted its advanced state of decay, and the filthy showrooms that were all but empty. It irked her to see it all. Now — if she could find a means of getting her hands on *that*! All was not lost yet — and there were still things to do. She would try *anything*. Why, the battle had only just begun!

Chapter Twenty-seven

'Sod off! D'you hear me, you buggers? Sod off and leave me be!' Lizzie Pendleton's high shrill voice carried from the roadside and into the room, where Laura was standing watching the proceedings. Lizzie Pendleton was being half-persuaded, half-propelled into the ambulance parked by the kerb outside her house, and she was loudly making her protests known to one and all. 'You've no right to take me from my own house!' She turned to stare at Remmie and Netti, who were approaching the ambulance, each of them carrying some personal possessions of the unwell Lizzie Pendleton. 'You! You and Laura! I never thought I'd live to see this day, Remmie Thorpe, when you turned a blind eye to such goings on! Or was it *you* who arranged it all, eh? Shoving a poor woman away in some awful infirmary! Well, you've not seen the last of me, I can promise you that.' She was still screaming abuse as the ambulance man closed the doors on her and his colleague.

He collected the clothes and packages from Remmie and Netti and said, 'Take no notice. All that shouting and threatening. Well, its mostly bluff and bravado. They're always the same, these old 'uns; don't take too kindly to leaving familiar surroundings.' He smiled at Netti, whose mouth was set in a grim line and whose thoughtful gaze was fixed onto the closed doors of the ambulance. 'You're not to worry yourself, Miss, she'll soon settle.' Glancing down at Lizzie's possessions which he had clutched in his arms, he added, 'These things'll help, familiar things and the like. So don't you worry none, eh?'

'I'm not worried.' Netti's voice was strangely quiet as she returned the man's concerned smile, before excusing herself and starting across the pavement to Remmie's house.

Laura couldn't hear what was being said by the small group gathered round the ambulance door, but she could still hear the echo of Lizzie Pendleton's last words, 'You've not seen the last of me.' Laura now murmured in reply, 'I'm sure we haven't, Lizzie Pendleton. Oh, I'm quite sure we haven't!'

Laura watched Netti as she approached the house. Behind her, the ambulance had moved slowly away down the road and Remmie had disappeared back up the path to Lizzie Pendleton's house, where Laura assumed he was making sure the house was secure. Following Netti's progress along the pavement then up the path to the front door, Laura thought how very pretty her sister looked. Netti had never been a girl for following the changes of fashion, and her individuality showed clearly in the long straight locks that hung down her back like a golden mantle and in the uncluttered style of her straight dark skirt and the clean simple lines of her pink short-sleeved blouse.

Laura had seen a growing difference between her and Netti, and she found more peace of mind in deliberately ignoring the obvious. As each day passed, Netti had matured more and more into the image of Katya Thorpe, and although Remmie never mentioned it, Laura had seen him gazing at Netti in unguarded moments, his eyes filled with an emotion she could not recognize, but which instilled in her a feeling of great sadness. She had long been of the opinion that she, Netti and Remmie had outgrown this house that still held the essence of Katya Thorpe and that seemed from time to time to bring out memories that were painful.

Laura resented Netti's dark quiet moods, for they widened the rift between her and her sister; although the distance between them was not of a measurable quality, and took nothing away from the deep love and devotion that Laura held for Netti and that she knew Netti felt for her. No, Laura secretly believed that Netti was one of those unique individuals remarkably talented and possessed of that artistic temperament which set her apart from others. Twice in these past weeks she had heard Netti at the piano and had been enthralled by her mastery of it — yet both times Netti had brought the melody to an end by crashing her fists down on the keyboard in great agitation, afterwards hurling herself from the room and out of the front door, to return some time later in a mood not easily recognized by Laura. And there had been the occasion when, going to Netti's room with the intention of consoling her, Laura had found several sheets of classical piano music strewn haphazardly across the floor, as though flung there in a fit of temper. Laura had thought of tackling Netti about it, but on reflection had thought it best ignored. It was probably only the temperament of a genius — and should it be more than that, well, Netti would always find her to be a sympathetic listener. Laura decided that for now, Netti wouldn't thank her for prying.

Laura pushed the nagging intrusion into her thoughts and hurried into the hallway where Netti was collecting her bag and music folder. Infusing a brightness into her smile that she did not feel, Laura said, 'Enjoy your concert, love. And don't give Lizzie Pendleton another thought. Promise?'

'It's not a *real* concert, Laura, just a piano recital by one of Miss Fordyke's old pupils who made it good.' Laughing softly, Netti stepped forward and embraced her sister. 'But I *will* enjoy it. And yes, I promise I won't give Lizzie Pendleton another thought.' Releasing herself from Laura, she added with a sly little smile, 'Hark at me! Some of *your* determination must have rubbed off on me, eh?'

Laura laughed out loud, retorting, 'Stuff and nonsense! You're stubborn enough for *both* of us when needs be.' She kissed her quickly on the cheeks and urged, 'You'd best get a move on, my girl, or they'll be waiting for you — and you'll have to face the wrath of the dreaded Miss Fordyke!'

Laura returned to the house and found Remmie seated at the kitchen table in a pensive mood. Thinking it wise to leave him to his quiet thoughts, she set about the washing-up and saw from the clock on the dresser that it was nearing five. With a long evening ahead, she mused.

'Laura. Come 'ere a minute, lass.'

Laura went to sit opposite him at the table. She said nothing, because although Remmie meant a great deal to her — and always would — she was still peeved and not yet able to fully forgive him for having dashed her plans for a business link with Weston and Favers. Yet although he had dashed her *immediate* plans, he had not dashed her hopes for the future. Yesterday morning she had posted a letter to Mr Craven, requesting confirmation of details regarding specific requirements on that vital first delivery. She knew exactly what was required but the letter was a skilful delaying tactic, and one which she knew would give her that extra time she so badly needed.

But Remmie was speaking, and as his words infiltrated her mood, they took on such significance that for the moment, everything else was unimportant. Her response was one of astonishment.

'You would *move* from here? You *really* would sell this house?' She never thought she would hear Remmie say such a thing.

For a while, Remmie did not answer but bowed his head. Then he pulled his thick frame up in the chair, looked into her face and said with conviction, 'It's time, lass. You'll find as you grow older that there's a time for everything. Well, it's time now to sell this 'ere house. When that Lizzie Pendleton took to banging on the wall in 'er vindictive hatred, well, it were like she'd wakened every ghost between us and the past. I'm thinkin' o' you, an' young Netti. I know you've mentioned us movin' from 'ere, an' I know it'll do none on us any good to pass that empty 'ouse next door, day in an' day out. What d'you say, lass?'

Laura grasped his fingers and squeezed them encouragingly. 'You *know* how I feel, Remmie. It's good for us to move, it is. Oh, and I'm so glad that you've decided.' He was right and she had been aware of it for a long time now. There *were* too many ghosts here, here and in Lizzie Pendleton's house, whether *she* was present or not.

'Can I leave it to you, then lass?' He seemed to sink before her eyes as he added, 'I'd rather you saw to all that business o' putting it on the market, people coming to look round, that sort o' thing.'

'Don't concern yourself with *any* of it, Remmie. I'll be glad to see to it. But where will we go? Have you somewhere in mind?'

For a while, Remmie appeared to be deep in thought. 'I'll not move away, not out of Blackburn and away from the shop. I'll not do that. Have *you* somewhere in mind, lass? Somewhere as Netti would like, somewhere as'd suit all three on us?'

Oh, had she somewhere in mind! Where else would she want to go, but out to the better part of town where the big nobs lived. She didn't hesitate in her reply. 'Cherry Tree, or Freckleton!'

Remmie did not show surprise at Laura's choice, for he had guessed what was in her heart. And hadn't he let the lass down badly when she'd come back from London? Oh, aye, and he'd been filled with shame ever since. He'd been secretly thankful when that business with Thackerey had all fallen through; but Laura had paid a higher price, and he felt the need now to make it up to her.

He laughed and shook his head. 'I *thought* you'd point us out in the direction o' them grand posh places, but to tell you the truth, Laura, I'm not rightly sure as me money'll stretch to such luxury.'

'What can you afford?'

'Well, I've reckoned on asking about eight hundred for this place, an' putting in another couple o' thousand. That's it! About three thousand all told. Now, see what you can do wi' that, eh?' He saw that Laura was about to speak and he added, 'Not a penny more, mind! I'm off to see Mitch; give 'im 'and with re-upholstering Taylor's chesterfield. It's fairly quiet Mondays, lass, an' you've a whack o' time owing you, so tek Monday off an' get on to it, eh?'

'Right.' Something to get her teeth into at long last. Laura's thoughts were running on ahead of her. If she had her way, it would be Freckleton, and wouldn't that be a move; Netti and Laura Blake, living in one of the grand houses out Freckleton way?

When Remmie called out from the hallway, 'If you're not in when I get home I'll see you in the morning,' Laura was so engrossed in her thoughts that she hardly remembered replying. And even as she heard him close the door, Laura's mind was alive with anticipation and excitement at Remmie's unexpected change of heart. And oh, she would make sure he never came to regret it. She knew *she* never would!

Chapter Twenty-eight

Laura put away the polishing rags and satisfied herself that the house was so spotless that she wouldn't mind the Queen herself coming to visit, then she looked out of the window and across the yard to the moors beyond. *There* was the real beauty of this place, she thought, the open moors and all their wildness. Wild beauty that came in many forms; richness in colour; or in the shape of dark intent like the one that had put her in the Infirmary! Oh, she wasn't fool enough to believe that the branches of a tree could be blown with such force as to knock her unconscious. Not in the modest wind that was blowing on that particular night. Oh no! She had thought long and hard about it ever since, and Laura had come to the conclusion that the wildness on *that* night had come in the shape of a demented creature, tormented by the devils that drove her; her own mother, Ruth Blake. The woman had gone now, and couldn't harm her again. Yet Laura cringed even now at the memory of Ruth Blake; almost as though sensing that even before the week was out, she would rise to darken Laura's life yet again.

Laura glanced at her watch. Netti and Remmie had been gone some forty-five minutes and it was now almost nine o'clock. Time for her to make the very best use of her Monday off, and to get this house placed, as well as to hunt for a new one.

It was a beautiful sunny day and Laura's equally sunny mood dictated that she should wear the pretty green paisley print dress with scooped neck and full swinging skirt. She had chosen not to wear her usual high-heeled sandals, in the event that in her search for a new home she would be called upon to do a lot of walking. Instead, she had donned a pair of dark green sturdier sandals with sensible heels. In passing, she reminded herself to take up Mitch's offer to teach her to drive.

Collecting her green leather handbag from the dresser, Laura made her way out into the hall. There, lying on the mat beneath the letter-box, was a small white envelope. She picked it up and would have left it on the telephone table in the usual way, but something familiar in the writing urged her to quickly open it.

As she scanned the words, her mouth opened in surprise and then closed to become tight-lipped in anger. It was from Jake Thackerey! Whoever would have credited him with the nerve to contact her again! Certainly not her; he was the last person she expected to hear from again. The blatant bloody cheek of the man! Laura read;

Darling Laura

It's taken me a while to put pen to paper; I'm so afraid of you rejecting me again. I don't blame you for not turning up at the airport. I guessed you had done it as a gesture, to pay me back for my behaviour. Now that you have, and in the process caused me a great deal of anguish, can we get together?

I do love you, and being tied in a hopeless marriage to Ria can never change my feelings for you. I have arranged the purchase of a flat in Leeds, where we can meet. It's convenient for both of us.

I'll be at the Lyton Hotel in Leeds on the 18th of August, less than a fortnight's time. Come to me there. *Please.*

Yours always, Jake.

Laura folded the letter and rammed it back into the envelope, bubbling with anger that surged through her. What on earth did he think she was, some kind of exchangeable merchandise! Did he believe she was devoid of any pride! She went back into the kitchen, where she withdrew a pad and pen from the dresser drawer and wrote,

To Ria Morgan,

As you can see from the letter enclosed, which I received this morning, it would take very little effort on my part to

332

deprive you of your husband. However, I have no wish to associate myself with Jake Thackerey in any way, and would therefore appreciate you putting a stop to his pestering of me.

Signed Laura Blake

She tucked the letter in beside that of Jake Thackerey and putting the whole lot in a new envelope, she addressed it to Ria Morgan at the gallery.

Twenty minutes later, Laura posted the letter on her way across town towards the new Land Agent office. She was in no doubt at all that her note to Ria Morgan and the letter she herself had received could infuriate Ria Morgan enough to carry out her threat and see Jake Thackerey behind bars after all. Laura hoped so, for he was despicable; a weak, worthless creature!

Laura went up to the Land Agent office, through the front door and found an elderly man at a desk, looking up at her. 'Good morning, how can I help you? You have a property to sell? Or are you looking to purchase one?'

'Both,' Laura answered, reaching into her handbag and taking out a piece of paper, which she placed on the desk before him. 'Here are the details of the property for sale.' She watched as he swiftly scanned the words. Then he looked up again, his hard-featured face softened by an admiring smile as he told her, 'This is certainly very detailed. However, we will need to visit the property.'

'Of course. Now, before we go any further, let me make it quite clear that we won't enter into price haggling on the sale of this particular house, you'll find it to be a large place, well-positioned and in excellent order.'

'Quite so, but it is the usual practice to add a few pounds to the asking price.'

Laura insisted otherwise, saying that the price asked was the price acceptable. On reflection, the man conceded. However, at Laura's interest in Freckleton property, he became adamant that the prices there were exorbitant. For the next hour, Laura and the agent browsed through property details, argued prices, held conversations with various people over the telephone, and drank endless cups of tea. At the end of it, Laura was exasperated that they had achieved nothing. The properties that had appealed to her were way out of Remmie's pocket, and though the agent assured her that a mortgage would be available, Laura instantly declined. That would be something Remmie would *never* entertain. Hadn't he always boasted that everything he owned was paid for on the nail?

Sifting through the last batch of Freckleton properties, Laura drew out a particular sheet to which her attention had been drawn. The details specified were her exact requirements; 'A grand old house of architectural interest, boasting nine rooms and having grounds extending to just over half an acre.' She knew of the house; it was the old nursing home just beyond Freckleton and on the way out to Lytham, no more than four or five miles from Blackburn town centre. *Nine* rooms! At first glance, it had seemed rather too grand and Laura wondered what Remmie's reaction would be to living in such a place. But then, she believed that people were only as grand as they let themselves be, and wouldn't they be the grand ones in a fine old place like that, eh?

Drawing in a sigh Laura laughed out loud and said, 'I'm almost afraid to ask, but what scandalous price are they asking for that?' She slid the sheet across to him. Seeing that she was referring to the Old Nursing Home, he removed the paper from the desk and put it away in his desk drawer. 'Ah, that was in there by mistake, I'm afraid. We've already had an offer on that one, and it's being considered by the Council. It's been going on for quite a time. Apparently the prospective purchaser has intent to use the property as a small select hotel, and the committee in charge of the sale are split in their views. Some of them object to the increased volume of transport that such an establishment would bring, and there is of course the argument that even under the description of 'small, select hotel', certain undesirable elements of society may be given admittance, or if refused, could cause disturbances that have not been seen in that particular area before. Of course, it's all under discussion at the moment, but I'm certain that it *will* be sold quite soon. According to our last report, the matter is all but resolved. It's simply the formalities now to be completed.'

Laura was intrigued, and it was with a sense of excitement

that she now asked, 'What *is* the asking price?'

Laura sensed his reluctance as he answered, 'Well, as it's been closed down for over two years now, it has fallen into disrepair. The grounds are completely overgrown and there's a great deal of work needed. All of this is generously reflected in the price; three and a half thousand.' He appeared decidedly uncomfortable, particularly when Laura declared, 'I'd like to see it.'

'It's all but sold, and as I said, it's in a state of disrepair.'

'Have contracts been drawn up and exchanged?'

'Drawn up yes, not yet exchanged.'

'Then it is *not* sold! And if it is not sold, then it's still on the market, and I, as a prospective purchaser, would like to see it, indeed I *insist* on seeing it!'

The agent fell back into his chair, his eyes on Laura's alert face, and between his appreciation of her astonishing beauty, her relentless drive and dynamic attitude, he regretted not having checked that particular batch of property details and not pushing the deal through more vigorously, in view of the fact that the Hampstead partnership, who had been valuable and lucrative clients of his for a very long time, had set their minds on a hotel on the site of that nursing home, and who were counting on *him* to push the deal through. But more than anything else he might regret at that moment, he regretted having opened up earlier than usual this Monday morning and having this indomitable woman walk into this particular office.

Within ten minutes, Laura was seated beside him in his little black Morris saloon, and after a further fifteen minutes of driving, they had pulled into the curving private drive that led to the old nursing home.

Laura loved the place at first sight. As they went up the drive, she could hear the birds singing in the chestnut trees, smell the scent of the rose bushes and enjoy the magnificent colours of many other proud wide-spreading trees and shrubs that swept away to both her left and right. The house itself was everything she had hoped; a fine proud old place of Regency architecture, tall marble fireplaces and high decorated ceilings, and rooms downstairs of immense proportion, light and spaciousness.

From the moment Laura left the car, mounted the wide

335

circular steps that led to the impressive deeply-panelled front door and then let herself into the spacious hall that boasted stately white columns and intricate mosaic floor, she made up her mind that here was where she wanted to live. Here and no place else!

Laura went from room to room, her enthusiasm causing her to almost run and make the man trying to keep up with her puff and pant in pursuit. The need for a considerable degree of renovating and repair was evident in the large areas of fallen ceiling and wall plaster, broken windows and rotting wood and various other obvious signs. But Laura was not deterred, because she was quick to realize that it was this very dilapidation that had reduced the price to within Remmie's capabilities. Of course, there would be money needed to carry out the repairs, but she thought that the actual labouring could be done by her, Mitch and Remmie. For a price like this, they could all of them give of their best.

Back at the office, she put in a firm offer of the asking price, together with the assurance that the premises would be used for the sole purpose of domestic residence. These points she directed to be put in writing and despatched at once to the owners.

When Laura stepped back out into the brilliance of a wonderful August day, she felt almost light-headed, certain in the exhilarating knowledge that this day had brought a marvellous opportunity and that the lovely old nursing home was as good as theirs. She could not however, avoid feeling a degree of apprehension as far as Remmie's reaction was concerned. A spacious nine-roomed residence of architectural interest and extensive grounds was not exactly what he'd anticipated when he had sent her out that morning. It was hardly the sort of place in which either he or his furniture would look comfortable. Laura knew that well enough; but she also knew that beneath that staid old-fashioned attitude of his, there still remained a sharp business sense. She was counting on Remmie being astute enough at least to recognize and appreciate the first-class investment that such a move afforded. She also had a sneaking instinct that the amazingly low asking price, even in view of the deterioration of the property, had been artificially manufactured by the agent and his possible inside contacts, to benefit a person of much greater consequence than her. Well, they would now discover that they were not about to have it all their own way!

Eager though Laura was to tell Remmie the news, she did not go towards the shop, but lost no time in returning home. There, she penned a long informative letter to the Council. She claimed to be the spokesman representing the residents in close proximity to the old nursing home. She described the anger and militant attitude of these same residents at the proposed plans to allow the nursing home to become a public hotel, the development of which would bring its own undesirable elements. She also pointed out that the matter would not be allowed to end with this letter, which they were to look upon as a forerunner to further and more constructive action. Lastly, she went on at great lengths about the forthcoming elections and the need of people to ensure that their interests were being well looked after; an end to which their votes would be usefully employed. She simply signed the letter, 'Elected spokesman', gave no specific address, and went straight down the road to the corner postbox, where she posted the letter to catch the afternoon post. She calculated that if all went well, both this letter and her offer should arrive at the Council's office together.

Taking the path onto the moors, Laura laughed softly to herself. That should give them something to think about, she mused, and with a bit of luck, should swing the whole thing in her favour. Oh, she felt good! It would be a marvellous thing to live in a grand old house like that, to have room to move, and to be referred to as, 'the people who bought that lovely old nursing home'.

The sudden intrusion of Mitch into her thoughts caused a momentary darkening of mood. He would either call her a snob, or he would receive the news with that infuriating silence that always made her feel guilty.

Oh, if only Mitch would accept her just as she was. If only he could appreciate the need in her to strive ever upwards away from the chaos beneath. But they were different, she and Mitch, and he had already found his contentment.

All the same, there was a part of her that would have liked his approval, for she couldn't deny the deep regard she had for his opinions.

337

Chapter Twenty-nine

The following morning Laura was filled with such energy and enthusiasm that she could only expend it by clearing every single item out of the window with the intention of cleaning and polishing them and afterwards completely re-arranging the entire window display.

Remmie had received the news far better than she could ever have hoped. At first, when she'd told him that on his behalf she had put in an offer for the old nursing home, his eyes had virtually popped from their sockets and he had nearly choked on the spare rib he was chewing. But before he could recover, Laura had swiftly delivered all the advantageous details, how it was a dream of a place and how she knew that if anybody could bring it back to its former glory, it would be him! That sly piece of flattery had brought an embarrassed smile to his face and made Netti snigger surreptitiously, and when Laura pointed out that his investment of three and a half thousand, plus renovation costs, would instantly double on completion of the work, he had stroked his chin and fallen into a silence, in which Laura could almost *hear* him thinking.

Finally, he had stood up, wiped his mouth with the back of his hand and declared swiftly, 'What does it matter *where* we live, eh?' Then he opened his arms to receive Netti in one and Laura in the other. 'So long as we're all together! And if we're to live in style, well, why not? Why not, eh?'

After that, there was excited discussion about their course of action and plans of attack regarding the jobs that needed doing. It was as Laura had hoped. Both Remmie and Netti, who seemed more happy for Laura's sake, offered their services wherever necessary. She believed that Mitch would do the same.

Mitch had confirmed her belief not ten minutes ago when

Remmie had imparted the news to him. Now he had come back into the shop after seeing Remmie off with a Queen Anne bureau, waited for by Squire Vernon of Salmesbury Bottoms.

'I never thought I'd live to see the day when Remmie Thorpe would sell that house of his.' Mitch came to stand by the window, his strong green eyes following Laura's every move.

'To be honest, Mitch, neither did I. But I feel it's for the best, don't you?'

'Let's hope so.' As Laura returned to busy herself amongst the items which she had already moved from the shop-window, Mitch watched her with eyes that brimmed with love for her, and with a heart which prayed that his Laura, the gentle sensitive creature he had grown up with, was not lost to him forever.

Mitch firmly believed that she was not, and he knew that beneath that sharp business exterior of hers, there still remained an essence, an intangible and intricate quality that was his Laura and that nothing could destroy; not hardship or poverty, not suffering or cruelty, not the blind ambition that drove her nor the money and power she craved. He believed with all his heart that this destructive fire raging within her would eventually burn itself out. And when it did, he prayed that it would be *him* to whom she would turn.

She turned to him now, her dark eyes glowing, her lovely face wreathed in that familiar smile that so haunted him, and in a voice that was soft as the breeze, she said, 'You *do* think it's good to make a fresh start, don't you, Mitch. *You* know the way he's been brooding over Katya.'

Mitch made no immediate move. Instead, he looked down at her face, his hungry eyes moving over her every feature; that burnished gold hair that was as fiery and wild as Laura herself could be; the smooth creamy texture of her skin that shaped her face into a perfect heart; the full plump mouth that was sensual and inviting yet forbidden to him. And those vivacious dark eyes that were capable of tenderness and love, but were all too often infused with the fire of ambition. He loved this woman, this rebel, with such fierceness that if he had been a lesser man, he might have forcibly taken her, quenched his thirst of her taunting beauty. He could understand now how a man could be driven to such a thing as Laura had been made to suffer; understand it yes, but forgive it? Never! And he was not such a lesser man. The quality of his love was born of endurance. And while there was hope, even the *smallest* hope that she would return his love, then he could be patient.

Laura had waited for his response and she looked hard at him, but now, beneath his desirous expression, she dropped her eyes. And at once, Mitch turned sharply away and went across the shop and out to the workroom, where he pulled on his overalls and lost his frustrations in the demands of his work. Laura stood for a while looking after him and for a reason she couldn't fathom, her heart, beating fiercely within her chest, seemed suddenly like a lead weight that rose to fill her throat and threaten to choke her.

Quickly now, before the day got busy and produced a stream of shoppers, she deliberately concentrated once more on the task of cleaning out the window, before re-arranging a more attractive display. Twice she went outside, to stand well back on the pavement and pass a critical eye over the mounting display, examining it first from one angle and then from the other. Each time she did so, Laura was completely unaware of the man who had lumbered along the street towards her, and whose drunken senses had caused him to stagger heavily against the wall, where he had stayed to watch her every move.

When Laura went back inside, satisfied that she could complete the display without further reference, Parry Griffin threw himself into as near an upright stance as he could manage, and on slow cumbersome footsteps, he moved towards the door through which Laura had just disappeared.

On hearing the door bell jangle, Laura hurried from the back store room where she had gone to replace her box of polishing rags and cleaning fluids.

'Good morning, Miss high an' bloody mighty.' Parry Griffin was leaning over the counter, his pink bulbous eyes leering at her. Laura was sickened at the sight, all the hatred and disgust she felt for this basest of creatures instantly rising to tremble in her icy voice. 'Get out! Out of this shop!'

'Oh! So it's *your* shop is it? Well now, I was under the impression as it belonged to Remmie Thorpe.' For an instant, he stopped and stared at her, seeming to be struck by her appearance. Then in a low voice that was close to tears, he murmured, 'It's not Ruth,' and lifting his head, he asked again, this time in a louder tone, 'It's *not* Ruth, is it, eh? It's 'er bloody ghost! Oh, I know you, Laura Blake. You don't like me, do you? Never 'ave liked me.' He was blubbering now.

The awful sight of him and the memory of how he had defiled her strengthened Laura's resolve to seek out revenge, to make him pay, and pay dearly. Summoning all of her self-control not to strike him with the nearest heavy object, she ordered him, 'I've told you to get out of here, Parry Griffin! And you'd better do it. Now! If you don't want to face the consequences.'

'Consequences? What bloody consequences might they be, eh? Now you look 'ere, it's Remmie as I've come to see, an' I'll not go till I've seen 'im! Remmie's the only one as'll 'elp me. An' I need some money, need it bad. Where is 'e? Fetch Remmie out 'ere!'

'He's not here! And if he *was*, you'd get no money from him, I can promise you that.' Her words rang out loud and clear, and their meaning was unmistakeable to the desperate man who heard them. Driven beyond reason, he sprang at Laura's throat, dragging her to the end of the counter where he pulled her to him, his bulging face red with rage and almost touching hers, his thick shapeless mouth open and dribbling saliva.

Laura felt the air being squeezed from her shrinking lungs and the knot that was her stomach filling to overflow. His mouth was on hers, wiping itself along her lips, across her face and down her neck. And his voice came to her in ever-darkening waves. ''Elp me, Ruth. For God's sake, what 'ave I done.' He was moaning now, his words a babble of confusion issued from a drunken incoherent mind. 'I wouldn't 'ave tekken Laura, it's *you* I wanted. I'm in trouble, money . . . what am I to do?' The tears were flowing fast down his face and in the instant that he was hopelessly overcome by his emotion, his fingers loosened their grip on Laura's throat. In that instant, Laura jerked herself from his reach, her chest heaving and contracting as she gasped air into her lungs. Blind to everything now and bereft of all caution, she grasped the heavy glass door-stopper from the counter and would have brought it down again and again on Parry Griffin's bowed

341

head. But as she drew her arm back, she felt the stopper being lifted from her hand and when she turned, her stark white face marked by tears spilt without her knowledge, it was to look into Mitch's face. There was such deep anguish and fury in his expression that Laura hardly recognized him.

Parry Griffin looked up, and when he saw Mitch coming quickly towards him, he drew himself up to his full height, and lurched forward, his thick fists doubled and lashing out in the direction of Mitch. In a moment, the fists were stilled as Mitch heaved Parry Griffin from the floor. Then without speaking a word, he lunged towards the door with his struggling burden, and manoeuvering the door open wide enough to take Parry Griffin's bulk, he hoisted him through it and he landed with a heavy thud on the pavement outside. Before closing the door, he issued a warning, delivered in such a way that the cowering man could not mistake its implications. 'If there's still some sense in that drink addled brain o' yourn, you'll not think to bother Laura again.'

Mitch came back to stand before Laura, his anxious eyes searching her still white face. He would have gathered her into his arms and poured out his need for her; a need that grew stronger with Laura's resistance. He would have rained comfort and kisses on her and held her close enough for their hearts to beat as one; but a streak of defiance in Laura's burning eyes told him that such a move on his part would not be welcomed. When he softly asked, 'Alright are you? He'll not be foolish enough to trouble you again.' Laura simply answered 'Yes. I'm alright, and thank you Mitch. I wanted to kill him.' Mitch recognized that particular tone in her voice, and he knew that she had gone into her own private world. A world that as yet, he had no part in.

Laura felt his hand running down the length of her hair. She made no move at the touch of his mouth on her forehead. When he walked away, she lifted her fingers to caress the spot that he had kissed. Then in a quick shivering movement, she hurried away to the back store room to wash her face, and wipe away the vileness of Parry Griffin's mouth on hers.

It was twelve o'clock when Remmie returned. The first Laura saw of him was when he came storming through from the back yard, where she guessed Mitch must have been wait-

342

ing for him. It was obvious from the expression of disgust on his usually quiet features that Remmie knew what had taken place, and it was equally obvious that he was bent on going after Parry Griffin with some degree of violence.

Laura did not want a confrontation to take place between Remmie and his vile brother-in-law for two reasons; one was fear that in the low mindless state that Parry Griffin had sunk to, there was a real possibility that he could harm Remmie. And secondly, since Mitch's ejection of Parry Griffin and the hurried departure of that obnoxious creature, Laura had concentrated on one particular matter; that of speeding Parry Griffin's descent into the gutter, and in doing so, speeding her own ascent into being a woman of property. The plan had germinated in the seething heat of her anger, an ungainly plan that blindly sought for revenge. Then as her anger gave way to cool objective calculation, she at once recognized the flaws in her plan, quickly eliminated them and finally the whole thing triumphantly emerged as a devious master scheme, which her instincts told her would bring about the fulfillment of a long awaited happening. At last, she could see the means by which her old enemies could be brought to their knees! And it would not serve her purpose to have Remmie and Parry Griffin locked in a situation that could end up with one of them being badly hurt, or worse still arrested.

It was with this in mind that Laura ran across the shop to grip hold of Remmie's coat sleeve and to tell him firmly, 'No Remmie. I'll not have you soiling your hands on him.' When it seemed as though Remmie might not heed her remarks, she rushed before him to stand by the door and block his way. 'Let it be, Remmie, please. I'm not harmed, and Mitch dealt with him. Let it be now, he'll not be back.'

'The bastard! I'll tear 'im limb from limb if 'e ever 'arms you.'

'He *won't!*' She sensed that Remmie's abhorrence of violence was winning him over, and she moved towards him and said quietly, 'He won't harm me. He's to be pitied really, and not worth getting yourself riled up about.' She linked her arm through his and would have drawn him away saying persuasively, 'Come on, I'll make you a fresh brew, eh?' But just at that precise moment, a burly man entered the shop and said,

'Me bloody wagon's broke down. I've managed to push it aways, but I could do with another pair o' hands to get it off the road 'an into yon sidin' agin the market.'

'Aye.' Remmie was at once alert and sympathetic. 'I'll fetch Mitch.'

Laura watched the three of them go off down the street to where the brown-coloured wagon was straddling the narrow road, and she breathed a sigh of relief. He wouldn't go after Parry Griffin now. But *she* would! Oh yes indeed, and if she went about it in the right way, he wouldn't even know what had hit him; until it was too late!

Now that Laura had devised the plan that would deprive her old enemy of all that he held dear, she was impatient to put it into motion. Oddly enough and fortuitously for her plans, there were few customers that day and when she had finished all the usual routine tasks at the shop, Laura approached Remmie, who on the surface appeared to have forgotten the business with Parry Griffin, though Laura suspected he was still quietly fuming about it, and asked him whether he would miss her for the last hour.

'No, go on lass, want to do a bit o' woman's shoppin', eh?' He smiled. 'Get yoursel' back 'ere by five-thirty mind. We've to drop that set o' chairs off at Yeldon 'ouse out Cherry Tree way.'

'I'll be back,' she promised, grabbing her bag and throwing her lemon cardigan loosely over her shoulders, then quickly leaving in case either Remmie or Mitch should find some reason to keep her.

As she made her way towards the town centre and the office of Mr Drew the solicitor, Laura was grateful for the fact that when she'd telephoned him earlier, he had agreed to see her almost straightaway. It was her assurance that it was merely a matter of consultation and should not take up more than ten minutes of his time that had finally persuaded him. He had protested at first that she would need to make an appointment for another day as he was a very busy man. Laura knew that to be true; he was the best there was, and it was for that reason alone that she had chosen him.

Because the shop had been surprisingly quiet, Remmie had donned his overalls and had gone to assist Mitch in the workshop. It had been then that Laura had telephoned the solicitor, and immediately afterwards had drawn up a letter. This letter, which was to be the subject of her talk with Mr Drew, was in her handbag. Laura had couched it in terms that were as formal and straightforward as possible. She wanted there to be no misunderstanding of its meaning; and most of all, she required that there could be no recourse as to the legal terms of its demands. It had to be water-tight and irreversible in every way.

It was a mere ten minutes walk at a brisk pace to Mr Drew's office, which was situated along the row of older offices adjacent to the Town Hall. As soon as Laura had announced herself to the reception clerk, she was whisked away up a narrow flight of steps and into the somewhat pretentious and heavily furnished office of Mr Drew.

After a brief introductory exchange during which Laura was irritated by the fact that her purposeful gaze was completely unable to draw any sort of real communication from the tiny bespectacled man, he gestured for her to sit, saying sharply, 'Ten minutes, you said Miss Blake. So how can I be of assistance?' Still he did not lift his eyes to look at her. Instead, he focused on her handbag, his eyes following the quick movement of her hands as she withdrew the letter. She then unfolded it and offered it to him, saying, 'I want to know whether this letter would stand up in court if needs be. Is there any way, any way at all, in which the debtor could avoid having to comply with the terms laid out?'

Laura watched as the thin little man closely scrutinized the letter in his hands. His narrow shrew features adopted a multitude of expressions as he considered the words over and over again.

In the quietness of her mind, Laura read them with him, for she knew every word by heart. At the top of the letter, she had set out Parry Griffin's name and address, stating that he was the debtor. Beside his details, she had given her own, stating that she was the creditor. The wording of the agreement read:

I, Parry Griffin, accept a loan of one thousand pounds from Laura Blake. I have given a personal guarantee against the loan; this to consist unreservedly of my shop in Blackburn

345

(together with all fixtures, fittings and stock) and my private house (to be offered with vacant possession).

The total ownership of the above properties will pass to Laura Blake, in the event that I cannot repay the total loan of one thousand pounds on or before a date which shall be three months from my receipt of the money.

If however, I am able to repay the loan in full, there will be no penalty incurred, and the house and shop will remain my property.

Still with his eyes fixed on the letter in his hands, Mr Drew asked, 'Have you spoken to this Mr Griffin regarding the contents of the agreement?'

'Not yet.'

'Is it likely that he will agree to such a proposition? Risking both his house and his shop?'

'Quite likely.'

'I wonder the man doesn't go to a *bank*. After all, with such security, they would hardly turn him down.'

'He doesn't trust banks, or officials of any sort.'

'And he trusts you?'

'That remains to be seen; but yes, I think he will trust me to be lenient should he fail to repay the loan.'

'And will you be?'

'No.'

For the first time, Mr Drew lifted his eyes to look at her. What he saw was a young woman of striking beauty, but with a steel glint in her eyes that offered no quarter. For a brief moment, he studied her face with the same thoroughness that he had employed examining the agreement. Then looking away once more, he asked, 'Is it possible that Mr Griffin will be able to repay the money within three months?'

'Yes. He's just as likely to have double that in one day, as he is to be broke the next.'

'So he's a gambling man?'

Laura was beginning to tire of the questions which she saw as being hostile to her purpose. Drawing her back up into a stiff posture, she retorted, 'Mr Drew, all I require from you is an assurance that this document and the terms stated will be binding on Mr Griffin should the need arise. And as you can

346

see, I am prepared to sacrifice three months interest on my savings in order to help this man, my uncle, out of his present predicament. I do *not* intend either, to charge him any interest on the loan.'

'Ah! So Mr Griffin is a relative?'

'That's right.' Laura had deduced that such a snippet of information might mellow his attitude, and she had been right. For now, his manner became more friendly and less inquiring, as he informed her, 'I shall of course need the deeds to the properties, if I am to act on your behalf in this matter. They must be deposited as security against the loan, but will of course be returned to Mr Griffin as and when he pays the sum owing.'

'Three months from the day he collects the thousand pounds! There will be *no* extension on that.'

'Of course, three months. I will also need to see Mr Griffin, to explain the terms of the loan and to witness his acceptance of them. He must be fully aware of what is involved.'

Laura rose and straightening the cardigan which had slipped from her shoulders, she asked, 'Is there any reason why I can't just present that letter to him, and acquire his signature? Is it really necessary for him to come here, to deposit his deeds?' The suggestion had worried her. She wasn't certain whether Parry Griffin would put himself through such an ordeal, for it was true that he had an intense dislike and suspicion of anyone in authority, even a solicitor.

'If you require, as you say, for the agreement to stand up in court, then the whole procedure needs to be conducted in a legal manner. It saves unnecessary battles and so on. But of course, your uncle will probably *not* find himself in such a situation, I'm sure?'

'Let's hope not,' lied Laura, adding, 'We'll do it *your* way then. I want the least possible opposition to my claiming rights to the property, should it prove necessary. And the agreement I have drawn up, will it suffice?'

'You do appear to have been extremely thorough. However, there are one or two additional pieces of information, which no doubt your uncle will provide. Have you any idea when he's likely to come in?'

That was a question, thought Laura, a question indeed, and

she could think of no answer that would prove satisfactory, so she said, 'All I can tell you is, if he should suddenly turn up on your doorstep, drunk or sober, *please* don't turn him away. He is *not* likely to make an appointment beforehand, I warn you.'

'I understand. But *you* must also understand that he must be *sober* when he puts his hand to this agreement.'

Laura was beginning to wish that she had never consulted this person. He was complicating what she had hoped would be a relatively straightforward matter. But if it was to be done, then it was best to do it right. Even if Molly Griffin didn't launch herself into full scale battle to stop Laura from collecting her dues, there was always Pearce. Pearce Griffin was no pushover, and although it appeared at the present time that he'd washed his hands of his father, there was no guarantee that he wouldn't be up in arms and out for blood, once he knew what Laura was up to. Yes, she'd do it properly and make quite sure that when the time came, the full weight of the law would be on *her* side.

A few moments later, she had left the solicitor's office, her fertile mind already setting up the next move in her merciless assault on Parry Griffin. She was to lodge one thousand pounds with Mr Drew. Then, somehow, she had to persuade Parry Griffin to go and collect the money from Mr Drew in return for his signature.

As she swung her way back to the shop, the warmth of the afternoon sun made the world a brighter place, and not for one moment did Laura doubt that soon, quite soon, Parry Griffin's shop and his house would be hers. She felt it in her bones, as Mabel used to say, and she could taste the bitter-sweetness of revenge and smell the success that would be hers.

Parry Griffin was a base person, a beer-swill who had used her like so much trash, who had impregnated her and left her with a child who was better off never knowing who his father was. That much at least, she would do for Tom.

In his act of debauchery on her, Parry Griffin had impregnated Laura in a way that he had not stopped to consider. He had instilled in her the deepest of hatred and a driving desire for revenge. And now, it was her turn to triumph, for time and fortune had brought about a new situation, where *he* would be the victim and Laura the aggressor.

Chapter Thirty

'By! That's a glorious morning.' Remmie looked at Laura, who was seated beside him, and slowed the car to a halt where the drive from the old nursing home joined with the road. He looked back through the rear window and beyond towards the grand but neglected building. 'You know, Laura, I'm never one for fancy things, but there's some'at about that place as fair draws a body to it.'

'I know just what you mean.' Laura twisted herself round to follow his gaze. Even though the big house was empty and had been for a long time, there was something still alive within its walls, an exuding warmth, love even and Laura wondered whether it was a legacy of all the care that had been given to its former residents, the old and privileged who had been fortunate enough to live there; and maybe even to die there.

Remmie resumed his driving position, then he rammed in the gear stick to engage bottom gear and amidst the ensuing roar, drove out onto the road, where he headed the car in the direction of Pleasington and the late Mrs Saviour's cottage. Keeping his eyes alert to the road in front, he asked Laura, 'Got the keys to the cottage, 'ave you, lass?'

Laura drew a bunch of keys from her pocket, holding them up for Remmie to see. 'Yes, I've got the keys. So stop fretting.' She laughed softly.'You must have asked that at least a dozen times since we dropped Netti off at Miss Fordyke's.'

'Aye, well, it's allus best to mek sure. By the way, what's gotten into Netti lately? She's never a kind word to say of yon Miss Fordyke; seems she's tekken a sharp dislike to the woman.'

Laura had noticed that herself of late, and she could only think it was Netti and *not* Miss Fordyke. The level of study required for the final exams had intensified, and if Netti was to do well and move on, then she would just have to buckle under. There was no room for halfway measures, and Laura suspected that the woman had come down hard on Netti since she herself had intervened. Well, that was alright, Netti could cope quite well with any demands made on her musical ability, of that Laura was confident, and it showed in the firmness of her voice as she told Remmie, 'No, Netti hasn't taken a dislike to Miss Fordyke, it's just that she's having to work harder lately. I expect she's feeling worn, edgy, that's all.'

Remmie fell silent for a while, lost in his own interpretation of what was ailing Netti, and his conclusion did not match Laura's explanation. When he spoke again, it was to change the subject. 'According to Mrs Saviour's daughter, there are a lot of genuine antiques in her mother's cottage, aye, an' a lot o' rubbish I'll be bound!'

'Maybe.' In Laura's mind there appeared a picture of the sad young woman who had come to the shop. 'But we must be careful to offer fair prices. That poor woman looked devastated by her mother's sudden death. And on top of that, being turned out of her cottage!'

Remmie didn't answer, other than to utter a supportive grunt.

'Remmie.' Laura's quick mind had moved on to a matter close to her heart. She still hadn't heard from the Land Agent regarding the offer she had made on Remmie's behalf for the old nursing home. 'I think I'll go along and see the Land Agent this afternoon, find out what's happening about the offer we've put in.'

'It's only Thursday, lass! The poor chap'll not 'ave 'ad time to get a reply yet. An' *we've* not sold *our* place yet. We don't want to get caught the wrong way up. We need a firm buyer ourselves, afore we can put pen to paper.'

'Oh, I think you'll find that couple who came last night were well pleased. I'm sure they'll buy from you.'

'Think so, do you? Well, you're never far wrong, but leave it till Monday, eh? Things'll more than likely all be sorted out one way or another by then.'

Laura knew he was right. She was too impatient, that was her trouble. 'Alright,' she agreed, 'I'll go and see him on Monday.'

Remmie appeared satisfied at that, as he smiled and concentrated on the road.

Laura relaxed too, taking pleasure in the changing scenery. They were in the heart of the country now and close to the open spaces of Pleasington. The main road had given way to narrow picturesque lanes that meandered first between banks strewn with the colour and variety of wild flowers; and then between flat open fields whose boundaries were lumpy stone walls that looked more attractive for their higgledy-piggledy construction.

Laura delighted in everything about the countryside; the grass that was brown from lack of rain; the breezes that blew unfettered by buildings and that could whisper upon an upturned face with the gentleness of a kiss, or whip themselves into a storm that couldn't be tamed, and raged and whistled until its strength had gone. Laura had always felt close to nature. It was proud and magnificent, even more so when untouched by civilization. There was an essence of these qualities in the old nursing home, in spite of the fact that for as long as she could remember, it had been a refuge for the old and infirm. She hoped, oh how she hoped that the Land Agent would come back with instructions from the owners that it should be sold to Remmie.

Settling back in her seat, Laura closed her eyes and allowed her thoughts to drift. White walls she would have, and deep burgundy curtains of the best velvet. In that splendid vast hall would hang a magnificent crystal chandelier, and along the wall that snaked upwards with the line of the grand stairway would be displayed the most exquisite oil paintings and watercolours. Oh, what plans she had! And it was all but in her grasp.

A particular anxiety that had played on her mind these last few days had been that of finding a way to keeping Weston and Favers in tow. At the moment delivery of a secretaire to them was an impossibility; at least of the quality they had specified. And while she was not about to admit defeat and lose that vital link she had created, Laura was in desperate need of time, time to locate someone of Mitch's capabilities, for she knew that the chances of Mitch himself building the secretaire were slim indeed. He was Remmie's man, and first and foremost his

351

loyalties were firmly rooted in Remmie's shop. And on this particular issue, it was as though the two of them, Mitch and Remmie, had ganged up on her. Her problem, however, had ceased to be a problem, at least for the time being, because this very morning she had received a letter from Mr Craven. In it, he had requested her forgiveness, saying that because of refurbishment of the entire showroom area, together with the outer shop front, he would not be able to take delivery of the said item of furniture yet. He had further requested that he be allowed to contact Laura on completion of the work, which he anticipated to take somewhere in the region of two months, with a view to arranging a new delivery date. Laura had replied by return of post, sympathizing with the circumstances that appeared to be causing him such inconvenience, and adding that she would of course comply with his request and delay delivery.

'Are you sure you'll be alright in that shop tonight, lass?' Remmie's voice infiltrated Laura's pondering, 'I'll not be back from yon pub till at least 'alf past eleven. Whatever I let mesel' get talked into that blessed domino competition for, I'll never know! I'm not a man for the pubs, and never 'ave been.'

'Of course I'll be alright.' Laura knew that Remmie was casting his mind back to Parry Griffin, and she dare not contemplate what his reaction might be if he knew the real reason behind her decision to stay late and empty out all the stock cupboards.

'Mitch won't be there either. 'Im an' Sally, they're tekkin young Tom to the pictures. According to Mitch, the lad's been in trouble at school; got a right quick dirty temper, so they say. Funny though, I can't recollect any o' Mabel Fletcher's brood being other than real nice little people. Still, we can't all be alike I suppose.'

Laura was glad that Tom had found a friend in Mitch. He would be an excellent influence on the boy. Yet Laura wasn't fooling herself that Sally came after Mitch solely for the boy's sake. Oh no, Sally was in love. Laura had seen it way back, and everything that Sally had done since only confirmed that she was desperately in love with Mitch.

Laura closed her mind to whether Mitch might feel a measure of love for Sally. She noticed the sign up ahead that indicated the turn to Pleasington, and sitting up in her seat, she kept a sharp look out for the back lane that Mrs Saviour's daughter had described. In answer to Remmie's concern about her being left alone in the shop until he collected her, she replied in a mock chiding manner which indicated that the subject was now closed, 'I'll hear no more if you please about me being late in the shop. There's a great deal of work to be done that I can't find time for during the day. It'll be done tonight, so there's an end to it!'

Remmie burst into great gusts of laughter that took Laura by surprise. And when he retorted, 'Well, if *I* were a bad 'un lookin' for some poor 'elpless lass to pick on, it's a fact I'd give you a wide berth! You've as fiery a temper as'd send anything scooting on its way, 'ooligan an' ghosts alike, poor sods. Aye, 'appen you're safe enough.' Laura's laughter fused with his, and when Remmie brought the car to a halt outside a tumble-down cottage, it was some time before he had composed himself enough to approach what was after all, a serious matter.

Laura never enjoyed rummaging in what had been somebody's treasured belongings. It always seemed like an act of sacrilege to her somehow. But today, with the trilling of birds filling the hedges and the sun lighting the sky to azure blue, and with Remmie's laughter still ringing in her ears, she felt a degree of contentment in her heart that she'd not felt for a long time.

Remmie saw her merriment, and he was pleased. God knows he'd spent many a sleepless night worrying about this lass by his side. She'd grown difficult to fathom, and she'd always been one for keeping her troubles to herself. There were women in this world he knew who seemed to draw tragedy in spite of themselves. Laura was such a woman. But by God, she was strong-willed, stronger of mind than any man he'd ever known, and where her loved ones were concerned, she was a fearful protector. And yet Remmie had come to the conclusion, that in spite of Laura's quick perception and fierce devotion to Netti, she appeared to be unusually blind to the girl's growing discontentment. He'd mentioned it, both to Laura *and* Netti, and they each in turn had scoffed at his fears.

Remmie alighted from the car and when he brought his

straying thoughts to order he saw that Laura was watching him. She smiled and asked quietly, 'Penny for them?'

'Worth more than that!' Remmie jokingly replied. He looked at her lovely face and as always he was reminded of his sister, Ruth. But this young woman standing before him now, astonishing in her beauty, was nothing like Ruth. His sister had always been weak in character and immoral with her men. Laura was neither. It bothered him that the only passion men seemed to stir in her was mistrust, or even hatred. There seemed to be an unnatural element in Laura's relationships with men, an observation that disturbed him more than he could ever bring himself to admit. There was Mitch for instance, a grand upstanding fellow who idolized her. She had never given anything in return and yet, Remmie sensed that in her heart Laura loved Mitch every bit as much as he worshipped her. It were a strange set o' circumstances an' it were all way beyond his understanding. Then there was that Thackerey person, weak and deceitful, a man that he himself wouldn't give the time of day to normally, but it seemed that Thackerey's quick understanding of business and his acquired position had rendered Laura insensitive to the poorer facets of the man's character. Well, it was a fact that he'd been more than pleased when *that* particular development had been aborted, for whatever reason! There was no doubt of it; Laura was a woman unto herself. Why, she could have taken any one of a dozen or more lads who'd panted after her. But she'd wanted none of them, rejected them as if they were the devil himself! Still, Laura would no doubt confide in him should she feel the need to. She must know what she was about; Laura was nobody's fool and that was a fact. All the same though, it did seem unfair that if there was to be a measure of heartbreak dished out, more often than not it was Laura who was on the receiving end.

Laura put her arm around Remmie's thick waist, and pulling him forward, she said, 'Come on then, let's away inside and see what treasures we can find.' Remmie's deep thinking moods always made her feel uncomfortable, and when he put his arm about her shoulders in a fierce hug, saying, 'You're all the treasure I want, lass, you an' Netti!' she recalled how deeply resentful she had felt towards him when he'd flatly

354

refused to expand the business any further. In a rush of shame, she reached up to kiss him. 'You're a good sort, Remmie,' she said, her heart warmed by the strength of his love, 'and I owe you so much, we both do.' It was so very true, and she promised herself that she would not be so quick to forget it in future — whatever the future might bring.

Chapter Thirty-one

'What's wrong, Laura?'Mitch had stopped on his way through the shop, and looked at her quizzically. When she didn't answer, he came to stand directly before her, so near that when Laura lifted her head, she found herself having to stretch her neck backwards in order to meet the scrutinizing look which he was giving her, and which immediately put her on the defence. 'Wrong? There's nothing wrong. Why do you ask that?'

'Just a feeling. Ever since you and Remmie got back from that cottage this afternoon, you've seemed, well, miles away, as though something was troubling you. Is there?'

Mitch made no move away from Laura, and with her back tight against the counter, she was unable to do anything other than to defend herself against the close questioning look with an equally close look of defiance.

'You're imagining things, Mitch. I've just been trying to work out the best way to go about these cupboards, stacked ceiling high they are, and most of it's rubbish.' How perceptive he was, she thought, and how attractive he looked in that light grey jacket that hung squarely on his broad shoulders, and the darker trousers that fitted perfectly right down to the turn-up over his highly polished black shoes. He smelled nice too, a sort of rugged earthy smell that reminded her of the moors.

Mitch seemed to catch the mood of her thoughts, and Laura watched the quick concern in those sharp eyes give way to a deeper, more meaningful expression. He bent his head towards her, inclining it to one side, his eyes softer now and caressing hers. She could taste the dryness of his breath as it mingled with her own, and almost involuntarily, her mouth moved to receive his kiss. Suddenly, she was speaking in a small voice that she hardly recognized. 'You'd better go, you don't want to keep Sally waiting.' Laura had meant her words to be delivered kindly; but there it was again, that sharp defensive attitude that only Mitch and Mitch alone could create in her. It was as though her voice had struck him with the force of a whip for he quickly straightened up and his eyes harder now, he said quietly, 'No, I wouldn't want to keep Sally waiting!' Then he was gone, and Laura was left still trembling from his nearness, the pride in her heart and the thought of Sally like a knife turning.

For the next few hours, Laura worked like a demon possessed. She emptied out all the cupboards, catalogued their contents and discarded any useless items. Then just as carefully, she returned the sound articles back into the cupboards, all properly cleaned and labelled.

She took her mackintosh from the back store room door, and put it on together with the headscarf that would afford her at least a degree of anonymity. It was dark as she let herself out onto the street, quietly closing the door behind her and slipping the shop keys into her pocket.

The street was all but deserted as Laura hurried on towards Parry Griffin's shop. She came to the cobbled square where, looking about, she satisfied herself that there was no one in the immediate vicinity. Then quickly stepping into the recess that led to the front entrance of the old shop, she went on silent footsteps to peer through the dirty smudges that shadowed the glass in the top half of the door. Yes, there was someone in the back room. The door leading to the private quarters was very slightly ajar, throwing a thin sliver of light out into the darkness of the front shop.

For a while, Laura just stood there, her heart thumping violently in her chest, and all the courage she had mustered throughout the afternoon and evening seemed to have deserted her. Her mind was awash with all sorts of ponderings. Would he be drunk? Yes of course he would; then *how* drunk? What violent frame of mind would he be thrown into at the sight of her? Recollections of past encounters with him tortured her mind. She could feel them as though they were taking place, at this very moment. The horror of how he had raped her, and more recently his hands about her throat, was all so alive in her mind that Laura suddenly found herself trembling.

She was afraid; there was no denying it. To admit herself

quite willingly to Parry Griffin's home ground seemed quite preposterous to her now. And yet, she told herself, it had to be done if she was to achieve what she must!

She drew herself together physically and mentally, and sucked in a series of deep gulping breaths. Then after a moment, when she felt more calm within herself, she deliberately set her features into a stern expression and at once tried the door handle. It was as she had imagined. He had not yet locked the shop up.

Almost on tiptoe, she edged her way into the shop, nudged the door closed, and proceeded towards the shaft of light at the back end. She went on carefully, for it was pitch black save for the thin light, and although she could not see about her, Laura felt as though her every movement was echoed and she sensed that the actual shop floor was bare of merchandise.

She reached the light and there was nothing for it but to announce her presence, so Laura lifted up her closed fist and in quick sharp knocks, she brought it against the door three times. She waited, but there was no answer. Again she knocked at the door, this time with more determination. When she still received no response, Laura pushed the door open and stood looking round the room. She had expected Parry Griffin would live in conditions not acceptable to a normal human being. But what she saw was far in excess of her worst expectations. In the middle of the floor stood a small wooden table, which had one chair pulled up to it. The table was completely littered with empty beer bottles, dirty plates and spilt fluids of various colours. In similar disarray was the floor, whose brown linoleum covering was torn in places and left sticking up with no visible attempt at repair. The stone sink and an adjacent tall cupboard on the far side of the room bore evidence of the same neglect, for the sink was piled with dirty crockery and all the cupboard doors were open to reveal tins and jars that had been half-emptied and left lying on their sides, a half-eaten loaf and various other items of food that looked as if they had been thrown into the cupboard rather than stacked. Against the wall to the right of the cupboard was a narrow iron-framed bed whose coverings were in a tangle, half draped on the floor.

Amongst all that filth and degradation, the one thing that struck Laura as being the most nauseous was the smell. It was a thick pungent smell of the vilest kind, whose creeping vapours seeped their way into Laura's head and throat, stimulating in her a terrible urge to vomit.

Laura stepped from the doorway and into the room itself. The very instant she had done so, the awful smell grew to envelop her, almost as though its intangible essence had materialized into solid matter. And even while the thought crossed her mind and every instinct in her body told her to flee from that place, he was on her and shouting, 'Well now! What's this, eh?' Parry Griffin's right hand was over her mouth, and with his left hand gripping her shoulder, he propelled Laura towards the table. He was laughing now, a deep rumbling roar that might have struck fear into a more timid creature than Laura. But she knew that the noise was the roar of booze and not the measure of the man. Outside, she had been mortally afraid, her fear fed by old and vivid memories. Yet strangely enough, her fear had vanished, and in its place was a riveting hatred and such desire for revenge that all else was driven from her mind.

Parry Griffin had thrown her into the chair by the table, and now he was leering over her, still laughing and saying, 'Thought you were the lads, Johnny Street's lot, thought you'd come to get me.' He was less drunk than Laura had ever seen him, and he was in a heightened state of fear. Parry Griffin, frightened! Frightened of what? She wondered. His words came back to her: 'Thought you were the lads come to get me.' 'The lads'? By that, Laura took him to mean his gambling cronies, and if they were the ones from out Mill Hill way, then he was in with a real bad lot. She'd heard tell by various men, in and out of the shop, that the men from the gambling quarters were not the sort to flinch at crushing a man's private parts if they found him hesitant in paying off a bad debt. They didn't take to welchers, and more than one mutilated body had been found floating in the canal before now. Oh yes! Parry Griffin was terrified. Laura could see it in his bloodshot eyes, and she could smell it on him, almost taste it. Fear was something she hadn't counted on, but she would be quick to use to her own advantage.

She got to her feet, stepped away from the table and moved slowly towards the door; all the while with Parry Griffin's eyes following her. He moved as though he might come after her, and it was then that Laura stopped. Lifting her hand in a gesture for him to stay away, she said, 'I've got a proposition, a money deal to offer you.' Her head was high and her eyes glittered hard towards him. To the man who watched her closely, her dark blazing eyes and challenging stance was a formidable sight, and something about her caused him to stand still and listen as she went on. 'Go to Mr Drew's office in town. He's a solicitor and he'll be expecting you. He has one thousand pounds of mine, and he has instructions to give that money to *you*, on one condition. You are to take with you the deeds to this shop, and to your house. Mr Drew will keep the deeds safe. He'll give you the thousand pounds and in return you'll be asked to sign a paper saying that if you do not repay the money within three months, then the house and shop will be forfeited.' Laura stopped, allowing her words to sink in. All the time she had been speaking, Parry Griffin had remained motionless, his hands flat on the table, his body leaning over it and his head tilted sideways to look at her. He had given no indication that he had either heard or understood what she had been saying.

Laura would have repeated her offer, but all of a sudden Parry Griffin had fallen back in the chair and letting out a burst of laughter, he spluttered, 'My shop and my bloody house! Jesus, d'you think I'm altogether brainless?' Then he roared with uncontrollable laughter which echoed round the room and deafened Laura until she thought he'd gone completely mad. As she stared at his wide open mouth and watched the lifeless eyes first disappearing beneath bulges of flesh and then popping open like bulbous marbles, something inside her suddenly gave way. Surging forward, she swung quickly behind the chair in which Parry Griffin was still rocking with mirth, and grabbing his hair with both hands, she yanked his head sharply backwards. At this, the laughter stopped and turned into a yelp of pain. And still Laura hung on to his hair, pulling it tight until it looked as though the roots might spring from his forehead. Keeping his head back in this way, and staying well clear of his arms which were flailing the air in an unsuccessful bid to grab her, she told him, 'So you thought I was the lads come to get you, eh? Well not *this* time, Parry

Griffin, not this time! But think, just think,' her voice became hushed, 'every time you hear a sound, it could be them; one dark night when you least expect it, they'll be on you, swift and silent. And you know what they're likely to do to you, don't you?' He was quiet now, save for a low whining whimpering, and Laura could feel him trembling. 'You can pay your debts, and in no time at all, you'll have won the money back to pay Mr Drew for the return of your deeds. Three months, think of it, you've got three whole months to use that thousand pounds, *double* it even! And I'll not charge you one single penny interest.' She released him and made her way to the door, where she turned. She looked back to see him rubbing his hands across his forehead and she said in a low forceful tone, 'Remember, Mr Drew the solicitor in town. Take your deeds, and he'll have the thousand pounds waiting. The choice is yours, and if you've any sense at all, you won't hesitate to take up my offer.'

As Laura left the shop, she could hear him shouting, 'You bloody bitch! You wouldn't dare do it if Pearce was 'ere. He'd soon put a stop to your soddin' games! An' I'll not be taking your money. So you can tell your Mr bloody Drew to give it back to you. I'll not be going anywhere near! I'll rot in the bowels of hell first! D'you hear me?'

Laura heard him. So he'd rot in hell first, eh? Oh yes, he'd rot in hell, and it would be *her* who'd put him there! And he reckoned he wouldn't go near Mr Drew's office? 'We'll see,' she murmured, hurrying back to the shop before Remmie arrived, 'We'll see.' She was not over concerned at his reaction. It was words. Just words. But he had mentioned Pearce, and if anything at all had unnerved her, then it was the thought of Parry Griffin's son, who could stir emotions inside her that were best left dormant.

Laura had left the light on in the shop, and once inside, she carefully bolted the door. Normally, she would have been satisfied just to slip the sneck; but something inside her urged extra caution. That Parry Griffin was unstable and his actions could prove equally unpredictable. Quickly now, she slipped off her outdoor garments and returned them to the back store room. She wouldn't want either Mitch or Remmie to suspect that she had left the shop.

Remmie returned first, and when he found Laura on her

knees amidst a pile of old books, he naturally assumed that she had been hard at work right up to that moment. 'By God, you're a glutton for punishment, Laura Blake, just never 'ave learned when to stop, 'ave you?' He saw the pink glow that lighted up her face, a glow that Laura felt inside, a heightened sense of Parry Griffin's predicament, and Remmie took it to be the flush of overwork. Laura got to her feet and watched, quitely amused, as he went away to the back store room, from which he reappeared in a moment, with her mackintosh and headscarf. 'Leave them books right where they are!' He held out the mackintosh while she shrugged herself into it. Then he thrust the scarf into her hand and ordered, 'Right! Away with you into the van.'

'You're an old fusspot, Remmie Thorpe,' she said with a smile, allowing herself to be all but frogmarched out of the shop.

On the journey to Ribble Road, Remmie chattered incessantly, about how he'd been bamboozled into playing that bloody silly dominos game, and how they'd lost shamefully anyroad. All this genial prattle ran above Laura's head, as her own thoughts took precedence. She wondered at Parry Griffin's state of mind, what was he thinking at this very moment? Tomorrow was Friday. If he wasn't driven to Mr Drew's office tomorrow, that would afford him the space of the whole weekend before he could take up her offer. That might be ruinous to her plans, for it would give him that extra time in which to see the pattern of her trap. Laura didn't like the way her thoughts were taking her. No! He was desperate. She would not even entertain the possibility that he would desist. He *must* go to Mr Drew's office and collect the money! And if it wasn't to be tomorrow, then no matter, because the space of a weekend could just as easily work in her favour. He'd be left to stew in his fear that much longer. He would respond favourably to her proposition, she was certain, for she had deliberately made it one that he could hardly refuse.

'Tired, lass?' Remmie had been quiet for a while, but now he cast a sideways glance. 'It's nigh on midnight, you know.'

'I am ready for my bed,' she replied truthfully, 'it's been a long day.' Yes, almost midnight — and Mitch still out when she and Remmie had left the shop. Mitch and Sally? Well, what did it matter to her? Those two were made for each other. They were both content with the basic pleasures of life and sought nothing grand. Well, that's not for *me*! she thought, not me at all.

The following evening, Laura phoned Mr Drew — five minutes before he closed the office for the weekend. And when in a matter-of-fact voice, he informed her that, 'No, Mr Griffin has *not* contacted me,' Laura was bitterly disappointed. So! It wasn't just Parry Griffin who would stew over the weekend. It was *her* also! Well, she would not allow it to dominate her thoughts, because she was still very strongly of the opinion that he *would* go to Mr Drew. Laura would not — *could* — not contemplate any other outcome.

All the same, that night, sleep was denied her. She could not help but dwell on the disquietening fact that Parry Griffin had found the discipline to stay away from Mr Drew's office, and that being the case, it crossed her mind that maybe, somehow, he had found in himself the strength to resist her, and her tempting offer. And if he had, then how in her heart could she honestly blame him? He was not *entirely* stupid. He must surely know what was at the back of her mind — what had been at the back of her mind these many years!

Laura churned all of this over in her thoughts. Yet she could not believe that Monday wouldn't bring her the news she wanted so desperately. Parry Griffin was not made of the kind of stuff that would allow him to leave a thousand pounds just lying there. No indeed! He was *not*. Her every instinct told her so.

Chapter Thirty-two

'You know bloody well I haven't got the money to pay!' Parry Griffin's voice bellowed down the telephone, causing Laura to hold the receiver a distance from her ear, and even then, she could still hear him shouting a stream of foul abuse that, had she been a delicate sort of female, might have offended her ears.

As it was, she waited for the torrent to subside, before bringing the mouthpiece to her lips and delivering a cool response. 'If, as you say, you cannot repay the secured loan, then there is nothing further to be discussed on that issue. I understand from Mr Drew that he wrote to you some days back, reminding you that under the terms of the agreement, and on the assumption that you wished to redeem the deeds to your house and shop, that the thousand pounds must be delivered to him no later than five pm on Wednesday the seventeenth of this month.' Laura deliberately paused here, allowing the implication of her words to sink home and to take her own pleasure in them. 'That was *yesterday.* You have not repaid the loan, therefore the consequences demand that you immediately relinquish ownership of the two properties. As from this morning, Parry Griffin, your shop and your house are both mine.' Laura knew that her words were harsh and her manner unyielding, yet she felt not the slightest mercy towards this man. His usage of her had stayed deep in her memory these past years, hardening that gentle part of her character that hitherto would have recognized and used a degree of compassion. This was her day of triumph; the day when both Parry Griffin and his wife Molly would know what it was like to be without a roof over their heads, to have their small measure of dignity taken away. Laura felt that even at that, they had been given the better treatment; for she had allowed Parry Griffin a breathing space of three months, a real chance to take her carefully accrued money for that period of time, without malicious interest charges, and without penalty of any kind had he repaid it. It was a straightforward business transaction, nothing hidden and nothing untoward. The ace up her sleeve had been her own assessment of the man's character, and just as she had firmly believed he would, Parry Griffin had dug his own grave. And as for that wife of his, well, Molly Griffin had cheated two young girls out of everything they held dear, while their mother was detained in an asylum and their father recently buried. No! Laura felt no regret at having paid her back, for she herself had not cheated as her mother's sister had done. She had beggared these two legally, and who could blame her if she was now savouring their downfall. To hell with the pair of them! And may they burn there forever!

'Laura, listen to me,' his voice, which had been vicious and threatening, was now pleading and did not move Laura, 'give me another week. Just a week! For God's sake, 'ave you got no bloody heart, woman.'

'No, I've no heart, Parry Griffin.' She interrupted, her voice cold and clipping, leaving him with no hope of cajoling more time out of her, and with no hope of redeeming what had been rightfully Jud Blake's in the first place. They said the devil came after his own, and Parry Griffin could hear him in Laura's final words, 'I have a letter of authority from Mr Drew. I'll be along to collect the keys and to see you and your wife out on the streets. Six o'clock tonight.'

'You'll not get though *this* soddin' door! Never! D'you hear me, bitch? Set one foot against this door, an' I swear I'll do for you!'

Laura raised her voice above his to tell him, 'Six o'clock! And if you refuse me access, it'll do you no good, because I'll just return tomorrow with the Bailiff. You've lost, Parry Griffin! And I can imagine how it must stick in your throat.' She gave an empty laugh. 'Six o'clock!' she said, and quietly replaced the receiver.

Upstairs in his bed, Remmie, drained by the ravages of an influenza virus that had kept him immobile this last week, strained his ears towards Laura's insistent voice as it came up the stairs to encroach on his fitful sleep. Hitching himself up on one elbow, he leaned towards the door and called out, 'Laura! Laura, lass.' His voice was croaky and failing, and Laura would not have heard his cry had she not been halfway up the stairs and making her way to his sickroom.

'Lie down!' she instructed him, as she came swiftly towards his bed, where she took him by the shoulders in a gentle but firm grasp, and eased him back against the pillow. 'You're not the easiest patient in the world, Remmie Thorpe! Fussing and fidgeting, giving a body no peace.'

'Ha!' he retorted drily. 'Look at the pan calling the kettle black. I shall need to go a long way to be as grumpy and fidgety as *you* when you've a need to keep to your bed!' He wriggled uncomfortably. 'Sit me up, lass. I'm as weak as a bloody kitten.'

When Laura had gripped him tight beneath the armpits and manoeuvered him into what at least resembled a sitting position, she sat on the bed to watch him for a moment before saying with some concern, 'Are you feeling much improved, Remmie?'

'Aye, lass, I feel I'm on the mend.' Remmie felt no such thing. He could not remember a time when he'd felt so low, when all the energy in him had seemed to melt right away, leaving him as helpless as a newborn babe. But it wasn't so much his own disposition that concerned him as the way Laura had been these last few days. He watched her now as she busied herself tucking the clothes in around him. She looked tired and too thin for his liking. How in God's name she'd managed these last few days, he would never know. She'd been up at the crack of dawn to get the housework done and to see to him. Then she'd gone off to the shop where she'd worked till one o'clock, when Mitch would run her home for an hour. During that time, she'd leave Mitch down in the kitchen, brewing a pot of tea and cutting a few sandwiches for both of them, while she went up to see Remmie, taking him hot lemon and home-made soup. When he'd had his fill of both, she'd wash him and see that he was comfortable, before going back downstairs to revive herself with a cup of tea, a sandwich and a few minutes quietly talking to Mitch about matters of business. Mitch had more than once suggested that she should stay at home for the rest of the day, assuring her most emphatically that he was well capable of keeping things going till Remmie found his strength again. But as he might have expected, Laura would have none of it.

'Who was that on the 'phone just now?' Remmie kept his eyes intent on Laura's face as he awaited an answer. He felt there was some urgent matter in her thoughts. He sensed something, a feverishness about her of late, that had nothing to do with his being laid up, or with her self-imposed punishing vigil. No; nothing at all to do with any of that, he was sure. What then?

'Oh, nobody for you to bother yourself about, Remmie.'

'It wasn't our Netti then?'

'No. When she rang yesterday, she said she'd not ring again, as she'd be home tomorrow night.'

'By! I was relieved when she took up Miss Fordyke's offer of a week in London to celebrate the end of all them blessed exams.'

'It wasn't just that, Remmie. I'm sure that shrewd old woman's *real* intention was for Netti to see what life in London would be like, when she's offered a place at the College of Music.'

'*If* she's offered a place!'

'No. When!' Laura emphatically corrected. 'By all accounts, the exams look to have gone well.'

'Aye. But like as not, it took as much out of Miss Fordyke as it did Netti. Odd that, her suddenly announcing her retirement like she did.'

'Yes,' Laura had her own ideas about that, and she felt none too proud of them, 'it *was* a bit out of the blue. Right! Well I'm away out for a couple of hours when I've washed these tea things up.' She put the crockery on the small wooden tray on the floor by the bed. 'You'll be alright?'

'Is it to do with that 'phone call just now? Sally Fletcher, was it?'

'Yes,' Laura lied, turning away to hide the surge of colour that heated her face. Some instinctive urge inside her warned against confiding in Remmie. She sensed that if he knew of the agreement between her and Parry Griffin, and that this very night she was going to go first to that man's shop then to his house to claim what was now *hers*, Remmie would rise from his bed like a bolt of thunder.

His gentle nature and heightened sense of fair play would never entertain the idea of an eye for an eye, a tooth for a tooth, and she was certain that he would move heaven and hell to stop her. But he would *not* stop her. Nothing and nobody would. The tide had turned in her favour, and far from checking it, she would urge it ever onward until it carried her to dizzy heights and dashed the Griffins of this world to the depths!

'Go on then, lass. It'll do you good to get yourself into the company o' that Sally Fletcher; she's a grand little thing.'

'Try and get some sleep. I'll be back as quick as I can.'

Downstairs, Laura pulled on her warm boots, wrapped herself into the thick tweed coat that had been Katya's and fastened the headscarf tight about her head. Then shivering at the onslaught of the cold as she opened the door, she stepped out into the murky hostility of the November night.

On the way to the tram stop, she asked herself what she would do if Parry Griffin, or even that wife of his, turned violent towards her. The she quickly emptied her mind of such speculation, and turned her thoughts to the nursing home. It was hard to believe that in just three weeks' time, all the renovations would be finished. They would never have been able to complete the purchase if she had not persuaded Remmie to take out that bridging loan. But the house and all of Katya's furniture was now sold, as was Remmie's wish. Everything had fallen to plan, just as she had promised Remmie it would.

It seemed to Laura that just lately her every move came up trumps. Even the delicate link that had been forged with Weston and Favers had been strengthened by her determined search and the consequential location of a first-class cabinet maker in Manchester. The secretaire had been delivered two weeks ago and had been well received by the scrutinizing Mr Craven.

Laura suspected that Mitch had become aware of her continued dealings with Weston and Favers. But like the man he was, he had not betrayed her to Remmie. She knew that it would only be a matter of time before she was forced to disclose several matters to Remmie. But when that time came, they would be presented to him as a *fait accompli.* After that, she was confident that he would be brought round to her way of thinking.

As she turned the corner, a sudden icy blast prompted her to grab her coat tight about her, and she broke into a run as she saw that the tram was just pulling in.

Chapter Thirty-three

'Evening! Street lights not working again, I see. It's allus the same; come the onset of winter and the Council's caught wi' their pants down.' The burly man gaffawed loudly, tipped his flat cap at Laura as he passed, and left her with a warning to, 'Mind 'ow you go then. Goodnight.'

'Goodnight,' returned Laura, before quickly proceeding on her way along Bent Street.

She had no liking for the month of November. The cold wasn't a sharp biting experience that nipped your nose and whistled sharply about your ears. It was a creeping dankness that seeped right through the pores of your skin. The days were bad enough, but with the coming of darkness, and the inevitable smoggy atmosphere, it was much more discomforting, especially when, like now, one or two of the street lights had given up working, throwing any intrepid traveller into thick darkness.

Laura shivered, her teeth involuntarily chattering inside her tightly closed mouth. Well, at least there was still the odd light functioning, she thought gratefully. And anyway, if people had any sense at all, they wouldn't be on the streets on a night like this. They'd be snug and cosy indoors, with their feet up against the fire. Ah, but *she* had important business to attend to; and even though her deeper instincts told her that she should have followed Mr Drew's advice about leaving the taking of possession to him, Laura had wanted to carry out that particular task herself, and thinking of it now set up a warm fire inside her.

Lifting her head up, Laura stared at the approaching figure, and almost at once she recognized the burly shape and cumbersome carriage of Molly Griffin. It took but a minute for the woman to arrive within a few feet of Laura. She halted, straddled across the path in such a way as to bar Laura's advance.

Even in the semi-darkness, Laura saw at once that Molly Griffin's eyes were swollen and sore from crying. When she spoke, her voice was filled with malice. 'I knew you'd be trouble! Saw it in you a long way back.' She cackled now in a peculiar slow-motion manner that alarmed Laura in spite of her defiant stance. 'No wonder your Mam was obsessed with the need to lay you under the ground all that time she was hid in my cellar. Ah!' Laura's look of surprise had not escaped her quick eyes. 'Never knew that did you? Oh aye! I kept your Mam well away, and if only she'd 'a been patient like I wanted, and listened to me, waited, we'd 'a done for you *proper*! But she were past waiting, that one.' She was gabbling almost incoherently, but then suddenly, she stepped forward to within a hand's breadth of Laura. 'You! You've tekken my man's shop! And the pitiful abode that I've looked on as my home.' In a quick thrusting movement which caught Laura completely off guard, she stepped back to throw a bunch of heavy iron keys which thudded hard against Laura's breast before clattering to the ground.

Molly Griffin gave out a loud gruff laugh, shouting, 'Tek the sodding things! I'll not give you the satisfaction of seeing me away over me own bloody doorstep, by God I won't! And to think that bloody coward told me nowt! I could mebbe 'ave thought of some way to outsmart you. Yesterday! That was the first I knew, when he brought 'issel to let me know. Well, he never was much of a man. He's in there now, blabbering and wailing like a babby lost its tit! But you'll not see *me* in such a state, much as I know you'd like to, Laura Blake. Oh no! I've cleared me things from yon house, and you're bloody welcome to it, 'cause I'm not without friends let me tell you.'

Laura suspected that she was lying, putting on a brave front. A woman of Molly Griffin's sort wouldn't have friends, unless of course they were of the same low mould as herself. Laura said as much now, her eyes almost black from the bitterness that filled them. She said in a low meaningful voice, 'You're scum, Molly Griffin, and I don't give a damn whether you've found a roof over your head, or whether you're forced to walk the streets in the day and sleep in the gutters at night!' The

371

other woman's eyes blinked away from the vibrant hatred that now faced her and struck the fear of God into her. She backed away, but as Laura collected the keys from the flagstones and straightened to pass the subdued woman, Molly Griffin sprang into life. She flung out an arm which struck Laura's breast, then gripped Laura's arm with her huge fist and said through clenched teeth, 'Yer Mam was right! You *are* a witch. But mark my warning, Laura Blake, you'll get your come-uppance, and there's not a night'll go by that I'll not wish you every kind o' sorrow. They do say as there's a bit of witch in *all* of us. Well, it's the witch in me, as curses you now!' She threw Laura from her, and in an instant was fleeing down the road and out of sight.

Laura thrust the bunch of keys into her pocket and muttered, 'It'll take more than the likes of you, or your silly curses, to keep me from my sleep at night.' Now she quickly went to Parry Griffin's shop doorway. Arching her neck to look along the streets towards Remmie's shop, Laura saw that there was a light burning, and she pictured Mitch going about the business of locking up. The thought of Mitch gave her strength, for the truth be told, although she harboured no regrets for the events of this day, she would be glad when it was all put behind her.

She proceeded cautiously, putting her hand inside the relative warmth of her coat pocket to satisfy herself that the note of authority from Mr Drew was safely there. Clutching the paper between her fingers, she held it firmly within her pocket and brought her free hand up, with the intention of knocking on the door. but it moved away beneath her touch, opening of its own accord and admitting her into the shop, which was bathed in darkness. Staying in the doorway, Laura narrowed her eyes in an effort to pierce the gloom.

Laura made no move to step inside the darkness. She had not anticipated this, and the fact that Parry Griffin hadn't forced her into a situation whereby she had to literally *fight* her way into his domain seemed totally incredible to her. Something, some sixth sense within her, warned against entering the shop, in just the same way as it had done on the one occasion that she had been here before. It was infuriating, how this man still had the power to strike fear into her. But old memories could be persistent enemies. Certainly, *she* had gained no peace of mind from their dogged presence, and quite suddenly, Laura was surprised to find herself wondering whether Parry Griffin had. But then, who could tell with a creature of his sort?

She took a deep breath, which she released in a slow calming manner, and took one tentative step forward and reached out to the wall on her left. She located the round protruding light switch, traced her fingers to the small solid bobble on the end of the lever and quickly flicked it down, immediately flooding the shop with light.

To Sally Fletcher, on her way to Remmie's shop, it was an odd thing to see Laura at Parry Griffin's door. She said as much to Mitch, whose company she often sought these days. Even before she finished speaking, Mitch was already at the door. So the rumours that had been rife lately might carry more substance than he'd allowed for? Dear God! What *was* going on? He turned to Sally, who appeared to be quite alarmed at his reaction that Laura was paying Parry Griffin a call. 'You stay here, Sally, I'll be but a minute.' Then without stopping to answer the anxious questions that Sally was already putting to him, he yanked the door open and bounded up the street towards Parry Griffin's shop, unaware of Sally's light steps immediately behind him. When she called after him, 'Mitch! Mitch, what is it? What's wrong?' he did not hear; for he could think of nothing other than that Laura was in mortal danger. To think she had actually taken herself into that man's place! Good God above, didn't she know that Parry Griffin was capable of anything, *anything*! Why, only recently he had made for Laura's throat. What had come over her to do such a thing as this?

Mitch rushed into the shop and saw at once that Laura was not there, so he swung open the door to the back room and stepped inside. For an instant, he was disorientated, coming in from the highly illuminated shop floor, into this small unlit room, save for the broad shaft of light that now streamed in from the shop.

He searched for the light switch, which he quickly flicked up and down. Blast! The bulb had gone. He moved into the room, and when his eyes grew accustomed to the semi-darkness, he searched frantically for Laura, calling, 'Laura! Griffin, are you in here, you beast . . .' The intended abuse froze on his open mouth, for hanging from the light flex in the centre of the ceiling was a figure.

For a moment, Mitch was unable to distinguish the identity of that limp still body, so obviously lifeless as he moved ever nearer.

'Laura!' Mitch swung round at the sound of Sally's cry, and what he saw brought such relief to his fearful heart that his throat constricted like a steel band tight enough to choke him. If he had searched to the right of the door for the light switch, Mitch would have discovered Laura was standing with her back against the wall, both hands spread across her mouth as though to stifle her own screams, and such a vacant expression in her staring eyes that made Mitch think she must be in a trance. He gathered her in his arms and instructed Sally, 'Back to the shop, Sally, I'll be right behind you with Laura. Phone the police.' He jerked his head in the direction of the body hanging grimly in the darkness, 'That must be Griffin, Lord help us.' He made no move towards the body, because judging by the sweet smell that lingered thick in his nostrils, the life had been gone from it for some time.

Sally nodded and swiftly made her way back to the shop. Laura looked up at Mitch, who had brought her into the lighted shop-front and was briskly rubbing her hands in his. 'We'll soon have the blood back,' Mitch said.

The image of that hanging figure was etched deeply into her mind, and now Laura found her tongue to murmur, 'It *is* Parry Griffin hanged himself, and oh Mitch, am I wicked to feel no pity for him?' Her voice broke into a small sob.

'No. You're not wicked!'

'But *he* was, he was . . . '

'Aye. He was, and a coward to take that way out. What in God's name could drive a man to such extremes?'

'*I* did.' Her voice felt flat and empty, in spite of the emotions which tore at her insides. 'Oh, Mitch, *I* drove him to it.'

'Quiet now, Laura. You've had a shock, a real bad shock.' He pulled her to her feet and supporting her against him, he said gently. 'Let's get you away to Remmie's. And we'll hear no more o' that damaging talk! The very idea that *you* drove him to it.'

374

Laura felt the iron strength of his arm as he pulled her into him, before propelling her out of that place and down the road towards where Sally was waiting at the door.

In the darkness, Laura lifted her eyes to gaze upon Mitch's countenance. She saw the firm set of his jaw and the strong green eyes turned now to smile on her, and she took great comfort from him. Yet she wondered what he was thinking at that moment; what he *would* think when he learned the truth of this night. She tried to tell herself that it would not matter *what* he thought. But Laura knew more than ever before, that it did matter to her what Mitch came to think. It mattered a great deal.

PART THREE

1959

TRUTH

Anger in its time and place
May assume a kind of grace;
It must have some reason in it,
And not last beyond a minute.

Charles and Mary Lamb

Chapter Thirty-four

The little woman jerked her head towards the far gate. "Ere's Laura now,' she told her attentive colleague, a woman of manly bearing. 'If you ask me, it should be Laura Blake walking up the aisle today!'

'Aye, mebbe, but Laura's not the marrying kind, I'm thinking. She's had no time for men these past years, worked like a dog, she has.'

'There's nowt truer than that! All the same an' all, I've an idea that she'll rue the day she let *this* one slip through her fingers!'

'Aye, mebbe. No amount of power or money can keep a body warm on a cold night. Teks a *man* to mek a woman feel good that way.'

Laura herself had entertained much the same thoughts of late, and they were running through her mind now, as she leaned forward in her seat, waiting for Remmie to pull the car in off the road. Since being a child, she had believed that money and position could buy anything. But she had since come to realize that one thing it could never purchase was peace of mind. The powerful ambitions that had long consumed her every waking thought, were now almost realized. It was a good time. A time for people with drive and confidence, and it was a time for looking forward; 1959 was proving to be the year of increased productivity, with local mills picking up on export, a narrowing trade gap to encourage them, and stable prices together with demand bringing more employment. There was an atmosphere of well-being, and people with more money in their pockets and the urge to spend it.

Laura had seen her own hopes materialize into reality. Yet deep in her heart, there was no contentment, for she still felt driven by the same fears and bitterness that had shaped the pattern of her life so far. At times, Remmie would shake his head and tell her, 'Whatever haunts you, lass? Don't drain yourself of everything that makes life worthwhile.'

'Don't worry about me, Remmie,' she would reply, 'I'm happy as I am.' But she wasn't, and she wondered if she ever would be.

"Ere we are then, lass.' Remmie in middle-age was still a good-looking man, but since Katya's death the light seemed to have gone from his eyes and the spring from his step. He seemed now to live in the shadow of Laura, looking to her for the strength that would keep him going.

She looked at him now, as he brought the car to a halt outside the church, his voice quietly condemning as he told her, 'You know, Laura, I still can't help thinking that Netti should have made the effort to come home. I'm sure she could have spared us at least *one* week from her summer holidays.'

'Well, I did try, Remmie,' Laura couldn't have agreed more, 'but with her final year coming up, she wanted to spend this holiday trekking Europe with her student friends.'

'I still think it were thoughtless of her. And you're far too generous with her, I've told you that 'afore!' Remmie slapped a hand impatiently on the steering wheel. 'Out you get then, lass.' He looked through the car window and across the lawn to where various people stood about in small, busy groups. 'Lots o' folk already here,' he observed.

Laura emerged from the car, and even in the intense August heat, she looked cool and elegant. She ran a hand down the fold of her blue dress. She liked blue. It usually made her feel good; but not today. No, not today.

She looked at the faces turned now in her direction. She smiled at them, and they returned the warmth in her gesture. Then as Remmie drove off to find a parking-place, she made her way up the narrow gravelled path leading to the church. She was not unaware of the buzzing of low voices as she passed. It didn't bother her. Not like it used to. She turned just once, before disappearing inside the church, where the voices of the two mill-women echoed down the aisle to where she sat.

'Lord knows what Jud Blake would think of his lass now, eh? Too good for the likes of us, dressin' like royalty, an' living in that great fancy place outside o' town.'

'Earned it though!' Laura was grateful for the thread of defence in the other woman's retort. 'Appen she does live a lot grander now, an' who's to blame her? She's not cut herself off altogether, else she'd not be here today, now would she, eh?'

They fell silent, and Laura settled back in the pew. Her eyes were drawn to the altar, and she thought how splendid it looked, all decked out in ceremonial regalia, as befitted a wedding service. She felt guilty that she didn't come very often to church. It was only the thread of Jud Blake's teaching that held her open-minded about things like faith, and belief in God. She would have liked to believe with all her heart, for there must be great comfort in such faith. And yet, so much had happened, and there was a part of her that felt betrayed and hurt. It was that part, and her own sense of guilt, that always seemed to put her on the defensive, denying her the comfort and reassurance which seemed so elusive. She didn't understand, and she didn't pretend to.

As the guests filed in to the church, filling up the pews all around her, Laura watched for Remmie, and his appearance gladdened her. It crossed her mind just then that he had been right about Nettl. She might have made an effort to spend a few days at home. It didn't seem the same without Nettl around and she had to admit that she sorely missed her presence, quiet though it often was.

The beautiful haunting tones of the church organ bathed the bride on her slow purposeful walk down the aisle. From her place in the pews, Laura gazed at Sally Fletcher as she passed, and her thoughts were a mixture of happiness and regret. How lovely Sally looked in the flowing white dress and lace headpiece that Belle Strong's nimble fingers had created. And how wonderfully happy she seemed.

As Sally approached the altar, Laura's quiet gaze fell on the man who turned to meet his bride. Mitch made a fine strong figure in his dark blue suit and crisp white shirt, and Laura's heart ached as she looked at the familiar face with its lean proud lines and honest expression.

She found herself smiling as he self-consciously lifted his hand to push the wayward fair hair from across his forehead. Then, in the same instant, his eyes came to rest on her face, and the steadfast and intimate gaze made her look away.

Remmie reached out to hold her hand and smile reassuringly, and Laura noticed the sadness in his kind brown eyes.

The music stopped. The vicar stepped forward, and the serious business of joining man and wife began.

Laura bowed her head and gave vent to her thoughts. Sally had been a good mother to Parry Griffin's boy, and she would be a good wife to Mitch. Laura knew that, and knowing it somehow helped. She lifted her eyes to look at the small dark head some way in front. It was her own son, Tom; but for all the world might know and for all he acknowledged her, he might have been a stranger: Or an enemy, Laura thought sadly. As it had these past years, the grotesque sight of Parry Griffin swinging from that flex materialized to sicken her, and Laura wondered how much more young Tom would hate her when he learned, as one day he surely would, that Parry Griffin was his rightful father, and that she, his mother, had driven the demented man to hang himself. The very thought of it caused Laura to shudder. Would she never rid herself of the guilt that she still felt? After she had come upon his body there had been no going back into that shop, not even when it was being looked over by prospective purchasers.

It had been fortuitous that the old council offices had come up for sale at that time, and the money she had raised on Parry Griffin's shop and the house provided a handsome down payment on these, her first business premises. Laura was convinced she could not have found a better site if she'd searched for a lifetime. Yes, it was certainly strange how things turned out.

Afterwards, when the bride and groom had gone and the guests began to file out, Laura found herself kneeling a while longer, for there seemed to be a kind of peace here that she could not find outside. It was a peace which she knew would be short-lived. Too much had happened in the past for her to secure peace in the future, and her mind refused to let the past go. There were other people too, who would not let it rest, and looking back now, she could understand it. After she'd sold Parry Griffin's shop and house and her dealings with him had become common knowledge, there had been many to condemn her part in it all, and there still were. Mitch and Remmie had both said their pieces, which were not sparing in their outright disapproval. Then they had fallen silent on the subject, but she sensed that they had not easily forgiven her. Yet time was a great healer. Most people forgot very quickly with new excitements. But it had taken Remmie and Mitch a long time to get over seeing that side of her character which Mitch had accused would, 'Shame the wickedest moneylender,' and Remmie had said was,'Hand in hand with the devil's doing'. But these two loved her, and in their love, how could they help but forgive her?

Laura by necessity had risen above the initial reaction and vehement attitude of some townsfolk, mainly because in the first place, like those of more sensible attitude, she saw the roots of all blame lying squarely in Parry Griffin's own destructive hands; and secondly, because the vilest tongue that wagged, spreading poison, was that of Molly Griffin, who had rented a run down property off the Alley, and who paid her way with the dues received from her constant stream of menfriends. It was a familiar sight these days to see Molly Griffin plying trade and selling her body openly in the market square. And strange to say, she appeared to thoroughly enjoy her new way of life.

Of Pearce Griffin there had been little news, save the odd speculation that he must either be abroad making his fortune, or he must be dead. And if he wasn't dead, then there'd be all hell let loose if he should ever make his way back to these parts and learn of the means concerning his father's suicide. Laura resisted this particularly disturbing line of thought, bringing her attention back now to the nigh empty church and the fact that it was time to leave.

She and Remmie were the last to leave the church, and when they arrived at the Working Men's Club where the reception was being held, Mitch was anxiously waiting at the door. Remmie shook his hand and warmly congratulated him, 'Where's that lovely bride, eh? I'm not missing out on me kiss!'

'She's with Belle, setting the presents out in the back room.'

'Right then!' Remmie walked on, before turning to tell Laura in a half-serious voice, 'And don't you be keeping him out here too long, lass! We mustn't forget our Mitch is a married man now.'

Laura smiled, but the truth of that remark made her feel uncomfortable. She turned to Mitch and told him, 'We'd better go in. Sally's bound to be wondering where you are.'

'Laura.' Something in the quietness of his voice deeply

383

disturbed her. 'I'll say this now, then never again as Sally's husband. I love you, Laura. I think Sally knows that, because I've never denied it, I never could. But a man can't wait forever. I'm turned thirty, and God knows you're as far from me now as you've ever been.' He looked down at her face, and Laura saw the despair in his eyes, and her heart went out to him. She let him go on, because even though his words should not be uttered, their profound sincerity brought great comfort to her. 'I will always hold you closest in my heart, Laura. But Sally and young Tom, they were there, loving me, needing me. I'll not waste such precious love and I swear to God, I'll take good care of them both.'

Laura knew he would, and when he bent to kiss her lightly before leaving, she felt that he was finally lost to her. Yet it wasn't regret that filled her heart. Oh, there was a *tinge* of regret, she couldn't deny it. But mostly, it was pride she felt. Pride and humility at this man's strength of spirit. And only now, when it was too late, did she begin to admit that the strange emotions he stirred in her could so easily be of a quality that was love. Looking back over the years, she remembered their school days and the early times in Remmie's shop. She recalled how they seemed always to be growing within each other's shadow, and that there hadn't been a moment in his company when the passions he created in her seemed to dominate their relationship: irritation and resentment when he interfered in decisions she might have made too hastily; anger and fear whenever he came too close. Had these emotions been a camouflage for her real feelings? Laura didn't know. But what she did have, as she made her way to the back room and Sally, was a heavy heart and pain of a kind that she had not known before.

'Laura! Laura Blake!' Turning at the sound of her name, Laura immediately recognized the elderly woman rushing through the crowded room towards her. There was a comfortable familiarity about the round dimpled face, the dark smiling eyes, and the shrill friendly voice. The cumbersome figure brought itself to a halt before her, and brushing a stray wisp of grey hair out of her eyes, the woman cried in a breathless voice, 'Well! You *are* an ungrateful little sod! Thought you were making your way to Clayton Street, to come and see yer old friend Tilly, eh? That were a bloody month back! Forgot, didn't yer? You *did*, didn't yer? Ooh, for all you're grown up now, an' the grand lady, I ought to smack yer bloody arse.'

Laura's memory was jogged, and it was with a warm heart and a rush of conscience that she hugged the indignant woman. 'Tilly! Oh, Tilly, how could I forget? And I *did*, you're quite right.' Laura had spent two frantic days in London on business, and her arrangement to go down Clayton Street to see Tilly had completely slipped her mind. Unforgiveable!

Tilly Shiner pushed Laura away, and eyeing her severely, she snorted, 'Don't want a bloody smotherin' now, do I?' Then in a mock reprimanding tone, 'I'm well aware as you've med your way up in the world, my gal! An' I'm right proud o' that, oh yes. I can remember the times you'd come down the mill streets, draggin' that bloody 'andcart be'ind you like a soddin' cross! Aye, till yer back were fair broke.' She sniffled hard and dabbed a finger at a threatening tear. Then forcing a laugh, she caught Laura by the arm, 'It's titled folks an' silver these days, eh? But you don't want to forget the days when you were glad of a legless chair an' a bloody old well-used piss-pot my gal!' She broke into an uproarious cackle that attracted the attention of other guests, as they craned their necks to pinpoint the cause of the commotion.

Laura appreciated the remark and was surprised to find herself laughing out loud also. It felt good. She grabbed Tilly by the arm and still laughing, propelled her towards the backroom. 'Behave yourself, Tilly,' she giggled.

Tilly shook her head and winked. 'I'm off back i' the chaos, afore all the bloody ale's been supped! Best part of a wedding is the suppin! An' think on, get them soddin' feet o' yourn to Clayton Street.'

'You can count on it, Tilly,' Laura promised, releasing her.

Laura watched Tilly go, and for a while she thought of her father and Ruth Blake. Then before all the bad memories could come crowding back, she hurried on into the backroom.

Sally and Belle Strong had just finished setting out the display of presents, ready for the guests to troop through, after all the food and drink had gone.

As Laura entered the room, Sally turned to ask, 'Have you seen Mitch?'

'Yes,' Laura replied, 'He was outside.'

'Thank you for that lovely clock, Laura. I don't think I've ever seen such a beautiful time-piece.'

It was a delicate thing, of silver and gilt, and Laura knew that while Mitch would think it too fussy, Sally would treasure it.

'Belle told me that the only thing you didn't appear to have was a mantel clock.'

'Oh, I wouldn't dare put it on the mantel piece, Laura. It might get broken there.'

Laura smiled. Sally wasn't much younger than her own twenty-eight years, and yet in spite of the way she had coped with everything after Mabel Fletcher's death, there was still a child-like innocence about her. And it had never shown itself more than right now. In her bridal gown, glowing with happiness and her great love for Mitch, she looked radiant. Laura envied her, because she knew in her heart that such joy would never be hers.

'Will you be content to live over the shop, Sally?' Even as she asked, she knew that Sally's happiness would be wherever Mitch was.

'Oh yes! If only you knew how proud Mitch is of that shop, the improvements he's made, and the way he decorated the flat. Oh, Laura, it's lovely. And it's thanks to you and Remmie.'

'I'm glad things have worked out well. When I got my own business and Remmie decided to take life a little easier, the next thing was to sell the shop and give me a hand. It went without question that Mitch would be given the first refusal to buy the old shop.'

'Well, it's his life, Laura. And now it's ours, Mitch's, mine and Tom's.' She half turned to address the dark-haired boy who had been working on the far side of Belle, and whom Laura had not seen. Now Belle had gone to fuss around the back of the display and the boy looked towards Sally. 'Tom, come here a minute, love.' Then when it looked as though he might refuse, Sally insisted, 'Tom! Please, just for a moment.'

Laura was suddenly afraid. 'No, no, Sally,' She protested, 'it's best left alone.' She would have turned and hurried from the room, but the boy Tom was coming towards them, and she was unable to move her feet, which suddenly felt riveted to the floor.

Tom was tall for his age, and watching him now as he approached, Laura saw that he moved with a proud confidence, so very reminiscent of Mitch. She supposed that the boy had modelled himself on Mitch and had looked to him as being the father he had never known. Looking at him now, Laura's heart began to race, and when he came to stand before her, she caught her breath at the shock which rippled through her. The boy was so like her own dear father. The strong lines and dark features of Jud Blake's face had been reproduced almost to perfection. The only startling difference were the eyes, because the dark eyes which stared at Laura now were cold and accusing, and they appraised her with blatant contempt.

'Tom,' Sally placed an affectionate arm around the boy's shoulders, 'would you like to show Laura the presents?'

Laura was glad that Sally had not referred to her as 'your mother', for somehow it would not have been appropriate. Aware of the nervousness in her smile, Laura took a step forward, saying quietly, 'I would like that Tom, very much.' Almost at once, she saw the intensity of his glare deepen, and squirming out of Sally's embrace, he backed away, his eyes never leaving Laura's face. And in a growl that issued through clenched teeth, he said, 'Well, *I* wouldn't! You're nothing to me, and never will be. I *know* what you did! You gave me away.' Laura's heart ached as Tom's voice began to tremble and his eyes sparkled with tears as he spun away to run from the room.

Sally hung her head and closed her eyes, saying, 'Oh, Laura, I'm so sorry.' She was looking up at Laura now and her eyes were shadowed with tears.

Laura was very angry that Sally be made to suffer such anguish on her wedding day. If anybody should be sorry, it certainly wasn't Sally, but herself, for ever allowing Sally to shoulder the burden that was rightfully hers. Yet Sally had wanted Tom, and had gladly devoted herself to bringing the boy up. Laura knew that the money she had paid to Sally's account all this time, for the boy's keep, had lain untouched. Money that at first Sally must have desperately needed, and that her pride had not allowed her to touch. Laura had long been of the belief that Sally was made of much finer stuff than she herself was, and that in itself augured well for both Tom and Mitch.

Thinking of the boy's behaviour just now, Laura saw that while he may not have inherited Parry Griffin's looks, he certainly had the capacity to hate. But then again, she reminded herself, Tom could have got that undesirable trait from herself. She hoped it would not be a passion that would be allowed to dominate his life, for if it was, then he was in for a great deal of suffering. And who should know that better than Laura Blake?

Laura leaned forward to straighten Sally's head-dress, and in a quiet whisper, she said, 'No, Sally. It's *me* that should be sorry.' She kissed the sad little face and told her, 'I love you, you know that, don't you?'

Sally's smile lit up her face as she flung her arms about Laura, 'Oh Laura, me Mam was right. You *are* "a good 'un".' Both of them laughing, they did not see Belle until she spoke.

'The boy'll be alright, 'e's young, and 'e's sensible.' She gave Laura a strange look. 'I'm not rightly sure *where* the blame for all of this lies. But one thing I will tell you, Laura, there'll come a day when *somebody'll* be dreadful lonely, an' shedding bitter tears.'

'Oh, Belle!' Sally's voice was reprimanding. Belle nodded her head in warning before ambling away.

Laura knew Belle's ways very well. These past years Belle had been brought to the big house as housekeeper, with dear Tupper as handyman. Mitch had been the instigator of this, for his own peace of mind, and the arrangement had worked out extremely well. Belle had a way of speaking her mind that hadn't altered with the years, and Laura knew that Belle's warning had been for her alone. And it hurt very deeply. Belle was right, and here was the loneliness she spoke of. A loneliness of her own making. It was just punishment.

Chapter Thirty-five

'You know, Laura, you really have done well for yourself. That's a handsome rewarding property, indeed it is.' Mitch leaned against the car as he looked back past Laura, and swept his eyes over the building which, before Laura's acquisition, had been a spacious and impressive block of offices used by the various departments of the local government.

Laura's eyes followed his, and there was unmistakeable pride in her dark glowing eyes as they encompassed the building which she considered to be the real tangible representation of the impossible dream that she had coveted for as long as could be remembered.

It was an imposing building of splendid Edwardian structure, with the square strong lines of that particular era. Set back from the pavement in its own flagged square, and with a sizeable rear access where loading and unloading took place, it was an awesome and advantageous property. Its geographical position in the busy main shopping street of Blackburn attracted potential customers of all types. Laura had quickly taken advantage of the fact that not all of these people were what Remmie called 'money-folk'. Having realized the rewards of catering to their various needs and tastes, she had cleverly utilized the building to create three spacious showrooms, each linked with the other, and therefore offering several services all under the same roof. Her formula had been an instant success, and from the first day of opening its doors to the public, 'Laurems' establishment had never looked back. Even the name 'Laurems', derived by Laura from the first syllables of both her's and Remmie's christian names, had a particular ring of quality about it that had caused more than one customer to comment favourably.

In the face of Remmie's foreboding noises, which he had

since been forced to swallow, Laura had set up a contract with the utility furniture manufacturers, and as she had so shrewdly anticipated, this cheaper lighter furniture was well received by young married couples just setting up home. The whole of the middle floor was devoted to this particular line, and had proved to be a very lucrative venture.

The ground floor, laid out with the most expensive and solid furniture of rosewood, mahogany and walnut, attracted the more discerning and wealthier clients. These were mainly the well-to-do property owners and 'Gentlemen farmers' who were buying up the small holdings hereabouts, and developing them into sizeable conglomerates. Their exclusive abodes were the scattered mansions which had once belonged to local squires and gentry. When they visited Laurems, it was obvious that money was no object.

Recently Laura had commissioned Mitch to supply her with the splended reproductions he created with such perfection. This had resulted in extremely beneficial profit both for her and Mitch, whose own trade had moved away from furniture sales towards a wider choice of merchandize, and who found his time these days taken up more and more with renovating and polishing. Certainly, Laura's business demands on him were increasingly heavy. His careful workmanship was fast becoming known, and customers were beginning to ask for him by name. Laura was as proud of his achievements as she was of her own, although Mitch had often reminded her that he'd been known well enough for his work these many years, and it was only her new breed of clients that had elevated him to instant fame.

Remmie seemed content to quietly involve himself wherever needed at any given time, and he drifted between Mitch's and Laura's concerns, giving a helping hand and offering the occasional advice, even though he no longer owned a part in either. His money had been sunk into beautifying his home, a place of magnificence and tranquillity and one which he had grown to love. His life and its whole purpose was devoted only to the happiness of his two young women, Netti and Laura. He wanted no more than to see them both established.

To Laura, it was all a new and exciting world, and she had eagerly reached out to enjoy a strata of society that she had never known existed, and like a cloak of many exciting colours, she had wrapped it around her, experiencing each new discovery with delight and wonder. Now it was as though she had known no other way of life, nor wanted any.

She had harboured two great ambitions all these years. One was to see Netti on the road to being an accomplished concert pianist; and only the other evening Netti had mentioned over the phone that she had been chosen to play a medley of her own compositions during an evening of college entertainment for some visiting VIP's. It seemed a wonderful opportunity and Laura had been thrilled; more so, she thought, than Netti.

The second ambition Laura had worked towards was to be a woman of property. She looked up now at the enormous grey stone building, and even beneath its superior shadow, she felt she was the stronger of the two. And this, she vowed, was only the beginning.

Only during the last eighteen months had she opened up the top floor of her establishment, and now it was completely taken up with a comprehensive range of soft furnishings, such as lamps, rugs and curtains. At the rear of this floor she had incorporated a small tea-room, done out with attractive paned windows of leaded light and furnished in medieval design, with dark oak ladder-back chairs with tapestry pallet seats and tables of solid oblong tudor design. The whole effect was one of comfort and delightful period atmosphere which never failed to receive a flow of favourable comments from its many visitors.

But if Laura was to say which facet of her business she enjoyed the most, it would have to be the auction rooms. These ran along the rear of the offices on the ground floor and opened out into the enormous open cobbled area at the back of the building. It was here on Thursdays that people delivered a fascinating catalogue of items for auction the following Saturday. Often, prospective sellers would request that someone come out to clear a house, or collect a particular item. This was Remmie's specific field, but more often than not, Laura would accompany him and even help load the things into the van should it prove necessary. Since her idea of auction rooms had come into fruition, Laura had not missed a single sale; and with a commission of ten per cent on every pound earned, this too had proved to be a success. Occasionally, there would be a sale where every item offered was the property of Laurems, purchased individually or in bulk form from a house closure. On these occasions, the profit margin was considerably higher.

For the first three years that the establishment was open Laura had ploughed all the money back into it; improving its appearance; purchasing items that she had not at first been able to afford; installing essential lifts to the various floors; and extending her stock. Now, however, *this* year had actually shown a fine credit at the bank, and Laura found herself thinking more and more about the possibility of a second larger establishment in Manchester. But it was early days yet and such a move would require a great deal more money than she had yet accrued. Still, it was a goal, and one towards which she would aim with increasing tenacity.

Laura had been so lost in her thoughts that she had all but forgotten Mitch's presence and it was only now, when he moved to stand by her side, that she became aware of him. When she raised her eyes to look into his she sensed that he had in fact been watching her closely for some time.

'Are you happy, Laura?' he asked.

Laura laughed gently, and not with cynicism. 'I have no complaints.'

Mitch's gaze deepened and Laura swiftly looked away. 'About these pieces you're finishing, Mitch. You won't let me down? This sale is really important.'

'And so was last week's, and did I let you down then?'

'No.' She looked at him, her smile an apology. 'No, Mitch, you didn't. But tomorrow's sale *is* special. It's the widest I've ever advertised and we've had requests from all over the country. We've also secured some rare paintings, which will probably attract some very discerning customers. And if they have to go away without a painting, they will no doubt console themselves with an expensive consolation prize; at least that's what I'm hoping.'

'And these "discerning" customers chasing paintings, especially the Yourelli one, well, one of them wouldn't be Jake Thackerey, would it? Are you hoping for *that*, Laura?'

He had hit on a nerve, and Laura wondered what his reaction would be if she were to tell Mitch that yes, she *was* hoping to draw Jake Thackerey out of the wormholes. In response to repeated adverts far and wide, she had only two weeks ago received a request from Ria Morgan for a sale catalogue on the impending auction. She had sent it immediately.

It had been clear from Ria Morgan's polite impersonal letter, that she had failed to make the connection between Laura and Laurem's Auction Rooms. This had given Laura a measure of satisfaction; until it came to her that Ria Morgan probably did know. After all, she was no fool.

Mitch was talking again now, and Laura felt threatened as he came closer. 'Jake Thackerey was bad news for you, Laura. I hope to God you've no feelings left for the man. You made small fuss that time, but I'm not blind.' The underlying anger left his voice as he said with concern, 'Be careful, Laura. You've never seemed able to protect yourself against his sort. In spite of what you'd have folk believe, *I* know you're not above being hurt, like the rest of us poor mortals.'

Laura remembered the way in which Jake Thackerey had hurt her, but it was not in the way Mitch thought, because Mitch, in his innocence, thought she had loved the man. Mitch was not aware of what really happened between her and Jake Thackerey. Maybe the time was ripe now for her to hurt Jake Thackerey where he would feel it most, in his pocket.

'You needn't worry on my account, Mitch, I'm quite able to take care of myself.' Yet she was not forgetting that this was Mitch, who had known her most of her life and who was not easily moved from his opinions, especially when they concerned her. So, choosing to change the subject, she brought his attention back to the matter of the auction. 'Will you have the Elizabethan card-table restored? Robert Ford was inquiring only last Thursday.'

'It's all but ready.' Mitch chose not to press the business of Jake Thackerey, and Laura was grateful. 'I've not clapped eyes on Remmie lately, not since,' he paused and then went on vigorously, 'since I've been made an honest man of. Is he keeping well?'

'He's alright. But I have to watch that he doesn't overdo things. It's as well that we've got young Jay to keep pace with the accounts.'

Mitch appeared to be deep in thought, then suddenly he declared, 'Right! Well, I'll get off then.' He climbed into his car, asking, 'What time did you say the auctioneers were due?'

'Sharp on eight in the morning. The sale starts at eleven, half-an-hour later than usual.'

'What do you reckon, three hours?'

'I'd say it should take till half-past two, at least. I'll expect you here about seven.'

Mitch nodded in agreement, glanced at his watch and remarked, 'It's gone eight, you know. I could just as easily have got things ready in the morning.' He laughed. 'A slave-driver, that's what you've become! Go on, off home with you, and try not to frighten every Tom, Dick and Harry on the road! Worse thing I ever did, teaching you how to drive!' He closed his car door, started the engine and with a final wave, he was gone, leaving Laura to wonder what she would ever do without him.

Drawing her car to a halt outside the grand entrance to the house, Laura got out and for a long moment she leaned back against the car, her eyes sweeping over the vast expanse of landscaped grounds. She was not surprised that Remmie had grown to love this place in spite of his initial reservations towards it, for the lovely old house had a wonderful character all its own. And these gardens, oh, these magnificent gardens, whose beauty even in the rapidly fading daylight was undeniable. They stretched before her now in all their glory, a bright moving sea of colour and scent, created by multitudes of plants, shrubs and trees; some lately introduced by her and Remmie, but most were aged, having matured with nature and developed undisturbed these past years. The high strong walls which ran around the perimeter and protected the grounds were alive too, smothered with climbing plants such as clematis, pyracantha, rambling roses and rampant honeysuckles; all of which had been carefully retrained and supported. The enormous expanse of lawn, that had taken a great deal of hard work to reclaim from the creeping neglect, shone now like a velvet green carpet.

Laura gave a deep lingering sigh, a feeling of tranquillity and happiness filling her soul, as it always did when she gazed at, or walked in these rambling grounds. They were different in character to the moors, where she often escaped to even now, but there was something especially captivating about *all* of God's natural creation that left no room for comparisons.

Making her way up the half-circular steps that led to the front entrance, Laura glanced about the forecourt, and it was with some surprise that she noticed the absence of Remmie's car.

As the hands of the clock moved from nine to nine-thirty, then ten, and finally eleven pm, Laura grew increasingly agitated. What on earth was keeping Remmie? He'd been gone since seven o'clock that morning! But that was over fifteen hours ago and there was still no sign of him, and he'd left no word with Belle, or so the big woman had said. Laura racked her brains. Where on earth had he gone? There were times when he *would* just take himself off, she knew that. But she knew also that more often than not he had gone to kneel at Katya's graveside. It was his mood when he returned which always told her. Yet she never made any comment; his grief was still too private. Never before though, could she recall him having left the house for such a long period, without her knowing more or less where he'd gone.

This morning she had suspected that his trip was *not* to the churchyard, but to Freckleton. She had caught sight of the letter that arrived in yesterday's post, addressed to Remmie and bearing the stamp of The Convent of Mary Magdalene. Lizzie Pendleton had been a patient there these past four years. It had recently crossed Laura's mind to go and see her, but although she did not hate the old woman any more, she found the prospect of talking to her and looking at her unpleasant, and so she had resisted the idea.

The letter to Remmie could indicate one of two things; either her old enemy was dead, or had expressed a wish to speak to Remmie. Whatever it was, Laura was sure that she herself had no part to play in it.

For the third time since arriving home, Laura wandered through the house, enjoying the satisfaction and pleasure it always gave her. The entire left side of the ground floor was given over to the more formal aspects of life. It consisted of Remmie's large office, where Jay spent many hours working with him on the accounts, and beyond that lay Belle and Tupper's living quarters, together with a private area that had been placed at Jay's disposal during the evenings she stayed over.

After anxiously checking out of every front window as she passed it in anticipation of Remmie's arrival, Laura came back to the entrance hall, a spacious open area, lit now by an enormous chandelier with a myriad of light-giving crystals that sparkled on the mosaic patterned floor.

'I hope you've not been traipsing all over them rooms!' Belle's voice boomed across the hall. 'Making a mess and touching things! *Hours* I've spent today polishing and shining, till I'm all but bent double an' set in a particular shape.'

She came to stand in front of Laura, her short dimpled arms folded across a well padded chest, and her grey hair struggling to burst free from the halo-roll into which it had been squashed. 'I feel a right bloody idiot done up like this! I told you when I came to work for you, I weren't wearing no daft silly uniforms! Put it on an' try, you said. Well, I've tried it! and thank you very much, but I'll give it a miss. I shall peel this lot off smartish, now I've let you know my feelings on the matter. An' you've got my word, I'll *not* be putting it on my back again!'

Laura had great difficulty in stifling her laughter. She had to admit that the sight of dear homely Belle in a straight, light blue skirt and white blouse that strained dangerously at the button-holes didn't exactly measure up to the crisp sharp image required. 'Oh, alright, Belle,' Laura agreed, 'as long as you promise that the next time we invite people here, you won't let yourself be seen about in that flowered pinny and your hair hanging down all over the place.'

'Here now! There's no need for you to go feeling ashamed o' *me*, Laura Blake!' she retorted, shaking her head. She started to walk past Laura in somewhat of a huff.

At the door she paused and said, 'Well, I'm off to get these things off. And that Remmie'll have to settle for a cold supper when he thinks to get himself on home! I've thrown his earlier meal out, he might have told me he'd be so late!' But for all her bluster, there was a note of concern in her voice.

Laura watched Belle hurrying away and she called after her, 'He didn't tell *me* either, although I expect he meant to.'

Belle halted and swung round to say, 'Hmph. So says you!' Then muttering beneath her breath, she stalked off in the direction of the kitchen. No doubt to make sure I haven't been interfering with her pots and pans, thought Laura with a smile. But at least the subject of Tom had been let lie, where it could cause no friction. In Belle's continued silence on the matter, Laura could see that Sally had taken a firm line, and she was glad.

Laura was surprised to find her thoughts coming back to Jake Thackerey, and she wondered whether that Yourelli painting might just attract him. If it did, would he come on his own, or would he bring that woman with him? The thought amused her, and with a wicked gleam lighting her eyes, she hoped that they *would* come those two, yes, she hoped they would condescend to attend the auction. It could add spice to the proceedings!

She was walking down the corridor now, and as she went, the bright expensive decor and luxurious space of it all pleased her. As always, she was forced to think of the narrow cobbled streets of her childhood, with their tiny houses, dark dreary rooms and outside lavvies. She had come a long way, but not, she considered, far enough, for this lovely old house belonged to Remmie and not to her. It was past time that she acquired a home of her own, as much as she loved dear Remmie.

She went into the drawing-room, an elegant room with high sculptured ceilings and an air of refined style, evident in the carefully chosen pieces of furniture, all of which were furnished in deep red mahogany. The Sheraton sideboard, matching sofa-table and long leather topped coffee table were complimented by the three piece suite of soft hide, luxuriant in a rich burgundy shade. The walls were the merest complexion of cream, as was the carpet and the table lamps, one placed on the coffee table and one either end of the sofa-table. In this room, on days when it was too bitingly cold to wander about in the garden, Laura would derive much pleasure from looking out of the tall glass door which led out onto the paved area which in summer was a magnificent sun-trap, and where Remmie sat for many an hour until the sum became so hot that it forced him back into the drawing-room for a cooling spell. Here in this lovely room, she and Remmie would sit discussing the work of the day, or ruminating on one of Netti's long welcome letters; or maybe they would argue about whether she should buy this or sell that. But they were nearly always of the same mind, and sometimes Remmie would give way and sometimes she would give way. But she always held his opinions in the highest regard, because he knew well the fundamentals of trading, albeit a restricted occupation for him these days. And apart from business, he was her friend, and she loved him.

Laura crossed to the small bar over by the french window, and poured herself a glass of wine. The bar had been installed for the benefit of the occasional visitor. Neither she nor Remmie had a taste for drinking, but tonight, she felt on edge, anxious, and somehow she thought a glass of wine might calm her down. Settling into one of the deep leather chairs, she glanced up at the clock on the mantelpiece. Eleven fifteen! Where in God's name was he? If she didn't hear from him soon, but no, he was alright, she was certain. These days he seemed so absent-minded. He'd probably forgotten to leave a message, and at this very minute was saying a jolly goodnight to one of his old cronies.

In fact, Remmie was at that moment within twenty minutes of home and Laura. It had been a long and tiring day, a day that had started with a short anxious letter from Netti some forty-eight hours ago, and finished with him leaving a less than happy niece in the roaring bustling city of London, some five hours drive behind him. If he had been allowed his own way, Netti would have been here in this car and on her way home with him right now!

He was satisfied though, that he had left Netti happier than when he had found her at midday. Her brief urgent letter had asked whether it was possible for him to pay her a visit, as she wanted to talk to him without Laura's knowledge. If it was possible! By! Didn't the lass know by now, that where she and Laura were concerned, he would make *anything* possible? Hadn't he given up his little shop so that Laura wouldn't feel guilty about setting up what was in effect competition to his own business? And hadn't he agreed to move from the house where he'd been happy with his Katya, so that Laura and Netti could have that grand place, which at first he'd resented and then come to love? It was a great comfort to him that he had such a legacy to leave the two lasses after he was gone.

But what to do about this present dilemma? Well, it was a

tricky business and there were no two ways about that! Here was Netti, just eight months from the final exams that would take her at long last away from the studying that she found so grinding, and into the world where she would make her mark, he was certain. But talking to Netti today, Remmie had discovered that the nearer she came to taking up her fine career, the more distressed she was becoming. She had moved out of the College accommodation and into a private lodging house with friends, whom he had not been invited to meet, because of Netti's insistence that he be shown Regent's Park and the nice little tea-room where they had taken a bite to eat. But Netti's distress had been painfully obvious to him during their time together.

Later, after they had talked, he had been successful in his hesitant request that she should give it at least until Christmas, when she would be home for a while, and they could all see what must be done. Netti had agreed, but she had confided her anxiety about 'letting Laura down'.

Remmie had dismissed such speculation as nonsense, but secretly, he too was anxious. Laura had made many sacrifices over the years to see Netti realize a brilliant musical career. Although he knew Laura to be a strong minded and iron willed business-woman; it was a plain fact that where Netti was concerned, she was very vulnerable. She loved her sister with ferocity and it was with that same fanatical ferocity that she had schemed and worked to get Netti where she was today. He himself had seen the danger signs though, and like a fool had let them wash over him.

Two promises had been exchanged today between himself and Netti. Netti had promised to give it another two months or so, until the Christmas holidays when she would be home. And he for his part had promised not to say anything to Laura. Oh, and to think that in her present frame of mind and rather than face Laura, Netti had lied about going abroad with her friends that summer, and had been in London all that time!

As he turned into the drive way, Remmie remembered the note that he should have left, explaining to Laura that he was at a friend's and wouldn't be home till late. He had discovered the note still in his trouser pocket, less than half-an-hour back, when he'd fished about for a hankie. Well, it was likely she would give him a dressing down for being so thoughtless. And quite right too! And no doubt Belle was waiting up to put in her twopennorth. Whatever he got, he deserved; but as likely as not, it would all blow over quickly on the swift production of the note in his pocket.

Oh, and how he wished this other blessed business would all blow over quickly. But deep down inside, he sensed that it would not. For the life of him, he couldn't see the outcome of it all, nor could he rid himself of the feeling that someone was bound to be hurt, and hurt badly!

There was something else too. He had guessed from Netti's attitude that there was more to this whole affair than met the eye. Yet when he'd broached this to her, she had swiftly dismissed the idea as being his imaginings. But they weren't! Netti was hiding something from him; he knew her well enough to be sure of it. So, between now and the Christmas holidays, he would pay her *another* visit. Only this time, he would not be so easily dissuaded from seeing where she lived, nor from seeing for himself the quality and cut of her friends.

Chapter Thirty-six

Laura was out of the house and on her way into Blackburn unusually early the next morning, leaving Remmie in bed sleeping off his late arrival home last night and recovering from the reproachful welcome he had walked into; especially from Belle who had made it quite clear in no uncertain terms that Remmie was 'not a youngster to be gallivanting about till all hours!' His response had been to grab her in a bear hug, twirl her round till she was breathless and then make off to his bedroom, leaving Laura smiling and Belle hurling abuse after him.

The market clock was chiming six am as Laura parked her car in the cobbled area at the rear of the auction rooms. She manoeuvred it well into the corner over by the high stone wall, where it was less likely to become an obstacle to what she hoped would be a constant arrival of vehicles later in the morning.

She let herself in through the service doors, locked them behind her, switched on the lights, then quickly made her way through the auction rooms and on into the ground floor showroom. Going over to the panel of switches, Laura flicked them all down, and at once the entire area was illuminated by the soft lighting from the chandeliers hanging low in the ceiling, which gave the whole area an atmosphere of intimate luxury and affording just the right setting for the expensive merchandize.

She stepped further into the showroom and stood for a while, allowing her eyes to take in the scene before her, a scene which had never once failed to instil in her a feeling of great pride and achievement. This floor, with its display of magnificent furniture, was her favourite. She moved forward now, going from setting to setting, each one a room on its own and

designed accordingly, with matching period furniture, complimented by expensive table-lamps, exquisite porcelain
ornaments and deep pile scatter rugs of pastel hues.

Whilst looking at the extent of her achievements so far, a
sudden image forced itself into Laura's mind. A sharp painful
image of the tiny parlour where she had watched her father's
futile struggle for life day after day, week after week. And
where finally, she had held him fast in her arms, unable to stem
the ebbing tide that had washed the life from his poor thin
body, leaving her with only the shell that had been her father,
and a heart unbearably heavy in its grief; a grief that had only
strengthened with the events that were to follow.

Laura felt that same grief now. But the tears that welled up
to fill her eyes were not allowed to spill. Swallowing the hard
persistent lump in her throat, she drove from her mind all that
would rise to haunt her.

Laura went up the stairs to the next floor, which housed
what was referred to as 'soft furnishings', vital accessories,
which according to Laura were the key factors in turning a
house into a home. To this end, she gave the purchasing of
such merchandize her own personal attention, and it was she
who supervised the finished displays.

Up on the top floor, Laura surveyed the clean sharp lines of
the vast array of furniture that provided the less well-off with a
nice home at prices they could easily afford, and which still
returned a reasonable profit. Remmie had prophesied doom at
what he'd called her 'female stubbornness' at pursuing such a
project. But when it had proved to be an immense success, he
had been forthright in his apology, recognizing once again that
she was a 'born business-woman'.

Laura left all the lights on because by now it was five
minutes to seven and it was a rule that her assistants, one
senior and one junior on each floor, and a floor manager who
moved from one level to the other, should be on the premises
no later than seven-thirty. Though the main doors were not
opened until an hour after that, she herself set the example of
arriving a good half-hour before any of them.

As promised, and using the key with which Laura had
entrusted him, Mitch walked into the auction rooms at seven
o'clock, his overalls already pulled on in readiness for work.

'Right then!' His tone conveyed the same eagerness. 'Let's check through the catalogue, and get the seating set up.'

'My! You're not about to waste any time this morning, then? Good!' Laura collected her own wrap-around overall which concealed all but the trim turn-back collar of her smart sage-green worsted dress. Then she stood before Mitch, and gave a mock salute, saying, 'Ready for duty, Cap'n.'

Mitch didn't reply, but smiled in that attractive easy manner which so often disturbed her. Then his smile broke into a laugh and he said, 'Come on! There's work to be done.'

Half-an-hour later, the room was set out and every item checked, when Jay came in.

'Ah! Just the person, Jay.' Laura watched as the young woman came towards her. Not for the first time, she thought how uncannily like Ria Morgan Jay was. The same slim petite figure, the small oval face and brownish hair. Yes, there *was* a striking similarity, but there it ended, for Jay's nature was gentle and caring. Laura had found her to be a person of high principles. She was also extremely efficient at everything that Laura set her to do. It was for this reason, and much to the indignation of her male employees, that Laura had given Jay a position of high authority, and in Laura's absence, any problems arising were referred to Jay's jurisdiction. It had been an unpopular decision with the men, who took it as a personal insult, especially the floor manager who pointed out to Laura with some considerable frustration that he could boast a wealth of experience in the trade and that he didn't take too kindly to consulting a person junior to his years, and a woman at that!

Laura had simply given him the choice of supporting Jay as over-manager, or leaving. She would, of course, supply him with exemplary references. He chose to stay, and when later, Jay reported that he was a great help to her, being quick and conscientious, Laura was glad that she had not admitted her innermost thoughts to the man; that she had little faith in the male of the species, and when she had to allocate someone to a post demanding absolute loyalty and keen business sense, she would select a woman to fill it every time.

'I expect you'll stay here until the end of the auction?' Jay asked now.

'That's right. So you're in charge up there, and unless

there's a dire emergency, I don't want to know.'

It wasn't long before the auctioneers arrived and as always the place became a hive of activity, with the porters lining up in lots the smaller items to be offered. The impressive wooden rostrum was brought in from the van and set up under the fastidious instructions of Mr Peeble, the auctioneer.

The cobbled yard was soon filled with tightly-parked cars, vans and lorries, their owners similarly packed into the rows of seats which had been carefully positioned earlier by Laura and Mitch.

The auction was due to start in fifteen minutes, and Mitch positioned himself in the side room, where he assisted the porters. Laura had spent the last ten minutes hovering by the outside door, her attention on the car-park and the entrance beyond. It didn't look as though Jake Thackerey and the woman intended coming, and the realization brought a rush of disappointment, which showed in her expression now as she turned to go back into the auction rooms.

Suddenly, from the corner of her eye, she perceived a movement and she swung round to see a car which had turned in at the entrance, and was now searching for a suitable place in which to park. Laura wanted so desperately for it to be them! She had never really forgiven Jake Thackerey for his treatment of her and for being the despicable coward that he was. Nor had she forgotten Ria, who had resorted to her own particular brand of cruelty and had enjoyed gloating over her triumph. Well, they deserved each other, those two. Mitch was wrong if he thought Jake Thackerey meant anything to her. He had simply been the means whereby her hopes might have been realized. That was all!

As the car drew to a halt she wasn't surprised to see that it *was* them after all. Ria was still the slim elegant figure that Laura remembered, and Jake Thackerey, now closing the door behind her, had lost none of his good looks, although Laura thought he looked like a man haunted.

As they walked towards the steps, not yet having lifted their eyes to see her, Laura stepped out to where she would be in full view once their attention was drawn towards the premises.

Ria Morgan saw her first, and it was evident from the naked shock on her face that Laura Blake was the very last person

404

she had expected to see. The sharp gasp of breath that she took and the sudden way she came to a halt, caused Jake Thackerey to look at her, and then to follow the surprised stare that was directed towards Laura.

He said her name quietly, but not so quietly that it didn't fill Laura's ears with pleasure. Laura felt that he would have bounded up the steps to her, but by that time Ria Morgan had regained her composure and she laid a restraining hand on Jake's, and said, 'Let's not forget what we came for, Jake.' Then, the two of them moved towards Laura, and her beauty was never more striking than in the smile with which she greeted them. It was a radiant, triumphant smile, and when she said, 'Jake, Ria, how lovely to see you after all this time,' she meant every word.

Ria smiled back and her surprise at Laura's elegant appearance showed in her eyes. 'I wouldn't have thought this kind of sale would have attracted *your* attention, Laura. Or have you landed an exclusive position with the auctioneers?'

'But how clever of you Ria. Yes, very exclusive. This establishment is *mine*! And the auctioneers are acting on my behalf.'

Laura thought she had never enjoyed anything as much as she now enjoyed the vacant open expression of Ria Morgan's face. Yet she was intrigued that Jake Thackerey showed no surprise. As she looked into his eyes, she saw that same desire that had darkened his eyes before whenever he'd gazed at her. He held out his hand and she took it to feel his fingers close around hers. 'Congratulations. I knew you would make it, Laura. I saw it in you a long time ago.'

'Thank you. The sale's about to start. You'd better go in.' She wasn't fooled by those dark hypnotic eyes. She stepped aside and gestured towards the doorway, and as she did so, two things happened. First, Mitch appeared in the doorway to tell Jake and Ria in a curt voice, 'If you intend bidding, I suggest you join the others.' Then, while she watched Mitch leading them into where the bidding was already underway, a voice spoke behind her, smooth and velvet in tone; 'Oh, Laura, still the beautiful witch.'

She turned quickly, and with a startled expression she looked towards the column against which a man was leaning, and with a trembling heart she recognized the handsome arrogance of Pearce Griffin. These past years had not diminished his dashing style, or the striking magnetism of his beckoning smile. He came towards her now, and they stood facing each other. As his eyes seemed to melt into hers, Laura imagined she felt like how a trapped animal must feel when finding its hunters moving in. It was still there! God help her, she still felt desperately attracted to him.

'Given you a bit of a shock, have I? Well, it was no more than you gave me, *and* the Thackereys just now.' For the briefest of moments, his dark eyes hardened and the smile left his handsome mouth, as he added, 'But even then, not so big a shock as I had when Molly got word to me about my father.' He stopped as though waiting for a response from Laura, but she didn't give him that satisfaction. Indeed, her chin was defiantly thrust out, and in spite of the anxiety she felt, her look was a challenging one. Their eyes met, but it was he who gave way, and with a swift disarming smile he went on, 'Still, like I told Molly, he only had himself to blame!' Laura wondered whether he really believed that, and somehow she doubted it. But she said nothing, and now he changed the subject. 'Those two, they never stop talking about you, well, perhaps not so much talking as arguing.' He nodded his head in the direction of the door, and Laura wondered how he had come to know them, and just how much they had put him in the picture. But now he was speaking again; 'Jake and me, we do a bit of business now and then. Came on hard times, didn't I? Found myself in their circle. Made myself useful.'

'Scum will always find their own kind!' she retorted.

He shrugged his shoulders and Laura let him go on. There was much she wanted to know.

'I hope they don't come up against too much opposition on that Yourelli painting. I'm not the only one that's been on hard times. That painting's the only reason they're here; it's a lifesaver. They've got a ready buyer, eager to part with good money for it.' He laughed, but it was not a sound of mirth, for it was marbled with spite. 'Good job he didn't know where to come for it, eh? Else he might have come himself and beat them at their own game!'

'How much can they go to?' A plan had already formed in

Laura's mind, and the attraction of Pearce Griffin was nothing compared to the attraction of getting her own back on those two. So they were down on their luck, eh? This was even better than she had hoped.

Pearce Griffin had lit a cigarette which he placed between his lips, and drawing on it slowly, he gazed down at her, a long intimate gaze, that rushed the beat of her heart. Then he looked beyond her and swept his arm in a wide half-circle. 'Now I can see how you came to own all this.' He looked at her again, and his voice was soft and enticing. 'You're shrewd, Laura, and more woman than I've ever met.' He laughed softly and said, 'You realize if *they* go broke, that leaves *me* without the means of support? I do enough for them to keep me ticking over. It's *not* much, but it keeps body and soul together.'

'What can they go to?' Laura was impatient now. She feared that the painting may already be under the hammer.

'Is it worth anything to *me*?' He waited for her answer, but when none was forthcoming, he just smiled and said, 'Two thousand. That's about their limit.'

Laura returned his smile and said, 'You really are a bastard, aren't you?' And then she left him and hurried inside. She was vaguely aware that he had followed her in, and now, still smiling, he was leaning against the inner door, watching her.

It took only a few minutes to find Mitch. He was supervising the order of catalogue, and at the very moment she drew level with him, he was already passing the Yourelli painting to the waiting porter. There was no time to be wasted. She waited for the porter to disappear, then seeing Mitch's questioning look, she said in a stiff urgent voice, 'Quick. Go out there and bid on that painting. Take the bid over two thousand pounds.'

Mitch's curious frown deepened into suspicion. 'What are you saying, bid on your own painting? And two thousand pounds?'

'Please Mitch!' she could hear the auctioneer's patter in the background. The price was already nine hundred. 'Don't waste time. I'll explain later. Just do as I ask!'

'By God, Laura. I don't know what you're up to.' Mitch caught her by the shoulders, only to release her again, his face alive with accusation. 'It's Thackerey, isn't it? You're trying to force the price up,' his voice had dropped to a harsh whisper, 'or are you trying to deny him the painting altogether?'

So he had guessed. She might have known that Mitch would be on to her game. 'So you won't do as I ask?'

'You know I won't! I wouldn't give the man a minute of my time. But I'll play no part in your dirty little games!'

'Then I'll manage without your help!' Laura turned from him and swept out of the room and into the hall, where the auctioneer had just called a price of one thousand four hundred. Laura stood for a moment, half-hidden by the screens. The bidding had slowed down, and judging by the expressions on the many faces in the room, Laura feared that the interest too had reached its peak. But then, the price was about right. It had reached her expectations. From the end of the third row, a head movement caught her eye. The new price was quickly called out. One thousand five hundred. The bidder relaxed and waited. Laura recognized him as Robert Ford, a good-looking elegant middle-aged man. He was a man of questionable morals, considerable wealth and powerful influence and he lived in a grand old place some miles away towards Lytham. He was well known hereabouts as a true connoisseur. His blue-blooded passion embraced an impressive list of women, an enviable collection of priceless treasures and ill-begotten reputation.

Laura caught his eye and smiled. He was a regular visitor to the auctions, and had been instrumental in introducing other, equally valuable clients. He didn't return her smile. His attention was directed towards the rostrum. His well-bred features, with a straight classical nose, fine-lipped mouth and distinguished greying temples, were intent on the purpose of acquiring the painting. He had obviously developed a taste for Yourelli paintings. But Laura knew that he would not increase his bid by much, if at all.

Jake Thackerey was staying in, and the price quickly rose to one thousand eight hundred. Laura could see the painting going to Jake Thackerey, and she was incensed by the possibility and by the smug anticipation on Ria Morgan's face. It crossed her mind to enter the bidding herself, claiming that she was acting by proxy on behalf of an interested client. She hesitated at such an intervention, but now, with Jake Thackerey's last bid of two thousand pounds seemingly lying unchallenged,

Laura felt she had no choice. But before she could put the exercise into motion, the auctioneer called out a new bid of two thousand one hundred. But who? *Who* had made the bid? Had Mitch changed his mind? She swung round to look behind her. Her sweeping glance told her there was no-one there. She scanned the rows before her, and as she did so, Jake Thackerey entered a further bid. The new bidder swiftly challenged, and she saw that it was Pearce Griffin.

It was quickly over, and while the next item was being offered, Laura made her way towards the outer door, indicating to Pearce Griffin to follow her. Jake Thackerey and Ria Morgan had also slipped out quietly, and met Pearce Griffin and Laura at the foot of the steps. Laura met Ria Morgan's hardened stare, and was shocked by the hatred in the other woman's eyes. Yet there were no screams of accusation or threats of revenge; just a hate-filled glare as she muttered, 'Bitch! You bitch!' Then she got into the car and looked at the floor. Jake Thackerey looked first at Laura, and then at Pearce Griffin, who shook his head and smiled. 'Sorry. But you know, I always did like to be on the winning side, and the truth is, Laura brings out the worst in me.'

Jake Thackerey didn't answer. Instead, he turned to Laura and addressing her in a quiet, controlled voice, he said, 'What I did to you, well, I can't blame you now. But this business is full of ups and downs. It's just a setback, that's all.' Then he looked back towards the auction rooms before addressing her again, and when he did Laura detected a note of warning in his tone. 'Enjoy all of this while you can. Nothing is ever as it seems.' He was deliberately looking at Pearce Griffin. 'Especially people. Isn't that right, Pearce? We *all* have our little secrets, eh?'

Laura wondered at his remark, but it caused her no concern. She met his gaze with cool arrogance and said, 'Good-bye, Jake. I don't expect to see you again. Now, you'll forgive me if I don't see you off, I have some business to discuss with Robert Ford.' She said nothing more and walked away to go back into the building. Pearce Griffin looked at Jake, raised his eyebrows in mock question, and quickly followed her.

Laura knew the impossibility of approaching Robert Ford while he was deeply engrossed in the bidding. So, conscious of the fact that Pearce Griffin was just behind her, she made her way to the small private office.

She sat by the huge desk, rising when Pearce Griffin opened the door and entered the room with a boldness that immediately irritated her. He closed the door quietly and came across the room towards her, saying in a voice filled with admiration, and Laura thought a little envy, 'You've come a long way, Laura, a long way.' Then in typical fashion, he approached her, saying, 'I thought you'd changed when I first saw you today. But you haven't, apart from the expensive clothes. You're just the same as you've always been, only more so. Everybody said you would get whatever you went after, and you've proved them right.' He moved closer, and in spite of herself, Laura took a delight in his nearness. 'You were always a good-looker. But you've grown even more beautiful.' He was stroking her hair now and his mouth was caressing her ear. 'You always did crazy things to me, you little witch, you know that, don't you. Nobody, no woman I've ever met, can rile me like you can.' He slid his arms around her and pressed his mouth over hers. When Laura felt his hand slide beneath her dress, to caress the warmth and stiffness of her nipple, she knew she should resist. Her every instinct recoiled against him. But lost in the swimming passion of his kiss, she could do nothing.

The moment was violently lost as the door was thrown open and they turned, startled, to be confronted by Remmie, his face displaying such anger that he seemed like a stranger to Laura. Quickly, she stepped forward, at the same time discreetly adjusting her clothes.

'Remmie.' But he looked beyond her to Pearce Griffin.

'Get out! We don't want you or your sort on these premises!' The echo of his words fell away into the silence that followed, during which Laura feared from Remmie's appearance that he might collapse. She ventured towards him, but he held out a restraining hand. 'I want him *out* of here!' And then, it came to her that he must know; he must know that this man's father had raped her. But no, he couldn't. She had told no one. Not even Mabel Fletcher.

She turned to Pearce Griffin and told him firmly, 'You'd better go.'

For a brief moment, he stared at her as though in disbelief, then slowly, a smile transformed his features and he walked away from Laura, saying to Remmie as he passed, 'Old feuds die hard, eh, Remmie?'

'Just get out!'

Pearce Griffin laughed softly and turned at the door to say to Laura, 'I'll be in touch.'

When he had gone, Remmie stood for a second, then as though his energy had suddenly flowed away, he sank into the nearest chair. Laura, wanting to ask him, but then *not* wanting to, in case she was wrong, came to sit on the arm of the chair. Sliding her arm around his neck, she said, 'What is it, Remmie?' suspecting that even he was surprised by the vehemence of his outburst.

He murmured in a subdued voice, 'I'm sorry lass, an' you're past old enough to lead your own life, but I wonder if you know what a rod you could be making for your own back?' He looked at her now, a long searching look that she understood, and then he warned, 'If that one means anything at all to you, lass, he means trouble! Them sort don't easily forget when one o' their own kind ends up the way of his father. No, you'd do well to steer clear on him. It fair breaks me up, lass, to see you mixing with that kind.'

Laura sensed the truth in his words and bent to kiss his greying hair. 'The answer's simple then. You *won't* see me mixing with that kind. He was here only because of the sale. That's all,' she said reassuringly.

'That the truth, lass?'

'That's the truth, Remmie.' And it was. She had no intention of ever seeing him again.

The sale went on longer than expected and it was approaching two pm when at last the auction rooms were empty. The showrooms too were busy, right up to five o'clock, when they closed for the weekend. When Laura eventually followed Remmie home at seven o'clock, the long day was telling on her. She was thankful to relax into a hot bath.

Remmie was unusually quiet, and when he eventually stood up and declared that he was off to his bed, Laura felt relieved. Yet, at the same time she was concerned. Remmie had not

411

been his usual self these last few days; almost as though he had some worrying matter pressing on his mind. She had not pried, because she knew Remmie from old. If he had anything to tell her, he would do just that, but only if and when he wanted to. And maybe it was nothing more than he was still missing Katya.

Not long after, Laura gratefully went to her own bed. On her way past Remmie's room, she looked in and, satisfied that he was fast asleep, closed the door and went on her way. Her thoughts had grown sad at the thought of that dear man. Poor Remmie, he was a lonely person these days, and however hard she tried to draw him out of himself, he seemed to slip away deeper into the memories he cherished.

The anger he had shown today when confronting Pearce Griffin had been his strongest display of emotion for some years. Again, she pondered on what could *really* have triggered off such a vicious attack. It was true that there had never been any love lost between the Griffins and Remmie. But as a rule, Remmie was a patient man who bore no grudges. Perhaps he was just at that age, she thought, when patience and forgiveness were trying virtues. Ah well, there was nothing lost. In fact, Remmie had no doubt saved her from making a fool of herself, as she was wont to do when subjected to the devilish charms of Pearce Griffin.

As for Jake Thackerey and Ria, Laura's conscience had bothered her after their departure. But they would bounce back again, she promised herself. Their sort always did. All the same, she hoped that by denying them a fat easy profit today, she had repaid at least some of the frustration that they had caused her.

Now as she entered the bedroom, a wicked smile whispered over her face. She hadn't come off too badly anyway. The affluent and waywardly charming Robert Ford had been glad to accept the painting at his final bid of two thousand two hundred pounds, so she had made more of a profit than expected.

On the whole, it had been a satisfying day, leaving her much to think about. Strange though, how the last thought on her mind before she went to sleep was Mitch.

Chapter Thirty-seven

Soft flakes of snow were falling as Laura watched from the window, her eyes beginning to ache from their vigil.

'Are you going to stand there all night?' Belle bustled into the room and went over to the small mahogany table by the settee and clattered the tray onto it. 'Come an' drink this coffee afore it goes cold like the last lot!'

Laura turned and smiled at the disgruntled expression on the little woman's face. 'Leave it there, Belle. I'll have it in a minute.'

'Hmph! That's what you said last time.' She straightened her back and lifted her chin. Scowling deeply, she went to the fireplace, where she irritated the fire with the long brass poker and then she marched out of the room, saying, 'She'll not be here any quicker with you glueing your nose to that window, my gel!'

Laura looked deeper into the growing darkness, and satisfied that there was still no movement along the driveway, she walked over to the settee, where she sat down and poured herself a cup of coffee. As she slowly sipped it, she thought of these last few months, and a frown traced itself across her forehead. Remmie was keeping something from her. She knew him well enough to be certain of that. Since the day of the sale, he had seemed unusually edgy. In spite of her questions, he still hadn't confided in her. But whatever it was that had happened and he insisted on keeping from her was obviously causing him some anxiety, because lately he had grown more quiet and troubled.

This evening particularly, before setting out to collect Netti from the station, he had seemed like a cat on hot bricks. But then, she reminded herself, so had she, because Netti was coming home for Christmas, and she was bringing a friend.

Much as Laura enjoyed the bustle and excitement of customers thronging in to spend their money at Laurems, she had looked forward to the holiday closure, when she, Remmie and Netti could spend that precious time together. And selfish as she was where Netti was concerned, Laura was slightly peeved at having to share her with this friend she was bringing. But she was excited, and until Netti's arrival, she would not be able to sit still.

She finished her coffee before going back to stand by the window again. Oh, she had missed Netti, and strangely enough, she seemed to have missed her bright company more since Mitch and Sally's wedding.

The thought of Mitch and Sally ... and young Tom ... brought a feeling of sadness which threatened to cloud her joy. They had each other, and their contentment stemmed from each other. Laura, however, could not erase that slight envy from her heart, for in the face of their apparent happiness, she, on the other hand, seemed to be oddly afraid and lonely most of the time. But when this feeling came over her she forced herself to think of the achievements in her life, and her spirits would lift. After all, she had much to be thankful for.

Lost in her thoughts, she hadn't seen the car drive up, and now there was a knocking at the front door. She heard the echo of Belle's feet across the marble floor and a flurried exchange of greetings, before she went quickly into the hall and caught Netti in a loving embrace. Then she held her out at arms' length. 'It's been a whole year,' she said, 'Let me have a look at you.'

What she saw was a lovely young woman, who had a calm, confident air about her. The long fair hair had been trimmed to the shoulders, and she was disagreeably surprised to note how much more striking now was Netti's likeness to Katya Thorpe. There was something else too. It showed in the hesitant way Netti had returned Laura's embrace, and it was there in the blue eyes that had grown a shade deeper looking at Laura now with a disturbing appeal. Laura stroked the hair from Netti's face as she had often done when they were both very much smaller. 'You look really lovely.' She smiled, and it struck her that Netti seemed unable to return her smile. 'Everything's alright, isn't it, Netti?' she asked.

'Of course. Why shouldn't it be?' Netti's quiet expression broke into a smile, but to Laura it wasn't convincing, and she had not missed the anxious look on Remmie's face as he took his coat off and shook the snow from it. Belle folded the coat over her arm, and looking beyond Remmie, she asked, 'Will I take yours as well?'

It was then that Laura became aware of the figure standing quietly by the door.

Laura thought later that her face at that instant must have been a study, and she could vaguely recall Remmie's eyes intent on her expression. But she had gained much practice in disguising her real feelings, so when Marlow Connelly held out his hand in friendship, Laura was able to take it secure in the knowledge that the shock she had experienced was not evident on her face. He was everything Netti had said he would be; he was tall, handsome, impeccably dressed and there was about him an air of quiet confidence. But what Netti had omitted to say was that Marlow Connelly was as black as the darkest night Laura had ever seen. 'It's nice to meet you,' he said most charmingly, his brown eyes curiously wary of Laura, whom he found to be far more beautiful than Netti had described, 'I've heard so much about you from Netti.' He released Laura's hand and turned towards Remmie. 'Netti's a lucky girl to have such a family.'

'Oh, Netti,' Laura was in her element at seeing Netti home again, 'it's lovely to have you home; what a holiday we'll have.' She had clasped Netti's hand in her own, and would have danced her towards the drawing room. But something in Netti's expression warned Laura to be still. When Netti then withdrew her hand, Laura was compelled to ask, 'What is it? Is anything wrong, Netti?' She could not rid herself of the feeling that there was some sort of conspiracy here, and everyone knew about it but her.

Before Netti was forced to give an answer, Remmie stepped forward to address Marlow Connelly. 'You an' Netti will want to freshen up 'afore dinner, eh?'

'I think that would be a good idea. Thank you.' There was no disguising the relief in his voice, or in the looks exchanged between him and Netti as he took her hand.

'Right then!' Remmie slid his arm about Laura's shoulders

and propelled her rather hurriedly towards the drawing-room, calling out behind him, 'Go on then, you two. Netti knows the way well enough, Marlow. Belle, ask Tupper to bring some logs in would you please? Oh, an' a fresh brew o' tea.'

'Huh! Could sink a battleship with the tea you drink, Remmie Thorpe!' was Belle's parting remark.

In the drawing-room, Laura rounded on Remmie as he closed the door behind them. 'Remmie! What *is* going on? Netti's keeping something from me, and you know what it is, don't you?'

Remmie sucked air in through his nose, rammed his hands deep into his pockets and then released the air through his mouth with a hiss. 'Aye, I do know, lass. I do.' He sat down on the settee and gestured for her to sit alongside him. Laura grew inpatient and fearful all at once, but she said nothing for the moment, and when he took her hand in his, she waited, her eyes intent on his face.

'Laura. There *is* some'at you'il 'ave to know, and it's best that I'm the one to tell you. I've known about it some time now, an' I know I should've told you afore. But I gave the lass my promise that I'd say nowt till she were 'ere this Christmas. There's a lot she wants to explain.' He sighed as though searching for the right words. Then his kindly eyes melted into a frown and he told her, 'The lass won't be going back to university, Laura. She's with child. She an' Marlow were married three weeks back.'

The silence that followed seemed to pound in Laura's ears, as Remmie's words repeated themselves over in her mind. Not going back? Married, and with child? No, that wasn't the case. Remmie had got it all wrong. Yet one look at Remmie's face told Laura otherwise. He had told her the truth, the devastating truth. What future now for Netti? She rose to her feet, and looking down at Remmie she asked in a strange voice, 'So it was all for nothing? All the scheming and penny pinching, working and hoping; all for nothing!'

Laura felt as though a cold hand had grasped her heart and was squeezing it mercilessly. All the emotions racing through her gave no heed to thought. She could not think logically, and all she wanted to do right then was to get out, out of the house to find some quiet place in which to think. She couldn't even trust herself to speak, for fear of saying something that she might later regret.

'I've got to get out,' she murmured and hurried towards the outer hall, with Remmie following.

'Laura! I know it's a shock, love.' Her face was grim, her manner distant, and so Remmie went on, 'Alright, lass. We'll talk when you get back, eh?' When Laura gave no agreement, his pleading gave way to anger. 'I'll not turn the lass out! This is *my* place an' Netti's, for as long as she needs it. Aye! An' 'er man's an' all! I'll tell you this! If you walk out on yon lass now, you needn't bother coming back!'

Laura looked at him, at this man whom she dearly loved, but the tears had risen to blur her vision and deny her a clear view of his face. And so, without speaking, she turned and left.

Outside, the snow was falling fast and her car didn't start easily. But once it sprang into life, Laura eased it along the drive-way and then onto the main road, where she followed the road into town. She felt no emotion and her thoughts had grown quiet, going over the years that had brought Netti to be studying at a university. And now, she was with child and had abandoned her music. The dreams which had been foremost in their lives since childhood, trampled. And why? Why? Laura found herself wondering about this man, this Marlow Connelly. What kind of man, white or black, would persuade a girl from a life-time's study to get her with child, and to cruelly dash her promise of a wonderful future? But Laura reminded herself that Netti was no infant. The choice had been hers and she had taken it. If Marlow Connelly was what she wanted, and if all these years and her brilliant gift for music had come to mean nothing to her, then there was nothing that Laura could do.

Laura drew the car to a halt outside The Bull, then as she walked into the reception area, her emotions began to change. She had received the news from Remmie, and it had rendered her numb. But now the numbness had softened, to lay bare the awful pain beneath, and with it came a cold resentment against this Marlow, against Netti, and yes, against Remmie for the words which had cut deep: 'don't bother coming back,' he had said. Well, she wouldn't!

Not sure of her plans, Laura booked a room for one night

417

only and having no wish to go straight up to the loneliness of her room, she headed for the bar. There were too many things on her mind for sleep anyway. Things that she could lose more easily in a glass of wine.

But half an hour and two glasses of wine later, Laura still could not rid herself of the dreadful weight of despair that had settled on her. So feeling utterly dejected, she went up to her room.

It was a pleasant enough room, with stark white furniture and a deep comfortable bed with a gaudy floral eiderdown that matched the curtains covering the window. With the pleasant effect of the wine still heavy on her, Laura had no clear recollection of actually discarding her clothes and getting into bed.

It was some time later when she was awoken by the presence of a man in her room, that Laura realized she had omitted to lock the door. Even more surprising was the fact that the man was Mitch. His expression was severe as he told her sharply, 'I know all about it. Remmie rang me, and I'm here to take you back.'

'Back?' Laura sat up to face him. 'Ah, then Remmie obviously forgot to inform you that he doesn't *want* me back! And you know all about Netti, do you? That she's given up her music, that she's come home married to a Jamaican, and carrying his child?'

Mitch opened his mouth as though to reply, and for a moment, Laura was sure that he was about to challenge her statement. But then he shook his head and in a controlled voice which belied the tight angry set of his features, he instructed her, 'Get out of there and get dressed. You're going back! There are some things you just have to get used to, like it or not. You've got responsibilities to Remmie, yes, and to Netti.'

Laura seemed suddenly to be completely sober. Responsibilities! Hadn't she already played her part in those responsibilities? Hadn't they lain across her shoulders these many years? Hadn't they swallowed up her childhood, her happiness and all her personal dreams? And for what, for Netti to throw it all away! And here stood Mitch like he'd always done, telling her what to do! All the old antagonisms rose in her now, and she yelled, 'You're blaming *me*, aren't you? You're saying it's *my* fault. Well you're wrong!' In her blind anger, she had got

418

up from the bed and was standing not two feet away from him, completely naked, her beauty never more vibrant.

It was the look in his eyes that quickened her awareness, a look of hunger as naked and revealing as her own flesh. His gaze travelled over her body, and when he rested his eyes on her face, she sensed such exquisite love, that some part of her deep inside began to cry. The thought came into her mind that it wasn't because of Netti or Remmie that Mitch had searched her out. It was because *he* needed to know where she was, and the thought of her being in another man's arms could drive him to despair. *That* was the truth! And it was so clear in those expressive green eyes. Yet, at that moment, when she could so easily have melted into his arms, when the feel of his manly strength about her would have been so comforting; she hated him! *He* was the one who had married! Just then, in that instant, she forgot how she had left him no choice. She forgot that never once had she professed to love him, while he on the very day of his wedding had opened his heart to her. Now, her only thoughts were that Mitch had let her down, had talked about *her* responsibilities, *her* selfishness, and she hated him. Lifting her clenched fists, she beat him viciously about the chest. '*You*! You've always wanted more from me than I can give. Always interfered, and when I really need you, you can't help me. Who cares if I *never* go back? Who the hell cares?' she screamed, breathless now in the hysteria of her relentless attack on him.

'*I* do! *I* care! God in heaven woman, don't you know what you're doing to me?' His strong fingers closed about her flailing fists, pinning them tight to his chest. As Laura looked up at him, the tears she had so often denied spilled unchecked down her face. And now, Mitch brought his face to touch hers, and when the warm moistness of his mouth covered her own, exciting within her a multitude of emotions, she knew without doubt, without reservation, that she loved this wonderful man with all her heart. She had *always* loved him.

Laura gave herself up to him, and he held her with such possessive strength that she thought her very bones would snap, and the kisses with which he claimed her became violent in their demands, as though she had unleashed a passion too long pent-up. Then, with that same violence, he thrust her from him, and when he gazed on her face, she could see that his passion had become marred by guilt, and she knew that once again, he was lost to her. This time, probably forever. When he said in a soft, low growl, 'It meant nothing!' she knew he was deliberately being cruel, and it saddened more than hurt her.

She looked at him and said nothing. Then with a deep sigh, he picked up the sheet from where it was draped across the edge of the bed, and roughly draped it about her nakedness. 'I'll wait downstairs,' he said without looking at her. 'I'll take you back, then I'll get home to Sally, where I belong.'

It could have been the thought of going back, back to live with Netti and to be reminded daily of what might have been, or it could have been the thought of Mitch going home to Sally, but whatever the cause, something snapped inside her, some fine thread of emotion that had been tested beyond endurance and which, for all her inner strength, she could contain no more. The love she had felt for him and the warmth it had brought disappeared now beneath her cool controlled voice. 'Go home to Sally. I'll find my own way.'

He offered no resistance, and when he spoke, his voice was sharp. 'As you wish. You know the way of things.' Then without looking at her again, he strode from the room, the anger still taut in his broad shoulders.

For a while after he had gone, Laura just stood, watching the door as though she expected him to return. But when he didn't, she kneeled before the bed, folded her arms to make a pillow, laid her head against them and sobbed bitterly. Her tears were for so many things, but most of all, they were for Netti. She herself had not been blessed with anything special other than her looks, which were tangible and quick to fade. Oh, but in Netti's fingertips, there was such timeless beauty and exquisite music, which could have raised her to the very heights, and which she had so callously disregarded.

Laura cried too for the boy Tom, who in his innocence had been made to suffer for Parry Griffin's evil deed. Through her mind ran all manner of thoughts; of Mitch whom she loved so desperately and whose deep loyalty would keep him rightly forever in Sally's arms; and dear gentle Remmie whose heart was ever filled with memories of his Katya, and who through no fault of his own now found himself divided between the two people he loved most in all the world.

A need arose in Laura, so acute that it became like a physical agony; she wanted, needed, someone to talk to, and the one person to whom she could have poured out her heart was gone. Mabel had been such a mountain of strength and a special friend; but she was gone from her.

Laura cried the agony out of her, and when the long overdue tears were spent, she got to her feet and went to the bathroom where she splashed her face with cold water. And at that moment, a name came into her mind, a name so unexpected that Laura's mouth fell open to emit a startled cry.

She went quickly to her coat and withdrew a letter from the pocket; a letter to Remmie from Lizzie Pendleton. Remmie had given it to her to read, for in it Lizzie had begged him to persuade Laura to come to the convent and see her, for she was convinced that soon she would be called on to meet her maker. Laura had not placed too much importance on such a sentiment, because Lizzie's woeful prophecies were an outstanding facet of her miserable nature.

Now however, for some inexplicable reason, Laura felt the urge to see old Lizzie Pendleton, a familiar and strong link with the past — however distasteful. Yes, she would go and see her. With that intention uppermost in her mind, she climbed back into bed. It was certainly strange how after all this time, and remembering the awful things Lizzie had said and done against Netti, the thought of responding to Lizzie's offer of friendship gave Laura a feeling of well-being.

She would go to the convent first thing in the morning. But before leaving, she would telephone Remmie and heal the rift between them. Netti and her new husband would no doubt have taken a very dim view of her walking out the way she did; yet in all truth, Laura had not found it in her heart to reconcile herself to what Netti had done. She felt that nothing would ever be the same between them again, although she prayed that it would.

Down in the reception area, the telephone was in constant use the following morning, so Laura decided to leave a message with the proprietor. It was simply to inform Remmie that she had gone to the convent to see Lizzie Pendleton, after which she would make her way home to him and Netti. Laura paid the price of the phone call, and thanked the proprietor for his assurance that he would make the call at the first opportunity. Then she paid the bill, went out to her car and followed the lanes out of town towards the Convent of Mary Magdalene. She felt no qualms at seeing Lizzie Pendleton, for if the old woman really was as ill as she claimed, then the time had come for peace between them.

Laura wondered whether Remmie might also make his way out to the convent on receipt of her message. The proprietor however, had made the call twice and each time the number had been engaged; he probably wouldn't try again. He was a very busy man.

Chapter Thirty-eight

'Arse'oles!' Lizzie Pendleton glowered from her bed at the black-frocked nun, 'I'll pray when I've a mind to, not when I'm bloody told! I 'int passed through them pearly gates yet. So piss orf! Go on you, piss orf!'

The nun approached Laura, her face blushing crimson against the stark white head-piece that flowed like a mantle around her shoulders. And Laura, who had so often recoiled in disgust at Lizzie Pendleton's colourful language, was now finding it increasingly difficult to stem her laughter. 'I'm afraid Lizzie's one of the crosses we have to bear. Go in please.'

'An' I 'int soddin' deaf neither!' came Lizzie Pendleton's rebuke, at which the nun smiled at Laura and quickly added, 'But she's a good Christian at heart.'

Laura trusted herself only to nod, and was thankful when the nun had departed, closing the door behind her. In the light of Lizzie's aggression, it had been difficult for Laura to accept the Sister Superior's words on welcoming her, 'I'm afraid Miss Pendleton has a very short time left. Stay as long as you wish.'

Yet now, as she moved forward into the small square room, simply furnished with a wardrobe, chest of drawers, a bed and huge wooden crucifix on the wall, Laura was visibly shocked. On the wall to the left of Lizzie Pendleton's bed was a tall narrow window, through which the morning light passed to light the old woman's face, revealing to Laura the truth of the Sister Superior's words.

Lizzie Pendleton was slightly propped up in her bed by the numerous bolsters beneath her head, and as Laura looked at the pale wizened face and saw the ghastly toll of her illness, it struck her how vulnerable and helpless her old enemy had become. Lizzie's eyes grew wary, as they quickly darted towards Laura. 'Don't stand there bloody well gaupin'! Fetch that chair and sit by me.' She waved a gnarled hand towards the far corner and the stand chair. Watching Laura closely as she went to fetch the chair, Lizzie went on, 'Smell the rot, can you?' She threw back the bedcovers and overwhelmed Laura with the awful stench that rose up. 'Gangrene! Wanted to cut me bloody leg off, they did.' Laura felt herself being yanked forward by the clawing grasp of Lizzie Pendleton's fingers about her arm. Then just as swiftly she let Laura go, and covered her face with both hands and fell into a convulsion of loud pitiful sobbing.

Laura gently brought the covers over the swollen leg, noting with horror that the small area of exposed skin above the thigh bandages was black in colour.

With Laura's arm about her shoulders, Lizzie Pendleton quickly gained control of her emotions and presently the sobbing ceased. She reached into the depths of her pillow and withdrew a small bottle of gin, and holding it out towards Laura, she said, 'I can twist that silly bloody caretaker round me little finger. Want some, do you?'

Laura shook her head, and sitting back in her chair, she watched as Lizzie swigged from the bottle. She supposed it was her duty to fetch someone, or at least report it. But she had no intention of doing so, for if it gave a measure of comfort to Lizzie Pendleton, then who was *she* to deny her small pleasures in the face of such a painful demise.

'You'll stay, won't you, Laura?' Lizzie Pendleton's whispered question was a plea. 'You'll not leave me, will you?'

So Laura gave her day to comfort this woman who had never shown Laura such consideration. Lizzie Pendleton unburdened herself of all that had corrupted her vision of Laura. She talked of Joe Blessing and of how he had used her. She recalled the times when she had been young and beautiful and she told Laura of Ruth Blake's cunning and beauty, which had been the cause of Joe Blessing deserting her and leaving her to bear the shame of Katya.

And as the old woman sped back over the years, emptying her heart of revenge and bitterness, it seemed to Laura as though she was shrinking before her eyes.

Many hours later, when it had grown dark outside, the nun

424

came in to wrap a blanket around Laura, and turning to Lizzie Pendleton, who had grown quiet, she whispered, 'Let her sleep, and try to get some sleep yourself.'

She didn't hear Lizzie's low murmur of, 'I will, I'm ready now.' And with a long searching gaze at Laura's sleeping figure, she smiled and slowly closed her eyes.

Chapter Thirty-nine

'What in God's name is she playing at? She can't just up and take off, without letting us know where she is!' Remmie paused long enough to stare at Mitch in exasperation, then shaking his head impatiently, he continued to pace up and down.

Mitch straightened up from the work-bench where he had been teasing the sharp edge of his knife in and out of the delicate damaged scroll-work in the leg of a piano. He placed it on the bench and rested the knife beside it and turned to say with some impatience, 'Remmie, you know Laura. She's stubborn and independent. She'll do what suits her and she'll be dictated to by *nobody*! As to where she is, well, your guess is as good as mine. But she'll be in touch, I've no doubt. Happen as not, she's taken herself off to some sale or another.' Then he said in a more thoughtful tone, 'The truth is, all this business with Netti came as a real blow.'

'I *know* that, Mitch. I didn't help though, did I? We should have *talked*, proper like, but I couldn't see her turn from Netti like she did. There were bad words 'atween us, Mitch, and Lord knows, I wouldn't have hurt her for the world. They're *both* my lasses, loved and cherished like me own.'

'Come on,' Mitch walked over to Remmie and slapped a hand on his arm, 'let's away upstairs. No doubt Sally can find us a brew of tea, eh? Look here now, don't fret yourself. Laura's an intelligent strong-minded woman. She knows what she's at, and if she's taken it into her head to disappear, and to think things out, then she'll not come back till she's good and ready, not Laura!' There was a suggestion of laughter in his voice, but when he turned to lead Remmie up the stairs to the flat above, his changed expression reflected the deep concern that Laura's absence had caused him. Remmie wasn't the only

426

one who had used cruel words. The memory of Laura in that bedroom, and the feel of her naked form tight within the circle of his arms had torn him apart and haunted him ever since. If he hadn't thrust her from him, he would have had to betray every vow that he held sacred. Sally didn't deserve that. But oh God! Laura couldn't know what she had done to him, and how desperately he loved her, worshipped her the way he had always done and always would. The longing for her became so great within him, that it forced a loud sigh from his lips, and instantly, he was aware of both Sally and Remmie watching him.

Remmie misunderstood the low moan, and his apology was immediate. 'It's wrong of me to burden you and Sally,' he glanced at the clock on the mantelpiece, noting that it was coming up to midnight, 'especially at this late hour. It's just that I can't settle. I was sure she'd turn up this morning. But it's been two nights now, and not a word! Oh, she's never done owt like this afore. I'm worried, real worried about her.'

Mitch went over to slap his hand on Remmie's shoulder and murmured, 'Look, I'll get myself out first thing in the morning. The landlord at The Bull might just know in which direction she took off. Now don't you worry, Remmie. I'll find her. Laureme hasn't yet opened its doors without her being there, and I'll lay you ten to one that she's getting ready for home this very minute, even as we stand here talking.'

Remmie nodded, a look of relief on his face. 'You're right o' course. And it'll do no harm if she has some time to herself.' He waved away Mitch's invitation to stay awhile, and after placing an affectionate kiss on Sally's forehead, he turned to leave. 'God forgive me, but I as good as showed Laura the door. And I'm telling no lie when I say it seems like a lifetime without having her about me. Netti did wrong. It were an awful bombshell, an' I'm afeared I 'andled it badly.' He turned to look at Sally first, and then at Mitch. 'You're both a regular comfort to me. I'm sure Laura's alright, and no doubt once she's home, things'll work out just fine. It were just a shock, as knocked 'er off 'er feet, eh?'

Mitch and Sally stayed quiet for a while, listening to the clump of his weary steps descending the stairs. Then Mitch said to Sally, 'Poor Remmie, it's to be hoped things *will* be fine when Laura comes home. She's his whole life.' And mine too, he thought.

Looking out of the window, he saw Remmie emerge from the shop, and the instant Mitch perceived that something was wrong, Remmie sank to the ground, his body lifeless.

Mitch's reaction was immediate and he dashed to the door, shouting back to Sally, 'Remmie's collapsed! Call an ambulance!' Then he leapt down the stairs without caution and rushed outside to where Remmie lay motionless, his greying hair now whitened by the incessant falling snow. 'Alright fella,' he told him, undeterred by the absence of recognition or response in the older man's face, 'alright. Help is on its way.' But even as he spoke, Mitch feared that this man, this dear gentle friend, was beyond the help of this world. Spiralling up amidst the anguish of his thoughts came the image of Laura. He caught the image close to his heart as though to comfort her, and the tears which swam in his eyes to blur his vision tumbled down his face to fuse with the blinding snowflakes.

'Dear God,' he murmured, gently and easily collecting Remmie's limp body into the strength and warmth of his arms, 'don't let them part as enemies. Don't burden her with that.'

But the man in his arms did not stir, and Mitch's heartfelt prayer fell away into the darkness and the sweet distant sound of carol singers.

Chapter Forty

Laura had spent the last twenty-four hours by Lizzie Pendleton's side. Just once she had made to leave in order to contact Remmie, whom she had expected to arrive at the Convent. But such had been Lizzie's panic at being left that Laura had stayed to comfort and reassure her.

And now Lizzie Pendleton was at peace, and in a strange way, Laura too felt as though a crippling weight had been lifted from her shoulders. Through the long hours, she had come to terms with what Netti had done. It was her intention to get home quickly, and she hoped with all her heart that Netti and Marlow Connelly would accept her apology for having turned her back on them.

She crossed the forecourt to her car, when she saw Mitch emerging from his own car, and striding towards her. His sudden appearance threw her completely off guard. Mitch here? He was the last person she expected, and his presence created in her a mingling of anxiety and pleasure. As his tall commanding figure came towards her, she thought how very handsome he looked in his long grey overcoat, with the collar turned up towards the dark trilby that was brought down at just the right angle. And recollections of being in his arms were still warm in her mind.

He was speaking now, and even before the words were uttered, something about his attitude and the anxiety in his expression caused a heightened sense of fear within her. 'It's Remmie, Laura, taken badly.'

Laura felt the strength of his arms about her and was never more glad of it. She gave no resistance as he propelled her towards his own car. Indeed, it seemed natural that she should go with him without question.

Once inside the warmth of the car and on her way home,

Laura put all other thoughts out of her mind. Her only concern now was for Remmie, and when she again inquired of Mitch as to her uncle's condition and he simply answered quietly, 'He's badly, Laura,' she knew at once that it was indeed serious. And when glancing sideways at her, he said, 'you'll want to go straight to Remmie,' quietly adding, 'we're not bound by visiting times,' her heart grew cold. She turned away, to look up into a sky that was rapidly growing darker and ominously heavy with snow. She dared not dwell on his words.

When she could no longer hold back the tears that pulled at her heart, he drew the car over to the side of the road, and gently gathering her in his arms, he murmured, 'Don't hold it back, Laura, we all need to cry.'

'No,' she muttered looking up at him, the tears still wet on her face, 'I'm alright.' Strange how she had always felt guilty about shedding tears, as though they were a sign of weakness. But she was so fearful for Remmie and she had been deeply stirred by the feel of Mitch's arms around her, and somewhere inside her there was a strong desire that was running dangerously fierce.

For the briefest of moments, Mitch let his eyes linger on her, and he silently asked Sally's forgiveness, because in that wonderful moment when he had held Laura close to his heart, he'd known such exquisite happiness that all thoughts of Sally had flown from him. And he knew, God forgive him, that no matter how hard he tried to make it otherwise, no matter how he might strive to build a future with Sally and Laura's son Tom, his life would always be painfully empty without this woman, who meant more to him than life itself.

'Will Remmie live?' Laura had to steel herself to ask that question, because she was so afraid of what the answer might be.

For a moment, Mitch gave no reply and Laura found the silence almost unbearable. Her worst fears were confirmed when he said in a soft anxious voice, 'Severe internal haemorrhage.' He laid his hand on hers and said, 'But we must hope, Laura, and pray.'

And pray she did, with all her heart, for the remainder of the journey.

Chapter Forty-one

Jay spotted Laura approaching from the far end of the show room, where she had been deeply engrossed in conversation with a representative of Mr Craven. Now the man had departed and Jay left her office to await Laura, who was quickly threading her way through the milling customers. She drew to a standstill before Jay and let out a long exasperated sigh. 'I've never known it so busy soon after Christmas.'

'You look washed out, Laura,' Jay said quietly, taking note of the dark rings beneath Laura's eyes, and her pale thin, almost gaunt face. 'You know, you'll have to trust me to take more of the responsibilities off your shoulders, at least until Remmie improves. If you're not careful, *you'll* be in that Infirmary alongside him! You can't go on the way you have this last week, arriving here almost with the dawn, then rushing yourself off your feet till late afternoon with hardly a break. Then back to the Infirmary until nigh on ten o'clock! You can't divide yourself in two, you know; and just *look* at you, you're not even stopping for a proper meal. Belle's worried out of her mind.'

'Goodness me!' Laura bit back a smile, 'That was a speech. But you're right, Jay, I know.' Laura realized that Belle must have been complaining to Jay and, of course, they were both right. She couldn't go on as she had been. Not only did she feel utterly drained, but there was that nauseating pain deep in her breast that had started the day before yesterday, and had given her little peace since. She supposed it must be a symptom of anxiety or something. Certainly, up until this morning, when the Matron had told her over the phone that Remmie was more comfortable, he had been a constant source of anxiety. So too was Netti's immediate departure on the day that she herself had returned home. Apparently, Netti and Marlow were staying with Mitch and Sally now, until they could locate a home of their own. To all intents and purposes, Netti was very bitter and holding Laura to blame for Remmie's collapse. It had hurt Laura deeply and she was in no doubt that any reconciliation between her and Netti was now out of her hands.

'I mean it, Laura,' Jay was insisting, 'Mitch's right, you are making yourself ill! You really must slow down!'

'Alright, I'll think about it,' Laura assured her, and she knew that she would have to.

On New Year's Eve Remmie suffered a further haemorrhage, a bad one, and gratefully taking up Jay's offer to keep a stringent eye on Laurems, Laura stayed constantly by Remmie's side.

Several times during her long vigil, she was aware that Netti, now beginning to show her pregnancy and swollen-eyed from crying, had crept into the ward. During this worrying ordeal, she had made no effort to communicate with Laura, and on the one occasion that Laura had approached her, Netti walked away without saying a word. When Netti had come into the ward, she always stayed by the door; silently watching, silently blaming. And then she just as quietly left to sit on the hard bench outside in the corridor and cry softly in Marlow's comforting arms.

Once, Laura's eyes strayed from the monitor that registered Remmie's heartbeat, and she had seen Netti looking lonely and forlorn, and her heart ached. Yet the grim foreboding expression with which Netti had received her attempt to smile had warned Laura that her sister was determined never to forgive her. It was on this particular occasion, after Netti had left the room, that Remmie regained consciousness. Laura leaned closer to hear what he was saying. 'Laura, young Tom, an' our Netti. Don't fret, lass, just keep loving them, eh?'

She wasn't shocked that he had known about Tom, but it brought a great sadness within her; bless him, Remmie had known, and had kept her secret safe. And then he had seemed to smile. But when the monitor sent out its warning signal, and the nurse hurried her to leave, Laura knew that it hadn't been a smile. It had been a grimace of pain, and when later she thought back on his last words, she realized how reflective of

Remmie's nature it was that his parting words should be of love.

That period of time closely following Remmie's death was one of great difficulty for Laura. Her grief threatened at times to suffocate her, but somewhere within her tremendous reservoir of strength, she found the will to control her emotions, and to throw herself vehemently into her work. Keeping busy certainly helped her to cope with the painful chasm left by Remmie's death, for it seemed that all her life that dear man had been there with his wisdom and love, to guide and cherish her and Netti, and the world was a darker sadder place without him.

After a while Laura was able to present to the outside world at least a semblance of disciplined calm. But inside, her heart was sore and, in addition, Netti's unbending attitude caused Laura many a sleepless night.

Remmie left Netti his private, but moderate, funds and gave to Laura the house, which he claimed had always been more Laura's than his. When the solicitor read out the words, written in Remmie's hand, 'I hope that lovely house will be a happy home for my two lasses over many years to come,' Laura's heart was filled with hope that Remmie's wish might bring Netti home.

But throughout the solicitor's meeting, when Laura had sought to capture her sister's attention, Netti had sat stony-faced and impassive. For the first time in her life, Laura was lost as to her next move. She had to win back Netti's love and trust, even though she now believed that it had been lost through her own fault. She realized that *nothing*, no, nothing was of the same importance as the bond between her and Netti, a bond that had grown slack beneath the pressure of ambition and selfishness, and a blind neglect on her part towards Netti. She could not accept that such a wonderful bond, that had seen her and Netti ever close through the bad years, could be finally broken.

Some weeks after Remmie had been laid to rest beside Katya, Laura took it upon herself to pay Netti a visit, which she considered long overdue. The awful silence between them must come to an end, she had decided.

433

Mitch had told her about the little terraced house along Whalley-Banks, which Marlow and Netti had rented and made into a cosy comfortable home. Now here she was, standing at the door of Netti's house, wondering how to break down the barriers that had driven them apart.

When the door opened and Netti appeared, Laura was struck at once by the beauty of Netti's pregnancy, which seemed to light her face with an inner radiance. But, as the soft blue eyes came to settle on Laura, she watched them harden and saw the tightening expression. The cold clipped voice that greeted her was not one that Laura recognized. 'What do you want?'

'I've come to talk with you.' As Netti took a step backwards into the passageway and raised her hand to close the door, Laura asked softly, 'Please. Please, Netti, let me come in.'

'Oh, so you want to come in? You want me to welcome you into my home the way you welcomed my husband into yours? No, Laura, you won't set foot in *this* house!' Her eyes became bright with angry tears. 'It's your fault that Remmie's dead, and I won't forgive you, I can't. Go away from here.' The door closed against Laura, and tears spilled down her face as she heard Netti's receding footsteps.

Netti was right. There was nothing more to be said. Yet as she drove away, she knew that there *was* more. She had seen it in Mitch's face that night when he had followed her to The Bull. And now, she'd seen it in Netti's face. There *was* something.

She pressed her foot down on the accelerator and nosed the car towards the centre of town and the shop. If Netti wouldn't tell her, then Mitch *would*!

When she reached the shop, and let herself in, Sally Fletcher was serving a customer, but she smiled a welcome as Laura entered. Then when the customer had gone, Sally came to greet her with customary enthusiasm, and Laura thought how happy and content she seemed and how marriage to Mitch appeared to have made Sally blossom.

'Is it Mitch you want, Laura? He's not back yet — gone to hand pick some timber from the sawmill.'

'Oh.' Laura felt disappointed. 'Yes it *was* Mitch I wanted to see. But it doesn't matter. It'll have to wait.'

434

'No. He'll not be long. He's been gone since half past twelve, and it's nearly three now.' Sally paused, and when she went on, Laura realized that Sally had guessed what was on her mind. 'Tom won't be home from school for a while yet. Come on, let's take ourselves upstairs, eh? You can wait for Mitch in comfort.'

Laura followed her, and when Sally stopped at the back store room and called for Marlow, who quickly appeared, looking so much at home that he might have been there for years, Laura turned away.

'Yes, Sally?'

'We're off upstairs. Will you keep an eye on the shop, Marlow?'

'Sure. There's not much more I can do here, till Mitch gets back with that mahogany.' As they moved away and on up the stairs, Laura could feel Marlow Connelly's eyes on her, and she wondered whether Netti would tell him about her visit. But of course she would; they probably told each other everything.

A few minutes later, Sally had made a brew of tea, and she and Laura were sitting by the table. Laura was astonished by the change in Mitch's old flat. It had been completely redecorated and furnished by Mitch with lovingly restored pieces of period furniture. The whole place had a wonderful 'lived-in' atmosphere, and Sally's final touches in the soft fabrics and curtains gave the sitting-room a bright airy look that belied the one small window looking out over the busy road.

Laura's eyes came to rest on the far wall against which stood a long sideboard, and lovingly displayed on this were a number of wood and gilt trophies. Laura stepped over to the sideboard, and Sally came to stand next to her.

'They're Tom's. He won all those trophies in the school's boxing team.'

Laura suddenly resented the pride inherent in Sally's statement, and she responded with a tone of reprimand, 'Boxing! You surely don't encourage *that*?'

Sally smiled patiently and explained, 'Tom needs no encouragement. Mitch and me, we'll not *dis*courage him though. He's good, and he enjoys it.'

Laura found it difficult to believe that anyone could actually enjoy boxing, and it disturbed her. And when Sally went on to say that Tom's teacher had told Mitch that Tom had what he called 'the killer instinct', Laura was horrified.

Sally laughed softly and went back to the table. Laura followed, not particularly consoled when Sally said, 'It's just a term they use. It means he has a natural aggression in the ring, a winning talent. Don't worry, Laura, Tom will make out fine.'

Make out fine, thought Laura, and without me. It was a bitter pill to swallow. 'Sally, I came here to ask something of Mitch. Something I feel he and Netti have kept from me.'

'Does it concern Netti?' Sally asked, and when Laura affirmed this, she went on to tell Laura how it had been Remmie's wish that Laura should not know of Netti's downfall, and of her search for Joe Blessing, who had died previously in a home for down-and-outs in London. It seemed as though Lizzie Pendleton's words had caused Netti far more distress than anyone knew.

Netti had been unable to settle to her studies and had gone from bad to worse. Marlow had found her when she was at her lowest, living in a commune, and already pregnant by a man who had deserted her. Marlow had taken Netti out of that place and married her against the wishes of his own family, who did not agree with mixed marriages. Sally thought Netti was a very lucky young lady to have as good a man as Marlow Connelly. After hearing the truth, Laura was quick to agree.

'I'm glad you told me, Sally. Thank you.'

'Will you go to Netti and try to patch things up?'

Laura shook her head. 'It's too late, Sally. It's up to Netti now.'

Before Laura made her way downstairs, Sally asked, 'You can see that Marlow is a good man?'

'Yes. I can see that. But what Netti did . . . leaving the University . . . living like that, in squalor. That wasn't the way. I don't recognize her, Sally. And now, I'm not sure I ever will.'

She didn't see Marlow Connelly on her way out and she didn't particularly want to. But as she stepped from the shop and into the street, she found herself face to face with Mitch. For a moment, neither of them spoke, although Laura had so much she wanted to say. And when he gazed down at her, his eyes alive with emotion, she saw her own torture echoed there,

436

and she realized just how much of their lives she had wantonly thrown away, and if she was being punished now, then it was only what she deserved.

'Hello Mitch.' Her voice betrayed nothing of her emotions.

'Laura. Problems?'

'No.' She smiled to herself. How right that he should link her name with problems. She'd certainly been that to him. 'No problems.'

He walked to the car with her, and when she was behind the wheel he stood holding the door open and said with a smile, 'Drive carefully. I know you can be reckless behind that wheel.'

'Well, it was *you* who taught me. And they do say you pick up your teacher's bad habits.'

He didn't reply. Instead, he brightened his smile and closed the door. She saw him in the mirror, just standing there watching her drive away, and she recalled the times that dear Remmie had expressed his wish to see them together. A wish dear to his heart, and one that she had so foolishly rejected.

What Laura did not see in her mirror as she turned out of the street was Sally, watching from the upstairs window.

All the way home, Laura thought again and again of Sally's words, and each time, her conclusion was the same. Netti had become a weight on her conscience, and yet she could not rid herself of the anger she felt at Netti's cowardice. Why hadn't she faced up to things? If she had really been so desperately unhappy, she should have come home. But then, Laura had to ask herself how *she* would have greeted such a decision. And in all truth, she had to admit that she would probably have persuaded Netti back to her studies. Nevertheless, Netti had degraded herself, and must accept part of the blame for things having gone dreadfully wrong. But there was nothing to be gained now from going over it all, for there was little to be done to change matters. Netti had chosen her future, and she had made it painfully clear that there was no place in it for Laura.

In spite of the fact that she pretended not to care, Laura couldn't find the enthusiasm for work, so she made straight for home, arriving with a heavy heart and a great sense of loss darkening her mood. Remmie's marked absence as she entered the drawing-room only served to heighten her loneliness.

Some time later, as Laura replaced the telephone after a

short discussion with Jay, Belle came rushing into the room to tell Laura in her brusque fashion, 'You've got a visitor.'

'Thank you, Belle. Who is it?'

'It's Pearce Griffin! I've put 'im in Jay's office. I did say you might be some time, but 'e said you would want 'im to wait.'

'He said that, did he?' Laura was surprised to find herself smiling. So, Pearce Griffin had turned up again, like the proverbial bad penny. She supposed he must have heard of Remmie's death, or she doubted whether even he would have had the blatant nerve to find his way back here. As she waited for Belle to bring him to her, Laura realized with some surprise that she *wanted* to see him and was looking forward to it with a considerable degree of pleasure. Pearce Griffin had been right, when he'd said that they were alike. To a certain extent, they might well be — in their early struggles, their blind ambitions and capacity for breaking other people's lives. And yet, in spite of a strong physical attraction she felt towards him, there were certain facets of Pearce Griffin's character that she despised, that always turned her from him with revulsion. But it seemed to her a strange yet true phenomenon, that whenever she found herself low in spirits and in need of comfort, Pearce Griffin invariably appeared.

She was still dwelling on that peculiar observation, when she entered the drawing-room and hurried forward to where he was standing by the window. The thought entered her mind that for a man turned thirty, handsome and charming as he was, it seemed odd that he should never have married. Had he been speaking the truth years ago, when he'd told her that he was keeping himself only for her? She hardly thought so. But now, quite suddenly, the idea held a certain pleasant fascination.

If he was down on his luck, as had previously been the case, it certainly didn't show in the well-tailored dark trousers and cream open-necked shirt, or in the expensive watch that caught her eye as he extended his arms to embrace her. 'Laura. It's been the best part of a year, and there hasn't been a day when you've not crossed my mind.' There was no sign of his usual stormy passion in the way he folded her into his arms. Laura was confused. There was something about his whole manner that she had never witnessed before; a kind of tenderness and genuine concern, and it left her unsure how to deal with him. But her suspicions rose to the surface when he released her and said, 'I'm sorry to hear about Remmie,' and quickly he added, 'Belle told me when she brought the tea.' He eased her into the settee and sat beside her, then he said in a soft but firm voice, 'With Remmie gone you'll be needing help. With a place like this and a vast establishment like Laurems you'll want somebody with experience.' Then came the words she had been expecting, 'I've no ties, Laura, and I want none, unless they bind me to you. If you need my help, you've only to say the word.'

Laura moved her head to gaze out of the window, thinking about what he had said. At least, he'd left the final approach to *her*. Even that was unlike what she might have expected from the Pearce Griffin of old. He seemed to have lost, or *pretended* to have lost, that drive and fire that had set him apart from the others. And yet, sitting here like·this, feeling the nearness of him, she was still inexplicably drawn to him. He had a way of reaching deep inside her, to stir and irritate unattractive passions that had only ever responded to him. She turned back to him, smiled and said simply, 'Thank you, Pearce. I'll bear that in mind.' No sooner had the words left her mouth, than she wondered what in God's name had made her utter them. Of course she would never bear such a proposition in mind. Pearce Griffin here! Working alongside her and taking Remmie's place!

Had it been any other time, she might have given him short shrift, excused herself and shown him the door. But today she felt more alone than at any other time in her life. Though she detested the very idea of it, the truth was that she *needed* Pearce Griffin. Laura would never have believed such a development possible. But right now, at this moment in time, Pearce Griffin was the only friend she had, and that revelation startled even herself, for it made miserable everything she had ever strived towards.

'You'll stay to dinner?'

'Of course! Thank you.' He seemed surprised at the suddenness of her invitation. 'But I'll need to use your phone. I came by train and got a taxi from the station. I'll have to ring The Bull and book a room.'

Laura suspected that her hasty decision was not a wise one. But the big house was lonely now without Remmie and Netti. 'That's no problem. You can stay here the night. I'll get Belle to prepare you a room.'

'Well that's marvellous.' He touched her hand and Laura felt the need to move away from him.

'I'll tell Belle.' She laughed softly, as she went towards the door. 'She won't like it! Not one for changes in routine, is our Belle.' Then as an afterthought, she asked, 'Breakfast?'

'Yes. And after that, I'll be away.'

Oddly enough, Belle didn't mind. In fact, she was quite taken with the idea. 'Do you good, a bit o' company,' she declared heartily, and Laura inwardly agreed.

It *did* do her good. The entire evening was as pleasant as any she had ever spent. All through dinner, Pearce Griffin behaved like the perfect gentleman, and then as they talked well into the early hours, Laura was surprised to discover that he was well-read and very widely travelled, although she wondered whether some of those travels hadn't taken him to Amsterdam as a courier for Jake Thackerey. When she said as much, Pearce Griffin laughed out loud, and skilfully skated around the subject.

'The Thackereys moved away, you know.'

'Oh. Did they go broke?'

'Not them. Too crafty for that. No, attached themselves to some fella — dealer in precious stones, I think. Last time I heard, Ria Morgan had the poor bloke eating out of her hand. As for Jake, well, he follows her about as though she had him by the nose.'

And that's *exactly* how she has got him, thought Laura. But what she said was, 'Good luck to the pair of them.' And Laura experienced a deep instinct that she would never again set eyes on either Ria or Jake. And she was glad.

Belle and Tupper had long retired to their rooms at the back of the house, and after the long evening that had stretched into the early hours, Laura finally decided she needed to get to her bed. She was still impressed, and to her own shame, somewhat disappointed that Pearce Griffin had made no attempt to take her in his arms the way he had always done. She wondered whether there was indeed after all, a real spark of decency in him, and he was duly respecting her grief for Remmie. But then another thought crossed her mind; maybe he didn't find her attractive anymore. After all, she was nearing thirty, and the fresh bloom of youth had begun to tarnish.

Evidently, that wasn't the reason either, because as she bade him goodnight, Pearce Griffin rested his hands on her shoulders, and searching her dark brooding eyes with his own, he told her, 'You're a very beautiful woman, Laura. I've always thought it strange how the years seem to enhance your looks,' and then he laughed softly, 'perhaps you're a witch after all. I meant what I said. If you need me . . .'

Laura needed him right then. But not in the way he had suggested. She imagined Sally and Mitch lying in each other's arms, and the pain it brought created in Laura a need to be that close to another human being. Pearce Griffin was here, and it was just possible that he might help her to forget.

Impulsively, Laura reached up to touch his hand, still resting on her shoulder, and for a moment as their eyes met, Laura thought he might take her in his arms. But he didn't.

'Goodnight, Laura.' His voice was dismissive and Laura thought she detected a trace of his old arrogance. She gave him a half smile before going out of the room and upstairs. Once up there, she went straight through the bedroom and into the bathroom, where she turned the taps on and absent-mindedly watched the water tumbling into the bath. A faint smile lit her face as she undressed, and beginning to feel amused and curious, Laura found herself wondering about the women Pearce Griffin had bedded. There must have been many, for he was essentially a woman's man; a man made for passion of the deepest kind, whether it be hatred or love. Laura wondered which of the two she stirred in him.

She took a long leisurely bath, luxuriating in the water and deliberately closing her mind to the things that always brought her sadness and pain. Yet, although she did not consciously acknowledge thoughts of Mitch, he somehow found his way into her heart. Then when the feeling threatened to spill over and engulf her, she made herself think of Pearce Griffin, and she was glad that he was here, in this house.

Stepping from the bath, Laura paused at her reflection in the long mirror fixed to the back of the door. What looked back at her was a slender figure of youthful proportions. Her finely structured features were overshadowed by strong dark eyes, scarred now by a haunting sadness. Her shoulder-length auburn hair had lost none of its natural lustre, and on the whole, Laura supposed she was still beautiful. But it was of no importance; not a matter to dwell on.

She did not towel herself down. Instead, she wrapped her bathrobe about her and sat at her dressing-table to brush her hair before sliding into the coolness of the sheets.

Laura must have been lying there for some fifteen minutes, not able to sleep, when the door opened and there, silhouetted against the light from the landing, was Pearce Griffin.

Once he had closed the door, Laura couldn't see him. But she could sense him moving towards the bed and she could hear the soft pad of his bare feet on the carpet. Then he was there, between the sheets with her, his searching skilful hands roaming her naked body. Laura gave herself to him, but not completely, for her mind was bathed with the image of Mitch's handsome features and wise loving eyes. And her heart cried out to him.

Later, with Pearce Griffin lying asleep beside her, Laura felt somehow comforted by his presence, and as she looked at him, her mouth moved into a faint smile. What was that old saying? 'Life sends us strange bedfellows'? Well, here's a strange one, and no mistake!

It was some time later before she felt drowsy enough for sleep. There was a gnawing fear inside her, a restlessness that seemed to deny her the peace of mind she so desperately craved. In spite of that, Laura had come to a decision. It was not the right one, she knew that. But how many of her decisions had been? She was convinced now that any chance she had for real happiness had been denied through her own actions. And surely, second-best was preferable to nothing at all?

As she moved to her side she felt the slight discomfort in her right breast she had experienced so often of late. But then, like now, it swiftly passed, and so warranted no further anxiety.

She closed her eyes and moved to embrace the warm sleeping body of Pearce Griffin, and somehow, it gave her a degree of comfort.

PART FOUR

1962

LOVE

But if he finds you and you find him;
The rest of the world don't matter.

Rudyard Kipling

Chapter Forty-two

'What do you mean, Tom?' Mitch had the boy by the shoulders, and on his face was a deep frown as he persisted, 'What do you mean, Pearce Griffin was asking you questions! What sort o' questions?'

The boy, who had grown in these last months to reach Mitch's shoulders, shook his dark head and set himself against the older man's anger. 'I dunno!' His manner, though surly, was not without respect. 'He wanted to know about you and Sally. He knows you're not my parents.'

'How? How does he know that?'

'He said his Mam told him years ago. It doesn't matter though, does it, Mitch?' There was a trace of anguish in his voice. 'He asked if I ever wondered who my Dad was. I told him no! I said *you* were my Dad, and Sally was my Mam. Ever since I were little . . . and I didn't want to know anything about anybody else!'

Mitch grabbed the boy to him in a rough embrace. 'And you did the right thing, lad! You did the right thing. There's only Laura who knows the name of your father, and that's her secret to keep if she wants to; and it's her burden, too, I dare say. But you've a set o' parents here, that'll always love you like you were our very own. You know that, don't you eh?' He held the boy from him, and smiled into his face. 'But if I was to tell you what was in my heart, lad, I'd say that to see Laura walk through that door and claim you as her son would gladden me no end, and that's a fact. Because as loud as you deny it, she loves you every bit as much as do Sally and I.'

'She only loves herself!' The boy broke away and looked at Mitch with unnerving directness. 'I don't *want* her to claim me. I want nothing at all to do with her! And if I thought she was ever coming for me, I'd run away right now!'

Mitch laughed gently, but it was a sad laugh, and when he reached out to tousle the boy's thick dark hair, his voice held a trace of sadness as he told him with an attempt at humour, 'You'll *not* run away! Not while you've still got some schooling, and not while you've a line o' lads waiting to box your ears.' When he saw the boy's face relax into a warm smile, he pushed him playfully, and said, 'Go on champ! Down that club and get some footwork in ready for that match next Saturday.' As the boy sprang forward to wrap his arms about Mitch's neck, Sally called out from the back store room, 'Come on, you two! Let's have you both about your work. And do that coat up, Tom. It's a freezing January wind out there!'

Mitch and Tom broke apart and turned towards her. 'Now look what you've done! Got us in trouble with the boss,' said Mitch.

The sound of laughter filled the shop. Then Mitch spoke again; but this time, his voice was not veiled by humour. 'Tom, you'll not go near Pearce Griffin again. I've never asked this before, but I want you to promise you'll stay well clear of him?'

'That's easy, Mitch.' Tom walked towards the door, and before he opened it to disappear down the street, he promised, 'You've got my word; I don't like him anyway. He just comes in the Club sometimes.'

Mitch watched him go, then made a low groaning sound as he turned to gather Sally in his arms. 'Oh, Sally, Sally, it's fearful how the past catches up on you, eh? The world strides on . . . with the Russians putting men into space would you believe, and the Americans about to follow suit. But things that affect the likes of mere mortals like you and me, well, they just won't let go, will they? You heard what Tom said?'

'I did, and we knew it might happen. Secrets don't keep forever, Mitch.' Sally crossed to where he was, and seeing the anxiety on his face, she asked quietly, 'You think Pearce Griffin is Tom's father don't you? You've *always* thought it. And if he *is*, and if he claims the boy, would there be anything we could do about it?'

Mitch looked up at the sorrow in her voice, and reaching out he pulled her into his chest, kissing the top of her head. He said but two words, but they were enough to bring the smile back to Sally's face. 'Tom's *yours*.'

446

'No,' she whispered, 'he's Laura's son. But I've loved him like my own, and if he went to Laura tomorrow, I would still be forever grateful to her for the happiness Tom's given me all these years.' Her face became shadowed. 'It's been almost a year now, since she married that Pearce Griffin. And she *still* can't see through him! What is it about that man that makes her so blind? And you're wrong in your thinking that she must love him, Mitch, for she doesn't. He's like a magnet, drawing her to him like a spider draws a fly. There's talk; he's known in the town for a bad 'un, drinking and gambling, and he's got an unhealthy taste for women.'

Mitch declined to comment on what was common knowledge, because he could not trust himself to speak of that swine, Griffin! He walked with Sally towards the back store room, but stopped in his tracks when Sally suddenly mentioned that she thought Laura had been looking ill lately.

'What do you mean, Sally?' He kept his voice steady.

Comfortable within the strength of her man's embrace, Sally did not look up, and so she couldn't see the concern on Mitch's face as she answered, 'Well, I'm not rightly sure. She insists that there's nothing wrong, but there *is* something, I just feel it. Oh, I wish Netti would relent in her hardness, because she's a heartache to Laura, that she is.'

Mitch said quietly, 'We'll be seeing Laura tonight at Mayers Abbey. I'll have a quiet word then.' For the rest of that day the only person on his mind was Laura.

447

Chapter Forty-three

'What a place!' Pearce Griffin glanced sideways at Laura, as he coasted the car up the tree-lined drive towards the magnificent home of Captain Lloyd-Freeman.

'It *is* beautiful. What a pity it's to be sold.' Laura sighed and her concern was genuine. 'I expect it will be left to fall into foreign hands, so many of them are.'

Mayers Abbey dated back to the time of Henry the Eighth. It was a huge sprawling place, boasting numerous rooms which in turn were filled with endless treasures. Duties and taxes had forced the impending sale, and this evening's Grand Ball preceded the auctions which would commence the very next morning. It was Captain Lloyd-Freeman's way of saying goodbye to the place.

The first person to greet Pearce and Laura as they entered the vast hall was the man himself. As he came towards them, a broad spreading figure decorated in past military honours, Laura felt no sympathy towards him. Oh, it was true that he was about to lose this grand place and its coveted treasures. But no doubt he would still end up a rich man. People of his privileged kind always did. Cossetted in childhood, not knowing real hunger or poverty, the Captain Lloyd-Freemans' of this world considered it agony of the worst kind if their stocks fell in value, or if champagne was not served chilled. Laura had little time for such people, in the same way as they had little time for the lesser mortals beneath them.

'Ah! Mr and Mrs Griffin isn't it, of Laurems?' When he smiled, his shoulders rose with the curve of his lips and deep wrinkles ran from his pale expressionless eyes downwards to meet the laughter lines around his mouth. 'Enjoy yourselves,' he told them, waving an arm towards the ballroom. 'As you can see, we have a full house.'

As they entered the ballroom and sat at one of the tables around the edge, Pearce Griffin and Laura made a striking couple. The slim, dark elegance of a formal dinner suit flattered the youthful figure and vitality of Pearce Griffin. Laura, dressed in an off-the-shoulder gown of soft flowing blue, with her natural elegance could have been mistaken for the lady of the house. The profusion of auburn hair had been attractively gathered to cluster high on her head, in a slim blue bandana. She wore little make-up, except around her lovely amber eyes, which quickly scanned the room, finally coming to rest on Mitch and Sally, who were already making their way towards them from the bar.

Laura thought Sally looked lovely. Her long brown hair hung naturally, and the soft cream dress with its pretty collar belied the fact that she was in her late twenties, but made her look like a teenager. But it was Mitch who commanded Laura's attention. His tall manly figure stood out from all around him, and he carried himself with pride. As he neared their table, his eyes were only for Laura, and the warmth of his gaze gladdened her heart.

Pearce got to his feet and deliberately ignoring Mitch, he addressed Sally at once, 'I can't possibly start the evening without a dance from you.' The band on the rostrum had started playing a foxtrot. Sally looked at Mitch, and when he gave an unsmiling nod, she moved onto the dance floor and Pearce immediately followed. Mitch looked back at Laura, and his expression grew serious as he told her, 'You look very lovely.'

'Thank you, Mitch.' Laura thought she could not stand the caring scrutiny of his eyes upon her. She turned and glanced at Pearce and Sally, who were lost in the throes of music. 'You don't want to dance do you, Mitch?' she asked.

'No. Not yet. I want to talk to you.' There was an intimacy in his voice that caused her pain, and yet she so desperately needed to hear that caress he could not disguise. 'Laura, is something bothering you?'

'No. Things are fine, just fine.' How she wished that could be true. For months now she'd been plagued by a discomfort in her breast. Hoping it might go away, she had foolishly ignored it. But now, it was impossible to ignore. She was worried, frightened, and she knew that in spite of her efforts otherwise, the anxiety was beginning to show. It showed in her loss of appetite and lack of enthusiasm as she tackled her arduous business demands. The sleepless nights, she knew, were beginning to show in her face. She had already made her mind up that very day, to go and see Doctor Faber first thing in the morning. Whatever it was, she had to face it. It was the only way. And after all, she assured herself over and over again, it would probably turn out to be nothing.

The music drifted into a waltz, and Mitch stood up. 'Perhaps you'll confide your troubles while we're dancing?'

On the dance floor, he took her in his arms, and held her close. She felt that life was suddenly beautiful, and if she was to lose it now, the only real regret she would have would be not having shared her life with Mitch. As he took her round the floor, his lean muscular body moving against hers, she felt for the very first time a small resentment towards Sally, and she was immediately ashamed.

Some time later, when all four of them were sitting at the table enjoying their drinks and discussing the impending auction, Pearce suddenly announced, 'I've been given the ultimate honour tomorrow.' He turned to look at Laura, and she hoped he had at least learned discretion. But when he went on, she knew he had not. 'Isn't that right, darling?' He raised his whisky glass — his fifth — and turned back to Mitch, and his voice, though vaguely slurred, also held a trace of arrogance. 'Laura is trusting me with a *blank* cheque book. She's off to see the doctor on some triviality, and I've been given the duties of buyer. Shows what complete trust she has in me, eh?' His look was for Mitch, and it was a challenging one.

But Mitch didn't reply. Instead, he shifted his gaze to Laura. He might have said something, but Sally was speaking anxiously, 'Is that right, Laura? You're going to see the doctor?'

Laura deplored her foolishness in giving Pearce her confidence, although she hadn't mentioned the *cause* of her visit to the doctor and she was glad of that at least. She simply told Sally, 'It's nothing really. Just this weather, I suppose. I hate these long drawn-out winters. They seem to chill me to the bone.'

'I expect you need a tonic or something,' Pearce interrupted.

'I hope the sale doesn't go on too long, though,' he was addressing Mitch now, 'I had thought to go down to the Club tomorrow to watch Tom. Good little boxer, that Tom.' He drained his whisky glass, and emptied the wine bottle into it. Then he turned to Laura, and he grinned as he said, 'I wonder *you* don't go and watch the boy. Oh, I tell you, if my dad was alive, he'd see Jud Blake in that boy at every turn.' He sat back in his chair and began to laugh, then he sneered and leaned forward again, to stare at Mitch. 'Hated Jud Blake, did my dad,' then he looked deliberately at Laura, 'but not his daughter, Laura. Oh no, not *this* beauty. He took a real shine to her! And it cost the bloody fool, oh yes, it cost him!' There was real hatred in his voice and Laura did not doubt that it was reserved for her.

Suddenly, Mitch was on his feet, and rounding the table he grabbed Pearce Griffin by the shoulder. As Laura looked on, she saw in Mitch's face a fury and passion, that only the deepest hatred . . . or love . . . could create. And she knew that Sally had seen it too.

'Take yourself outside!' Mitch growled, yanking Pearce Griffin from his seat. 'Or I'll help you every inch o' the way!' And that was just what he had to do, for when Pearce Griffin got to his feet, he swayed dangerously and hurled abuse and insults at the two waiters who came towards him with offers of assistance.

Once outside, Laura and Sally stood by, while Mitch roughly bundled the protesting Pearce Griffin into the front passenger seat of Laura's car. A few minutes later, the car headed towards the shop with Mitch driving and Sally and Laura in the back.

'What about your car?' Laura asked, filled with shame that Pearce should have ruined a lovely evening.

Mitch didn't answer, and Laura thought he was still too filled with anger. Sally replied softly, 'Don't worry about it, Laura. It can be collected tomorrow when Mitch comes to the auction.'

'Oh, Sally. I am sorry.'

'Don't be. It's alright.' Then her voice dropped so that only Laura could hear. 'Laura, why *are* you going to the doctor's?' Then she quickly added in a rush of concern, 'I'm not being

451

nosey. I've watched you for some weeks now, and I *know* you've been worried, desperately worried. Please Laura, if I can be of any help?'

Laura knew that in Sally she had a good friend, and right now she did need someone in whom she could confide. For some moments, she was silent, and then she took Sally's hand and whispered, 'Thank you, Sally. I know that if I need to, I can count on you.' She didn't want to talk anymore, and Sally seemed to understand.

The remainder of the journey home was silent. Now and then, Pearce would mumble, or throw his arms about, and Laura would remember what he'd said, and she realized that he had no doubt learned that Tom was her son. She hoped he wouldn't suspect that Tom was his half-brother. She didn't want any such connection to be made, for the boy's sake. But then she recalled his words about Parry Griffin not liking Jud Blake, and liking his daughter, and she wondered if somehow, he had already begun to put two and two together. The thought disturbed her deeply.

It was still on her mind when they pulled up at the shop, and Sally alighted. When she turned to close the car door, she smiled reassuringly at Laura, and her softly spoken question was a pointed one. 'Will I see you tomorrow?'

'Yes, Sally. I'll ring you.' She had already decided that whatever the verdict, she *would* confide in this dear, warm-hearted friend.

'Right. Now don't you forget.' Leaning back into the car, she kissed Laura lightly on the cheek, then she turned to Mitch and asked, 'How long will you be?'

'Fifteen minutes, maybe twenty.'

'I'll put the kettle on, and wait up then,' she said, withdrawing her head and closing the door. Laura thought how trusting Sally was, until it crossed her mind that a man like Mitch would never give a woman cause to be anything other than trusting. And she loved him all the more.

Some twenty minutes later, after depositing Pearce on the drawing-room settee, Laura was driving Mitch back home.

'You could have taken the car yourself,' she told him. 'Jay could have brought Pearce over in the morning to collect it.'

'No. It's better this way. The less I see of Pearce Griffin, the

452

better. He riles me up to murder, at times!'

'I know, I know.' She moved her hand from the steering-wheel, and would have reached out to touch him, but she thought better of it, and returning it back to the wheel, she concentrated on negotiating the narrow cobbled road to the shop.

When they drew up at the door, she didn't stop the engine. She felt the need to hurry away from there, from that cosy home that was filled with the close love of a family, and where all those years ago, she had known great affection with Netti and Remmie. Now, Remmie was dead, and Netti was just as lost to her.

'Goodnight Mitch,' she said softly, 'and thank you. I couldn't have managed him on my own.' Oh God! She didn't want to leave him. She wanted to feel those strong comforting arms about her, and to know the feel of his mouth on hers. Just that, and she would be able to face the doctor in the morning without fearing the worst.

Just for a moment, when Mitch turned his loving eyes towards her, she felt in her heart that their thoughts were alike. He didn't take her in his arms, and he spoke no words of love. But his eyes were filled with a great longing, and when he tore his eyes from her, he bowed his head and uttered, 'Oh, Laura, Laura.' It was a cry from the heart, and it gave her all the strength she needed.

He didn't look at her again, and when he was standing on the pavement and she was driving away, she did something she had never in her life done before. She prayed to God, and asked him for the strength she knew she would need.

Chapter Forty-four

In an effort to suppress her mounting terror, Laura scanned the local newspaper while the trim white-smocked receptionist went to announce her arrival to Doctor Faber, a specialist in his field. But the pages were a blur — her mind was too full and too anxious. When the receptionist returned to take her through to the consulting room, Laura replaced the newspaper on the table and forced her attention to the matter in hand. It must be faced, she reminded herself squarely, faced and accepted, however reluctantly.

Yet the words still came as a shock when the doctor finally spoke, 'There's no doubt about it, Mrs Griffin. I'm afraid you'll have to go for tests.' Doctor Faber walked from the cubicle, where Laura was sitting on the edge of the examination bed. It was high up from the floor, and she had to inch forward until her feet contacted the stepping-stool below. She did not look up when he spoke. Instead, she slowly buttoned up her silk blouse, and rather than dwell on the implications of what the doctor was saying, Laura deliberately concentrated on the feel of real silk against her skin. It was a real luxury, and the soft brown colour suited her. Now, her fingers touched the small oval locket that had been Mitch's present to her on her twenty-first birthday. It came as a shock to realize just how long ago that had been. Over ten years now! And more than double those years since they had been at school together. The memory caused her to smile to herself. How they used to fight!

'Mrs Griffin.' Doctor Faber was sitting at his desk now, and the young nurse, looking smart and efficient in her crisp clean uniform, smiled at Laura. Then she indicated a chair which had been positioned directly in front of the desk. 'If you'd sit here, please,' she said. Laura got down from the bed, and walked across the consulting room. She sat in the chair, and was immediately irritated by the unnatural brightness of the January day, which came in through the slatted window to play on her eyes.

'Now then,' Doctor Faber was smiling again and when she looked up, he lowered his head and peeped at her over the top of his glasses, 'I don't want you to be alarmed. Because more often than not, these things turn out to be nothing more serious than harmless cysts. But it's always as well to get them checked out.' She made no reply, and he went on, in a quieter voice, 'You were right. There is a long deep shape beneath your right nipple.' He looked down and scribbled on his pad. 'I'm giving you something for the discomfort.' He whipped the top sheet from the pad, and handed it to her. 'Get these from the chemist. Follow the instructions. Oh, and if you have any problems, don't be afraid to come back. You should hear from the Infirmary in a few days. They won't waste any time, my dear. By the way, have you received a knock on that breast?'

Forgetting Molly Griffin's spiteful act in throwing those keys, Laura shook her head and he went on, 'Just a thought.'

Laura asked in a small voice, 'These tests?'

'Nothing to worry about. Just an overnight stay, and then a couple of days for the results.'

'And if the tests,' she breathed hard, then finished, 'if they're positive?'

'Now, you're not to think the worst. There's no use in me going into lengthy details, not until we have the results of the test. Don't you worry. You'll be well looked after.'

Laura walked across the car park, and for some time she just sat in the car, trying to think. What had he said? A long deep shape beneath her nipple, a harmless cyst? She kept trying to recall exactly what the doctor had said, word for word. But for some ridiculous reason, her thoughts kept going back to the words of a song that had been Remmie's favourite. It was an old Irish love song called 'I'll take you home again, Kathleen'. It surprised Laura to think she had even remembered it.

When she finally started the car up, it had been her intention to head for the shop, and Sally. A glance at the small facia clock told her that the auction at Mayer's Abbey would be well under way. Pearce had shown no after effects from his excessive drinking the night before, and he had gone off that

455

morning in the pick-up, quite unconcerned about the whole matter. She was satisfied that Jay could look after things in hers and Pearce's absence. Thinking back on it later, she really could not remember changing direction, and when she found herself way out on the moors, it was with some surprise.

It was a bitterly cold day, and out there in the bleak expanse of the moors, the wind was low and spiteful, moaning like a soul in torment searching for a place to rest. Laura got out of her car, and walked along the tufted grass ridge which ran up the slight rise towards the field of heather, and then down again, into the brook.

When she reached the brook, Laura sat on a boulder at the foot of a tree, and she let her troubled mind relax to follow the run of bright sparkling water that danced and gurgled in and out of the half submerged stones. The tidal wave of sickness and fear which had threatened to overcome her, for a while was stayed, and in its place there came an uneasy peace.

After a time, she made her way back to the car and drove quickly to work. There was much to be done, and she needed to see the place alive with people, people who had come to spend their money at Laura Blake's establishment! Also, there was that delivery to be arranged for London. The suppliers were already two days behind schedule, and it seemed they would take notice of no one but Laura herself. Well, if that delivery was not on the way after the roasting she'd given them yesterday, she would have no alternative but to carry out her threat of taking her business elsewhere.

It was eight o'clock when Laura finally brought the car to a halt at home that evening. Jay alighted and said, 'I was concerned about that delivery, but thank goodness it's on its way. They soon jump when *you* get on their backs, and that's a fact!' She laughed, and followed Laura into the hall, adding, 'I'll finish that work off for the accountant. I'll leave it on the desk for you to check before I submit it to him. Then I'll be on my way.'

'Thank you, Jay.' Laura watched her go towards the office, but she made no move to follow her. Instead she went straight to the drawing-room, where she found Tupper piling up the coal in the scuttle, and Belle on her knees beside him, just as quickly emptying the scuttle to replenish the fire. The two of them looked up at her, and as always, Tupper appeared agitated and grabbing the neb-cap from his head, he quickly picked up his coal-bucket and shuffled past Laura, muttering,' ''Ow do, Miss Laura, I'll be off to fetch more coal.'

Laura touched his shoulder as he passed, and with a warm smile she assured him, 'Thank you, Tupper, but there's no need. Go and get your cocoa, the pair of you. Leave the fire till tomorrow.' The sight of the cheery blaze gladdened Laura. Pearce had wanted her to have the fireplace blocked in, but she had refused; it gave the room a heart.

Belle wedged another big lump of coal into place, then replaced the scuttle beside the hearth and put her hands to the small of her back and straightened up with a groan. 'You've 'ad a phone call; bloody phones, mek me nervous!' She was already on her way to the dor, still muttering.

'Who was it?' Laura asked, taking her coat off and slinging it over a nearby chair.

'Sally. It were Sally. I telled 'er you were out, an' she said she'd ring back later.' Without waiting for Laura to comment, she went on, 'Like a brew o' tea would you, afore I gets me 'ead down?'

'Love one please, Belle.'

'Sandwich?' She scowled at Laura. 'Went out wi'out your breakfast this morning, didn't you, eh? Oh, there's not much you can 'ide fro' me, my girl!' Then with an angry shake of her head, she was gone.

When the phone rang, Laura assumed that it must be Sally. But it wasn't, and just for a fleeting second, when the female voice asked, 'Is Pearce Griffin there, please?' Laura was reminded of Ria Morgan. She couldn't be certain, although she had spoken to her on the telephone many times, soon after first meeting Jake.

'I'm afraid he's out.' There was a silence before Laura inquired. 'Is there a message, or a number where he can ring back?' The reply was a low incoherent mumble and then a decisive, 'No. Thank you,' and the receiver at the other end was replaced.

It could have meant nothing, and the fact that the woman

457

sounded like Ria Morgan was probably pure coincidence. But all the same, it preyed on Laura's mind. Yet, what course of action could she take? If she faced Pearce with it, and the caller turned out to be none other than a customer, how would it look then?

The door opened and Belle came in, carrying a plate of heaped-up sandwiches and a pot of tea. She put the tray down on the table by the settee. 'Come on! Get yoursel' over 'ere,' she instructed Laura. 'I'm not budging till you do!'

Laura decided to put the matter of the phone call out of her mind, at least for now, and she gratefully accepted the cup of tea which Belle held out to her. 'You have one, Belle,' she invited. When Belle declined the tea, but came to sit by Laura all the same, there was something about her expression that told Laura she had a question on her mind.

Belle's look was direct and her voice, although kindly, was equally firm. 'Look 'ere, lass. I might be a loud, vulgar little sod who enjoys bullying folks,' she reached out to touch Laura's hand, 'but I'm right fond o' you, you know that?'

Laura grasped the little woman's hand, and shaking it gently, she said, 'Of course I do, Belle, and I'm "right fond" of you.'

'Aye, you an' me, well, we go back a long way. An' all I'm saying, lass, is that me bark's worse than me bite. An' if you ever feel the need,' she slapped a hand across the expanse of her shoulder, 'that there's broad enough for crying on.' Then she stood up, and in a smart voice told Laura, 'There's eyes an' ears all over Blackburn, an' they likes nowt better than to follow the fortunes o' Laura Blake as was. You see, lass, folks'll allus 'ave a soft spot for you. For all you've come up in the world, you've never deserted your old friends . . .' She shook her head at the look on Laura's face. 'Oh aye! Tilly Shiner won't be forgetting the way you kept 'er family fro' starving when 'er old fella were out o' work poorly.'

Laura remembered poor Tilly's dilemma, but she had no idea that her discreet help in the way of cash and moral support was common knowledge. Certainly, she herself had never mentioned it to a soul. She made no comment, and Belle shook her head again. 'You've more friends than you know, Laura, an' *old* friends are allus the best.' Laura laughed and told her in a rush of embarrassment, 'Be off with you, Belle.'

But when Belle reached the door and turned, she had something else to say, and she said it with quiet warning, 'It's the *new* so-called friends as need watching, with their eddycation and pretty faces! Aye, you think on this, my girl, they needs watching!' Then with a flounce and a shake of her head, she went, letting the door close noisily behind her.

Laura had been moved by Belle's sincere words, but mystified by her parting remarks. She thought for a moment to go after Belle and pursue the matter. Recalling the description of whoever it was she should watch, Laura was amazed to find herself thinking of Jay. What nonsense! She actually laughed out loud. Then she finished her tea, picked up the telephone and called Sally. While she listened to the monotonous ringing tone, her thoughts turned to the reason for her call, and her mood darkened. She would tell Sally the way of things. But she would tell no one else, and she'd trust Sally to do the same. Because in her heart, there was the strongest hope that the tests would prove negative. Beyond that, she dared not think.

Sally was shocked by the news, but she quickly disguised her dismay, assuring Laura, 'It'll be alright. You'll see, Laura. I know it's only natural to assume the worst. We all do. But everything will be alright, I promise you.'

A few minutes later, when Laura put the phone down, she sat for a moment, mulling over Sally's words. Even though she recognized that Sally couldn't know the outcome any more than she or the doctor did, the mere fact that Sally had never been known to break a promise gave her a measure of comfort. She wondered whether Sally might be sitting by her phone right now; sitting there just as *she* was, and wondering how she had dared to make such a promise. The thought caused Laura to smile a little. She supposed that Sally's faith was a good deal stronger than *hers*.

During the course of the following week, Laura was called into hospital. No one but Sally knew, and she kept Laura's confidence. The story was that Laura had gone to London on one of her usual business trips.

Laura was quickly released, and Sally went to the big house to see her.

'How long before we'll know?'

Laura told her, 'A few days, they said.'

But it was less than forty-eight hours before Doctor Faber telephoned. She was to report to the Infirmary immediately.

Chapter Forty-five

'God in Heaven, Sally! She's *got* to be told!'

'No, Mitch. I won't have it. Look,' Sally came and stood in front of the chair where Mitch sat, his fist still clenched against the table where he had brought it down in anger, 'I know you think it's for the best. But Laura's been so ill these past two months, and she still is. Please, go and see Pearce Griffin. Tell him what you suspect. Threaten him with telling Laura. And if things really are as bad as they seem, then you're right; she *will* have to know.'

Mitch rose from the chair, and kissed her. Then he sighed noisily, and asked in a quiet voice, 'What sort of monster is he, Sally? It's taken Laura *years* to build that business up.' He wandered to the window, where he looked out over the busy road, and Sally watched him, her eyes filled with a sad kind of understanding. She walked over to his side, and he put his arm about her and drew her close. 'You know, Sally,' the sorrow in his voice seemed to come from deep inside, as he went on, 'I don't think *any* of us can ever really know how much Laura sacrificed, for that business. When her father died, and then her Mam took from her, she could have gone any one o' three ways. She could have starved, sold herself on the streets, or fought tooth and nail to better herself.' He paused for a while, gazing over the vast sea of roofs and chimney-pots that shadowed the streets of Laura's childhood.

'All those hard early years when she tatted these streets for a living, always worrying and fighting, fighting every inch of the way to bring Netti up, and to give her the things which Laura denied even herself.'

To Mitch it was remarkable that a slim chit of a girl like Laura had always managed to ride over every rotten deal that plagued her. 'Oh, I'll not deny that she pulled some crafty deals

461

herself, on her way to the top. But that business is all she's got. And I'll not stand by and watch that husband of hers bring it to ruins,' he left Sally's side, and striding purposefully across the flat towards the door, he told her angrily, 'not for his fancy women and his gambling, I won't!'

'Be careful, Mitch,' Sally's voice was a quiet warning, 'he *is* Laura's husband. And these past months she's been content to leave the running of the business to him and Jay. She might not take too kindly to your interfering.'

'That's because she doesn't know what's going on!'

To this, Sally said, 'Or doesn't *care*,' which made Mitch pause and stare before quickly making his way downstairs and out towards his car. This was something that had never even crossed his mind.

A half an hour later, after being told by the floor manager at Laurems that Pearce was working from home, Mitch pulled the car up outside the house, and when he climbed the steps to the front door, Belle welcomed him. After a brief embrace, during which he was chided yet again for allowing young Tom to take up boxing, Mitch inquired as to Pearce Griffin's where-abouts.

'You may well ask, son,' Belle said quietly, 'It's not *my* busi-ness to poke me nose in; it wouldn't do no good any 'ow just yet! But when Laura's better, I intend to tell 'er just what's been going on 'ere. Aye! A shame an' a sin, I calls it!'

'Where is he, Mam?' His question sounded more like a command, and Belle, who had thought to keep Mitch out of it all for now, could do nothing but stand aside and thumb towards the wide stairway. 'Up there, 'im *and* that little vixen!'

Mitch cleared the stairs two at a time to the vast expanse of landing, where he stood, not sure which way to go. And then he heard, coming from the door to his left, a low murmuring and giggling, like children at play.

His sense of decency caused him to pause, but then the thought of Laura spurred him to cross towards the door, and when the grip of his fist failed to open it, he put his shoulder to it, and with brute force he thrust his weight forward until the door gave way, opening to admit him with some considerable vigour into Laura's bedroom. And there before him were Jay and Pearce Griffin.

462

Mitch's intrusion had been so quick and unexpected that their joy in each other was still alive in their faces for a fleeting moment, before it turned to amazement, and then to fury on Pearce's face.

They were both stark naked sprawled across the bed; she lying in a diagonal line, her arms above her head and face turned towards Mitch; Pearce Griffin lay still wedged between her small white thighs, his mouth still open from the passion of a kiss.

Now he sprang from the bed, grabbed a robe from the chair and flung it around him. 'What the bloody hell's going on? Get the hell out of here!'

Jay jumped from the bed and grabbing her clothes, she made for the door, clutching them in front of her, her face a fearful expression. Mitch sprang forward, and with a speed that belied his size, he grabbed Pearce Griffin by the neck. The fury in his face came out in his voice as he yelled, 'You filthy bloody swine! I ought to choke the life out o' you!'

The other man's arms were still free, and clenching his fist, he swung it hard to land heavily on the side of Mitch's head. This only inflamed Mitch, who took his right hand back, and still holding Pearce Griffin by the throat, he slammed his fist forward, and as it made contact, there was a groan and a splurt of blood from Pearce Griffin's mouth coloured the carpet.

Jay was screaming now, and the sound caused Mitch to turn towards her. Flinging the struggling form of Pearce Griffin back onto the bed, he yelled, 'Get out, you little fool! Tampering with business accounts is a prison offence. Take yourself off, and don't show your face round these 'ere parts again! D'you understand?' She nodded and he waved his arm impatiently. When she'd gone, he turned back to Pearce Griffin, and the look of loathing on the other man's face told Mitch that there was murder in his mind.

'I'll have you for this, mark my words, one way or another, I'll have you!' Flaring his nostrils he finished, 'And I'll have words with the police.'

'You will, eh?' Mitch leaned forward, to meet Pearce Griffin's hostile glare. 'Now, that should be interesting! And will you tell them how you and that . . . tart . . . have been doctoring the accounts, in Laura's absence? Will you tell

463

them how you've managed to get yourself in real bad with the big boys who don't take kindly to gambling debts? And how you've cheated and robbed your own wife's business, and took a succession of other women into her bed?' With each accusation, Mitch's voice grew more angry, and now he stepped forward menacingly. 'And all that, while she was lying close to death in Blackburn Infirmary?'

'You don't know what you're talking about!'

'No? You've not been as careful as you might have been. You and Ria Thackerey, conducting God knows *what* sort o' deals in The Bull. And stuff going from Laurems at a *quarter* of its worth. You're no bloody good, Pearce Griffin, and what made Laura marry you, I'll never know. But you'll not cheat her no more, because it's time she were put wise about you.'

'She married me because she *loves* me! That's why.' Now Pearce Griffin was on his feet. 'What's the matter, eh? Can't understand why she'd prefer another man to you, can you, eh? But it's not the first time, is it? She likes the Griffin men, always has.' The look of suspicion on Mitch's face urged him to taunt, 'That lad you call yours, that Tom. D'you think I don't know what's going on. Tom's my half-brother. That were a secret well hid, eh? But I'm no fool. My dad spawned him. Took Laura fresh and virgin, he did.' A sadistic laugh echoed across the room, and he went on, 'He liked 'em struggling, did my dad.' He said no more, for his words ended in a splutter, as Mitch yanked him from the bed, to heave his hefty fist into that mouth, that had spoken such vile and terrible things. And in his awful mental pain, Mitch would have kept on hitting out. But when Belle's hand touched his arm, and her kindly voice asked, 'Is 'e worth it?' Mitch seemed to come to his senses, and looking down at the creature on the bed, he stared hard for a moment, then without a word, he turned away and went out, towards the fresh, clean air beyond that room. He didn't even hear the hate-filled words that followed him, 'Keep looking over your shoulder, Mitchell Strong. You'll pay for this!'

Chapter Forty-six

Laura turned her head on the pillow and looked out of the window. She liked to watch the sky. It reminded her of the moors, and somehow it helped her to forget that she felt like only half a woman. It was an angry sky today though, and the wild March wind was throwing the clouds into chaos. Like life, she thought, life was like the wind, blowing us first this way, then that, and taking delight in seeing us lose our way, or bump into other poor creatures who were trying to find theirs.

'Oh, Mrs Griffin!' Laura hadn't heard the portly grey-haired nurse come in. Without spite, she wished she would go. And no doubt she would; but not before giving Laura a lecture on the value of finishing her meals.

'Look at that,' she gestured towards the untouched food on the tray, 'you've hardly *touched* your dinner! And no breakfast at *all* this morning. This won't do! It won't do at all.' She tutted loudly, her false teeth making a clicking sound. The orange bowl she was carrying was half-filled with water, and she put it beside the tray on the mobile table at the foot of the bed. Then she wheeled the table over the bed and right up to where Laura was half-sitting. She swished the bottom curtain round to screen the bed from the door and took the soap and flannel from the bedside locker and dropped them into the bowl. 'Let's get you looking ship-shape and lovely, ready for your visitors,' she told Laura briskly.

Laura didn't reply. She didn't even smile, though normally, she would have done. Sometimes, she felt glad of the opportunity to exchange a few sentences, but this evening, a kind of weariness had settled on her, and she felt no inclination to talk.

She was aware that her arms and face had been washed. Now the nurse was soaping her legs, and telling her, 'You're off to the bath in the morning. That'll be nice, won't it, eh?'

465

Laura wondered why nurses always thought it necessary to talk to grown people as though they were children. But she nodded all the same. They meant well, and they were kindly enough folk. As the nurse chattered on, Laura found herself responding, and she began to relax within herself. But when it came to washing the upper part of her body, she became conscious of its odd uneven form; her left breast firm and rounded; her right side conspicuously flattened and swathed in clinical white dressings.

The nurse flicked a brush through Laura's tangled auburn hair. 'What I'd give to have such beautiful hair, Mrs Griffin.' She replaced the brush in the drawer. 'There! As pretty a picture as ever I've seen. Ten minutes to visiting time.'

'Thank you.' Laura nodded her head and the nurse collected her paraphernalia, and then she was gone.

Laura looked around the room. It was a nice enough room, bright and cheerful, with pink-patterned curtains and vases of fresh colourful flowers. But she would have preferred to stay in the long, crowded ward into which she had first been admitted. It had been Pearce's idea to have her moved into a private ward. His decision seemed to have been triggered off by the doctor's warning that her breast would probably have to be removed, and by that unmentionable word, cancer. Thinking back on it, Laura imagined that it was as though Pearce wanted to hide her away, something to be ashamed of. Then she was filled with remorse that such ungrateful thoughts should have entered her head. The whole thing must have been as much of a shock to him, as it was to her. When they were wheeling her down for the operation, it had not been finally decided that the surgeon would carry out a full mastectomy. Even though she had reluctantly signed the paper, giving them her consent, she prayed with all her heart that it would not come to that. But when she came round later, surrounded by tubes and drips, she knew instinctively that not only was her right breast gone, but that her very life was in danger.

During the long weeks that followed, a series of infections and complications dragged her illness on, until at one point she had found herself praying to be left alone, to die in peace. Now, over two months later, her health and strength returned, and the time for her to go home was less than two weeks away.

466

But going home meant nothing to her, and each day that brought it nearer seemed to pass too swiftly. At first she had welcomed the news, and a sense of gratitude had filled her heart that she was still alive. But then, she looked at the quality of her life, and it seemed as though everything she had attained was just a cruel mockery of the precious things that in her blind ignorance she had thrown away. When she had first seen the awful mutilation of her body, her mind had screamed and raged in protest. But then, her fury had given way to a great stillness inside her. She felt no pain, no hatred or anger; only a belief deep inside that she was being punished, and rightly so.

But she kept these thoughts to herself, confiding in no one, not even Sally, who had been a constant visitor, and staunch friend.

The sound of many hurrying footsteps alerted her to the fact that the visitors had been allowed in, and were making their way to the various wards leading off from the corridor. Then, as her own door opened, Laura quickly grasped the edges of her bed-jacket, pulling it together across her chest, in an effort to disguise the deformity that she was so conscious of.

She fleetingly hoped that it might be Netti coming to see her. She knew from Mitch that her sister had spent many anxious hours at the Infirmary during the weeks they had feared for her life. But Laura had been unaware of this at the time, and now she desperately hoped for a reconciliation between them. Netti was seemingly not of the same mind, for once Laura was considered out of danger, Netti had stayed away. It was only then that Laura realized just how deeply she had hurt her sister. But by the same token, Laura realized that it would have to be Netti who made the move to break down once and for all the barrier between them.

Her visitor was unexpected, and as Laura raised her eyes to look into Marlow Connelly's face, a confusion of fear and embarrassment caused her to immediately lower her gaze.

Marlow Connelly closed the door and approached Laura, and as he did so, they exchanged a quiet smile. Laura found herself wanting to know him, to understand this man who had loved Netti enough to defy his own family. When she spoke, it was with warmth. 'Hello, Marlow.' Her anxious gaze moved towards the door, and he, quick to notice, placed his gift of flowers onto the table at the foot of Laura's bed, and said softly, 'No, Netti didn't come. She won't, that's why *I'm* here.'

Laura indicated towards a chair by the far wall and asked him to bring it forward to sit on. Then when he was seated before her, he smiled gently, and Laura realized that he too was embarrassed. 'I'm glad you're well now,' he said. Laura nodded and thanked him, assuring him that she did indeed feel well, and all the while curious as to the real reason for his visit.

It soon became obvious that his only purpose was to bring Laura and Netti together again. And when he told Laura, 'I want you to know that Netti did not desert you,' Laura's heart warmed to him, and she was thankful that it was he who had found Netti in her trouble, for so much harm could have befallen her.

'I know,' she said, 'Mitch told me, and it meant a great deal to me.' A tiredness entered her voice. 'She still hasn't forgiven me, you know, I wonder if she ever will.'

Marlow leaned forward and Laura saw the concern in his dark eyes. 'I really don't think you know Netti, not in the way a sister should. You've punished yourself all these years, you know, Laura. Netti never wanted fame and fortune. She's a timid soul at heart. And when you love someone like you love Netti, you need to discover what's important to *them*, even if they make mistakes and learn the hard way.' He paused and Laura held out her hand. 'Please,' she begged 'go on.'

'You meant well, I know that. But you drove Netti into doing something that she came to hate. It got so she didn't know who she was or what she wanted. You know, Netti would have done anything for you, Laura. But then, when you bribed her friend to keep away from her . . .'

'Oh! Netti knew about *that?*' Laura's immediate reaction was one of surprise and horror. But she remembered the girl concerned, and she was not surprised anymore. A tight smile etched itself onto her mouth, and the smile held no laughter as she asked, 'Will she *ever* forgive me?' Her voice tailed away in a sob.

'She forgave you, Laura, when you were too ill to know it. Netti loves you very much and always will.'

'But she won't come to me?'

'Just give her time.' He rose from the chair and went to look out of the window. And for a long moment, he was quiet.

Suddenly the ache in Laura's heart became unbearable. As the scalding tears ran down her face, she felt Marlow's comforting arms about her, and he said, 'I'm sorry. I didn't come here to hurt you, I came to assure you of Netti's love.'

His words were a comfort to Laura, and she knew that if Netti did come back to her, it would be because of this man. A few minutes later he left, leaving Laura with the promise that things would work out fine. As he walked out of her room, Sally and Belle walked in. But although she was delighted to see them, Laura could not concentrate on their meaningful chatter. Her mind was still on the man who had just left, and on her sister.

Later, when Sally and Belle had gone, Laura couldn't rid herself of the feeling that Sally was on the verge of confiding something to her. It crossed her mind that Sally might be pregnant. The thought brought Mitch into her mind, saddening her, even in her joy for Sally, and almost without thinking, she had lifted her hand to touch the place where her breast had been. And she thought of Tom; Tom, who was her own flesh and blood. The memories pained her too much, and so Laura forced herself to wonder why Pearce had not come to visit her. But then, she reminded herself, he had been left to cope with the business, and she knew just how demanding that was; how at the end of a long busy day, all you wanted to do was fall into bed exhausted. And, according to Jay, Pearce was doing an admirable job.

Chapter Forty-seven

Pearce Griffin laid the expensive green corduroy coat with a deep fur collar over the chair, then he came towards the bed and leaned over to put the case down by the locker. Before he straightened up, he quickly kissed Laura on the mouth, then he sat in the chair; and when he looked at Laura   she thought that he seemed almost like a stranger. And when he remarked, 'So you're coming home tomorrow?' she thought, just for a moment, that it wasn't gladness in his voice, but fear.

Laura nodded in reply to the question that warranted no answer. But the question she now put to him was direct, and a result of the feeling that had disturbed her from the minute he had entered the room. 'Is everything alright?'

He looked up quickly, and his voice was almost too sharp as he answered, 'Of course everything's alright. Why? Is there any reason why it shouldn't be?'

She could think of none. But her deliberate gaze upon his face seemed suddenly to irritate him, and he hurriedly got to his feet and started to pace alongside her bed. 'I suppose I ought to tell you that Jay's gone ...'

'Gone? Where to? Why?' There *was* something wrong. She knew it.

'Nobody knows *where* she's gone.' He halted at the head of the bed and, reaching down to touch her hair, he said in the soft persuasive voice that she knew so well, and could still churn her insides, 'I don't think we need to worry about Jay.' He leaned over towards her and as she lifted her face, he brought his mouth down to cover her lips, and she was surprised that his kiss failed to stir anything within her. She supposed the fault was not his. Somehow, no matter how hard she tried, she could not forget the awful truth, that part of her womanhood had been taken from her. It wasn't a matter of physical shape, but something far deeper, and she wondered if she would ever be able to cope with it. When Pearce straightened up from her, she even imagined a look of revulsion on his handsome features. But as he sat down to look at her closely, his smile was ready enough, and she chided herself for the uncharitable thoughts in her head.

'Did Jay say *nothing* to you, about wanting to leave?'

'Not a word, ungrateful bitch, and when I checked the books, I found she hadn't been doing her job properly for some considerable time.'

'What do you mean?'

'Oh, nothing that couldn't be rectified. Just sloppy work,' he reassured her.

'That's not like Jay. It might be a good idea to let the accountant check them over.'

'Well, yes, I had that in mind. I'm sure he'll find everything in order.' He paused and reached inside his pocket for a black leather wallet. He withdrew a slip of paper from it, and when he held it out for her to take, Laura saw that it was a bank-cheque. 'I went into the bank this morning, darling. We need to shift a few thousand from the deposit account to current trading, but the idiots insist on having *your* signature. I tried to explain the position, but you know how pig-headed they can be.'

Laura was more than surprised. There had been ample funds in the trading account. When she spoke, it was in a quiet, quizzical tone. 'They *aren't* idiots. They're only acting on instructions.'

Pearce reached out to touch her hand. His voice was matter-of-fact as he told her, 'I know they are, and it's just as well they *are* vigilant.'

'Why should we need to transfer money? There was the best part of four thousand pounds in the current account, and more money due in from sales.'

'The money isn't in yet from the sales. I spent all last evening, chasing it up. It's on its way, don't concern yourself. As for the four thousand, well it's still there, less living expenses. But I'm off to Manford Hall auctions first thing in the morning, and we don't want to miss out on any unexpected bargains, do we, eh?'

Laura didn't want to argue with *that* philosophy, because she had been around this business long enough to know that the unexpected was always just around the corner.

'How much had you in mind?'

'Well, I thought ten thousand, just in case, eh?'

Laura's business instincts rose to challenge the figure. She leant over to pick up a pen from the small locker drawer, and scribbled onto the cheque and signed it. As she did so, Pearce saw in Laura a glimmer of her former self. It worried him.

'You won't have need of *ten* thousand.' She watched him closely as he glanced down to scrutinize the cheque.

'Only *three*!'

'You'll find that to be plenty, I'm certain, Pearce.'

'And if it isn't?'

'Then use some of the trading account. We'll square matters up when I get home tomorrow. Don't worry now.'

Laura was pleasantly surprised to find that her interest in the business was still keen. But then such a thing was surely only natural, when it had been her life for so long. And after all, what else was there now?

Pearce folded the cheque carefully and slipped it back into the wallet. He was smiling in his most charming manner as he said, 'You're right of course, darling. Three thousand should be plenty. We'll cut the coat according to our cloth.' He pointed to the case by her bed. 'There should be everything in there that you need. Belle packed it.' He laughed, a low sinister noise. 'Old sod wouldn't even let *me* touch it!' He made no attempt to come back to the bed and the odd look which he gave Laura made her feel somewhat uncomfortable. In that instant, Laura knew exactly what he was feeling. Pearce Griffin, who idolized perfection and beauty, was *repulsed* by her.

Some deep instinct told Laura that never again would Pearce Griffin take her in his arms, or whisper of her loveliness. Of all the times she had felt lost or lonely, Laura had never been more so than at that moment.

Laura enjoyed little sleep that night. Her mind had been too filled with questions, and her heart too heavy with fear. She seemed to have lost all faith in herself, and the way ahead was too fraught with doubts and insecurities.

But now, as she lay in her bed, looking out of the window and watching the rain spill down the roofs and into the guttering, a new determination began to fill her heart. She had never been a loser, and she didn't intend to start now. What did it matter if she was destined never to know the fulfillment of real love? She had lived without that, and she could go on doing so. And if her naked form was less than perfect, she could learn to live with that too, in time. There was so much more to occupy her mind, than fulfilling the body's desires and wasting time on regrets. She still had Laurems, and that would be enough.

This new sense of purpose cheered her spirits and sharpened her appetite, and when her breakfast arrived, she actually enjoyed it.

She knew deep down though that she was fooling herself, forcing the awful depression out of her system before it completely destroyed her. She *had* to convince herself of her own strength; she knew that in the final analysis, nobody else could help her. It was with these thoughts uppermost in her mind that she greeted the surgeon. And now, she *wanted* to be allowed home, and she told him so.

'That's good, my dear, and I can't see any reason why you shouldn't go home today, as planned.' The nurse had removed the dressings from Laura's right side, and the surgeon leaned forward to inspect the scars. Laura looked away. She still couldn't bring herself to look on the horror of her body. It was a gesture that hadn't escaped the sharp eyes of the surgeon. Straightening up, he watched the nurse as she replaced the fresh dressing, and then he turned to look at Laura. 'I was in the *war*, you know. Oh yes, medically discharged in 1943.' He thrust his hands deep into the pockets of his white coat, and a far-away look came into his eyes. For a moment, Laura thought he had forgotten all about her. Then, with visible effort, he dismissed his thoughts and looked at her with that direct stare that only doctors seemed to have. 'No sense dwelling in the past. The war ended over twenty years ago. But what I am saying to *you*, my dear, is that I witnessed some of the most horrifying wounds you can imagine. Medical science has come a long way since then, and you would be amazed at some of the things they can do.' He gestured to the emptiness which

473

had once been her breast. 'We'll fix you up with some appointments, get you fitted out, so as no one could ever tell the difference.' He slapped the end of the bed, smiled at her and said abruptly, 'No problems! You can go today.'

Just like that, Laura thought. She wanted to laugh out loud. 'No problems', he had said. What would *he* know? And yet in a way, she knew that he was right. Worse things did happen, and not everybody was given a second chance. She had always despised self-pity and cowardice in other people, and she must not let such weaknesses devour *her*. She was in her thirty-second year; not young, but not old. Although she despaired of ever experiencing the sort of happiness that Sally and Mitch had found, there would be compensations. There surely *had* to be?

The rest of the time went quickly up to her planned departure, and at half-past two, she was already dressed for going home. Standing by the window, she scoured the driveway leading from the Infirmary and out to the main road, and gradually, as three o'clock came and went, she began to feel impatient. Surely to God, he wasn't *still* at the bloody auctions, knowing that she was waiting for him to fetch her home. Smarting with anger at such callousness, she hurried out of the ward and down the long corridor to the telephone at the top of the stairs. She rang her home number, and for what seemed ages she waited, to no avail, for someone to pick the phone up at the other end. She decided that Belle was probably at the shops, and Pearce was no doubt on his way to collect her, so she returned to the ward to resume her vigil at the window.

Half an hour later, at ten to four, she noticed a familiar car driving up to the doors beneath her window. But it wasn't Pearce who had come to collect her; it was Mitch. As always, when she saw Mitch, her heart was gladdened. But this time, the pleasure was overshadowed at the possibility that something untoward had prevented Pearce from coming to collect her. For a fleeting moment, her instincts made her shudder, and she dared not think of the implications of Pearce's absence.

When Mitch came into the ward, and stood for a moment just looking at her, she ran her eyes over the strong lean features and those all-expressive eyes, filled with such honesty and wisdom. He looked so handsome, dressed in the long grey overcoat with a deep collar upturned against the cold March weather. And when he smiled at her and lifted his arms to run both hands against his wind-blown hair, she thought how natural it would be if she went to stand before him, and he was to lower those arms to embrace her. Such was her pain at that wonderful thought, that she felt angry, and wished he hadn't come. She was about to say so, when he came towards her, his voice low and gentle as he took her hand in his. 'Ready for home?' he asked. Then he did something that made all the pain and fears more bearable. He reached out those long, work-worn fingers, that could persuade the most delicate and beautiful carvings from the ugliest of wood, and with gentleness that Laura had long recognized, he gave the lightest, most loving of touches, against the emptiness where once had been her breast. At least Mitch had once seen the full beauty of her nakedness, even if it had been in anger, and even though he would never now fold her lovingly within his arms.

He didn't speak again until they were in the car and driving away, and that was to tell her that Pearce wasn't home yet. But before he had turned from her to collect the case from the foot of the bed, their eyes had met, and there was no need for words. When she was following him carefully down the wide marble steps, she realized that nothing else would have mattered, if only she had been going home to a life with Mitch.

As they neared the house, Laura sensed by his very silence, that Mitch was searching for the right words to tell her something. But he betrayed nothing of his thoughts, until the car had come to a stop on the gravel drive-way. Then he turned towards her and said, 'Sally's waiting inside.'

Although Laura saw nothing unusual in Sally's concern to welcome her home, she knew it was more than that. Ever since Mitch had come to the Infirmary, and during the drive home, it had been on Laura's mind to ask him about Pearce. Yet, she had not been able to, for she couldn't rid herself of the feeling that something was terribly wrong. But now she did, and it was with a question that voiced all of her suspicions, 'Pearce isn't coming home, is he?' She didn't look at Mitch, but focused her gaze towards the front door, where Sally was standing. When she saw the desolate look on Sally's face, she turned to look at Mitch and asked in a small weary voice, 'There's more, isn't there?'

He didn't answer. Instead, he clenched his fists and thumped them against the steering-wheel. Then he opened his door, and went round the car to help her out. He drew in a long sharp breath and held it for a while before releasing it. 'By God, Laura! You married a right bastard.'

Chapter Forty-eight

'Oh no!' Netti quickly crossed the small parlour to where her daughter was playing on the linoleum. She swept the toddler up in her arms and clutched her to her chest, as though to protect her from the terrible adversities that life often saw fit to deal out. Her blue eyes bright with tears, she stared at Marlow as though in disbelief. '*Everything*? He's robbed her of everything?'

Marlow moved to where she was standing, and taking the child from her arms, he said gently, 'The accountant is over there now, and Mitch. They're waiting for the police. Sally's just got back. She sent me to take you to Laura.' He looked at Netti and waited for her response. For a while there was none, and he urged, 'Netti, Laura *needs* you. She'll never admit it openly, but she does need you. You're the only family she's got, and you know what it took for her to build that business up.'

'Oh, Marlow. I feel so ashamed,' Netti said, her voice low and tremulous.

'Just get your coat on. We'll take little June over to Sally's.'

By the time they arrived at the big house, the police were just leaving, and the man in the green car they had just passed on the driveway, Netti and Marlow took to be the accountant. After parking the car at the foot of the steps leading to the front door, Marlow followed Netti, who had already left the car and was hurrying towards the house. Turning once to look after the departing vehicles, she remarked, 'Thank goodness *they've* all gone!'

Laura was seated in the deep armchair that had been pulled up to the cheery, blazing fire, her feet resting on the stool where Mitch had thoughtfully placed it. Belle had just poured a cup of tea, which she handed to Laura, and said, 'A

477

wicked shame! The bugger ought to be hung, drawn and quartered!'

'Please, Belle.' Laura didn't want to hear any more; not tonight. It was all too much to take in, and suddenly, the many nights without sleep had caught up on her, and she felt bone-weary and close to tears.

Belle said in a more subdued voice, 'Me an' my mouth! I'm sorry. After what you've been through, you need to rest, lass. And I should know better. I'll leave you be, an' I'll go and see our Mitch in the office, see if he wants a cup o' tea, eh?'

Laura looked up, and her soft smile was reassuring. She didn't want this dear woman to feel hurt. She hadn't meant that. She would have said as much, but as she looked up a movement at the door caught her attention, and she saw that it was Netti; her Netti whom she thought was lost to her. And when Netti ran forward, to stop before her and whisper, 'Oh, Laura, Laura, forgive me, please,' she could hardly see her for the tears that welled up in her eyes to blur her vision. She held out her arms, to clasp Netti to her, and as they embraced, Laura's mind sped back over the years. Eighteen years it had been, and more, since this lovely young woman in her arms had been a small child. Now, she was grown, a wife and mother, and it crossed Laura's mind that of the two of them, Netti was far richer. Because her riches were of the heart. No amount of power or wealth could buy love and happiness; they were gifts, and they needed to be cherished.

When Netti stepped back, her hand surreptitiously wiping away the tears from her face, Laura looked beyond her to the two men who had witnessed the scene from the doorway. The look she gave Marlow was one of gratitude, for she recognized the part that he had played in all of this. The two men stepped forward; Marlow to put his arm around Netti and draw her to the settee opposite, and Mitch to come and stand with his back to the fire, facing the three of them. His gaze fell on Laura's upturned face and he said in a solemn voice, 'So, it's worse than we feared. The cheque you signed, altered to draw out your entire funds, and the swine already guilty of emptying your trading account. And barely enough assets left to pay the scandalous bills he left behind, and all in *your* name!'

'And I was fool enough to believe him, when he said the

478

money from the sales wasn't in. I believed everything he told me. What a blind fool!' Laura could see no way out of the catastrophe that Pearce Griffin had made for her.

'You're no fool, Laura.' Mitch's voice was softer now. 'Scum like Pearce Griffin make a living out of conning folk! It's what we can do now, to get back what he's stolen from you. The police are straight onto it, and we've given them all the information we can about his old haunts. So it's really up to them. Your accountant will arrange for any monies owing to you to be collected in. Balance that against monies owed by Laurems,' he sighed noisily before finishing on a note of depression, 'and hope the considerable mortgage repayments already way overdue can be kept up till things improve.'

'It's bad,' Laura murmured, 'and there's no use denying it, or raising any false hopes.'

'Nobody's denying it, Laura,' Mitch replied quietly. 'But we've to try every which way, before we go down. And if it comes to that, I've a bit o' money put away, and I can take all the restoring jobs on without pay.'

'And we can put a little money in the kitty, Laura,' Netti offered. 'We've still got some of Remmie's inheritance.' Netti looked at Marlow, whose approval was immediate.

'*Any way* we can help,' he agreed.

'No!' Laura's reply was emphatic, and as she spoke, she thanked God for those around her. 'I'll not let *any* of you throw good money out the window. And that's what it would be. Four or five payments on the mortgage,' she waved an arm in a gesture of hopelessness, 'would swallow up your money. No!' Her voice faltered, and she would have welcomed a long, deep sleep. 'Let it go,' she finished, 'Let it go.'

'You know we'll not do that.' Mitch spoke softly, and when he looked at her, it was with an intimacy that only she could understand. Even after Laura had drawn her eyes from him, Mitch continued to look at her lovely face, so pale and thin, and those wonderful dark eyes that were still scarred from the extent of her illness. And oh, how his heart cried out to smother her with love that had been born from the first haughty look she had given him, and that had grown over these long years to torment his every waking thought.

'But what *can* be done? . . . What can *we* do?' asked Marlow.

Mitch looked at this dark-faced man, whom he had come to regard as a friend. 'I don't know Marlow. I only wish to God there *was* something we could do.' His voice was deep and full of bitterness. Suddenly, he stepped forward, a look of excitement on his face. 'There is *one* thing we hadn't thought of.' He turned to Laura, 'Will you do as Sally asked? Will you come and stay at the shop for a few days? You're not well enough yet to be on your own.'

'No. I'll be fine, honestly. And I won't be on my own, Mitch. Not with your Mam and Dad here.'

Netti rose from the settee to come and stand beside her. She took Laura's hand and said quietly, 'And *I'll* be here — if you want me to stay?'

Laura's answer was to smile up at Marlow and tell him, 'It would be lovely to have you all here, Marlow.'

So it was arranged. Netti and her family would move in with Laura for a few days.

Chapter Forty-nine

'Where are you going?' Laura got to her feet and facing Mitch, she demanded again, 'Mitch, *where* are you going?' From the look on his face and the determined set of his jaw, she feared that Pearce Griffin's possible whereabouts were known to him, and in Mitch's heart there could well be murder.

Mitch looked beyond her towards Netti, and he said, 'Take care of her. We'll not be above a couple of hours.' Then as he and Marlow departed, Mitch muttered, 'We've some gutters to scour, looking for a rat!'

Less than twenty minutes later, having driven into the heart of Blackburn and then through the narrow cobbled streets of the older part of town, then out towards the Mill-Hill area and the night spots of ill-repute, Mitch and Marlow parked in front of a run down cinema.

The old picture house had been taken over some years after the war by a number of characters who could only be described as perpetrators of everything corrupt. As those characters had moved on or died, so others, of more evil intent, had moved in. Such was their cunning, that even the vigilance of the police had failed to close the place down.

But there was one man, who had stayed. A man of whom all others lived in fear. A man called 'Johnny Street'; so named because he had first built up his empire on the streets. An empire that had brought him uncountable wealth, and a huge house on the outskirts of town. The cinema was his place of business, and all those who needed him would be sure to find him here, in this hive of drug-peddling, prostitution and gambling.

'Are you *sure* this Johnny Street might know Pearce Griffin's whereabouts?' Marlow walked abreast of Mitch, as they made their way up the broad steps that led to the front entrance. Mitch nodded. 'I'm sure.'

After the third and most insistent knock, a thin, wiry man with shifty eyes opened the door. He looked them up and down, as though mentally calculating their business, and he seemed particularly interested in Marlow's black face. Then he pulled the door half-closed behind him, and in a brisk impatient voice, he asked, 'What is it you want?'

Mitch stepped forward. 'We'd like a word with Johnny Street.'

'Oh? What about?' As the thin man spoke, a second man of hefty build emerged through the doorway. He didn't speak, but just stood there, his eyes flat and staring.

'I'm looking for a man called Pearce Griffin. It's common knowledge that he's got business with me. And I'll leave no stone unturned to find him!' said Mitch.

The thin man didn't answer. But Mitch was quick enough to see the darting movements of his eyes, and as the second man lunged forward, Mitch dived into him and a scuffle followed, during which time Marlow took hold of the thin man, who made small effort to struggle loose. Now Mitch, whose capable build and years of lumping heavy furniture had given him formidable strength, had the big man against the wall, one arm bent up his back, and a sliver of blood leaking from his mouth, where Mitch had landed a vicious punch. The man let out a twisted moan as Mitch grabbed him by the throat, and in a fierce but low voice, he said, 'You tell Johnny Street. If he's hiding the man I'm after, I'll swing for the pair of 'em! An' I'll haunt this filthy place till I get what's needed to close it down.' Then his features contorted with disgust, he tightened his grip on the burly man's throat and almost lifted him from the ground and slammed him hard against the wall. Then gesturing for Marlow to follow him down the steps, he looked back to yell at them, 'So tell the big man I'll be back.'

As they got into the car and accelerated away, they didn't see the man who came out of the doorway. Dressed in a dark suit of expensive cut, he was a figure of grotesque proportions, and turning to the two men, he gave them a shrivelling look. Then rolling the cigar about within his mouth, he said in a flat voice, 'Useless bastards!' As he spoke, the fat heavy jowls rippled against his broad white neck. He lifted his foot and jabbed it forward to kick the door, which flung open. To the man who was standing within its shadow, he said in a sinister threatening voice, 'You're in to me deep. But if you bring trouble on my back, you'll get yours broken!' He took the cigar from his mouth, before looking hard into the shadows where the man lingered, and said, 'Whoever he is, *deal* with him. D'you understand?'

The man in the shadows was Pearce Griffin. He nodded, the big man laughed out loud. He replaced the cigar in his mouth and jerked his head towards the other two men; one of them all the worse for having met Mitch. They followed the big man back inside, and the sound of his laughter echoed behind them.

Chapter Fifty

'They shouldn't have gone there!' Laura felt refreshed after a good night's sleep, and she was facing Netti, her eyes bright with concern, 'You don't dictate to those sort of men. They're dangerous, and even Pearce Griffin, rotten as he is, must have more sense than to get mixed up with *their* sort.'

Netti listened, but she said nothing for a moment. Instead she held out her hands; in one was a glass of water and in the other, two small tablets. As she took them from her, Laura wondered at their reversal of roles. For all those years she had tended Netti, cared for her the only way she knew. And now, here was her sister tending *her*, and they had never been so close.

Netti watched Laura take the tablets and in a quiet meaningful voice, she said, 'Mitch intends to find Pearce Griffin.'

'Well, he won't find him by beating up Johnny Street's men! All he'll find there is more trouble than he can handle. Where is he now?'

'He's at the shop, Laura. They both are, him and Marlow.'

Laura, obviously relieved, settled herself back into the chair. 'And let's hope they have the good sense to *stay* there!' She looked down lovingly at the fair-haired toddler playing on the carpet by the window, then she laughed and said, 'Mitch always was quick to temper.'

Netti laughed also, and came to sit beside Laura. 'Oh, what I'd have given to have been there and seen Mitch paste that big one, eh?' They laughed again at the thought of it. But then Netti's face grew serious and she told Laura, 'It's good to know they haven't beaten you, Laura, and in spite of everything, you can still laugh.'

Laura thought that by 'they', Netti probably meant the traumas of life itself, which had come close to stripping her of

484

all that kept her fighting. Yet, Laura knew now that while there was a breath left in her body and friends around her, she would *never* lose her fighting spirit. Such things could stay unspoken between her and Netti and still be understood. So Laura simply asked, 'What time is the accountant due?'

Netti glanced at the small marble clock in the centre of the mantelpiece, then before she could answer, the sound of the door-bell echoed from the hallway, and soon after, Belle ushered the accountant in. In the early days, the onus had been on Laura, to visit *his* office. Then, when she prospered, it became the expected thing that *he* should visit Laurems. Netti collected the child from the carpet, and going out of the room, she told Laura, 'We'll be in the kitchen.'

Laura nodded, and going to meet the man, she held out a hand which he took in a firm shake. When they were seated, facing each other, he swung his small black attaché case on to his lap.

'Things are in a more serious position than I had anticipated,' he said.

'Tell me the worst, then.' Laura had half-expected this. But expecting it did not make it any easier. Opening the attaché case, the accountant withdrew a sheaf of papers.

When a full hour and endless cups of coffee later, the accountant rose to go, Laura's worst fears had been confirmed.

She had never looked on accountants as being capable of compassion, but it was there on his face and in his voice as he said, 'I can arrange a bank loan.'

'No.' She stood to face him, and together they walked towards the door. 'Something Remmie always told me. Start on borrowed money and you're heading for disaster.' They had stopped at the door, and she smiled. 'It seems I've already *got* the disaster. So I'll start from there, with the best resource I've got; *me*!

For a moment, this man of high finance in the hard, cold world of business, looked into those shrewd dark eyes that had so often unnerved him. Here was a woman of substance, a woman who was a born fighter. 'Well,' he said at last, opening the door and following Laura into the hall, 'at least when this place is sold and the creditors are paid off, you should have *something* left.'

'And if I *have*,' smiled Laura, thinking back to the days when she had tatted the streets as a child, 'then it will be more than I first started with.'

'Good-bye then, Mrs Griffin.' He waited until Laura had collected his hat and coat from the recess, and when she handed them to him, he concluded, 'I'll keep you informed.'

Just then the telephone in the drawing room began ringing, and excusing herself, Laura hurried towards it. She supposed it was yet another client who had not yet been informed of Laurems' untimely closure. She had deeply resented such a move. But as had been pointed out, there was no money with which to purchase, and the pitiful remainder of stock would fetch a far better price in a final sale.

The irony of such an occasion had not escaped her. How often she herself had gathered with the rest of the scavengers, to pick at the bones of someone else's tragic auctions. It seemed like poetic justice, that those same scavengers would be invited to hers.

The woman on the phone was *not* a client, and when she asked for Pearce Griffin, Laura detected that the woman had been crying; and she wondered whether she had heard that voice somewhere before.

'Pearce Griffin isn't here.'

'Is that Laura Blake?'

'Yes.' Laura would have corrected the woman's error, but she held no pride in the name that had usurped that of her father. 'Who are you?'

There was a pause before the woman, ignoring Laura's question, asked one of her own. 'Where is he? I've not heard from him in weeks.' The voice began to rise and the words came tumbling out one after the other. 'I've kept my mouth shut, like he said. But I've *got* to talk to him! He'll look after me, he will, I *know* he will. He always has.' She was crying now, and for a moment, Laura was lost for words. Who in God's name *was* this woman? Another of Pearce Griffin's indiscretions, perhaps left with a child by him? Such a thing would not have surprised her. Nothing that man stooped to would ever surprise her again.

When the woman spoke again, Laura learned something that not only surprised her, but positively shocked her. But when the shock had run its course, a tremendous feeling of relief followed, for the woman's answer to Laura's repeated question, 'Who are you?' was a bold angry statement, 'Well if *he* won't talk to me, *I'll* talk to you. I'm Nora Griffin, and Pearce was *my* husband long before he was yours, and legally *still* is!' Laura could hear the woman's voice ranting on in the background, now crying, now threatening, and she felt like crying herself, yet she didn't know whether it was from humiliation, disgust, or pure, wonderful gratitude. So she had never legally been Pearce Griffin's wife, for he was *already* married.

Chapter Fifty-one

A few days later the business was all wound up, and the big house which had been Remmie's pride and joy and for Laura a symbol of conquest over degradation and poverty, stood empty. The few items of remaining stock were ready to be auctioned. Laura had turned all responsibility for that and for the sale of the house, over to the accountant, and she had temporarily moved in with Netti and Marlow. In a strange way, even in spite of the spasmodic discomfort from her wound and the occasional surge of weariness, Laura had begun to feel more quiet and contented within herself than she had ever been. It was as though a great crippling weight had been lifted from her shoulders, and she didn't have to struggle anymore.

The feeling made her remember a saying she had heard somewhere; 'Once you stop struggling against drowning, it can be a sweet experience.' Well, she certainly did not intend to drown! But for now, she was content to enjoy being around Netti and her family, and to leave the accountant and the police to do their jobs.

Leaving the big house for the last time had cost her a few tears though. Yet, she had been encouraged by Belle and Tupper's childish eagerness to return to their caravan lifestyle. And as Belle was quick to point out to Mitch, 'It's only temporary, lad, till Laura finds 'er feet agin!' Yet Laura suspected that Belle and Tupper were overjoyed at returning to their beloved freedom. It had only been Mitch's insistence that had prompted them to accept Remmie's offer of employment in the first place, but they had stored their precious caravan for a day such as this.

The old pendulum clock on the wall of the tiny parlour struck seven o'clock, and as Laura rose from the armchair, Marlow came in from the front passageway followed by Belle.

Belle was staying with little June, while the rest of them went over to Sally and Mitch's place for supper. Tom had gone to stay with Tupper in the caravan, and it hurt Laura to know that even now, Tom still hated her. Hated her so much that he could not stay under the same roof as her, not even for an evening.

'I'd better go and get ready,' Laura told Belle.

'Aye. Go on, lass.' She waved an arm towards Marlow, who was rubbing his hands against the fire. 'You'd best move *yoursel'* an' all.'

Laura walked up the dark staircase, past the room where Netti was soothing her child, and into the small bathroom at the far end of the landing, and all the while, she was thinking of Tom. Then her thoughts turned to Mitch, and she wondered at the future and the long empty years without him. It had been dear Sally's idea to bring them all together tonight for a dinner party. Laura had feigned eagerness, but in truth, she would rather not have gone. To sit at the same table as Mitch, to witness that special comradeship that existed between him and Sally, and to be so close to him yet so far away, would be more painful than anything she had endured. But she herself had played a part in creating the situation, and now she would have to live with it. She knew that. She accepted it. Yet it still hurt and would go on hurting.

Later when she stood before the dressing table in Netti's daughter's small room, which was temporarily hers, Laura looked into the mirror, and deliberately let the bath towel fall from her shoulders, slither down her body and onto the linoleum. The image that stared back at her from the mirror was of a woman mentally tired and physically scarred, yet still striking in her beauty. And as Laura looked at her body, she deplored the times she had shared it with Pearce Griffin. The solicitors had confirmed he was never her husband, therefore adding bigamy to the many other charges against him. She became aware that her eyes were smarting, and that tears had begun to slowly trickle down her face. They blurred her sight, but she could still see the deformity of her own form; the wide angry scar that swept upwards in a flat arc towards the pit of her arm. And she hated its ugliness.

'Don't cry, Laura. Don't cry.' She opened her eyes, which

had been closed in anguish, and she fell into Netti's arms, where she sobbed as though her heart would break, and when she could sob no more, she raised her head and saw that Netti too had cried with her and her heart was eased.

Laura even managed a small laugh, as she said, 'You'd better ask Marlow to lend me a couple of his thick woollen socks, until I get my falsie.'

'Oh, Laura.' Netti's chin dimpled into an uncomfortable smile, and wiping her tears, she picked the towel up from the floor and draped it about Laura's nakedness. Then she held out a sheer, full-length petticoat for Laura to see, and told her softly, 'Look, I've filled and shaped the right breast with cotton wool. I used a pair of your brassieres as a guide. So now you can wear your favourite silk blouse, and not feel self-conscious.'

Laura looked at the altered petticoat, conspicuously swollen where she herself was flat; then she looked at Netti's face, which was bright with encouragement, and on an impulse, she began to giggle. Netti too looked at the misshapen petticoat. In a moment their laughter filled the room, and to Marlow who heard it, it was a wondrous sound.

Chapter fifty-two

'Do you think Laura's coping alright?' Sally looked up from her pillow into Mitch's sleepy face, and he moved in the bed to draw her closer to him.

'It's hard to tell with Laura,' he replied, his eyes now open and thoughtful, 'she keeps things deep, always has. God only knows what she's been through.' The pain in his voice caused Sally to lovingly press herself into him, as he went on, 'But she's made o' good stuff. She'll pull through.' He reached down to kiss the top of her head. 'That dinner tonight. It were a good idea o' yours. Bless you.' He tightened his arm about her, then closing his eyes, he gave his innermost thoughts to Laura.

After he had fallen asleep, Sally lay for a while, watching him and loving him. She knew that even while he slept, she shared him with another. But it was no matter. She had never deluded herself that he could stop loving Laura; for she knew that he never would. Laura was too much a part of him. His feelings for her were deep within him, and much as he might try to deny their existence, he could not. But he had looked after the wife he had taken, and together, they had shared a very special kind of love. She was content that she could have found no greater happiness elsewhere, and with that warmth filling her heart, she pulled herself closer into his arms and fell asleep.

Outside, the night was dark and filled with shadows. Only the moon silhouetted the figure as it lifted itself over the back-yard wall, and silently descended the other side. Then moving swiftly, it approached the rear of the shop, skilfully opened the window and disappeared inside. Leaning now against the window, the figure turned and the light of the moon picked out his features; they were the features of Pearce Griffin, wild-eyed

491

and like a man out of his mind.

Quickly, he unscrewed the top from the can he was carrying. On stealthy feet, he moved about between the bulky furniture and timber, pouring the thick stinking liquid, which formed a coat over furniture and floor alike and dripping into every nook and cranny.

When Pearce Griffin had drained the can of its pungent liquid, he stepped back towards the window and prepared to escape. Then he threw the lighted match behind him, and all at once, there was a whoosh and an instant explosion of awesome force. Within seconds, the whole place was like an inferno, the light of which paled the moon.

From the surrounding streets, the sound of the explosion brought people from their beds, and in a short time they had gathered to watch the fearful red and yellow flames that roared into the night. Their one united thought was to save the family still trapped inside. As the firemen fought against the licking heat, the men prayed and the women wept; for it seemed there could be no hope.

Yet hope there was, for Sally and Mitch were saved that night. Mitch sustained burns on his neck and shoulders and Sally was badly shocked and suffered from deep inhalation of the black crippling smoke. Yet both were brought out alive and swiftly despatched into the skilful care of doctors at Blackburn Infirmary.

During the four agonizing days which followed, it became painfully clear that Sally was losing her fight for life. Mitch was wheeled to her side in order to offer her a degree of comfort and encouragement. Hour after hour he sat close to the woman whose love for him had been like an anchor in the storm of his troubles. He lovingly held her hand, saying nothing, and just occasionally allowing his desperate feelings to show on his face. At these times his head would bow to his chest, the tears would flow unchecked and the broad strong shoulders would stoop and shake in a terrible convulsion of deep sobbing, now and then interspersed with the question, 'Why? Dear God above, why?'

For Laura, who also kept vigil, it was a sight to wrench the heart from her. From Tom, in his inconsolable grief, there emerged the deepest hatred. For in his confused and sorry heart he believed it was *Laura* who had brought all this about, *Laura* who had caused them all such anguish, *Laura* who had brought down the wrath of Pearce Griffin on them all; he, whose dark deed was exposed in the light of day, when his body was found. Yes, Laura! And for as long as he lived he would never forgive her!

It was a week to the day after the fire, when Sally opened her eyes and serenely smiled at Mitch, and then quietly gazed about the room. In that moment, the whole place was lit up by the soft beauty of her gentle smile. His hopes cruelly raised, Tom ran from the room in search of help, returning some moments later with the white-coated man whom he believed could work miracles.

In the meantime, Laura had eagerly grasped Sally's outstretched hand, and her eyes scalded by the tears which ran down her face, she had softly encouraged that dear woman to cling to that delicate life's thread which kept her to them. Only once did Sally speak. 'Take care of each other,' she said. Both Mitch and Laura heard the whisper, but neither found consolation in it.

Now, Laura retreated to the back of the room to make way for the doctor, her gaze falling once more on Mitch, who himself was under no illusion about Sally's momentary awakening, for every sense in his being warned him that already dear sweet Sally was moving further away, and there was not a thing in this world to bring her back. Amongst the pain and helplessness ravaging his heart had come a realization so stark that it shook him to his very core. He *loved* Sally! Loved her in that special way he had not thought possible. Oh, it was undeniably true that his *soul* had always belonged to Laura, and that never had he wanted another woman in the same way. He had loved her with a fever which even now held him in a grip from which he saw no escape nor, God help him, *wanted* one! Dear God, was it true that a man could love *two* women at one and the same time? He felt like a man torn apart, wrenched in two opposite directions, and seeing no peace in either. And the guilt he bore where Sally was concerned, that searing guilt, was almost more than he could bear.

When the doctor shook his head and moved away and Tom

ran to cradle the now lifeless form of Sally in his arms, crying to Laura, 'I hate you! *You're* to blame. Get out! *Get out!*' Mitch could not bring himself to look at Laura's shocked face, but he brought his wheelchair even closer to Sally's bed and clasped her fingers tight in his. Without looking up, he groaned, 'Please, leave us, Laura. Do as he says, please.'

Laura, already reeling from Sally's passing and Tom's onslaught, caught her breath in a sob, before silently leaving the room and the people she loved more than words could say.

Only when the door clicked shut behind her did Mitch look up, after which he collapsed into such dreadful sobbing that his sore heart might have split in half.

There followed for Laura the most desolate two days of her life when, without food, without sleep, and against Netti's desperate persuasions, she punished herself to the limits of her endurance; tormenting her mind with thoughts of Sally, of Tom, and of Mitch, damning whatever wickedness there must be in her to have brought all this about, and blaming herself for the unforgiveable way she had both loved and betrayed those nearest to her.

She found a degree of solace in the wild windswept moors which so often before had brought her comfort. Yet this time it was an uneasy comfort; for hour after long hour she wandered in pain and memory of things that might have been, of foolish pride, wanton emotions and the terrible waste of so much loyalty and love in so many hearts. And oh, how she prayed for forgiveness and for the strength to go on. Yet search as she might for such relief, there came none. Instead, Laura became filled with a dreadful urgency, a restlessness within her which demanded that she go from that place, find a new life and make a fresh start, learning from all the mistakes she'd made.

So compelling became this urge that inside the hour, Laura had sped away from the moors to inform Netti of her decision. She would leave immediately following Sally's funeral the next day. No, she had no idea where she might go, but she would keep in touch. In spite of Netti's misgivings, there was no dissuading her.

'I won't let you do it, Laura!' Netti was beside herself with anxiety, for she had seen Laura's state of mind and health deteriorate of late.

But for all her sister's pleading, Laura stayed adamant. 'I must go, Netti. I *have* to — don't you see?'

And even though she would have it otherwise, Netti understood Laura's decision.

But Laura had not reckoned on that immense love which had spanned a lifetime and which had taunted her these many years — weaving a bond so powerful that even she could not sever.

All who adored Sally went to the church of All Saints, where they paid their final respects. Afterwards each came from the churchyard to light a candle at the altar where she had lain only moments before. Then, heads bowed and hearts heavy, they wended their way home.

For a long time, Laura knelt on the soft red cushions, her fingers clasping the golden hand rail which fronted the altar. Her head lowered to her hands, her eyes closed and silently weeping, she said her own special farewell to Sally; her mind drawn back over the years to that day when she had gone to Sally's mother — the day Tom was birthed. How terrified she had felt, how alone and helpless. And Sally had been there by her side, easing the pain and giving her a semblance of hope. Then afterwards, oh, what a unique friend Sally had been to her.

Laura's thoughts returned to the church and to the service beautifully conducted by the priest. She remembered also how both Tom and Mitch had kept their backs to her, and how when they were leaving, neither one of them had so much as glanced at her. It was as though she didn't exist. And it hurt. Yet it was no more than she deserved, Laura told herself.

She wiped away the tears which blinded her and looked up to ask, 'Dear Lord, will you forgive me?' Then she got to her feet and walked down the aisle towards the vestibule. At the door she turned to say quietly, 'Good-bye, Sally.'

Twenty minutes later, Laura sat in the waiting room at the railway station. Her train would be along any minute now; her means of departure, and, she hoped, her means of escaping from memories too painful to live with. She heard the train approaching and made her way out to the platform, suitcase in hand and eyes peeled against the billowing steam which puffed from the front to form an impenetrable barrier, clouding the compartment doors from her vision.

Suddenly a vision emerged through the clouds of steam. A man of unmistakeable build and stance; that same man who had been the pivot of Laura's emotions as far back as she could remember, and who even now set her heart pacing so that she didn't know whether to run or to stay.

Now, the two of them were within touching distance; Laura looking up with tearful eyes and a full heart, and Mitch looking down at her, his gaze a mingling of pain and love. For a long moment no word was spoken, but now the tears were falling down Laura's face, swimming in her eyes until she could hardly see.

When Mitch spoke, it was with great tenderness. 'I can't let you go, Laura,' he murmured, reaching down to take the suitcase from her. 'Sally wouldn't want that. She knew, you see. She *always* knew.'

Chapter fifty-three

The summer had come and gone and it was the last blaze of autumn when Laura stood looking at what was left of the shop.

Bollards had been placed around it and along the front were notices telling people that it was dangerous and under order of demolition. Looking now at the stumped and blackened timbers, Laura could see that she and Mitch had made the right and only decision not to build on this site. Things could never be the same. She thought of Pearce Griffin's charred and mutilated body that had been found in the store room, and Laura knew there would always be ghosts to haunt this place.

She recalled Sally's contentment and her love for the little shop, and she remembered all the happy times that she herself had spent there. But that was all in the past, and it was only the future that mattered now. She and Mitch would set up a rewarding business in the fine old Victorian house they had found out towards Freckleton. But now, and for the rest of her life, Laura knew that her ideas of 'rewarding' would be very different from what they had once been. This time, she had her priorities right. Whatever made Mitch happy, would make her happy too.

They were fortunate, she knew, to be making such a wonderful new start. They had enough money, what with the little left from the sale of her own depleted assets and, more surprisingly, that helpful inheritance from Lizzie Pendleton. Laura paused for a moment to think of that; for it still struck her as odd that Lizzie should have named only Laura Blake in her will. It had come as a shock. But as Mitch had remarked, 'Folks do strange things when their turn comes to face the Almighty.'

Laura stood for a while longer, until the sharp October wind cut through the warmth of her outdoor coat. Then as she made to turn away towards the car parked at the kerb, Mitch appeared from the direction of the market. He had been inspecting the rear of the shop and as he arrived at her side to gather her shivering form into the warmth of his embrace, he remarked, 'I'm glad we paid a last visit before the old shop's to be brought down.'

Laura was happy that his memories of the shop were good ones, and that Mitch, like she herself, was able now to put away the bad things that had happened. Theirs was a future with wonderful promise, and the deep love they had found in each other negated everything else. Money, power, and all the blind ambitions that had raged within her, born out of bitterness and hatred, those things were of no consequence. Not now, and not ever again.

'Happy?' Mitch was looking down at her now, and Laura lifted her gaze towards him. The love in her smouldering eyes was the reply he sought, and it was there also in the kiss they quickly shared.

Suddenly aware of a small group of people approaching from the Market Square, Mitch tightened his grip on her and urged her towards the car. 'Let's be going,' he said, with an intimate smile. 'We've a wedding to attend tomorrow, and I wouldn't want to miss it for the world.'

And neither would I, thought Laura happily, neither would I.

The wedding had been fixed for four o'clock. Tupper was to take Mitch straight to the Registry Office, and then he would go on to Whalley-Banks to collect Laura and Netti.

When he arrived at the Registry Office in the town centre, it was in a smart shining black hired car, with Laura seated in front, secretly amused by Tupper's obvious pride in his 'new fangled' vehicle, and Netti in the back, her fair hair bobbed in a most attractive fashion and her blue eyes shining with the excitement of her role as maid of honour.

As the car eased to a halt outside the entrance, Laura looked to the foyer, where Mitch was standing, and she thought how proud and handsome he looked in his dark suit. The patch of burn that straddled his shoulder and reached up towards the side of his neck was a scar that he would always carry; a legacy from Pearce Griffin's hatred. But now only the tip, that still looked angry against the white collar of his shirt, could be seen. In time though, it would fade to be hardly noticeable. Yet Laura could look at it, and not see it. She had learned that scars didn't matter.

Mitch turned as Laura approached, and on his face there showed a deep pride in this woman, whom he had loved from the very first moment he had seen her, when he was just a boy. He had always believed that this day was meant to be. As Laura made her way towards him, her slender figure dressed in a fitting two-piece of deep pink and her lovely auburn waves subdued beneath a cream-coloured beret, she ran her dark smiling eyes over the people who had come to see her married. They were good people, plain and unpretentious. People she had known for almost all of her life, old friends tried and trusted, who had come to wish Jud Blake's eldest daughter all the luck in the world, for they felt she deserved it. Beside the big-hearted women, stood their daughters; some of Laura's maturity and some of tender years. They had all come to see this woman, Laura, because they had heard of her beauty and of her hardships; hardships that she had conquered, to become an influential and wealthy person who had kept the company of titled folk. And when they saw her, they were not disappointed.

Laura felt comfortable with these people, and when she and Mitch walked happily through the gathering of well-wishers and guests, she knew that at last, she had found her place. She was here by Mitch's side and here she would stay, and together they would build a new life.

The ceremony was short, yet when she and Mitch emerged to face the barrage of confetti, Laura could remember every single word as though they were engraved on her heart, especially when the registrar had asked Mitch; 'Do you, Mitchell Strong, take this woman?' And without hesitation he had answered, 'I do.'

Suddenly, she found herself in Mitch's fast embrace and his mouth was on hers, claiming her as his wife. It was a meaningful kiss, hard and warming and it fired in her a surge of passion as strong as his own.

So quickly lost in each other were they, that the roar of

appreciation which rose from the onlooking guests escaped them for the moment. Then, embarrassed but laughing, Mitch took her by the hand and led her to the front waiting car, that would take them back to Netti's house and to a long evening of celebration. After that, they were to spend a few days amidst the lovely scenery of Howarth; then home, to start afresh and build a new life together.

'Treat 'im with a firm 'and, lass.' The laughing face of Tilly Shiner thrust itself against the car window, and Laura laughed out loud at the woman's words. 'If 'e don't be'ave isself, smack 'is arse! They're never too big for a good paddling, I'll tell you.'

Mitch caught Laura closer into his arms. 'You wouldn't dare!' he said, and there was a particular gleam in his eye as he bent to whisper his mouth along her neck.

As the car drew slowly away, amidst loud cheers and instructions from the long-married, Laura swept an anxious glance over the happy faces that lined the way. She was searching for one face in particular; the face of a young man, her son. The son that in her pain and immaturity she had abandoned as a new-born babe. And if he never forgave her, she could not blame him.

Tupper eased the car onto the main road, and as he did so, Mitch leaned forward. 'Stop the car, Tupper,' he called out.

Laura followed the direction of his gaze and saw Tom, standing some way back from the road and partly hidden by a willow tree.

When he saw the car slowing, Tom stepped out towards it as though he might greet them, and Laura prepared to rush from the car as it stopped. But after staring into the back of the vehicle where Laura sat, Tom quickly turned and hurried out of sight.

Laura was left thinking of the hatred alive in his eyes. And all she could murmur was, 'Mitch, oh, Mitch!'

As Tupper drove on, Mitch caught Laura in his arms, speaking but two words, 'One day,' but they gave her hope.

Now Tupper sought to bring her comfort, and in the mirror Laura could perceive the kindness in his ageing eyes as he reassured her, 'The lad'll be fine with me an' Belle for a while. Then you'll see, 'e'll search you out of 'is own accord.'

Strangely, Laura believed this to be so. 'Thank you Tupper,' she said. Tom was hurting, she knew that, and all she could do was wait, and hope. Time would tell and God had been good to her after all. He had brought Netti back to her and he had given her Mitch. There *was* a chance that Tom would eventually come to forgive her and to look on her with affection. Odd, she thought, how life could be likened to an angry sea, the might of which drove a body along like a helpless vessel searching for harbour. When all the while, that tormenting sea was our own emotions, and the peace we seek is always within ourselves, if only we know how to find it!

That night, when Laura and Mitch found themselves together and alone at last, Laura stood at the foot of the bed, unsure, half-afraid and trembling. When Mitch came to place his hands on her shoulders in that protective way he had, Laura lowered her eyes from his probing gaze, at the same time chiding herself for behaving like a young virgin bride, for she was a *woman* and she knew what it was to be in a man's arms. But this was different, she told herself; this was *Mitch!* For some inexplicable reason, she had never really learned how to behave with him. He had an uncanny way of seeming to see inside her, to read her every thought and know her every mood.

Of a sudden, Laura felt painfully aware of his nearness and a sense of panic began to take hold of her. Then, as Mitch bent his head to rain the most gossamer of kisses on her face, the feeling was gone and in its place came a surge of love so intense that it took her breath away. In a moment, Mitch was tenderly peeling away her clothes, then his own, and all the while murmuring to her in a soft persuasive voice. Sinking to his knees, he rested his hands on her thighs, his moist mouth lightly placing kisses, travelling with excrutiating slowness upwards on her exposed nakedness, sending exquisitely unbearable sensations through her every nerve-ending.

Now he was on his feet, locking her to him, moaning her name over and over and rocking her back and forth, his eyes burning into hers. As Mitch swept her up into his arms, Laura wrapped her arms about the warm tautness of his body, and when together they slid onto the softness of the bed, their eyes locked in a loving gaze which neither could tear away; not a word was uttered, but a torrent of emotion poured between them.

501

When the fleeting touch of Mitch's fingers swept over her body, Laura shivered with ecstasy. And when his mouth covered her mouth and his strong broad frame began to move rhythmically against her, she heard herself moaning aloud. There came into her whole being such soaring exhilaration that she knew at long last how real love felt. This merging of bodies, of spirits and minds; *this* was real love, glorious and wonderful. And Mitch was truly her man — had *always* been her man! And now, she would never let him go, for they had a lifetime to make up.

Epilogue

On an evening in November some two years later, a young man left the building of Laraby's Stadium in London. He had just won his first open fight against a man the critics said could not easily be beaten. It was an important step in his chosen career, and he was feeling good.

It took a little over ten minutes for him to walk the distance from the stadium to his flat nearby. Passing through the main entrance, he glanced into the postbox allocated to him, and collected the rolled-up newspaper. It was the *Blackburn Telegraph*, his one remaining link with home.

As he turned to climb the stairs towards his rooms, the light from the street lamp outside shone through the hall window and lighted the shape of his strong features. Tom had grown to be a fine young man. But there was a haunted expression about his lean handsome face, and the straight serious mouth was not easily moved to laughter.

Tom walked across the room, to sit in the deep armchair by the empty fire grate. He unrolled the newspaper and turned to the items of local interest. At once, his searching eyes found the insertion of a birth notice. He read the words twice, as though not able to believe them the first time.

Strong
Mitchell and Laura Strong are proud to announce the birth of a son to them, on the 15th October 1964. The newly born, christened Mitchell Jud, is the second son, after Tom.

Tom stared again at the words, 'a second son, after Tom', and a pang of conscience alerted him to the fact that he had not kept in touch with Mitch, who had been a father to him for as long as he could remember. And yet, even now, there was regret in Tom's heart that he knew nothing of his real father. All of his questions were still unanswered and in spite of his determination not to let that fact disturb him, it had continued to do so. His own mother had disowned him, and he still could not find it in his heart to forgive her. Laura Blake had brought him into a harsh world, and then she had deserted him. Why? He had never found out, and now he wasn't sure that he even wanted to know.

All he did know, was that ever since that awful day when Mabel had told him who his real mother was, he had felt like a person without a past or an identity. Laura Blake had made him feel like a nobody. Well, he would prove her wrong. He was going to be a great boxer, a celebrity with a real place in the world; and with a backer like Lady Gabrielle, he needn't trouble himself over finances.

Now, with his mouth set in a strong determined line, Tom walked over to the sideboard, where he placed the newspaper into a drawer. A fleeting concern shadowed his dark eyes as he thought of Laura's years. But then he remembered that Blackburn mill-women continued to produce children well into their fortieth and even their fiftieth year. And Laura Blake was as strong and stubborn as they came! He had often wondered what made her so.

Going into the bathroom, he turned the bath taps on and peeled off his shirt to reveal a broad muscular back. So many times he would have liked Mitch to be close at hand; so many times when his face was running with blood beneath his opponent's onslaught, he had looked beyond the ropes, searching for Mitch, and many times for Laura, his mother. Afterwards, when his strength had returned and the barriers within him had been erected once more, he would chide himself for his foolish weakness and drown his sorrows in a world of merriment.

He took off the last of his clothes and stepped into the bath and slithered into the warm soothing water, where, closing his dark angry eyes, he pictured Laura. Laura, with her wild auburn hair, proud defiance and deep brooding eyes. She was a magnificent woman; she was his mother, and for that at least he felt an irresistible pang of pleasure. At the same time though, he took pleasure in the thought that right now at this very moment, she might be suffering for him, in the same way that he had suffered for her. Who was his father, and *why* had Laura Blake given her own son away? Why? These haunting questions never left him, but the answers were as elusive now as they had been all his life!

Afraid of the emotions beginning to rage within him, Tom quickly brought his mind to dwell on other urgent matters. In eight months time, he would face his biggest challenge yet. He was scheduled to meet Sergio Ferrari in the ring! And by God he meant to win! He *had* to win, because that particular fight would be the one to launch him into the big-time. And in Bill Tyler he had the very best of trainers, so it seemed there was little to stand in his way.

But that was eight months away. And for now, tonight was all important too. Gabrielle would be waiting for him in half-an-hour, and although Lady Gabrielle was a good deal older than him, she was enough of a challenge to keep any man happy! In fact, Tom had often seen in her a resemblance to Laura Blake; a woman of real passion and depth, and just occasionally, an unleashing of ruthlessness.

Tom supposed that if he had anything at all to thank Laura for, it was for instilling in him the craving to win; that 'killer instinct' Bill Tyler said all the great fighters had. It was certainly true that once inside that ring and faced with his opponent, a vicious compulsion to triumph, whatever the odds, was released in him.

He often thought that the ultimate victory he could attain would be to become rich and famous, but for one reason only! So that on that day — which he sensed was an inevitable part of his future — the woman who had so callously renounced him, would learn of his accomplishments. And it was his intention that for the remainder of her life, Laura Blake would be made aware that the hands of the clock had turned full circle! For it would be *he* who had renounced *her*!

In the meantime though, he meant to have one hell of a time. For the next few weeks, he had a lot of living to do!